MW00472319

Berlin Finale

Heinz Rein was an influential German novelist writing before and after the Second World War. He became a major figure in the 'rubble literature' period, and his famous novel *Berlin Finale*, published in 1947, was one of the first bestsellers in the tumultuous German rebuilding period. He abandoned East Germany for the West in the 1950s.

Shaun Whiteside is a distinguished translator of both German and French literature. His translations for Penguin include Sigmund Freud's *On Murder, Mourning and Melancholia*, Norman Ohler's *Blitzed*, Friedrich Nietzsche's *The Birth of Tragedy*, Sybille Steinbacher's *Auschwitz* and several novels by Georges Simenon, including *Maigret's Doubts* and *The Saint-Fiacre Affair*.

HEINZ REIN

Berlin Finale

Translated by Shaun Whiteside

PENGUIN BOOKS

PENGUIN CLASSICS

UK | USA | Canada | Ireland | Australia
India | New Zealand | South Africa

Penguin Books is part of the Penguin Random House group of companies
whose addresses can be found at global.penguinrandomhouse.com.

Penguin
Random House
UK

First published by Dietz Verlag, Berlin in 1947.
This translation is based on the edition published by Schöffling & Co.
Verlagsbuchhandlung GmbH, Frankfurt am Main in 2015
This translation first published in Penguin Classics 2019
001

Translation copyright © Shaun Whiteside, 2019

The moral right of the translator has been asserted

Set in 10.5/13 pt Dante MT Std
Typeset by Jouve (UK), Milton Keynes
Printed and bound in Great Britain by Clays Ltd, Elcograf S.p.A.

A CIP catalogue record for this book is available from the British Library

ISBN: 978-0-241-24559-0

For Erich Weinert

'The bullet in the middle of the chest, the brow split wide
That's how you lifted us high in the air on a bloody board!
High in the air amidst wild cries, so that our tortured gesture
Might be an eternal curse to him who ordered us to kill!'

Ferdinand Freiligrath, *The Dead to the Living*

Pre-finale

'Eris shakes her serpents
All Gods flee
And thunder clouds hang
Heavily on Ilium'

Schiller, *Cassandra*

Berlin, April 1945

Lisbon, San Francisco and Tokyo were destroyed by earthquakes in a matter of minutes; it took several days for the fires of Rome, Chicago and London to be extinguished. The fires and earthquakes that raged upon the spot on the earth's surface marked by the geographical intersection of 52 degrees 30 minutes northern latitude and 13 degrees 24 minutes eastern longitude lasted almost two years. They began on the clear, dark night of 23 August 1943 and ended in the rainy grey of 2 May 1945.

It was at this spot, thirty-two metres above sea level, that the city of Berlin lay nestled in an Ice Age dune until that night when destruction began its baleful course. It had risen from a fishing village to a fortress town, to the seat of the margraves and prince-electors of Brandenburg, to the residence of the kings of Prussia and the capital of the imperial and republican German Reich. It had come into being with the advance of colonizing German tribes into the settlement zones of the Wends and Slavs, and had lain for centuries far from the tribal territories of German culture. It had become a bulwark in the German colonial nation, an outlier of the old German West and an outpost of the new German East, and was late in entering the Reich and still later in becoming the centre of German history. It consists of a multiplicity of small, middle-sized and large towns, of villages, settlements, farms and barbicans that lay scattered between the Havel and the lake-land to the east of the Marches, and merged together towards the old fortress towns of Berlin and Kölln. The scourge of history worked very sparingly here, there were few traces of its rise and its transformations, but they refined an ambiguous appearance with certain noble features

3

that were firmly engraved upon the city's core. There are innumerable traces of the city's downfall, which began as soon as it was elevated to the capital of the Greater German Reich. Devastating conflagrations, storms of steel and carpet-bombing have transformed the city's lively face into the grimace of a death's head.

On 23 August 1943 the city was dealt its first wound when 1,200 British Air Force planes launched their first great strike. The southern suburbs of Lankwitz, Südende and Lichterfelde were rendered into a smoke-blackened island of death in the middle of the sea of life. But this time it was not sea engulfing the island, it was the island ousting the sea, because soon it was no longer alone. Everywhere, in Moabit and Friedrichstadt, around Ostkreuz and in Charlottenburg, at Moritzplatz and around the Lustgarten, islands of death appeared, their shores advancing further and further and amalgamating, until at last the whole city became a land of death with a few patches of water that still contained a trace of life. Each attack broke a piece from the structure of the city, destroyed property and lowered living conditions.

Whole districts were turned to barren rubble. Large factory sites, flanked by unused chimneys, became a wilderness of shattered hangars and rusting machinery, pipes, metal bars, wires and joists. Many streets were still lined with the façades of buildings that looked like living houses but were now nothing but cynical backdrops. Mutilation has left other districts so disfigured as to be unrecognizable, filling them with wheezing, struggling life. The stumps of their mutilated buildings rise naked and ugly among the heaps of rubble, they loom like islands from the sea of destruction, torn and shredded, the spars of roofs which have been blown away like ribs stripped of skin, the windows as blind as eyes with permanently lowered lids, occasionally blinking glassily, the walls bare, having shed their plaster, looking like ageing women whose faces have been ruthlessly wiped of foundation and rouge.

In other parts of the city the destruction is less complete, but in those rows of houses the war's claws have torn great gaps, often revealing a surprising view of the inner courtyards of buildings. Having escaped the airstrikes, they are visible from the streets for the first time, and so can no longer hide their ugly countenances behind the shoddy flamboyance of their external façades; in a sense, the hurricane of explosions has raised the curtain on them. These streets hold all degrees and varieties of destruction, from total annihilation to shelters cobbled together from cardboard and cellulose. There are houses whose roofs have burned away, and others consumed by flames up to the first floor, and some that have been emptied by the blasts, their window frames, shutters and doors ripped from their bodies, the dry skeletons of the roof beams protruding like bones from corpses. There are flats that hang like swallows' nests above the exploded façades because the bombs fell at an angle, and basements that have survived the pressure of the collapsing houses. Only smoking stove-pipes among the piles of rubble suggest that people are vegetating in there as if in a fox's den. The anatomy of the houses presents itself unadorned, the stairs and the partition walls, the lift shafts and chimneys are like bones, the gas and water pipes like arteries, the radiators and bathtubs like entrails. The remains of life are wasting away amidst the jungle of ruins, and nature alone begins to clothe the naked destruction, covering the piles of debris with greenery.

The wide network of the public transport system, woven from the many tram and bus lines, the overground and the underground, the Stadtbahn and the Ringbahn, the local and suburban trains, has been torn to pieces, provisionally repaired with the most makeshift of patches. The timetables change from one day to the next because the destruction of platforms, overhead wires, tunnels, viaducts, bridges and stations has led to restricted services, cancellations and diversions.

The typical features of the city, those classically bourgeois buildings clustered around the island on the Spree and the swiftly flowing axis of Unter den Linden, which once lent it its characteristic features, created by the masterly hands of Schinkel, Schlüter and Eosander, Rauch, Knobelsdorff and Langhans, have been erased even before Speer's drawing-board architecture could supplant it. Its landmarks now are high-rise bunkers, accumulators of anxiety, inhalers of flight, olive-drab lumps of concrete with anti-aircraft guns which, heavy as gigantic mammoths, stamp down the grass of the Friedrichshain, the Humboldthain and the Zoological Garden, no conciliatory feature mitigating the brutal functionality of their architecture. To these are added the many bunkers, both below and above ground, in the squares and by the stations of the city centre, in the estates and leafy colonies of the periphery, and their most primitive variety, the slit trenches, carved into parks, patches of forest and the embankments of the suburban railways.

At the beginning of the war the city had 4,330,000 inhabitants, but in April 1945 there are only 2,850,000. The men have been conscripted to military service, they have been recruited to the Todt Organisation, to the Volkssturm territorial army, they have been sent elsewhere with their factories. The women have fled to areas supposedly safe from air attacks, the old and the sick have been evacuated, the young called up for work duty, the schoolchildren lodged in rural evacuation camps, and the Jews removed. The decline in population is in fact far greater than that, because among the 2,850,000 inhabitants of the city 700,000 are foreign forced labourers from conquered and subject countries, Ukrainians, Polish, Romanians, Greeks, Yugoslavians, Czechs, Italians, French, Belgians, Dutch, Norwegians, Danish, Hungarians and those Jews and inmates saved from the death camps in the east because they were fit for work. They are crammed in barracks on the desolate stretches between the city and the suburbs, in sites cleared of bomb damage, usually along the railway lines, hastily thrown up and surrounded by barbed wire fences. They bear a striking similarity to the emergency settlements that stand grey and bleak between patches of woodland and allotments, except that here (as everywhere else) the barbed wire is replaced by the invisible network of a system of surveillance and control, calculated down to the tiniest detail.

The ministries have left Berlin, they have been 'transferred', or moved to 'temporary quarters', the offices on Wilhelmstrasse are being dismantled, freight trains are being loaded night and day with files, cabinets and boxes, but also with furniture, household effects and suitcases. Senior ministry and Party officials have fled, leaving only the so-called 'intelligence centres', but there are plans for them too, and the extensive 'Thusnelda transport operation' is already in progress, with the special trains 'Adler' and 'Dohle' in Lichterfelde West and Michendorf, and numerous private cars.

Beneath the roar of the air-raid sirens, the muses fall silent. In the brief intervals between power cuts and air-raid warnings, all that emerges from microphones and cinema soundtracks are the voices of the illegitimate sisters of those muses, although the heroic bass of Mars is drowned out by a hysterical descant of compulsory frivolity; the little troop that consists of *Comrades, Kolberg, Hallgarten Reconnaissance Unit, Johanna the Black Hunter* and *The Great King* stand lonely among the interminable armies of *Young Hearts, A Happy House, My Colleague Will Be Right With You, The Ideal Husband, All Around Love, The Woman of My Dreams, It Started So Well, Long Live Love, The Honeymoon Hotel, The Greatest Love, The Man Who Was Sherlock Holmes, Women Make Better Diplomats, A Man for My Wife, Fritze Bollmann Wanted to Go Fishing, Love Letters, Easy Blood, Nights of Madness, Don't Talk to Me About Love.* The flagging thrust of *Fridericus Rex* and the *Horst Wessel Song* mix with the *Königswalzer*, the music of the weekly newscasts, the tormented laughter and the wailing sounds of the sirens mingle into a horrible cacophony.

In this city of ruins, whose body is burnt and broken, whose entrails are shredded and torn, people live pressed closely together, they lead a life more terrible and difficult than the lives of soldiers, devoted entirely to battle and danger. Beneath the constant threat – and it is no less of a threat – from explosions and fire, asphyxiation and entombment, the people of this city still lead a kind of private life, and carry the pitiful ballast of civilization around with them. They need to look after themselves and their families, they need to work and at every second they expect that they will have to interrupt whatever activities they happen to be engaged in, whether it be sleeping or making love, drilling or calculating, cooking or shaving, and devote themselves to a fate that gives them no chance of escape. They lead a nomadic, troglodytic life, they allow the seed of a neurosis that may well be incurable to grow within their children, and surrender them to illiteracy. They watch the substance of youth being consumed in labour camps and anti-aircraft batteries, and the sense of a meaningful, orderly life dying away while their children are raised as warlike nomads. They have already moved so far from their origins, they have allowed their humanity to wither and atrophy to such an extent that at last they are merely machines which react willingly to the gentlest pressure of a finger or a phrase. It is the phlegmatic quality of people who have become fatalistic, who have rid themselves entirely of their own will and stubbornly continue along the path on which they have embarked, impassively accepting orders and special assignments, and praising as heroism their inner and outer indifference, and as perseverance their readiness to suffer; they ceased long ago to be the 'reckless race' described by Goethe. Beneath the ashes of their numbed souls there still smoulders the hope of divine providence announced by the mouth of the Antichrist, that famous covenant with God to which Hitler and Goebbels, Fritzsche and Dittmar are now so keen to refer. They know that fate, as unstoppable as a flood from the Volga and the Atlantic Ocean, will not halt at the gates of their city, but no spark of revolutionary zeal comes alive within them, no unleashed rage bursts the chains of duty, no cry of despair stirs the pangs of conscience. The disasters that the British and American Air Forces are delivering so masterfully in the airspace above the city absorb all capacity for thought, they send their victims off in search of refuge, food and clothing, ration coupons, food cards and bomb-damage certificates. They leave those who have been spared busy with repairs, safeguarding their belongings and struggling to reach their workplaces. The forms of civilized life are shattered, apartments have turned into dark caves since the protecting shell surrounding the sensitive cortices of the city, the telephone and electric cables, the gas and water pipes and the sewerage system, is torn and frayed. The people of the city have returned to the pump, the stove and the tallow candle.

There is something frantic about their movements, about their language, any unusual sound that springs suddenly from the flowing monotony makes them flinch and listen excitedly. They have only one single topic of conversation: the situation in the air, whether the Reich is free of enemies, whether any bomber units have flown in, where they are headed, whether they are flying away again. Everyone who leaves his apartment says goodbye to his family like someone undertaking a long and difficult journey into the uncertainty of an unknown and dangerous country, everyone carries with him a suitcase, a rucksack, a full briefcase or a shoulder-bag, since the alarms often take them by surprise and force them to seek refuge somewhere far from home.

But it is not only the danger of war from the air that weighs down on the people, another menace has added to the weight of that burden: the front lines. Since the crossings of the Rhine in Remagen and Oppenheim, the Western Allies have reached the Elbe in a surprise incursion across western and central Germany, the Soviet armies have advanced as far as the Oder from the bridgeheads of Puławy, Warka and Baranów, through Poland and eastern Germany, but even though the western front is constantly shifting, Berlin has turned its face to the east, where the Soviet armies wait menacingly beyond the Oder.

It is the unease before the storm that lies over the city, an unease caused by the uncanny peace that spreads behind this last barrier in the east of the city, it is a restless peace, in which the railway trains and columns of motor cars from the Russian hinterland, from Chelyabinsk, from Sverdlovsk, from Gorky, from Magnitogorsk, from the collective farms of the Urals and Kuznetsk, advance towards the Oder. There is no one in the city who doesn't know that each day the lull before the big storm is being used to put new gunners in the firing position, to drive new tanks into place, new aeroplanes are preparing to launch, new divisions are reaching their combat zones. Those far-off worlds, the Soviet Union and the United States, have come frighteningly close, the distance between the Stars and Stripes and the Red Flag has shortened to the distance between Frankfurt an der Oder and Magdeburg, and in the middle lies the besieged city which – once protected by the waters of the Volga and the English Channel – seemed an unattainable hinterland, the stump that is Berlin. The enemy armies are still beyond the big rivers that form the final obstacle, but they are already bringing in their fleets of planes and severing their last thin threads of life. They are preparing for the final onslaught, which could break out at any moment, across the Oder and the Elbe, rolling towards the city with the force of an avalanche.

The city's stump has been turned into a makeshift fortress which is preparing to defend itself. Anti-tank ditches have been carved deep into the areas on the outskirts, communication trenches run diagonally across fields and allotments, one-man trenches have been dug into railway embankments, hillocks and patches of woodland, gun emplacements and anti-tank barriers block all access routes, immobilized tanks are buried at crossroads, flak artillery has been adapted to fire at ground-level targets, factories have downed tools, electricity, coal and fuel are now unavailable; the clerical and manual workers stay busy on the city's edge, digging yet more trenches and lining up barricade after barricade. In the streets, in the restaurants and cinemas, in shelters and railway waiting rooms, patrols of the Wehrmacht, the SS, the Todt Organisation, the Gestapo and the police go in search of those unwilling to work and deserters: once again the Party has mobilized all means within its power to force each individual to do his part.

And to the east and west of the city the fronts rise up like a dark curtain of clouds. They seem like storms in the distance, no rumble of thunder can yet be heard, lightning still lurks behind the wall of clouds, but a whirling wind heralds the approaching storm, an oppressive, sulphurous yellow brightness spreads, a stormy closeness weighs upon the city. A fearful sense of expectation has taken hold of the city's inhabitants, they oscillate between hope of a miracle that has been repeatedly promised and presented as imminent by the Party leadership, and the paralysing horror of a terrible end. While exploding and incendiary bombs fall on the city, just as pitch and sulphur once rained on Sodom and Gomorrah, the little groups of the resistance movement wait with painful longing for liberation, because they cannot free themselves by their own power.

PART I

Unease Before the Storm

'We must now think and act like Friedrich the Great.
But if we perish, the whole German people will perish
with us, so gloriously that even after one thousand years
the heroic downfall of the Germans will occupy pride of
place in world history.'

Dr Joseph Goebbels
Reich Minister of Public Enlightenment and Propaganda
to journalists, March 1945

I

In the early hours of the afternoon on 14 April 1945, the door of a restaurant on Strasse Am Schlesischen Bahnhof opens as it has never been opened before. It is not thrown wide open, or simply pushed open with the feet, as some guests like to do, nor is it hurled aside boisterously or with great force, or simply opened unceremoniously. No, the door is opened slowly, almost carefully, only a narrow chink, the gap between the door frame and the large window next to it is just wide enough for a slender young man to be able to slip through. He hastily closes the door, darts his eyes around the empty restaurant and then, as if afraid that someone might get in his way, makes quickly for the furthest, darkest corner. Here he slumps heavily onto a chair with a deep, almost audible sigh, leans back for a few seconds and closes his eyes, but then, with a mighty effort that runs through him almost like a shock, opens his eyelids again and says loudly, 'A beer!'

In his thirty-year career in hospitality, the landlord of this pub has served many a curious character so he is especially good at gauging his customers. He can tell at a glance a thug from an opportunist thief, a full-time lady of the night from an amateur prostitute, a con man from an ordinary card-player, he knows immediately when he is dealing with a brawler and when with a harmless drunk. He draws his conclusions, if that is what one wishes to call his rather instinctive cognitions, from behaviour and clothing, attitude and gesture, language and expression, and in the case of this individual – who has just pushed his way through the door, huddled shyly in a dark corner and exhaled with relief as if he had just jumped into the last lifeboat, whose eyes are filled with harassment and anxiety, whose movements are nervously alert, whose clothes have been assembled at random and are not exactly by the very best tailor, clothes in which in all likelihood he doesn't belong, because the young man's hands are not well kept, long, slender hands with pliant, nimble fingers – it is plain that a number of things do not quite add up.

The landlord, as he froths the beer in a mug and then brings the full weight of his massive body out from behind the bar, studies the solitary guest again, the ski-cap with dirty fingerprints on the right-hand side, the mud-splashed boots which he has quite clearly not taken off for days, his threadbare green rucksack: it is quite clear. The young man is a deserter.

When the landlord sets the beer down in front of him he says, as if in passing, 'So, where are we off to, young man?'

The man thus addressed gives a start and blinks uneasily. 'Off to?' he asks back. 'Why should I be going off somewhere? Do I look like a traveller?'

The landlord chuckles.

'You shouldn't take these things so literally, young man,' he says. 'It was just a question. You have to talk to your customers, don't you?'

As he speaks he sits down opposite his guest and looks him in the eye with unconcealed curiosity.

'Of course,' the young man confirms, but it isn't hard to tell from his face that he has no wish to be entertained, that the conversation might even be an annoyance to him. He drains the beer in one great swig and hastily pushes the glass towards the landlord. 'Same again!'

'Of course,' the landlord says, but gives no indication of wanting to get to his feet, his little eyes between swollen lids will not let go of his guest, and constantly circle him.

The young man turns awkwardly away and begins to read the posters on the walls. 'One Volk, one Reich, one Führer!', 'Boa-Lie, the deliciously refreshing drink', 'We will never capitulate!', 'So appetisingly fresh, Bergmann Privat', 'No entry to Jews!' He turns away, repelled, takes the *12-Uhr-Blatt* from the newspaper hook and begins to read.

Wehrmacht Senior Command: Focus on the Central Section
Severe street-fighting rage in the Danube city – Weimar falls.

The headlines spread, bold and black, like victory fanfares. He skips the report, apparently interested only in the front lines around Berlin.

Führer's Headquarters, 13 April
From the front to the Bay of Pomerania no combat operations of any significance are reported. The enemy are continuing with their preparations to attack in Silesia and on the lower Oder. Naval battleships were sunk . . .

'Here,' says the landlord and taps the table a few times with his index finger. 'There's something I'd like to ask you.'

The young man flinches briefly, but he doesn't look up from the newspaper.

Between Ems and Weser . . .
In Wittenberge on the Elbe reconnaissance fighters are in combat with our bridgehead troops on the western shore. Further to the south the Americans are advancing against Magdeburg.

'Stop pulling faces!' the landlord says, his voice a strange mixture of command and request. 'How long have you been on the road?'

The young man casts another quick glance at the headlines.

'A ruined continent sends its curses to Roosevelt.'
'The war-makers judged by fate.'
'Great consternation in London.'
'Mass murders on his debit account.'

Then he lowers the paper and stares at the landlord with his eyes wide open.

'How do you mean, sir?'

'If you've done a bunk I want to know!' the landlord says impatiently.

'I don't know what you mean,' the young man says, and sets the newspaper aside again as if it bothers him now, then he sits up stiffly, puts both hands on his knees and leans forward. His attitude suggests tension and a readiness to pounce.

'Don't try and fool me, son,' the landlord says, and twists his fat, flabby mouth into a broad grin, 'you've done a bunk, you're on the run, you've hightailed it, you've skedaddled or – to put it another way – you have deserted.'

The young man leaps to his feet and hastily pulls a revolver from his coat pocket. 'I'll blow your brains out if you try to hand me over to the cops,' he yells breathlessly.

The landlord leans back comfortably in the chair, rests his chin on his chest and looks up from beneath raised eyebrows. 'Put that thing away,' he says calmly. 'You don't need that here.'

'I don't trust you,' the young man says agitatedly, and keeps his finger on the trigger. 'I don't trust anybody, these days everyone is . . .'

'Not everyone, son, not everyone,' the landlord cuts in. 'Put that thing away and sit down again.'

The young man sits uncertainly back in his chair, but he doesn't put the revolver away and observes the landlord's every movement. 'Who are *you*,' he asks, 'that you are so special?'

The landlord laughs loudly. 'I'm Oskar Klose, pub landlord. My name is up there in big wide letters for everyone who knows how to read. And who are you?'

'No, no,' the young man says, 'you can't talk to me like that. Sounding me out here and then . . .' He shakes his head, takes a money bag out of his coat and leaves a five-mark note on the table. 'Pour the beer.'

The landlord flicks the note contemptuously back. 'Why don't you trust me, son?' he asks.

'Why should I trust *you* of all people?' the young man asks back. 'Trust is a plant that no longer flourishes in Hitler's Germany.'

'Now you've given yourself away, son,' Klose says, and rests his fat hand on the young man's arm.

The young man automatically shakes his hand away. 'Stop that, or . . .' he adds threateningly and sets the gun down again.

'But that's enough nonsense for now,' Klose says angrily and strikes the table with the flat of his hand. 'I'm trying to help you . . . and you . . . You're fed up with all that crap, right to the brim, that much is obvious.'

'I bet I'm not the only one in Germany,' the young man adds.

'No, you certainly aren't,' Klose says. 'And you can believe that I hate that brown-shirted shower like the plague, you can trust me. Or do you think you're the first one to find his way to my bar because he threw that damned uniform in the dirt and did a bunk, whatever the consequences?'

'You're not telling me anything I don't know already, Mr Klose,' the young man says. 'But there is so much betrayal and spying . . .'

'It happens, it even happens a lot,' Mr Klose the landlord admits, 'but at my place . . .' He shakes his head. 'Sit down again, there's something I'd like to tell you.'

The young man sits down on a chair again, but he sits right on the edge, alert and ready to pounce, still not letting go of his revolver.

'I fought in the First War,' Klose begins. 'Of course, I mean I had to fight. I was a bad soldier, not that I'm a coward, I've often proved the contrary in my life, but it didn't enter my head that we little people are supposed to let the big bosses smash our bones to bits, and once you've got thoughts like that in your head, you can't be a good soldier. Isn't that right?'

The young man nods. 'That's exactly how it is, but . . .'

Klose waves his words away. 'You can have your say afterwards, just let me talk first. They tied me to the post a few times, you don't forget that kind of thing as long as you live, and much else besides, like for example the way the brownshirts smashed windows after what they call the "seizure of power", and beat me black and blue, because Solidarity and the Fichte Sports Association used to meet at my pub and because I always donated to Workers' International Relief and the Red Cross and the Iron Front, but I'm sure none of that means a thing to you. How old are you?'

'Twenty-two.'

Klose shook his head regretfully. 'You didn't grow up in normal times, that is, it wasn't all that normal even before . . . But when you started thinking, the troublemakers had already glued up your brain. And what's your name?' The young man hesitates before answering, and plays awkwardly with the revolver.

'Come on, out with it, lad,' Klose says encouragingly.

'Joachim Lassehn,' the young man says at last.

'Very nice,' Klose says with an ironic bow. 'And I'm Oscar Klose, fifty-eight years old, widowed, owner of this grand coachmen's pub, but you know that already. And what's your trade?'

Lassehn laughs bitterly and shrugs with resignation. 'Trade?' he asks. 'How could I learn a trade? Have a think, Mr Klose, then you'll see that your question, forgive me, is nonsense. In Easter forty-one I did my school-leaving exam, then I enrolled at music college, studying piano, I finished a term there, and then I was called up for labour service. It was incredibly hard for me, because I'm not especially manly, and my hands' – he holds his slender, deli-cate hands out to the landlord – 'are more designed for playing the piano than for shovelling. And from labour service I went straight to the army. How could I have a trade?'

'You're right, Joachim,' Klose agrees, 'it was a silly question. Go on?'

'It won't take long, Mr Klose,' Lassehn replies. 'Basic training in Münster, occupation in Norway and then off we go playing Chase the Soviets. I'd soon had enough, you can believe me. I don't know if I'm a special kind of person, but I didn't really connect with my comrades. They always thought everything was being done right and well and took everything at face value, but perhaps we shouldn't judge them too harshly, because they were brought up to be unable to make judgements, to stick rigidly to the rules, to idolize. Six years of Nazi school, four years of Hitler Youth, one year of labour service, and then the papers and the radio are constantly hammering away at our brains, you can hardly be surprised . . .'

'Nothing suprises me any more,' Klose says, but he doesn't smile, an angry, pinched expression has appeared on his benign, broad, jowly face. 'You're right, son, damn it all, but now tell me something about yourself. Obviously, they'd have worked out pretty quickly what was up with you.'

'Of course,' Lassehn confirms, 'they bullied and tortured according to all the rules of Prussian military art, whenever they could, particularly when they caught me handing out a Soviet flyer.'

'What kind of a flyer' Klose asks.

'One written by German soldiers in Russian captivity, I can still remember pretty clearly what it said:'

Front-line soldiers! German men and women!

Our sacrifices are senseless and pointless. Our comrades are dying for a completely hopeless cause.

There are two Germanys: the Germany of the Nazi freeloaders and the Germany of the workers, the Germany of the animal robbers and murderers and the Germany of honest hard-working people.

A chasm gapes between these two Germanys. The second people do not need the enslavement of other peoples, but its own liberation from Nazi serfdom.

The German people do not need to become the masters of foreign territories, but the masters of their own country. They must cleanse their own house of the Nazi plague, which condemns them to hunger, deprivation and endless wars.

Through the fall of Hitler our people can and will be able to take the fate of Germany into their own hands.

They will create a new Germany in which the people will be masters in their own house.

'That was more or less what it said.'

'I know it, son,' Klose says.

'You know it?' Lassehn says, amazed. 'Were you out there too?'

'No,' Klose laughs, 'but Moscow broadcasts in Germany on short-wave thirty-one metres.'

Lassehn nods. 'So that's how. But let me go on. One day, when I refused to execute Russian POWs whose only crime was to carry a Communist Party membership card or to be Jewish, or simply because they looked intelligent, that was, as they say, it. I ended up in a punishment unit.'

Klose nods. 'I know, the suicide team, digging up mines, defusing squibs, building bridges under enemy fire and so on. Right?'

'Right!' Lassehn agrees. 'Even then I tried to run off and join the Reds, but it was impossible, the SS kept too sharp an eye on me. Then in December forty-three I was wounded at Voronezh, at first it seemed to be a simple bullet to the thigh, but the wound got worse because they'd neglected to give me a tetanus jab. For weeks there was a danger that my right leg would have to come off, or at least I lay there for months, first in Harkov, then in Kovel, and finally fetched up in Ratibor, when our magnificent Führer was on his way home with that great victory march of his. When the Russians were launching their major attack at the Baranov bridgehead, our hospital was ruthlessly cleared, and anyone who wasn't exactly on the brink of death was decreed fit to fight. In Ratibor a reserve division was set up, and I was assigned to that. The division wasn't even fully equipped when the Russians entered the Upper Silesian industrial zone. We ended up at the front, just as we were, some of us unarmed, without warm clothes, everything was at sixes and sevens – and I decided I wasn't joining in, I threw the shooter away, got hold of some civilian clothes from an abandoned farmhouse and set off. It was a hellishly difficult business to get to Berlin, it's crawling with military police thugs and swarming with Gestapo, and they're very quick to turn you in these days. Well, at least I'm in Berlin now.'

Klose had been listening carefully. 'All very lovely, son,' he says, 'but what happens now?'

Lassehn shrugs his narrow shoulders. 'I don't have any particular plan,' he replies. 'The war can't go on for much longer, our men are completely finished. Once the Russkis get going at the Oder . . .'

'That's exactly what I think,' Klose agrees, 'but let's leave high strategy aside for a moment and address the burning question of the day. Where are you going to stay? Where do your parents live?'

Lassehn lowers his head. 'My parents died in the big raid on Lankwitz in forty-three,' he says quietly.

There is a short pause. Klose shrugs slowly as if to express regret, then he gets up and turns on the radio. 'Let's see how things are in the air,' he says.

'. . . at the gong it will be two minutes past two. Here is the air report. Over Reich territory there are no hostile fighting units. I repeat. Over Reich territory . . .'

'The impudence of it,' Klose says, 'over Reich territory. That should be over what's *still left* of Reich territory.'

'. . . no hostile fighting units. The army report follows. Führer's headquarters, fourteenth of April. Wehrmacht Supreme Command . . .'

'Let's see what they're going to serve us up with today,' Klose says.

'The most important bit is the front line at the Oder,' Lassehn says, 'the calm – there . . .'

'Shut up!' says Klose. 'Just listen!'

'At the front leading to the Stettin Lagoon, in the Bay of Danzig and in Kurland no particular combat operations have been under way.

On the Elbe the enemy managed to gain a foothold after violent battles with weakened forces south-east of Magdeburg on the eastern shore of the river. In central Germany the Americans have advanced further with attacks to the north and the south-east. Reconnaissance units have explored the zone around the Saale near Halle and the zone around Zeitz.'

Klose contemptuously switches off the radio. 'We know the rest,' he says furiously, 'we know it all too well. "The attack was victoriously repelled, but sadly the town was lost."' He turns again to Lassehn, who is propped up on arms spread wide on the table and looking stiffly down in front of him, and taps him on the shoulder a few times with an outstretched index finger. 'Don't let yourself go, son,' he says, 'don't go soft on me.'

Lassehn looks at him through glistening eyes. 'It's over, Mr Klose.' Klose sits down again.

'Have you absolutely no relatives in Berlin?' he asks.

A small, hesitant smile plays on Lassehn's face.

'Relatives? No, or rather I do, in fact . . .' He pauses noticeably. 'A woman, in fact.'

'Please don't beat around the bush, Joachim,' says Klose, smiling sympathetically. 'You mean a fiancée or a girlfriend, a little sex kitten for cuddles. Am I right?'

'Not this time, Mr Klose,' Lassehn says seriously. 'As I said: a woman. I'm actually married.'

'Lad, lad,' says Klose, and shakes his head. 'Whatever for?'

'A strange question, Mr Klose, and a difficult one to answer.'

'Great love and all that, I get it.'

Lassehn shakes his head very slightly. 'Great love?', he says thoughtfully. 'I don't know if it was great love. A few months before I was injured I went on leave, I was very alone. I have no friends and have always been a bit of a loner, my friends were Bach and Beethoven and Chopin. Until then women played no part in my life at all, then I met her, and all of a sudden I was overwhelmed by loneliness and the hateful duty of having to go back to the front . . . You know, Mr Klose, when you're that far up the creek in the end you don't care about anything, but when you've wiped it off and reacquainted yourself with cleanliness, the idea of having to go back into it . . . So I just needed someone for me who could be something like a target for my thoughts, desires and longings, within me there awoke a burning desire for female tenderness, the desire to disappear entirely into another human being, it was . . .'

Lassehn breaks off and looks quizzically at Klose. 'I hope I'm not boring you, Mr Klose, I'm sure you're not used to . . .'

'I'm used to all kinds of things! Just go on talking, my boy,' Klose says encouragingly. 'You speak almost like a poet, it's different and I'm enjoying it, so keep going.'

Lassehn nods gratefully. 'It's good to be able to express myself for once. Yes, so it wasn't just that, it was also to some extent a desire to have somewhere for one's thoughts to go, when you were lying out in snow and dirt and ice again, when life seemed more worthless than everything else in the world, when the only words you ever got to hear were rough yokel conversations, about scoffing and boozing, about women and about . . . Come on, you know yourself, Mr Klose, you were a soldier. Yes, then I met Irmgard and fell in love with her, as I would probably have fallen in love with any other girl, simply because I was ready. I should imagine she felt something similar, and the same evening we had agreed that we would marry while I was still on leave. Things like that go through quite quickly when they've got the papers to hand, and they didn't look too closely at leave marriages. Well, we got married, and it didn't change much in either of our lives, I went back to the front, my wife stayed living with her aunt and went on doing her job . . . Yes, that's it in fact.'

Klose rocks his head back and forth. 'Lad, lad,' he says at last and exhales noisily. 'Just for a bit of . . . you do know you don't actually have to get married?'

'But Mr Klose,' Lassehn protests, 'I've already told you it wasn't that.'

'You aren't about to change my mind, son,' Klose says energetically. 'Wasn't there another way of winning her over?'

'That did have something to do with it,' Lassehn admits, 'but it wasn't the crucial thing.'

'So how old is this little wife of yours?'

'Twenty-three.'

Klose nods a few times. 'She'll have enjoyed being the young bride. And besides' – Klose looks Lassehn closely in the eye – 'I can imagine that you're quite a handsome fellow when you're clean-shaven and nicely turned out, there's something of the artist about you, and girls like that. Well, she married you. And what is marriage nowadays? These days people get married the way they used to strike up friendships, it doesn't even matter. Marriage today is worth just as much as the whole Nazi state. But there's one thing

23

I'm completely clear about: you barely know your wife, it couldn't be otherwise.'

'You're right, Mr Klose,' says Lassehn, 'the few days we still have left . . .'

'Yes, I get it,' Klose laughs, 'out of bed, into bed and in between honeymoon sweet nothings. You know your wife's legs, her bosom, her cute little nose and other lovely things, but you haven't the faintest notion what's going on in her mind. Is that true or am I right?'

Lassehn looks at Klose in surprise and nods. 'It's amazing, Mr Klose, how you can . . .'

Klose chuckles. 'Nothing is amazing, but old Klose doesn't come from Dummsdorf, he comes from Rixdorf, and only clever little boys are born there. I understand you, music student Joachim Lassehn, you wanted to do some proper living before you went back to Vorenezh, before you allowed yourself to be thrown back into the lottery drum of death. I felt exactly the same when I came home on leave from France, I cooked up a storm and threw all my money around till there wasn't a cent. When life and death are as closely bound together as they are in wartime, you draw on life as if it were a spring, you don't want to waste a single drop. You've probably been a bit more civilized about it than I was, but if you look closely it was the same thing.'

Lassehn sits there in silence.

'You've gone very quiet, son,' Klose says. 'What are you thinking about?'

'About the words of our battalion commander when we first went into battle,' Lassehn replies.

'And what did that jolly uncle tell his beloved little kiddie-winkies?' Klose asks.

'That war is the father of all things,' says Lassehn, 'that only in war does the personality develop and show true human values.' He laughs, a short, jerky laugh, as if divided into small, mocking exclamations, his boyish face, deeply etched with manly wrinkles, is angry and menacingly tense, his almost gentle blue eyes have the severity of a lowering bird of prey.

'It doesn't seem to have got through to you,' Klose says. 'Your sole human value probably seemed to have become very questionable, isn't that right?'

'Yes,' Lassehn begins, 'during the war I discovered I had capacities whose existence I hadn't previously been aware of, namely the capacity for revenge, murder and homicide. Then there was one of our lance corporals, a so-called ethnic German from the Sudetenland, his words felt like pincers, his orders were like shoves to the back of my neck . . .' Lassehn clenches his fists, which have rested quietly on the table until now.

'He was never off your back,' Klose finishes his sentence and nods. 'I know that one, my boy, something comes loose inside you and tautens until one day the spring goes off.'

'Yes,' Lassehn agrees a little more calmly, 'then patience, stubbornness and submission fly away, a feeling of revenge runs through you like a searing pain and makes you unconscious . . . It was a moment like that, the rage surrounded me like a fog, I threw back my rifle stock and struck out blindly and furiously.' He takes a deep breath and lets his hands relax.

'So?' Klose asks.

Lassehn sits there motionlessly. 'He skilfully dodged me and I struck air,' he replies slowly.

'And after that?'

'Nothing,' Lassehn replies. 'He took a knife from the side of his boot and wanted to lunge at me, but all of a sudden there was a Rata fighter plane above our heads and it dropped a few bombs. You know, Mr Klose, the Russians have this kind of flying bomb, small-calibre but highly explosive, and one of those fell right next to us and a splinter tore the lance corporal's chest open . . .'

'Boy, you were lucky,' Klose says. 'I wouldn't have thought you were capable of going for a superior officer with your rifle stock . . .'

'I said that before,' Lassehn says excitedly. 'I'm a peaceful man, Mr Klose, I abhor all forms of violence, but . . .'

'It's fine,' Klose says, and rests his right hand on Lassehn's arm. 'Now let's talk about the present again. Where does this beloved spouse of yours reside?'

'In Charlottenburg,' Lassehn replies, and sighs deeply.

'So what's up with the young husband?' Klose asks. 'He's sitting around here rather than going home. Are you scared to?'

'Yes,' Lassehn explodes, 'that's it exactly.' His face is serious, his mouth twists with mute despair. 'Imagine the situation again, Mr Klose, my wife believes that I am at the front, and now I turn up suddenly as an outlaw, secretly, dirty and in a state of dissolution, a deserter, a traitor to the fatherland. So I know how she's going to respond to that!'

'It isn't good for a person to think too much,' Klose says. 'Come on, Joachim, that's ridiculous . . . She's your wife!'

Lassehn jerks his head up. 'Really? Is she my wife?'

Klose shuts his eyes tight. 'What's that supposed to mean? A little while ago you said it was all fine, with the register office and everything, and now you're saying something different. You have some explaining to do, young man.'

'You see, Mr Klose, it's like this,' Joachim says slowly. 'Irmgard is my wife, legally and . . . and in another sense as well, you understand, but apart from that there's nothing between us, absolutely nothing. I haven't seen her after the few days of our marriage, and that's almost two years ago now.'

Klose sucks air through his teeth. 'So that's what this is all about. Hm, hm, now I get it, young fellow, all you really know about your wife is what she looks like, how she kisses and what she's like in bed. Christ, Joachim, this is hilarious.'

Lassehn shakes his head indignantly. 'I don't see anything silly about it, Mr Klose, the whole matter is deadly serious, because I am not a superficial person, believe me.'

Klose turns serious again. 'You're right, Joachim, forgive my merriment, I meant no harm. But now it's dawning on me, someone comes home, he's taken off his grey field uniform, he no longer believes in the final victory, and he doesn't dare to go home because his wife may be a Nazi witch and she'll clap her hands in horror over her loyal German cake-hole. Have you never written to each other?'

'No, we have,' Lassehn replies, 'although not very often, but I didn't get an image of her from those letters. Irmgard only wrote about small everyday matters or refreshed memories of our brief time together, otherwise her letters were always rather short. But apart from all that, there is something else.'

'Something else? Yes, good grief, what is it?'

'You said before that all I really knew was what my wife looked like.'

'So?'

'I don't even know that, Mr Klose,' Lassehn says gloomily. 'It's about two years ago now, I've never seen her before or since, over two years her picture has been completely covered over with war and injury, misery and death. At first I still had her face clearly in front of my eyes, but the picture faded more and more, I tried desperately to recall it, but it was in vain, I simply couldn't do it. And it may have been the same for her. It's quite possible that we could walk past each other in the street and not recognize each other. I know the score of the *Moonlight Sonata* off by heart, I could write out every note of the *Appassionata*, but I don't know what my wife looks like. So now you know everything.'

Klose listened, his face frozen. 'Lad, lad,' he says after a while. 'That is quite something. What am I supposed to do with you two pretty little doves?'

'I don't know the answer to that myself,' Lassehn replies, 'but one thing is clear to me, that I have to be careful, I have to approach my wife as a huntsman approaches a dangerous creature which, if startled, can become a murdering beast. Not a pleasing simile, but a fitting one.'

Klose has been listening, shaking his head. 'Lad, lad,' he says. 'What's your wife like? Is she good-natured, or a harridan? Do you think she's the kind who would grass you up?'

'I really don't know, Mr Klose,' Lassehn replies, 'and that's why I didn't go straight to her.' He pauses and thinks. 'She is good-natured, at least that's the impression she made on me, but what her actual essence is like . . . I really have no idea.'

'Well, then we'll have to think about what we need to do, little man,' Klose says and gets to his feet. 'Listen, young fellow, if I suddenly turn the radio on for no reason, it means danger.'

II

Night has fallen on the ruined city of Berlin. The slender sickle of
the moon shines brightly in the deep-blue sky, star sparkles by star,
it is a night that could have been made for reflection and contemplation, for peaceful sleep and happy dreams, but those things no
longer exist in this city. A suffocating fear of the inescapable creeps
from the darkness of encroaching night, a feverish horror of waiting clenches the heart. The great silence of the night, once a gentle
hand, has become a terrible threat, people force themselves not to
make a sound, not to ignore the calls of the sirens that still ring in
their ears even when they are silent, they circle in the brain, they
are always there like memories of a terrible dream, because day by
day and night by night the terrible dreams are becoming a crushing, fiery reality. Here there is nothing but the fear and horror of
nocturnal threat, fever-dreams, anxious waiting, shallow sleep,
always listening for the wail of the sirens, extreme recklessness in
the fight for their own lives in the pounding of the bomb-proof air-
raid bunker, there is no peace here now after the haste and the
work of the day, no resting in soft beds. Here tens of thousands of
people already sit tightly pressed together in the bunkers and halls
of the underground. Millions wait ready to leap for the infernal
concert of sirens, suitcases stand ready, steel helmets, gas masks
and protective goggles lie within reach, radios blare, but no one is
listening to the music or the words. Neither does it matter very
much whether it is Beethoven or Lehár coming from the speakers,
Rilke or Goebbels, they let everything flow inside them, listening

only for the moment when music or language are faded out, the speaker's voice sweeps aside a curtain and takes the stage and announces its ominous 'Attention, attention, this is an air-raid warning', or the triad sounds on the radio and the Berlin division command post delivers its report. Then the city starts up, the ghostly trams driving through the extinct canyons of the houses, and the S-Bahn winds like a ghost train between the rows of ruins, for fifteen minutes of life. People hurry to the bunker with suitcases, rucksacks, bags, blankets, bed-rolls, prams, they dash down the steps to the air-raid cellar, crouch on narrow benches along the walls and listen, senses tensed, their whole bodies focused on their ears, their brains are like selenium cells that trigger certain reactions to certain sounds. High above the earth, meanwhile, are the aeroplanes, searchlight arms grab for them, the anti-aircraft guns thunder into the air, red, yellow, green cascades of light fall to the earth, payloads fall bringing death and ruin, constructions of steel and powder, wiping out everything they touch. When the long-drawn-out cries of the sirens ring out above the burning city, people spill from the caves and holes, they sigh with relief at having saved their possessions, preserved their lives, once more escaped destruction for the rest of the night.

In his restaurant Klose stands behind the bar waving his arms around. 'Come on, come on, gentlemen,' he calls, 'That's enough, there'll be an air-raid warning in a minute, they're already in Magdeburg, on their way to Brandenburg. So let's get a move on, gentlemen.'

'What's on the way?' one of the guests asks. 'A small squadron?'

'The usual,' Klose replies. 'Couple of dozen fast ones, the unit has turned off towards central Germany.'

'Well thank God for that,' the other man replies.

'What are you thanking God for?' Klose asks. 'I expect you were thinking, let the bombs fall on everyone else's heads, at least my precious life has been spared, isn't that it?'

'Charity begins at home,' the other man insists.

'Good national comrade you are,' says Klose, 'people like you will keep the Führer going.'

'I've had it with national comrades, Klose,' his interlocutor replies, 'each man for himself, the National Socialist *Volkswohlfahrt* for all of us.'

'Great flying weather,' says another guest as he pays his bill.

'Don't talk rubbish, Krause,' Klose replies, 'it's always flying weather for them, you should have worked that one out by now. They come in broad daylight and when the moon is shining, in rain and snow and the deepest night, no blade of grass, no Göring is a match for them, however many little girls he recruits for the army.'

'Say what you like, it's mean of them, harassing us night after night,' says a railway worker.

'It's total war, Transport Minister,' Klose says and shrugs. 'Nothing you can do about it. What do you think our lot would do if they could do whatever they wanted . . . But let's get out of here now, people, and close the door quickly behind you so that the light doesn't fall on the street.'

When the guests have left the restaurant, Klose shuts the place up, lowers the shutters and goes into the back room. Lassehn is lying on the sofa there, fast asleep, his breathing the only sound in the little room with the old-fashioned furniture, he is lying on his side with his face to the wall, he has taken off only his coat and spread it over him, he has put a sheet of newspaper under his boots and even kept his ski-cap on.

Klose stops by the sofa and looks at the sleeping young man.

'Hey,' he says, and shakes him gently by the shoulder. 'Air-raid warning.'

Lassehn turns away from the wall and blinks dazedly into the light. 'What's up?' he asks, his tongue thick.

'In a minute . . . there goes the siren. Air-raid warning, my lad,' Klose says. 'What shall I do with you?'

'There's a big bunker not far from here,' Lassehn says and sits up, 'over by Wriezen Station.'

'No, son,' Klose says quickly, 'you can't go there, they're checking everybody very closely, they'd nab you straight away the way you look, but I can't take you to my shelter, the warden has the eyes of a hawk, he's already got my number, no, no, that would be that for you, and me too and everyone else, perhaps . . . So, right, let's forget that one.'

'Couldn't I stay upstairs, in your flat, I mean?' Lassehn asks hesitantly. 'I could promise you that nothing . . .'

'I know,' Klose interrupts him, 'you don't look to me like the kind of bloke who steals from other people.' He pauses, then nods. 'Right, then, stay upstairs. I wouldn't go to the basement either, but the air-raid warden insists that all residents are down below when the alarm goes off, particularly the loose cannons like myself. You see, he's scared that somebody might give signals to the pilots. As if they needed them! I've also left a few newspapers on the table for you, you can take a look if you feel like a read. It's worth it.' He pauses for a moment and whistles the first few notes of the 'March of the Toreadors' from *Carmen*. 'OK, catch you later.' He claps Lassehn on the shoulder and leaves the room.

Lassehn is left on his own, and immediately becomes aware of the extent to which he has put himself under Klose's wing, so much so that he already feels something like a sense of security. The simple, undramatic way of looking after him, apparently quite casually, even though he just turned up by chance at his pub a few hours ago as a complete stranger and an outcast, did Lassehn good. The perfectly natural way he took care of him, gave him food and cigarettes and cleared a place for him to sleep, without even wasting a word on the subject, or praising himself as a benefactor and wearing his goodness as a flower in his buttonhole, all that did Lassehn good as well, and for that reason he now feels doubly forsaken. It is not fear that afflicts him, only a feeling of infinite abandonment in a silence that clings, as if he is now completely alone, as if all the inhabitants of the city have sought some kind of refuge from which they promise themselves protection, and he alone is helplessly exposed to the British bombers.

He turns to the wall and tries to get back to sleep, but he can't, his thoughts have been stirred up now, they thump in his temples, hammer in his pulses, chase the blood through his veins. Sleep won't come again, the weariness, the great weariness that is more a longing for silence and peace and safety than physical exhaustion, is pounded to pieces by his thoughts. Lassehn listens to the silence, but everything is quiet, incredibly quiet, the night is woven of gloom and stillness.

Lassehn rolls onto his back and thinks about the past. The image of his parents appears in front of him. His father with his little pointed beard, cool eyes, thin, dark-blond hair, always a little unapproachable, meticulously correct, entirely the official, always ready to give to the state that which belonged to it. His mother, small, slightly stout, quick with her tongue and quick on her feet, kind, always informative and understanding, and he, a bad school student, not because he was lazy or stupid, but because he didn't fit with the rigid discipline of school and the Hitler Youth. He was a musician, only a musician, and that almost manic tendency made everything else collapse into insubstantiality and rendered insignificant the demands and necessities of life. The daily battle with school and his struggle with his father, who refused to admit that his son was going to become a musician, his resistance against the mass organizations, against the uniformity of thought and submission, against service in the Hitler Youth and, at the same time, dependence on it (because without a good mark for leadership he could never have enrolled at music college). Until then he had never been able to savour the joyful experience of becoming one with music, something else had always got in the way, imperiously demanding attention.

The deeper he descends into his memories, the darker the shadows that fall upon him, the more painful the features revealed. He closes his eyes to dismiss the images of the past, but they force their way through his closed eyelids. He had to do his labour service and become a soldier, at the same time laying aside his old life. His old life being Beethoven and Rilke, the Havel lakes and singing academy, peaceful shades of evening among tall pine trees and a path between swaying cornfields. In that life there was a sky unsullied by the little clouds of exploding shrapnel, fountains of soil flying into the air and flaming, smoke-filled cities. And what remains of that past? His parents were burned to death, pitifully, helplessly, and dumped in a mass grave in Baumschulenweg, while he himself, always a loner who never belonged to the much-vaunted 'people's community', has now freed himself from it completely, he has taken a step that cannot be reversed. But where does this path that he has embarked upon lead to? Where is his guiding star? What is his destination?

Lassehn struggles bitterly for clarity, he desperately resists the nihilistic insinuation that life is neither destiny nor providence, neither predestined by fate nor dependent on the benevolence of the power that he is still minded to call God, instead there was absolute meaninglessness. How did it happen, though, how did he escape? He had often considered the possibility, and rejected it just as often, before it matured into a clear plan and a firm intention, he was waiting for the right moment, he lay in wait for it, and there were many right moments, but they did not coincide with his availability until one day, marching through a field, he stumbled and fell and one of his puttees was untied. He stayed behind to sort it out, and when he stood up again the unit was already twenty metres ahead of him. He watched after the last man and stood where he was, and the twenty metres had turned into thirty, and still he hadn't moved, and then it was fifty metres, and it was as if he was petrified, and then it was a hundred metres. He wanted to get moving but the last man was just disappearing behind a bend in the road. Then he had drawn his outstretched foot back and pressed it firmly against the moss, he had been suddenly filled with defiance and all at once he knew: this is the chance, he hadn't been lying in wait for it, it had been waiting for him, and had grabbed him when he heedlessly tried to pass by. He had first walked, then run into the forest, and at last he had thrown himself into the undergrowth, when his lungs had given out. As if in a daze he had peered into the swaying tips of the pine trees until the cold stirred him once more. That was how it was, it was not a brave decision, he had allowed himself to be impelled, and it was necessity that drove him further along the path he had taken.

At first his flight was only a leap from a train dashing headlong to perdition, the saving of his raw, naked life, but he doesn't feel like someone who has been saved, someone who has solid ground beneath his feet once more, because with every hesitant step that he takes into unknown territory his uncertainty grows. He lacks the robust nonchalance of an inveterate soldier, he feels cornered wherever he happens to be. Again and again the question of the meaning of his action arises, now transformed from mere thought to reality, suddenly separated from forced membership to a national community. He has become autonomous and has no idea what life has in store for him. All that is certain is that he has broken the bridges behind him, and again and again he feels utterly amazed that such a thing could have happened. Often he feels like a dead man walking through the realm of the living, he no longer has a part in anything, neither in joy nor in suffering, but that isn't even what oppresses him so, for he has usually gone his own way in the past. But he feels empty, burnt out, music is nothing but a memory of beautiful, far-off days, the memory of his wife has faded like an old photograph. Has nothing survived but the fact of vegetating away, the satisfaction of the most primitive needs, hunger, thirst and copulation?

Lassehn lies there like a sick man, closed in on himself, but there is no pain in him, only a dark sense of loss. Pain would have made his blood twitch and burn and erase his thoughts, but this feeling of being lost in the bottomless depths of horror is not pain, it sends his thoughts dashing into the void again and again. He feels as if there could be nothing more in his path, as if nothing more could plunge into his heart. Apart from music there has never been anything there, none of the fiery, dramatic speeches has ever made an impression on him, militaristic ideas always disgusted him, and he always escaped from spiritual and physical violence into music. But all of a sudden he knows that it's too little, that the music was only a way out, an escape from reality, that in fact he always felt within himself the compulsion to flee.

Lassehn opens his tightly closed eyelids, slings aside his coat and jumps to his feet, runs to the mirror and stares in horror at the dull glass. So this is what's left of him? Take a good look at yourself, Joachim Lassehn, a good, long look, this is you: hollow-cheeked, with a chiselled, vertical wrinkle above your nose, deep-grey shadows

under your eyes, short, bristly hair, thick, dark-blond fluff on lips, chin
and cheeks, skin stretched taut over the bones of your temple . . .
Lassehn stares penetratingly into the face in the mirror, pulls down
his skin with the jagged knife of self-laceration, frees the flesh from
the skull and sees the death's head with empty eye sockets and
bared cheekbones.

Lassehn raises his fist to shatter the vision, but his hand falls
weakly down. What is he? A dead man who can't bear the sight of
his own skull, stripped of all living accretions? A dead man (albeit
this side of Lethe), who doesn't dare to give up the last pitiful scrap
of life? A dead man who knows he is already beaten, but still tries
to avoid the scythe-stroke of death that will finish him off once and
for all?

Lassehn slumps onto a chair and hides his face in his hands, his
lungs wheeze as if after a violent run.

'No,' he says quietly. 'No, no!' he cries out to himself and jumps
to his feet. 'No!' he roars at his reflection, and turns his back to him.

Then his eye falls on the newspapers. What use are newspapers
to him? He shrugs. What does it matter what they write in their
papers? But he flicks through them briefly, *Angriff, Völkischer Beobachter, 12-Uhr Blatt, Deutsche Allgemeine Zeitung, Berliner Morgenpost,
Das Reich*, odd that pub landlord Klose seems to think it important
for him to stir about in this mishmash of opinions. But was there
not a strange smile playing around his lips when he nodded at the
newspapers? Lassehn doesn't even pick the papers up, and only
now does he notice that certain articles are marked in red.

I want to see what's so interesting and important that it attracted
your red pen.

There's the *Berliner Morgenpost* from 2 March.

Defiant Stronghold of Weapons and Hearts.

An example for the entire German people: the spirit of
Königsberg – fights to the last blow of the rifle stock!

Eastern Prussia, 2 March.

The spirit that unifies the soldiers and population of Königsberg
may be heard in a proclamation by Kreisleiter Wagner, which says

among other things: 'Just as the defence of the stronghold of Königsberg has been reinforced, the losses of the Soviets and the difficulties they are experiencing with their supplies have increased. With each day we come closer to the hour when our armies will step up and sweep the Bolshevik hordes out of Germany. Until then we will do everything we can to become better trained, tougher and more resilient.

So use every free minute of training in guns and their care! Your gun is your life! Mastering your weapon is your victory! Anyone who abandons his gun or his anti-tank grenade and leaves it in the way of the enemy is a traitor and must die! Use every minute to disassemble and improve positions! Every time the spade cuts deeper into the earth your life is closer to being saved! Dig yourselves in straight away and claw your way into every clump of homeland earth. Sweat spares blood! Fight like Indians, battle like lions!

Every means you use to hold the position and destroy the Bolsheviks is sacred and correct. There is no turning back! Anyone who is unwilling to fight and runs away will perish! Beat all cowards, smart-alecs and pessimists! If a Führer or Unterführer weakens, then let the bravest assume leadership! The crucial things now are not age or official position but courage and resolution. The Bolshevik infantry is a ragbag of trash. When they feel fire on their faces, the battle is almost won. Do not waver at the sight of the tanks! Destroy them with the anti-tank grenades or let them run over you! Infantry reinforcements strike together!

The Führer says: the last battalion on the battlefield will be a German one. We must have the strength and pride to be a part of that battalion. So I appeal to your passion. Men! Soldiers! The fate of our mothers, wives and children is placed in our hands, the fate of our city and the freedom of our Eastern European home! Volkssturm men! The sun will not go down on us! Hail to our Führer!

Lassehn picks up *The Reich*, the issue dated 11 March.

'The Turning-point' by Reich Minister Dr Goebbels.

The article is too long for him, he only reads the passages marked in red:

> History offers no example of the courage of a people, unbroken to the last, being overwhelmed at the last minute by raw force. At the crucial moment an inexplicable power of destiny always kicks in at the right moment, which means that the eternal laws of history can be ruled out of court.
>
> The spiritual power of a people can be very precisely calculated in advance, but of course only by those who are capable of such a feat.
>
> We have an advantage over the enemy that he is not able to off-set. Depending on the state of things, it can fully take effect only after a certain amount of time has passed. We must wait for that time to come, however many sacrifices it takes. It will bring the definitive turning-point of the war.

So Goebbels wrote that four weeks ago. And what did the Reich Boozer-in-Chief Ley have to say on the matter? The night edition of *Angriff* of 17 March published his article:

> 'Journey to the front line at the Rhine' by Dr Robert Ley.
>
> Now the Rhine has actually become the front line once again, and German men must defend it to the death. By that I do not mean that the Rhine represents Germany's destiny. The thing that I said about Berlin still applies: we will fight before the Rhine, around the Rhine and behind the Rhine. We fight as long as we have a breath within us, wherever it might be. Spaces, rivers, cities and provinces have nothing to do with it.
>
> Beneath the thundering guns of Meiderich, amidst bombs and shells, our work continues. The chimneys smoke, the hoisting cable makes its familiar hum, the tracks roll and people become accustomed to artillery fire. They are used to so much suffering, they have experienced so much pattern-bombing and now they have had enough of the shells as well. At any rate: they are still working.

Under the heaviest artillery fire, so that the soldiers have guns to fight with. Anyone who is not otherwise required and has a free minute digs trenches, builds anti-tank barriers or exercises with the Volkssturm. A glorious people, these Germans on Rhine and Ruhr – all of them, workers, engineers and works managers, form a single community of fate and defence. I am proud to be one of them.

I arrived in Cologne on the right bank of the Rhine as Gauleiter Grohé was the last to cross over in the rubber dinghy.

Anyone who thought they would find a broken man was mistaken. On the contrary! Full of fanaticism and wild hatred as before, when we both began the battle for Cologne, he said to me: 'Now that we have encountered those cowardly dogs over there I am more convinced than ever of our victory.' Now I knew that the old fanatic and National Socialist Josef Grohé, whose fists flew dozens of times in brawls of various degrees of severity, and acquitted himself excellently, would give the Americans hell to pay today.

We will reconquer it all for a second time. Not a single square metre of German soil, no person of German blood will be left to them. They will have to make reparations for all the crimes they have committed against Germany. They will be given nothing, and nothing will be forgotten, an eye for an eye, a tooth for a tooth!

Lassehn, repelled, lays the newspapers aside. He feels and senses it, yes, he knows he didn't do what he did just to preserve his life, to save himself from the general chaos of downfall, but that there is also something else that impels him with irresistible force, an incomprehensible energy that feeds on a source that lies deep within him, which he does not know. Isn't there something from which one might draw inspiration, for which heart and soul might blaze? He cannot think of an idea that carries his life and forces its way towards a goal, he knows only rejection of the idea that they had tried to force on him with pathos and brute force, he knows only revulsion because he sees blood dripping on the well-tended hands and shiny boots of that idea's supporters, he knows only resignation because he has entered the machinery that crushes like an insect anyone who even tries to break out of the formation.

There must be something worth living for, but he doesn't know what it is, it has been withheld from him or counterfeited, lies and slander have been sown so deeply within him that the weeds of prejudice have overgrown his capacity for thought.

Lassehn looks in the mirror again and runs his right forefinger along the contours of his face, it runs gently over chin, cheeks, lips, nose, forehead, ears, and that calm contact of his own finger makes him feel strangely good, as if it is instilling breath within himself again, as if that touch has re-established contact with life.

'No,' he says again and shakes his head, a faint smile curls his pale, bloodless lips. He isn't dead yet, he's only seemingly dead, he has had life breathed back into him through the mysterious power of an unknown idea. The time that lies between the beginning of a flight and the start of a new light is no longer a dead, empty gap in the deepest trough of his life. It is like a musical pause after a painfully fading coda, a quiet bar in which energy collects into new chords, which leads from the border of deadly resignation into a defiant will to live. He knows that he will now fight for knowledge, but it is not yet clear to him where he will find it and who will convey it to him, but right now that does not concern him.

His thoughts leaped directly to Klose, and now his faintly curving lips really turn into a smile that wrinkles his nose and draws two distinct lines towards his chin.

Klose is in fact the only person in Lassehn's field of vision who was not washed over or torn down by the wave of National Socialism, from whom all the high-sounding speeches and refined propaganda tricks slid off ineffectually, who has been corrupted by nothing. Lassehn doesn't know that there are still such people, since he hasn't met one, neither does he know where Klose's resilience comes from and why his capacity for resistance is so unbroken, but he guesses that the roots of that power must reach back into a time when he, the college student Joachim Lassehn, was not yet consciously thinking. He knows nothing of that time, or only what the teachers, the youth leaders, the propaganda officers, the newspapers and the radio broadcasts let him know, and that was . . .

His chain of thought is suddenly interrupted. All at once the anti-aircraft guns suddenly bark and hammer away, a mighty roar is slung into the silence, the fine, singing notes of the planes drifting above them and the wail of the falling bombs as they hurtle to the ground. The ground vibrates, the house shakes to its foundations, the blast forces its way through all the cracks and chalk-dust trickles from the walls.

For a few minutes Lassehn listens to that infernal concert, then he picks his coat up from the floor and lies back down on the sofa. Events outside do not concern him, he pushes his ski-cap over his eyes and pulls his coat up around his neck.

A few moments later he is fast asleep.

III

When Lassehn wakes up again, he doesn't know whether he has been asleep for only a few minutes or for many hours. A cloud of exhaustion still weighs down on him. He wants to abandon himself to sleep once more, when a voice reaches his ear. It is not Klose's voice, that slightly droning, rather rough voice with its Berlin accent, it is a cultured, harsh, matter-of-fact, rather mannered voice, the voice of a practised and experienced speaker.

Lassehn pushes aside the cap covering his eyes and raises his head, but he can't see anything, he has to sit up to turn his head, and then he sees . . .

Klose is sitting by the radio, but he is not alone, there are two other men there, sitting right by the radio, with their heads leaning forward and their hands behind their ears as if they are listening. They have hard, angular faces, their muscles tense with resolution and defiance.

The voice that woke him is coming from the speaker, it is clear and unrhetorical, it makes no attempt to sound beautiful, it calls a spade a spade, it pours bitter, stinging mockery over the Nazi gods and turns them into bestial, belligerent, bloodthirsty philistines.

Never before has Lassehn heard such language. His heart starts thumping wildly, an iron circle settles around his forehead, he blinks uneasily and looks anxiously around. He would like to ask, but instead he listens as if under a spell. He holds his breath so as not to waste a single word. The voice over there comes from a completely different world, a world not held in the iron vice of violent

41

rule. Lassehn wants to shout, there is something inside him that calls out to be shouted, joy, hope, liberation, hatred, torment, but all that issues from his throat is a hoarse croak.

Klose turns round and puts his finger to his mouth, while the two other men remain in their position without looking up.

'Soldiers' radio, western station, on short wave forty-one and thirty-two metres. Our news broadcast . . .'

A crackle in the speaker, Klose has turned off the radio. Lassehn swings his feet from the sofa and gets up, brushes his hair with his hand and straightens his jacket, then he stands uncertainly in the middle of the room.

'Come here, Joachim,' Klose calls and waves to him, 'let me introduce my friends.'

Lassehn walks slowly over.

'Don't be shy, lad,' Klose says encouragingly, and points at the two men in turn. 'This is Dr Walter Böttcher and this is Friedrich Wiegand, former trade union secretary.' Lassehn makes two stiff, clumsy bows and murmurs his name.

'Sit down, son,' Klose says, 'and don't be such a stranger, I've already told them both about you, you little deserter.'

'Mr Klose,' Lassehn says pleadingly and settles heavily on a chair, 'please don't use that term all the time.'

'Why not?' asks Dr Böttcher and looks carefully at Lassehn. 'Being a deserter is no shame, Mr Lassehn, on the contrary. By deserting you have shown more courage than your comrades, who are presumably still stubbornly doing their duty. I am in fact of the opinion that your desertion is not an act of cowardice, because by deserting you have cast off your hated bonds and will no longer be abused, because you don't want to make yourself guilty of the crimes that are being committed on foreign people and on the German people. The true cowards are the others who carry out all orders, however cruel and violent, and thus kill off their conscience. By old Prussian standards they are dutiful and courageous, but only because they are cowardly, because they lack the courage to put an end to it all and resist. That's how you must see it, Mr Lassehn.'

'Thank you, Doctor,' Lassehn says quietly and looks Dr Böttcher in the face. 'It is hard to find your bearings, there are no standards, no guidelines.'

'Your generation, Mr Lassehn, is in a regrettable situation,' Dr Böttcher says gravely. 'We, particularly Wiegand and I, and our mutual friend Klose, have talked about it often and reached the conclusion that no young generation has been as unhappy as yours. The magnitude of your misfortune will only become apparent in its full horror after the collapse, which is only a matter of a few months away. Your generation will lose the ground beneath your feet because of the shattering of its foundation and plunge into the void. It will stand there empty-handed and with a disappointed heart, it will recognize the betrayal and the seduction to which it has fallen victim, but it will also recant all other ideals and every new faith it is offered. It will look at anyone who claims to offer leadership or who speaks of a vision of the world with deep suspicion and contempt and it will, consciously or otherwise, measure using the standards it has been brought up with.'

'These young people, Doctor, of whom I too am one,' Lassehn objects, 'have known nothing else. The contempt for everything that existed before National Socialism has become its flesh and blood, and even if one day it should recognize the worthlessness of National Socialism and the criminality of its leaders, it does not mean that it places any trust in the spiritual and political leaders from the time before 1933.'

'You are completely right,' says Wiegand, joining in with the conversation. 'At first it may be less a matter of immediately presenting this young generation with ready-made old ideas, or even new ones, and more one of making them forget what National Socialism has allowed to seep into it from many dubious sources, ceaselessly and with searing acids.'

'It is clear, people,' says Klose, 'that what is drummed into you in your youth is fixed within you as if with a barbed hook. When I went to school, Old Kaiser Friedrich and Bismarck were still glorified, and to be quite honest I didn't think critically about them until much later.'

'It was the same for all of us, Klose,' says Dr Böttcher, 'but in the Kaiser's Germany there was an opposition, there were certain freedoms, there were ways of getting hold of other information. But our young generation today has no opportunity to do that, it is excluded from everything that lies outside the circle of National Socialism, it encounters everything as if through a distorting mirror, the so-called National Socialist view of the world is filtered into it ready for use as an elixir, and all the things of this world, whether they be German history or stamp-collecting, biology or dance music, are interpreted for it in this sense.'

Lassehn sighs deeply, and helplessness and torment appear in his eyes. 'What does it say in *Faust*?'

'Oh happy he who still can hope
To rise again from this great sea of error,
What we do not know is the very thing we needed
And what we know we cannot use.'

'That's exactly how it is. I envy you, Doctor, I envy you all, for your . . . How should I put it? Yes, in a way I envy your age.'

Dr Böttcher laughs bitterly. 'Yes, that's how it is. Probably for the first time in the world youth does not feel superior to age, it is not proud of being young. When you just said, Mr Lassehn, that you envied us our age you didn't phrase it quite correctly. It is not our age that now appears so desirable to you, it is the knowledge and experiences that we accumulated at a time when National Socialism had not yet limited thought to a few primitive phrases. Admittedly this knowledge has not yet seeped into the consciousness of most of your generation, because it is still covered over with war and the frantically confident speeches of Hitler and Goebbels, but one day the war will be over and Hitler and Goebbels will no longer be there, once the great silence falls upon them and there is no one there to tell them everything they are doing is right, when their mistakes are held up to them on all sides, only then will they recognize that their youth has been shamefully betrayed, their capacity for enthusiasm scandalously abused, their thinking misled.

Then the great vacuum will open up in front of it, because while the older generations can still flee into older visions of the world, into socialism, into communism, liberalism or democracy, the Church or some philosophical system, the youth will stand there spiritually naked. Do you have any idea of what will come after the inevitable defeat, Mr Lassehn?'

Lassehn shakes his head. 'No, Doctor, how could I,' he replies. 'In the past Hitler's Germany always struck me, in spite of everything, as being an orderly state . . .'

'. . . built on unscrupulous betrayal and held together by the violent application of force,' says Dr Böttcher.

'Certainly,' admits Lassehn, 'but if that order should fall, when all the repressed instincts and passions are liberated, only chaos can rule.'

'There is no doubt,' Dr Böttcher says thoughtfully as if weighing every word, 'that our war is driving us into the greatest disaster of our history, but then again we do have some experience with losing world wars, Mr Lassehn. After the war of 1918 an army of millions returned home, men who had known nothing for years but trenches and army brothels, murderous hand-to-hand combat and the satisfaction of only the most primitive needs, who had been horrifically degraded in a spiritual and physical respect and who had only atavistic memories of a normal life. These men, and among them there were many hundreds of thousands who had gone straight from the schoolroom to the battlefields, and who knew just as much or as little about life as you do today, returned home one day too, and a wave of coarseness and vulgarity, murder and violence ran through our country, but there were also forces there that ordered chaos and tamed the forces unleashed.'

'The tamers were later overwhelmed by the tamed, my dear Doctor,' Klose says. 'Your fault . . .'

Dr Böttcher silences him with a sudden movement of his hand. 'Let's not judge our faults and yours for the umpteenth time, my dear Klose,' he says. 'What is important here is to make it clear to this young man – who has never believed anything, or had the opportunity to believe anything, and who seems to be refusing to believe anything in future as well because, quite unconsciously I have no doubt, he is still filled with Nazi terminology – that even after this war a new order will arise in Germany, not *even though* but *because* National Socialism will have disappeared.'

'I cannot imagine, Doctor,' Lassehn says dubiously, 'that a way might lead into an orderly life, a life with cleanliness and freedom, music and love. What might the nature of that order be?'

'We don't yet know,' Dr Böttcher replies, 'in the end it will depend on the final phase of the war. But to return to the starting points of our conversation: even then there were many people, mostly from the middle class, who simply couldn't imagine Germany losing the war, because it would mean the downfall of their world. Well, the world did not collapse, all that collapsed was a certain world of the bourgeoisie.'

'But it only seemed that way,' Wiegand suggests, 'the capitalist and agrarian ruling class only disappeared from view, they went on living, modestly at first, reticently, they were barely apparent, but in silence they carefully preserved all of their spiritual and material components, before gradually deploying them again with all their full weight, since they had been left astonishingly untouched, and in the end they became the basis for National Socialism. This war, whose final act we hope we are living through now, is basically only a continuation of the First World War, which left Germany floored in a material sense, but also politically untouched.'

'That is the great accusation to be levelled against the victors of Versailles: they did little to encourage democracy in Germany,' Dr Böttcher says, nodding, 'with their politics they created a situation whereby the politically immature German people confused cause and effect, some of them rejected democracy, some didn't know how to use it, and slowly but surely they slid into the arms of militarism and nationalism in its various guises. That must be prevented this time, and I am completely clear that it will be possible only with the help of our present supposed friends.'

'But we must be clear about one thing,' Wiegand says when Dr Böttcher pauses briefly. 'The soldiers who will return this time are not soldiers like the ones after the First World War, coarsened, degraded, disappointed, embittered and weary. These soldiers have passed through the school of the so-called National Socialist philosophy, in their awareness of belonging to a master race they have committed unimaginable acts of cruelty and laid whole nations waste, they have fully enforced the maxim that might is always right. If soldiers in the First World War to some extent killed their uniformed opponents in self-defence, man against man, the soldier of this war, in the awareness and belief in his racial superiority and his people's claim to superiority, murdered not only the soldiers on the other side but also countless people of every age and sex and robbed them of their possessions. This spiritual attitude will not be removed without further ado by military defeat. It will go on affecting people for a long time to come, at least until they learn to see that it was not strategic errors that led to their Führer's defeat, that it was not war that was an error, but that the whole so-called movement was a crime in itself.'

'You speak of the coming defeat as if it is an inevitable fact, gentlemen,' Lassehn says. 'Don't get me wrong, I don't hope for victory, because I am clear that in the event of our victory we could develop into a dangerous race of human beasts of prey, but just wish to establish that . . .'

'Good God, Joachim,' Klose interrupts him almost angrily, 'the Soviets are at the Oder, ready for their last leap against Berlin, on the other side the British and the Americans have crossed the Siegfried Line and the Rhine, and even reached the Elbe in places, and you still have doubts?'

'I don't even consider the territorial element to be the crucial one,' Dr Böttcher says, commanding their attention with a gesture, 'what is of far greater moment is our absolute material inferiority. Are you not aware that the famous anti-tank grenade is only a surrogate because we lack heavy anti-tank guns? Are you not aware that the Luftwaffe is often unable to take off for want of fuel? Have you not seen that the American and British Air Forces can bomb any point they wish to hit unhindered and at any time of day or night? Are you not familiar with the fact that the very last reserves, half-children and elderly invalids, are being sent to the front as part of the Volkssturm? Do you not see these ridiculous anti-tank barriers in the streets of Berlin, which are supposed to stop the enemy, who have swept over the Atlantic Wall, the Siegfried Line and all the great rivers as if they were playthings?'

'He believes in the miracle weapon,' Klose says with a smile.

'You are not far off, Mr Klose,' says Lassehn. 'I don't believe in it, but I do fear that those people at the top are preparing something terrible. There are so many rumours about whether it is the V-3 or some kind of weapon of desperation, gas shells or bacteriological war . . .'

'Good God, Joachim, music student,' Klose laughs, 'you're going to fall for that one? Yes, if they had any of those things in the making . . .'

'You shouldn't laugh, Klose,' Wiegand says seriously. 'I admit quite openly that there are moments when Goebbels' and Fritzsche's stubborn confidence strangles me like a garrotte.'

Dr Böttcher nods.

'A few months ago Goebbels wrote the following sentences in *Reich*: "We recently saw modern German weapons at the sight of which our hearts stood still for a moment." That sentence has, I admit quite openly, pursued me into my dreams.'

'It isn't easy, I would even say that it is very difficult, to put oneself in your spiritual state,' Dr Böttcher says. 'You have neither a firm spiritual basis, nor are you rooted in another vision of life, you reject National Socialism, the state-prescribed and compulsorily enforced philosophy, but have no other, because you have never encountered one. Do you believe in God?'

Lassehn shrugs. 'I don't know, Doctor,' he replies, 'I really don't know. I'm not exactly religious, but I wasn't brought up as an atheist either. In my parents' house faith was to some extent a good, reliable middle-class prop that could be taken out of mothballs when necessary, it was part of the family reputation, it was faith without obligation and basically without content.'

'So you don't believe in God,' Dr Böttcher establishes matter-of-factly. 'Philosophical systems apart from the Rosenberg myth might be unfamiliar to you, yes, for heaven's sake, what then is the point of your life? Simply the fulfilment of material desires and nothing else?'

'No, Doctor,' Lassehn replies, 'I have seen the point of my life as lying in music.'

'The phrasing of your answer already shows that that is no longer the case, or at least that you have begun to have considerable doubts about the matter.' Dr Böttcher pushes his glasses a little way up his forehead with two fingers. 'Music,' he continues quietly, 'music is one of the most precious gifts of the human spirit, but it alone cannot be the content, the goal of life. Music alone is too little, it must be rooted in something. There is no thing in itself, my young friend.'

'For as long as I was able to practise it, music left me entirely fulfilled,' Lassehn disagrees. 'There was no room for anything else in me, and it is to music that I attribute the fact that I could not be infected by National Socialism. You can't convince me . . .'

'You are still very young, Mr Lassehn,' Dr Böttcher replies mildly, and rests his hand lightly on Lassehn's arm, 'and I do not want to use my age as argument in any way, but I am sure you will believe me when I claim to have more experience and greater insight into things. You say that your complete absorption in music left you able to resist the National Socialist infection. But I believe that you, entirely obsessed by music, would also have been able to resist any other influence. Did you in the past consider art as a thing in itself?'

Lassehn nods.

'However, Doctor, art is a task in its own right, it has no particular purpose.'

'Oho,' Dr Böttcher says emphatically, 'are artists not embedded in their environment, are they not shaped by their influences, are they not subject to universal laws? Yes or no?'

'Perhaps,' Lassehn admits reluctantly, 'but in their art they rise above the everyday.'

Dr Böttcher smiles indulgently. 'You think you are elevated above everyday life, Mr Lassehn, but you are every bit as much a part of it as everyone else. Art does not stand outside or above the laws of life, the artist's independence is a mere illusion, even art is not apolitical and must ossify without the load-bearing support of an ideal or a faith in the aesthetic. You will never be able to play Bach to perfection without the gift of feeling your way into his naïvely trusting thought, never will you be able to grasp Beethoven's sonatas in all their depth if you do not understand the revolutionary hothead, you will always remain a mere technician if your own attitude of mind and soul does not breathe life into his scores.'

Lassehn has lowered his head. 'Where is the way out, Doctor,' he asks quietly. 'You have shown me the spiritual limbo of my situation, and for years I have had the oppressive feeling that life was trickling through my fingers like sand. But you have not yet told me how I can get out of this situation. You and Mr Wiegand and Mr Klose have your political and philosophical foundation. Won't you let me share in that?'

'It isn't as easy as it was with the Nazis,' Dr Böttcher says with a smile, 'that you join the Party and get the philosophy free of charge with all its proscriptions, rules of behaviour, regulations of implementation et cetera delivered free to your door. Our philosophy, Mr Lassehn, needs to be worked upon, it cannot be learned, but I would be happy to engage with you, but above all I will entrust you to the protection of our friend Wiegand, who has more time than I do. I am a doctor and have a big cash practice, but Wiegand too lives underground.' Lassehn jerks around. 'You live underground?' he asks hastily. 'I'm going to have to do that too . . .'

Wiegand holds both hands up against the storm of questions that threatens to break over him. 'Slowly, slowly, Mr Lassehn,' he says solicitously. 'You doubtless want me to give you advice on how to do this. Well, the answer is in fact quite simple. There is no diagram to follow, you have to act as the situation requires, be fundamentally suspicious, always keep your eyes open and mind your tongue. When did you run away from the . . . ah, you don't want to hear that. Since when have you been on the road?'

Lassehn thinks for a moment. 'Since the . . .' – he throws his head back – 'since the twenty-second of January.'

'That's almost three months,' Wiegand says, 'so you can't say you're completely inexperienced.'

'Certainly,' Lassehn agrees, 'but during all that time I've been travelling, I roamed the country roads and above all the forests, I joined the columns of foreign workers and mingled among trails of refugees, but I don't know how things are in Berlin, because I haven't been here since September forty-three.'

'We recommend extreme caution, Mr Lassehn,' Wiegand says seriously, 'checks have been stepped up over the last few days. Haven't you read the latest proclamation, calling the population to be alert?'

Lassehn shakes his head.

'I'll leave you the *12-Uhr-Blatt*, you can read about it,' Wiegand continues. 'We've been talking about you, you can stay alternately with Klose and with me.'

'With you?' Lassehn asks, perplexed. 'But don't you live outside the law yourself?'

Wiegand smiles through pursed lips, 'Yes, but there are very different ways of living underground. You probably imagine that you're either constantly crouching in some dark cellar or creeping through the streets with your head lowered. No, my dear chap, you can't keep on doing that indefinitely, but quite apart from that it depends on why you are living underground. A wanted criminal is also living undergound in a sense, because he doesn't want to go to jail, a Jew hidden from the Gestapo is also living underground to escape transportation to the east and thus certain death, a soldier who has, like you, abandoned his unit because irresistible longing calls him home or because he can no longer bear the bloody madness of war is also living underground because he can't reverse the step he has taken without facing the rope.'

Wiegand pauses and looks quizzically at Dr Böttcher.

'So in which way are you living outside the law?' Lassehn asks.

Wiegand hesitates before answering.

'In a legal way,' Dr Böttcher laughs.

'You can tell the boy everything,' Klose says, 'he's genuine, I can tell, he'll keep his mouth shut, he's not going to rat on anyone.'

'Legally outside the law?' Lassehn says, amazed. 'I don't understand.'

'I could extend the paradox,' Dr Böttcher says. 'He lives outside the law in an illegally legal way, but of course you can't get your head around that. Wiegand is properly registered with the police, his papers are all in order, he even has an army documentation book that has passed through various checks, he even works for a major company, the Karlshorst locomotive depot. Everything in his life is in excellent order.'

'So where's the illegality?' Lassehn asks.

'Ah, you little lamb,' Klose laughs broadly. 'Friedrich Wiegand is only known as Friedrich Wiegand to us, for the world out there, for the police, for the military authorities and the other authorities his name is . . . what's your name, Fritz?'

Wiegand has not quite overcome the suspicion that is still alert within him, he smiles and nods slightly.

'Franz Adamek,' he says.

'I get it now,' Lassehn says, and smiles along with the other men. 'You live in legal illegality. But why do you live illegally, why do you live underground?'

'You will learn that too, Mr Lassehn,' Wiegand says with some reluctance. 'I used to be a trade union secretary, and played an outstanding part in a number of strikes, I believe I may say. When our beloved Party comrade, Prime Minister and master forester Hermann Göring set fire to the Reichstag on the twenty-eighth of Feburary 1933, I was arrested for the first time. And that happened again on different occasions: all political functionaries were taken into custody, as they so sweetly put it, that means they were put in a concentration camp. Then, when the greatest Führer of all time began riding eastward on the twenty-first of June, a similar action was due, but this time they didn't arrest me, because I had got wind of it and went underground, I became an illegal. Is that enough for you?'

Lassehn shakes his head. 'Not quite, Mr Wiegand,' he says. 'I have another question that doesn't strike me as unimportant. Why did you not go on living underground? Did you not put yourself in great danger when you went on living under a false name and probably at a different address?'

'You are completely right,' Wiegand replies, 'the danger of being recognized is ever present, and I also know that I'm on the Gestapo wanted list. But that does not deter me from carrying on with my illegal activity.'

Lassehn thinks for a moment. 'Illegal activity,' he says then, 'with the emphasis on activity, I see.'

'You've got it,' says Wiegand, and the smile on his lips is mirrored in his eyes for the first time. 'I said that you can live illegally for various reasons. I do it for political reasons, because even if I wasn't about to be put in a concentration camp, I could hardly have moved, as I was under constant surveillance, it wouldn't have been possible for me to meet my political friends, I couldn't have continued to . . .' He pauses and bites his lips. 'In short, every step I took was keenly observed.'

'And you continue to live undisturbed under your false name?' asks Lassehn.

'Insofar as one can live undisturbed these days,' Wiegand replies. 'I move lodgings from time to time, so that no one gets a glimpse of the way I live, no one has a chance to become familiar with my habits, and so that I don't become known in any particular area, which would only restrict my freedom of movement. The worst mistake of those who live illegally is that of lulling themselves into a sense of security, thinking that you're unobserved, or that you're not attracting attention. Experience has taught me that everyone observes everyone, that everybody suspects his neighbour, whether it's because he fears he's being spied upon or because he himself is a spy, quite apart from those creatures who, without actually being spies, like to make themselves tools of the Party, to demonstrate their loyalty and reliability. Today everyone wears a mask that he only takes off when he is alone, even in the smallest circle of the family people weigh their words very carefully if children are around. A great deal of misfortune has been created by children innocently repeating the thoughtless words of their parents. I know one case in which a whole group was arrested because an allusion by one of our comrades was passed on by his six-year-old son.'

'I suggest we bring this training course in the theory and

practice of the illegal life to an end,' Dr Böttcher says, and looks at his watch. 'It's nearly midnight.'

'Then it's time for me to go,' Wiegand says and gets to his feet. 'I have to be up at six tomorrow.'

Dr Böttcher rises from his chair as well. 'And I have a full day's work ahead of me tomorrow. Will you let us out by the front door, Klose?'

Klose nods. 'That would be better, then you'll be on the street in a moment, and won't need to pass through the courtyard.'

Lassehn is still sitting irresolutely in his chair.

'What about you?' Wiegand asks.

'The boy will stay here tonight,' Klose replies. 'And do you have anything particular planned for tomorrow?' he asks, turning towards Lassehn.

'I wanted to go to Charlottenburg tomorrow,' Lassehn replies hesitantly.

'That's right,' Klose says. 'You wanted to sound out your young wife. Well, you're right, maybe that'll be a nicer place for you to stay, with a bit of love and everything.'

Wiegand shakes hands with Lassehn. 'Goodbye, Mr Lassehn,' he says simply, 'will we meet again here at Klose's house?'

Lassehn shakes his hand firmly, he likes the question, it sounds like proof of trust. 'Yes, of course,' he replies eagerly.

Dr Böttcher holds his hand out to him as well. 'Goodbye, young man, stick with Klose and he'll see you right.'

Klose closes the door of the restaurant, he turns the key very slowly and, without a sound, carefully opens the door and looks out into the quiet, dark, nocturnal street. 'The air is pure,' he says, turning round. 'Goodbye.'

Dr Böttcher and Wiegand dart outside on tiptoe. In a few seconds they have disappeared into the darkness.

IV

On Kurfürstenstrasse there is a house that is clearly different from the other houses nearby. It is not a four-storey block of flats, but an imposing building, it does not have an ordinary front door, but a portal with mirrored doors framed by a pair of Ionic columns, it houses not flats but great halls. The building was once the seat and meeting point for many different masonic lodges. People came here to spend a few hours of unforced, relaxed conviviality. The slightly dusty, slightly ridiculous but, as might be imagined, extremely secretive rites of the fraternal lodges were celebrated here with dignified seriousness, and charity work was also practised on the quiet. But once these official ceremonies had been wound up, and the usual gregariousness began, with coffee parties followed by dancing or cabaret evenings with dilettante contributions by the members, or solid rounds of cards with quarter-pfennigs at stake, then anyone who had arrived here innocently and with no preconceptions would never have found himself thinking that the people here in front of him were members of the dangerous and nation-destroying masonic lodges. Instead he would have had the impression that a nice middle-class choral society or skittles club was enjoying a sociable evening together. He would have seen dignified old and elderly ladies sitting at tables, and heard modest gossip being talked, seen beautiful young women and pretty girls gliding across the parquet with nicely turned-out men and well-behaved boys, and last of all, in the side rooms, he would have seen the older generation of men sitting playing poker or skat, and here too, as elsewhere, delicate threads were being spun, matches made and deals struck. The people coming and going were absolutely harmless, their only spleen directed at the fact that they called themselves not a club or an association but a lodge or a fraternity.

When the incredible happened, and someone from the Viennese underworld was appointed Chancellor of the German Reich by the senile Field Marshal of the First World War, some things changed in this house on Kurfürstenstrasse. No more did delicate ladies' pumps or dignified patent-leather shoes slip across the parquet, they were replaced by the tread of solid knee-boots and crude military footwear, now sharp, clipped, peremptory, nasal voices rang out through the rooms, and where once consultations were held on the support of members in need, referred to as brothers and sisters, now a giant spider began to weave its ever-growing, deadly net. The portly chairmen of the association, known as incumbents of the chair, had disappeared, and now tall, slender men with hard, angular faces and cold eyes sat in the rooms, they wore grey uniforms, stars or bars and the two SS runes were affixed to their black collars and on the forearm of their jacket sleeve a black diamond.

The Reich Security Main Office of the SS had occupied the building on Kurfürstenstrasse. The intelligence service – Sicherheitsdienst, or SD: that was the harmless term for the powerful apparatus that had unlimited funds, was accountable to no one, was liable to no law and ignored every court, and whose sole task consisted in securing the power of the National Socialist Party with all means at its disposal, and ruthlessly destroying all opponents. From here the Sicherheitsdienst extended its feelers, vertically, horizontally, in every direction, into every dimension.

There was no area of life in Germany, and particularly in Berlin, that was not kept under surveillance from here. It was from here that the army of spies was dispatched and swept into every channel of public and private life, here that the flood of all reports, notifications and denunciations were collected. Nothing was too insignificant for the accountants and paymasters of death not to be registered here, noted in files or processed into files. From here the concentration camps were constantly fed with new human material, the law-breakers of the People's Court were constantly given fresh victims. In this building the dignity of man was an unknown concept, and the freedom of the individual was replaced by compulsion into the community. People were divided into those who were for and those who were against the National Socialist state; all of those who were not for it or who were merely suspected of not being so were seen without further ado as opponents and treated accordingly. All the procedures that would not have shamed the cruellest judge of the Inquisition were dreamed up here, with the deployment of the services of all available technical experts. It was here that technical monstrosities were conceived to make possible the destruction, both profitable and unbridled, of millions of creatures judged to be of inferior race, and hence unworthy of life.

Kurfürstenstrasse, formerly one of the many streets in the old West Berlin that had nothing special about it, became a household name. There are many streets in Berlin which have, sometimes wrongly, become household names. So, for example, Ritterstrasse became synonymous with import and export, Ackerstrasse for the lumpenproletariat, Tauentzienstrasse for the sophisticated demi-monde, Münzstrasse for the underworld, Lindenstrasse for social democracy and General Pape Strasse for round-ups and physical examinations. National Socialism alone retained the right to make street names synonymous with deadly terror, Prinz Albrecht Strasse, Burgstrasse, Kurfürstenstrasse, Grosse Hamburger Strasse – summonses from here spread fear and horror, because being accused generally meant being sentenced to detention in a concentration camp. Testimony was equivalent to an accusation of complicity.

In one of the rooms in the building on Kurfürstenstrasse there sits a big, stout man, he wears the uniform of the SD, four silver stars flash on his collar, the features of his broad, slightly bloated face are remarkably taut, his left cheek is split from mouth to ear by a great scar, his white-blond hair is slightly thin and carefully parted at the side, his pale-blue eyes have something of the colour of a chill winter sky.

This man, to whom all intelligence officers in the Berlin companies are accountable, is Sturmbannführer Wellenhöfer, director of the intelligence department of Berlin central office. He is feared because he has the reputation of being an ice-cold intellectual, a relentless sleuth, a ruthless go-getter. He is known to have access to no emotions, and to know no consideration. His smiling expression, which he displays both to his inferiors and to all visitors, and even to the unfortunate victims of his tracking dogs, is a calculated mask designed to lure others out of their reserve, and persuade them into confessing intimacies and indiscretions. Only someone who looked very closely at Wellenhöfer and gazed him attentively and fearlessly in the eye would recognize that his smile is not real, it is in a sense only applied to his face like a mask, through which only the eyes peer undisguised. Lips and eyes are not congruent in their expression, because while smiling wrinkles lie around the mouth and the teeth even flash now and then between the lips, there is a cold gleam in the eyes. Although Wellenhöfer demands short, clear, factual reports from his inferiors, tolerates no circumlocutions and abruptly dismisses any polite phrases, he lets the people who have the misfortune of being interrogated by him tell their stories at random, he never interrupts them, he even sometimes encourages them a little, but otherwise he maintains an agonizing silence. He knows that his victim will become more eloquent the longer he remains silent, and that the moment is eventually bound to come when the narrator will say things that he didn't want to say. When this moment has come, Wellenhöfer pounces like a hawk, plunges his claws into the flesh of his victim and doesn't let go until he has pulled out everything still hidden within. Wellenhöfer is a man who leaves nothing to chance. He runs all operations of any consequence himself, or at least directs them with precise instructions. He has an infallible eye for what is significant and would sooner forgive a big mistake committed in the heat of combat than an act of carelessness or failure to obey an order.

On the morning of 15 April 1945 he is sitting opposite a civilian. It is not difficult to tell from his posture that a massive burden lies on his bent back, he is sitting on the outer edge of a chair, his arms are pressed tightly against his sides and bent in front of his chest, his fingers play nervously with the buttons of his waistcoat, his head is drawn deeply back between his shoulders, his gaze is uncertain and leaps from point to point, but he assiduously avoids the eye of the Sturmbannführer.

This man is Reichsbahn Senior Inspector Deiters, the intelligence delegate of the Karlhorst depot of the Deutsche Reichsbahn. It isn't the first time that he's been in this room with Wellenhöfer. Since a series of malfunctions had occurred at the Karlhorst depot, which can only be put down to sabotage, he has been repeatedly ordered to Kurfürstenstrasse. Every time he has been asked by Wellenhöfer, in increasingly harsh tones, whether he had still not managed to catch the perpetrator or perpetrators, or at least prevent the continuation of the acts of sabotage through keen surveillance. Repeatedly Deiters had not only had to answer in the negative, but even to admit that here, once again, a locomotive has been rendered useless, that a coal crane has become inoperative, that the number of incidences of overheating is increasing all the time and that one day even the transfer table in the big workshop has been so badly damaged that a number of locomotives were blocked and unable to leave the depot. Once the perpetrator had almost been caught while planting explosives in the smokebox of one of the steam locomotives, but at the last moment he had been able to defend himself against his pursuer with a monkey wrench and had disappeared into the darkness of the great hall. Still, and this was the only positive aspect of the nocturnal scuffle, they had come a step further since they now knew that the perpetrator was without a doubt a German because he had, when he had been caught closing the smokebox, uttered a curse between his teeth, one that no foreigner could have used. But that had been all, in spite of the tightening network of surveillance and control they had not advanced a single step further. It was only clear that the perpetrator was to be sought among those employed in the factory, because apart from his precise knowledge of the work terrain with its locomotive halls, wagon sheds, boiler houses, crane plants, workshops, signal systems, water cranes, clinker pits, tracks and points, the form of the sabotage had also revealed an excellent knowledge of the subject, because with a minimum of effort a maximum of destruction had been achieved.

Even if the big depot was not brought to a standstill, since there were enough fallback procedures in place, considerable disruption still occurred.

The perpetrator, who must also have had access to the central locomotive control room, had preferred to render unusable precisely those trains intended to bring supplies to the eastern front.

Now Deiters is waiting for the results of the SD investigations, after further pursuance of the matter was taken out of his hands early in February. 'I called you here today, Mr Deiters,' Wellenhöfer begins the conversation, 'to tell you that we are almost certain that we have identified the perpetrator.'

Deiters sits bolt upright.

'Really?' he says, almost breathless. 'Congratulations!'

'Thank you,' Wellenhöfer says carelessly, looks at him with cool contempt and lights a cigarette.

'So who is it, if I may ask?' Deiters asks. 'You must tell me, after all, so that I can take my own measures.'

Wellenhöfer blows the smoke from his cigarette playfully in front of him. 'You have absolutely no measures to take, Mr Deiters,' he says in a cold and cutting voice. 'You will do what I tell you to do, no more and no less.'

'Of course,' Deiters says and smiles awkwardly, 'I was just saying.'

'Your opinion is absolutely undesirable to me, and of no interest whatsoever,' the Sturmbannführer continues in the same tone. 'I have called you here today, not to hear your unimportant opinions, but to give you orders and precise instructions.'

Deiters shrinks under his sharp, aggressive tone. 'Of course,' he says quietly. 'May I be permitted one question, Mr Sturmbannführer?'

'You may,' Wellenhöfer replies contemptuously. 'And I will draw your attention once again to the fact that Mr Sturmbannführer does not exist as a form of address. It always amazes me that as a Party member you are not more familiar with the customs of the SS. So what do you want to know?'

'Has the perpetrator already been arrested?' Deiters asks now.

'Arrested?' Wellenhöfer asks back. 'I fear that you have lost your mind!'

'I . . . I don't understand, you said . . .' Deiters stammers.

'I am well aware that you understand nothing,' Wellenhöfer continues. 'Arrested! Had he been arrested straight away, the proverbial bull would have entered the china shop. No, my dear fellow, you don't arrest a chap like your perpetrator, you let him run around freely for a while and observe him, because a customer like this always has an entourage. We will go in for the attack when we have the whole gang, not before.'

'But until that happens,' Deiters summons the courage to object, 'he can do all kinds of damage.'

'Do you take me for an idiot?' the Sturmbannführer roars, lowering his head like a bull and placing both hands firmly on the desk. 'Of course the man needs to leave the depot, he must be transferred to a position where he can't stir and agitate and do damage, where he is under constant supervision. That's why I summoned you here today, to . . .'

The phone rings and Wellenhöfer picks up the receiver. 'Siering is here? Tell him to come straight to me.'

He hangs up and turns again to Deiters. 'Untersturmführer Siering is the man who brought the matter to its temporarily successful conclusion. You will hear very shortly.'

Some minutes pass, Wellenhöfer appreciatively smokes a cigarette down to the butt, Deiters leans back in his chair, stares blankly in front of him, when there is a knock he gives a start.

A young man is standing at the door.

'Heil Hitler! Untersturmführer Siering reporting for duty!'

Wellenhöfer returns the greeting and points to the chair. 'This is Senior Inspector Deiters from the Karlhorst depot,' he says, casually waving in Deiters' general direction.

Siering nods to him cursorily and sits down.

'My suspicion has become a hundred-per-cent certainty, Sturmbannführer,' he says.

'Good, Siering!' Wellenhöfer nods with satisfaction. 'Thank

you, after definitive and successful completion of the investigations I will put you forward for promotion.'

'I am honoured,' Siering says.

Wellenhöfer waves his words away. 'It's fine,' he says. 'But now I would like to hear once again a complete report on the results of your work.'

'In the presence of this gentleman?' Siering asks, nodding towards Deiters.

'It doesn't matter,' Wellenhöfer replies, 'we need to bring him into our confidence anyway, and your report will give him a rough idea of how we are supposed to work in such cases. So fire away.'

Siering leans back and folds his arms over his chest. 'The first thing to do was to mark out the circle of suspects, and draw that circle tighter and tighter,' he begins. 'At first I established the times when the different acts of sabotage were committed, and that produced a certain result: all acts of sabotage were performed in the shift from ten in the morning until six in the evening. Only manual workers, clerks and officials who worked during that period were taken into consideration, and with the exception of some office workers who only work by day, that was all of them.'

'So not all of them, in fact,' Deiters suggests, 'I'm sure you won't have suspected the executive staff.'

Siering swings round and looks at Deiters as if noticing his presence for the first time.

'Why not?' he asks. 'Fundamentally everyone is a suspect, even you, Senior Inspector.'

'But please . . .' Deiters says defensively.

'Don't interrupt me,' Siering says roughly, 'I don't want to talk to you about my working method, and I need only refer you to the twentieth of July.' He turns his back on Deiters again, and addresses the Sturmbannführer. 'So I shall continue. The dates of the acts of sabotage already considerably reduced this great circle of suspects, because the dates yielded the following: the acts of sabotage were only carried out at night, and at very regular intervals of about three weeks, that is, they accumulated in one week, then there was a pause of fourteen days in which everything continued in an orderly fashion, and then they began again, stopping after a week, again for fourteen days. It could not be a coincidence. The solution to the apparent mystery presented itself to me when I got hold of the duty rosters of the Karlhorst depot. The circle in which the perpetrator was to be sought became considerably smaller, by precisely two-thirds.'

'Excellent!' Deiters cannot help interjecting.

'Yes, excellent,' Wellenhöfer says sarcastically. 'It never occurred to you, you dyed-in-the-wool expert. Continue, Siering.'

'I had a fixed circle of people that I now had to deal with,' Siering goes on. The foreigners were ruled out, as the perpetrator, on the occasion when he had almost been caught, was said to have cursed in fluent German. I must say quite openly that this information did not seem to me to be nearly as valuable as the Senior Inspector likes to claim. What convinced me much more firmly that the perpetrator is a German was the thorough, systematic nature of his work, a quality which I would hesitate to attribute to the Belgians, Dutchmen, Serbs, Italians and whoever else is swarming around in the depot. If the circle of suspects had also become considerably smaller, it was still a large number of people, forty-seven in all. An unremarkable confrontation between the train driver who had scuffled with the saboteur and these forty-seven people led to nothing. Further investigation and detailed interrogations removed several more people from consideration. I might mention here only the two workers involved in de-clinkering the locomotives, who were kept busy all night and were able to keep an eye on one another, and the stoker who fills the stoves in the boiler room, the train driver and the stoker of the Teckel, the depot locomotive, who also keep checks on each other, and I also dismissed from the circle of suspects a number of officials who had already retired but volunteered themselves, and some doubtless dependable Party members. Through the application of this deductive method the number of suspects had dropped to eighteen, but after that it remained constant. So I had no other option but to subject these eighteen people to precise investigation. I looked into their domestic circumstances, I talked to their neighbours and concierges, and even made myself directly known to them. So suspicion was in the end narrowed down to a few people, but suspicion is not proof, and if I had simply issued a warrant against the six people whom I considered to be likely suspects, perhaps the actual perpetrator would have been among them, but we would not have tracked down the rest of the gang to which he doubtless belonged. I will not trouble you, Sturmbannführer, by listing every individual clue relating to one individual or another, I shall only say that those six people were all loners who had no family and came from elsewhere, some of them from territories currently inaccessible to us. The police registration cards were entirely blank and offered no clues, except that I was struck by the fact that one of them had moved house unusually often. To avoid being over-hasty and drawing false conclusions, I investigated all seven of his previous addresses and discovered that his frequent change of residence did not occur because he had been bombed out, for example, as one might have assumed, and neither was he dismissed by his landlord in six of those cases, but he gave up the room voluntarily. He always gave a good impression, he was described as a quiet man who kept himself to himself, who never received visits of any kind, and people were extremely surprised when he gave up his room one day for no reason. A few days' observation produced no results, and the regular evening air-raid warnings kept thwarting my plans. I'm not mentioning the elements of suspicion against the other five people, I just wish to show how and why I . . . happened upon this particular person.

'When I had access to the personnel files of these six individuals again yesterday afternoon, and flicked through them again and again, reading everything through very carefully, perhaps to extract a clue from some seemingly trivial detail, I read that for this . . . for this particular man for the period between the sixteenth of January and the seventh of February a sick note had been given, by one Dr Walter Böttcher, of 14 Frankfurter Allee, diagnosis: sepsis. This Dr Böttcher is not unknown to us, but we have had nothing to reproach him with for years, the fact that our man had consulted him could be entirely a matter of chance, because he lives near Dr Böttcher, on Lebuser Strasse. On the other hand, of course, one might also argue that the man in question lives near Dr Böttcher deliberately, probably seeing him as a kindred spirit. Now, one likelihood is worth as much as another.' Siering breaks off, he has talked himself into a state of excitement, his cheeks are bright red and his eyes have the look of a hunting hound, he runs the fingers of his right hand between the collar of his uniform and his neck as if his collar is suddenly too tight.

'You tell a good story,' Wellenhöfer says benevolently, nodding to his inferior. 'You crank things up like a thriller writer.'

Deiters confirms his words with a vigorous nod of the head. He too is in a state of suspense.

'I couldn't stop thinking about the sick note,' Siering continues at last, 'I read it again and again, and then it came to me in a flash, I took out my notebook and ran through the dates of the acts of sabotage, and then I had it: in the period between the sixteenth of January and the seventh of February there was a week with the shift in question, the one from the twenty-first until the twenty-seventh of January, and during that shift, for the first time, nothing had happened since the start of the acts of sabotage. Now it was clear!' Siering exhales as if freed from a heavy burden. 'But I wanted to be completely sure,' he continues hastily. 'This morning, when the landlady of the man in question had gone out, I gained access to the flat and carried out a search of his room. I must say: the man is entirely neutral, there was not a single belonging that would allow one to draw conclusions about his character, not a single monogrammed piece of underwear, no picture of family members, absolutely nothing, but it was precisely that neutrality that put the seal on my suspicion: I believe the man is an illegal.'

'And what is the man's name?' Wellenhöfer asks.

'Franz Adamek,' Siering replies.

'Good heavens,' Deiters exclaims. 'Adamek? Unbelievable, a quiet, thoughtful man, a good worker, unbelievable!'

Wellenhöfer completely ignores his remark. 'Franz Adamek?' he says. 'Never heard of him. Does he have any kind of record?'

'No,' Siering replies, 'I've looked through all the wanted lists, but the name doesn't appear anywhere. Of course, it isn't necessarily his real name.'

'That's true!' Wellenhöfer agrees. 'If your suspicion is correct, and the man is living outside the law, then of course he will be doing so under a false name.'

'I am confident that I will be able to draw his real name out of him,' Siering says. 'We could . . .'

Wellenhöfer raises his hand. 'Just one moment, Siering,' he says quickly. 'Before we go on discussing the matter, I would like to dismiss Mr Deiters.' He turns to the Senior Inspector. 'Listen very carefully to what I am about to say to you, Mr Deiters, you must give me your personal assurance that my instructions are carried out to the letter. Adamek must be transferred immediately, you will have him informed of his transfer by a random third party, because you already know too much to be able to tell him without giving the game away. I do not believe you have the requisite acting talent.'

'As you wish,' Deiters says meekly. 'I will transfer him to the boiler room, as he is constantly . . .'

'You have no decisions to make in this matter,' Wellenhöfer cuts him off abruptly. 'Adamek will no longer be doing shift work, you will put him in a column that always works outside, under a very strict and dependable foreman who won't take his eyes off him. Do you understand me?'

'Yes, sir,' Deiters replies. 'I will see to it.'

'Please do!' says Wellenhöfer, the harsh tone of his voice contrasting with his words, which are an order rather than a request. 'And now you will leave us on our own.'

Deiters considers himself dismissed, he rises to his feet, bows to Wellenhöfer and Siering and raises his hand in the Hitler salute, then leaves the room.

Wellenhöfer looks after him darkly. 'Inadequate excuse for a human being,' he says irritably. 'You have to chew their food for them if you want anything to happen.' His face brightens when he looks at Siering. 'You will continue to keep Adamek under supervision, I'll give you two good people to do that. I want to learn who

Adamek keeps company with. You have full freedom to do as you please, Siering. Your hands will not be tied. You know what that means?'

'Of course, Sturmbannführer,' Siering says with a nod, and rummages in his jacket pocket. 'Here is a picture of Adamek, I took it from the personnel files of the Karlhorst depot.'

'Let me see,' says Wellenhöfer, and takes the photograph. He frowns and holds the picture away from him. 'I know that face,' he says slowly, 'I'm sure I know it. But where from?'

'It's not the sort of face you'd forget,' Siering says.

'That's why,' Wellenhöfer observes thoughtfully. 'Damn it, where do I know this rogue from?'

He sits there motionless for several seconds, blinking uneasily.

Siering sits quite still, reluctant to disturb the concentration of a superior officer.

Then Wellenhöfer brings his fist down on the table with a thump. 'Now I know,' he says loudly. 'When I was in charge of a unit in Sachsenhausen I ran across this piece of filth. I can't remember his name right now, but we'll have it very soon.' He lifts the receiver and dials a number. 'Archive?' he says into the phone. 'Wellenhöfer here. I need the list of prisoners in Sachsenhausen between 1934 and 1936.'

He hangs up again. 'I remember him very clearly, he was some kind of trade unionist, one of the radicals,' he says to Siering with a certain excitement in his voice, the thrill of the passionate huntsman who has good lighting conditions, and who might at any moment see a rare deer walking into his sights. 'This man Adamek, or whatever his name is, was one of those characters who can't be defeated however hard you thrash them, who have such a damned superior expression on their mugs that my blood boiled at the sight of them and I thrashed them at every opportunity. And in spite of everything I could never knock that sense of superiority out of the bastards.'

'I'm familiar with that, Sturmbannführer,' Siering agrees. 'There's something about those swine that we can't get at, and the devil knows what it is and what it's about. In Dachau I once had a vicar who had criticized the Führer from the pulpit, I stood in front of him and said to him, "Listen, vicar! Say quite loudly and clearly, 'Heil Hitler!'" The vicar looked straight at me with big eyes, then said loudly and clearly: "Praise be to Jesus Christ!" Wait, you piece of filth, I thought, you're going to learn this lesson, and I lashed him across the face with my riding crop, leaving stripes of red. "You are to say 'Heil Hitler'", I roared at him. This vicar stood there motionless, only his fat cheeks wobbled up and down, and he didn't even wipe the blood from his eyes. "Praise be to Jesus Christ!" he repeated loudly and clearly. Then I hit him again, and issued the order again, and he answered the same way again, and that happened at least twenty times, Heil Hitler and Praise be to Jesus Christ, in between blows to the face, until the bastard finally toppled over and kicked the bucket, but while he was giving up his vicarish ghost he babbled, "Praise be to Jesus Christ!" again. I must say quite honestly that I admired the chap's attitude, but that was exactly what goaded me and made my fury all the greater.'

Wellenhöfer nods. 'Adamek was exactly that kind of guy,' he says, 'I made him clean out the latrines with his hands, he had to scour the SS men's quarters with a handkerchief-sized cleaning cloth until it shone, but I couldn't get that look of superiority out of his face. That chap's face irritated me so much that in the end I tied him to the vaulting horse with my own bare hands and gave him twenty-five great, loud blows, but the swine didn't even shout. Then he fainted, and when a cold shower had put him back on his feet he looked at me as if to say: you can destroy my body, but not my mind. I would have beaten him to death next time, I'm sure of it, but I was transferred to Buchenwald, which was just being set up at the time. Damn it all, I remember the fellow, it's just his name . . . But we'll have that very shortly, the list is on its way.'

There is a knock at the door, an SS man comes in, salutes, hands over a list and disappears.

Wellenhöfer opens the list and begins to read. It's very quiet in the room, the only sounds Wellenhöfer's quick breathing and the rustle of paper. Siering sits there excitedly and watches Wellenhöfer's finger wandering from line to line. Then the silence is suddenly broken.

Wellenhöfer throws the list on the table, jumps to his feet and claps his Untersturmführer heartily on the shoulder.

'You've landed a big one, Siering,' he says. 'What do we care about the little saboteur at Karlshorst, this Franz Adamek has been a wanted man since 1941, he was also supposed to have been involved in the twentieth of July.'

'So who is he really?' Siering asks excitedly.

'The bastard's name is Friedrich Wiegand!', Wellenhöfer replies triumphantly.

15 April, 10.00 a.m.

The Berlin Stadtbahn is an eleven-kilometre viaduct supported by countless arches; it runs through the heart of the city from east to west in a four-lane thoroughfare. The houses and factories huddle up to it, their rough, soot-blackened firewalls are a huge balustrade with gaps built in at Jannowitz Bridge, Alexanderplatz, the Stock Exchange, Friedrichstrasse Station, the Zoological Garden and Savignyplatz, through which the business of the city crashes in a great wave against the viaduct. Only between the stations of Tiergarten and Bellevue, crossing the Charlottenburger Chaussee known as the east-west axis, the fleeting glance takes in more significant details, the Tiergarten, the Brandenburg Gate, the Victory Column, Charlottenburg Bridge, before the dark chasm of the firewalls closes over it again.

Lassehn has boarded the S-Bahn at Silesian Station for Charlottenburg.

He is paralysed with shock as he looks at the disfigured face of the city and sees smoke-blackened walls, blind window sockets, twisted iron joists, charred wood, mountains of rubble, dangling power lines, gaping streets.

The Stadtbahn is a ghost train, Berlin has become an inhabited Pompeii, a city which has already rotted away in many places, and in others is suppurating from freshly opened wounds.

The two angular, bulky high-rise blocks close to the entrance of Alexanderplatz Station have remained strangely unchanged, their white towers, once showy and gleaming with glass and concrete and snow-white plaster, now have a merely shabby elegance made of cardboard, wood and dirty grey concrete. Just past the exit of the station a stretch of almost complete destruction begins, in fact extending all the way to Charlottenburg. Lassehn looks into grey, dark chasms, closed off by fallen walls, and the car parks of long rows of wrecked cars, formerly brightly lit streets with balconies on which geraniums blossomed, with neon signs and cars gliding over smooth, mirrored asphalt. But behind Lehrter Station there begins the hideous wasteland of the former Hansa district. It was destroyed completely in one night, going up in a single, huge con-flagration beneath an overcast, rainy sky.

Lassehn is stunned.

In those thirty minutes that the journey takes from Silesian Sta-tion to Charlottenburg, he becomes aware for the first time that this city is his home, and he has not previously seen it as anything remarkable, he has taken its gifts for granted, as if things could not be otherwise. Now he understands that much is irrevocably lost, and since the end of the war is not in sight, still more will fall into rubble and ashes.

One question burns in him, and he cannot find the answer. What is it that enables people to tolerate and endure such an exist-ence, which they euphemistically call life? Is it really a belief in a big idea, divine providence, that enables them to do so? Or is it only the iron compulsion that ruthlessly crushes those who do not comply? Or merely the small chance of saving one's own small self from the general chaos?

Lassehn studies the faces of his fellow passengers. They are slack, weary faces which reflect only hopelessness and resignation, but there are also hard, grim faces, with wrinkles and harsh edges that allow no easy smile. He remembers an article that he read recently in the newspaper, which he picked up by chance, he looks in the faces once more and takes the newspaper from his coat pocket, his eyes slide over the lines. Yes, there it is:

We have become a people on the defensive. We work, we work and fight, wander and trek, suffer and endure, and we do so with mute dignity. No weakness may befall us, not for a second may we waver. We must remain firmly on our feet, even if we bleed from a thousand tears and scratches and the body of our people is riven with countless wounds. Later they will be our scars of honour. Then the nation will bear for all time the face of the warrior.

The man who wrote that is not some hack, not some propaganda unit reporter, giving vent to his inner warrior poet, no, the article is by no less a figure than Dr Joseph Goebbels and published on 11 February 1945 in the *Reich* under the headline 'A People on the Defensive'.

Lassehn keeps looking attentively at the faces, but he sees nothing there of mute dignity, of the honour of being able to endure the wounds of war and bear its scars, the pride of belonging to a nation of warriors and not one of well-fed, peaceful civilians. He can read nothing in those faces but despair and stubborn defiance, a reluctant flinching from fate, whose shadow is already falling upon them, a wrangling with destiny that refuses to accept defeat. Admittedly they had not at first agreed with the war, they did what they saw as their duty, but their enthusiasm had not been fired. The army columns did not march singing as they did in 1914, accompanied by music and decked with flowers, through the streets to the railway stations, the women and girls did not cheer them as they had back then, and no flags fluttered in the windows. It was still a war that began with an invasion and at first found little resonance on the ground. After the victory over Poland, however, people began to come to terms with the fact of war, and what the authorities had not succeeded in doing, could not have succeeded in doing at the beginning of the war (because everything had been done secretly and in a clandestine fashion, and because even with the most elegant distortion of the facts it could not be turned into a war of self-defence), namely the creation of consensus and a certain amount of enthusiasm, did occur when Denmark, Norway, Holland, Belgium, France, Yugoslavia and Greece fell, military and political success seemed to prove the leaders of the Reich right, and also the rich bounty flowed in from the conquered nations (after the seductive bubble of the pre-war years had left no doubt about the rightness of the National Socialist management of the economy), then people came to agree entirely with the war, it was their cause, they suddenly believed in themselves, and it also seemed wise for them to stick with the winning side.

When the German Army advanced as far as Moscow, the whole of Europe seemed to have been brought low and Great Britain was seen as a remote island destined for oblivion, then even the last doubters joined in, then the crowd of the just had hopelessly turned into the minority. The great mass of the people stuck with the victors, a gigantic propaganda machine using all the means of lying and mass psychology had left them numbed and immune to outside influences, by making common cause with a criminal gang they had become chained to it for good or ill, chained to it so tightly that its fall must become their fall, retaliation against one was retaliation against both, so that all decisions taken against them were seen not as decisions but as side-effects or the result of the fortunes of war, and finally, when the setbacks started coming thick and fast, they were seen as inescapable fate. For that reason those people also endured all the setbacks which began with the winter battle outside Moscow, continued via Stalingrad, El Alamein and the elimination of the U-Boat force, culminated in the landings in Italy and France, the loss of the Romanian oilfields and the advances on Warsaw, Aachen and Budapest, and finally led to the Elbe and the Oder and to massive daily air raids on the Reich.

That is the situation of these April days. Even though all predictions have been proved false, hopes repeatedly dashed in spite of all reassurances to the contrary, even though the material superiority of the enemy is in fact all too apparent to be ignored, and their strategy is putting ever-greater pressure on the Reich with deadly certainty, the great mass of the people still refuse to believe in defeat and downfall. Every optimistic word from Goebbels in the *Reich*, every rumour inspired from above and whispered with significant expressions is greedily received, even now when, at the terminus points of the suburban railways in Erkner, Strausberg and Königs Wusterhausen, with a half-way decent wind they can hear the thunder of cannon at the eastern front. What is this almost grotesque faith based on? Is it only rooted in fear of Bolshevism and the Western democracies?

Again and again Lassehn studies the faces around him, but he can read nothing in them, the faces are not only hard, they are frozen.

In Charlottenburg Lassehn leaves the S-Bahn. The station is nothing but a wreck, the roof is covered over and the twisted joists stretch into the air, the structures of the platforms are shattered, the waiting rooms burnt out and destroyed, the whole enterprise is a makeshift operation, and around the station stands a horrific backdrop of ruined houses.

Lassehn crosses Stuttgarter Platz, from which all life seems to have fled, and walks dazedly into Kaiser-Friedrich-Strasse. Scruffy children, squealing wildly, climb over the piles of rubble and into the bomb craters, as nimble as mountain goats on broken walls and barricades, familiar with the colours of the dead city, charcoal-black, rust-red, heedless of the fact that tears and blood, curses and prayers hang over these fields of ruins. War, which once we brought to foreign lands, he thinks, has returned to us like a boomerang and retaliated, it is making us pay for Warsaw, Rotterdam and Coventry. The terrible logic of a vengeful justice!

Then he stops in front of a house. Was this not where his wife lived? The white sign with the number has been hit by a ricochet and is now indecipherable, and the houses nearby have been destroyed. Lassehn is still unsure. Was there a bookshop in the building? He can't remember, he only lived here for a week, after all, at last he decides to go in. When he tries to open the door and puts his hand on the handle, it is pushed back up from inside and thrown violently open. Lassehn quickly steps back.

A lady comes out of the door, she gives Lassehn a fleeting glance and mumbles an apology, then she walks past him. Lassehn stands there paralysed, as if an electric shock has run through him. Was that not Irmgard, his wife? He has to summon all his strength to turn his head and watch after the lady. The figure seems familiar to him, but there are tens of thousands of women and girls in Berlin who look like that. And the way she walks? No, Lassehn doesn't know how she walks, he has only ever walked beside his wife, there has never been an occasion when she walked in front of him, there is not a single detail that has stayed clearly in his memory. Were Lassehn challenged to confirm that the lady he met on 14 April 1945 at 11 o'clock in the morning in the doorway of number 46 Kaiser-Friedrich-Strasse was his wife, he would be unable to deliver such an oath. She does bear a certain resemblance to the image he has vaguely preserved in his head, but no more than that. Does the cause lie in his deficient memory, or has his wife changed so much that he can no longer establish the identity between memory and reality?

Lassehn stirs himself at last and enters the dark hallway into which not a shimmer of light falls, the front window is boarded up and the light switch doesn't work, he feels his way towards a door, through the frosted glass of which a faint beam of light penetrates the darkness of the hallway, and knocks. It happens to be the concierge's lodge.

A small, squat woman opens the door. 'Yes, what it is?' she asks, holding the handle in her hand and apparently determined to get rid of the visitor as quickly as possible.

'Excuse me,' Lassehn says, 'does Mrs Lassehn still live in this house?'

'What is her name?' the concierge asks back.

'Lassehn,' says Lassehn.

'Doesn't live here,' says the woman.

Lassehn smiles thoughtfully. 'If she no longer lives here,' he says in a patient voice, 'then she used to live here, at least until September 1943.'

'No, no, young man,' the woman says resolutely, 'there you're absolutely wrong, I've been the concierge here for twenty years, I know my trade. What was the name? Spell it for me again.'

'Lassehn,' Lassehn replies. 'Ell ay ess ess ee aitch en.'

'Never heard of her,' the woman says stoutly, 'certainly never lived here.'

'But my dear Mrs . . .' Lassehn looks at the sign on the door, caught by a beam of light from the window – 'my dear Mrs

Buschkamp, Mrs Lassehn definitely did live here, or may live here still. I myself . . .' he pauses, something holds his tongue, warning him not to give up his anonymity.

'You yourself done what?' the woman asks quickly.

'I once visited her here myself,' Lassehn finishes his sentence. 'But I don't remember . . .'

Mrs Buschkamp looks at him pointedly. 'How old is this Mrs Lassehn of yours?'

'Twenty-three,' Lassehn replies.

'Ain't no twenty-three-year-old woman here,' Mrs Buschkamp says firmly. 'Whose flat's she supposed to have lived in anyway?'

'At the front of the building,' Lassehn says, 'with her aunt, a woman . . . something to do with Meyer.'

Mrs Buschkamp lets go of the handle and opens the door a little more.

'Step in, young man,' she says amiably. 'This one's interesting. Here's a chair.' She goes on. 'You don't look as if you're all that keen on standing up.'

Lassehn thanks her and slumps heavily on the chair.

'Now let's think about the case of Mrs Lassehn with the aunt called Meyer,' Mrs Buschkamp says convivially, 'I'm interested in this one, because I know everyone. Hardly anyone I don't know goes in or out of here. But Lassehn? No such person, young man, never heard of her, not in my house.'

'But I know for certain . . .' Lassehn objects. 'Her first name is Irmgard.'

'Irmgard?' Mrs Buschkamp says thoughtfully. 'Good heavens,' she shrieks after a moment, and laughs loudly. 'You mean Irma Niedermeyer, of course, I do know her, she's out right now. You must have bumped into her a minute ago. She just left!'

Lassehn is paralysed, he feels as if an iron hand is crushing his chest. So the lady he bumped into a few minutes before at the front door was his wife! She didn't recognize him! She stood in front of him for a heartbeat, murmured a fleeting apology, she glanced at him and didn't recognize him, she showed not the tiniest spark of recognition. Lassehn conceals his bewilderment behind a smile of agreement.

'Yes,' he says, and tries to give his voice an indifferent tone. 'Irmgard Lassehn, née Niedermeyer, that's the lady.'

'Irmgard Lassehn, née Niedermeyer?' Mrs Buschkamp repeats in astonishment. 'Blimmin' heck, that's true,' she adds, and smacks her forehead with the flat of her hand, 'Irma got married, it was sometime in the middle of 1943, I completely forgot about it. And no wonder . . .'

'What is no wonder?' Lassehn asks.

'Well, God knows, it's not really a marriage,' Mrs Buschkamp says contemptuously, and shakes her head energetically. 'A soldier goes on leave, smiles at a girl and takes her to bed and they get married so the child has a name.'

'A child?' Lassehn asks.

'No, I was just saying,' says Mrs Buschkamp, 'it's just a manner of speech. It's a very modern sort of marriage, on the quick, not binding, change permitted, they know nothing about each other, but get married they do, off they go, the Führer needs his soldiers. Oh mighty God, how great is your animal kingdom, there's no shortage of idiots.'

'Forgive me . . .' Lassehn protests, feeling wounded. He is about to explain to this kind woman the reasons for his marriage, but then he quickly thinks again. He forgot for a few moments that he is a deserter, that he mustn't come out of the shadows.

'Have I stepped on your toes?' Mrs Buschkamp asks and looks carefully at Lassehn. 'Who are you anyway, young man?'

'My name is Kempner,' Lassehn replies, 'I'm a friend of Mr Lassehn, just an acquaintance, in fact, I wanted to see . . .'

'Just a moment,' Mrs Buschkamp interrupts him, 'the music's gone quiet again.' She listens in to the next room. 'There'll be an air-raid announcement in a minute. Such rubbish, you can't get anything done any more . . . "Attention, attention, this is an air-raid announcement. Large squadron of enemy aeroplanes approaching over the North Sea towards Schleswig-Holstein. I repeat . . ."'

'Well, then we'd better get everything ready,' Mrs Buschkamp says, and looks at the street, 'the bunker unit is already on the way.'

Lassehn is hurt, he remembers what Klose said, about public shelters being subject to keen checks. He still has his *Soldbuch*, but no leave pass, and he isn't wearing a uniform, any Wehrmacht or Gestapo patrol could mean the end of him. 'Where can you take shelter when there's a warning?' he asks.

'At the station there's a public air-raid shelter, but they only let you in with a ticket,' Mrs Buschkamp says, 'but there's another one further over by Pestalozzistrasse. It's not that far.'

'Where do *you* go?' asks Lassehn.

'I'm staying here in my house,' Mrs Buschkamp answers proudly, 'the Buschkamps don't leave their house alone with all those old people in it. Fine thing that would be.'

Lassehn listens with an interested expression, but it has nothing to do with him. The situation he has got himself into by denying himself and the fact that his wife walked past him as if he were a stranger irritated him, it may be his only opportunity to find out something from an uninvolved third party about his wife, and about himself. 'To come back to the question, Mrs Buschkamp,' he begins again, 'a moment ago you suggested that Mrs Lassehn had only known her husband for a short time . . .'

'Yes, that's exactly how it was,' the concierge replies. 'You must forgive me if I tidy up a bit while we're talking, but I need to have everything ready when the thing goes off.'

'Have you known Mrs Lassehn for a long time?'

'A long time? Depends what you mean, since she's been living here in the house, about six or seven years,' Mrs Buschkamp replies. 'She's a pretty girl, very decent, but otherwise . . .' She shakes her head as she takes a coat out of the cupboard and hangs it on a hook ready to hand.

'What do you mean?' Lassehn asks excitedly.

Mrs Buschkamp turns round all of a sudden. 'Are you interrogating me, young man?'

Lassehn gives a forced laugh. 'Not in the slightest, my dear Mrs Buschkamp,' he assures her, 'I'm just asking, with no particular intent.'

Mrs Buschkamp narrows her eyes. 'With no particular intent?', she asks incredulously. 'Anyone who believes that needs their head examining. I can vouch for what I say, I don't weigh my words, but I also want to know who's asking me questions. Old Buschkamp isn't stupid, my dear boy, you've got to get up a bit earlier if you want to pull a fast one on me.'

'I've told you before, my name is Kempner,' Lassehn replies, 'I'm a distant acquaintance of Lassehn. And since I was in the area . . .'

'Whether you want to tell me your name is Kempner or Schulze or Müller or whatever,' the old woman says firmly, 'I couldn't care less, the name doesn't mean anything. You are expressing yourself very vaguely, young man. Are you perhaps from some kind of information office?'

The suspicion is so surprising that Lassehn is at first completely startled, but then he laughs with relief. 'Information office?', he says with a smile. 'Not at all, it's just personal interest . . .' Mrs Buschkamp takes a step towards Lassehn and looks at him steadily. 'First Lassehn is a friend of yours, then he's a fleeting acquaintance, and now it's personal interest,' she says, and shakes her head vigorously, 'it doesn't add up. Or do you fancy Irma?'

Lassehn holds up his hands. 'You're mistaken, Mrs Buschkamp.'

Mrs Buschkamp winks mischievously. 'Well, well, well, young man,' she says cheerfully. 'Well, it's none of my business, but you wouldn't have a chance with her.'

Lassehn has to get a grip on himself to keep from sighing with relief. 'So is she faithful to her husband?' he asks.

Mrs Buschkamp shrugs. 'Well now,' she replies. 'You've misunderstood me, I meant *you* wouldn't have a chance with her.'

'Why not?' Lassehn asks sadly.

'You'd need to look different,' Mrs Buschkamp says, 'you'd need to look dashing, like a cavalier from a fashion rag, or even better in an officer's uniform. Irma is very fussy! She . . . oh, damn it, the music has gone again.'

The music from the speaker has faded, after a few seconds of frightened silence, in which all that can be heard is the monotonous hum of the electricity, the announcer speaks. 'Attention,

attention, this is an air-raid warning. The bomber squadron announced as approaching Schleswig-Holstein is flying towards north-west Germany. Further bomber squadrons approaching Lower Austria. I repeat . . .'

Mrs Buschkamp puts a shoulder bag, a gas mask and a steel helmet at the ready. 'This is it,' she says seriously. 'You should get out of here, Mr Kempner, and make sure you're home when the siren sounds. Where do you live?'

'By Silesian Station,' Lassehn replies. 'Will I make it?'

'If you're lucky,' Mrs Buschkamp says. 'But didn't you want to pay a visit to the Niedermeyers? It doesn't make much difference whose cellar you're hiding in.'

'If Mrs Lassehn has gone out . . .' Lassehn objects.

'Look at this one,' Mrs Buschkamp says and props her hands on her hips. 'I said you fancied that Irma. Don't you want to ask about him?'

'Yes, of course, where . . . where is Mr Lassehn?' Lassehn asks, stammering.

Mrs Buschkamp chuckles. It sounds like the cry of a jay.

'Funny that you've only just thought of asking *that* question. So you don't know? That . . . I keep forgetting his name . . . so Irma's husband is a soldier, he was in hospital somewhere in Upper Silesia, God knows where he's crawling about these days, Irma hasn't had a letter from him for a few months.'

'When was Mr Lassehn last on leave?' Lassehn asks. He would like to ask more penetrating questions, but he doesn't have the courage, he fears this feisty woman's keen eyes and sharp tongue.

'On leave? I'll give you on leave!', says Mrs Buschkamp. 'Not at all, the young bridegroom slept at his young wife's place for eight days and since then not a peep. That's a marriage for you! They've barely sniffed each other and already they're getting married, I call that a dog's wedding. So, was that the siren going off? No, it was just a tram, we're already half crazy, we give a start every time there's a noise.'

Lassehn nods a few times. He doesn't know how to ask the questions that are trying to spill out of him without arousing suspicion.

'He was a nice young man, too, Irma's husband was, I only saw him two or three times,' Mrs Buschkamp continues, 'pretty fellow, a bit soft-looking, not really right for Irma.'

'Really?' Lassehn objects. He is filled with a strange tension, as if through the voice of this down-to-earth woman a neutral judge were delivering his verdict.

'I was surprised at the time,' Mrs Buschkamp goes on, 'when Irma turned up with that boy. Don't get me wrong, Mr Kempner, I thought the young man was very nice, but he wasn't a match for Irma, he was actually too good for her.'

'In what way?' Lassehn asks, confused. 'I had a sense that . . .'

'Oh nonsense,' Mrs Buschkamp interrupts. 'You're practically a boy yourself, what do you know about such things? You see, Irma is a confident girl, she knows exactly what she wants, she needs a man who's at least ten years older than she is who can show her how to do things, you understand, in *every* respect. And this . . . Now, what's his name again . . .'

'Lassehn,' Lassehn says helpfully.

'That's right,' Mrs Buschkamp says, 'and Lassehn was the right medium for her, she could definitely do what she liked with him. The first time she came here with him I was standing outside the front door shouting at the street kids. Well, and when I saw him arm in arm with Irma, I thought to myself, what sort of boy is she bringing home? He looks as if he's never even been with a girl.'

Lassehn flinches at the clarity of the woman's vision.

'I wouldn't have given him another thought if she had only taken him to bed the once, maybe she wanted to find out how a boy like that . . . Well, you know what I mean. But even today I don't understand why she married him, and I'd eat my hat if she didn't have very special reasons of her own.'

Lassehn holds his breath with tension, he's aware that this strange woman knows far more about his wife than he does. Certain thoughts that often tried to raise a warning voice, but were always silenced, now take shape, but he hasn't the time right now to look at them in detail, piece by piece, and connect them up with each other. The voice of this woman, a stranger who is really talking now, and who seems to want to get everything out of her system, leaves him no time, because with each new sentence she suggests new perspectives that had previously been completely hidden, and weren't even vaguely present.

'I must say, I felt sorry for the lad,' Mrs Buschkamp continued, undeterred, 'he must have put all his feelings into it, and when the eight days were over he probably had nothing to show for it but a pair of weak knees. You know, Mr Kempner, I'm a simple old woman, but I've got eyes in my head and there are things I don't like. When I saw the two of them, it always seemed to me that Irma was just tolerating him and that was that. Yes, when she went with the others, with the Luftwaffe captain, she was a long way away from love, she fluttered her eyelashes at him, she wanted to get into his trousers . . .'

Lassehn feels as if an ice-cold hand has clutched his heart and is pressing it with bony fingers. The woman's voice comes from very far away, he can't form a coherent thought, his brain is alternately filled to the brim with thoughts and then completely empty again. He stands up and looks out of the window, he feels he has turned pale to the roots of his hair, but he doesn't want to let the woman see, he grits his teeth to resist the questions that are trying to spill out of him and manages to hold them back. All that issues from between his teeth is a hoarse croak, which he masks with an artificial cough.

'Ah, yes, who knows where love is going to strike,' Mrs Buschkamp goes on.

Lassehn has now recovered himself to the extent that he can ask a question in a calm voice, but he is still looking away from her because he hasn't got the muscles in his face under control. 'Was Mrs Lassehn, or rather the then Miss Neidermeyer, engaged to the Luftwaffe captain?', he asks.

'Engaged? No, she never wore a ring,' Mrs Buschkamp replies, 'but she was head over heels in love with him, handsome fellow he was, a real man. You see, and I don't understand this, a little while later she married for the exact opposite, a sweet boy that she had to train up. That's why I'm forever saying that Irma must have had a special reason for finding another boy and even marrying him.'

'How do you mean, Mrs Buschkamp?' asks Lassehn, pressing his fingers tightly together to keep control of himself. 'Did the Luftwaffe captain . . .'

'. . . never came back, he just never came back,' Mrs Buschkamp finishes his sentence. 'There are plenty of pretty girls in Berlin, they all want a taste of love before a bomb falls on them. It's not like in the old days, when girls did a lot of thinking beforehand. When they have to bear in mind that their wonderful life in Hitler's Third Divine Reich could come to an end at any moment, they want to know what it's like to be a woman, just once, even if it's just a moment of pleasure between two air-raid warnings. We've come a long way, haven't we?'

Lassehn has turned round again and nods a few times to show his agreement, but right now he is not interested in general observations, his attention is focused on one very specific point, which he must now address with a question, whatever the result. He summons all his inner strength and at the same time tries to maintain a look of indifference. The question chokes him, it takes his breath away, it wells up inside him like a geyser, nothing can hold it back.

'And for what reasons, Mrs Buschkamp,' he says very slowly, matter-of-factly, because that's the best way he has of suppressing the insecurity in his voice, 'do you think Miss Niedermeyer married Lassehn even though her heart was still full of love for someone else?'

'You put that very nicely, young man,' Mrs Buschkamp says, 'old Goethe couldn't have put it better. Yes, sometimes you hear people say things, and then you find out it was Mrs Buschkamp as said it first. Here it comes, Mr Kempner, the next air-raid announcement.'

The music that was slipping past Lassehn's ear constantly and unnoticed is interrupted once again. Then the announcer's oleaginous voice rings out: 'Attention, attention, this is an air-raid announcement. The large combat unit reported as approaching north-west Germany is now heading towards the area around Hanover and Braunschweig. Combat unit over Lower Austria flying south. Another combat unit approaching West Germany. I repeat . . .'

'Well, it's nearly time,' says Mrs Buschkamp. 'Here, look out the window, the way they're running to the bunker. If the radio says north-west Germany, they're half mad, and when it says Hanover-Braunschweig, they go completely insane.'

'And what do you do when the siren goes off?,' Lassehn asks.

'Corpses on leave, waiting for the undertaker,' Mrs Buschkamp goes on. 'How they can bear it . . .'

'Well, they do bear it,' Lassehn objects.

'I'm an old woman,' Mrs Buschkamp replies, 'nothing throws me these days, and I don't think my life's all that valuable, but young women with little children who go to the pub all dolled up as if it was peacetime, they're the ones who suffer. And believe it or not: the elegant ladies around here sense curse the Americans and the British for daring to drop bombs on us. The Nazis aren't to blame, and the Führer will soon show them.' Mrs Buschkamp breaks off. 'There it goes, the cuckoo!'

'I beg your pardon?,' Lassehn asks. 'The cuckoo? What cuckoo?'

Mrs Buschkamp looks at him uncomprehendingly.

'I only arrived in Berlin yesterday,' Lassehn apologizes, 'hence my ignorance.'

'There's something not quite right about you, young man,' says Mrs Buschkamp, and narrows her eyes, 'but for now I've got no time to put my finger on it. You see, there goes the anti-aircraft radio station again.'

Three notes issue from the speaker, always the same three notes: it is the feared triad of death. And then another voice is heard, not the practised voice of the radio announcer, but the harsh, clipped voice of an officer.

'Attention, attention, gun position of the Berlin anti-aircraft unit. Here is a report about the situation in the air. The spearhead of the large unit of hostile bomber planes is now heading eastward towards Magdeburg-Stendal. The mass of the large enemy formation is following in the areas between Magdeburg-Braunschweig and Hanover-Braunschweig. Public air-raid warnings are being given for the western territory of the Reich capital.'

'The fat's in the fire,' Mrs Buschkamp says furiously.

Lassehn has been temporarily diverted from the question that burns inside him, but now he advances towards it again. 'You wanted to answer another question for me, Mrs Buschkamp,' he remembers.

'Really, did I?' Mrs Buschkamp asks back.

'Yes,' Lassehn says firmly, 'the question of why Miss Niedermeyer, Irma, as you call her, married young Lassehn out of nowhere, you hinted a moment ago that you had guessed the reason.'

Mrs Buschkamp comes very close to Lassehn, who is standing behind a chair and holding on tightly to its back. 'That's a question of conscience, Mr Kempner, and one that interests you a great deal. But as you claim to be a friend of Lassehn's, I'll tell you so that you can tell the lad. I do the Niedermeyers' laundry, and it struck me that there was a particular piece of Irma's laundry that was missing a few times. Do you understand?'

Lassehn looks blankly at Mrs Buschkamp. 'Quite honestly, no, Mrs Buschkamp,' he says. 'What does that have to do with laundry?'

Mrs Buschkamp shakes her head at his naïveté. 'Well, then I'll have to make myself quite clear, young man,' she says. 'I think that Irma only married that young man, that Lassehn, because she was pregnant by her vanished lover, the captain. So now you know.'

Lassehn seems numb. 'You think . . .'

'I've got no time to think,' Mrs Buschkamp says abruptly. 'Don't you hear it? The siren!'

VI

The American daylight bombing raid rolls in, above Berlin and the surrounding area. As if on manoeuvres, the squadrons, units, flights, detachments of bombers and fighter planes fly into the territory above Berlin. Conveyor-belt masterpieces of the human brain and human technology, surrounded by the flashes from the anti-aircraft guns and the bursts of fire from the fighters. Flying arsenals whose cannon and machine guns are aimed in such a way that there are no blind spots, and in whose body light- and dark-skinned men are crouched, American students, workers, drugstore salesmen, clerks, farmers, waiting and lying in ambush since the helicopter propellers began to turn on the airfields of Great Britain, and the few seconds in which the object of this hunting raid appears in their sights.

The three million inhabitants of the city are cowering now in cellars and trenches, standing pressed close together in the bunkers and the underground stations of the underground and the S-Bahn, the fire brigades of the city and its greater surroundings are on standby, the fire-fighting teams in the factories have hydrants and grappling irons, picks and axes at the ready, the police are on extreme alert, the Morse machines in the police stations tap away ceaselessly, the barrels of the anti-aircraft guns are aimed steeply at the sky.

In the streets are the empty trams and buses and laden carts whose unyoked horses have been stabled in a hallway.

It is spookily empty and silent, every now and again a motorbike dashes through the silence, the firing from the batteries in the outer air-defence zone roars and thunders. The city has held its breath, the blood is congealing in its veins, its pulses thump anxiously, under a clear blue spring sky with a few white clouds, a deadly feeling of expectation has settled above it.

There it lies now, this great city, 880 square metres, stretching into the landscape of Brandenburg, surrounded for a huge radius by far superior and magnificently armed enemies, and even the sky above it is occupied by hostile forces. Nothing protects it, no hand of God lies protectively over it, no obfuscating cloud, no black dark of night. The many anti-aircraft batteries are no more use than the few fighter squadrons or the many observation posts that stretch from the border of the Reich into the city itself. The anti-aircraft radio stations, the stations of the police and military surveillance report without interruption about the size, course and location of the enemy, they pursue them persistently from square to square on the map. But it all has only a Platonic value because nothing can avert or halt or even delay the attack, unstoppable and undeviating, like a long-distance runner with a stopwatch running around and around a track. The formations follow their own route, they leave white vapour trails in the cloudless sky, they mark out the target area with strange signs that point earthwards like frozen lightning bolts, they open their hatches, the bombs plunge down on houses, stations, factories, streets, bridges, upon the just and the unjust, the living and the unborn. They make the air tremble with explosions, with the cries of stones and people, and the great city lies there helplessly offering itself up to the annihilating blows.

Lassehn sits in the air-raid shelter of number 26 Kaiser-Friedrich-Strasse. He has found a remote corner where barely a beam falls from the lamps, the events around him don't affect him, he is quite far away, he recognizes every detail, hears every sound, feels the vibrations, but he perceives it all with the indifference of a completely uninvolved bystander. The long shelter is divided into two cellars. Some light bulbs screwed into unshaded fittings give off an unpleasantly bright, cold light among the vaults, benches stand along the walls, bunks stand along the transverse walls, there are also benches between the pillars, later additions. In every gap and corner there are places of all kinds to sit, wicker chairs, leather armchairs, stools, footstools, footrests, couches, sofas, children's chairs, cane chairs. Along the walls packages are stacked as if in a left-luggage office, black, brown, yellow, grey suitcases made of leather, corduroy, vulcanite, cardboard, some bearing stickers from happier times, 'Grand Hotel Bellagio', 'Hotel Carlton, Budapest', 'Bellevue Terminus, Engelberg', 'Weisser Hirsch, Schwarzburg', bulging straw mattresses, rucksacks that looked as if they had been filled for giants, cardboard boxes, boxes of every size, men's suits, coats, dresses, skirts and jackets, furs hang in a long row from a coat-stand. The cellar is crammed full, every seat is occupied. Back in 1940, when the air raids brought lengthy alarms but caused little damage, going to the air-raid shelter was almost a kind of popular entertainment, card players and discussion groups had met up there, children had opened up playgrounds among the rows of benches, the whole thing had been almost perfectly safe, and almost a way of bringing the members of the house community into contact with each other. The fanfares of special announcements and choruses of 'Wir fahren gegen Engelland' had thundered from the speakers, a headline from the Völkischer Beobachter had been enough to make them feel that National Socialism's claim to power was their very own birthright. The enemy air force had been dismissed with a con-temptuous shrug, they all thought they could avoid it, and lively discussions had often been held about what was, theoretically, the best place to be. Some maintained you were safest near the entrance to the cellar of the house next door, others closest to the exit, still others thought the wall that formed the foundation of the house facing the courtyard was the best place, while some preferred the seats near the reinforcements of the walls. Opinions were no less different when it came to the course of action to be pursued in the event of danger. While some throw themselves flat on the floor as the bombs approach, others stand up stiffly, in response to the shock waves some quickly exhale all the air in their lungs, while others hold their breath.

In this cellar there are only two people watching everything that is happening with stoic calm, Mrs Buschkamp and Joachim Lassehn. However, the source of this calm is quite different in each of them, because while in Mrs Buschkamp's case its cause lies in natural fearlessness, for Lassehn it is complete apathy.

At first the two cellars are still dominated by the nervous activity that usually comes in the first few minutes after an alarm. They are filled by people taking their seats, by the residents of the building greeting one another, storing away their luggage, closing the ventilation flaps. Then suspicions about the supposed destination of the enemy formation are exchanged; the important thing being to know from which direction the squadron is coming, but it is all done almost automatically, with the mechanical routine of a procedure carried out a hundred times.

But when that activity is over, a weird quiet starts to spread, all senses wither except the sense of hearing, only the ear still lives. No one is aware of the mouldy, fungous smell of the cellar, no one feels the cold rising from the stone floor, no one sees the tense, distorted faces in the cold light of the bare bulbs. A suffocating silence presses people's throats together. In the silent stillness the heavy breathing is the only sound. Everyone is listening as hearts race in faster and faster bursts and hands flutter to the sounds that trickle down into the cellar from the world above, and even though the cellar is below street level and has no windows, the iron doors of the gas locks and the air flaps are firmly shut. The fine, even song of the four-propeller planes, the roar of the anti-aircraft guns can still be heard, and the unpleasant hissing, wailing and shrieking of the plunging bombs, and even though after four years of war from the air it is general knowledge that the bombs that can be heard falling have already done their destructive work, because the bombs are faster than the sound produced by their air suction, they all hunch their shoulders, the blood seems to freeze in their veins, their fingernails dig deep into the balls of their hands, the tension in the mind has reached a level that almost sends it plummeting into abject submissiveness. As if etched by an invisible stylus, lines of horror are drawn on faces. A deafening crash rends the air. The cellar begins to shake in waves, as if in an earthquake, a dragging feeling penetrates the bodies from below. A terrible shock wave drives the air in a swift blast through the closed doors and hammers against eardrums, roof tiles rattle onto the cobbles, windowpanes shatter, bursting stones splinter, the house's joints seem to creak, the bulbs flutter, their light becomes fainter, at last only the filaments are glowing. They recover, go out, some women scream shrilly, children begin to cry, another one whimpers quietly, an old woman kneels by her bench and prays loudly: 'Our Father, who art in Heaven!'. One of the few men shouts in a voice that is loud but no longer firm, 'Shut up! Shut up!'. And again and again come hissing sounds, vibrations, shock waves, impact, and then all of a sudden it is over as it began. The first waves of the attacking unit have flown over the district. The lights flicker on again, then the place is bathed in primal brightness. The women sob a few more times and blow their noses violently, then they look at each other, and in their eyes, alongside distraction, there is a sense of wonder that death has only touched them, only brushed them with its icy breath, but still left them alive.

Lassehn is unmoved by all of this, none of it has reached him, not the danger, not the release from the anger, not the screams of the women or the demand for silence. He sits in a niche built into the wall, his feet are stretched out in front of him, and his head is lowered so that his chin is touching his chest.

He tries to order the thoughts that have crashed in on him, but it is a difficult thing to do, because they have rolled up into a solid ball that is not easy to disentangle. He can't find the beginning, so he forces his thoughts away from the present and the immediate future, and pushes open the door to memory. At first it's only a tiny crack, but soon it's gaping wide, when the flow of thoughts strikes against it. Much that seemed indistinct, incomprehensible and mysterious at the time, which crouched over experiences like a shadow, perceptible and yet intangible, today becomes crystal-clear and hurts with manifest ruthlessness.

The images glide constantly past, they are not equally sharp, some have already faded, some seem unlit, but many stand out clearly against the dark background. This dark background was the mood of Joachim Lassehn, back on leave, born of the despair of having to waste the best years of his life to no good end. This despair was not only the consequence of the demoralizing battles at Voronezh and Orel, it had already begun when he had to turn up for labour service, when they tried to grind all individuality into a particular form, to suppress any independent thought, to direct mind and body entirely towards the military goal. Lassehn was not repelled so much by the strains of work and the monotony of the training as by the suppression of every unregulated impulse; and what labour service had begun with the pretext of toughening-up and social levelling had been continued by the military. The perpetuation of these phrases was no longer considered necessary, here they marched directly towards their goal of physically toughening the young man and intellectually making him a submissive tool, before leading him as quickly as possible onto the battlefield.

In Norway Lassehn found himself transferred to a hostile environment, admittedly no shots were fired and there was no combat, because the underground resistance of the Norwegians was a matter for the Gestapo and their quislings, but even though he belonged to the winning army, in fact Lassehn was the humiliated one. It was unbearable to look into the proud, unfriendly faces of the Norwegians, to see them ostentatiously getting up straight away and leaving the coffee house as soon as a German soldier crossed the threshold, or the seat next to him remaining empty on a crowded tram. He was ashamed of his superiority and constantly amazed at how naturally his comrades felt that wearing the light-grey uniform with epaulettes and insignia made them feel superior. He despised the uniform that he had to wear because it was a target for hatred and contempt. He couldn't walk through the streets with the imperious stride of the conqueror, defiantly looking at the faces of the conquered people. He did not understand his comrades, who could swim calmly in this sea of hostility, and even feel good. The fact that Norway was not at the front line far outweighed all the manifestations of ill will, if they were perceived at all.

Then came the deployment of the regiment on the eastern front. Even though Lassehn abhorred the combat that would now replace the surveillance of an oppressed people, the battle ahead of him felt initially like a liberation. Yet the feeling of relief was short-lived, because the eastern front too had a hinterland with a hostile population. To his horror Lassehn was forced to acknowledge that war did not only consist in fighting against a hostile army, but that the very meaning of that war seemed not to be to bring peace to the country beyond the front, but rather to fertilize it with the blood and corpses of the remaining population – those who were not deported, as war booty, to be used as slave labour – preparing the ground for the benefit of the settlers of the colonial eastern territories who would arrive in due course. He could not shake off the experiences he was forced to go through and then turn to more cheerful matters. What little inclination he possessed to accept life and hope for the future had been sucked away by the war. When he became aware of this, he seriously considered suicide, but at that point he was allowed to go on leave. Leave meant not only getting away from orders and commands for a few weeks, shedding the crusty scab of blood and filth and allowing the pores of his skin to open by breathing air that was not thick with the smell of corpses. Leave also meant being lifted out of the communal life of the trenches and being able to follow a rhythm of his own once more. He found Berlin changed, the officially endorsed flight after the destruction of Hamburg had put the city in a wildly feverish state, and the first three major British night raids had fallen upon it like infernal storms. When Lassehn had left the Lichterfeld tram at Lankwitz Station, he walked along Leonorenstrasse with a sense that things wouldn't be all that bad. But when he reached the junction with Kaiser-Wilhelm-Strasse he had stopped, bewildered, because he was suddenly in the middle of a dead city in which all traces of life had collapsed into piles of rubble. Then he had walked on in a daze, automatically putting one foot down after another, his boots had crunched on shards of glass, his feet had stumbled over heaps of rubble, they had directed him past Lankwitz Church into Gallwitzstrasse across Havensteinplatz to Seydlitzstrasse, and death and destruction had constantly intruded upon him. He had looked right and left, and from the blackened ruins the images of the incinerated past had risen, the sedate, bourgeois life, assembled from opaque respectability and untroubled comfort, snobbish superiority and the inferiority of the parvenu. It had all been there: the advertising columns with their enticing promises, the thé dansant and the Philharmonic Orchestra, the midsummer ball and the heavyweight championship, shops with brightly coloured enamel signs, Spratt's dog biscuits and Juno cigarettes, Fromm's rubber goods and Chlorodent toothpaste, telephone kiosks with stylized receivers and signs saying 'Keep your conversation short', green meadows and urban trees, lindens, chestnuts, acacias, and flats, flats, flats in long new buildings, two, two and a half, three, four rooms, self-contained, with stove, and central heating, hot running water and Junkers gas boilers, rubbish chutes and communal aerials, with old-fashioned and modernist furniture, with pictures of the Führer in dining rooms and pictures of dancing fairies above the beds, with bookshelves, Goethe, Schiller, Lessing, Ulhand, *Mein Kampf, The Myth of the Twentieth Century, Via Mala, The Wiskottens, Debit and Credit*, and flags, flags, flags, red with a white circle and the black swastika inside, from the little pennant between the double windows to the metre-long household flag from the skylight. It seemed entirely logical to Lassehn that that he couldn't find his parents, that the block of flats on Seyditzstrasse had burned down and his parents had suffocated in the cellar with many others and their bodies dumped in Baumschulenweg with countless others. Lassehn had stood completely cold, inert and emotionless by the long, uniform rows of graves, hardly bigger than molehills.

To confront the past and prove to himself that he still had some kind of relationship with her, he had gone to Prager Platz to visit Ursula, his mother's youngest sister, whom he loved with the forlorn adoration of a nephew several years younger. It had been a gloomy day, evening had fallen early, and it was only upon leaving the underground at Nürnberger Platz that he had realized that Ursula was no longer living in Berlin. But out of defiance he had still climbed the steps to Nürnberger Strasse, had crossed Prager Platz, that round square that looked as if it was surrounded by giant gravestones, and turned into Aschaffenburger Strasse, that burnt-out stone canyon with heaps of rubble and backdrop walls in which empty windows stared like dead eye sockets. It was dark, and impossible to make anything out, but just as, sitting at the piano, he didn't need to trouble his memory of the score to play, he found, even in the darkness and in the midst of the destruction, the house whose steps he had climbed so often, and never without a beating heart. He climbed through the cave that had once been a hallway and was now like a dried-up, stony river bed, and then stood in front of the garden house, as the rear of the tenement was known here in the west, and if a veiled, pale moon had not wandered ghostlike through the ruin and illuminated the charred beams with painful clarity, he might have thought the house was still standing. For minutes he had stared unwavering into the cold, bare house, in a corner where deep black shadows stretched. That was the corner where the baby grand had stood, he had sat there, and there had also been an armchair that she had sat in and listened motionlessly, and he had always had to play the same pieces for her, Beethoven's *Ecossaises* and Weber's *Perpetuum mobile* or, if they felt particularly solemn, the *Appassionata*, music from another world, from a distant star. When he had finished she had risen to her feet and run her hands gently over his hair. The bright light of a passing car had darted across his back for a matter of seconds and broken the enchantment, shedding too bright a light on the blank walls and the dead tree stump and abruptly turning the gentle face of the past into the grimace of the present.

So that was the grim background, labour service, Küstrin, Stavanger, Orel, Lankwitz, Baumschulenweg, Aschaffenburger Strasse. Not a patch of light in the darkness, not a friendly sound emerged from the backdrop, no memory of friendship or tenderness went with him, only the music was still there, but it sounded quieter and quieter within him. It was drowned by shouts, by roars, by thunder, it vibrated unattainably far and high among the spheres. The young soldier stood alone in the big city, loneliness had suddenly been dropped over him like an enormous bell jar. Life pulsed all around, only he was excluded, his brittle nature, his taciturnity would not let him participate, join in with unhesitating open-mindedness, plunge himself into the frenzy of a hysterical bustle of enjoyment, he couldn't do it, it was not in him, it was against his nature. But the idea of having to return to the eastern front, subjected once again to the coarse conversations of his comrades, the bloody haze of battle and idiotic orders, the suffering faces of a tormented population, without having even the smallest point of reference at home, someone he could waste his thoughts on if they threatened to become crusted with blood and revulsion, made him more open and receptive than he had ever been before, but the engine of his receptivity needed feeding from within.

That time coincided precisely with Lassehn's meeting with Irmgard Niedermeyer. He sat opposite her in the S-Bahn and hadn't even noticed her at first; he had chosen a seat at random and sat down. His eye went to the rows of houses that stood endlessly along the tracks and whose windows sometimes allowed a brief glimpse into the flats, but then, as if drawn by some magical force, he turned his head from the window, and his eyes met those of the girl who was sitting diagonally opposite him and who hastily turned her head away when Lassehn's eye came to rest on her. Something in Lassehn immediately opened up, grief dissolved into a painful longing for tenderness and care, for a still point and a target for his thoughts. He studied the girl's face, it was narrow and slightly pale, her dark-brown hair fell over the round forehead with a soft wave, the mouth had a tender, passionate curve. The girl's face was shadowed by sadness, but a hint of promising joy and lust were recognizable in her features. Every now and again a hesitant little smile played upon them, which slightly curled the corners of her mouth and sent bright little sparks flashing in her eyes. Lassehn absorbed every feature of that face, he inhaled it like a suffocating man breathing deeply to pump fresh air into his lungs. An enormous yearning to give and receive tenderness grew within him, he couldn't take his eyes off the girl, and now the reverse was true as well, her face turned slowly towards him as if an invisible hand were turning her head in his direction. Lassehn did not turn away or cast his eyes down and their eyes came to rest firmly on one another.

Both faces were tense and serious, their gaze interrupted only by the occasional blink. Lassehn could not have said whether that look lasted a few seconds or many minutes, and when at last they looked away, a little smile appeared upon their faces. Lassehn closed his eyes with happiness, his heart thumped all the way to his temples, and when he opened his eyes again he was welcomed by the girl's eyes, and now nothing stood in the way of that look, no embarrassment, no shame.

When the girl got out, Lassehn also left the carriage as if anything else were impossible, he was jostled as he got out and lost sight of the girl for a few seconds. He was immediately filled with a burrowing excitement, he ploughed his way through the crowd with long and thoughtless strides – then saw her by the steps leading to the exit, she stood there and looked at him calmly – she was waiting for him. Lassehn held out his hand, at the same moment it struck him as ridiculous and simple-minded and gauche, but he didn't know how to behave, how to speak, he had never addressed a girl in the street before, he had had absolutely nothing to do with girls apart from some insignificant little flirtations. In labour service and during his time in the army he had always refused to join in with the vulgar pursuits of his comrades, and had had to endure a degree of mockery and a certain suspicion of strangeness. Some acquaintances had remained superficial because he did not have the gift of small talk, serious notes always quickly crept into his conversations, and if they were not echoed they were very soon followed by silence. So he was not unacquainted with girls, but they had always seemed puzzling and hard to understand, he had not sought out their company and in the end had had no opportunity to seek it, particularly since he was not the type for fleeting friendships and non-committal erotic connections.

And now he had been struck by a look that did not lure him towards a superficial flirtation, but in whose depths something fated seemed to gleam, a smile had been directed at him that seemed to spring not from coquettishness but from seriousness and melancholy. A girl had simply got to her feet and waited for him as if it was the most natural thing in the world, she had taken his hand, they had passed through the station barrier together and walked across a few streets. At first there were no words between them, only that look and the feeling of their joined hands. He had felt the girl's pulse beating in his hand and a great feeling of happiness had swept over him as if he were being freed from the cold loneliness of his life. He began to talk, slowly at first, with careful, considered words, his speech was like a stone that won't move initially but starts rolling once it has been set in motion down a slope.

Lassehn gave everything of himself that afternoon. After a brief separation he met the girl the same evening, it was like a miracle that he could not grasp. The next day they appeared at the register office in Charlottenburg, eight days later they married, and another eight days later Lassehn had to go back to the front. Those two weeks were intoxicating, but joy was mixed with pain, beauty contorted with horror, separation loomed over their union, but perhaps it was that dualism that created their curious inebriation. For the first time Lassehn was entirely absorbed in another person. He immersed himself entirely in her, he felt the heartbeat of a girl, a woman, his wife, against his chest, her hot, quick breath on his mouth, her warmth in all the pores of his body, it was a drunken pleasure, insatiable in its bid to give oneself entirely to the other person and at the same time possess them entirely, which extinguished all other thoughts, concentrating the will completely upon itself. The mystery of the opposite sex had revealed itself to him for the first time. The days were now a quivering wait for night, and night a wait for morning which would reveal a head of tousled dark hair on his shoulder. Lassehn was often ashamed of his happiness, which allowed him to lie in a white bed beside a soft, warm body when his parents had just died a terrible death, but he always managed to justify himself in the end. Did he not have to go back to the front, did he not have the right to live his life to the full before he did so?

The memory rises hotly in Lassehn, hot and painful, but the pain that seizes him now is different from the one that was once the musical accompaniment to his happiness. It is the pain of recognition that even that happiness was not real. Now that he has acquired fresh knowledge, much that seemed mysterious, which he attributed to his inexperience of the unpredictable nature of women, now appears in quite a different light.

In the past he had always ignored the memories that are now assailing him, but those memories are too concrete for him to avoid, they force him remorselessly to analyse, to draw up checks and balances, they imperiously call for understanding and conclusions. Lassehn did not feel that his wife understood him, he had an unconquerable need for tenderness, for a soft hand to stroke his hair gently, for blissful peace on a beloved shoulder, for the beating of her heart and the rushing of her blood, but she didn't understand that, when he was blissfully happy and only wanted her near him to find confirmation for himself she pulled him to her with brutal tenderness, suffocated him with caresses and did not yield until everything ended in a wild embrace. But Lassehn's need for unerotic tenderness did not always end like that, sometimes his wife withdrew from him for no reason, shook off his presence like an unnecessary item of clothing and gave him a look that was empty and inessential and fell upon him as if he were an unimportant stranger.

Lassehn had probably felt at the time that the sexual connection alone could not establish complete contact between them. Increasingly he had a sense that his wife had not laid the book of her life so open before him, but all of those hints and suggestions had remained so small and trivial in comparison with the great passion that time and again overwhelmed them. But now it was becoming apparent that those hints and suggestions had taken root and now, in the light of an entirely new consideration, are proliferating in confusion. Much that had remained unnoticed then, or dismissed with a shrug, is now gaining in significance. Why had Irmgard insisted on marrying straight away? At the time Lassehn had seen it as an entirely natural demand, it had even, in fact, corresponded with his own desires, though the suddenness of it surprised him. But today he is becoming aware of the discrepancy between that demand and Irmgard's normal attitude to such matters. That attitude was free, and unburdened by traditional ideas, she was also, as she sometimes hinted in passing, by no means unexperienced in erotic matters, and had had other relationships before marrying him. So why had she only granted him an embrace once they were legally united, while with other men she had not insisted on that requirement? At the time Lassehn had sought an explanation for her favours, and found it in the idea that she was unwilling to be exploited, not being aware at the time of how platitudinous that point of view really was. Now he knows – and the recognition is a deeply painful one – that it was not the right to material support that was due to her as a soldier's wife, that it was not even that she was wearied of erotic vagabondage, but merely an attempt to legitimize her unborn child by another man by marrying him.

But why me, of all people? Lassehn wonders desperately. Why from the great mass of men was I the one she chose? Have I only been a means to an end? Had she only given herself to him so uninhibitedly, and suffocated his hesitant references to responsibility with outbursts of passion so that she could dispel any doubts that might later arise? Had it all been a calculation? Hadn't there been a bit of love involved as well, given that the other reasons, perhaps the true cause, could never have produced such an effect? Every question immediately yields another, the chain of ideas never breaks.

But if it was love, couldn't she have said so openly? Would she not have felt the obligation first of all to come clean about the past, by being open and unsparing about herself and about him, rather than entering into a new relationship with a lie, or at least with a guilty silence? But that had probably been cowardice, stronger than honesty, and perhaps also fear that everything – having only begun – might already be over. At any rate, and Lassehn came at last to this conclusion, things are by no means as unambiguous and clear as Mrs Buschkamp likes to see them, her interpretation is also a little too simplistic. Lassehn is one of those people who do not believe in essential wickedness, he sees weakness, carelessness, fear, cowardice and incapacity as supposedly smaller sins, and does not know that it is the sweetness of that first embrace that still quivers within him. Lassehn feels his way tentatively through his emotions as if through a jungle, in which every step must be conquered and every path freshly hewn, but this is the path he must walk, because at the end of it stand truth and clarity. Whatever happens he must speak to his wife, the sooner the better. He must know whether the journey on which he embarked with her on 21 September 1943 leads to a common future, or whether it had already come to an end when he went off to the eastern front two weeks later.

Then a question hits him like a stone. Where is the child that Irmgard was carrying?

VII

Lassehn gives a start when a hand grips him hard by the shoulder.

'Who are *you*?,' asks a hoarse, raw voice.

Lassehn hears the words as if from a great distance. He was so immersed in the past that it takes him a moment to re-emerge into the present. Now the coarse words bring him and his thoughts back into the present.

'I'm sorry?,' he asks mechanically.

'I want to know who you are,' the challenging voice repeats impatiently.

At last the veil that the past had wrapped around him is torn, and Lassehn becomes aware of where he is: in the air-raid shelter of 26 Kaiser-Friedrich-Strasse in Charlottenburg. And in a flash he is also aware of his situation: a deserter with inadequate papers in a city that is keenly searching for soldiers who have fled the battle-field, a deserter, surrounded by strangers, any of whom could give him away, any of whom could be a spy, only out of fear of being accused of helping a deserter, not handing him over. Even though the whole edifice of the state is shaking and tottering and Party, Gestapo and Wehrmacht are all writhing in agony under the anni-hilating blows of a superior adversary, their power is still stretched around everyone like a ring of steel. The fear of terror is still great enough to give every threat the desired intensity, every order unconditional obedience. Behind everyone there still stretches the black shadow of the SS, the horror of the concentration camps and the death sentences of the People's Courts. The man standing in front of Lassehn is dressed in civilian clothes that are also military, steel helmet, windcheater with belt and gas mask, knee-length boots and breeches, blue armband and Party insignia.

Lassehn reaches for the revolver in his trouser pocket, he wants to have the gun ready to fire in any eventuality. As he stays in his half-reclining position, every muscle in him tenses as he contemplates the possibility of flight.

'What right do you have to ask me that?' he asks.

'I'm the air-raid warden for this building,' the man replies.

'Very interesting,' Lassehn says casually. 'I don't care, as far as I'm concerned you can stay that way.'

A vein stands out thick and red on the man's forehead, but he manages to contain himself. 'I am responsible for the safety of the shelter,' he says, 'and I am also the Party Block Warden. So, who are you?'

'My name is Kempner,' Lassehn says now. 'Is that enough for you?'

The man ignores the question. 'I want to see your papers,' he demands.

'I haven't got any,' Lassehn says, 'I lost all my papers when I was escaping.'

'When you fled?' the air-raid warden asks in surprise. 'Who were you fleeing?'

'The Russians, of course,' Lassehn says, and tries to look nonchalant. 'Had to leave everything at home, the whole place was topsy-turvy.'

The man gives him a penetrating look. 'Where from?' he asks curtly.

'From Neumark,' Lassehn says, 'between Soldin and Lippehne.'

'And no papers?' the man persists. 'People always have papers.'

'Not always,' Lassehn disagrees, 'if you're working in the fields . . .'

The man shuts his eyes tight, you can tell that behind his forehead the thoughts are chasing after one another. 'Since when have you been travelling?'

Lassehn rocks his head back and forth. 'Well, for fourteen days, perhaps three weeks,' he replies. Why is he asking all these questions?, he thinks.

'Listen, there's something wrong here,' the warden says after a short pause.

Have I given myself away? Lassehn wonders. It all sounds quite credible, I could really believe that this is what happened. 'What seems to be wrong?' he asks, and measures the distance to the cellar exit with his eyes.

'You said you'd been working in the fields,' the other man says, 'when you suddenly had to leave.'

'That's right,' Lassehn replies. 'And why . . .'

'You were working in the fields in the middle of March?' the man asks again. 'In snow and ice? Were you picking potatoes or harvesting carrots? You don't even believe that yourself.'

Lassehn gives a start, he can see that his excuse was a serious mistake, the thoughts in his head begin circling unbearably, it's as if someone were slowly lifting off the lid of his skull.

The man walks right up to Lassehn. 'What's up now?' he asks menacingly. 'Either you identify yourself, or you come straight the station after the all-clear. Meanwhile you'll sit here quietly.'

'Out of the question!' Lassehn says and slowly stands up, taking the safety catch off the revolver in his trouser pocket. 'You haven't the right . . .'

'Don't be impertinent!' says the man. 'Haven't the right? Everyone these days has the right to arrest suspicious people. Haven't you heard of deserters, spies and foreign agents? And in any case, this is ID enough!' And he points at his Party insignia.

'That is . . .' Lassehn is about to object, he is about to say that even an insignia isn't a form of legitimation.

'What's going on here?' a woman's voice says. Mrs Buschkamp has joined them, and grasped the situation with a glance.

'What do you want with my nephew, Mr Exner?'

The air-raid warden turns round hastily. 'Is this your nephew, Mrs Buschkamp?' he asks in astonishment.

'What else?' says Mrs Buschkamp. 'Turned up yesterday, the lad's half dead, leave him in peace.'

Lassehn responds to the concierge's intervention first with astonishment, then with relief. Even though he doesn't know what has prompted her to do this, he is still grateful to her for helping him out of his precarious situation. Once he has reached the cellar steps he is no longer afraid, but inside the shelter, where outstretched legs, prams, suitcases and electric ovens are ready to impede one's flight, it's dangerous.

'Why didn't you say straight away that he was your nephew?' the man asks.

'You didn't ask,' Lassehn replies, and slips back into the resting position. If the situation has relaxed a little, he still has to be on his guard, as his suddenly acquired nephew status presents him with new problems that he will have to solve carefully, as general attention is focused on him and the Block Warden's suspicion has only been distracted, not entirely dispelled.

'Go on sleeping,' Mrs Buschkamp says to Lassehn, 'you must be exhausted.'

'Are you assuming responsibility for the young man?' Exner says.

'Course I will,' says Mrs Buschkamp. 'Now clear off, it'll be the all-clear soon, and he'll be able to go back to bed.'

'Doesn't look that way,' says another man coming down the narrow passageway, 'all kinds of formations are headed this way.'

Exner turns towards the speaker. 'Where are they coming in from?' he asks. The expression on his face has changed very quickly, the menace that leaped from his eyes and caused his chin to jut are being replaced by fear that makes his cheeks quiver and casts a dark shadow into his eyes.

'From Potsdam and Luckenwalde,' the other man replies, 'they're probably flying in from the south and south-west.'

'Let's listen to the police radio station,' Exner says.

They both leave, and Lassehn is no longer the focus of interest, the other waves of American bombers overshadow his insignificant little person. He puts the catch on his revolver and pushes it back into the depths of his trouser pocket.

'Mrs Buschkamp,' he says quietly and looks gratefully at the old woman, 'thank you . . .'

Mrs Buschkamp makes a quick, defensive movement with her

hand. 'Daft sod,' she says loudly, 'what were you doing annoying Mr Exner?'

'But . . .' Lassehn says, trying to defend himself.

'Shut up,' Mrs Buschkamp snaps at him. 'Are you trying to cause your old aunt problems?'

Lassehn smiles and nods, he understands at last that Mrs Buschkamp is a new aunt for him, and that for her this new relationship is not without its dangers, a single false note could place not just him but also this old lady in very great danger. He is in no doubt that the scene has etched itself on the consciousness of the assembled residents of the house, and will be the sole topic of conversation once the daylight raid is past. He watches after the old woman, who is now returning to her place by the entrance that links the two cellars, she sits down, takes a pair of glasses from her coat pocket and starts reading a battered book. What moved this woman, a stranger, to speak up on his behalf, putting herself in danger that could become acute at any moment and whose consequences are unpredictable? What made her do that? Pity? Kindness?

Lassehn is inclined always to assign all that is good in people to their emotional components, to explain it with reference to the innate goodness of the human psyche, he doesn't know, or it has not revealed itself to him sufficiently clearly for him to recognize it, that impulses like pity, helpfulness and loyalty can also spring from a particular set of convictions. Nationalism has stripped many words of their noble content, so that even the notion of convictions still has a whiff of National Socialism about it. Lassehn has known since yesterday that there are certain sets of convictions which National Socialism has not been able to eradicate, and which it has not been able to distort even with the most skilful turns of phrase, but he does not suspect this feisty old woman, with her slightly pinched eyes and her quick Berlin tongue, of having them.

So why did she come to his assistance? Just out of human kindness, pity, goodness? In the few years during which he has had to rely on himself, Lassehn has met no one who possessed these qualities, instead he has only ever encountered harshness, selfishness and suspicion. Every man seemed to be an island, an island without a beach on which a strange boat could wash up. And now, two days in a row, two complete strangers have taken him under their wings, a pub landlord from Silesian Station and a concierge from Charlottenburg, strange parallelism of events. Do they allow us to draw conclusions about the people of this city?

Lassehn looks around from under lowered eyelids. The fear has fled a little from people's faces, at intervals you can still hear the deep growl of the four-propeller engines, but there are no more explosions, the unbelievable tension of the first fifteen minutes, when bomb after bomb was falling nearby, when everyone clutched their bags more tightly as they prepared to jump, ready to push anyone ruthlessly aside to get to the exit, has now dissolved into effervescent chattiness, into small activities that smack of nervousness.

Relationships between people, which had recently been close to hostility, become conciliatory again, neighbours who are rivals in the struggle for life reacquire more human features, but it's all a thin layer of plaster.

If the bomber squadron dropped another series of bombs nearby, that plaster would fall away immediately, revealing the wild instincts beneath. But wave after wave of planes flies over the western part of the city without dropping anything, and from the announcements on the police radio station it is soon clear that the bombers are already flying away, which makes it very unlikely that bombs will be dropped. The greater the distance between the city and the departing squadrons, the more human the faces become, and occasional laughter can even be heard ringing out in the cellar. Even though it is clear that the Americans can fly large raids every day, and even though nothing is more certain than the nocturnal attack of several dozen British mosquitoes, people know they have been spared for now, they believe that the unbearable burden placed upon them has been lifted, and that awareness revives them. It allows them to make plans for the next few hours, even to arrange to meet and go to the cinema that evening. As incredible as it seems, in half-dilapidated houses, in streets blocked by rubble and anti-tank barriers, the cinemas are still operating, they reel out their performances during the few hours when the electricity ban

is lifted, but even then they are seldom able to show the whole programme all at once uninterrupted because the phrases of the
newsreel announcers and the chatter of the shadows on the screen
are drowned out by the sirens. Lassehn knows that as the spirits of
life revive, interest will be focused on him once more, and since he
feels no great need to clash again with air-raid warden Exner, he
gets to his feet and walks with a swinging stride and in a deliberately casual posture, not too quickly, but not too slowly either,
towards the exit.

'I'm going out for a cig,' he says to Mrs Buschkamp as he walks by.

Some men are standing smoking in the room just outside the
cellar, and with a fleeting glance Lassehn sees that Exner is engaged
in animated conversation with a big man in a brown Party uniform. Everything in him urges him to flee as swiftly as possible,
but he controls himself, he only quickens his step a little, and only
when the twists of the cellar stairs have hidden him from view does
he charge up the steps, push open the cellar door and stand in the
courtyard. A cloudless blue sky stretches over the great gap surrounded by houses, it is very quiet, a deep peace has settled over
the big city at midday, as people dart like rats down underground
passageways.

In the hallway Lassehn lights a cigarette and draws the smoke
deep into his lungs. Should he go now? He only came here to see his
wife, to talk to her, to consider the possibility of their living
together, of finding a place to live, until . . . yes, until when?

Lassehn steps outside the front door. The street has been emptied, as if a magnet had sucked all the life from it, he looks along
Kaiser-Friedrich-Strasse, towards the north-east there hangs a
dark, greyish-black wall of cloud, slowly rising into the sky.

Strange weather, he thinks, it's a spring sky, light blue with a
bright sun, small, white clouds, and beyond it the dark-grey, threatening bank of storm cloud which whirls and seethes and twitches,
and there is no wind, hardly a breeze. Strange weather! But suddenly an icy feeling of terror runs through him. The thing that is
rising over there is not a storm cloud, that is smoke and haze, deso-
lation and destruction, death and ruin, that is the terrible trail of

war which now stretches from Egypt and the Kazakh Steppe, from Narvik and Crete to Berlin. So that's what it looks like. While only sideswipes fell here, over there the full, targeted force of the bombers came raining down.

Lassehn gives a start when the front door opens behind him. His hand immediately reaches for the revolver in his trouser pocket, these days it has become an entirely instinctive movement, but he quickly puts the revolver back and is almost a little ashamed. Mrs Buschkamp has stepped outside.

'Ah, it's you,' Lassehn says.

'Yes, it's me,' says Mrs Buschkamp. 'What are you doing standing outside the front door? Do you want the Party bigwigs to come after you?'

'I'm just thinking about something,' Lassehn says.

'But not in the street,' Mrs Buschkamp says firmly. 'Too much air in your belly? Or do you want them to hang you?'

Lassehn shakes his head, he's almost irritated, the woman's care and attention are nearly becoming a little too much. 'Look over there,' he says by way of distraction, and points towards the threatening cloud.

'That's nothing new, I don't even bother looking at that any more,' Mrs Buschkamp says. 'We've all been through it all, and I've even been in the middle of one of those, nothing bothers us these days. But now . . .'

Sirens cut three long, harsh notes into the deadly silence that spreads like a shroud over the city.

'All clear,' Mrs Buschkamp says. 'Well, you've got away with it again.'

'It's all a matter of luck,' Lassehn says, for the sake of saying something.

Mrs Buschkamp looks at him with quick, appraising eyes.

'Come to mine first,' she says. 'Be quick, before the others creep out of the cellar.'

Lassehn follows her hesitantly.

'Thank you,' he says, when he is sitting opposite her in the concierge's lodge.

'It's fine,' Mrs Buschkamp waves the idea away, 'I don't want anything in return.'

'Why have you done this?' Lassehn asks. 'You don't even know me.'

Mrs Buschkamp looks at him thoughtfully. 'Do you need to know someone to pull him out of the water?' she asks.

'No,' Lassehn admits, 'but you had no reason . . .'

'Save your breath, lad,' Mrs Buschkamp exclaims angrily. 'Are you saying you would have let me perish?'

'I don't know,' Lassehn says honestly. 'Damn it all,' he says, tearing furiously into himself. 'You're quite right, if you're indirectly reproaching me, Mrs Buschkamp, this Nazi system which supposedly trains up everyone to be a hero and a dragon killer has in fact turned us all into pitiful cowards, cringers before any shit-brown uniform, toadies at the sight of every piece of enamel. All humanity in us has been suffocated, all individuality flattened out, and if humanity in Germany has not quite died out, it's only because the bastards haven't yet had time to squeeze the little remaining decency and justice out of us.' Lassehn is amazed by his own outburst, but he feels liberated, and somewhat justified in the face of this clear-eyed old woman.

Mrs Buschkamp looks at him seriously and thoughtfully. 'You put that very nicely, Mr Kempner, that's exactly how it is, I couldn't have said it so well myself.' A violent twitch runs over her wrinkled and furrowed face. 'It would make you weep, all the things the criminals have made of us,' she says. 'Have you any idea how mean and wretched I feel for having said Heil Hitler every now and again? But they put you under so much pressure that sometimes you really have no choice, but inside we're still the same, you can depend on that! It's lucky they can't peep inside us.' She taps her chest and laughs scornfully. 'They can't break people like us, and they can't persuade us either. You're still a young man, Mr Kempner. This is all you've ever known, but what you've learned should be enough, if you can see further than the nose in front of your face.'

Lassehn nods. 'Certainly, but – forgive me if my question is intrusive or bothersome – why are you opposed to Hitler's rule?'

Mrs Buschkamp gets to her feet and props her hands on her hips. 'So that's your next question?'

'I'm interested in your reasons,' Lassehn says emphatically, 'to some extent I'm a student, how . . .'

'Well, then take a look around you,' Mrs Buschkamp says quickly, 'then you'll see reasons enough, but you didn't need to wait for war to hate that gang. Christ alive, were you blind? Didn't you see them persecuting the Jews, crushing our trade unions, dragging the best of our comrades to the camps and shooting them if they tried to get away? Didn't you see a whole people having to hold its nose, that the capitalists had us all under their thumbs disguised as socialists, and that they're destroying everything in their path with their damned war?'

Lassehn is surprised by the woman's outburst, her calm, detached air has made way for flaming fury, her face twitches, deep folds have formed among her wrinkles. If Lassehn didn't understand everything that has poured forth from the old woman, he does know one thing for certain: that this flood has its source in a just sense of rage.

'That's how I see it by and large,' Mrs Buschkamp continues. 'And what does it look like on the ground? What does it look like for the little man, the simple proletarian? Look at me, I'm just sixty, and I'm spending my last days on my own, they took my husband to the Volkssturm eight days ago, my daughter and her kids were evacuated, her husband is missing, my other daughter was transferred with her factory to western Prussia, God alone knows where she is now, and my son . . .' she breaks off and sits down again. 'You see, Mr Kempner, you've worked for a lifetime, you've toiled and slaved, you've brought up a son, you've sent him to Beuth University so that he can become a technician, maybe an engineer, and then . . .' her voice lowers and becomes almost a whisper – 'and then one day a letter arrives, and it says: "For Führer, Nation and Fatherland, died a heroic death at Marsa Matruh." I know exactly what that means, it means that they buried him in the desert sand, maybe they even put up a little wooden cross, and at the next sandstorm it was gone, blown away. That's how it is, Mr Kempner, you've brought up a boy, you've put everything into him, love, care, pride, hope, also vexation and annoyance, a lot of work and money, you were proud that he'd achieved something and you'd contributed to it, and then one day it says: died a heroic death. That's it, gone, died a heroic death, the Party sends you its deepest condolences. For Führer, Nation and Fatherland. What a stupid thing to say. What did he die for? For something good? Then I might accept it. But for this? For them? Buried in the desert, a plaything for the hyenas, food for jackals?' She sits there frozen, her hands lying limply in her lap.

Lassehn is shaken, he walks over to the old woman and rests a hand lightly on her shoulder, for a moment he is almost even tempted to let his hand run over the dark-brown hair already run through with grey, but then he thinks better of it, it's too familiar.

'I understand your pain, Mrs Buschkamp,' he says quietly. 'You have sowed life and harvested death.'

Mrs Buschkamp jerks her head up again, for a few seconds her gaze is quite blank, but then she shakes herself from her stupor.

'But don't believe that I'm going to die of grief, oh no, Mr Kempner, I'm cut from different cloth.' She laughs loudly. 'He didn't die in vain, my Werner didn't, he left me something that keeps me going. And you know what that is? It's hatred, a very great hatred that no one can take away from me, a bitter, deadly hatred of those bandits who call themselves the government and the Party. But don't think I didn't hate that rabble before, of course, I always hated those fellows, but back then it was in a way a general hatred, the way you might hate dogs or bugs, you're not hating a particular dog or a particular bug. You hate the species, you see, and that's how it is for me. After my Werner's death my hatred turned into a very personal hatred, for every Nazi I know, and you can rely on that, I won't forget a single one of them if things change. The little Hitlers who boss us and bully us day in and day out, who slap us in the face if we let slip a single word about their proud Greater Germany, who stand by our doors listening to hear if we've tuned into a foreign station, who control all the lists, how much each of us has donated for winter relief, and check whether everyone's got that cleaning rag dangling out of the window, who are always making sure that we say "Heil Hitler". Those little Hitlers, like Exner here and a few other rogues, I hate them very personally. I'd like to see those bastards dangling because they're almost more to blame for our misfortune than the ones at the top, because what could the ones at the top do, Adolf, Club-Foot, Hermann, Heini the Undertaker and whatever the hell their names are, what could they do if the people down at the bottom didn't join in? They could do nothing, that's what. And what do you have to say to that, Mr Kempner?'

Lassehn shrugs. 'I haven't thought about it all as much as you have . . .'

'Thought? Did you say thought?' Mrs Buschkamp interrupts. 'There's nothing to think about, it's all about feeling, you can see that if you've got eyes in your head and take the trouble to open them. You don't look to me as if you were born stupid and never learned anything, and you don't look like a farmer to me either. With that face and those hands? Exner only believed that story you told him in the cellar because you're my nephew. You can tell there's something not right about you by the tip of your nose, you can't hide it, not you.'

Lassehn is startled. 'Do you think so?' he asks hastily.

Mrs Buschkamp laughs briefly. 'You see, that question gives you away already! What's up with you? Do you really have no papers?'

'I do,' Lassehn replies. 'I've got papers, I've even got real ones, but they're incomplete.'

'So?' Mrs Buschkamp looks at him quizzically.

'Sometimes incomplete papers are worse than none at all,' Lassehn replies.

'Hang on a second,' Mrs Buschkamp says suddenly, 'incomplete papers are worse . . .' She shakes her head violently. 'No, I don't get it.'

Lassehn hesitates for several seconds. Should he tell the old woman the truth? Is he obliged to do so? But then he makes his mind up. 'It's like this,' he begins slowly, 'I have got my *Soldbuch*, but no leave pass, and that means . . .'

The old woman's eyes gleam. 'Now I've got it,' she says and

nods. 'You're one of those fellows. And still you're running about in plain clothes. You've skedaddled, you've done a bunk. Am I right?'

Lassehn just nods, even though he knows that this woman isn't a threat to him, he can't bring himself to say a word because she knows his secret.

'I'm impressed, Mr Kempner, I'm really impressed,' Mrs Buschkamp says admiringly. 'But you should clear off now, Exner might be on the way, that brown-shirted bastard, he might be coming after you, and that's something we want to avoid.'

'What about you?' Lassehn asks the question that preoccupied him a little while before. 'Have you never done something? . . .'

Mrs Buschkamp waves the idea away.

'I'll sort out Exner, don't you worry about him. But if you have nowhere to stay, then come to old Ma Buschkamp, she'll put you up. And now if I were you I'd make myself scarce . . .'

Lassehn nods. 'But I actually wanted to see the Niedermeyers . . .'

'There's no one there now, Mr Kempner,' Mrs Buschkamp says. 'The old aunt certainly isn't at home, as soon as she hears the words north-west Germany she's straight out of there and into the bunker at the Zoo, and Irma was just leaving when you arrived, there's nothing to be done, you'll just have to come back later.'

Lassehn turns to go and holds out his hand to the old woman. 'Thank you, Mrs Buschkamp,' he says warmly. 'I'll definitely be back. Goodbye!'

'Goodbye, Mr Kempner!'

The phrase 'Mr Kempner' is like a slap in the face for Lassehn, it hurts him deeply because he hasn't told the old woman the whole truth.

VIII

Ethnology of a Small Town in Germany

'People have voluntarily given up their nobility, they have voluntarily brought themselves down to this lower step. They flee in horror from the spectre of their inner greatness, they acquiesce in their poverty, they decorate their chains with craven wisdom.'

Schiller, *Don Carlos*

The character of a place is determined by certain facts. It may have emerged from the landscape or from certain features of the landscape, the presence of a ford, a confluence of rivers, the crossing of roads, the abundance of nature, the fertility of the fields. Or else it has simply been founded, it owes its existence to a not entirely risk-free speculation if its birth occurs not in the depths of the earth but in the spartan office of an estate agent, when the seed that generates it and the ovum that receives it do not belong to the primal forces of nature, but are the fruits of a commercial spirit, which sees in the soil only parcels of land, in the forest only wood and in the rivers only the stretches of shoreline that bring in revenue, and balances everything out accordingly. The spirit which is manifested in the begetting of such places, and which acts as godfather at their baptism, accompanies them along their subsequent journeys. A village or a city are not just material, stone and wood and iron and asphalt, they have been moved and assembled by the human spirit, it leaves its mark on them, they absorb it into their pores and send it back out again. This inter-action grows weaker or stronger over time; either the material overwhelms the human being, or the human violates nature.

Eichwalde, on the suburban line from Görlitz Station to Königs Wusterhausen, is the result of a project that sprang from the brains of businessmen and property speculators. There is no tradition here, no heritage, no agricultural necessities have played any part here, all that mattered was its proximity to the transport network and the proximity of the big city. The town was arranged according to a predetermined plan. Many things remained at the stage of publicity and enticing promises, since the rapid urbanization of the settlement seemed to render their fulfilment otiose. From the outset the planners had aimed to attract a certain social stratum of the population, officials, senior executives and mid-ranking businessmen. This group drew its economic power from the industrial proletariat, but otherwise remained remote from it and above all did not want to be disturbed by the sight of workers – and later of the unemployed – in its residential areas, but was also unable to afford the exclusiveness of the haute bourgeoisie of Wannsee and Nikolassee, Dahlam and Grunewald. They looked down on the neighbouring town of Schulzendorf, whose houses had largely been constructed by the building workers themselves over months and years of difficult labour during their leisure time after work and on Sundays. It was contemptuously sneered at as the 'bricklayers' estate'. But they had not been able to prevent the influx of non-bourgeois elements entirely, since anyone was eligible to purchase new land. So into this middle-bourgeois milieu there trickled a number of existences which, in Marxist terminology, belonged to the labour aristocracy. Still, however, the population of Eichwalde – a few exceptions aside – formed a homogenous whole, and that homogeneity was essentially down to a single cause: landed property. It is the landed property of the middle and petit-bourgeois people who have attained ownership through work, luck and other favourable circumstances, who cling firmly to it, defend it with every means to hand and look down contemptuously on anyone who has not managed to do the same. That here – where the terror of expropriation reigned – there could be no room for socialist ideas, should be clear to anyone familiar with the character of such settlements.

In this place – and here Eichwalde stands in for hundreds and hundreds of places, villages, small towns, settlements, hamlets, parishes, communities – people live for themselves, here each person sees himself as having a particular individuality, but it is the individuality of sheep, sheep that are not herded closely together, but driven a large distance apart. The restriction of their space for economic movement corresponds to the constricted nature of their intellectual world. Subservience and reverence for political and military strong men is complemented by their contempt for the weak, the oppressed, the fallen. It is here that National Socialism finds its most fertile breeding ground, when it turns out that it is entirely socially acceptable, that even bankers, industrialists and senior military officers, university professors, poets and artists wear the Party badge, and the term 'workers' party' is only one of many decoys used by the man from Braunau. If these people had previously followed one of the thirty-three parties in the Weimar Republic, and thus a misunderstood democracy, now they are now gripping with both hands the strong rope of a new kind of authority. The undisputed authority of the monarchy was followed by a vacuum in which all authorities, government, Church, family, became unstable, offered no solid footing and finally dissolved, while social respect and economic certainty were lost. As a result, people unhesitatingly projected their own sense of inferiority upon the nation as a whole, and it became the norm of behaviour. The unfortunate German inclination towards the doctrinaire, the categorical and the exclusive is in harmony with the claim to total power of the National Socialist tyrants. People willingly allow themselves to be crammed together and levelled out into a so-called 'national community'. Then they play their own part in the process of adjustment by appropriating the terminology of the regime, which contains, in a horribly intensified form, all the ingredients of what might be seen as the German character: national pride and a sense of community, militarism and an entrepreneurial spirit, pioneering work and anti-Semitism. The constitution of a new middle-bourgeois class now seems assured, after the rise and power of the working class has raised it to the same level and thus robbed the petite bourgeoisie of its claim to a position on the last-but-one rung on the social ladder. The authority of God's mercy has been – after the interregnum of a period without authority – replaced by the claim to power of a new autocracy, which is only hesitantly recognized, since it comes from within the ranks of this class, and then greeted enthusiastically because it is successful. At the same time the credulous middle and petite bourgeoisie, who have come worryingly close to the level of the proletarian masses through the loss of their property and savings as a result of inflation, spot the chance of economic growth, and when has a bourgeois heart ever resisted the blandishments of economic growth? They see the boost in the economy and hear the cries of work and bread, they laugh at the warning voices prophesying that the very same boost can be twisted into a terrible dance of death, that they will one day be destroyed by that work and choke on that bread. They do not feel the fetters that National Socialism places on its subjects as being such, because German submission to *raison d'état* and orders from above is raised to a new level by elevation to the noble race, the right to self-determination, and personal freedom is compensated by the primacy of the German people in the world. Dazzled by the economic successes of the illusory boom, the petit-bourgeois masses devote themselves to National Socialism and identify with its goals, making them their own and over-emphasizing them with the pride of the parvenu. They deprive themselves of their own decision-making capacity, and renounce any independent moral thought, since the Führer is always right. And since no one else speaks, they slip at last into a psychic trauma, in which their complete intellectual and mental violation is accomplished. The pendulum of the German sense of being has always swung back and forth between self-contempt and self-over-estimation, and the action in one direction is now followed by the reaction in the other. They sigh with relief at dissolving into a nation of brothers, who all belong to one and the same Party, or at least act as its followers. The inversion of all values into their opposite, their grotesque distortion and the disparagement of all ideals that even call into question the hegemony of the Nazi programme, all of this is accepted without objection, people enter a form of tutelage that is followed by an inconceivable intellectual alienation. The deployment of hatred as the governing idea of the state is greeted enthusiastically, the accumulated resentments of the petit bourgeoisie are discharged against political, religious and racial minorities. They listen as if enchanted to that mighty voice which, with impudent sarcasm, declares the intellectual achievements of 4,000 years of world history to be invalid, which moves each stone in Germany and turns each wheel, which sets the armies in motion and ploughs the world's waves, to which all is owed and which is always right. At the same time these people are not aware that loyalty has become a lack of character, respect has become servility, obedience slavery and service of the state the practice of denunciation.

Where Eichwalde passes into the parish of Zeuthen, in a small, short side street there is a cottage, narrow and with a pointed roof, not in fact any different from the other houses in the surroundings, it is built far back from the street, and is surrounded by a few tall pine trees, while towards the street it is shielded by a clump of spruce. This house, as unremarkable as it may appear from the outside, has long been at the centre of general interest, until that interest, a mixture of curiosity and gossip, was covered over by other, greater events, since gossip and curiosity cannot be permanent conditions. On a number of occasions public attention has been drawn repeatedly to this house, and its obscure past was remembered. Nothing stays so clearly in the mind of the petite bourgoisie as the recall of things that diminish others and thus elevate one's sense of oneself, and nothing is better suited to making one appear complacent in the eyes of the ruling party, and to be seen as a loyal citizen, than to join in the boycott of those disliked by the regime.

The house in question belongs to the former trade union secretary and Reichstag member Friedrich Wiegand. But he has only rarely been able to delight in his own home, and in the idyllic peace and quiet of the Brandenburg landscape not at all, since he moved into his house at a time when the most severe labour struggles were being fought out, racing from one tariff negotiation to the next, from Berlin to the Ruhrgebiet, from the North Sea coast to Upper Silesia, from Saxony to Baden.

These years were followed immediately by the rule of National Socialism, which for Wiegand meant only persecution and arrest. He was arrested for the first time on the day of the Reichstag fire, then released after twenty-seven months and placed under very close surveillance over the following years. Whenever there was any internal and external crisis in the Hitler regime, he was imprisoned again and interned in concentration camps. Shortly before the invasion of the Soviet Union he chose to go underground, since police surveillance and the constant checks of the Gestapo left him with no freedom of movement and clandestine work took up the whole of his being. Wiegand disappeared from Eichwalde, he simply wasn't there any more, no house search brought any clues to his whereabouts, no surprise nocturnal raid led to his discovery or pointed to his trail.

His family had stayed in the house, his wife and four children. His wife, Lucie Wiegand, is one of those wives who stick by their husbands for good or ill, not because custom and morals decree it, and not out of habit or natural persistence, but because an irrepressibly strong emotion and an unshakeable faith in the cause for which he fights binds her to him. Not for a second has she wavered, she has never in moments of weakness struggled with a fate that has frequently robbed her of her husband. Neither has she ever tried to play her husband Friedrich Wiegand off against the politician Friedrich Wiegand – on the contrary, she has always taken strength from him not to give in. She has never thought of persuading him into the Nazi camp to escape the dangers that threaten him, and thus attain some kind of peaceful existence.

Socializing with criminals in the Nazi state is not necessarily dangerous, but socializing with so-called enemies of the state and politically unreliable elements (and of course with Jews) is considered a serious felony.

A magic circle soon formed around the Wiegand family which no one dared to enter, as the floodlights of police surveillance illuminated everyone who even dared to approach that circle. But there was no one there who would have risked such a thing, since it would have run contrary to the efforts of the German bourgeoisie not to stand out or make oneself unpopular in any way. The hatred that had raged in most of the residents of the settlement suddenly came to light and flared up.

Lucie Wiegand had proudly endured the ostracism imposed upon her after the takeover of the government by the Nazis, she had made no attempt to break through the ring of silence placed around her, and not returned any greeting that she was given in a secret or a furtive way. She had always had little to do with the bourgeois world that surrounded her, her points of contact with it had only ever been general and superficial. She didn't miss the social contact, and the ostracism caused her no pain, but she revealed the cowardice and dishonesty of the bourgeoisie in her immediate vicinity, to whom she had suddenly become unacceptable.

Lucie Wiegand is a delicate woman of medium height, she is still as slender as a young girl even though she has had four children, her narrow face, whose beauty is only slightly dimmed by the shadow that care and suffering has thrown upon her, has the delicate complexion of strawberry blondes. The physical charms are equal to those of the soul and the mind. Just as her body, in spite of its delicate constitution, is unusually resilient, so too is her spiritual and mental attitude determined by the strong will not to bend to any external compulsion, and even in her darkest hours she has never been bowed by what is normally known as fate, but has always organized her life in a positive way, she has not, like most women, frittered herself away on trivial matters, but always had one great goal in mind. When in the spring of 1941 there was a purge against a series of former Communist and Social Democratic functionaries, and against left-wing bourgeois and Catholic politicians, and Friedrich Wiegand expected to be thrown into a concentration camp, she immediately agreed to live underground when that presented itself as the only way out.

Constantly surrounded by hatred and persecution, encircled by hostility and contempt, she saw her life as neither a disaster nor a gloomy fate, since it had to a certain degree been of her own making, by her political conviction and her desire to maintain it. But her life was shadowed by deep tragedy. It was the tragedy of parents in Germany who were hostile to Nazism for political, religious or other grounds, but who had to look on with impotent rage as the upbringing and intellectual guidance of their children was taken completely out of their hands and forced in a direction whose consequences were clear to them, but about which there was nothing they could do. Apart from that, life had one special surprise in store for Lucie Wiegand.

Robert, their oldest son, was a reckless over-achiever, he had an intelligence that translated all ideal values into material reality. The virtuous disposition was only a rung on life's ladder, a thing that one appropriated or pushed away as circumstances demanded, the content of the disposition was unimportant as long as it served the goal at hand. This curious feature of the boy's character had had very unpleasant consequences at school, and brought him reprimands from his parents, but it had at first remained to some extent in the private sphere. But that changed immediately when National Socialism came to power and forced its way with all its demands and blackmail into all the pores of public and private life. The boy suddenly found himself isolated and the target of sneering and hateful remarks, and he soon had to acknowledge that his parents could only give him personal consolation, but were unable to give him any public help or leap to his assistance. Even though he was a good pupil – he was at the time in the lower third of the upper school in Eichwalde – he found his progress hindered or at least inhibited, since now some teachers were taking masks from their faces and trying to win themselves a good reputation with Party officials and the new mayor with their particularly severe treatment of the 'red rascal'.

Since any form of caution was alien to the boy where his own person was concerned, and where reflection only formed an obstacle, and since public recognition was more important to him than inner confirmation, the thirteen-year-old took a step that abruptly separated him from his parents: he became a member of the Hitler Youth, which was not at the time the compulsory organization for

German youth that it later became. But he did not just do that: he publicly disavowed his parents, he moved away from them, and was soon the keenest member of the group.

Lucie Wiegand – at this point her husband had just been arrested for the first time – was by no means the kind of woman who would have smacked her son for his wilful behaviour or heaped him with reproaches; instead she tried to use persuasion. She understood that the boy did not want to stand apart from his bourgeois environment, which with its waving flags had made itself dependent on the new people's tribune, that he couldn't bear to see others writhing in enthusiasm and devoting themselves to mass psychosis while he himself had to stand on the sidelines as an uninvolved and rejected onlooker, that he had fallen prey to a serious inferiority complex. But all of her words bounced off the boy's determination not to play the role of a pariah, but to enjoy equal status and equal respect among the others.

Even when Wiegand was released from the concentration camp and came home, and learned of the transformation in his son, nothing changed, the boy refused to respond to reason, he strode off along his chosen path with an iron resolve that he had inherited from his father, and willingly allowed the poison of National Socialism to seep into him just as he greedily absorbed and appropriated everything that might serve and benefit his new role.

It was a short step from rejecting his parents and their ideals to treating them with contempt. In the end his parental home was merely a place of shelter, of food and drink, and what in fact remained in terms of emotional fragments had been entirely removed through the systematic undermining of parental authority by the Hitler Youth. Lucie Wiegand suffered indescribably under this change in their relationship. When she looked into her son's hard face, when she felt his cold eyes sliding over her and her husband, a wave of horror ran through her: was this her son, whom she had conceived in love, and who had grown in her womb? Then in her mind she ran through all the stages of his development, from his first time at her breast until the present day. What diabolical force had possessed the boy, that everything good she had tried to plant within him was suppressed in favour of an almost manic ambition?

Time and again she tried in every way she could to breach his walls, appealing to emotions and giving voice to reason, but she could get nowhere near him, his membership of the Hitler Youth released him from all family relationships, from respect and from gratitude. In her despair she even played the materialistic card, but the seventeen-year-old merely laughed scornfully and looked down at his mother standing there in front of him, small and delicate, with helpless eyes and drooping shoulders, he looked at her with a superior demeanour and a contemptuous expression, because the term 'Thousand-Year Reich' had just been coined.

The older Robert Wiegand grew, the greater was the tension between him and his father. When the Gestapo took Friedrich Wiegand away again during the Austrian crisis in 1938, his son cynically observed that it might have been better to keep his father constantly imprisoned before he brought misfortune upon the whole family; he wasn't going to change, he simply lacked the good sense to understand the new way of things, and he didn't want to either. An enemy of the state was an enemy of the state, and the fact that he happened to be his father changed nothing in that respect.

After Robert Wiegand had left school and completed his year of labour service, he joined the SS as a volunteer. Now, in April 1945, almost three years have passed since he last set foot in Eichwalde. Lucie Wiegand can only think back with horror at his last period of leave, of which he only spent half at her house, because she was forced to acknowledge with a shudder that something which her son had at first seemed to appropriate only superficially as a means to an end had in the meantime become flesh and blood and the most essential part of his life. If a conciliatory trait had appeared rarely, but every now and again, in the boy, with his uniform he also seemed to have put on an armour which tears, reproaches and grief, pleas and curses, bounced off ineffectually; by wearing the uniform he seemed to have acquired a right that exculpated him from any personal bonds, and obliged him to become completely insensitive towards human fates. He had in the end reached the final spiritual state in which there was no more room for individual thought and feeling. And again Lucie had faced the terrible question of whether this boy, who talked about racially inferior people as if they were bothersome vermin, about the necessary debasement of the biological potential of the enemy as if discussing the eradication of harmful plants, was really her son, who had once entered her in the form of a seed and had been nourished on her blood. That night she cried for a long time, not out of grief but out of shame. She tested herself and ruthlessly exposed her own thoughts, but she could find nothing to blame herself for. She and her husband had always done everything they could to make the boy turn out like them, but the external compulsion had been stronger, but – and this had also become clear to her during that night – it could not only have been pressure from without. There must have been something else, some kind of ferment at work in Nazi theories which replaced the protective shell that had been imposed upon people for many centuries and which had masked the wild instincts of the cannibals of the jungle, which awoke the barbarian within and laid bare all the wild instincts, imperiousness and the drive to conquer, rapacity and bloodlust, rape and arson, and spurred and spurred them on. The unhappy mother's feverish imagination saw her son advancing in cold blood on the tormented inhabitants of the conquered Russian territory with his sub-machine gun and riding whip, throwing burning torches into peaceful villages, carved in his face, which still bore the innocent features of the child he had once been, she now saw the mark of Cain of the SS runes. It was simply inconceivable that her own son should wear the same uniform as those criminals who had taken her husband away so often and even now, from time to time, entered their domestic world at night, turned everything upside down, insulted her with the worst obscenities and took out their fury over the failure of their searches on the objects they found, casually sweeping a vase from the credenza or slinging the dog into the corner with a swift kick.

But in her despair over the psychical cretinism of her son she derived some comfort from her other three children, twenty-year-old Ernst, sixteen-year-old Katharina and thirteen-year-old

Rosemarie. Even though they were younger than Robert, and had been exposed to Nazi influence at a younger age than their brother, even though they had barely known anything else, the parental counterweight had managed to achieve a certain balance. But it had not been possible to exclude the Nazi influence entirely, since the image of the world given to them by their parents was riddled with holes. The two girls in particular, for whom emotion was the gauge of things, were unable to escape this influence, but a solid core of doubt remained within them. But emotion also enabled them to renew and cement that core time and again, since it would never have occurred to them to doubt their mother's integrity, and the very fact that the teachers had always presented their eldest brother to them as the glowing example of a convinced and fanatical Nazi meant that their doubt was repeatedly enriched.

At the age of fourteen, Ernst Wiegand had suffered a complicated fracture which had left him with one leg much shorter than the other, which had freed him from labour service and excused him from the military. He was a curious mixture, a dreamy idealist and at the same time a solid realist, he escaped from harsh reality into an unearthly romanticism, but he also dissected the phenomena of the present with keen logic and surprising discernment. He trod his path like one whose steps find only occasional purchase, and who can see the edges of the path for the briefest of moments, but whose feet cannot find solid ground and whose eyes cannot see how the road continues. He was attracted by much in the teachings of the Nazis, failing to recognize that they used the great heritage of German culture only as a preamble and a shield, that behind Goethe, Beethoven and Kant there marched the endless ranks of eternal soldiers, of imperialist slavers and murderous racial theorists, that at every available opportunity culture was worn without any particular obligations like a Sunday suit (because a murderer in tails is still a murderer), that they impudently faked and twisted their traditional intellectual legacy for their own purposes, with the manners of horse traders. But Ernst Wiegand did not succumb to the Nazi ideology, because what in his sisters assumed the form of a doubt, a mutable but fixed component of their mental attitude, was for him already an (admittedly quite patchy) accumulation of recognitions. Everything that he had always acknowledged as true and right was firmly anchored within him, and in the few hours that he had spent with his father at secret assignations during his years underground he had been full to bursting with questions, and had used that short period of time to cram in as much knowledge as possible. A bright light always emerged from those meetings, they became a place of anchorage for the shipwrecked vehicle of his hopes, the light that his father always lit within him went on glowing until it was overshadowed once again by the official propaganda machine. Ernst Wiegand was driven mad by everything, he believed his father, but he also believed certain things that had been inculcated into the people as eternal truths, as an inalienable tradition and the justified claims of a great nation, it went beyond his powers of imagination to conceive that anything delivered with utter conviction and a respectable demeanour, from pulpits, lecterns and podiums, might be nothing but lies and betrayal, fakery and slander. So because the one ruled out the other he constantly oscillated between that which was to some extent innate within him, and repeatedly reborn in him, and that which pressed upon him with the brute force of conviction and an intransigent faith in the Führer; he sometimes caught himself falling prey to the prejudices so insistently preached and the assessments constantly repeated and he had to summon all of his logic to master them. Yet he could not keep a small remnant from staying within him like a viscous sediment.

He thoroughly despised his elder brother Robert, and his contempt turned to hatred the last time his brother came home on leave, when he delivered the scurrilous observation that it would be better if their father never returned from hiding. Only the fact that Ernst was transferred to Silesia with his firm that same day – he worked as a precision engineer in the electrical industry – prevented the two brothers from coming to blows. His sudden departure spared him a defeat that he would never have been able to deal with, because not only was he physically weaker than his brother, he was also his intellectual inferior. Ernst's rejection of National Socialism, a matter both of instinct and superficial knowledge, would have had to face the robustness and brutality, power-drenched, self-confident and certain of victory, of the future master of the world. All of his arguments would have been stifled by bloody cynicism and demolished by the dogma of the racial theory that excluded everything else.

In April 1945 Lucie Wiegand was alone. Her husband lived in hiding, only half an hour's train journey away and yet impossible to contact, her older son was fighting somewhere on the eastern front, she knew nothing of her younger son, as he was with his firm in a factory that had in the meantime been overrun by the Russians, her sixteen-year-old daughter was doing labour service in Pomerania, and thirteen-year-old Rosemarie was in an evacuation camp in the Sudetenland. She herself had been called up to work in an armaments factory, and had to do nine hours of the most tedious work every day near Scharzkopff in Wildau. Her features are etched with the weary, exhausted expression seen on the faces of hard-working women, but there is a gleam in her eyes, it comes alive more and more every day and becomes a glow, because the millstones of the Allied war machine are crushing the front lines with terrible force. When the catastrophe at last engulfs everyone, it will bring one cheering thing with it: the end of Hitler's accursed Reich.

IX

The change of shift at the Karlshorst depot is over. Between the tracks of the railway and the S-Bahn, and the many sidings, the long rows of fast, express and goods trains, shunting locomotives, points and signals, signal bridges and signal boxes, those coming off their shift stream to the Rummelsberg depot. They walk fast, because a few minutes ago the sirens wailed loudly again to announce the public air-raid warning, and everyone wants to get home quickly before the full alarm sounds.

Friedrich Wiegand is in no particular hurry, he doesn't care whether the alarm forces him to take refuge in a cellar or a shelter here or somewhere else. He has a home, but it is closed to him, he has a wife and children but he isn't allowed to see them. He doesn't think about that now, however, he is preoccupied with something quite different, so he walks slowly, he lets others overtake him and ignores their warning cries. If you walk at a fast pace you can't think, and thinking is precisely what he has to do now. He has to think clearly about certain things, that is much more important than avoiding an air raid or mulling over the question of which air-raid shelter is safest or whether there's enough time to reach a bunker. The danger that threatens him from the air doesn't scare him, there's another danger, not yet discernible, not yet tangible, but it is there, it is in the air, the atmosphere is saturated with it. Wiegand does not lull himself into a false sense of security for a moment, he can never quite abandon caution, it has become a habit to him, and it weighs each word, guides each gesture, it governs his relationship with his surroundings and determines his actions. But it is not a petty fear for his life, it is his concern about the task he has set himself, this task that requires the greatest devotion and earns no applause, no acknowledgement, one that is its own reward.

The destruction or temporary disabling of locomotives, the cutting of signal wires, the decommissioning of major points, the burning of coal bunkers and not least the bringing of flyers and proclamations to many places in the depot is the work that Wiegand has been doing for a long time. It requires a high level of manoeuvrability, because he always has to be where he is least expected, he must always concentrate the whole of his attention to act at the right moment without arousing suspicion or being caught. He relies entirely on himself, it is a constant battle for the opportunity, the favourable moment, against chance and the pack of hounds on his heels. He has the advantage of knowing the huntsmen, the men from the plant and rail security service, which received reinforcements some months ago and which guards the grounds day and night, but the guards act with the stubborn thoroughness of functionaries, they go on their rounds loyally and dutifully, they always appear at particular points at the same time each day, so that you could almost set your watch by them. Every few days they search the workers and the office employees, now in the locomotive workshop, then again in the rail depot, another time by the cranes or by the exits, but the only things that come to light are contraband cigarettes or alcohol or a rucksack full of coal or wood with which the thief planned to improve his coal rations. No, Wiegand isn't afraid of huntsmen like these, they are too stupid and unimaginative, as criminal investigators they work as monotonously as if they were working a piece of iron on a lathe or selling train tickets. More dangerous are those colleagues who would like to earn a promotion through espionage and bragging, or the ones who are in the Party or the SA and now sense the menacing calamity that threatens their whole existence, their property and their lives, who would like to strangle everyone who isn't 100 per cent in favour of National Socialism, who would like to force everyone to fight and even die with them, who will allow no one to survive the catastrophe by which they are already mesmerized, which is advancing towards them on giant strides and already casting its shadows over them. But these people are not Wiegand's equals. Over the last few years he has learned to tame and train his tongue, to allow his face to fall into hypocritical wrinkles, and hypocrisy and the habit of telling people what they want to hear are the prime requirements of the Third Reich.

But for some time now there has been something new. It has not escaped Wiegand that for a few weeks a young man he has never seen before has appeared in the depot. Of course there is nothing unusual about new people turning up in the depot, but there is something quite special about this young man, he doesn't wear the uniform of the Reich railwayman, sometimes he is dressed in inconspicuous plain clothes, and then he is usually accompanied by inspectors and senior inspectors of the plant output, or else he wears a blue overall that is still quite new and shows no traces of work, no bare patches, no tears, no mending and no oil stains, and then he roams around like a hunting dog that has lost its scent, or strolls about harmlessly, but his eyes are constantly darting about. He presents himself as an engineer who is supposed to be getting to know the depot, and he doesn't play his part badly, he even has some knowledge of engineering, but it is just a role that he is playing. Wiegand has soon worked out that he is anything but an engineer, he seems more like someone who knows a few Latin quotations but not the simplest declension or conjugation because he has no knowledge of the language itself.

So why is this young man wandering about the depot? During these weeks when the whole workforce of the Reichsbahn is being exploited down to the very last man, is there really time to allow a young engineer to act as some kind of volunteer, like a junior manager from a partner depot? Unlikely, very unlikely. It is no secret that the mood in the Karlshorst depot is extremely bad, with the advance of the Allied armies, but since the Russians have reached Küstrin and Frankfurt an der Oder the foreigners have become increasingly recalcitrant, they often stay away from work without any explanation, they are becoming rebellious, and only a few weeks ago a foreman was beaten half to death by a gang of Eastern workers who could no longer bear to watch him sadistically tormenting a group of Ukrainian women who had to do extremely difficult work on the tracks. Were they going to set another example here, were a few men going to be sent to the camps? The fellow smells like a spy, and he can't hide it with the perfume of benevolence and sympathy with the workers, there's something of the police informer about him, he's a good actor, but only to the superficial observer. Over the years of living underground Wiegand's eye has grown keener, he can't see ghosts, but he can see behind masks and listen out for undertones.

Or . . . struck by a sudden suspicion, Wiegand pauses. What if the presence of this chap has something to do with his own sabotage work and the distribution of those flyers? Wiegand forces his memory to concentrate on a particular point.

How did that happen? The lad has also approached him, there's no doubt about it, the conversations, most of which only lasted a few minutes, weren't exactly forced, but equally they weren't quite natural either, they always started out with some kind of technical question and then immediately leaped to the war and the situation in general, then the young man always hinted that he had had enough of the war, and that the Führer ought to call the whole thing off before all was lost. Wiegand had only smiled inwardly, he was decades past the stage of reacting to provocative phrases, so he hadn't been tempted to join in, had instead cursed the bloodhound Stalin, the alcoholic Churchill and war criminal number one Roosevelt, stressing his confidence of victory and his trust in the new weapons that were about to be put into action, but even though Wiegand had only expressed himself in positive terms, the young man had come to him another two or three times. Had he attracted suspicion after all?

Wiegand runs through his behaviour over the past while but can't find anything suspicious that would have lifted him out of the crowd, he has always gone to work with extreme caution, he has never had a witness, never a confidant, he has always worked alone because he sees that as the best guarantee of going undiscovered.

Only once was he nearly caught, he still remembers that night very clearly, all the details have fixed themselves firmly and inextinguishably in his mind. It was during an air-raid warning, a few dozen Mosquitoes had dropped bombs and blockbusters, immediately after the pre-all-clear Wiegand and some others had left the air-raid shelter, the lamps on the tall masts above the sidings hadn't yet been lit, the emergency lights were still on in the locomotive workshop, a few spare, blue-glass bulbs had dispersed a gloomy light around the long, dark hall.

He knew that a locomotive had just been made ready to drive on track 5, an ammunition train had been left in Erkner because of mechanical damage and Karlshorst had to supply an 03 as a replacement, it was already under steam and only needed watering. The hall was still deserted, there wasn't a soul. The only sound was the monotonous stamp of the air compressor and the hum of a few night fighters circling pointlessly above the city. He jumped impetuously onto the train, with a wrench he struck back the levers that held the smoke chamber shut and threw a high-explosive cartridge between the flue tubes. Just as he was about to shut the door of the smoke chamber and push the locking lever forward again, someone who had apparently slept through the alarm in one of the trains grabbed him by the shoulder from behind. Fear numbed Wiegand like a blow to the heart, but only for a few seconds, he didn't fight back, but knocked his attacker down with a wrench and disappeared into the darkness. When the all-clear sounded a few minutes later he was standing at his workplace. Of course there had been a big investigation, but it had yielded no results, not a hint of suspicion had fallen on him, and otherwise he had never given himself away.

No, Wiegand shakes his head and walks on, it's out of the question that . . . And yet, something inside him errs on the side of caution. But for now he won't have any chance of committing acts of sabotage, since from tomorrow he has been transferred to a track-building column. However unpleasant that transfer might be, he is reassured, because if he was suspected of being the saboteur they would probably have left him in the depot to catch him *in flagrante.*

When Wiegand reaches Lebuser Strasse, the sirens are piercing the air with a long wail. All clear! So the American squadrons have changed direction and not flown towards Berlin.

Number four Lebuser Strasse is a bleak, grey, discoloured stone box that no longer deserves the term house, in fact it never did, it rises five storeys high, massive and crude, among its equally botched neighbours and lines a small, dark courtyard, its asphalt warped, battered and full of holes, with rubbish bins spilling over. It is divided into the front part, two side buildings and a rear wing, every corner is exploited to the maximum. The architect saw comfort as a waste of space, because it brought the rent down. There is a musty, stuffy atmosphere in the building, which was created by a capitalist desire for profit and a subservient, complacent architect.

Wiegand is lying on the sofa, he is very tired, and would like to sleep for a few hours before going to Klose's, but sleep doesn't come, even though weariness lies heavy on his eyelids and his limbs are like lead. It isn't just the thoughts circling incessantly within him and keeping him from sleep, it's something else, something that keeps him awake. The hostile caution with which every German meets foreigners, the hypocrisy with which he arms himself, the shy rejection that he puts on like armour, these things are very much Wiegand's own. He is a sober and realistic thinker, he pays no heed to omens and premonitions, he isn't superstitious in the slightest, but he reacts to the finest stimuli of his instinct, he is aware of the tiniest deviations and the most delicate vibration of his compass needle. There is something in his room that makes him uneasy, something, something. But what?

He picks up the *Morgenpost* and scans the Wehrmacht report, as always he reads the news from the eastern front first, but nothing is happening there.

Between the Drava and the Danube . . . The brave defenders of Breslau . . . Between the mouth of the Neisse and the Oderbruch the Soviets have carried out numerous attacks, which were supported by a heavy tank presence particularly to the west of Küstrin. Our divisions fought off the Bolsheviks and in fierce fighting destroyed

98 tanks. Artillery effectively halted the concentrations of troops and the attacking enemy forces with heavy fire. From the plain to the west of the Vistula . . . Sambia front . . . Holland . . . between Ems and the Lower Elbe . . .

South-east of Magdeburg grenadiers pushed back the Americans who had advanced over the Elbe. Further south counter-attacks were under way against other local bridgeheads.

Ruhr . . . Bergisches Land . . . western and southern Harz . . . south of Bernburg a large American fighting unit forced its way across the Saale. The troops advancing on Leipzig and Chemnitz were halted by reservists and containing troops.

Wiegand sets aside the paper, he is unsettled about something, he straightens his torso and looks around, but everything is in the right place, nothing has changed. But there's something . . . Suddenly Wiegand knows what has startled him: the room smells of tobacco, not insistently, but perceptibly. Wiegand knows very well that he hasn't smoked here for days, the smell that floats in the room tells him that someone has been smoking here very recently. Clouds of tobacco that settled here a long time ago smell differently, there is something musty and stale about them, but this smell is unmistakeably fresh. Wiegand slips from the sofa, walks around the room and sniffs around like a dog with his nose in the air.

No, he's not mistaken. Someone has been smoking in the room very recently, he even thinks he can sense that it isn't one of the usual cigarettes, a Stambul or a Juno or one of the new rationed varieties, but one with a sweetish Virginia smell. Who has been smoking here? There's no point wondering about something if there's a chance of discovering the truth. Wiegand leaves his room, crosses the corridor and seeks out his landlady in her kitchen.

'Has anyone been asking after me, Mrs Schmitz?' he begins.

'No, Mr Adamek,' the woman replies.

'And no one was waiting for me in my room?'

'Not at all, Mr Adamek,' Mrs Schmitz reassures him. 'No one has been here.'

Wiegand stands there uncertainly for a moment, he doesn't

know whether and how he should take his questions further, but then he quickly decides he has to get to the bottom of things, too much depends on it.

'Do you smoke, Mrs Schmitz?' he asks first.

Mrs Schmitz looks up in surprise and lets the stocking she is darning fall into her lap. 'You ask very odd questions, Mr Adamek,' she says dubiously.

'Odd or otherwise,' Wiegand replies impatiently, 'please answer my question.'

'If you really want to know,' Mrs Schmitz says, slightly insulted, 'I don't smoke, I send the few cigarettes on my women's ration card . . .'

Wiegand waves her words away. 'But someone has been smoking in my room,' he says firmly, 'yesterday or today.'

Mrs Schmitz sets aside her darning with a resolute gesture, as if to open a completely new phase of the conversation. 'What are you getting at, Mr Adamek?'

'I'm not saying anything, Mrs Schmitz, I'm just asking,' Wiegand replies.

'Then I'm sorry, I don't understand your question,' Mrs Schmitz says.

Wiegand pulls himself together. 'I would like you to tell me who has been smoking in my room today or possibly yesterday.'

"No one has been smoking in your room, Mr Adamek, no one has been here,' Mrs Schmitz says emphatically. 'Or do you think I have a boyfriend and go to your room, of all places, to . . . Please, Mr Adamek.'

'You misunderstand me, Mrs Schmitz,' Wiegand says, calming the excitable woman. 'I don't suspect you at all, far from it, but I need to know who has been in my room.'

'I don't know,' Mrs Schmitz says and shrugs, 'I really don't know. Is it so important to you?'

A matter of life and death, Wiegand thinks, but of course he can't say that to the woman, he hasn't been able to look behind the mask that everyone wears in Hitler's Reich, and previously he hasn't been interested. Questions usually produce counter-questions, and he has no intention of lifting even a hem of the camouflage coat that he has to wear, for this woman he is the railway worker Franz Adamek from Ratibor, who is getting divorced from his wife, that was what he told her when he rented a furnished room from her in September 1944, and he has added no further information to that. He avoided all attempts by Mrs Schmitz and her husband, who was sent off to join the Volkssturm a few days before, to set up a kind of house community, and apart from a few general phrases when they have happened to meet they have barely exchanged two dozen words.

'It isn't as important as all that,' Wiegand says, 'but I would have liked to know. You know my wife always spies on me . . . Were you away for a long time yesterday?'

'Yesterday evening I was with my sister on Fruchtstrasse for a few hours,' Mrs Schmitz replies, and looks at Wiegand with a surprised and questioning eye. 'Do you mean that in my absence . . .'

Wiegand doesn't answer the question. 'And did you notice anything? Was anyone hanging about here on the stairs or outside the front door?'

Mrs Schmitz shakes her head. 'No, I didn't see anyone . . . unless you mean something like the key turning heavily in the lock, when it usually closes so easily . . .'

'The lock didn't work?'

'That would be taking it too far,' Mrs Schmitz thinks, 'but it was difficult, as if someone had been fiddling with it. Do you really think someone tried to get into the flat?'

'I think someone not only tried, but was in the flat, in my room,' Wiegand says stoutly. 'So now the matter is resolved, there is nothing missing. Good evening, Mrs Schmitz.'

The matter is far from resolved, Wiegand thinks as he leaves the kitchen and goes back to his room, it is only just starting, and we will have to establish once and for all whether anything is missing.

When he enters his room again he can smell cigarettes very clearly. He begins to look systematically through all the containers in which he keeps his things. Everything is still very orderly, but not so untouched and in such neat order that Wiegand wouldn't notice that it has been moved by the hands of a stranger. Since living underground, Wiegand has assumed the habit of committing to memory how he leaves his things, and now he can see quite clearly that everything has been touched and then put back in its old place. The stranger who has gone through his belongings has taken the greatest trouble to leave everything as he found it, but he didn't quite succeed, because Wiegand knows very well that it was not the *Nachtausgabe* but the *Berliner Morgenpost* that was on top of the pile, he deliberately left the lining of his right jacket pocket poking out, and now it has been put smoothly and neatly back, he also notices that the mattress of his bed is sticking out a little more over the side, and that the bed sheet has only been loosely stuffed back in, and there are other clues, only tiny trivia, but they indicate beyond a doubt that a thorough search has been carried out by a very smart sleuth. And he has also taken something with him, an identity card that is two years old and which Wiegand no longer needs because the Reichsbahn has introduced new IDs in the meantime.

When Wiegand has thoroughly searched his room, he sits down in an armchair, crosses his legs and considers what he knows. Someone has secretly entered the flat and very thoroughly searched his room, a stranger at the depot has taken a keen interest in him on a number of occasions. Might there be a connection between those two things? The question is not unimportant, in fact it is of great importance, because it contains another question: does the search relate to railway worker Franz Adamek or former Reichstag member Friedrich Wiegand? At any rate it is clear that he is under suspicion, suspicion of something, and in the Third Reich suspicion alone means Gestapo and the camps. It is, however, unclear why he hasn't yet been arrested, a lack of evidence has never prevented the Gestapo from arresting someone, the gentlemen from the Prinz Albrecht Palais and Kurfürstenstrasse aren't as highly strung as that, and if he's being allowed to keep walking freely around, there must be a reason for it, it wouldn't happen without some particular intent. There isn't time right now to discover that intent, he needs to act quickly and resolutely.

Wiegand sits very still for a few more minutes and looks into the gloom outside the window. He can feel the net that has been thrown over him almost physically, he feels it on his skin, contracting and snaring him, taking his breath away. But he isn't anxious, he has forgotten what fear feels like in the difficult years of the Nazi terror. He didn't know it in the past either, when he had to put himself at risk at demonstrations or in beer-hall fights, but no net is so tightly woven that there isn't a way of slipping out of it. You just have to find the gap.

Wiegand gets to his feet and packs his things together, there aren't many of them, they fit comfortably in the middle-sized suitcase that he takes from the wardrobe. When it is completely dark, he will leave the flat and not go back into it, and he won't go to work tomorrow either, there's no point putting himself unnecessarily in danger and waiting until the Gestapo's fist comes crashing down on him with all its weight.

Wiegand is under no illusions: they are on his trail, and he has to erase it.

X

These days getting from Charlottenburg to Silesian Station is more difficult, more awkward and almost more time-consuming, at any rate it is more laborious and tiring than a journey from Berlin to Königsberg once was. The S-Bahn, which only runs now for certain sections of the route, or on only one track, has been completely cancelled since the raid, and even the underground isn't running, or after only a few stations they say, 'Everybody out!', and whether and where and when it will start running again is unknown and difficult to find out. The trams, whose timetables change from day to day, have only run irregularly since the daylight raid on the western and south-western suburbs, to Spandau, Lichterfelde, Wilmersdorf, Halensee, Grunewald. No lines are running in the direction of the city centre and Moabit.

Lassehn has initially allowed himself to be carried along by the stream of people moving eastward. At Wittenbergplatz he has joined a group of three people, two men and a woman, who were making for Alexanderplatz. Their acquaintance came about quite casually, since after the air raids people have become rather more open than before. But there is no real friendliness in that openness, it is only a reaction to the danger that has been survived once more, a great sense of wonder and a kind of gratitude for the life that has been saved. It has nothing to do with the much-vaunted people's community, it is only a kind of reassurance upon which one lays claim when the feeling of being alone or an encroaching danger become so overwhelming that one can no longer endure it alone, it is the liberating feeling of having re-established a connection with the herd. For a short time, in one's fellow man or one's neighbour, one greets once more a creature of a related species, the rat race, the fight for a seat in the bunker or the S-Bahn, in the queue outside the grocers' shops or for the favour of the Party bosses, is laid to rest.

The air raids (and war in general) have joined people not into Goebbels' national community, but more into a kind of loose guild of people under threat. The emotion felt by these people before and during an air raid can be compared more or less with that of a school student who is relieved to discover that it wasn't only his essay that was given a poor mark, but that almost the whole class performed badly. Having survived the danger, once life re-emerges from caves and cellars into the smoke-dimmed daylight, people are governed by a feeling comparable to the one that travellers have towards each other once they have charged shoulder to shoulder onto a train and are now sitting opposite one another in the compartment, when the joy at finding a seat is still echoing within them and they now see someone who was a dangerous rival a moment ago as simply a harmless fellow passenger with rights equal to their own.

Lassehn had taken up position outside Wittenbergplatz underground station, whose entrances are closed, and the expression of bafflement on his face is too obvious to be ignored. While he stood irresolutely by the bars wondering whether it was worth waiting, two gentlemen and a lady walked up to the bars, darted a quick, practised look into the bleak interior of the ticket hall and then turned round again. The lady glanced briefly at Lassehn and then stopped in front of him.

'You could be waiting there for a long time,' she says amicably.

'Don't you think the underground . . .' Lassehn wonders.

'Are you from out of town?' the lady asks rather than answering.

Do I look that way?, Lassehn thinks quickly and nods.

'Come on, Lisa,' says one of the two gentlemen, 'it's already late enough.'

'Give me a minute, fatso,' the lady says, casually waving away his demand. 'Where are you trying to get to?' she says, turning back to Lassehn.

'To Silesian Station,' Lassehn says. 'I was wondering if the underground is still . . .'

'No point waiting for that, young man,' says the man the lady just addressed as fatso. He has a broad, red face with wobbly cheeks and a massive chin. 'Come along with us,' says the other man, 'we're going to Alexanderplatz.' He is a gaunt man of medium height with a pair of dark horn-rimmed spectacles, perhaps a teacher.

'If I may . . .' Lassehn says politely. He looks directly at the lady, she has bright, friendly eyes and her mouth is painted dark red.

And now Lassehn walks with them down Kleiststrasse, where there is barely a house that hasn't been destroyed, on either side nothing but burnt-out ruins, the intersecting streets are blocked by rubble. They walk first along the promenade and then, where the underground rises to the station at Nollendorfplatz, along the carriageway. Berliners have long assumed the habit of walking along the carriageways, as the pavements are often impassable, covered with rubble and debris, and also because it is less dangerous, for it is not uncommon for the looming walls to collapse all of a sudden. Lately people in the city have been telling of how on Müllerstrasse a ruined house fell on a tram, killing more than forty people, but the newspapers have not yet reported this misfortune.

Lassehn listens to his companions' conversations, he himself does not join in, he has soon discovered that the lady is married and her husband is in Italy where he is an army paymaster, that she works in something that she calls the government office, and the red-faced man is one of her colleagues. While the gentleman in the horn-rimmed glasses is a total stranger to them, their acquaintance is based solely on their shared occupancy of a public air-raid shelter, and only their common destination has made companions of them. The lady essentially dominates the conversation. Lassehn is amazed that there are so many words about things which, given the ruins and the constant threat from the air, should have sunk into utter insignificance. While Lassehn's gaze wanders constantly to the shattered walls, the smoking piles of rubble and the mountains of debris, he studies women with troubled faces carrying rubble out of their houses in buckets, or waiting stoically for water by the street pumps. While his boots crunch on shards of glass and slip along the tram lines, the three of them stride through the ruined streets with complete indifference, their eyes reflect neither horror nor surprise, and Lassehn finds himself wondering whether these people are even capable of greater emotions. It is as if the profusion of great events, whether negative or positive, has covered their souls with the calluses of complete insensitivity, and only very small emotions can penetrate them, that their brains have room only for extremely personal concerns, eating, drinking, sleeping and copulating, extra rations and air-raid reports.

Lassehn only occasionally catches a few words of their conversations, but he can't do anything with them, they awaken no associations, something quite different resonates within him. Given the destruction that is an almost permanent presence in the street, the superficiality causes him a nearly physical pain, and in the end he cannot hold back from making an observation during a pause in the conversation.

'I wonder,' he says, struggling to keep a note of reproach out of his voice, 'that you can walk so unperturbed among these ruins. Personally I'm terrified . . .'

The red-faced man turns towards Lassehn in surprise and looks at him as if only now noticing his presence.

'I don't understand,' he says, 'this is completely normal . . .'

The man with the horn-rimmed glasses interrupts him. 'Normal, certainly, but only for those of us who have experienced the growth of the destruction . . .'

'The growth of the destruction?' Lassehn replies 'But that's . . .'

'. . . a paradox, you mean,' the man with the horn-rimmed glasses says. 'Yes, of course, that's what it is, a mocking paradox, because growth and destruction are contradictory concepts, but let's leave that aside for now. What I meant was, and this is how you must understand my words, that we have witnessed house after house, street after street, district after district collapsing, because it didn't happen all at once. It wasn't, if I may use the comparison, a quick surgical strike, it is a great wound from which the pus goes on flowing again and again and further and further. When we saw the first ruined houses with their torn flanks, the twisted iron joists and the splintered beams, we were just as horrified as you seem to be now, because the first destroyed houses were gaps in the middle of life, but now life vegetates in the midst of destruction. Destruction has now become so great and so extensive that a ruined street is nothing special and barely worthy of attention. You can hardly imagine it.'

'Of course, if as an outsider one is suddenly placed in the midst of this ruined Berlin,' the lady says quickly, almost breathlessly, as if afraid that she won't have the chance to speak, 'of course you are horrified. But we also live, as you can see, in the midst of the rubble, and in the pauses between the air raids.'

'Is that life?' Lassehn wonders. 'Is not every action overshadowed by the coming dangers, by . . .'

'Oh nonsense,' the red-faced man cuts in roughly, 'don't get all poetic on us, lad, it doesn't fit this place. We're still alive . . .'

'And we still love,' the lady says, and laughs slightly hysterically. 'Take pleasure in life . . .' she hums a few bars of the song, but soon falls silent again.

However, the conversation has paused, both the lady and the red-faced man seem to have grown thoughtful, and the other gentleman has in any case always been more of a listener than a speaker.

Lassehn hadn't paid particular attention to the lady, he had only taken in her appearance with a fleeting glance, and had only really noticed her fiery red mouth, while now her laugh and the intimate tone of her voice draw his full attention to her. She is of middle height, well upholstered, as they say, and her suit is tailored in such a way that it emphasizes all the charms and assets of her figure, admittedly she is wearing rough ski-boots and thick, rolled-up woollen socks, but that is more than made up for by her very short skirt, which reveals a pair of slim and shapely legs. Lassehn's eye, which carefully rises from the lady's feet, now comes to rest on her face, the pretty face of a woman who is no longer quite young, with a small nose and full lips, precise eyebrows and bright, round eyes whose long, dark lashes reveal the experienced hand of a cosmetician. Her light-coloured hair, only a curl of it visible under her tight, dark-brown turban, is almost white-blonde. Her age is difficult to determine. Lassehn thinks she must be in her late twenties or early thirties, but he isn't quite sure, because he has no experience in such matters.

All in all, Lassehn decides, she is someone with a strong and even dangerous seductive power, every movement, every glance contains a barely restrained sensuality. She repels and attracts Lassehn to the same degree; she has all the qualities that stimulate the senses, and none of the charm of a young girl.

'You are unusually cheerful, madam,' says the man with the horn-rimmed spectacles. 'Where does your good mood come from?'

'From trivia, nothing but trivia,' she replies, laughing. 'The fact that the weather is nice today . . .'

'. . . and offers an excellent view to the Americans,' the red-faced man joins in.

'. . . and half a pound of extra butter that I got yesterday . . .' the lady goes on.

'. . . for a hundred and seventy-five marks,' the red-faced man says.

'. . . and the fact that I've still got my flat,' the woman continues her list.

'. . . which could have gone up in smoke today,' the red-faced man insists.

'. . . and doubtless a field-post letter from your husband,' the man with the horn-rimmed glasses ventures to add.

The lady looks at him almost dismissively. 'Yes, of course, certainly, that too,' she says hastily, but it doesn't sound as convincingly delightful as the butter and the fine weather.

Meanwhile they have reached Potsdamer Bridge, and here again there is little but rubble, ruined houses and mounds of debris. But the destruction is somehow contained and cleared. The rubble doesn't just lie around on the pavements, it has been carried inside the ruins, the battered bricks have been lined up neatly in the gaps of the burnt-out façades, posters and signs announce the new addresses of the destroyed firms and factories, half-faded chalk inscriptions announce 'everyone's alive' or 'we're still alive', or the Berlin address book of 1945 is listed, 'Otto Schulz, now 74 Hauptstr., with Pfeiffers' (someone who wanted to stay nearby), or 'Baensch family to Basdorf, 26 Summterstr.' (they chose instead to leave Berlin). But there are also inscriptions in fresh white oil paint: 'Our walls may break but never our hearts', or 'Führer, we follow you', or 'We will never surrender!'

North of the bridge there rise the remains of the round square, the semicircle of a building, collapsing before it was completed, the arch of the windows boarded over, still wrapped in the spider's legs of the scaffolding, defiant witness of an upstart desire to build, which blindly erected and tore down houses for centuries, to construct its Babylonian temple.

'I must say, gentlemen,' the red-faced man says, 'I'm incredibly hungry.'

'Let's go to the Bayernhof,' the lady says quickly, 'they may have something decent to eat.'

'I agree!' says the man with the horn-rimmed glasses.

'It's a date!' says the red-faced man.

Lassehn doesn't say anything, he wants to leave this company now, he is absolutely starving but he has no food cards, and visiting a restaurant strikes him as too dangerous. The special patrols of the Wehrmacht, the Gestapo and the OT prefer to go to restaurants – when they don't go to cinemas – to hunt out deserters, Jews and other illegals who can't afford the horrendous prices of the black market and have to fall back on the fixed-price menus in the local restaurants. But the company of the lady with the red lips (and Lassehn can't take his eyes off that tantalizing mouth) holds him back. Before he can make his mind up, he is already being pushed through the revolving door, and finds himself standing in a spacious restaurant, very simply furnished, with wood panels, polished wooden tables and farmhouse chairs, and which yet manages to create an almost distinguished impression.

There aren't many customers in the restaurant at this time of day. The red-faced man and the lady seem to know their way around, and make their way to a table in the area elevated by a few steps at the back of the restaurant. Lassehn has allowed himself to be dragged along, even though he doesn't know how things will go from here, he guesses that he may be putting himself in danger, but in fact there is danger everywhere, and here there is a woman with a tantalizing red mouth and an enticing, alluring body. She walks up the steps to the platform, her skirt rises to the backs of her knees and stretches tightly around her hips, and now Lassehn sees the lady the way men tend to see a woman, gone is the veil that the clothing spreads over strong thighs, a slender torso with wide hips and an abundant bosom. Lassehn is befuddled, tormented by an ardent longing for feminine tenderness, his blood shoots wildly into his heart and flows through his veins.

Then he is sitting next to her, with the two gentlemen opposite. The red-faced man seems annoyed that the lady has ended up sitting next to Lassehn, but he struggles desperately to look indifferent and casually takes a wallet from his jacket, gives the waiter an order and hands him his food card, the man with the glasses and the lady have set a few banknotes on the table and wait for the waiter to come to them.

Only Lassehn sits there, not knowing where to look, now that he is among people and his loose connection with the three people at his table is assuming a kind of social form, he feels doubly abandoned and helpless. All the others, sitting here with a sense of their inalienable civic rights, papers and food cards, they all have a flat or at least a room, a human being to give them shelter or support, in spite of war, worry and death. They are all sitting here with their bourgeois dignity, as they once sat at *Rheingold* or in Kempinski's, a little more modest, but essentially unchanged, he alone sits there like an outsider, he feels like a tramp who has wandered unwittingly into an elegant party.

'And what would you like, sir?'

Lassehn starts from his contemplation when the waiter bends down slightly towards him. 'The fixed menu, please,' he says.

'I'm very sorry, sir,' the waiter says, straightening again, 'but we don't serve the fixed menu in the afternoon.' Lassehn is distraught, he curses his carelessness in coming here with the others. 'Then forget it,' he says, it's supposed to sound indifferent, a phrase uttered in passing, but even he notices that the effect is meek and pitiful, he tries to smile, but all he manages is a spasmodic twitch at the corners of his mouth.

The waiter raises his eyebrows arrogantly. 'But I can bring you a glass of beer, sir?' He says it quite correctly, but it sounds as if he has said, 'Oh, you poor bastard, you don't even have the five grams of fat you need?'

'Just a moment,' the lady says now, rummages hastily in her handbag and puts two brightly coloured little coupons on the table. 'Bring the gentleman the same as me.'

The waiter assumes an expression of confidentiality. 'The gentleman will surely . . .'

But the lady cuts him off abruptly. 'No speeches,' she says in a commanding voice, 'just see to it that we are served quickly.'

The waiter's face immediately freezes expressionlessly again, he takes the coupons from the table and quickly disappears.

'You seem to be richly blessed with coupons,' says the red-faced man, his voice raw with barely repressed fury.

'Whether richly or not,' the lady replies quickly, 'is it any of your business?'

'Of course not,' the red-faced man says and catches his lower lip between his teeth. 'Don't you have any food cards?' he says, turning on Lassehn.

'No,' Lassehn says apologetically, 'I only arrived in Berlin yesterday.'

'But you must have food coupons,' the red-faced man continues his interrogation.

'It all happened so quickly . . .' Lassehn tries to explain. He feels himself growing very cold inside, he touches his trouser pocket with his elbow to check that his revolver is there, and with his eyes he gauges the distance from the entrance, only about forty metres, and the passage in the middle is wide, but at various tables on either side there are officers and two labour service leaders.

'Leave the gentleman in peace,' the lady says imperiously. 'I can imagine that fleeing the Bolsheviks like that is no small matter, Mr . . .'

'Joachim Lassehn,' says Lassehn, he smiles with relief and bows slightly to the lady and the two gentlemen.

'Elisabeth Mattner,' the lady says and smiles approvingly at him.

The two gentlemen also say their names, but Lassehn doesn't hear them, and he isn't interested in them anyway, but he greedily absorbs the fact that the lady's first name is Elisabeth. It's always been like that when he's met a girl, he isn't able to rest until he knows her first name. You can't do anything with a surname, it sounds wooden and always formal, absolutely impersonal, but a first name is music, it can be varied, you can let tenderness, longing and hope flow into a first name, you can dream of a first name, you can whisper it, and this lady's first name is Elisabeth.

The red-faced man still won't leave him in peace. 'It's very strange for a young man like you to be running around in civilian clothes,' he says doggedly.

Now that Lassehn knows the lady is on his side, he grows bold. 'Do I owe you an account of myself?' he asks.

'Bravo!' cries the lady. 'You tell him!'

The other man's face turns even redder, a vein in his temple swells fat and blue. 'I wouldn't mind having you arrested,' he hisses through his teeth, and a menacingly flickering light appears in his eyes, wide with hate.

Lassehn wants to put his revolver on the table the way he did yesterday afternoon at Klose's, but of course that is out of the question here. Stay calm, he whispers to himself, stay quite calm, you can only get yourself out of this situation with calm and impudence, not by being soft and yielding. 'And what good would that do you?' he asks.

The man with the horn-rimmed spectacles, who has taken a newspaper down from the hook and been reading it, tries to intervene. 'Let's not argue, or our food won't taste nice,' he says. 'I'm sure you have papers, Mr Lassehn, show them to us and everything will be fine.'

'You're just jealous,' the lady hisses at the red-faced man before Lassehn can say anything. 'Don't do anything of the sort, Mr Lassehn, you don't need to.'

'Jealous? Ridiculous!' the red-faced man says, his mouth twisted. 'And by the way, don't poke your nose into matters that don't . . .'

At that critical moment the waiter brings their food, he serves them slightly awkwardly and asks if things have gone quickly enough.

Lassehn sighs with relief, at least he has gained some time. As he eats he realizes what the lady, this woman Elisabeth, has just said: the red-faced man is jealous! Jealous? Of him? Until now he had interpreted the lady's attitude as one of general, impersonal friendliness. Might it be more than that? Didn't they only get to know each other an hour ago? Get to know each other? That's putting it strongly, they walked a little way together, that's all. So it can't be friendship. And love? Of course it can't be love, love doesn't look like that, love grows out of a gentle seed, love is quiet and peace, loneliness and pain, but this woman Elisabeth is jolly and disputatious, no soul has appeared in her eyes. Lassehn racks his brain as he eats his soup, but he can find no explanation, because he doesn't know that there is also an animal lust that requires only the body and nothing else.

Suddenly he feels something touching his foot, he looks carefully under the table and sees that the lady's right foot is resting close beside his left one. It could be chance that her foot is touching his, he tries to take his foot back, but he is so confused that he presses his foot against hers, and then he feels the counter-pressure. Even though it is foolish to assume that the warmth of her foot is communicating itself to his, because she is wearing coarse skiing-boots and he is wearing solid knee-length boots, a hot shock runs through him, as if she had touched his body with her hand. Lassehn studies her face over the edge of his plate, but her face hasn't changed, it bears the same nonchalant expression as before, perhaps with a little extra hint of excitement.

But right now his attention is claimed by the food, he consumes it with the concentration and gratitude of one who hasn't had a proper meal for weeks, he has to control himself not to wolf down his soup at speed, and not gulp the vegetable dish with the aromatic potatoes in one great bite, but even though he is holding back, he has finished long before the others. The meal has created a certain distance between him and his adversary, the red-faced man, but the end of it diminishes him again, he feels the red-faced man constantly staring at him, and hides behind the *Deutsche Allgemeine Zeitung*, which he spreads out in front of him. His eye falls on an article about the new air-raid warning technology.

> The consequence of the military development is that enemy planes cannot, as before, be registered a long time before they fly into the Berlin alert network. Because the front line is so close by, the time between the start of the air-raid warning and the arrival of enemy planes over the Reich capital has become shorter. The military agencies responsible are doing everything they can to ensure that the period between the start of the air-raid warning and the start of hostilities is no less than ten minutes. Particularly at night, all technical possibilities are exploited to ensure that the air-raid warning is started in time. Understandably, the closeness of the front line has led to more frequent warnings, since fighter aircraft are able to enter the Berlin alert zone more frequently.

He gets no further, because the red-faced man addresses him again.

'You seem to be extremely hungry, young man,' he says casually, and there is something like a smile on his face, but it doesn't look real, a malicious gleam in the back of his eyes reveals that he has drawn the smile over his hostile intentions like a curtain.

Lassehn doesn't respond, and lights the last of the five cigarettes that Klose gave him for his journey that morning.

'At least you seem to be well supplied with cigarettes,' the red-faced man continues to probe, he has finished his meal and pushes his plate far away from him, as if he needs room for the argument that is beginning.

Lassehn goes on smoking his cigarette, the thoughts chasing around in his brain. If only he knew how to escape this unpleasant red-faced fellow without at the same time losing his connection with this woman Elisabeth. 'What do you actually want from me?' Lassehn asks and frowns with displeasure, he can still feel the pressure of Elisabeth's foot against his, and that boosts his confidence.

The red-faced man rests both forearms on the table and looks keenly at Lassehn. 'There's just one thing I'd like to say to you, young man,' he says slowly, emphasizing every word. 'There are all kinds of rogues wandering about in Berlin at the moment, deserters, saboteurs, spies, the communists are suddenly very active again, and the Jews are getting cheeky again . . .'

'You exaggerate, sir,' says the man with the horn-rimmed glasses, 'it isn't as bad as that.'

'What do you know?' the red-faced man says, spinning round. 'The danger must not be underestimated, and that is why it is the duty of every decent German to make all suspicious and unreliable elements harmless, and any ways and means for doing that are acceptable.'

The man with the horn-rimmed glasses narrows his eyes. 'You don't need to lecture me about the duties of a decent German,' he says excitedly.

'Opinions differ about what constitutes decency . . .' the red-faced man begins.

'Certainly!' says the man with the horn-rimmed glasses. 'But if being an informer is considered decent . . .'

Now the red-faced man turns round to face him squarely. 'I reject that term completely,' he says threateningly. 'It seems that I will have to take an interest not only in this young man, but also in you.'

The man with the horn-rimmed glasses crumples visibly. Lassehn realizes that he has said too much in the heat of the moment, that he would like to take back his words or at least water them down retrospectively, because he knows as well as anyone else that behind everyone today who appeals to the sovereignty of state there is a consistently brutal power that crushes everything that might stand in its way or hamper it. It is easy for anyone who wishes to get rid of an enemy, out of hatred, jealousy, revenge, envy, an interest in profits, wounded pride or simply a delight in doing evil, to see to it that they perish.

'You misunderstand me, my dear sir,' the man with the horn-rimmed glasses says, 'you misunderstand me fundamentally.'

Lassehn is aware of a stale taste in his mouth. The man with the horn-rimmed spectacles is doubtless a decent citizen in his private life, blameless and in all likelihood efficient at his job, but he is a weak character who ducks immediately when someone else clenches his fist, who allows cruelty and injustice to happen and salves his conscience with the commonest of all excuses, that he couldn't change anything.

'So?' the red-faced man says slowly. 'As a rule I understand very well. When the enemies of our Reich, which we have sacrificed so much to defend, now believe that their time has come, they are thoroughly mistaken. My opinion is not crucial, and I don't want to use it to tip the scales, but I recommend that you read the most recent article by Dr Goebbels in the *Reich* and the leading article by Dr Ley in the *Nachtausgabe* . . .'

'Quite right,' the man with the horn-rimmed glasses says eagerly, 'the article "Without Luggage" was particularly . . .'

The red-faced man looks at him with contempt. 'So do you think that men like Dr Goebbels and Dr Ley,' he goes on, 'could write with such expressive force and such bravura if they were not them-selves convinced of the absolute rightness of their words?'

Oh God, Lassehn thinks, sitting here and having to listen to all this and not being able to say a word, not simply to be able to stand up and say, 'Animals! Idiots! Cursed fools!', oh how pitiful and cra-ven we have become, how have we been put in fetters, how have our tongues been stilled and then our brains jammed, our charac-ter bowed and our manly confidence broken, while cowardice and hypocrisy have thrived, how shabby our character has become.

Now the lady joins the argument for the first time. 'There I must agree with fatso,' she says, 'even though the situation looks rather difficult at present, it will soon change.' She lowers her voice to a mysterious whisper. 'I know from a very reliable source that over the next few days we will be deploying our V-3, and then . . .' She doesn't finish the sentence, but there is in her voice a tone of confidence and hope, and her eyes gaze into the distance, as if she could already see the German armies back at the Volga and the Atlantic.

'You can't believe how much we are all waiting for that, my dear lady,' the man with the horn-rimmed spectacles says immediately, almost rolling his eyes.

You cowardly bastard, Lassehn thinks furiously, if you can't say what you mean then at least keep your trap shut, but don't just pretend, to let this fat fool give you an alibi.

'A little while ago I didn't have the impression that you were such a good National Socialist,' the red-faced man says, still suspicious. 'Your statements before were very . . . well, let's call them incautious.'

'I am infinitely sorry if you have gained a false impression of me, sir.' The man with the horn-rimmed spectacles practically writhes with willingness to please.

But the red-faced man is no longer listening, his attention has suddenly fled, neither is it focused now on Lassehn, but on two men who have just come in through the revolving door and are walking along the passage in the middle. An excited, evil expression appears in his eyes, Lassehn follows that expression and stares at the men, but he can't see anything striking about them, unless it's that they look a little foreign, like Italians or Hungarians. As they pass Lassehn's table, the red-faced man is practically bouncing up and down with excitement, his hands are firmly pressed to his fat thighs and his head is drawn in between his shoulders as if ready to strike.

'What's up with you, fatso?' the lady asks and watches after the two men as they sit down at the last table in the furthest corner of the restaurant.

'If they aren't Jews I'm a Bantu Negro,' the red-faced man replies without taking his eyes off the two men. 'I'll teach them to walk around without their star and play the Aryan. Curse them, that gang of bandits!'

Lassehn claws his fingernails painfully deep into the balls of his hand. He has had as much sympathy for Jews as he has had antipathy, as indeed he has for other people. He has never transferred that antipathy to the generality and sympathy to the individuals who seemed worthy of it. Since he is used to making his assessments and judgements on music and the term 'Jew' only assumed concrete form when he was almost thrown out of his grammar school for playing a Mendelssohn scherzo as an encore after thunderous applause in a school concert, he has always felt that universal defamation to be particularly contemptible. For a few seconds he hears within him that Mendelssohn E minor scherzo, which begins with a few staccato notes before moving into sparkling runs of sublime purity, but he can't take the melody to its conclusion and is dragged painfully back to earth.

The red-faced man has risen to his feet and pushed his chair noisily back. 'I'll teach those two,' he says firmly. 'Will you join me?' he asks the man with the horn-rimmed spectacles.

The man with the horn-rimmed spectacles nods eagerly, but gets up only hesitantly from his chair.

'Are we authorized?' he asks cautiously.

'Every German is authorized,' the red-faced man replies gruffly. 'Or do you want to issue an arrest warrant, or ask somebody or other for permission? They're fair game! But if you're afraid . . . please do!'

'No, of course not,' the man with the horn-rimmed spectacles says hastily, 'of course I'm at your disposal.'

'So, why not do it straight away?' the red-faced man says and smiles crookedly. 'Let's go!'

Lassehn's hand twitches towards his revolver, but he pulls it back, it's pointless, he wouldn't be able to help the two Jews, he himself would go down with them, because the restaurant has filled up in the meantime, and there are lots of SS officers and a few NCOs among the guests. He feels wretched when he sees them both approaching the last table, but then he is distracted.

'Come on, Mr Lassehn,' the lady says, getting to her feet and hastily buttoning up her suit jacket. 'Let's go, then we won't get involved in whatever those two are up to.'

Lassehn gets slowly to his feet, he sees the red-faced man and the man with the horn-rimmed spectacles approaching the last table, but he can't make out what is said, the hubbub of voices in the restaurant is too loud.

'Come on, hurry up,' the lady urges. 'What does it have to do with us? Don't you fancy walking alone with me?'

Even though Lassehn inwardly feels a part of the scene in the background, because instead of the two Jews it could just as easily have been him, the deserter Joachim Lassehn, his face flushes when he sees the lady's red mouth, which is slightly open in a promise of pleasure. He presses some money into the hand of the waiter, who has noticed that they are about to leave, and follows the lady as she walks quickly towards the revolving door, he turns round one last time but he can't make anything out.

Then the revolving door receives him and he is standing with the lady in Potsdamer Strasse.

XI

15 April, 8.00 p.m.

By the time Lassehn gets back to Klose's place near Silesian Station dusk has already fallen, the time when the declining day and the ascending night meet briefly. Lassehn is somehow invigorated, he has taken his first steps in Berlin, admittedly quite uncertain and hesitant steps, guided by chance, if one can see an air-raid warning, a humane old woman and a woman's enticingly red mouth as chance. But steps they were, and a child making its first attempts to walk and keeping its balance against its swaying surroundings could not be more delighted. He is absolutely clear that fortune has favoured him, and from the solid ground beneath his feet to the all-engulfing abyss it was but a short step.

Because it's Sunday, Klose hasn't opened his restaurant, and on the shop door, which is closed with a sliding grille, there hangs a sign: 'Beer sold out'. Lassehn has to walk down the dark hallway, and collides with a man who is walking down the hallway from the courtyard and almost knocks him over. Lassehn has a ripe curse on the tip of his tongue, but he keeps it to himself, chat and back-chat can lead to arguments, and Lassehn must avoid everything that might make him stand out, for good or ill. So he reacts with neither words nor deeds, but continues on his way across the courtyard into the side building that contains the rear entrance to Klose's restaurant.

'Ah, the global traveller,' Klose greets him as he opens the door.

'Didn't quite work,' Lassehn says while they are still on the stairs, 'I . . .'

'Not here, my boy,' Klose interrupts him. 'Come in first. The

156

walls have ears,' Klose says when he is sitting at the table with Lassehn, 'you've always got to remember that, but now tell me what's been happening.'

'I've experienced a lot of things, Mr Klose,' Lassehn replies, 'but the important one was . . .'

'What about your young woman?' Klose interrupts and winks with a smile. 'Didn't she take you into her bed?'

Lassehn tells him, haltingly, constantly searching for words to circumscribe what he has to say, he doesn't want to lie, but neither does he want to admit the truth, which strikes him as humiliating.

Even though Klose is aware that Lassehn is keeping something from him, he doesn't press him. 'So it actually happened as you suspected it would,' he says thoughtfully. 'You didn't recognize each other. So what are you going to do now?'

'I absolutely have to speak to her,' Lassehn replies. 'After all, she is my wife, I have rights to her and she to me, and besides . . . there's also something that absolutely needs clearing up.' Lassehn is thinking about the child that was already alive in Irmgard when he met her, and which later mysteriously disappeared.

'So you want to stay with me for the time being?' Klose asks. 'Or what were your plans?'

Lassehn stares stiffly at the ground in front of him. 'If it's possible, Mr Klose,' he says hesitantly, 'I would like to stay with you.'

Klose puts a hand on his arm. 'If it isn't possible, it will be made possible. Do you know what solidarity is?'

Lassehn looks at Klose, on his face a mixture of embarrassment and questioning. 'Not really,' he answers, and then, as if speaking to himself, 'solidarity, that comes from the Latin *solidus*, meaning authentic, genuine, hard, solid, real . . .'

'Whether it's Latin or Greek or whatever it is I don't actually know,' Klose says, and his face is full of unusual, almost solemn seriousness, 'but I do know that it comes from the workers' movement, and it means that each man defends his fellow, leaps to his aid when he is in trouble, that's what we mean by solidarity.'

'But they have that in the field as well,' Lassehn adds. 'I've seen cases when . . .'

'Of course, I don't need proof, I was a soldier too,' Klose interrupts, 'but you can't compare the two. You're a soldier out of obligation, soldiers are forced into a community, they have no other possibility but living communally and standing up for each other, but with us it's different, we have found our way together voluntarily, what is compulsion for soldiers is for us a way of thinking, and it all has its roots in free will.'

'I'm not one of you,' Lassehn objects.

'Don't talk nonsense,' Klose says, returning to his abrupt way of talking, 'everyone who opposes fascism is one of us, whether he's a deserter or a saboteur, whether he secretly distributes flyers or practises passive resistance. You're not a Nazi . . .'

Lassehn shakes his head. 'Of course not, you know that, Mr Klose.'

'It wasn't a question, just an observation,' Klose continues. 'Everyone who isn't a Nazi, for whatever reason, is one of us, Wiegand, for example, became a Communist and Dr Böttcher a Social Democrat, and you can meet others here, Catholic priests and people who were once tepid democrats, but now they all belong together, the common enemy has brought them together at last. Before, it would have been unthinkable for Wiegand and the Catholics to share the same initial premises, they were far too dogmatic for that, one with, the other without God, each holding his own perspective to be the only true one.'

'And today there are no differences?' Lassehn asks.

Klose shakes his head. 'The differences are still there, and they are not denied, but they are no longer extreme oppositions, they are no longer necessarily mutually exclusive.'

'I still only half understand,' Lassehn says with a regretful shrug, 'I lack too much that would help me follow you, I feel as if I'm arriving in the middle of a play, and since I don't know the beginning I only understand half or not at all, but I have noticed one thing, which is that Mr Wiegand and Dr Böttcher don't quite agree.'

'That's true, my boy, that's very true,' Klose says, 'but to some extent they are brothers who have cheated each other out of an inheritance, and neither of them wants to admit his own mistakes, and they're each looking as if mesmerized at the mistakes the other has made, they reproach their past and forget that they shared a father. Now they remember that they do, and that's good.'

Lassehn nods. 'I'm one of them, even though I don't know how I got there.'

Klose makes a dismissive gesture with his hand. 'You know that very well, son, just think about it very hard, the mistake, or more precisely the shortcoming, is due to the fact that it did not arise from a particular conviction, and that's why you're so uncertain. But as long as you know where you belong, or at least know the way there, then you're getting somewhere. But let's address the practical side of the matter, that's important too, isn't it?'

Lassehn nods, he feels a little awkward, because he's grasped that the actual difficulties are starting, he's been travelling until now. He had a goal and allowed himself to be driven towards that goal, he walked sometimes on his own and sometimes with the columns of refugees, he slept in barns or abandoned houses or in mass dormitories, he stole food or ate at soup-kitchen centres where no one asked him his name or any other information, but now in a sense his flight has become stationary, and the important thing is to bring something like order and a system into the life he is now beginning.

'But you want to eat and drink,' Klose goes on. 'Have you got money, son?'

Lassehn nods again. 'About two thousand marks,' he says.

'That's not much these days, given black-market prices,' Klose says. 'What else have you got?'

'A few items of clothing, some underwear and odds and ends, but they're at my wife's.'

Klose drums his fingers on the tabletop. 'Well, let's see how we manage, tomorrow I'll get you some Reisemarken, otherwise I always manage to get hold of something.'

'Mr Klose . . .'

'Fine,' Klose says, waving him away, 'we'll do that, I've got contacts, you won't starve, lad.' Lassehn sighs deeply. 'If only the war would end soon, so that I wasn't such a burden on you.'

'You can rely on the fact that they won't make it through the summer,' he says firmly. 'You'll survive those few weeks or months, because in the end it's down to you. There are people who live underground for years, some without money and often without contacts, they wander aimlessly about during the day or sit in cinemas, they sleep in trenches or ruined houses. That's no life, always being chased, always hungry, every loud footstep, every braking car and every attentive glance by anyone at all could mean betrayal and death . . . It's probably a little easier for the illegals right now, in fact, with everything topsy-turvy.'

Lassehn rests his elbows on the table and supports his head heavily in his hands. 'Mr Klose, it isn't just being worried about a bit of food and sleep that's making me impatient,' he says, breathing slowly and heavily, 'it's the impatience of waiting to leave this uncertain existence, saying goodbye to all the misery and starting again . . .'

'I understand,' Klose says, 'I understand quite clearly, you want to start tinkling the ivories again, your Beethoven and Schubert and whatever all their names are.'

Lassehn shakes his head violently. 'No, Mr Klose, you've misunderstood me this time,' he says. 'What Dr Böttcher said to me yesterday has gone through my head again and again, and I've seen that he was right, music on its own isn't enough, he said. You see, and this is why I want to find a foundation to build my new life on.'

'And what about music?' Klose asks.

'It'll have to be a background accompaniment until it harmonizes completely with my future life,' Lassehn replies.

'That sounds great, lad,' Klose says and smiles mischievously. 'Let's hope that our beloved Führer starts playing some pretty harmonies quite soon, that would be the loveliest harmony of all, but first of all we're going to have a few noisy diss . . . diss . . .'

'Dissonances,' Lassehn says, coming to his assistance.

'That's the one, have a few dissonances, with thunder and lightning and crashing waves, but not on the Rhine, rather on the Spree and the Panke, making the wall rattle. Man, when you see it like that, people putting up anti-tank barriers in the street, it's lucky that the city was bombed, at least they have plenty of rags and iron, they're spoiled for choice.'

'So do you think Berlin will be defended?' Lassehn asks.

'Of course, they'll let the people fight to the last,' Klose says bitterly, 'they'll stop at nothing. You've held the *Völkischer Beobachter* in your hand, you must have read Heini's latest proclamation.'

Lassehn shakes his head.

Klose takes the paper from the hook, puts it in front of him and points to an article. 'There, read that, then you'll know what you need to know.'

Lassehn pulls the paper over and reads:

A decree from the Reichsführer SS

Every town will be defended!

Reichsführer SS Heinrich Himmler has issued the following order: the enemy is attempting to use deception to persuade German towns to surrender. With fake armed reconnaissance vehicles he is attempting to intimidate the population with the threat that if the town is not handed over they will be shot by tanks or artillery that will shortly arrive. Every village and every town will be defended and held by every means possible. Every German man responsible for the defence of his town who fails to uphold this fundamental national duty will forfeit his honour and his life.

'Now you're in the picture,' Klose says when Lassehn looks up again.

'But there are hundreds of thousands of women and children and old people in the city,' Lassehn objects. 'Will they at least be allowed to leave?'

Klose shakes his head. 'Where to, Joachim? Have a think, it's all full of refugees from the east, and besides the railways can't handle it, the Americans and the British are systematically destroying the whole railway network, they're running out of rolling stock and it's getting worse by the day. They're nearing the end and the rogues up there know that very well, they're not that stupid.'

'So why don't they just call it a day?' Lassehn says desperately. 'It would be more decent than sending lots of innocent people to certain death.'

'Now hold your breath, Joachim,' Klose says. 'You might be a good musician, but you're a very stupid person. Don't be cross with me for being so blunt, but I speak as I find. You suffer from the deep-rooted failing of the Germans, they're good musicians and efficient bookkeepers, skilled engineers and industrious street sweepers. They are erudite connoisseurs of the cultures of all eras and they know all about all kinds of complicated things. They're unusually efficient and hard-working, curious and talented, but . . . yes, now comes the big but, my dear boy, but they can't see beyond their own noses, the musician can't see beyond his piano, the street sweeper beyond his broom, the bookkeeper . . . well, and so on, their navel is the centre of the world. We Germans are in fact not a part of this world, the world is built around us, to complement our incomplete appendage, the rest are merely dilettantes and beginners, that has been drummed into the Germans in every key for so long that they just believe it and pass on that belief from generation to generation.'

Klose pauses for a few seconds, he has been speaking quickly, perhaps a little agitatedly, and now he has to catch his breath. 'A simile occurs to me, one that Dr Böttcher once mentioned, and which fits perfectly: he compared us Germans to a stamp collector who pays attention to all the details, to watermarks, type of paper, perforations, colouring and whatever all else there is, and who forgets the beauty of the stamps, who breaks them down and dissects them into their details under the microscope, but ignores the whole, and then calls that scientific stamp-collecting, philately, he grasps nothing of the actual essence of the stamp. And the Germans are like that in every field, we can't see the wood for the trees, we lose ourselves in trivia and minor details and leave the leadership to the political specialists, who must be able to do it because they're specialists. We're a bloody strange people!'

Lassehn has been listening as if under a spell. 'Yes, that's occurred to me too, Mr Klose,' he says when Klose pauses to light a cigarette. 'Today, on Barnimstrasse, near the Königstor, I observed a group of men building an anti-tank barrier, across the road, but with a little gap for the traffic to get through, they were ripping the cobbles out of the ground, they rammed two rows of joists in vertically and covered the gaps over with wood and metal. In fact I don't need to describe that to you, because I'm sure you've seen things like that yourself. I'm not just telling you because of the technical details, but to some extent because of the psychological anomaly. The men who were doing this work were probably convinced that a defence of Berlin would be a terrible misfortune, they had probably understood that the conquerors of the Siegfried Line or the great Russian rivers would not be defeated by a few ludicrous anti-tank barriers. The men were quite tired and ill tempered, they were in no particular hurry, but they did their work with staggering conscientiousness. They checked that the joists had been rammed hard enough into the ground, they engaged in lively discussions about whether the outside walls were strong enough to withstand the pressure of the masses of sand and stones and so on. Elsewhere – probably on the Brauner Weg – an anti-tank barrier had just been completed, and I must say, the workers at that spot were no different from the ones in Barnimstrasse, they kept walking around the finished barrier and tested its firmness, they were proud of their work and were praised and clapped on the shoulder by a Nazi boss who had probably directed and supervised the work. Was it not clear to these men that with these barricades they were building they were probably pulling down their own houses and destroying the rest of the city, if it was really to be defended?'

Klose nods a number of times, the smile has vanished completely from his broad face, making way for a gloomy expression. 'You've been very observant, Joachim, and unfortunately it's true, it needs to be said that the German workforce has largely failed, it has worked industriously and conscientiously in the armaments factories, as if for its own cause. You need only have seen people after the air-raid warnings, when the trams and other modes of transport are cancelled or there is a hold-up due to congestion, pushing and jostling their way into the S-Bahn and U-Bahn stations, cursing each other and often even fighting just to get to their factories in time or at least as quickly as possible. Lad, I can tell you, it's shaming, you could despair and wonder whether they've all lost their reason, whether they don't realize that every shell unturned, every rivet unhammered, every piece of iron unpulled must shorten the war.' He brings the flat of his hand crashing down on the table. 'It would drive you mad that a handful of crazy demagogues and charlatans have managed to make an entire people obsessed with their idea.'

'The Nazis,' Lassehn says, 'managed to equate National Socialism with the German people, to universalize the view that the collapse of National Socialism must inevitably also mean the collapse of Germany and the German people. Several of my comrades have declared to me quite openly that they didn't sympathize with National Socialism, but they found themselves in a dilemma and had to defend Germany, and I must honestly admit that I thought similarly and haven't quite shed the last remnants of that way of thinking even today, that I hoped, if not in the end for a victory, then for an honourable compromise . . .'

'A compromise with Hitler?' Klose exclaims. 'Never! Churchill, Stalin and Roosevelt will never engage in negotiations with these word-of-honour contortionists and constant treaty breakers, quite apart from the fact that the question is completely outmoded today, since the others have their fingers around his neck. No, no, my dear boy, the German people can only regain their honour when they rid themselves of this Nazi horde. But how did we slip into this conversation? What were we talking about before, Joachim?'

Lassehn has to gather his thoughts, the conversation has taken a turn and achieved a significance that make its original source irrelevant. 'I said,' he begins after a while, 'that it would be more decent for the Nazis to bring things to a timely end . . .'

'Yes, that was it,' Klose says. 'How can you assume decency on the part of the Nazis? Can't you tell that that round-headed idiot with the pomaded hair from Braunau, that great fat lump and the club-footed dwarf are drowning out each other's screams out of sheer horror because there's no turning back? That they are quite deliberately dragging Germany into the abyss because they have no way out? Haven't they stated quite clearly that if the National Socialist Party should perish, they will drag the entire German people with them into the abyss because otherwise they would be abandoned to the sadistic tyranny and slavery of the Bolsheviks and the Western plutocracies? No, son, decency isn't a word in the Nazis' vocabulary.'

'I keep imagining,' Lassehn says, 'what it will be like here, artillery fire, street battles, tank battles, air raids, and all of that in the middle of a city with a civilian population . . .'

'Not to mention the Gestapo, the SS, and crazed functionaries . . .' Klose adds.

Lassehn shudders. 'I simply can't believe it,' he says.

Klose puts a hand on his shoulder. 'My dear boy,' he says and narrows his eyes, 'in spite of everything, you don't seem to know what the Nazis are capable of. Do you know, for example, what they did in Breslau? They put an airfield right in the middle of the city, a real working runway . . .'

'In the middle of the city?' Lassehn asks in disbelief. 'But that's impossible.'

'Impossible?' Klose says with a short, dry laugh.

Lassehn nods. 'I mean . . . even technically that's impossible.'

'You innocent angel! For the Nazis nothing is technically, let alone humanly impossible. Let me tell you how they did it. First they set fire to the houses and churches, then they blew them up and carried away the rubble and iron, and then women and foreign civilian workers had to flatten the runway, fill in the cellars and craters and roll them smooth, all under heavy artillery fire. You're amazed, young fellow, are you not?'

Lassehn shakes himself. 'Shocking!'

'Yes, it is shocking. And you know what happened in Kolberg?'

Lassehn shakes his head.

'These gentlemen wanted to re-enact 1807* there, Gneisenau,

---

* In 1807 the French Imperial Army laid siege to the Prussian-held fortress of Kolberg. The siege, which lasted from April to June, was lifted with the signing of the Peace of Tilsit.

Schill and old Nettelbeck, heroic defence, freely based on Veit Harlan. You really don't know what happened in Kolberg?'

'No, how should I . . .'

Klose grits his teeth like a beast of prey preparing to pounce.
'Yes, of course, why should you? They all say that, and strike their
innocent German chests. How should I and what can I do about it
anyway?'

'Mr Klose . . .'

Klose waves his words away. 'It's fine. Just stick your head in the
sand and whatever you do don't learn from the facts.' He pauses for
a moment and throws his cigarette stub irritably into the ashtray.
'So Kolberg was also defended, even though the city was bursting
with refugees from East and West Prussia, there were over a
hundred thousand people in the city, where only forty thousand
normally live, the streets were crammed with thousands of wagons, but the gentlemen in charge paid no heed to them. The order
was: *The whole city is to be defended!*, so it was defended, and it was
only when tank shells struck the city that they began to clear it.
'*Smooth evacuation*', the *Völkischer Beobachter* later wrote. Do you
know what that looked like?'

'How should . . .'

'Yes, that's right, how should you, I know. Then I'll tell you what
that smooth evacuation looked like. The city was surrounded on
all sides, as the Party and all the authorities had fled on speedboats
the SS took charge. The only gap in the encirclement was the
sea, and now the SS drove the people like cattle, in storm and snow
and rain, the harbour under constant artillery fire and attacks by
low-flying aircraft; they were loaded onto small boats, because
the transporters lay at anchor in the roads, fifteen kilometres from
the city. Over twenty thousand people lost their lives, Joachim,
in the capsizing overloaded boats, in the street battles, in the explosions, in the mass executions by the SS of all those who refused to
leave the city. That was what it was like, son, and that is also what
it will be like here in Berlin, mark my words.'

Lassehn stared at the floor in front of him. 'And now the black
storm clouds hang menacingly outside our city, their shadows fall

upon it already, and yet we act as if we haven't noticed anything, the people go on living their lives apathetically, they go on working and leading what remains of a private life, the police and the authorities still make their rulings and demand that their instructions be obeyed, and that all happens as naturally as if it were bound to go on like that for ever, today, tomorrow, the day after.'

'Yes, son, that is the much-praised perseverance,' Klose says, 'but in fact it is neither perseverance nor courage, it is a stubbornly phlegmatic attitude and a fatalistic indifference, that is the great talent of the Germans, to pretend something to themselves and almost to believe it. And if the T-34s or the Shermans roll over Alexanderplatz tomorrow, then they will take that into consideration, ensure that they heed all the traffic regulations and calmly get on with their lives, as long as they have saved a scrap of private existence.'

'That sounds very pessimistic,' Lassehn says.

'There is no option but to think pessimistically about the bourgeoisie and all those who are part of it,' Klose replies, 'and it is also the bourgeoisie that still clings to Hitler and his state because it senses that with the fall of the Third Reich the bourgeoisie is finished as an autonomous class. They didn't even blame Hitler for the war, it's only because he's now losing it that they're suddenly starting to have reservations. What's wrong, Joachim?'

Lassehn has craned his neck, listening.

'I think someone's knocking at the door, Mr Klose,' he says.

Klose gets up and takes a few steps towards the door leading to the corridor. 'You're right,' he says, 'you disappear into the tap room, just in case.'

XII

15 April, 8.30 p.m.

When dusk falls upon the urban canyons and grey islands grow in the sea of clouds that fills the sky, Wiegand leaves his flat. He stops, apparently irresolute, outside the front door and lights a cigarette, but that is only an opportunity to look around, he calculates that a spy might be lurking somewhere nearby to keep an eye on him, but he sees nothing, at this time of the evening there aren't many people in the street, only some very cautious individuals are already on their way with their belongings to the high-rise bunkers in Friedrichshain.

After Wiegand has smoked his cigarette to the butt, he walks slowly up Lebuser Strasse to Grosse Frankfurter Strasse, stops a few times and sets down his suitcase as if it's getting too heavy for him and glances cautiously behind him, but can't see anyone. However, the gloom would not encourage a pursuer, the streets are unlit, only every now and again does a faint beam of light emerge from a front door.

On the corner with Grosse Frankfurter Strasse Wiegand stops again, he has heard footsteps behind him, he wants to let them get closer and overtake him, so he busies himself with a cigarette and glances back to Lebuser Strasse again. A man with a rucksack walks past him and turns into Grosse Frankfurter Strasse, he stops outside the ruined 'Filmstern' cinema, rests a foot on a pile of rubble and busies himself with a shoelace. Wiegand looks down the street once more, but again there is no one to be seen, it is very quiet now, he thinks he heard the footsteps of several people a moment ago, but only one man has walked past him, the same man with the rucksack who is now standing uncertainly outside the 'Filmstern'. Wiegand picks up his suitcase again, he originally wanted to go straight to Klose's, but now he decides to take a few detours and shake off anyone who might be pursuing him, he turns into Grosse Frankfurter Strasse and walks slowly along it towards Strausberger Platz. Huge piles of rubble obstruct the pavements, no houses have been spared here, over the last few months the area has been hit by one massive blow after another, after previously having been barely affected, a few blockbusters had had a devastating effect during the night, by day volley bombing had rained down, because here in the blocks at the rear of the tenements and factory buildings, surrounded by residential blocks, there was a diverse precision-engineering and electro-technical industry, and a large number of textile workshops, all working for the arms industry.

At Strausberger Platz Wiegand stops again. On Strausberger Strasse a Line 1 tram is about to set off after reaching its terminus here, since the tracks on Grosse Frankfurter Strasse have been torn up, and the driver furiously rings the bell, probably because a handcart refuses to come off the tracks. The sound of the bell produces a strangely flat echo in the half-ruined street; the audience of the second-last performance, the only one that is guaranteed with some certainty to run undisturbed between the end of work and the beginning of the air-raid warning, is emerging from the cinema opposite, between Kleine Markusstrasse and Krautstrasse, and for a few minutes the street is filled with a hubbub of voices and a lively clatter of heels. Then the silence falls all the more heavily back into the darkness. A dull light glows from Böers' chemist's shop, and the wind rattles the loose window frames of the branch office of the Deutsche Bank.

The gloom has thickened in the meantime, darkness has almost spread over the city, the few inhabited buildings are placed like huge, dark boxes in the picturesque mountain range of stones and rubble, only the strips of light in the blacked-out windows or a banging front door revealing for a moment the view of a blue light bulb indicate that there is life inside. A group of men come from Weberstrasse, but there are also two or three women among them, laughing brightly and fending off advances, the conversation is noisy and unrestrained. For a few seconds Wiegand listens to the melodious French sounds and envies the people their insouciance. He is still standing in Strausberger Platz outside the café where he met his wife a few times as he couldn't risk making the journey to Eichwalde. He looks around, but the man with the rucksack has disappeared.

Wiegand slowly climbs down the steps to the underground and buys a local ticket, and when he turns round to glance at his watch, a man with a rucksack is passing through the barrier. These days there are a lot of men with rucksacks in Berlin, but Wiegand thinks he recognizes him as the man who came out of Lebuser Strasse a short time before and then stood outside the 'Filmstern'. He might of course be mistaken, but at any rate he will behave as if he were being watched by the man, and there are various tried-and-tested tricks to shake off a troublesome pursuer. Buildings with a passageway that leads to another street, shops with paternoster lifts, jumping onto a moving train or, last of all, going up to the pursuer and politely pointing out that his pursuit has not gone unnoticed.

Wiegand walks up and down the pavement a few times. The man with the rucksack is sitting on a bench reading the *Nachtausgabe* without looking up, he lets the train for Alexanderplatz go past, but an attempt to join it would in any case have been pointless, since it was full to the gills. It is the last half-hour before the evening alarm, most of the underground trains are almost empty, only a few individual lines are overcrowded, and one of those is Line E from Friedrichsfelde to Alexanderplatz. Alexanderplatz exerts the greatest gravitational force on the anxious souls of the north-east, since not only does it have two secure underground bunkers, it also has an underground platform which, being two storeys below ground level, is considered bomb-proof in the truest sense of the word. The evening alarm has become a constant part of life. It is not seen as an unknown, it is an event firmly built into the course of the day, which is almost unimaginable without it.

The evening is quite naturally divided into the time 'before the alarm' and the time 'after the alarm', just as history is divided into 'before the birth of Christ' and 'after the birth of Christ'.

Wiegand stops in front of a noticeboard, the paper still smells of printer's ink, and particularly important passages are emphasized in red:

Compulsory registration of refugees

Over the past weeks many national comrades have sought protection in the interior of the country; manual workers, office workers and functionaries have lost their jobs, soldiers the connection with their offices or units as the result of enemy activity. To make them active once again in the defence of our people, the following orders have been issued.

1. Leave, except in cases of illness, is initially granted only for acts of courage.
2. Exemption on grounds of indispensability of all men from enemy-occupied territories is cancelled.
3. All members of the Wehrmacht who are not with their offices or units, including soldiers on leave and on missions, must immediately report voluntarily to the relevant offices (garrison commander, garrison headquarters, local police or regional war office).
4. All other people who have left their domicile since 1 January 1945 must immediately upon being assigned to accommodation voluntarily perform the following acts of compulsory registration at their new place of residence:
   a) All Germans must report to the police registration office of their new place of residence.
   b) All non-registered men born between 1884 and 1929 must also report to the military registration office or local military garrison of their new place of residence, showing their military papers.
5. People who have been compulsorily registered receive salaries from the public coffers only once compulsory registration has been performed. The food kitchens, supply authorities etc. are instructed only to issue food cards and make payments once proof of registration has been shown.

6. Anyone giving shelter to someone obliged to register must show by presenting the stamped registration document that compulsory registration has occurred. If these papers are not immediately presented, the person providing shelter must report to the police registration office.

7. Anyone knowing of individuals suspected of avoiding compulsory military service must immediately report to the nearest police department.

    Violation of compulsory registration is a criminal offence. But anyone neglecting to report in order to avoid compulsory military or labour service will be seen as a deserter and treated accordingly. Punishment will be applied not only to the guilty party, but to anyone who has helped in any way.

Wiegand reads with an ironic grimace, he recognizes this proclamation as what it is: the last gasp of a defeated system that is still trying to prolong the agony using the same means that it has always used: after introductory phrases the blow to the stomach and the hand in the wallet, the threat of punishment and last of all the order to denounce. Wiegand is so immersed in his reading that he has ignored the arrival of the approaching train and turns round in surprise when the train enters the station and the brakes screech against the wheels. He gets into a smoking carriage and sits down calmly on the red-leather upholstery, the man with the rucksack seems to have gone into a different . . . no, there he is, he boards the same carriage as Wiegand, except that he uses the door at the other end of the carriage and stops in the shelter of the side wall which closes off the middle row of seats. His cover is imperfect, because the carriage is almost entirely empty.

At Memeler Strasse Station a group of Ukrainians board the train, wearing the blue badge of the *Ostarbeiter*, and use the rare opportunity to sit in the underground without being jostled or stared at, they bring the stale, musty smell of the barracks with them, the aroma of rarely aired clothes. It is as if, while working in the fields or walking in the streets, they had fallen into the hands of modern slave drivers, pressed into Sauckel's army of forced labourers and transported in cattle-trucks to Germany. Wiegand has always seen them as the oppressed brothers, but he has also been forced to observe that some workers see them only as workhorses placed under their dominion, and the example of the foreign forced labourer has made it clear to Wiegand more than any other the extent to which the National Socialist way of thinking about the master race and inferior human beings has taken hold of the people, the depth to which the poison of racial madness has eaten into the brains of the nation. The contemptuous treatment, the stupidly superior attitude of many German workers, the lack of any feeling for the situation of the abused Russian people has startled him again and again. But he has often also experienced his colleagues seeing the *Ostarbeiter* as class-comrades oppressed in a special and different way, bringing them relief and helping them to find a sense of direction in a strange world and protecting them against the prejudices of the foremen or other horse traders. Of course, that can only happen under circumstances of the greatest possible caution, since works security and the factory troops, the political inspector and the intelligence officer cut short all so-called attempts at fraternization from the outset, or choke off any initial approaches, constantly use the threat of the Gestapo and ruthlessly dispatch the spokesmen of the Russians to a labour camp from which nobody returns except in the rarest of cases. And still, no amount of espionage and arrogance has been able to prevent an understanding between class-conscious workers and their Russian comrades. 'Tovarich' is by now a common form of address.

Wiegand lets his eye wander over the broad, good-natured faces of the Ukrainians, and has almost forgotten the man with the rucksack, who is still standing by the door and now busy trying to light a pipe. When the train pulls into Petersburger Strasse he glances quickly at Wiegand, and when Wiegand stays in his seat, he too sits down on the bench at the back of the train and unfolds his newspaper again.

Now Wiegand wants to make his move, he wants to leave the train at the last minute before it sets off again, but he can't put his plan into action because the train doesn't move at all.

'Everyone out! Air-raid warning!'

The cry of the platform conductress rings out dully in the arches of the railway station.

Wiegand picks up his suitcase and gets out, he deliberately fumbles around by the barrier for a long time so that he can be the last to leave the station. There are barely more than three dozen people going through the barrier, the man with the rucksack is one of the last, and even he seems to have postponed leaving the station for as long as possible.

The Frankfurter Allee is a single, dark canyon, the sky is black, not one star is embroidered into the dark shroud of the sky, it is so dark that Wiegand can barely see five paces in front of him. He takes his chance walking down Petersburger Strasse, a massive rubbish dump rises on his left, and the row of houses only begins a few hundred metres further on. Wiegand has some difficulty making out the white arrow and the white letters 'LS', he sets down his suitcase and stops by the door to catch his breath, the gentle rise of Petersburger Strasse to Baltenplatz has left him slightly breathless. A gloomy silence has fallen on the street, the piercing hiss of a heavy freight locomotive roars from the Ringbahn. Down Warschauer Strasse, from the direction of the bridge, comes the rattle of a motorcycle, the faint, blacked-out beam of its headlight spreads through the darkness.

When Wiegand is about to pick up his suitacase again, a hand rests on his shoulder from behind, he spins round and finds himself facing the silhouette of a man of small rather than medium height.

'You can't stand around here,' the man says in a harsh and peremptory tone, he has a thin, croaky voice. 'Go to the shelter immediately!'

'Let's not get worked up,' Wiegand replies and picks up his suitcase. 'Where is the nearest cellar?' He shines the beam of his torch into the hallway and sees for a moment a brown uniform and shiny knee-length boots.

'Have you lost your mind?' the man roars at him. 'Put that torch out immediately!'

'You aren't exactly being polite,' Wiegand says, and walks into the hallway. 'Show me the way to the shelter.'

'Straight down the hallway, right in the courtyard, first door.'

The voice delivers the words like a verse repeated a thousand times. 'But get a move on!'

Wiegand is tempted to punch the man in the brown uniform in the teeth, he has been ordered about too many times and had to choke back his internal explosion. But this time the opportunity seems favourable, there's only him and the man in the brown uniform in the hallway. He has already clenched his fist and turned half the way back, but then he violently regains control of himself, he mustn't act impetuously, and in any case the man with the rucksack might be somewhere nearby.

In the air-raid shelter, a long, twisting space with lots of columns, he sits down on a bench that is not directly lit by a lamp. He isn't bothered about any of this, the hubbub of voices, the loudspeaker that alternates between insignificant music and reports of the state of combat, conjectures about the goal of the British units. As far as he is concerned, visiting this air-raid shelter is only one stop along his flight, which actually began on 30 January 1933 and finally forced him into hiding.

His thoughts wander backwards and then thrust again into the future. He isn't the kind of man to immerse himself in the past, as if into a warm bath, or refresh sentimental memories to brighten up the bleak, grey colour of the present. For him the past is the sum of experiences, it serves to acknowledge errors and also to shape the future, a future that must soon become the present and towards which both emotion and intellect impatiently strive. Wiegand himself can't quite believe how close he came to venting his fury in the hallway a moment before. If he has survived twelve years of Hitler's dictatorship so far, and reined himself in many times, he isn't about to put himself in unnecessary danger right now.

He has learned to be silent when silence is required, and to talk when talking is necessary. He thinks of the day when he was released from Sachsenhausen after two and a half years. He had not despaired in the camp, even though the abuse and humiliations were almost unbearable and no end to the torment was in sight. The concentration-camp inmates weren't prisoners who had been put in jail or a penitentiary for a certain amount of time established by the judgment of an ordinary tribunal, for whom the certainty of freedom came closer with each passing day, the concentration-camp inmates were in a state of timelessness, the grey days flowed into uncertainty. Today he knows what in those days he only guessed, that that uncertainty is part of the infernal system, because in the writing room in Sachsenhausen he happened upon a memo-randum from the Ministry of the Interior which said:

The prisoner must under no circumstances be told the duration of his imprisonment, even if the Reichsführer SS and the head of the German police or the head of the Security Police and the SD have already estab-lished it.

Even now, after almost ten years, he feels a shiver down his spine when he thinks back to that life, that life led an inch from the edge of reason, almost in the shadow of death, and a hot wave of rage wells up in him time and again when he thinks of the martyrdom of Ernst Heilmann, Member of Parliament of the Social Democratic Party, who for some reason was particularly hated by the bandits of the SS, and with whom they played a brutally cynical game, put-ting him in a kennel, making him wear a collar and fixing him to a chain, forcing him to crawl on all fours, to eat from a bowl without using his hands, to bark and sit up and shape figures out of his own excrement. Wiegand has forgotten nothing, not the terrible beat-ings and the hours of roll-call, the hangings from lamp posts and the sadistic torments, but still he has never felt a second of hopeless-ness and despair until . . .

Yes, until the day of his release. It happened quite suddenly, quite out of the blue, it surprised him almost more than his arrest during the night of 28 February 1933, when the Reichstag went up in flames. Before he had really come to his senses he was already standing outside the barbed-wire fence, and in front of him lay open countryside, with no fences, no posts, no roll-calls, no beatings. He was in a daze, he didn't know how he had reached Oranienburg, he had run out into freedom as if intoxicated, but he hadn't run quickly away, he had put one foot slowly in front of the other as if walking on unsteady ground. In Oranienburg he had boarded the S-Bahn and travelled to Stettin Station, even though he should have changed at Gesundbrunnen. First he had run back and forth among the streets of north Berlin and the city centre, he had looked around and stared into the eyes of the people, and the initial apprehensiveness that had settled on his chest like stale air had turned to horror.

He could hear that there was still laughter and jollity, that insouciance and nonchalance still lived, and in the end he had acknowledged that that had existed too, while the barbed wire of the concentration camps had cut deep into the flesh of innocent people. During those moments he became painfully, deeply aware that life had gone on and stepped over them, and that it would go on even if thousands, tens of thousands, hundreds of thousands more hung like men crucified in the fences of the camps. While people whose only crime had been to refuse to submit to National Socialist exclusiveness writhed in torment, blood, fever and excrement, they would laugh their high-pitched laughter and wipe from the corners of their eyes a moment's emotion over Zarah Leander's glycerine tears. While they would sway to the music of *Blonde Kathrein* and produce sublime feelings at the sound of the Horst Wessel Song, Rilke's *Book of Hours* would carry them to unearthly heights and they would believe in Hitler's proclamations about Germany's vocation in the world, they would know nothing or claim to know nothing about the pustule in their midst, and if they did become aware of something they would shake it off as one shakes dust from one's clothes. In that bitter hour Wiegand understood that the people had made peace with their new master and their new order long ago, even if it was the order of an enormous prison.

That realization had brought him to despair for the first time, he had walked along the streets of the city and asked himself over and over again: Why? What was it all for? 'There are days when I am pursued by an emotion, blacker than the blackest melancholy – contempt for humankind,' Nietzsche's terrible words from the *Antichrist* had tried to whisper to him, but he had not in the end succumbed to them.

Wiegand thinks of the long series of victims, beginning with Karl Liebknecht and Rosa Luxemburg, continued via Eisner, Rathenau and Erzberger, taking in Scheer, Mühsam and Klausener and ending with Breitscheid and Thälmann. Neither does he forget the infinite number of nameless links in the chain, which were joined each day by new victims of National Socialist justice and Himmler's barbarism, who died terrible deaths, hanged, guillotined, tortured, drowned, shot, gassed, slaughtered, massacred, fatally infected. What happens in the prisons and penitentiaries, the concentration camps and labour camps and at the fronts is nothing but murder, cold-blooded and ingenious murder.

Wiegand has probably noticed that a man has sat down very close to him, but he has taken no further notice of that man. Suddenly he feels a hand on his arm, not a grip but an intimate contact, he turns to the man and looks into the wrinkled, weathered face of an elderly worker with the eyes of a sparrow-hawk under thick, dark eyebrows.

'This is a strange coincidence, Comrade,' the worker says quietly.

Wiegand is dumbfounded for several seconds but he gives no sign of it, he has learned to control every muscle in his face. There is neither fear nor dread in him, he has good, correct papers with him, which have withstood precise checks on several occasions, he is Reichsbahn worker Franz Adamek from Ratibor. What startles and puzzles him for a few moments is being called comrade. A worker is calling him comrade, not national comrade or Party comrade, just comrade pure and simple, after twelve years of Hitler's terror, pressure from the Gestapo, spies and corrupt sets of ideas. Nonetheless, Wiegand is too reticent, the years in hiding have not passed him by without leaving a trace, they have left him with an almost psychotic caution.

'What do you mean?' Wiegand asks.

'A curious coincidence,' the worker says again.

'What is a curious coincidence?' Wiegand asks.

'That we should meet here, Comrade,' the worker replies, almost with a hint of impatience.

'I still don't understand,' Wiegand says frostily. 'What are you talking about?'

'Of course you don't remember me,' the worker says, 'but I know you very well, except that your name escapes me right now.'

'I'm sure you are mistaken, sir,' Wiegand replies.

The worker gives a start and a shadow of displeasure runs across his face. 'I'm not mistaken,' he says, his voice losing its vigour. 'It's you, and yet it isn't you, because . . .' He doesn't finish his sentence, and turns away with a gesture of his hand.

Wiegand explores his memory, but he can't remember the man. That doesn't necessarily mean anything, because he used to speak at hundreds of meetings and his picture appeared in newspapers and magazines from time to time, it's actually strange – and only at that moment does he realize – that nobody has never recognized him or said that they did.

'You are mistaking me for someone else, my dear sir,' he says, and hopes that this is the last word on the matter.

The worker turns to him again and looks him quizzically in the face. 'No, I'm certainly not mistaken, you don't forget a face like that, particularly when it's connected with such memories, but I can see that I had far too good an opinion of you . . .' He doesn't stop talking, his voice simply seeps away into a furious grumble that is caught in his bushy moustache.

'Who are you talking about, sir?' Wiegand asks.

The worker twitches at this form of address. 'Yes, of course,' he says sarcastically, and a contemptuous smile plays around his lips, 'the comrade has become corrupt as well, he has cosied up to the Nazis, perhaps he has become one himself. Did he maybe end up with a nice position on the Labour Front? The hell with it.'

'Won't you explain to me . . .' Wiegand begins.

'Yes, I will, you wretch,' the worker says bitterly. 'I called you comrade, and the word contained everything, confidence, solidarity, a set of beliefs and hope, and you called me sir and sir again. It's clear that you don't want to be reminded of it, that you were once a comrade, that you believed in Marx and Engels, in class struggle and historical materialism and workers' solidarity.'

'Stop,' Wiegand says furiously. 'You don't know what you're talking about, and you're talking far too loudly.'

'I don't care,' the worker says angrily, but brings his voice down a little. As he speaks, folds and gulfs, lines and corners appear in his face, in which all his thoughts slide back and forth as if on tracks. 'It's all been pointless, those twelve long years of perseverance, when even someone like you makes common cause with the criminals. It would make you want to take a rope and hang yourself.'

Wiegand feels his heart thumping painfully, the words of this unknown worker are producing a bitter division inside him. There is the caution he has produced a hundred times, warning him not to get involved, ordering him to stay hard and dismissive, but again there is also a feeling of connection, of affection, of fraternity towards this man, who spent twelve years resisting the phrases of Robert Ley, who refused to let his socialism be watered down either by the addition of the word 'national' or by the concessions of organizations like 'Strength through Joy' or 'The Beauty of Labour'. And there is something else that is almost more important: can he allow this man's disappointment to take root? It is not about him, Wiegand, it is about the fact that he, the workers' leader, has seriously disappointed a worker who remained staunch for twelve years. He gives him a sideways glance. No, this is not a spy or a traitor, his words sounded too genuine, his behaviour is too convincing. While he is choosing his words, the other man goes on talking.

'Now I know who you are, highly respected national comrade and perhaps also Party comrade in the National Socialist Workers Party,' the worker says, and looks Wiegand scornfully in the face. 'You are Mr Friedrich Wiegand, former revolutionary trade unionist and now boss in the German Labour Front . . .'

The man's scorn causes Wiegand an almost physical pain. 'Stop that,' he says severely. 'You are talking far too loudly, I am Reichsbahn worker Franz Adamek.'

The worker looks steadily at Wiegand. 'The same old story,' he spits contemptuously. 'Someone who wants to erase his past is furious with the man who forces himself to remember it.' He presses his lips tightly together. 'But be under no illusions, you are . . .'

'I am Franz Adamek and no one else,' Wiegand says quickly. 'Do you understand?'

'No, you are . . .'

Wiegand grabs the worker firmly by the arm. 'Be quiet,' he whispers. 'No one is to know who I really am, you know because you recognized me by chance. Now do you understand?'

The worker gives him a darkly penetrating look for few seconds, his eye is focused rigidly on him, then a flicker of understanding twitches in his eyes.

'In hiding?' he asks excitedly.

Wiegand nods. 'Now you'll understand that I can't have everybody chatting to me, and I also think . . .'

'It's fine,' the worker says, 'let's not waste another word on the subject.'

'And how do you know me?' Wiegand asks.

'I knew you before, always from a distance,' the worker answers, 'but in April or May 1932 you came to us, the Frister factory in Oberschöneweide, you spoke at a strike meeting when they were going through the place with a stopwatch and wanted to cut our wages. I'll never forget how you inspired my mates, at the time I was in the Frister workers' council, I even sat next to you. Of course you won't remember, it's too long ago, but you were in great form at the time, Friedrich Wie . . .' He clamps his hand over his mouth. 'I'm sorry, I'm not supposed to say that. What's your name now?'

'Adamek, Franz Adamek,' Wiegand says. 'And what's your name?'

'Richard Schröter,' the worker replies. 'I thought they'd finished you off in the camp long ago. What are you doing now?'

'I work in the Karlshorst depot,' Wiegand replies, 'or rather I worked there until this morning, but I'm not going there any more.'

'Bad atmosphere?'

Wiegand nods. 'Very bad. What about you?'

Schröter smiles, his lips pursed. 'I've had myself written off sick,

I'm not working for the war effort. You can do it if you know how, you just have to want to and have a good doctor, and I've got one, if they have a medical check he'll give you a salt injection, or you take a decent dose of Pervitin, and they won't have a clue about what strange thing ails you.'

'And otherwise . . .' Wiegand says.

'You don't think I'm sitting at home twiddling my thumbs?' Schröter says quickly. 'You don't know what we're capable of. Have you heard about flyers, about sabotage and everything? There's a small group of us . . . watch out, brown peril on the way!'

A small, gaunt man comes down the corridor in the brown uniform of the Nazi Party, a brown jacket with light-brown collar points, two gold braids and three gold stars, a swastika armband with a tress of golden oak leaves, a brown holster, brown riding boots and shiny brown knee-length boots. Beneath his brown cap with its blue edging is a pinched, wrinkled face, bulging eyes with brown rings underneath them, a pointed nose and a small, dark moustache. He walks slowly down the corridor, his eyes darting into every corner.

All of a sudden there is a deadly silence in the air-raid shelter, no one says a word, some people force themselves to smile subserviently, others pretend to be asleep. Outside the dull, hollow crash of the anti-aircraft guns.

'Heil Hitler, National Comrades!' shouts the brown-clothed man. It is not a greeting, it is the order to bow before this exclamation.

'Heil Hitler!' the tribute comes from many mouths, clear, murmured, whispered, spat, some people only move their lips, but no one fails to deliver the tribute.

Wiegand is choked with impotent rage. Having to watch sixty or seventy people, manual workers, office workers, shop workers, women, men, old men and old women, children, be silent and duck down as beaten dogs skulk and whine their submission, subordinate themselves, fall in line, smile subserviently, just because some puny man with the face of a ruler wears his brown uniform through the corridors. Having to watch as otherwise honourable people suddenly become hypocrites, toadies, arse-lickers and cowards, because behind that shit-brown uniform there is still an uncanny power, master over death and life, better or worse, is beyond Wiegand's power.

The brown-clothed man stops in front of Wiegand. 'You're a stranger here! Who are you? Are you carrying papers?' he snaps.

Wiegand silently takes his Reichsbahn papers from his pocket and holds them out to the brown-clad man.

'Stand up when I'm speaking to you!' the man barks, and looks first at the papers and then at Wiegand's face.

Right in the mouth, Wiegand thinks, in the mouth, you damned brown toad, I'm not going to stand up in front of you. He sits where he is, the muscles in his cheekbones are playing constantly, his teeth hurt, they are pressed so firmly together. 'And here is my military passbook,' he says, and holds out the little dark-brown book.

The brown man takes the military passbook and flicks through it.

'Exempt? Why exempt?' he asks.

'Reichsbahn,' Wiegand replies, 'it's just as important as the front.'

The brown-clothed man snaps the book shut again and gives it back to Wiegand. 'Why don't you stand up, Adamek?'

An ungovernable feeling of defiance rises up in Wiegand, he has to summon all his will to stay calm, his hands twitch with suppressed rage at not being able to go for the throat of the enemy, who is within grabbing distance. Yes, he will stand up, but in a very special way. He leaps up, clicks his heels together and brings his hands down against the seam of his trousers. 'Reichsbahn worker Adamek reporting for duty!' he shouts into the cellar.

Suppressed laughter rolls around the cellar, and someone burst out laughing loudly. The brown man turns crimson, his wrinkled cheeks twitch up and down, he stands there uncertainly for a moment and then takes a step back. 'Be quiet!' he roars.

It is immediately deadly silent, some people even fearfully draw their heads between their shoulders. The brown-clothed man stands there with his legs spread and studies the faces from narrowed eyes, then he turns to Wiegand, who is still standing there as stiff as a ventriloquist's dummy, hands against the seams of his trousers, and gives him back his papers. 'You haven't heard the last of this, Adamek!' he says severely.

'At your command!' Wiegand says, and puts his right hand to his cap by way of salute.

'Stop it, damn you!' the man shouts at him, and turns round, walks away a few steps and turns round again. 'You're in good company,' he hisses. 'This anti-social character, Schröter ... gentlemen, we will speak again!'

The brown-clad man walks slowly on and stops in front of a young woman. She is sitting quite still, with her head leaning against the wall and her hands slackly in her lap, her face, once doubtless radiantly beautiful, is lifeless, her eyes are wide open, but in them is the expression of someone ignoring the here and now, and instead gazing into the past or the future.

'Heil Hitler, Mrs Franke!' the man says. 'Back again?'

Perhaps it's supposed to sound benign, but the effect is almost inquisitorial.

The young woman goes on sitting there motionlessly, only the expression in her eyes changes, she looks confused and puzzled.

'Where is your little daughter?' the man asks, slightly impatiently, he isn't used to his questions going unanswered, everyone has to give him an answer straight away, because in Hitler's Germany there isn't a patch of earth that isn't a parade ground or a human being who isn't a soldier.

By now the young woman's facial expression has come to rest, it has returned to the present, to the air-raid shelter in the house on Petersburger Strasse, and now it falls on the man in the brown uniform. The young woman's head moves very slowly away from the wall, her hands rise from her lap and hold her head carefully as if it were a precious, fragile vase, her slender, nervous hands tremble, her index fingers press against her ears as if to block out the surrounding noises, as if any sounds in them had to come from within.

'Why don't you answer me?' the brown man asks, his voice

having almost regained its earlier harshness. 'As your cell administrator . . .'

He gets no further. The young woman takes her hands from her face, her eyes blaze with grief and rage. 'I apologize for not yet having reported to you,' she says, her voice wavering up and down, her chin quivering as she seeks to control herself. 'Something has changed in me. I will never report to you ever again!' Her voice becomes more resolute, it is still broken, but it has stopped wavering.

'National Comrade Franke, I must ask you . . .' the brown-clothed man begins.

'Ask me, ask me as much as you like,' the young woman says. 'I have had enough now, I want to bring this madness to an end, to an end, an end, an end!' Now she is speaking loudly, her slender hands clench into fists. 'Don't interrupt me, I'm talking now, you people up there have done enough talking, we were only allowed to listen in silence, but now I'm not going to keep my mouth closed any more, now it's spilling out of me and now *you* must listen to *me*. You ask where my daughter . . .'

'I warn you, National Comrade Franke . . .' the man tries to interrupt.

The young woman sweeps his words away with her hand. 'My daughter lies buried, somewhere between Schneidemühl and Kreuz, frozen as we fled, frozen in my arms. Do you know what that means, Party Comrade? Having to watch my child's body slowly freezing, one limb dying after another, the life escaping from that little body, the heartbeat becoming fainter and fainter until at last that delicate creature, who had smiled one sunrise before and formed her first clumsy phrases, cold and motionless, frozen dark blue and lying, eyes broken, at my breast from which she had drunk her life . . .' The young woman's voice fails, it is as if the words are dripping as slowly and heavily as tears, and a sob rises into her throat.

'Calm down, my dear Mrs Franke,' the brown-clad man tries to interrupt.

But the young woman's words can no longer be stemmed, the flood of words, previously held back and pent up by terror and anxiety, has now torn holes in the dam, sweeping away all caution and reticence. 'And why was that? I will tell you, and it isn't a Jewish horror story and it isn't enemy propaganda, because I was there and I saw it with my own eyes. The Party bosses secretly claimed the only train for them and their wives, they fled at dead of night when word came in that Russian tanks were twenty kilometres away from the city. Then we set off on foot – because you had already made things too hot for us – home to the Reich, in ice and snow, women, children and old people, we struggled through the thick snow and we braced ourselves against the icy wind while the Party bosses, their wives and all their suitcases steamed comfortably westward. And that was what it was like wherever went, the bosses were off and away in their cars, they kept the clearance orders in their pockets until they themselves were ready to flee, and then they proudly announced that "their" population had held out steadfastly and bravely until the very last moment. All that was left for us was the public trucks, at temperatures between fifteen and twenty below zero. What do you think, my dear cell administrator . . .'

The brown-clad man tries to dam the flood of words.

'National Comrade Franke, I . . .'

'Have you heard what happened at the stations?' the woman goes on excitedly. 'When a train came at last, a wild charge began, and anyone who hesitated was lost under the boots of a raging crowd, which was half mad, or entirely mad with fear. Children fell under the wheels and were crushed, they were torn from their mothers' arms and trampled, literally trampled into a shapeless pile of flesh and blood and clothes. And then the journey, the airstream came at us from the front, the east wind was behind us, and both together dragged the last warmth from our clothing, so that we felt completely naked. When the train stopped in the open countryside we got out to bury the dead beneath the earth, six children and four old people, but we had to leave them there because the ground was frozen stiff and hard as stone, so we piled them together into a mound, shovelled snow over them and put a few pine branches on top. It was a Christian burial, Mr Party Comrade, I can assure you of that, there was no proud grief about it, only curses directed at the Führer and the Party, and if there is a God in heaven, then he will make you perish just as miserably.'

'Of course I didn't know that, National Comrade,' the man says. 'I can understand your agitation . . .'

'You understand nothing,' the woman rages at him. 'You don't understand, and the others up there don't understand either, you cold-snouted dogs, otherwise you would have called the whole thing off long ago.'

'I don't want to hear any more,' the man says furiously. 'I will put what you have just said down to your agitated state.'

'I am agitated,' the young woman says loudly, 'but I know exactly what I'm saying. For far too long we have been quiet, and you have taken our silence for agreement, if anyone bears the blame it us for having tolerated you for so long. Take a look around, you friend of the people, the way they are all sitting there, dazed and intimidated, even though they are all full to bursting with rage. They don't even dare to murmur or nod their agreement when someone screams the truth in your face. Do what you like, but I'm not taking back a word of what I've said.'

'I'm asking you to be quiet,' he roars at her. 'Or . . .'

'I'm not afraid of anything any more,' the young woman says and leans her head back against the wall, her voice has fallen to a whisper, she closes her eyes, tears spill down her face. The brown-clad man turns round, stands there uncertainly for a moment and looks into the cellar, then walks quickly towards the exit. When he has left the cellar, the voices whir about like flies, curses and curses rise to the surface like bubbles, everyone knows what they would do with the Party big shot.

'I'm anti-social,' Schröter laughs grimly, 'because I don't fly that swastika rag, because I don't take part in winter relief, because I'm not in the Labour Front. Anti-social! That bunch of rogues, that

Himmelstoss* of the brown-shirt army! But no, he's furious, one fellow's made a fool out of him, and a woman has trodden on his corns, it's unheard of!'

'Who is he?' Wiegand asks.

'That's Otto Hille, the cell administrator and now also the commissarial director of the Baltenplatz local group, one of the most dangerous Nazi bastards running around in Berlin, he has a whole heap of people on his own personal conscience. Let me tell you a few things about him.'

---

* The sadistic corporal in *All Quiet on the Western Front* by Erich Maria Remarque.

XIII

Biography of a National Socialist

> 'It is on account of cowardice, laziness and stupidity that
> such a large proportion of humanity prefers to remain in
> tutelage, and why it is so easy for others to set themselves up
> as their guardians.'

Kant

This is the biography of the cell administrator and provisional Local
Group Leader Otto Hille of Berlin O 112, 65 Rigaer Strasse. First of
all it seems necessary to examine the structure of the NSDAP and
its many sub-organizations. Here we should clearly distinguish
between two organizations, the first from the Party's genesis to its
government takeover, the second from its government takeover to
its fall. Here the last section will not be explored in detail, since in
this phase of development the entire German people more or less
voluntarily allowed the Nazi avalanche to roll over it, and because it
is less psychologically fertile. National Socialism, its terrible magnitude and its uncanny power, its ruthless cruelty and absolute
amorality, can be understood only if we analyse the characters and
temperaments, the desires and goals, the interests and reasons of
the people who joined the Party before 1933, because they were
the ones who gave the Party its physiognomy, its principles and
its content, which were transmitted entirely unchanged to the
second phase of the Party's history and never lost their validity.
Regardless of disguises and circumlocutions, regardless of all cultural whitewashing and diplomatic elegance, the authentic
substance always shimmers through. On this point Hitler was

doubtless right when he said the Party must always act according to the laws it was based on. Those laws were betrayal, murder, terror, cruelty, amorality, and loyalty to those laws, having followed them everywhere and at all times, is in fact the only loyalty that can be attributed to the National Socialists.

As heterogeneous as the elements that came together in the Party might have been, before it became the Party of state, they can still be brought down to one common denominator: all of them were misfits, or on the point of becoming misfits. First of all there were the soldiers who are unable to find their way back into a peacetime occupation or have never had one, and the officers whose profession has suddenly shed its halo and no longer gives them the opportunity to fall in line and at the same time to issue orders, eternal NCOs, accustomed to giving orders without needing to assume responsibility, since they receive their orders from above. Then there are the countless people whose civilian careers have run into the ground, and who never seek the cause within themselves, in their inadequacy or their laziness, but always in others and in the disfavour of fortune. This category includes the permanent idlers, the eternal students and those who have failed in their attempts to train as bookkeepers or foremen. Then there are those marked by nature, whose inferiority is coupled with a herostratic need for validation, and the members of the criminal gangs who are given the opportunity on their very own turf to climb into the political arena. They all decided to become politicians because the Führer had done so, and because it seemed like the easiest and least strenuous way of getting to the top.

They were joined by the masses of the petite bourgoisie and the middle class. They were without political ambition and precisely what the Führer had once contemptuously referred to as a 'pile of interests'. They clung to National Socialism as their only hope of saving the tottering, bursting building of the bourgeois social order against collapse and restoring its stability. Last of all we should also mention a horde of political desperados, all those whose political *arrivisme* had not been satisfied in other parties, who had not established themselves as they had planned, or who had been thrown out for usually quite unambiguous reasons.

This conglomeration of mercenaries and gangsters, a bourgeois mania for ownership and failed existences, the losers in life's battle and those persecuted by fate, a morbid urge for validation and racial arrogance, this strange and unnatural creature represented the type who claimed to be *homo teutonicus novus* and the bringer of a new culture, who managed to force every area of the varied life of a talented people into the Procrustean bed of a miserable political primer and condemn it to intellectual onanism. What was added later, which was heralded as thesis and dogma by scientific hangers-on and philosophical nonentities, to be passed on as an axiom from generation to generation, was only a retrospective justification and motivation. It was used only to place the mask of the upright citizen over the grimace of the barbarian. What really existed in terms of honest idealism and naïve faith remained without any influence on the so-called philosophical line and was only tolerated on the margins with deep mistrust. The essence of the Party was immutable and irrevocably rooted in the motley band of adventurers, deracinated bourgeoisie and disreputable lumpenproletariat, and not least in the herd of the apolitical petite bourgeoisie and the middle class, following inertly and insensitively on, which saw itself threatened by monopoly capital and feared sinking into the industrial proletariat.

The cell administrator and provisional Local Group Leader Otto Hille can be seen as the prototype of a National Socialist from the period before 1933, he is what is known as an 'old fighter', whose Party membership card has a number below 100,000 and whose Party insignia is framed by a gold wreath of oak leaves. In his character he combines the essential features that mark out a real National Socialist: brutality and emotionlessness, impudence and arrogance, obstinacy and a lack of imagination. The data of his biography, unimportant in themselves, are elevated to a universal level by virtue of the fact that they fall under the sphere of influence of two wars and the unlimited display of power of the biggest criminal organization of all time.

Otto Hille, Hitler's brown-clad mercenary, is not presented here as an individual. One does not become as he is on the basis of one's own character, one is formed that way by a barbarous age. That is why he is shown here as a type whose separate features may not occasionally match all those of his Party comrades, but may, stripped of their outer shell, capture their essence.

Hille, born in Berlin in 1885, grows up in the cramped conditions of a petty-bourgeois parental home, he is the son of a dairyman, a pale, fair lad who begins early on to take pleasure in forcing weaker schoolmates under his sway, and shows tendencies to exhibition-ism. Since he is the only son, he is expected to become something 'better', to climb the social ladder by at least a rung, he is sent to a *Realgymnasium*, a grammar school with a scientific bent, but he fails his fourth year, he has no interest in learning, he prefers to stand behind the counter in the dairy, pouring milk, weighing but-ter and cheese and doing sums unusually quickly. Early on he learns to deal with money, and not all the coins that pass through his hands find their way into his father's till. *Non olet*,* those words are almost the only ones that have stuck with him from his Latin classes, and which will accompany him throughout his life. His apprenticeship in an estate agent's office lasts exactly four and a half months before he brings it to an end by simply not going in. He cannot be moved by threats or pleading to continue his apprentice-ship. As he stands his ground, his parents, who were already the weaker parties, give in, despairing that their son's social rise is fin-ishing before it has begun, it is the despair of the petit bourgeois who despise their own class. The young man hangs around in the shop and in the street, he helps in the dairy from time to time when he needs money, and sometimes disappears for weeks at a time, returning to the paternal milk churns in a very reduced state. By the time he joins the Hunters' Battalion in Lübben at the age of nineteen he already has numerous affairs, a case of gonorrhoea and a charge of passing on venereal diseases behind him.

The habit of universalizing from personal experiences and assum-ing one's own mentality as a given in others, but seeing deviant

---

* *Pecunia non olet*, 'money doesn't stink', a phrase attributed to the Roman Emperor Vespasian.

experiences as random and different mentalities as abnormal – Hille has made that habit very much his own, it leads quite naturally to the overestimation of his own person, and makes him despise those around him. Just as Hille generally judges women on the basis of his own experiences with frivolous females, so he assesses his time in the military according to the results it produced in him. Because the skill of the NCOs takes him as a young lad in poor condition and straightens him out, making him accustomed to rigid order and thrashing him into shape, he is convinced that the army in general and German compulsory military service in particular are an excellent form of schooling. The soldier's life, with its relentless constraints, the monotony of its daily routine and its heedlessness of the concerns of the day, suits him very much. The fact that one can live without an initiative of one's own, and only with reference to orders and regulations, is the most surprising discovery of those years. When he has served his two years he capitulates, and now he himself is master of the barracks yard, which is only a small one but it is enough for him. It is the simplest life one could imagine: one is given orders and passes them on in a harsher tone, one receives tellings-off and passes them on with double the force to one's subordinates, everything is precisely prescribed and regulated, the timetable is precisely fixed, there is nothing to think or think about, everyday needs are adequately satisfied and anything that is missing has to come from his father's dairy.

Hille is happy to go to war in 1914. Although there is a possibility of staying in Lübben as an instructor, he insists on being sent to the front. It has nothing to do with courage, bravery or enthusiasm, because war in the parade ground of Lübben is certainly less dangerous than in France or Poland, and even NCOs feel considerably happier as armchair strategists than as heroic corpses in a mass grave. Hille has his particular reasons, he has got married in the meantime, or perhaps one should say he has had to get married, since a daughter of a civilian in Lübben has found herself in an interesting condition thanks to him, and her parents insisted on the marriage. Hille, who had been more than comfortable with life lived among men, with occasional outings to prostitutes, is happy to grab the opportunity to defend the fatherland at the front, to escape the burdens of family life.

After the war Hille cannot at first understand that his days of playing soldiers are over. There is an opportunity to go to Rossbach or Ehrhardt or Lüttwitz, but that is a particular kind of playing soldiers, it is too erratic, too adventurous, it constantly requires initiative and decision-making powers, and Hille will have nothing to do with that, he is in favour of service regulations and drill books, and if that isn't possible then he would rather not have anything to do with it. He has only a petty-bourgeois desire for adventure, the longing for excess and transgression remains latently present, but it never entirely overwhelms a desire for subordination. Transgressions – excesses – certainly, but only if they are ordered or prescribed, the pleasurable sensation of upbraiding and tormenting people, kneading them in one's hands like wax, only reaches its climax when one knows that one is protected from above, and responsibility has been transferred to higher regions. He loves freedom and immoderation, but they must happen only sporadically, and must be grouped around a solid core to which he can flee at any time. Since it can no longer be the barracks, it will have to be his parents' house again.

He moves to Berlin with his family, his wife and three children, and takes over his father's dairy on Weidenweg. This happens in such a way that his wife occupies the position of his mother, who has died during the war, she looks after the housekeeping and the shop, she worries and struggles and toils while Hille doesn't worry about a thing. In the atmosphere of the eastern part of Berlin the spirit of his youth again envelops him, the conversations of the adolescents and their suggestive songs, the evening gatherings in Petersburger Platz and the Weberwiese, the secluded little cinemas and the primitive cafés whose only attraction lay in their faint lighting and poor visibility. Hille is by now thirty-five years old, but he still hasn't really emerged from puberty. He begins to live a dissolute lifestyle, hanging around in dubious bars with equally dubious girls, he eagerly visits racetracks and knows the horses in

Ruhleben and Mariendorf, Hoppegarten and Karlshorst almost better than he knows his own children, he throws himself into the speculating frenzy of early inflation, and busies himself with all kinds of things – but not with regular, honest work. When his wife pours the heavy milk churns into the containers early in the morning he is still asleep, and when she closes the shop at midday he is just getting up, and rages if his food isn't ready on the table. But the roots of the soldier's life are too firm within him, his instability and inconstancy lack superior authority, he tries to join the police but is turned down; at last, following the general flow, he becomes a member of the Social Democratic Party. Very soon he realizes that he has gone to the wrong address, they debate and vote, and it isn't what he's after, he only feels comfortable where he is given orders and no responsibility, his interest remains meagre, and when he is told one day that he will have to be excluded from the party if he doesn't change his way of life he leaves of his own accord, taking with him a very poor opinion of soft and spineless politicians striving for a form of state that they call democracy, in which everyone is supposed to have the same rights and duties. That is too much for his NCO's brain, the concept of state is inseparably bound up with the concept of orders, in fact the two are synonymous. He is not even satisfied with the association of former Lübben Hunters or the Kyffhäuser Veterans' Association, the familiar noises issue from throats raw with alcohol, and sometimes there is some disorderly marching, but there is nothing behind it, no power or vigour, only drunkenness and sentimentality.

Hille roams through life like a hunting dog, always with his nose to the ground and his ears pricked. What goes on around him doesn't affect him unless it is directly related to him. Elections and Reichstag sessions, factory councils and constitutional issues are empty concepts as far as he is concerned, Rathenau's* murder means less to him than a disqualification of Rastenberger,† and the

---

* Walter Rathenau, 1867–1922, liberal German Foreign Minister murdered by right-wing zealots in 1922.

† Julius Rastenberger, a famous jockey at the Hoppegarten racetrack.

conference of Locarno is far less important than the weight of Nebukadnezzar in the Big Easter Prize at Karlshorst.

Towards the end of 1923 Hille has his first run-in with the law, it begins with Clärchen's Widow's Ball on Auguststrasse and ends in criminal court III in Moabit. He has a fight with a man over a girl when dancing, the argument continues in the street, Hille knocks his adversary down with one blow of his fist, the other man falls badly with the back of his head against the edge of the kerb, fractured skull and death, arrest and a court case are the consequences. Hille has a lenient judge and is sentenced to a year's imprisonment for accidental homicide contrary to the law on self-defence while in a state of inebriation.

Hille serves his sentence in Plötzensee. He is a model prisoner, not because he is contrite and regrets destroying a human life, but because the old Prussian order has taken hold of him again. If it were not a prison, the big red-brick building between the cycle track and Spandau Canal would be his ideal place to live, it is full of order and discipline, precision and cleanliness, the fist of authority, which one would not have expected from the easy-going Weimar Republic, is in evidence here. There is even the possibility of promotion, and Hille soon becomes a trusted inmate. As soon as he feels he has got his hands on even the merest hint of power, he becomes ruthless and severe towards his fellow prisoners, who are now his subordinates, and becomes a supporter and spy to the prison warders. This works best on the corridor whose cells are under his control, everything goes like clockwork, and by the time the year is up Hille is almost sorry to have to return to a civilian life without authority and without orders.

But he soon finds the place to which his character and inclination suit him. At first he won't have anything to do with the new Party, he isn't happy with the attribute 'socialist' or the class denominator 'worker', for which the words 'national' and 'German' only partly compensate, and he hasn't got the slightest interest in politics, he was alarmed by his experiences during his one-year membership of the SPD, but soon he sees that the new Party with the long name is doing a quite different kind of politics, here there are no debates and votes, here the orders are issued and delivered from above, here everything is thought out in advance, here everything is done under the motto 'The Führer is always right'. The very fact that the man at the head of the party is a Führer – a leader – and not a chairman proves that everything is done in a different way here from the other twenty parties. Hille's surprise soon turns to joy when he notices that there is also a warlike style of ruling and acting here, that people don't ask about his lifestyle and his previous life – apart from the Aryan purity of his gonorrhoea-infected blood – but only whether he will blindly obey and carry out orders. That is the right thing for Hille, so he becomes a fighter for Adolf Hitler, the unknown corporal of the First World War and the godlike field marshal of the brown-clad host, and just as Hille once parroted phrases and value judgements during training classes without the slightest concern for their content, now he willingly absorbs the new political terminology without thinking about it. He knows what he needs to know, he says what he is told to speak, and that is quite enough.

Now life begins again, there are marches and parades, orders and obedience, people bow to his authority and he has the prospect of soon being one of those who issue the orders. In the SA he is soon a staff sergeant, shortly afterwards is promoted to squad leader, and as he kept his wing in Plötzensee in an excellent state of discipline and order, his squad is soon known in the district between Ostkreuz and Zentralviehhof as the most spirited and combative unit in the battalion. The first political brawls with the communists now begin in the magnificent beer halls in the east, and street battles on the edges of Friedrichshain and amidst the allotments between Eldenaer Strasse and Landsberger Chaussee. If Hille had stayed in the background where possible, at Souchez and Le Mort Homme, since the French were always very good shots, now he is right at the front, since these are unarmed opponents who have barely any experience of war or none at all, and in any case Hille is usually under the influence of alcohol and wants to impress his comrades' wives. His heroic misdeeds soon make him look ready for more important tasks: he is put in charge of an SA battalion, and when Dr Goebbels comes to Berlin to take over the leadership of the Berlin district of the NSDAP, Hille and his unit are appointed personal bodyguards to the new Gauleiter. When Hille announces the presence of his battalion and makes his stiff salute, he is startled at first, then he wants to tear furiously into the miserable little Jew boy with the club foot who is playing a mean joke on him, but his military discipline is stronger than his impulse, and that is his good fortune, because the little man with the Jewish appearance is in fact the new man that the Führer has sent to conquer Berlin. Hille is disappointed, but he quickly discovers Aryan traits in the doctor's face, and when Goebbels delivers the first speech to the gathered Berlin SA in the Sportpalast, Hille is convinced that the Führer has made the right choice. He laps up the slogans and ready-made phrases of the new Gauleiter, and when he is sitting in the battalion's local pub with his trusty followers, gulping down yet another beer, he speaks enthusiastically about Goebbels as a man whose 'face is full of determination'. From now on the SA-man Hille is a constant companion of Dr Goebbels, whether in the Pharus Halls on Müllerstrasse or on the tennis courts in Wilmersdorf, in the Friedrichshain auditorium or the Neue Welt in Hasenheide.

Before we come to the summit, the highlight of Hille's career, we should also mention that early in 1931 he withdrew from public life to Plötzensee prison for six months, after adding a little touch to a betting slip, which the judge interpreted as forgery; it also seems necessary to say a few more things about his private life. A person's public life develops out of their private life, the political and intellectual features of a person's character do not come out of nowhere, it is more of a synthesis of innate disposition and environmental influences, which are initially manifested in his private life. Any political single-mindedness and philosophical pose which at first appear indistinctly and are, for the reasons from which they emerge, difficult to recognize, are illuminated as if by lightning when one rummages around in the private backdrops of the great heroes and political geniuses.

Since his return from the First World War Hille has not touched a regular piece of work, he has allowed himself to be carried along in the stream of that agitated time without thinking about the direction or the speed of the stream, until he is washed up on the shallow brown Nazi shore. Having previously spent his time between racetrack and pub, his trail now leads from the pub to the meeting room and back from there to the pub. He is a tireless fighter, less out of passion than from a dislike of his home, where he is merely a bed lodger and often not even that. His wife is merely a domestic animal, obliged to work and sort everything out for him, to create the material basis for his life as a political idler, and look after their three children. Even though Hille thoroughly despises his wife and can't forget the fact that she first locked onto him only because he actually got a bit too close to her between two dances in the dark garden of the Lindenhof in Lübben, he sleeps with her every now and again, becoming suddenly violent if she refuses to be accommodating in any way or put up with the fact that he isn't worried about getting her pregnant yet again. Hille has no tender feelings or gentler impulses towards his wife, and is quite clearly incapable of them in any case.

Hille makes no attempt to expand the narrow economic foundation offered by the dairy business or indeed to do any other work, he is now every inch the politician and moves along the same line as most of his comrades in the battalion, who are unemployed either out of inclination or incapacity. In the end Hille has succeeded in transposing a piece of barracks-yard existence into his present life, he can now do his brawling under cover of the swastika flag of a political idealism and compensate for his feelings of inadequacy with a belief in his racial superiority. His hatred for Jews – like other of his views, experiences and opinions – is based on highly personal experiences which he carries over to all Jews. It may be interesting to present these experiences as a way of finding out how Hille draws logical conclusions, and thus characterize his intellectual disposition. When his wife fell pregnant again, the Jewish doctor who lived around the corner on Thaerstrasse and was treating his wife took Hille to account, asking him to ensure that his wife no longer had to lift the heavy milk churns, and also recommended that he ease off on her a little in private. Hille refused to allow such an intrusion into his conjugal life and unhesitatingly forbade the impudent Jew access to his house. The miscarriage that his wife suffered a short time later, leading to a serious condition in her lower abdomen, was an unforeseeable coincidence and only attributable to her increasing sickliness. The second experience that reinforced Hille's hatred of the Jews was one that he had with the owner of the building that housed the dairy, and who had the misfortune of being called Levinsohn. This insolent Hebrew crook had had the audacity to remind Hille that his rent was overdue and, when he ignored the reminder, to bring a legal case against him.

So his character already displays all the features which the Hitlerian side of the German spirit would later apply to almost the whole of Europe.

The year 1933 is in fact the highlight of Hille's life. The intoxication of power, the triumph over all enemies are overwhelming feelings, they later make way for calm, even upward development, the complete absorption of the people and the saturation of the whole life of the nation with the brown lye of National Socialist ideas. In 1933 Hille runs the boycott against Jewish shops on Frankfurter Allee, he himself organizes and guards the security cordons around the department stores of Tietz and Brünn. He leads his battalion in the heroic action on Grenadierstrasse, in which some old Jews are beaten up and have their beards shaved off, but then he disappears from the street. He is appointed a major in the SA, but soon leaves the active unit, since the SA is soon seen as not being entirely respectable, and as the proletarian organization of the Party. Now Hille devotes himself entirely to Party work, he becomes a block warden and then a cell administrator, and even practises a profession: he becomes an adviser in the district management of the German Labour Front. Admittedly he brings no specialist knowledge to the task, and still less industriousness, and neither does he have the intention to acquire the former or display the other, but the work effectively does itself, an efficient secretary does everything for him, he only has to put his name at the bottom of documents, and in any case he has always been of the opinion that the number of possible errors diminishes of its own accord the more he is able to reduce the volume of work. It is all so easy, and there is nothing that has not been precisely regulated or organized, everything is controlled down to the very last dots on the 'i's, one need have nothing but a good memory for when and how the many regulations, implementations, commands, guidelines, decrees, injunctions and orders are to be applied. But the most wonderful thing is the great lack of responsibility because everything is decreed from above, one is only an executive organ, not only is initiative unnecessary, it is even undesirable, because everything must be identically aligned and synchronized. Everything happens in conformity with something, in conformity with duty, in conformity with order, in conformity with instructions, in conformity with command, except that the phrase 'in conformity with conscience' is excluded from this vocabulary. Hille takes his office as an instrument of power that is guided from above and applied downward with full force.

It is a wonderful life for Hille, the natural subaltern. He speaks at meetings, and nothing could be easier. The speeches are often delivered ready-made in manuscript, but their themes are always precisely outlined, and all one needs to do is learn them by heart, but even that isn't difficult because the content of the speeches – apart from the respective events of the day – is always the same, and the newspapers and radio provide enough points of reference that one can use quite safely, since they all derive from the same murky sources.

At this point we must ask the question of whether Hille is in fact convinced about what he pretends to say and believe, for which he is supposedly fighting and working. The answer is not difficult. Of course he doesn't believe it, he isn't that stupid, he knows himself very well and can also to some extent judge the figures who have been thrown up to the top by the brown wave. They are all former battalion comrades or friends from other battalions who now occupy positions in the state and the judiciary, in the offices of the Party and the Labour Front, old fighters, as they call themselves, and then even officially receive this title, whose only fitness for the job is their set of beliefs and their Party membership card. He knows that many of them are degenerate characters, drinkers, con men, incompetents and idlers, and when he looks at himself in the mirror he can't help grinning at his reflection at the thought of his own career. This knowledge of his own shabbiness and that of his fellows only produces in him a boundless contempt for the mass of people who have allowed themselves to be lured in, and who are still caged, still allowing themselves to be duped and obeying the horde of brown-shirted martinets. Hille has recognized the suggestive power of repetition that creates faith, and just as his Führer begins each speech by saying that he was once an unknown soldier before he decided to become a politician, Hille always reminds his listeners that only National Socialism keeps the German people from tumbling into the abyss, that only a horde of tireless and selfless men guided by great ideals have swung the wheel of history around at the last minute. The countless slogans and commonplaces provided by the training letters and the journal *Arbeitertum* slip smoothly from his tongue, and in the end he almost believes them himself. When Hille stands on the podium on a shop floor or in a meeting room and lets his eye wander over the crowd while his tongue once again mechanically forms the clichés delivered a hundred times before, he must struggle to control himself to keep from directing a scornful snigger at the faces raised in devotion to listen to him. Anyone observing him speaking from close by can easily tell that even in moments of great excitement he remains quite cold and inwardly uninvolved, because he has performed this role many times before and is sure of its success. The feeling of power increasingly becomes the instrument that he plays more than any other, its maintenance and reinforcement the goal of his political work. The question of what the power is based upon is unimportant, whether it be founded in the disturbing menace of the Gestapo or in the fear of economic disadvantage, the bayonets of the newly established Reich Army or the hearts of the people, when he strides through the crowd and it parts to let him pass. When he carries the banners through the streets and all hands are raised in the Hitler salute, he doesn't care in the slightest whether it is done out of respect or fear, the only important thing is that it is done. What an intoxicating feeling it is to be esteemed, admired, respected, revered or even feared and hated. Both respect and hatred prove that he is no longer an insignificant somebody or other, but that he is elevated above the crowd and that he has been granted permission to look down.

Hille's political rise leads to deep changes in his private life. The dairy on Weidenweg was sold in 1933, and he has moved to a sumptuous four-bedroom flat on Kniprodestrasse, whose dining room alone is worth several times the value of the dairy, including equipment and goods and the adjoining flat. This new apartment is the property of a Reichstag member, who is criminalized twice over by being both a Social Democrat and a Jew; on the night of the Reichstag fire he is arrested and transferred to Dachau concentration camp, and shortly thereafter he is transferred from life to death. The man's brother, who claims a right to the inheritance, is persuaded to renounce it, with threats and allusions to the fate of the flat's late owner, and to pass the flat on to Hille at a ridiculously low price. Small and large matters are treated in an identical fashion: the adversary is placed under pressure, first of all you apply your velvet-gloved paws to the backs of their necks, saying not 'I will do . . .' but 'I could imagine that . . .', not 'I know . . .' but 'if I remember correctly . . .' If the neck is not prepared to bow, then you become more forceful, you threaten and you blackmail until your adversary yields. But once you reach that point at last, everything is entirely legal, the formalities of civil law are respected with scrupulous precision, and it is an outrageous calumny to claim that Germany is not a state based on justice and integrity. A sales contract is drawn up between Hille and the legal heir to the man who died in the concentration camp, a notary is present to witness it, and Hille pays the purchase price in valid banknotes of the German Reich, which makes him the legal owner of an Aryanized four-bedroom flat. One further advantage of the move is that he can free himself from his old surroundings on Weidenweg, where he is too well known, and even if Kniprodestrasse is only ten minutes from Weidenweg, they are ten Berlin minutes, or almost as much as if two villages in the country were several hours' journey apart. Still, here too there is a voice that wants to know about his previous convictions, but Hille is having none of that, he brings the slanderer before the court, and lo and behold, Hille's police record is as pure as the driven snow. There is no magic, no sorcery at work, it is just one of the tricks of the Third Reich, which is not of course discussed in court. According to a secret decree issued by the Ministry of the Interior the previous convictions of meritorious Nazis are to be wiped from police records.

Now Hille has become a citizen who maintains and represents the state, but he himself does not believe in his civil respectability, he is still dominated by the same impulses and makes politics with the same means, except with different nuances; he no longer drinks in pubs these days, but at Gerold's or Kempinski's, his erotic outings are no longer to Mulackstrasse or Steinstrasse, or to the freelance prostitutes on the edges of the Friedrichshain, but to the demi-monde of Friedrichstrasse and the Kurfürstendamm, he no longer stands by the paddock in Karlshorst or Ruhleben, but sprawls importantly in the stands by the finishing line. He is even proud of his wife, when the silver Cross of Motherhood is hung around her scrawny neck at a National Socialist People's Welfare evening, and if he really couldn't care less about his five children, they still prove that he has personally put the Führer's population policy into action for many years.

Hille is a loyal follower of Adolf Hitler, and one of the many guarantors of the Third Reich, which has elevated him socially, and which he must defend for his own sake. For the first time in his life he sees the course of his life ahead of him, all the way to his old-age pension, but before that goal is reached there are still little side streets here and there that lead to the promised land of eternally unsatisfied desires.

At first the outbreak of war awakens contradictory feelings in him, it throws the even sequence of his life into chaos, a vague premonition rises up in him and sometimes chokes him on restless nights unveiled by alcoholic fog. But the premonitions and doubts are stifled by the sudden victory over Poland, they lose consistency with the subjection of the Nordic nations, of Holland, Belgium and France, and they fall into complete oblivion when the thrust of the German armies, which had gone into the battlefield to win back Danzig for Germany and open up the Polish Corridor, brings him to Moscow and Alexandria. Hille imagines the holy German Empire of European nations coming into being, from Narvik to Gibraltar, from Archangel to Baku and with secure outposts in Aden and Dakar. He completely agrees with his colleagues and fellow Party members that nothing can resist the triumphal procession of the armies and generalship of Adolf Hitler. But then things suddenly stop advancing, they even start going backwards, in Russia and Africa, at first they are only tactical retreats, adjustments to the front, shortenings of supply lines, evasion manoeuvres, but Hille is still an old front-line fighter, and his experiences from the First World War put him on his guard. Are there not surprising parallels with the First World War? The unstoppable victory march into the heart of enemy countries, then a stand-off and finally a series of retreats, the material superiority of the enemy with their swarms of tanks and planes, the failure of the submarine war and finally the loss of allies? The front lines are still far away, but this time the arm of the war reaches far over the front and all the way home. It is not only the enemy aircraft that darken the German sky, they are now joined by the voice of truth and the conscience of humanity, which, in spite of all the jamming transmitters blocking the enemy radio stations, forces its way through the ether and penetrates the fog that has settled around people's minds.

Even more than the external enemy, Hille begins to hate the enemy within the country, the denier, the sceptic, the defeatist, because each of them undermines the foundation on which he has firmly based his life. Every no, every dose of scepticism breaks a pebble away from that foundation, worse than rape and murder are the offences which are described in the jargon of Freisler's* People's Court as subversion of the war effort and enemy propaganda. The

---

* Roland Freisler, 1893–1945, German jurist and Minister of Justice.

breakdown in human relationships had begun during the time of struggle, the war had speeded it up, the uninterrupted chain of military setbacks is aimed entirely at a new goal: rendering harmless those people who do not put all their energy into achieving the final victory. No means is too small for him, no path too devious, now he only wears his brown uniform on certain occasions or for official reasons, otherwise he goes hunting. He sits with a detached expression and pricked ears in barbers' shops, in restaurants and on the underground; he mingles with the workers who swarm outside the factory gates at the end of the working day, striking up conversations wherever he goes; he creeps up stairs and listens outside doors; he hands countless people over to the Gestapo, listeners to foreign radio stations, Jews who have escaped transportation and who are living underground, people who make discouraging remarks about the leadership of the Reich, soldiers who speak about the bad atmosphere at the front, women standing in queues who curse the Nazi bosses. On Elbinger Strasse he shoots an American pilot who has escaped from his plane with a parachute, and at the same time hands over to the Gestapo two women and a man who stood around the American to protect him; he arrests an old worker who is passing on an English flyer that had been thrown from a plane. Hille is a man obsessed, he seems to have been afflicted with lycanthropy, but now he is nothing more than a ham actor playing out his closing scene while all around him the shabby backdrops are being dismantled, and who is well aware of how unbelievable his role truly is. While outwardly, when he is not actually hunting, he continues to display an unshakeable conviction in the coming victory, his optimism is crumbling away, he feels the ground trembling under his feet, he sees everything being called into question. He clings desperately to any favourable news, he falls like a parched man on the *Reich* to drink some hope from Goebbels' leading articles, but doom is getting closer and closer, apparently inexorably, it is already reaching out its hand for him. Even the award of the War Merit Cross and his promotion to provisional Local Group Leader only lift his mood temporarily. Hille is filled with rage, hatred and a desire for vengeance, the will to destroy everything that lives burns within him, he knows that he is lost, that he does not have the escape route of the big shots who have for some days now been driving packed and laden cars westward along the military road to safety. He cannot cope with the fact that others should live while he must descend into the underworld, so now he is shaking off all his bourgeois respectability like loose plaster, the concept of community is dissolving like smoke, and the Nazi beast is running amok through the streets of Berlin.

XIV

15 April, 10.00 p.m.

Klose opens the door to the flat.

'Yes, what's . . . Oh, it's you, Fritz. Come in.'

Wiegand comes in, takes off his hat and coat and puts his suitcase down in a corner.

'What's up?' Klose asks. 'A suitcase? Has something happened?'

He goes over to the door leading to the restaurant and opens it. 'You can come to the back room, Joachim.'

'Nothing has happened yet,' Wiegand replies, and sits down heavily on a chair. 'But I think they're after me. Good evening, Lassehn.'

Lassehn has come in and held his hand out to Wiegand. 'Good evening, Mr Wiegand.'

'Is the doctor coming this evening?' Wiegand asks, and turns to Klose. 'Did he call?'

'Not yet,' Klose says and looks at his watch. 'It's still early, it's just ten. But now I'd like to ask what's up, Fritz.'

Wiegand talks in short, clear sentences. 'So, now you know, Oskar. I'd like to stay here tonight. Can you arrange that?'

'Should be fine,' Klose answers quickly, 'I've got an old army bed in the back, we can set it up here or in the kitchen. Are you sure no one followed you here?'

'Pretty sure,' Wiegand replies. 'There was a man with a rucksack, with an indefinable facial expression, you know, like someone trying to seem perfectly harmless, and strangely enough he was going the same way as me. It could have been a coincidence, I didn't see him again after the air-raid warning. I've been careful, Oskar, believe me, I know how much hangs on it.'

'Did you meet anyone outside the front door or in the court-yard?' Klose asks.

'Meet anyone? No, there were a few young lads standing in the hallway,' Wiegand replies.

'We'll have to be bloody careful,' Klose says, 'Sasse, that bastard, was making a few suggestive remarks yesterday in the air-raid shelter . . . That'll be the doctor!' Two short and two long rings sound in the corridor. 'Will you open the door, Joachim?'

'Of course!' Lassehn jumps to his feet, he's glad to make himself useful, even if it's just by opening a door.

Then they sit around the table, Klose, Wiegand, Dr Böttcher and Lassehn. Klose has dealt some cards, Wiegand and Dr Böttcher each have ten cards in front of them, Klose holds ten cards in his hands, fans them playfully and brings them back together again. In the middle of the table are two cards face down, and each of them has some money beside him, a few notes and a pile of coins.

'What's going on?' asks Lassehn, who has watched the cards being dealt with astonishment. Mixed with that astonishment is a fearful supposition that these three men may be nothing more than politically minded card players.

'We're having a game of skat, son,' Klose says, and grins from ear to ear, 'a perfectly harmless game of skat, do you understand?'

'To be quite honest, no,' Lassehn replies.

'We always have to reckon with the possibility,' says Dr Böttcher, who is sitting next to Lassehn, and who rests a hand gently on his shoulder, 'that a stranger may arrive, a check or a raid or whatever, and if that happens skat cards are to some extent our alibi. Playing skat hasn't yet been forbidden.'

Lassehn smiles, having understood. 'But I have . . .'

'No, you have no cards, Joachim,' Klose says, 'first of all skat is a game for three players, and secondly you have no papers to show. We have to hide you anyway. Do you see?'

'Completely,' Lassehn says. 'Where should I disappear to if . . .'

'Out the front,' Klose says, nodding towards the door that leads to the restaurant, 'and then into the cellar.'

'Is something going on?' Dr Böttcher asks.

'Not exactly, Doctor,' Klose says, 'but prevention is better than cure, and in any case Wiegand has definitely gone underground this time.'

Dr Böttcher turns round suddenly to Wiegand. 'Are they on your heels, Wiegand?'

'I assume so,' Wiegand replies.

'Who are they after?' Dr Böttcher goes on. 'Franz Adamek or Friedrich Wiegand?'

Wiegand shrugs. 'I assume it has something to do with my work in Karlshorst, but I can't dismiss the other possibility. In that case . . . yes, I've got to warn my wife whatever happens.' He says nothing for a few seconds and frowns. 'Lassehn, you could do me a big favour.'

Lassehn leans solicitously forward. 'I would love to, Mr Wiegand. What can I do for you?'

'I would like to ask you to go to Eichwalde tomorrow and bring my wife a message. But you have to be very careful, because my house may be under strict surveillance. Do you think you can do that?'

Lassehn nods. 'Admittedly I've never been to . . . What's the name of the place?'

'Eichwalde, a stop beyond Grünau. From Grünau you can take the Görlitz suburban railway or tram 86 to Schmöckwitz, I'll tell you exactly tomorrow.'

'Your underground status throws up very new prospects,' Dr Böttcher says thoughtfully. 'First of all we need to find you a place to stay.'

'That question has already been answered, my dear Doctor,' Klose says. 'Wiegand is staying at mine.'

'And the young man?' Dr Böttcher asks, looking at Lassehn.

'. . . is the third man,' Klose replies, 'it'll be fine.'

'I think it may be dangerous to have two people staying at your place,' Dr Böttcher suggests. 'I'm also of the opinion that we should have our meetings somewhere else, but most of all it is fundamentally wrong, my dear Klose, for you to keep your restaurant shut on a Sunday. If someone comes through your door, there's nothing unusual about that, but if people often use the back door, that might attract attention. We're making a serious mistake if we think we are already in safety, it's wrong to assume that with one foot in the grave the gang will give up and let things take their course. Precisely the opposite is the case, they're like mad dogs now, they won't think twice about taking down a few innocent bystanders. So we've got to be particularly careful, and, most importantly, if one of us should be arrested, there should be no discernible connection with the group.'

'Today I nearly had an opportunity to make contact with another group,' Wiegand tells them. 'In an air-raid shelter on Petersburger Strasse I met an old comrade who I didn't know, but who – by his own account – knew me from the old days.'

'And why didn't you establish contact?' Dr Böttcher asks.

'This man is probably reliable,' Wiegand replies, 'but I don't know if he's clever and cautious enough, and I didn't want to do anything without first discussing it with you.'

'I think it's the right thing to do,' Dr Böttcher says, 'but on the other hand we must leave our isolation a bit more, it is urgent that we extend our radius of action and consolidate our work. In my opinion we need to concentrate our forces, because we are heading towards the end on giant steps. You want to say something, Mr Lassehn?'

Lassehn had attracted their attention with a timid hand gesture. 'Yes,' he says, 'if I might interject something, Doctor . . .'

'Please do,' says Dr Böttcher and nods encouragingly.

'Fire away,' Klose bids him, and looks at him with an expectant smile.

'I'd like to take part in your underground work,' Lassehn says seriously.

'My dear boy, this isn't some romantic game of hide-and-seek, Indians and trappers and so on,' Klose says, no longer smiling. 'It's a damned serious and dangerous business, where you risk . . .'

'One moment, Oskar,' Wiegand interrupts him, 'that alone isn't the crucial thing, and Lassehn is certainly aware that our work is a matter of life and death. Before we even consider your offer to take part in our work,' he says, turning to Lassehn and staring hard into his eyes, 'I have to ask you why you want to do it, if you are driven by a desire for adventure or if your way of thinking calls for it?'

Lassehn holds his gaze. 'It isn't a desire for adventure, Mr Wiegand,' he replies. 'My need for adventure is amply satisfied, believe me, but a way of thinking . . .' He resolutely lowers his head and tries to catch Wiegand's eye. 'But I know what drives me: my hatred for this accursed Hitler regime.'

Dr Böttcher nods to him.

'Hatred is a good motive, Lassehn, but it must be fed with conviction,' he says with a hint of indulgence in his voice. 'Have you also considered who you want to sit at a table here and work with?'

Lassehn looks at him questioningly. 'I think it would be with you, Mr Wiegand.'

'That isn't what I mean,' Dr Böttcher cuts in, 'I mean what crimes you would be committing if you took part in our work? High treason, undermining the war effort, violation of the Treachery Act, violation of the Decree for the Protection of People and State, propagation of foreign information and . . . I don't need to tell you any more than that. For each of those crimes they will ruthlessly put a rope around your neck if they catch you. Are you clear about that?'

'Completely,' Lassehn confirms with a nod, and for a moment a smile crosses his face. 'In fact, one crime more or less doesn't matter, because by deserting I have already forfeited my life.'

Dr Böttcher gives Lassehn a penetrating look. 'And you don't want to rejoin your unit as a straggler?'

Lassehn shakes his head. 'No, I've burned my bridges once and for all, so there can be no way back, Doctor. I don't want to be overdramatic about it, but I must tell you that something has grabbed hold of me, I would almost call it a holy rage. Before there was only revulsion, resistance and detachment in me, but that isn't enough, now I have the urge to act, I feel as if a veil has suddenly been torn away.'

'The boy is sound,' Klose says, 'and while he may be a little bit shy, he has courage, and he won't be fooled too easily. Just look how quickly he took out his gun yesterday and wanted to fire a bullet into me . . .'

'You wanted to kill . . .' Wiegand begins in amazement.

'I had no idea who I was dealing with,' Lassehn apologizes, 'because Mr Klose . . .'

'Good God, Joachim, get to the point,' Klose interrupts, laughing. 'I'd just worked out that he'd run away from the front,' he says to Dr Böttcher and Wiegand by way of explanation, 'and he was afraid I might give him away. It was your right, son, I was very impressed! That's my motto, if I get nabbed, I'm taking a few of the brothers with me.'

'Have you finished, Klose?' Dr Böttcher asks slightly impatiently. 'I'd like to get to the subject at hand.'

'Off you go,' says Klose, he isn't insulted and laughs broadly.

'I was saying just now that we need to concentrate our work and at the same time put it on a firmer foundation, I think the most urgent task is to achieve influence over the Volkssturm. If there is a battle for Berlin, the Volkssturm can't fight in our interest and everyone's interest, and not in their own interest, because they are woefully under-equipped and have no combat experience, they would simply be rolled over. Even if it was a good and just cause, it would be a pointless, hopeless battle, all the more so in that every bullet we shoot, every shell we fire, means identification with the most barbaric system in the history of the world. We must explain to the men in the Volkssturm that . . .'

'You will explain nothing at all to them,' Klose interrupts. 'It would be a waste of breath.'

'We need to explain to them,' Böttcher continues unperturbed, 'that the war needs to be concluded as soon as possible to save what there is still to be saved; if our city isn't to end in complete carnage, they have to understand that they won't defend their wives and children by fighting, but by throwing down their weapons; and, starting at Volkssturm level, find a way to get to the Wehrmacht. It is self-evident that we always have to sound out our opponent, as boxers put it, you need to be delicate, find the right people and say the appropriate words. I think theoretical discussions are pointless, the right thing to do is to approach each individual in person, he will draw general conclusions unless he's particularly anti-social, all by himself. Did I express myself comprehensibly?'

'Entirely,' Wiegand confirms.

'As plain as the nose on your face, Professor,' Klose says.

Dr Böttcher nods. 'I would suggest that you only use the best people for this task, one slip could be deadly for everyone. But we always have to resist the resigned and depressing opinions that always end with the sentence "There's no point". At present we can't judge whether our work has a point and a meaning; we are too much in the middle of things, we will know the truth eventually, but even if it turns out to be pointless and meaningless, we are obliged to go on because our conscience demands it. There are only three possibilities: firstly, to work in armaments or fight with weapons, and so become complicit with fascist crimes; secondly, to act as a resigned bystander or wait, that is, to aid the crime; and thirdly, active opposition. For us there is only that third possibility. If we are accused of conspiring against our own fatherland, I can only reply that if this is our fatherland, this state ruled by Hitler and Himmler, then I'm no longer a German. A country in which freedom, humanity and justice are outmoded concepts can never be my fatherland.'

Dr Böttcher pauses and clears his throat. 'We need to say that to those who have become indecisive, or who are about to become so, and besides, the facts are unambiguously on our side. I expect the Russian offensive over the next few days, and without a doubt it will reach as far as Berlin. Why do you look so downcast, Mr Lassehn?'

Lassehn has wrapped his arms around his knees and lowered his eyes. 'I can't yet take part in this work,' he says candidly. 'I don't yet dare to.'

'We wouldn't have involved you anyway, lad,' Klose says resolutely, 'but there is still more to be done, for example tomorrow . . . Oh, yes, tomorrow you want to go to Eichwalde for Wiegand.'

'But not until the late afternoon,' Wiegand says, 'by day it would be better if he didn't show his face.'

'Well, then, that's all fine,' Klose says, 'then tomorrow he can pick up some flyers and bring them to you, Doctor.' He turns back to Lassehn. 'Right, on with our entertainment.'

Lassehn is about to reply, but Dr Böttcher interrupts. 'Our friend Klose likes to express himself with a certain amount of humour, he has his own names for things, but I wish once again to draw your attention to the seriousness – and also to the importance – of our work. Please bear one thing in mind: you don't owe any answers to anyone you don't know very well. The Gestapo have thugs everywhere, they disguise themselves so skilfully that they can barely be recognized. At this opportunity I would like to describe to you an episode that will give you an idea of how cleverly the Gestapo works.'

Dr Böttcher closes his eyes for a few seconds and then firmly stubs out his cigarette in the ashtray. 'A few months ago a man came to my surgery, about thirty-five, tall, strong, strikingly well fed, he had a sick note from the Berlin Public Transport Company and he complained about stomach pains. I gave him a thorough examination but couldn't find anything. Now with stomach conditions that isn't unusual, there are illnesses that are extremely difficult to establish, even an X-ray doesn't always provide an exhaustive explanation. This man, whose name was Altenberger, was at first a patient like any other, he came to see me regularly, I would give him a prescription, and he only told me what was absolutely necessary. I was annoyed, because I could find no precise diagnosis and wanted to send him to a specialist, but he didn't want that, I had been recommended to him, and he trusted me. There is nothing unusual about that either, I have often experienced that kind of thing, because patients are unpredictable, and trust in your doctor is often a better treatment than the best medicine.

'After this man Altenberger had consulted me a few times, on his fifth or sixth visit he started discussing political matters; at first he spoke quite generally, before becoming clearer, even though I did nothing to encourage him. He cursed Hitler and the damned war, and he clearly expected me to join in. Now I am unusually careful and reserved, and I'm not given to expressing my opinions. I criticized the way he was talking. Of course, there was a chance that the man was genuine, but there were various things about him that struck me as odd, so I maintained my discretion.'

'Listen carefully, Joachim,' Klose cuts in, 'you might learn something.'

'The way someone expresses his disaffection is actually an infallible sign,' Dr Böttcher continues, 'because there's cursing and cursing, whether it is done with conviction or according to a predetermined plan is something that most spies don't bear in mind. Cursing doesn't just consist of words, the eyes and the voice, the facial expression and body movement are part of genuine cursing, or else they remain somewhat uninvolved, you see, and in the case of this fellow Altenberger the eyes didn't join in at all, there always seemed to me to be something cold lurking in the background, and his movements and facial expressions looked as if he'd learned them, exactly as if he had stood in front of a mirror and rehearsed it all.

'But in spite of my adverse response the man wouldn't let go, he kept on and on, and in the end he stopped cursing and instead said quite openly that he was trying to make contact with resistance groups or people who were living underground. I asked him why he came to me with this request, and pretended to be shocked. He replied that people were most likely to express themselves to a doctor, and I was known as a man with no time for National Socialism. I told him furiously that I had no idea how I had acquired that reputation, but he merely laughed. I refused to speak like that, and hoped that I could get rid of him in that way, but the man came back and went on consulting me, but never again did he utter a single superfluous word. It was quite clear that he was trying to win my trust.

'I became indecisive, because if he really was a genuine opponent of fascism, of course I regretted turning him away, and since I am very thorough in everything I do, and always get to the bottom of things – qualities that every doctor ought to have – I once asked him in passing who had recommended me to him. He couldn't quite remember, he said, he thought it had been one of his colleagues. Now at that time I had a few transport workers and office staff as patients, and even in the past transport workers had come to my surgery, so it was entirely possible.

'Anyway, I decided to look into the matter, it wasn't just a question of making sure an informer had nothing on me, I would also have to reorganize my whole operation, given that many of our people came to my practice as patients to receive instructions and material. Altenberger's sick note bore the address 10 Neue Königstrasse. When I had to make a patient visit on Weinstrasse it occurred to me that Altenberger lived not far away, so I dropped by his address, and it turned out that 10 Neue Königstrasse had been completely destroyed, as long ago as November 1943. There was still a possibility that the personnel office had accidentally put his old address on the sick note. As everything on either side of Neue Königstrasse had also been destroyed, and there was no one I could ask, I went to the police station on Jostystrasse and asked for Gustav Altenberger, whose personal details I had on his sick note. Unknown, never lived here, was the information, there was no one of that name in the list of residents.

'So the matter was quite clear. Now I put it to the test. The next time he complained of severe stomach pains, I prescribed him something which, in those doses, would cause unusually severe cardiac disturbances, because I wanted to know if he was actually taking the medication.

'When he reappeared two days later I asked him how the treatment had gone, and he assured me that it had been excellent.

'Now I knew for certain that the man was not ill in the slightest. He wasn't taking the medications I had prescribed for him, he only came to me to get access to a resistance group and then expose them. Now the question arose of how I could get rid of him without making myself suspicious. I did the most sensible thing in such situations, I let him run himself into the ground, that is, I went on treating him for his supposed stomach condition and didn't react to any of his remarks. In the end he probably acknowledged the pointlessness of what he was trying to do, but he still tried to make me fall into another trap by asking to be written off sick, but I refused to accede to his request, as I couldn't find anything wrong with him. And in the end I ensured that he stopped coming.

'My decision not to let myself get involved may be considered justified by the fact that I recently saw Altenberger again, wearing an SS uniform with the ominous SD insignia. So you can see that it's impossible to be too careful. Having shaken somebody's hand a few times isn't nearly enough. Unfortunately there are some among us who are too trusting; if they encounter a face a few times, it belongs to an acquaintance, and of course it immediately slackens the reins otherwise imposed by caution. The need for trust is absolutely understandable and very estimable, but in the present circumstances it is completely inappropriate, you must have the gift of looking inside people, to tell what is genuine about them and what is fake.'

'You're just frightening the boy, Doctor,' Klose says as the doctor pauses for a moment.

Lassehn shakes his head and waves his hand dismissively.

'If it frightens him,' Dr Böttcher replies, and looks seriously at Lassehn, 'then he shouldn't get involved. I just want to make him aware that each of us is in a sense walking a tightrope, and will plunge to our deaths if we don't keep our balance precisely. I want to say the following, Lassehn: don't try to improvise, but act precisely according to the instructions given to you, unless an unforeseen situation or threat arises, and then you will have to decide for yourself. Do we understand each other?'

Lassehn nods. 'Perfectly, Doctor. I have only one last question. How do I identify myself to third parties, or how do I make it clear to them that . . .'

Dr Böttcher smiles.

'We won't just give you a password, we'll give you a whole bunch of keywords as well by way of identification, and Klose will give you thorough instructions.' He pauses for a second and then addresses Wiegand again. 'Now I have something else to discuss with you, my dear Wiegand. Didn't you say just now that you were close to making contact with another group?'

'Yes, but I hesitated,' Wiegand replies. 'It's one Richard Schröter from 12 Petersburger Strasse, he's . . .'

'He's a good man,' Dr Böttcher says with a smile, 'he's even very good, he's quite well known under the name of Rumpelstiltskin.'

'You know him?' Wiegand asks, surprised.

'Very well, he isn't just my patient . . .'

'So you're the good doctor who gives him Pervitin to swallow before he has to go to the slave-drivers of the AOK.*'

Dr Böttcher is slightly put out. 'So he told you that?'

'Yes, but only in passing, and only when it was clear who and what I am,' Wiegand replies. 'Are you unhappy about that?'

The concerned wrinkles on Dr Böttcher's forehead have quickly smoothed themselves out again.

'Where you're concerned, Wiegand, not at all, we are not just waging our little war against Hitler and Himmler with guns, flyers and sabotage, but also with injections and forgeries. Schröter is absolutely impeccable, on several occasions he acted as a go-between for me and another group that called itself "Ringbahn". They did good work, and among other things the fire at Knorr-Bremse was down to them.'

Wiegand frowns again. 'Knorr-Bremse? Then they are adorning themselves with false laurels, because that fire was caused by a bombing raid.'

Dr Böttcher nods. 'That seemed to be the case, but there were only a few stick-type incendiary bombs and a phosphorus canister, nothing at all in the larger grounds, and it was only because the anti-air-raid defences weren't working properly, the water hoses had been cut through and the hydrants filled with sand, that the fire was able to spread to the extent that it did.'

'Very good,' Klose says, and rubs his hands. 'The lads are quite right.'

'Schröter is coming to my surgery tomorrow,' Dr Böttcher says to Wiegand. 'Do you want to come along? Then you could talk to

---

* Allgemeine Ortskrankenkasse – the general health service provider.

Schröter about various things, because he's also in contact with the "Scala" group in the west.'

'Fine, I'll come,' Wiegand says. 'What time?'

Dr Böttcher thinks for a moment. 'At about six,' he says. 'Take a seat in the waiting room and I'll see you last.'

'Let's do that,' Wiegand says, 'and otherwise . . .'

The bell in the corridor rings stridently.

'Someone at the door,' Klose says, and jumps to his feet. 'Damn it all, who's turned up at this time of night?'

'Cool head,' Wiegand says.

'Warm feet,' Klose adds. 'Come on Joachim, you disappear. Let's see who's paid us the honour.'

XV

Klose comes back into the room with a man. It's as if the two had been brought together as a demonstration of contrast. Klose is of medium height and portly of physique, the other man unusually tall and gaunt, Klose is dressed in casual civilian clothes, while the other man wears the stiff brown uniform of the political function-ary, Klose speaks slowly and without hand gestures, while the other man speaks over-hastily and waves his arms wildly in the air.

'This is Mr Sasse, our block warden and air-raid warden,' Klose says with a gesture that is more of a demonstration than an intro-duction. He stands slightly behind their uninvited guest and casts warning glances at Dr Böttcher and Wiegand.

'Heil Hitler, gentlemen!' the brown-clad man says and raises his right hand in a salute.

Dr Böttcher and Wiegand murmur a few vague words through half-closed lips.

Sasse turns back to Klose. 'Your blackout isn't working quite correctly, Mr Klose. Let's take a look at what's wrong with it.' His voice has a benign tone, like that of a teacher pointing out a pupil's minor errors, having already forgiven them.

While Sasse goes to the window and tests the blackout roll by pressing it firmly against the window frame, Dr Böttcher and Wiegand pick up their cards and fan them out. It looks as if they had been interrupted in the middle of a game.

'It would appear that your blackout is adequate,' Sasse says, and turns back to face the room, 'you should apply some grips or battens at the sides so that the paper fits firmly.' As he speaks, his eyes run through the room, pierce every corner and peer into every cranny, they study the two men and for a few seconds they linger on the door that leads to the restaurant.

'I'll sort it out,' Klose says, still standing, and carefully watching every movement of the brown-clad man.

Sasse acts as if he doesn't notice Klose's expectant and forbidding attitude, he simply sits down at the table, in the seat that Lassehn has just left, he picks up his brown cap and runs his hand over his bald skull.

'A little game?' he asks cosily, and nods encouragingly to Dr Böttcher.

'People need entertainment,' Klose says, and stands behind his chair, resting his hands on the back. You didn't come here because of the blackout, he thinks, you just wanted to snoop.

Dr Böttcher tries to let his face settle into obliging wrinkles. 'Our little game of skat,' he says. Red is trumps, he thinks, and you brown rogues come in with a score of fifty-nine. Wiegand forces himself to smile weakly and looks at his watch. 'It's nearly eleven, we were about to play our last three hands.'

'Don't let me disturb you, gentlemen,' Sasse says, looking from one to the other, 'I'll sit here and kibitz, if that doesn't bother you.'

No one says a word.

Dr Böttcher gestures vaguely.

'Well, then, let's get going!' cries Sasse.

Klose sits down hesitantly and slowly picks up his cards again, then gives Dr Böttcher and Wiegand a challenging look. 'Right, then,' he says, 'I'm first, say something, Fritz.'

The three men begin to play, the fourth sits there as an onlooker. Everyone knows that people are really playing a game of hide-and-seek with their true intentions, the three know that the brown-clad man hasn't come because of the blackout and stayed because of the game of skat, the brown-clad man knows that these three men are anything but harmless card players.

They play stubbornly and carelessly, they keep lowering their cards and pausing, but Sasse keeps instructing them to get on with the game, and there is something that sounds like mockery in his voice. He looks at the cards and keeps giving advice, he looks at the hidden cards and comments long and loud on every hand. Any normal card player would have complained long ago and energetically refused to tolerate his presence, but these three players let him get away with it, they don't answer his questions or rebut his objections, they play very mechanically, they bid, pass, take tricks and follow suit, but it is all done without noticing, far from their thoughts.

The game reminds Wiegand of the sarcastic orders of the SS guards in the concentration camp, who tied a prisoner to the rack and whipped him while the other inmates stood there motionlessly, lined up neatly in the old Prussian military tradition, to attention, with their hands extended along the seams of their blue-and-white striped trousers, and were forced to sing 'Take Joy in Life'. And just as he cannot leave the game under the observant eye of political functionary Sasse, because he must maintain the fiction that they are actually playing a game of cards here, neither could he refuse to sing in the camp, because when two SS men were taking turns to bullwhip the bound prisoner, others, like dogs following a shepherd, crept around them, peering carefully and paying close attention to the mouths of the inmates, ready to lash out as soon as anyone dared not to sing the song about the joy of life.

Wiegand clearly remembers that look, passing quickly from one mouth to the next, like that of a beast of prey convinced of its place in the food chain, turned on him and the others; but in one respect this situation is totally different. Back then, during the whipping ritual in Sachsenhausen, everyone knew what was going on: there the beasts in human form, here the inmates, their souls almost extinguished in the swamp of brutality and wickedness, and in the atmosphere of complete abandonment, in which every muscle quivered with rage suppressed and forced violently back into the body. The roles were clearly assigned, error was impossible. The hatred and fury which had sprung nakedly out of their eyes in the camp are now masked by specious cordiality and feigned harmlessness. A heavy tension settles over the four men, and without a word being exchanged each of them feels the situation coming to a head and rushing towards its decisive phase.

Dr Böttcher is in a state of slight unease, but he observes himself and the others with the cool reasoning of a psychologist unwilling to waste the opportunity to study rare objects in an unusual situation, his face is controlled, his eyes mostly peer over the edge of his glasses with the searching gaze of the scientist looking through a microscope, he plays calmly and reflectively, and when it is his turn to play he sets his cards down slowly on the table.

Klose is completely calm, his stout figure leaning backwards in his chair, he doesn't make any rash decisions, his phlegmatic temperament lets things take their course, an ironic smile plays around his lips then rises to his eyes. He draws his cards quickly and throws them down rapidly on the table.

Wiegand's face is tense, with a smile that is completely unnatural. He looks stiffly at his cards and hurls them down on the table with an almost contemptuous movement. Even though he is gripped by a terrible excitement he is quite calm, because he is resolved to do anything at all.

Sasse sits on the edge of his chair, his hands resting on his knees and his body leaning forward, a smile is fixed firmly among the folds and wrinkles. He speaks constantly, not because he needs to talk or because the game is interesting, but in order to provoke the three players, to disturb their calm, to make them nervous and prompt them into making statements or actions that will give him the opportunity to expose this game of skat once and for all.

But nothing happens, the game goes on, the tension keeps on condensing into a black storm cloud rising from the horizon.

Even though he has the authority of an all-powerful state, Sasse is the most uneasy of them all, the atmosphere that he has created is becoming unbearable. He clearly feels the tension within him stretching beyond endurance until it is about to snap, so he can wait no longer. Even though he doesn't need to weigh his words, he wants to achieve the greatest possible effect with them, he wants to sneak up slowly on the target he has set for himself, and he can't do that if he is too agitated to think or speak properly.

When another round has been played and Klose shuffles the cards, the first words are spoken casually, apparently without any hidden intent.

'And there was a light in your window last night during the air-raid warning, Klose,' Sasse says.

Klose goes on calmly shuffling the cards. 'That's impossible, Mr Sasse,' he says without hesitation, 'I always take out the fuses before I go to the cellar.'

'Then you neglected to do so yesterday,' Sasse insists. 'You must have had your reasons, I should guess?' Klose is still shuffling the cards, but now he slowly cuts the pack. 'I don't know what you mean, Mr Sasse, I'm short-sighted in my right eye.'

Sasse claps him cordially on the shoulder. 'A little girlfriend in your bedroom, you old sinner?' His smile is still there, but the excitement within him almost erases it from his features, and a malicious glimmer in the back of his eyes reveals that the smile has been skilfully donned as if by a gifted actor. 'Stop that nonsense,' Klose says gruffly and shakes his hand away, he sets the cards down on the table and passes them to Wiegand. 'Cut!' he tells him.

Now any hint of a smile has vanished completely from Sasse's face, leaving only a pinched expression of malicious anticipation. 'But there was someone in your flat,' he persists, 'I know that very well.'

'Then you know more than I do,' Klose replies, and starts dealing the cards.

Now Sasse's face turns bright red. 'Don't evade the issue, Mr Klose,' he says, his voice struggling to maintain the tone of friendly conversation. 'You see, I'm responsible for everything that goes on in this building. You do understand that, don't you Mr Klose?' Klose shrugs and doesn't reply, he picks up the cards, fans them and brings them back together again. 'Go on talking to each other,' he says, turning to Dr Böttcher and Wiegand.

The slight flush on Sasse's face quickly turns deep red.

'Enough of this play-acting,' he says loudly, his voice now harsh and peremptory. 'I want to know who was in your flat last night during the air-raid warning.'

Dr Böttcher lays the fan of his cards face down on the table. 'I'll pass,' he says to Wiegand and then turns to Sasse. 'Won't you let us get on with our game, Mr Sasse? If you have things to sort out with Mr Klose in private, do it tomorrow. It has nothing to do with us.'

Sasse looks furiously at Dr Böttcher. 'You keep your nose out of this,' he snaps. 'The three of you belong together, you're all a big happy mischpocha.'

Wiegand lays his cards slowly on the table and pushes his chair back slightly so as not to be impeded by the table. 'Let's call it a day,' he says.

Sasse leaps to his feet and pulls his revolver from his holster. 'Sit where you are!' His voice is shrill with fury and agitation. 'Or I'll shoot you down on the spot like a mad dog!'

Any ambiguity has fled, making way for the excitement of open combat. Faces reveal themselves like a landscape lit by a beam of sunlight from behind a cloud. The three men sit there at a table, still in front of the cards that they have used as cover from undesirable questions, as a pretext for their meetings, and a few metres away, leaning against the credenza, stands a tall man in a brown uniform with a revolver in his hand, his brown cap still lying on the table like a straggler surrounded by the enemy.

Wiegand bites his lips, he is sitting closest to the Nazi, but there are still three or four metres between them. Dr Böttcher and Klose are sitting in unfavourable positions, there is a table between them and the brown-clad man, and in any case they have pushed their chairs too tightly under the table to be able to jump to their feet unprepared.

Dr Böttcher looks at Wiegand and they agree with a glance, he knows the important thing now is to get a conversation under way, or subject themselves to an interrogation, and that either or both must be extended ad infinitum to gain time and weaken the Nazi's attention.

Klose's broad, comfortable smile has frozen into a menacing mask, his eyes are narrow slits, his lips reveal his gritted teeth, hard folds run from his mouth to his chin, which seems to have shed its former bulk.

'Who was here yesterday?' Sasse barks again. 'Do you think

we're asleep, you fat boozer? I've been keeping a close eye on your place, three people went in, and there are only two here now. Where is the third?'

For a moment Klose looks as if he is thinking. 'Oh him,' he says at last. 'He left ages ago, he was just bumming cigarettes.'

'Claptrap,' Sasse says quickly, 'I don't believe a word. He didn't come out again, I was watching you very closely.'

'There's no one here but us,' Dr Böttcher says.

The brown-clad man doesn't even look at him. 'Klose, where's the boy? I want to know.' His voice has become a little milder. 'Perhaps it's all completely harmless, but I want to know what's happening here.'

'Nothing is happening here,' Klose says, and brings his hand down on the table. 'Leave us in peace.'

'That would suit you,' Sasse says with a broad, sarcastic grin and fumbles with his pistol. 'Will you spill the beans, you fat, greedy bastard?'

Klose's lips part. 'Kiss my arse,' he says calmly, 'there's no one else here.'

Sasse's eyes dart around the room again. 'So there's no one else here?' he says in a measured voice. 'And who owns the ski-cap on the sofa?'

'I do,' Wiegand says quickly.

'Codswallop,' Sasse replies. 'You were both wearing hats, you can't fool me. You gang of rogues, I'll unmask the lot of you, I have my doubts about all three of you, the Gestapo will loosen your tongues. That must be a rare bird you have in your nest.'

'There's really no one here, my good man,' Dr Böttcher begins, 'I . . .'

'Shut your mouth!' Sasse roars. 'I don't believe a word you say, not a word. You sit where you are, just like that, and not one of you is to move. I'll shoot straight away!' He looks around the room once more and checks their faces in turn. 'Right, then, let's make a phone call.' He reaches out towards the telephone on the credenza.

Gain some time, Dr Böttcher thinks, just gain some time, he stares fixedly at the door leading to the restaurant, which is out of

Sasse's range of vision because it's behind him. Dr Böttcher has to force himself not to look at the door so as not to draw the Nazi's attention to it. 'I think we've had a misunderstanding of some kind,' he says.

Sasse lets his outstretched hand rest on the receiver. 'It will all sort itself out, my dear fellow, the men from Prinz Albrecht Strasse are very good at clearing up misunderstandings.'

'They certainly are,' says Dr Böttcher, looking over the rim of his glasses at the door again. The latch moves slowly downward, millimetres at a time. 'I don't know who you think we are, Mr Sasse.'

Sasse laughs sarcastically, his hand is still on the receiver. 'I think you are rogues, tramps and traitors, if you really want to know,' he roars, 'in fact you should simply be shot without further ado.'

Dr Böttcher draws Wiegand's attention to the door with a movement of his eyebrows. Wiegand tenses his muscles, his joints are twitching like those of a runner at the start of a race, his expression is one of grim resolution, his teeth are grinding hard against one another. 'Forget this nonsense,' he says. 'You don't even know who we are.'

Sasse laughs his mocking laugh again. 'I don't care what your names are,' he hisses through his teeth, 'but you are friends of Klose's and that's enough for me. You thought you were safe, didn't you, Klose?'

'You brown piece of shit,' Klose growls.

'An honest word at last,' Sasse exclaims. 'Well, wait, my lad, I'll see you dangling yet, we'll order a specially strong piece of rope for you, you red swine.'

Dr Böttcher looks at the door, which is opening very slowly, already he can feel a cold draught. The Nazi will notice it soon as well, he thinks.

'What do you keep staring at?' Sasse asks, half turning round.

Dr Böttcher suddenly feels his heart beating fast and hard . . . now he's got to . . .

Wiegand leans forward, he sees the door opening a crack, and crouches like a cat about to pounce.

Then it happens. The door flies open, Lassehn is standing in the doorway, there is a short, sharp bang, a little cloud of smoke, the

Nazi totters, reaches into the air with both hands and drops sideways, pulling a few bowls from the credenza, glass shatters, a dull crash, the floorboards echo for a few seconds. Then all is still.

Klose is on the Nazi like a tiger. 'He's done for,' he exclaims. 'You did well, Joachim.'

Lassehn is still standing in the doorway, his face is pale, but stiff and resolute, although now there is a violent twitch running around his mouth, his features slacken, his arms fall limply down, he leans exhausted against the door frame and looks at the brown-clad man and Dr Böttcher, who is now bending over him. 'Is he dead?' he asks excitedly.

'No,' Dr Böttcher replies, 'sadly no, three centimetres lower and you'd have got his heart.'

'Damn it all,' Klose says, 'now we've got this fellow to deal with.'

Lassehn steps through the doorway and looks down at the Nazi. He is still holding the revolver, there is shock and horror in his eyes, he is trembling feverishly. 'And what happens now?' he asks in a blank voice.

Wiegand pulls the door shut and rests a hand on Lassehn's shoulder 'Stay calm, Lassehn,' he says, 'stay calm, we have to be quick and resolute. Is the wound fatal?' he asks, turning to Dr Böttcher.

Böttcher has taken a pack of bandages out of his medical box, removed the wrapper and made a plug of white cotton wool that he stuffs into the wound. 'Not necessarily, as far as I can tell right now,' he replies. 'However . . .' He breaks off and shrugs.

'What? Tell us, Doctor,' Wiegand urges, 'we have no time to lose.'

'A quick operation might save him,' Dr Böttcher says.

Klose snorts. 'God alive, Doctor, how do you imagine that?'

'I can't,' Dr Böttcher replies. 'I know what you're getting at, Klose. If he stays alive . . .'

'. . . we're all done for,' Klose completes his phrase. 'Clear as mud.'

'You want . . .' Lassehn begins, his lips quivering, he looks at the Nazi lying by the credenza, his bald, white skull is almost a ghostly glow in the shadows.

'No sentimentality,' Wiegand says sharply. 'The question is this:

it's him or us, there is no middle way. If *he* lives, then *we're* for it. Or do you think he'll spare us? The first word he utters will mean certain death for us.'

Lassehn's face is white as snow. 'That wasn't what I wanted,' he says.

Dr Böttcher pulls Lassehn into the room and pushes him down on a chair. 'If it wasn't what you wanted, you shouldn't have shot him. Apparently you haven't yet found the right attitude towards . . . well, let's say, towards your deed. You acted out of self-defence, Lassehn, isn't that clear to you?'

'Self-defence?' Lassehn looks at Dr Böttcher, disbelief and hope battling it out in his eyes.

'Even justified self-defence,' Dr Böttcher says excitedly, 'not according to National Socialist laws, but I can't imagine you obey those?'

'I know no others,' Lassehn says. 'Which laws am I supposed to have acted on?'

'The natural law of self-assertion and self-preservation,' Dr Böttcher replies. 'If you hadn't shot the man, then you and the three of us would have been hanged in cold blood. Is that clear to you?'

Lassehn nods with relief. 'Certainly, but I've only wounded him . . .'

Wiegand intervenes firmly in the conversation. 'No long speeches and academic discussions, now, gentlemen, we've got to be quick and reckless. I hope no one heard the shot.'

'An old couple live in the flat above,' Klose says, 'they will have gone to sleep ages ago, and I'm sure they won't have heard a thing, on the right there's the hallway, on the left the chemist's and there's no one there at night. I don't think anyone will have heard anything, and in any case the nights are unsettled enough . . .'

'That's what I wanted to know,' Wiegand says quickly. 'Give me the gun, Lassehn . . .'

Lassehn hesitates, he is still holding the gun in his hand.

'Give it to me,' Wiegand insists, walks up to Lassehn and takes the gun from his hand. For a few seconds he stands motionlessly by the Nazi, who is still lying on the floor, his body bowed and his legs bent, one hand on his head as if to protect himself, the other strangely twisted on his back. It is curiously quiet in the room, the only sound the men's breathing.

'Do it,' Klose says with an impatient gesture. Wiegand looks at Dr Böttcher, he is quite calm, the hand holding the revolver isn't shaking.

'In the temple,' Dr Böttcher says, 'put the gun right against his head, it will silence the shot and there won't be a spray of blood.'

Wiegand bends over Sasse and puts the muzzle of the revolver to the side of his forehead, he can't find the temple straight away, it's too dark in this corner of the room. Then the Nazi moves slightly, the cold steel against his temple prompts a reflex, his hand twitches and slips from his head to the floor. It is only a short, dull sound, but it cuts through the silence like a crash of thunder, Wiegand recoils a little, the gun slides away from its target, but he regains control of it, puts the muzzle back in place and fires. A dull explosion and a quick cracking sound, the Nazi's body rears slightly and then crashes back down, his legs straightening as if to kick something away.

'Gone, finished,' Klose breaks the silence. 'And now?'

'In Berlin right now there shouldn't be any problems in getting rid of a corpse,' Dr Böttcher says in a clear voice. 'And it's dark tonight as well. Where do you suggest, Klose?'

Klose thinks. 'We should take him out,' he begins, and then laughs grimly. 'As a matter of fact, isn't that what we've just done?'

'Seriously now,' Dr Böttcher says disapprovingly, 'we need to make sure they don't find him straight away, so that we can hide our tracks. Where should we take him to?'

'There are plenty of ruined buildings on Koppenstrasse,' Klose says seriously. 'It's not far, a hundred metres, maybe a hundred and fifty.'

'I know where it is,' Böttcher says. 'Will you give me a hand, Lassehn?'

Lassehn has been sitting motionless and apparently indifferent on the sofa; now, at Böttcher's request, he gives a start. 'Pull yourself together, Lassehn,' Wiegand says severely. 'How many times have you killed people anonymously as a soldier, people more innocent than that man there, Russian farmers or workers or students, and now you're losing your nerves because you've shot someone who wanted to slit your throat? Yes, my dear boy, there's no time for silly emotions here, or for inconsistency, you'd have been better off staying with your unit and being ordered to kill, carrying out instructions and relying on that thing called duty. But then you didn't want to do that either!'

Lassehn shakes himself violently back into life.

'You're right, Mr Wiegand,' he says, 'it was a shock.'

'Reason on its own won't help you,' Klose says and shakes his head a few times, 'you also need to know how to use it.'

'No long conversations,' Dr Böttcher says energetically. 'We'll take the man away now, and you can clear everything up, Klose, remove any bloodstains you happen to see. We'll carry him between us like a drunk, and the third man supports him from behind, then if we bump into anyone it will look as if we're carrying home a drunken friend. But first I want to seal up the wound to his head. Wiegand, bring my medical bag.'

Dr Böttcher works quickly and deftly, he twists a plug of cotton and stuffs it into the head wound with pincers, then sticks two strips of plaster over it at an angle. 'Right, that'll do,' he says, and gets back to his feet.

'I'll open the front door,' Klose says, 'then you don't need to walk through the courtyard.' He takes a bunch of keys from his trouser pocket and unlatches the door to the restaurant, but stays in the doorway.

For a few seconds the men stand there irresolutely, avoiding each other's eyes. Even though they have often dealt with corpses, with mutilated and shredded cadavers, one professionally because he is a doctor, and the others out of habit because they were soldiers, they hesitate to touch the dead man, their respect for human life, even that of the enemy, is too great for them to be able to forget that this man in his brown uniform was still standing here a few minutes ago, untouched by thoughts of death.

'Right, then, off we go,' says Wiegand. 'Come on, Doctor. Lassehn, lift him with your hips. Can you do that?'

Lassehn gulps violently, he has an unpleasant taste in his mouth, but he sees that he has to lend a hand – after all, he started this. 'I'll manage,' he says. 'We had to touch worse things in the field.'

Dr Böttcher nods to him, then they lift up the Nazi's body, Dr Böttcher and Wiegand reach under his armpits, Lassehn hoists him up by his belt. Then Dr Böttcher and Wiegand put his arms around their necks, they have to support Sasse's torso by wedging their hands under his armpits because the Nazi is significantly taller than they are, but even that way his legs still drag, his head slumps forward and rocks back and forth. This movement of the bald white head suddenly reminds Lassehn of a grotesque figure from an advertisement that they used to see in shop windows, a thin man with big, round, bulging eyes, a bald head and thick, pouting lips that moved mechanically while his head rocked back and forth like an upside-down pendulum, and one hand tapped on the glass with a stick.

Klose picks up the brown cap from the table and crams it over the dead man's head. 'Off we go to Valhalla,' he says.

The lifeless body seems to weigh a ton, it has to be dragged and pulled rather than carried, after only a few steps both men have broken into a sweat, but they have no other choice, the corpse must be removed.

Klose gently opens the door to the restaurant and carefully pushes aside the grille. 'It's all quiet,' he says, turning back to the others, 'not a soul in the street.'

'Let's carry on straight to the corner,' Wiegand says.

Then they're in the street, it's pitch-dark, they can hardly see a few metres in front of them, only over by Silesian Station is the darkness broken, a few faint lights shimmer through the window-less ribcage of the station hall, the sound of steam escaping from a locomotive comes from the ramp of the railway post office, for a few seconds a car's headlights send narrow beams of light into the blackness of the street.

The hundred metres from Klose's restaurant to the corner of Koppenstrasse seem endless, they have to trudge the distance metre by metre, the corpse becoming heavier and heavier, Wiegand

and Dr Böttcher have long since given up supporting the body under the armpits, they have grabbed the dead man's arms, which are draped around their shoulders, with both hands, so the corpse is literally hanging around their necks. Lassehn is left to push the body that dangles between Dr Böttcher and Wiegand.

There is no one to be seen, the street is deserted, the only sound the even tread of a policeman under the viaducts on Koppenstrasse.

At last they have reached Koppenstrasse, there is barely a house still standing, everything burnt out, entirely destroyed by fire.

'In here,' Wiegand says in a low voice.

They are standing by a gap that was once the doorway to a house, the entrance is blocked with stones and rubble, but this is the right place. Dr Böttcher and Wiegand release themselves from the dead man's embrace, let him slip to the ground and pause, panting, for a few seconds.

'Stay here, Lassehn,' Wiegand whispers, 'and take the other arm as well.'

Dr Böttcher reaches for the other arm of the dead man, which is passed to him like a relay baton. Wiegand grabs the corpse's feet and brings them level with the edge of the cellar, then they push the body slowly over the edge.

'Now,' Wiegand says quietly.

They let go at the same time. The corpse slips down into the cellar, rolls a few metres and comes to rest, carrying a few stones down with it, they clatter dully and then it is still. The dead man has disappeared into the shadow of the night.

Wiegand and Dr Böttcher listened to the sound and stood there motionless for a few seconds, then they climb back over the mounds of rubble. When they stand in the nocturnal silence of the street they feel as if they have emerged into daylight from the grim darkness of a catacomb.

XVI

Even where the city is most densely populated idylls can still be found. Where house presses closely against house, the apartments are crammed as tightly together as cells in a beehive, the court-yards are only narrow fireplaces, and the streets reduced to mere canyons. Where family lives side by side with family, human close to human. In the houses facing the front, where large families dwell in miniature apartments, and in the buildings to the rear small-scale industry carries on in dark, smoky, run-down factory halls. Where the many cafés, pubs, restaurants, dance halls, bars, foyers, billiard halls and cinemas are sprinkled like freckles over the dark face of the workers' district, and questionable pleasures, prostitutes who have seen better days, rejects of the smarter districts, offer fleeting satisfaction for a small reward. Where the pavements spill over with people and the carriageways are crammed with vehicles of every kind, handcarts, delivery vans and enormous goods trains, horses and carts, cyclists and trams. Where it is never quiet, not even in the depths of night or first thing in the morning, where turmoil, haste and urgency form the element of life, and everything is purposeful, bare, matter-of-fact reality. Where the city comes together into a dense, impenetrable core and the houses are not lined up along the streets, but the streets seem to be carved into a rock built with houses. This is where idylls are found. There are no flower-covered meadows or shady forests and no charming river walks or gentle hills. There is none of that here, it wouldn't fit the place at all. But there are corners which, even if they are not exactly born to blush unseen, still breathe rather more quietly, their hearts beating at a more moderate rhythm.

One such corner is the passageway that leads from Grosse Frankfurter Strasse to Weberstrasse. Here a breach is cut into the dark line of houses on Grosse Frankfurter Strasse, a narrow alley-way runs between blackened, ugly fire walls. After a few metres it turns to the north-east and then opens up onto a square on which St Mark's Church stands. Here, in the barren midst of asphalt, granite slabs, pebbled roadway and cobblestones, there are two lit-tle islands of earth on which sparse greenery sprouts. This little alley, which doesn't even have a name and is identified only as 'pas-sageway to Weberstrasse', has only pedestrian traffic, no wagons rattle down here, no cars dash, the streams of the big city flow by to the north and south, the voices of the city, noise, shouting, hub-bub, are heard only from a long way off, bouncing faintly against the walls and seeping away.

Lassehn has never been to this part of the city before. Now that he passes this way for the first time, everything is dead. It is the deadly silence of a city killed by aerial and incendiary bombs and blockbusters. The silence of the little alley known as 'passageway to Weberstrasse' has also spread to the adjacent streets, trams no longer ring their bells along Grosse Frankfurter Strasse, the whoosh of cars and the roar of lorries has fallen silent, people's voices have gone mute, over the smoke-blackened walls and the mountains of rubble silence has settled like a shroud. Only here and there does a spark of life still glow in the stump of a building that has chanced to escape complete destruction, only losing the plaster of its façade and its upper storeys, where people still lead a ghostly life between hecatombs of the slaughtered, burnt and suf-focated dead, who lie beneath the ruins, the quick, hungry rats darting among them.

How even the most terrible images may fade and, in the end, barely attract a glance, in fact barely enter the consciousness – Lassehn has experienced that while passing through this eastern part of the inner city. He has come along Andreasstrasse, Lang-estrasse and Markusstrasse, he has crossed Wallnertheaterstrasse, the Brauner Weg and Blumestrasse, but straight ahead and to his right and left he has hardly seen anything but burnt-out, bombed and ruined houses, ravaged, smoke-blackened rows of buildings, and breathed in the revolting smell of burning, mixed with the miasma of escaped gas. It has been like striding over a field of graves where the air seems to stand still. Only fleetingly has he been touched by the idea that the abysses and chasms, the craters and heaps of these stony mountains were once houses designed by architects and engineers on a drawing board, built by bricklayers and carpenters, plumbers and fitters, roof and floor layers, and finally inhabited by people. All the material possessions carried into those houses and all the experience that settled in them like a patina were shaken to pieces and scattered in just a few minutes into the chaos of a pile of glowing bricks, wood and iron.

The adaptability of the human spirit is one of the most significant, but also one of the most terrible gifts of man, the deadening effect of habit can take hold of him so completely that terrible things are no longer terrible, gruesome things no longer gruesome, the fearsome no longer fearsome. A ruined house, a torn-up carriageway no longer prompts an unusual reflex in the retina; they cease to convey a sense of agitation to the brain.

Lassehn has observed this quite matter-of-factly, and pushed aside the images that tried to cram their way into his brain, he has concentrated entirely on the task he has been given, which has eased and smoothed his journey through the sea of ruins. When he reached the corner of Markusstrasse and Grosse Frankfurter Strasse, he stopped for a few seconds before he discovered the passageway that Klose had precisely described to him. Klose told him much else besides, and Lassehn had to commit it all to memory in great detail, because nothing must be written down. He looked cautiously around several times before crossing the deserted carriageway of Grosse Frankfurter Strasse, and then he turned hesitantly into the alley of 'Passageway to Weberstrasse'. His delay is based not on fear, what holds him back is his amazement that there is still life in this chaotic wasteland of stones and rubble. He entered the little alley, climbed over a few piles of rubble on his right, forced his way through a gap in a wall that had half collapsed, and then stood by a flight of steps leading down to a cellar, its roof piled high with mounds of rubble. Lassehn stopped again, assailed by doubts about whether he had understood Klose correctly, he ran through all his directions once more and finally reached the conclusion that he was on the right track. Then he climbed down the cellar steps and in the end found himself standing in a dark room that was damp and smelled of mildew. Only after a while, once his eyes had grown accustomed to the dark, did he discover a niche, and in it a door. He knocked on the door, two short knocks and one long.

Then the door opened, a small, squat man held the latch in his hand and didn't say a word.

Lassehn handed him a piece of newspaper, the man held it and matched it carefully, almost pedantically, against a scrap of newspaper that he had taken from his breast pocket, and only when he established that the two pieces fitted precisely together did a strange conversation unfold between Lassehn and the man.

'What do you want?'

'I am to pass on greetings from Uncle Otto.'

'I don't know any Uncle Otto.'

'Not even the one from Halberstadt?'

'Halberstadt?'

'Halberstadt in Saxony.'

'Oh, he's the one you mean, what does he want?'

'Seeds.'

'How many?'

'Six hundred.'

'Have you brought a bag?'

'Yes, here it is.'

The door has fallen closed again, endless minutes pass, during which Lassehn casts his eyes around the place. He sees nothing, in the cellar there is only darkness, cold and wet, a penetrating smell of burning and an unreal silence. Then the door opened again, his bag was handed back to him, for a moment Lassehn was able to glimpse the cellar, where in the light of two faint bulbs he saw an apparatus that is probably a hand-press.

'Here is the bag,' the man said, and quickly closed the door again.

'Thank you,' Lassehn replied.

'Greetings to Uncle Otto.'

'I'll tell him. Goodbye.'

'Goodbye.'

Lassehn turned round to go when the voice called him back.

'You're new!'

'Yes.'

'Good luck, Comrade!'

A hand was extended to him, Lassehn took it and felt a brief, firm handshake, then the door closed again.

And now Lassehn is standing back in Grosse Frankfurter Strasse. In spite of the oppressive surroundings he feels inspired, and he knows very clearly why that is. It is that man's firm handshake, his familiar tone and the word 'comrade', it is the contents of the brief-case, which he doesn't know, but which makes him part of the group which, he now knows, calls itself the resistance movement. He has probably heard of it before, but it was just a name, every now and again he imagined something like a partisan division or a gang like the one led by Karl Moor in Schiller's play *The Robbers*, but now he can't help smiling at himself. Now, in the middle of the twentieth century, there are no impenetrable forests, no closed-off tracts of land, neither are there people or groups who can live out-side the community. The net of official surveillance and registration has been cast over everyone, and the system of food cards, which was created at the start of the war as a new and effective instru-ment of control, has tightened the meshes of the net so narrowly that it forms an excellent complement to the police and military registration apparatus. The present-day revolutionaries no longer retreat into the woods to lead a more or less romantic life like Karl Moor and his companions, they are – and Lassehn has finally worked this out – Janus-headed creatures, they have bourgeois pro-fessions, because they are forced to adapt to the organization of state and outwardly submit to its demands, if they don't want to be stripped a priori of all opportunities to get rid of it. This produces the paradoxical situation whereby even the sworn enemies of the state must somehow work for it, be active on its behalf, must in fact encourage and support it through their work, through their compulsory membership of associations, because they cannot avoid paying their taxes and making their donations (and even the donations to the Winter Relief Fund and the Red Cross, the National League of Germans Abroad and the Reich Colonial League, even for collections of bones and waste paper, are the price for modest security), use its terminology, because more than anyone else they need to be careful not to stand out. Anyone who stands out also forfeits what freedom of movement the Third Reich has left its citizens, they must build magnificent façades on which the emblems of the state are visibly apparent. Those façades are the Potemkin villages of the Third Reich. The enemies of the state differ from those loyal to it only by the fact that they try to keep to a minimum the fulfilment of their civic duties. The ones living underground, like Lassehn, barely take part in conspiracies, and they cannot because they can show neither valid papers nor employment in civil society as an alibi.

Lassehn walks along Grosse Frankfurter Strasse, he lingers for a few minutes by the huge craters blown in the U-Bahn on Strausberger Platz, then continues on his way. Walking has become strolling, nearly nonchalant and serene; for the first time since he has been back in Berlin he feels almost at ease. The spring sun burns pleasantly on the back of his neck and chases the sluggish blood intoxicatingly around his veins, strangely even the complete destruction all around him seems less terrifying. Today Lassehn no longer finds it unusual, almost suggestive, in fact, that the girls swing their hips and even manage the occasional smile.

Stretching ahead of him now is Grosse Frankfurter Strasse, which extends from Strausberger Platz into a magnificent, broad street with a central promenade, which points straight out of the city towards the east. Nothing remains of the former greatness of this street, however, only its situation reveals that it was once a central axis of Berlin. Here too the black grimaces of the burnt-out buildings grin on either side, the fleshless skeletons of the railway buildings stretch like cages crashed to the ground, among heaps of debris. The old people's homes and hospitals between Lebuserstrasse and Fruchtstrasse are also nothing but ruins; the Rose-Theater, the playhouse of the petite bourgeoisie of Berlin East, no longer exists. Where Grosse Frankfurter Strasse becomes Frankfurter Allee there is the Frankfurter Tor, but the name is now nothing but an allegory, there is no gate, nor any construction resembling a gate, it is just a memory, and then only for the very old or for local historians, of which there are, strangely, many in the giant city of Berlin. Other residents of the area no longer know that the intersection between Grosse Frankfurter Strasse and Frankfurter Allee is still called Frankfurter Tor.

The Weberwiese at the crossroads of Memeler Strasse, Frankfurter Allee and Königsberger Strasse has abandoned its actual task of supplying oxygen and peace in the stone and ozone-poor solitude of Berlin East. It was never beautiful or even well looked-after, it was always a place for poor people, and while the term *'Wiese'* – a meadow – may once have been justified for this square in former decades, for a long time now it has not even been a patch of ground that might prompt thoughts of growth and harvest, only a bit of sand with a few pitiful bushes and a number of old trees, and now it is not even that. They have dug it up in honour of the war from the air, they have drilled into it and raised molehill-like mounds on it that look like giant coffins and are officially called slit trenches.

Lassehn is so immersed in himself – his legs have walked all by themselves – that he only comes to when he walks into a big mound of rubble. A glance at the number of a house shows him that he has already overshot his goal. Quite by chance his eye falls on a squad of soldiers who are busy building an anti-tank barrier. An advertising column whose top part has splintered away is being filled with sand and stones, and joists are being rammed into the ground, the gaps between them filled with twisted company signs, grilles, beams and boards, and a truck keeps bringing new joists and iron bars. But Lassehn is interested in none of that, it isn't the first anti-tank barrier that he has watched being built, his eye is caught by the young lieutenant who seems to be in charge of the squad.

Caution warns him not to linger, but to move on immediately, even if the young lieutenant was once a good friend and school-mate, that doesn't mean anything, people are unpredictable these days, the false emotion of a misunderstood sense of duty and hon-our (not to mention slimy submissiveness and hypocritical servility) has obstructed and distorted people's minds.

Lassehn reluctantly decides to walk on, the possibility of saying a few words to someone who belongs to his former life is too tempt-ing. After a few steps Lassehn stops and turns round, glancing behind him, and from that point there is nothing more to be done. His eyes meet those of the young lieutenant, their eyes fix on one another and now Lassehn can no longer tear himself away, he stands there as the young officer strides towards him.

'Is it possible?' the young officer exclaims. 'Joachim Lassehn!'

Lassehn nods and extends his hand. 'Dietrich Tolksdorff,' he says emotionally, 'so it's really you?'

'Of course it is, old boy,' Tolksdorff says, and energetically grips Lassehn's outstretched hand. 'What a coincidence! How are things, Joachim?'

Even though the question is merely an empty phrase, it catches Lassehn completely unawares. What answer is he, the deserter, supposed to give to his former friend, the lieutenant? 'Not too bad,' he says, avoiding the question, but he knows he will have to say more than that. At school Tolksdorff was top in maths and Latin, those disciplines in which logic is an essential component.

Tolksdorff studies Lassehn critically. 'You're dressed very oddly, Joachim,' he says.

Lassehn shrugs. 'I had a task to perform, one that I couldn't really do in uniform,' he replies. 'What about you?' he asks, to head off any further questions. 'Why aren't you at the front?'

Tolksdorff shrugs as well, a slow, resigned movement. 'The front is everywhere now, Joachim,' he says, 'and I took a bad knock at Nettuno, so I'm not much use for deployment at the front. At the moment I'm a trainer with the fifth intelligence division in Nedlitz, but right now we're being deployed here.' He nods to the anti-tank barrier currently under construction.

'Is there still any point in it?' Lassehn asks, looking his old friend firmly in the eyes.

Tolksdorff turns his head to the side. 'It isn't up to a soldier to ask the point of things,' he replies, 'he is given his orders and he carries them out. You're a soldier too, Joachim, even if you don't look like one right now, so I don't understand your question.'

Lassehn shakes his head. 'I am a soldier,' he says firmly, 'that is true, but not out of ambition or vocation, while you . . .'

Tolksdorff turns slowly back to him. 'Well? You can speak openly, Joachim.'

'You're a soldier by inclination, so you accept military orders as the supreme law,' Lassehn continues slowly. 'Don't you?'

'You're mistaken,' Tolksdorff replies, 'I'm a soldier because our fatherland needs me.'

'To abuse you!' Lassehn cuts in.

Tolksdorff looks at him in astonishment. 'Excuse me?'

'To abuse you, I said,' Lassehn says. 'Or have you not yet realized that an enormous abuse is being perpetrated on you, on you and me, on your people and all of us, our whole people?'

Tolksdorff looks at the ground in front of him, then quickly grips Lassehn's right arm. 'Come on,' he says, 'we can't stay here, let's sit down for a few minutes.' He points to a few large blocks of stone that have been blown out of a house and are obstructing a ruined portal.

Then they sit down side by side in the half-ruined hallway, with a view of several factory courtyards now stripped of life. Lassehn in his worn, dark-brown winter coat, black trousers with no turn-ups which Klose gave him this morning, with a ski-cap and his shabby boots contrasts strangely with Lieutenant Tolksdorff, who is wearing his impeccable light-grey leather coat, made-to-measure riding trousers and high black boots. But he is far from downcast and is no longer tormented by the feeling that his own way of doing things is contemptible. He has completely shed that emotion, which took hold of him at first, and something new has taken its place, it is as yet nameless and formless, but it is there, and that something makes him feel superior to his former friend.

'You say they're abusing us,' Tolksdorff begins. 'I won't even say that you are completely wrong, but I am of the opinion that discussion of the matter is very unimportant right now.'

'Excuse me?' Lassehn says furiously. 'I think . . .'

Tolksdorff shakes his head. 'Let me finish, Joachim,' he says. 'The discussion of this question is unimportant right now, and I also want to tell you why it is. At the moment it isn't a matter of abuse, justice or injustice, it's just about Germany, about our lives. That must be clear, isn't it?'

Lassehn pauses for a moment, then shakes his head. 'It's about our lives, it's about Germany, that much is true,' he replies, 'but the premises are false. It's precisely because it's about Germany that we need to finish it off, straight away.'

'Finish what off?' Tolksdorff asks. 'How do you imagine that? What are we going to finish off?'

'The war, of course! Or do you want the areas that have been spared so far to be rolled over, stamped into the ground and destroyed as well?'

'Joachim, you don't know what you're saying,' Tolksdorff replies. 'We're fighting precisely to keep that from happening.'

Lassehn laughs briefly. 'You still believe that, Dietrich?' he asks. 'The game's up! Can't you see that what once sounded like music to your ears is only a croak?'

'Comparisons like that prove nothing,' Tolksdorff says dismissively. He takes two cigarettes from the outside pocket of his coat and hands one to Lassehn, then he flicks open a lighter and holds the weak flame in the hollow of his hand.

Lassehn bends over Tolksdorff's hands to light his cigarette, and only then does he look carefully into his friend's face. Just now it was the well-known, familiar face of his former classmate, with the narrow skull, the high forehead, the clever brown eyes, the straight nose above a narrow mouth, but now that he looks more closely at his features he notices that while the basic shapes have remained unaltered, new, unfamiliar lines are drawn on them, and another expression has taken root there. The joie de vivre and hope for the future, the openness and freshness of mind have gone, to be replaced by resignation and stubborn defiance, and not even forced optimism can conceal them.

'Comparisons like that prove everything,' Lassehn says, picking up the conversation. 'Wasn't that same tune played over and over at Stalingrad, at the bridgehead over the Kuban, at Mius and Warsaw, at Tobruk and Nettuno, in Normandy and at Aachen? Keep going, keep going and weather the storm! And what was the result of that? We're now taking lessons in Hitlerian strategy on German soil, now it's the turn of Kassel, Chemnitz, Bratislava, Königsberg, Frankfurt an der Oder, and tomorrow it will be Bremen, Munich, Rostock and finally Berlin!'

'Stop it, Joachim,' Tolksdorff pleads. 'It can't come to that!'

Lassehn laughs bitterly again. 'But that's not up to you, Dietrich! You lot can't stop the enemy!'

Tolksdorff raises his head again and turns slowly towards Lassehn.

'You lot, you say, you lot, do you no longer consider yourself part of it?' he asks urgently.

'No,' Lassehn says curtly, 'I'm not part of it any more, and I don't want to be.'

There is a long silence between the two young men, they sit closely side by side on the blocks of stone, and threads seem to have been spun between them, woven out of their former friendship, but now all of a sudden a gulf has opened up between them, so wide that the threads are bound to tear.

Tolksdorff is the first to break the silence. 'You've always been a decent chap, Joachim,' he says, 'I don't understand what makes you speak like that.'

Lassehn looks at him closely. 'And you've always been far too clever, Dietrich, not to understand what's going on all around us. You have eyes in your head, and logical thinking was always your strong point. Or have you gone blind and let them glue up your brain?'

'Shut up!' Tolksdorff says gruffly.

'You must be able to see that any further resistance is madness,' Lassehn insists. 'You can still save a lot if . . .'

'You, you, you're always saying you,' Tolksdorff exclaims, 'I can't bear to hear it any more. We're powerless!'

'Exactly, powerless! That's the right word,' Lassehn says, 'outwardly powerless and inwardly even more so, but if you are or we are, because this time I have to include myself, it's our own fault. We've been lied to and deceived, our credulousness has been abused and we have been reduced to robots . . .'

'Joachim,' Tolksdorff says, and his voice has lost its edge, it is quiet and pleading now.

'Maybe you don't want to hear it,' Lassehn rages, 'because it takes away your peace of mind, Dietrich Tolksdorff, it drives a spike into the armour of phrases that you've cocooned yourself up in so that you don't have to think?'

'Shut up,' Tolksdorff says again. 'You mustn't think me stupid enough not to recognize that our foundation, which seemed unassailable and inviolable, unshakeable and secure, as if for all eternity . . .'

'. . . for a thousand years,' Lassehn says sarcastically.

'Yes, for a thousand years, it seemed to be built for all eternity,' Tolksdorff continues seriously, 'that foundation has been shattered. Do you think I could ignore the fact that our situation is becoming increasingly hopeless?'

'Now I've got you, Dietrich,' Lassehn says triumphantly, 'it couldn't be otherwise, because the fact that you have listened to me without losing your temper has already proven that you are broken inside and no longer believe what you pretend to believe. That's the only reason I have dared to speak so openly.'

'I would rather bring the conversation to an end, Joachim,' Tolksdorff says wearily.

'Out of the question, that would be cowardice in the face of a friend,' Lassehn says firmly. 'I have at least one more question to ask you.'

'And what might that be?'

'Even though you've recognized all this, you're still going along with it?'

'Are you doing anything else, Joachim?' Tolksdorff asks.

Lassehn looks at him steadily. 'Yes,' he replies. 'I've stopped going along with it, for a few months now.' He is about to add that he has moved from not-going-along-with-it to being active, but changes his mind as it seems too risky.

'You've . . .' Tolksdorff begins, but he doesn't finish his sentence, he can't bring himself to utter the word.

'Yes, I've deserted, I've abandoned Hitler's bloody flag,' Lassehn says firmly, 'and I will tell you why I did. Because I could no longer go along with that madness, because I didn't want to be guilty for the crimes that were committed on foreigners and on our own people, and are still being committed every day and every hour. I admit that this recognition has to a certain extent come to me *post festum*, or only now been awoken in me, previously it was repressed by the cowardice that refuses to look things clearly in the eye. I ran away because of personal emotions, so to speak, but they have found a retrospective justification in this recognition, and I assume responsibility for that too, but you assume responsibility for nothing, Dietrich.'

'That's not true, Joachim,' says Tolksdorff, loosening the belt of his coat and undoing the buttons. 'I have assumed responsibility for Germany, my boy, I have been awarded the Iron Cross first and second class and the German Cross in gold. Does that mean nothing?'

Lassehn has only cast a fleeting glance at the decorations. 'You have misunderstood me, Dietrich,' he says, 'I haven't called your love of the fatherland into doubt, but it has, as I must repeat, been abused, it is as I just said: you aren't taking responsibility for anything. You think you're doing your duty by protecting a state which, if you don't despise it, you at least reject, but you haven't the courage to accept this fact and draw the conclusions from it. For all the military courage that you have squandered on an unworthy object, you are a moral coward, because you are doing nothing to change your present situation even though you have grasped it. Whatever you say and whatever you do, you do even though you know better.'

Tolksdorff has been visibly shaken by Lassehn's words, his

young face is in turmoil. 'But I can't stab my people in the back,' he says desperately.

'It won't be our people that you stab in the back,' Lassehn says quickly, 'it will be this state.'

Tolksdorff shakes his head. 'But it's the same thing.'

'No,' Lassehn says firmly. 'That's exactly what it isn't. Germany is not identical with National Socialism, and neither is Hitler's state with the German people.'

Tolksdorff buttons up his coat again, he does it slowly and with pedantically precise movements to gain time. 'It's a hopeless situation,' he says at last. 'Both possibilities are equally terrible, Germany losing the war and winning the war, that has been clear to me for a long time, but I have resisted that recognition, and basically I still do, I simply can't believe that German statesmen and generals can be so irresponsible as to sacrifice a whole people simply for their own sake.'

'You must believe it,' Lassehn says harshly. 'There's no getting around it. I have never been a National Socialist, you must remember that I had lots of problems with that at school, and I was never really clear why it was so. Even today I basically know only that my aversion is made up of many different components.'

Tolksdorff is breathing heavily. 'Being against something isn't a philosophy,' he objects. 'Why did most of our generation become National Socialists and remain so, even today? Because we know nothing else, we were given no other support in a spiritual void. If we lose that foothold now . . .'

'The famous bird in the hand,' Lassehn mocks.

'And what have you done?' Tolksdorff asks. 'You haven't fallen under its spell?'

'I've retreated completely into myself,' Lassehn replies, 'I've closed myself off from everything they tried to cram into our brains to disrupt our way of thinking.'

Tolksdorff shakes his head slowly. 'You can't do that,' he says. 'But perhaps my judgement is too subjective, I couldn't become spiritually rootless like that. And the fact that you could, Joachim . . .'

'You're forgetting music, Dietrich,' Lassehn reminds him.

'You're right,' Tolksdorff says. 'You were always so much of a musician that you didn't need anything else.'

Again there is a short pause. Lassehn listens to a tune that sounds inside him, Tolksdorff nervously presses his fingertips together.

'You always speak in the past tense,' Tolksdorff resumes the conversation at last, 'just as if you wanted to suggest that something in you has changed. Am I right?'

Lassehn nods. 'Yes,' he says firmly, 'I have overcome the intellectual vacuum, as you called it just now, and even though the life of an illegal deserter is incredibly difficult and fraught with dangers, I still have the feeling of having cast off an unbearable burden and liberated myself.'

'And what caused that transformation?' Tolksdorff asks.

Lassehn smiles. 'I can't give you a precise answer, I just fell in with some men who are against National Socialism.'

'There are many such these days,' Tolksdorff says.

Lassehn nods. 'Certainly, but these men aren't like that,' he replies. 'I've expressed myself badly and ambiguously. These men aren't moving away from National Socialism as lots of people are doing today, because the cause seems clearly to be going wrong, and because they want to create an alibi for themselves for later on. No, they are resolute opponents of the Nazis, not for personal, but for philosophical reasons. They are filled with the power of a conviction that cannot be lured away with a decoy or broken with a threat.'

Tolksdorff has been listening with a mixture of excitement and disbelief. 'And you've joined them?'

'Yes,' Lassehn replies, 'and I also know that I was right to do so, and above all I know that you don't do anything if you don't do everything, that you don't risk anything if you only take your risk halfway.'

'I've never been averse to learning things,' Tolksdorff says. 'For example, I've often thought about what it is that gives the Russians their almost superhuman endurance and their almost irresistible strength. I have never really believed that it was just the submachine guns of the commissars, as people are forever trying to tell us. But on the other hand I could never work out where these people got their strength from. It was just unthinkable to discuss such questions, it would have been like suicide even to ask them.'

'We have come to see all the concepts that don't conform with National Socialism in a warped and twisted form,' Lassehn says, 'the prejudices against socialism and democracy, parliamentarianism and pacifism have been planted in us so firmly that we ... I can't think of the right comparison.' He pauses and shuts his eyes for a few seconds. 'I could only introduce a comparison from music, you know that I always translate or condense everything into music.'

Tolksdorff nods. 'Yes, I remember very clearly,' he replies with a smile.

Lassehn can't help smiling now too. 'The prejudices are anchored as firmly within us as a tune that we learned wrongly and sang wrongly when we were very young, and even if we later sing that tune correctly from the score, the old tune goes on playing within us, we often prefer it to the real one. And it's exactly the same with prejudices, they poison our thoughts and go on working away within us even when we have convinced ourselves of the opposite. Slander as much as you like, something always remains within us, that's exactly the method the Nazis use, so with certain names and concepts we link certain ways of representing them, Stalin – a hangman, Churchill – a drunk, Roosevelt – a slave to the Jews, pacifism – a softening of the bones, parliamentarianism – chitter-chatter, democracy – broken-backed politics.'

Tolksdorff has risen to his feet and is pacing uneasily back and forth. 'And what is this new insight of yours, Joachim?' he asks, and gives Lassehn a penetrating look.

'It hasn't quite matured into an insight,' Lassehn replies with a shake of the head, 'you don't acquire recognitions as quickly as that, but I know there are things worth living for, something has opened up within me and led me away from my inner instability. Of course it's still vague, but it's there.'

Tolksdorff stops in front of Lassehn. 'A shame you don't know what it is that's inspiring you.'

Lassehn looks up. 'Why a shame?' he asks with surprise.

'Because I . . .' Tolksdorff is slightly embarrassed. 'Because I would have liked to know your new perspectives.'

Lassehn lowers his chin to his chest, an idea has just come to him, something fantastically bold, it seems to him, but perhaps not entirely impossible. 'What would you say, Dietrich,' he says slowly, thinking of Dr Böttcher, 'if I were to introduce you to somebody . . .'

'Fine,' Tolksdorff says firmly. 'I'd be very interested,' he adds with a hint of doubt. 'When and where would our debate be held?'

Lassehn shakes his head. 'I'm not in charge of this gentleman's timetable,' he says carefully, 'and besides I can't say in advance whether he would agree with me bringing an officer to the house, but I'll ask him. Where will I find you?'

'We still have a few days' work to do here,' Tolksdorff replies, 'and then I might be able to . . .'

'He's very close to here,' Lassehn interrupts. Only three blocks away, he thinks, only three houses, but there is a whole world between them.

XVII

At the end of the air-raid warning, when the sirens wail loudly again, Lassehn leaves Dr Böttcher's flat. The cheerful mood that filled him just now, when he took his first steps into his underground life and walked along Grosse Frankfurter Strasse in the bright April sunshine, is still with him, and might even be stronger than before. Furthermore, he has every reason to be satisfied. First of all, he delivered the flyers safe and sound and thus successfully accomplished his first task at the service of the 'Berolina' resistance group. He was also granted permission to visit Dr Böttcher with Tolksdorff over the next few days, and he had enough to eat for lunch, and a good meal. Even for a young man like Lassehn, inclined towards the spiritual life, this is not to be sneezed at, particularly when ample, good and regular meals have become a rarity.

But the main reason for his carefree mood comes from elsewhere. Lassehn runs his hand gently over the spot where he has put his wallet. His wallet now contains not only his military passbook, which, without his leave papers or marching orders was practically worthless, but a military passbook with discharge note and indispensability certificate. His picture has been mounted into this military pass with amazing skill, the circular stamps that run over the corners of his picture line up almost perfectly with the edges of the stamps printed in the pass, and one would have to look at it unusually closely to discover the minute deviations. These papers, along with a gun in his trouser pocket, give him more of a sense of security than a clear conscience and honest intentions could ever do.

Lassehn is now itching to put the perfection of his papers to the test, he feels an urge for adventure, exactly what Klose advised him against. He walks provocatively close to a Wehrmacht patrol, standing with steel helmet and gorget on the corner of Frankfurter Allee and Samariterstrasse, but the two military policemen pay him no attention at all, they stand as if rooted to the spot, with stubborn faces and arms clasped behind their backs, among the whirl of passers-by.

Lassehn walks past them again and then yet again, but with the same lack of success, in the end he gives up and walks further eastward along Frankfurter Allee, his destination is the S-Bahn that crosses Frankurter Allee between Pettenkoferstrasse and Möllendorffstrasse, and whose bridge is oddly known as 'the connector'.

When Lassehn joins the queue at the ticket counter he has already almost forgotten about his papers, he is preparing himself for his new task, and that is his trip to Eichwalde. He has never travelled along the stretch to Königs Wusterhausen, he doesn't know the eastern part of Berlin at all, he only has dim memories of an outing in a steamer on the Müggelsee, but that is a long time ago. When his parents still lived on Schönhauser Allee he only preferred the northern suburbs of Tegel, Frohnau, Birkenwerder, Bernau and Lübars, and later, when his parents moved to Lankwitz, he hiked through the western edges of the Grunewald to Werder, from Pichelsberge to Falkensee. It is an unquestionable fact that Berliners don't like to cross the whole city to get to the surrounding countryside, they like to go straight from the area where they live into the open, there is barely a Berliner who knows the whole surroundings of his home, unless he is an almost professional hiker.

When Lassehn has bought his ticket he stops by the railway map in the ticket hall, and first looks for his present location, the Frankfurter Allee S-Bahn station, and then examines the eastern suburban lines to Strausberg, Fürstenwalde and Königs Wusterhausen. As the ticket hall is quite dark, he walks up close to the map and runs his finger along the red line from Görlitz Station to Königs Wusterhausen. He has just reached Schöneweide when someone addresses him.

'So, my friend, where to?'

Lassehn turns around and finds himself face to face with a small, thin little man who is trying in vain to increase his height with a bowler hat.

'To Eichwalde,' he replies. 'I have to change at Treptower Park, isn't that right?'

'Correct,' the little man replies, 'and then again in Grünau. Come with me, I'm going almost the same way.'

Why not? Lassehn thinks. Now that his papers are in order he doesn't want to avoid people any more. Quite the contrary, he seeks out their company, he keeps his ears pricked at all times, pushes his way into all kinds of gatherings, he's interested in everything that people are saying, and what goes unsaid between the words.

The platform is thick with people, and even if an empty train pulled in only some of the waiting people would find a seat.

Lassehn stands helplessly in the middle of the platform.

'There's no question of me coming with you,' he says.

'Don't say that, my friend,' says the little man. 'If you take a good run up and put your back into it, you'll be on there in a second.'

'But if everyone did that . . .' Lassehn objects.

'Not everyone does, pal,' the little man says and winks smugly. 'People are divided into those who jostle and those who allow themselves to be jostled. I'm one of the jostlers. What about you?'

Lassehn shrugs. 'I absolutely have to get to Eichwalde today,' he says.

'There's no absolutely these days,' the little man says. 'Or rather there is. We must be absolutely victorious, says the Führer. Or maybe not?'

'He's said lots of things,' a worker chimes in and laughs sarcastically. 'It hasn't always been true, but he's always been right about one thing. Give me ten years and you won't recognize Germany. That's pretty much for definite.'

'It's all factored in, he said,' the little man says, 'the odd miscalculation isn't so important, we can deal with those. Isn't that right, pal?'

'And we're the ones who come out of it looking like idiots,' the worker says.

'We've been idiots from the start,' says the little man, 'if we'd had our wits about us that lot wouldn't have won the lottery. Or what do you think?'

'I'd thank you to keep your trap shut,' says a tall, fat man. 'The Führer would have been fine, except that he couldn't trust bastards like you. You lot should be reported for coming out with things like that, when everything's at stake.'

'So have you got something to lose, fatty?' the little man laughs. 'When you've been bombed out of your house you might change your tune as well.'

The fat man alters the tone of his voice, now he isn't just talking to the little man, to Lassehn and the worker, he's speaking to everyone standing nearby. 'Be reasonable, my national comrades, we must be victorious . . .'

'Or else you're stuffed,' a voice butts in.

'What do you mean, you, national comrades?' the fat man says. 'We all belong together, we are a united community.'

'That must be Goebbels' big brother,' the same voice adds.

Everyone laughs, and the fat man falls grimly silent.

Lassehn is amazed by such candour, it is the clearest indication that the Party's authority is in decline. The expressions used, in secret and also sometimes openly, would have been unthinkable in public only a year ago. But the curious thing is that opposition and rebellion go no further than these phrases. They are the product of passive aversion, not combative antagonism, because even though the National Socialist regime is on its last legs, it still holds in its clenched fist the threads of the powerful net that has been cast over the German people and forces everyone to turn their own tiny cog in the infernal machine of the Third Reich.

The debate concludes when the train enters the station; the passengers leaving the train force themselves through a tiny gap that opens up reluctantly in the wall of people, then the crowd surges towards the doors. Even though Lassehn doesn't make any particular effort, he is carried along as if by a whirlpool, it's impossible to escape it. It's as if the vacuum produced inside the carriage by the passengers were sucking in new people like a bell jar.

When the train sets heavily off, Lassehn is almost wedged in, he can't move a muscle, or move a centimetre in either direction.

The little man with the black bowler hat is standing right beside him, grinning at him with satisfaction. 'So, you see, my friend, you made it after all.'

Lassehn smiles back. 'Luck, I have no idea how it happened.'

'Lots of people don't,' the little man says ambiguously. 'This train is entirely symbolic. Or maybe not?'

'Really?' Lassehn says. 'Why would that be?'

'We all forced our way violently on,' the little man says, 'and now we're on and we can't move, we're stuck sitting or standing wherever we are, and we can't get off.'

'You're talking nonsense,' a man says behind the little fellow, 'if you want you can get off at the next station.'

The little man sticks to his comparison. 'It's not quite true,' he replies, 'I can only get off if you let me, and if I really do, how am I going to look? Crumpled and half dead, and they've practically ripped my clothes off. That's what we'll look like when we get off . . . well, when we get off that other train. Or maybe not?'

'You'll get yourself thrown off,' a sharp voice says over the luggage net, 'if you don't shut your trap pretty soon.'

The words are followed by an awkward silence.

'Well, the Ostkreuz is a lovely part of the world,' someone says at last.

'Which the British and the Americans are about to flatten,' the little man says. A medium-sized, broad-shouldered man tries to push his way to the door. 'I've got to see the chap with the big mouth,' he says.

'Not worth it,' the little man says quick as a flash, 'I'm not that much to look at.'

'Shut up,' Lassehn says to the little man. 'You're making people uncomfortable.'

The little man nods. 'I know,' he says, 'but I can't keep my mouth shut now, they've been force-feeding me too much nonsense for too long. Or maybe not?'

Lassehn is about to say something, but the train pulls into Ost-kreuz Station.

The medium-sized man pushes his way ruthlessly to the door and taps the little man and Lassehn on the shoulder. 'You're getting off when I do!'

Lassehn is slightly startled. Did I say something? I just tried to calm down the little man.

'Of course,' the little man says. When the train stops he gets out and disappears into the crowd in a fraction of a second.

The medium-sized man tries to follow him, but the human wall on the platform has suddenly closed firmly behind the little man. The other man curses and stays close to Lassehn.

'Who is that man?' he asks.

'I don't know him,' Lassehn replies, 'he spoke to me a little while ago at Frankfurter Allee Station, I'd never seen him before.'

The middle-sized man looks at him suspiciously. 'Let's have a look at your papers,' he says.

Lassehn hands him his passbook. This is the test that he had been hoping for a little while ago, but he feels his heart thumping violently. 'And who are you?' he asks.

'Any German is authorized to arrest suspicious people,' the medium-sized man says harshly. 'You don't seem to be aware of that.'

'Why am I suspicious?' Lassehn asks.

'Because you were in the company of an individual who has unfortunately escaped me,' the medium-sized man replies. 'And besides, I'm from the secret state police, if you must know,' he adds, showing an oval yellow metal tag fastened to a chain, which he has taken out of his pocket.

'And what can I do about . . .' Lassehn is about to object.

'Don't talk so much,' the Gestapo officer interrupts him gruffly, and flicks through his military passbook. 'Is that all?' he asks. 'This is my indispensability certificate,' Lassehn replies, and hands him the pink piece of paper.

The Gestapo officer reads it through and opens the passbook again. 'What's your name?' he says immediately.

'It's all in there,' Lassehn replies. It's lucky that Dr Böttcher insisted on my learning the contents of the papers by heart, he thinks. Good papers aren't enough on their own, he said, you also have to know their content very precisely, or do you think the bloodhounds aren't aware that lots of fake papers, or even real papers, fall into the wrong hands?

'Answer my question!' the Gestapo officer orders.

'Horst Winter,' Lassehn says.

'When were you born?'

'18 May 1920, in Strasburg, Uckermark.'

'Where is your time book?'

'The company has it.'

'Which company?'

'It's all in the document,' Lassehn says with feigned impatience.

'Which company?' the Gestapo officer insists.

'Argus Engines in Reinickendorf.'

The Gestapo officer growls something to himself and closes the passbook. 'Clear off,' he says irritably, and gives Lassehn back the passbook and the document, then he walks along the platform with a questing look and climbs down the stairs to platform E, where a train to Mahlsdorf is just pulling in.

Lassehn has passed the test, and he is seized by a feeling half of pride and half of relief, like the one he felt after doing his school-leaving certificate. He looks at his watch and establishes that he still has plenty of time, he stays away from the crowd and only now does he see where he is. He is standing on interchange platform D of Ostkreuz S-Bahn station, which rises like the central gallery of a theatre above the vista of railway tracks that seems to have been poured into the middle of the cityscape and is surrounded by houses in all directions, the side rows are formed by the twin curves of the Ringbahn leading to platforms A and B, the stalls are the two platforms for trains to Erkner and Hahsldorf, the railway tracks and the sidings, then it spreads out towards Warsaw Bridge, before running eastward for two four-track stretches that lead out of the city.

Lassehn stops by a noticeboard with a single weathered, tattered poster hanging from it, and starts reading, more out of boredom than interest.

Announcement.

On the orders of the Führer, in agreement with the Reich Minister and the Head of the Reich Chancellery, the Reich Minister of the Interior and the Director of the Party Chancellery it is hereby decreed:

I. Drumhead Courts Martial are to be instituted in Reich Defence Districts.
II. The Drumhead Court Martial consists of a criminal judge as chairman as well as a political leader of the NSDAP and an officer of the Wehrmacht, the Waffen SS or the police as assessors.
III. Drumhead Courts Martial are responsible for all crimes through which German fighting power or determination to fight is endangered.
IV. The outcome of the Drumhead Court Martial may be the death sentence, acquittal or a transfer to the ordinary judiciary. Confirmation is required from the Reich Defence Commissioner, who will immediately determine the time and manner of enforcement. If the Reich Defence Commissioner is impossible to contact and immediate enforcement is unavoidable, prosecuting counsel will assume responsibility for the task.

That's another real Nazi law, Lassehn thinks, all so much waffle. What does 'endangering German fighting power or determination to fight' mean? A dismissive remark, neglect to pass on information, refusal to dig a trench, failure to use a weapon? And if the Reich Defence Minister is unavailable – and how often will he not be? – then the judge is also an executioner, and no appeal procedure is provided for.

'So, hasn't your bad uncle done anything for you?' a voice crows suddenly beside Lassehn.

Lassehn looks to the side and smiles at the little man, who stands grinning beside him. 'There you are again,' he says. 'Speed isn't sorcery.'

'. . . said the Mosquito bomber and flew from England to Berlin and back in a few hours,' the little man adds, and pushes himself through a gap in the human wall. 'Here comes the next train. Let's get aboard, come on.'

This time getting onto the train is quite straightforward, it isn't too crowded.

Lassehn leans against the wall of the train between the seats and the door, the little man stands next to him and looks carefully into his face. 'Your papers must be perfectly in order,' he says, 'or that fellow wouldn't have let you go. Or maybe not?'

'Of course they're in order,' Lassehn replies confidently. 'Did you doubt it?'

The little man shrugs. 'With young lads like you . . .' He doesn't finish his sentence, and clicks his fingers a few times. 'There are all kinds of soldiers on the move. Or maybe not?'

'On the move?' Lassehn asks.

'Come on, don't be so slow,' the little man says and nudges Lassehn with his shoulder. 'They've run away, not from the enemy, but from their own units, they've fled the swastika, they have no desire to die a hero's death at the eleventh hour.'

Of course, I'm not the only one, Lassehn thinks, and looks out of the window. For a second he has a view of the Rummelsburger See with the bleak-looking jetties that stick out into the murky water like toothless black stumps, then the train crosses Stralauer Allee with the Osthafen, its giant cranes and the coal depots, and immediately after that he is crossing the big Spree Bridge with a dull rumble.

'You'd rather think than speak,' the little man says. 'Such people must exist. What do you do for a living?'

'I'm a music student,' Lassehn answers absently. 'Don't we change here?'

The little man nods and looks quizzically at Lassehn. 'Music student?' he asks as they get out and walk to the other side of the platform. 'Does such a thing exist in total war?'

Lassehn thinks of his new papers. 'You asked my profession,' he replies, 'not what I'm working at now.'

'So, what are you doing now?' the little man asks.

'I'm doing labour service at Argus,' Lassehn replies with some indignation. 'Is there anything else you want to know?'

The little man laughs. 'You're as sensitive as a virgin at her first time,' he giggles. 'You'll have to wean yourself off that one, my friend, these days you need a hide like the shell of a tortoise that everything bounces off. Or maybe not?'

Lassehn leaves his answer dangling.

'I've become completely insensitive,' the little man goes on, 'if it doesn't actually pierce the skin I don't feel it, I don't let it get to me.'

'Not everyone can do that,' Lassehn disagrees, 'it's a question of temperament.'

'Nonsense,' the little man says contemptuously. 'You're a queer fellow if you still have feelings after six years of war. Feelings are a luxury, we can't afford that kind of thing, with our poor health. Or maybe not?'

'You mean . . .'

'Listen to me, music man,' the little man continues benevolently. 'Just now, when I got out of that sweat-room of ours, an old man was run over, on the corner of Pettenkoferstrasse. Do you think a single soul cared that an old man was lying in the road with blood pouring over his face and white beard? "Why didn't the old fool look where he was going?" a woman said as she passed. And another murmured, "What was he doing round here anyway?" They all gave him a wide berth.'

'And what did you say?' Lassehn asks.

'Nothing at all,' the little man replies calmly, 'but what I thought was: one more food card down. And so partly by way of consolation I added: maybe the old man would have been killed tonight anyway when the Mosquitoes pay their evening visit. That's just how it is these days. Or maybe not?'

Lassehn breathes heavily. 'Did the old man die on the spot?'

'I don't know,' the little man says casually, 'I have no time to worry about such things. You know, I'm glad if I get home before the warning. These days everyone's next. Or maybe not?'

Lassehn shakes his head wearily.

'Now you're probably thinking: Christ, what kind of beast have we got here. And perhaps I really am, I could sometimes spit in my own face, but if you want to emerge more or less safe and sound in the middle of all this brown shit, that's how you have to be. Or maybe not?'

Lassehn is growing tired of his companion's uninterrupted chit-chat, he just shrugs and looks at the sparse greenery of Treptow Park, which reaches the edge of the S-Bahn line. Treptow – the name awakens memories of his childhood, the door opens hesitantly onto a time that seems worlds away. Treptow, it sounds like a gentle, melancholy tune that one might hum in memory of a loved one who had passed away, and who had suddenly reappeared in all their majestic grandeur.

'Do you live in Eichwalde?' the little man presses stubbornly.

Lassehn irritably shakes the question away, he tries to find a pretext for getting rid of the little man, but nothing occurs to him so he frowns forbiddingly, he wants to cling to his memory undisturbed. Treptow meant Zenner's beer garden, the observatory and the Plänterwald, it meant the abbey, the big playground and the Altes Eierhaus, and it meant the carp pond, the Hellas rowing club and the Spree tunnel; Treptow was surging, foaming life. On wide expanses of green the working people of Berlin camped out, sleeping, eating, chatting, playing, laughing, cursing, singing, playing music. Under a cloud of cries, squeals, cheers, shouts, giggles, among the outspread blankets on which the families sat as if on islands, naked children tumbled around, skimpily dressed girls with swaying hips strutted about, dignified men strolled in serious dark suits. With a bright sun shining down on everything, Treptow, that is a scrap of youth, carefree and protected, a Sunday symphony of joy and expectation, of open light-heartedness. There were the giant pots and cups carved in stone, as if made for all eternity. There were the bags of cakes which contained a favourite for everyone, sponge cake for his father, millefeuille for his mother, *Bienenstich* for him. There were the thrilling trips on the steamer to the Liebesinsel, one of the few occasions when his father came out of himself and gave a sense that he too had once been young. Then at last there was the big Wednesday event, Treptow in flames, huge fireworks, stars shooting up from the earth, opening up in every colour of the rainbow and magically creating whole pictures against the dark background of the sky, exploding and sinking back into the night.

Lassehn is overwhelmed by emotion, it chokes him and forces his thoughts back into the past. Here he is, standing in the middle of the unsettled, cursing crowd on a platform of Treptow S-Bahn station, the terrible backdrop of war rises all around him, but Lassehn sees none of it. The present is blanked out by the past, his mother's kindly face appears in front of him, the happy little wrinkles constantly around her eyes and mouth, which she could never quite banish even if she seemed to be angry. The serious, almost always rather severe face of his father appears in front of him, that face that seldom relaxed because it wasn't given to taking life easy. Now he studies the features of Ursula, his mother's younger sister, who was only a few years older than him and had lived at their house for a while. Her girlish face appears in front of him, clean and serene, under a shock of dark-blonde hair with a centre parting; and he sees himself, a slightly shy and awkward boy in whom his father's gloom predominates, his mother's cheerful nature shining through only rarely, in whom quite early on everything becomes music which drowns out anything else . . .

'Watch out, the Grünau train is coming,' the little man says and nudges him.

Lassehn surfaces back to the present, he stands close to the little man, because he is still a little dazed. It's strange how we manage to encapsulate the past and carry it around with us, without realizing, like a photograph in a wallet, and how it only takes a chance association to bring it back to life and allow the characters to step living from the picture.

'You were miles away,' the little man says when they have boarded the train and the doors have closed automatically.

Lassehn nods. 'Treptow brings back all kinds of memories from my youth,' he says.

The little man laughs brightly. 'Good heavens, you're talking about youth? Are you an old man or something, to talk about youth? You can't be more than twenty-five. Or maybe not?'

Lassehn looks over little man's shoulder, the train is just coming around the bend, and running along the track that goes to Görlitz. 'You're right, and then again you aren't right,' he says slowly, 'in years I am still a young man, but my youth is still far behind me, it is over once and for all, there has been too much in between, and nothing remains but memories.' My parents lie in a mass grave, he continues in his mind, music is a distant dream, women a disappointment . . .

The little man rests a hand on his arm. 'You seem to have been through all sorts of things,' he says. 'You owe it all to our Führer. But I won't ask you any more questions, you don't seem to like it.'

The train is now running along the railway embankment amidst wide expanses of allotments and anti-aircraft placements, sports grounds and new housing estates. Here the city has transformed its severe traits, but it no longer bears the cautiously smiling features of petty-bourgeois ambition, proletarian industry and the carefree delight in the body, the war has brutally invaded, debasing the sports grounds for military purposes. Beyond the allotments the silhouette of the city, with its factory chimneys, cranes, towers and gasometers, stands out against the darkening sky of evening.

When the train pulls in to Baumschulenweg Station, the little man says, 'Ruins wherever you spit, and more and more of it going to hell every day. And still it won't end . . .'

'Not until . . .' Until those dogs themselves have been brought low, Lassehn wants to say, but he holds back the words, the little man might be genuine, in fact he probably is, but Klose has dinned into him that he should never be lured into saying anything that might bring him under any kind of suspicion. The activity of the undercover operator, Klose said, doesn't consist of constantly opening your trap, because your word goes up in ineffectual smoke in an instant, but your flyer raises doubts, it penetrates people's certainties and gives heart to the waverers.

The little man is about to launch into a new question when the door is thrown open and a few young men noisily enter the compartment, wearing blue-grey uniforms and ski-caps and the red, white and red swastika armbands of the Hitler Youth, their caps set crookedly on their ears. They immediately fill the carriage with their conversations, less concerned with the words than with the volume, and they constantly laugh, but there is no real merriment spilling from their young mouths, only the desire to draw attention at all costs, the awareness that they are allowed to be loud and noisy without being told off. The uniform, which on the one hand commits them to strict discipline, on the other grants them an unhampered coarseness which everyone else has to put up with. They look around to check on the impression that their behaviour is making, not caring whether that impression is a good or a bad one, whether they are prompting admiration or revulsion, their only concern is to exploit this rare opportunity to rise above the mass and to test their superiority over everyone not wearing a uniform.

Lassehn whispers to the little man to ask what sort of young people these are, he has never encountered the uniform before.

The little man laughs. 'These are the new German heroes of the Luftwaffe,' he answers, not keeping his voice down, 'a mixture of heroism and pant-shitting cowardice. Or maybe not?'

'Are you talking about us?' asks one of the Luftwaffe assistants, coming and standing menacingly in front of the little man.

'I don't have to say a word to you, you brat,' the little man says dismissively, and turns back to Lassehn. 'What time is it, by the way?'

Lassehn tells him and tries to look as indifferent as possible. The new conflict that is already beginning is unpleasant, he wants to have nothing to do with it, he just doesn't want his mission to be endangered by anything.

When the train pulls in to Schöneweide Station shortly afterwards, and the little man gets off, saying, 'See you, pal,' he sighs with relief.

XVIII

A dark-grey limousine is driving along Köpenicker Strasse, constantly accelerating, ignoring the simplest rules of the highway code, overtaking on the right or driving up to the far-left side of the opposite carriageway, not stopping for the outstretched arm of the traffic policeman or for red traffic lights.

Past Schlesiches Tor the city begins to thin out, it shakes the grim expression from its features, running it through with the hopeful green of the parks and the rust-red and slate grey of the trees. When the car reaches the straight section of Strasse Am Treptower Park it starts driving at great speed, roaring along the S-Bahn underpass at Treptow Station, darting past the old trees of the park like shadows, and then turns into Köpenicker Landstrasse. For a few minutes it gets caught up on Berliner Strasse in Niederschöneweide, where the city once again contracts into a compact mass and lies like a clenched fist in the open expanse of the landscape. But where once dark smoke rose from the chimneys into the sky, and everything was covered in the sulphurous fumes of the chemical industry and the sickly vapour of treated hops, there is now deadly silence and a smell of burning, only rows of ruins and half-derelict workshops, Carbonated Drinks Company, German Brass Factory, Kali Chemicals, Shultheiss-Patzenhofer Brewery, Telephone and Cable Works.

At Schöneweide Station, where a tank is buried by the freight outlet, its gun barrel extending menacingly towards the east, the car turns into Grünauer Strasse and then dashes, engine wailing, under the railway bridge of the branch line to Spindlersfeld, and into the main eastward artery, Berlin's longest road, the Adlergestell. The car devours the straight segment of that road, racing against the S-Bahn, which runs to the right beside the railway embankment, a red, green and yellow flash clattering over the gaps in the track with a hum of electric engines, then following the Adlergestell as it pulls away from the S-Bahn with a slight northward turn.

From here on the Adlergestell is cut into the Grünauer Forst, the trees shimmer, shady and rust-red in the bright sun, the mossy ground smells of an awakening spring, but the driver of the dark-green Adler limousine doesn't notice that. Both his hands grip the steering wheel, his eyes, shaded by the cap pulled low over his forehead, stare fixedly at the dark strip of asphalt ahead of him. A menacing fold is carved deep above his nose, rising above his eyebrows and forming sinister runes among the wrinkles on his brow.

SS Untersturmführer Siering is in a particularly bad mood, a fidgety unease runs through him all the way to his fingertips. He has spent a disagreeable morning, he stood in front of Sturmbannführer Wellenhöfer and delivered his report, but it was a report which, for all its contorted explanations and justifications, could only be articulated in negative terms, and which concluded with an admission that the trail of Adamek alias Wiegand had gone cold. An air-raid warning had kept the surveillance man from doing his job, and Adamek-Wiegand had vanished from his flat the previous evening, neither had he reappeared, so however careful they had been, they had not been careful enough. As everyone knows, there is nothing more annoying than to discover that one's own cleverness has been outdone by the cleverness of others, that the snare one has delicately set is closing, but only as an empty knot, and the booty one hoped for has slipped away. Sturmbannführer Wellenhöfer listened in silence to the report, his face frozen. When Siering had finished speaking, Wellenhöfer rose to his feet and walked to the window, he looked for a long time at the ruined houses as if he were seeing them for the first time, and ignored Siering, standing stiffly to attention by the desk. Siering has known his boss for long enough to be aware that this is not a good sign. Wellenhöfer is not a man who dwells on things past, whether good or bad, he is capable of forgetting a dozen successes over a single failure, a series of failures over a successful operation. When at last Wellenhöfer turned round, lighting a cigarette without offering one to Siering, he paced up and down a few times, then at last he glanced at Siering, his face contorting into a harsh grimace. 'Siering, bring me Wiegand!' Wellenhöfer said no more than that, but in those few words everything had been decided. Siering knows that the Sturmbannführer didn't say those words casually, even though it sounded that way; he had taken measures, he had put guards on Lebuser Strasse and sentries in the grocers' shops where Adamek alias Wiegand's cards were registered, he posted a few people in and around the Karlshorst depot and finally ordered surveillance of Dr Böttcher on Frankfurter Allee, but essentially he expected little from these measures.

For that very reason he is now travelling to Eichwalde, where this man Wiegand's wife lives, his foot never leaves the accelerator and he stays almost constantly in fourth. It isn't that he is in a particular hurry to get to Eichwalde, he knows a few hours here or there won't make any difference, because startled deer don't leave their lair again straight away. But his furious driving corresponds to his inner state, a person's essence is not only captured by his handwriting, not chiselled ineradicably in his features, it reveals its unmistakeable and immutable stamp in all his actions. The whole of Siering's brutality and ruthlessness cannot be understood in a more exemplary fashion than in his way of driving. The constant violation of the rules of the road, the waste of fuel caused by such extreme acceleration, the violent application of the brakes and the reckless crossing of busy junctions are an absolute indicator of his total lack of respect for both lifeless material and living creatures. Siering takes out his fury on any inanimate objects and human vermin which might get in his way. He dashes along the Adlergestell through the Grünauer Forst, engine humming and klaxon sounding constantly, he doesn't slow down even at intersections or side roads, grimly baring his teeth when a few people are able to escape with their lives only by leaping to the side.

When the first houses of Schmöckwitz appear, Siering slows down and stops at the filling station which marks the road to Eichwalde and Zeuthen. He asks for the town hall, is given directions and puts his foot down again. A few minutes later he turns left off Bahnhofstrasse and stops in front of the town hall. It is a bright, solid building, it doesn't exactly reveal the artistic hand of an architect, more the clumsy paw of a decent and respectable master who understands his craft.

Here, in room 17 of the town hall in Eichwalde, in the district of Teltow, in the administrative region of Potsdam, sits Police Lieutenant Kiepert, a tall, imposing man with a slightly round face, fair, prematurely greying hair, good manners and a brisk bearing. He is one of the many millions of Germans for whom National Socialism may have become an element of life, but who have still preserved some small private views that do not cohere with National Socialist doctrines, and to which they are devoted partly out of habit and partly out of obstinacy, and who interpret these caveats as individuality.

In these individuals, who blindly carry out all orders and uncompromisingly recognize the authority of the state, conscience has not died out entirely, but to some extent it stirs only outside of office and within extremely narrow circles and it is silenced with the categorical imperative 'orders are orders' or 'the law is the law', and does not raise the question of whether orders and the law are a human right or a divine commandment. The order which gives the inherited sin of a corrupt tradition equal status to divine commandments relieves the individual of any personal decision-making, it is the regulation that lightens his conscience, at the same time turning him into a mesh in that net that has been stretched with mathematical precision over a people which has always apathetically and obediently allowed both good and evil to roll over it.

Kiepert is one of those people who only joined the National Socialist Party in 1933, and who are, to the casual onlooker, good National Socialists, but who by no means possess the brutal consistency of the old fighters and Party members from before 1933. Neither are they clearly aware that they are far more guilty than those other people, because they are acting for the sake of their lives, their advancement and also their comfort, against their better knowledge and against the voice of conscience. They see themselves as individuals because they have reservations about this or that National Socialist dogma, and have no idea that they are still falling for the horse-trading tricks and have slowly but surely succumbed to the standardization of thought. In the end they really come to believe that Hitler is the man of providence and the Germans are the chosen people, and they abandon their last reservations when war throws up the question of being or not being. Without being aware of it, and perhaps without even wanting it, they are by now so firmly bound up with the Nazi regime that the loss of the war and the collapse of the Party would also mean disaster for their own lives. Thus the Nazis have succeeded once and for all with their conjuring trick of putting their Party and the German people on the same plane and, even though the Second World War prompted no enthusiasm, there is no less inner willingness on the part of the bourgeois and petit-bourgeois parts of the population than in the mass delirium of 1914.

Police Lieutenant Kiepert would be extremely disobliged were one to describe him as a man given to brutality and excess, he might only smile in pitiful disbelief at such an accusation. In general terms, in fact, he is an open and companionable man who leads a harmonious family life and never gets too close to anyone. He is barely aware that he has allowed himself to be degraded to the tool of a tyrannical state, a cruel form of police-enforced justice and a monstrous policy of oppression. If he probes his conscience from time to time, and subjects his behaviour to an inventory, he feels entirely guiltless. Even if he executes the occasional order with inner reluctance, and cannot quite withhold a feeling of compassion for the victim, he still feels no guilt; he frees himself from his own scruples, arguing that if there is any guilt here at all, then it lies in the orders upon which he has no influence, and which it is not within his remit to criticize. Sometimes he also feels rage about those who bring him into a kind of conflict of conscience by virtue of their mere existence. At any rate, Kiepert believes he is satisfying his conscience by separating his private life entirely from his public activity, by being blameless in one and correct in the other. He has no sense that what he calls fulfilment of duty is nothing but active participation in Nazi crimes, passing through the stages of carelessness, complicity, encouragement and aiding and abetting. To orient his professional activity according to the principles that hold for his private life would be an absurd idea.

Kiepert is the typical product of a citizen of the Third Reich, a synthesis of personal honour, weak character and unconditional compliance to all the demands of the state. It is the schizophrenic character of the normal German citizen, the negation of the unity between social and individual being, and finally the constraint, imposed from above, of a racial consciousness which makes it possible for an entire population of millions of hardworking, order-loving people to be debased into an army of helots, for technology unleashed against the whole of humanity to move with the even mechanism of a robot.

At this quiet time of the afternoon, Kiepert is sitting in his office, the town hall is still, since there are never many visitors after lunch. He flicks through the papers in front of him, trivial and insignificant applications and denunciations. A while later he hears quick footsteps echoing in the corridor, and a moment later the door is flung open. Kiepert is about to hurl a harsh remark at his impetuous visitor, but he leaps quickly to his feet when he glimpses the two SS runes on the collar and the SD lozenge on the right sleeve, and another glance at the three stars on his epaulet identifies the SS man as an Untersturmführer.

'Heil Hitler!'

'Heil Hitler!'

The greetings sound like blasts from a trumpet.

'Untersturmführer Siering from Reich Security Head Office.'

'Police Lieutenant Kiepert. Please have a seat!'

Kiepert closes his office door while Siering sits down, crosses his legs and disdainfully studies the police lieutenant. Kiepert sits down at his desk again and pretends to put his papers in order, while at the same time thinking very hard about what reason there might be for this undesirable visit by the SD man from the RSHO. Even though he is actually a colleague from a different faculty, he feels uncomfortable. No one likes to have anything to do with the Gestapo, even he, Kiepert, prefers to stay out of their way. All the more so when dealing with such a wild go-getter, who comes charging in without knocking and inspects you with his eyes, whose hard, determined face and cold eyes are a threat in themselves.

In the Third Reich there is no one who has a clear conscience in every respect, and even Police Lieutenant Kiepert has to run through his memory quickly to see whether his own flawlessness might be . . . Damn it all, did he not speak to the Jew Wiener last week, the only one in the town, and even shake his hand? Did he not warn the foreman at the Ratthöfer sawmill to be a little more humane in his treatment of his workers from the east? Did he not . . . All trivia, atavistic impulses of human weakness, twitches of a disposition that had not yet quite hardened, forgivable lapses into humanitarian folly, and hence undesirable and forbidden, nothing but trivia, but they can weigh as heavy as deadly sins when seen through the keen lenses of hard-line National Socialists, and brought to light with the probes of the Gestapo.

'How may I help you?' Kiepert asks, and struggles to give his voice a harsh and unselfconscious tone.

'How may I help you? How may I help you?' Siering tears into the police lieutenant. 'That is how fishmongers and haggling Jews talk!'

Kiepert is hurt by the Untersturmführer's outburst and flinches, his face expressing the wounded dignity of the police officer, the police enforcement officer in a town of 6,000 inhabitants. The other man has no right – and hopefully no cause – to talk to him like that, because as a police lieutenant he is on equal ranking with an SS Untersturmführer, but that is of course only true on paper. In fact every SD man, even a simple Sturmmann, is his superior not in terms of rank, but in terms of power. For that reason Kiepert says nothing and chokes back the sharp remark that had been floating on his tongue, particularly since he still doesn't know why the other man has come.

'I come on a special mission,' Siering says and pulls a small, colourful package from his pocket, pinches a cigarette out of its paper wrapping and lights it. Then he sets the pack down on the edge of the desk and leans back and inhales his first few puffs.

Kiepert glances quickly at the pack and tries to read the writing on it. It is a pack of North State Blue. Where did the bastard get those, he thinks, English cigarettes, nowadays, in the sixth year of the war?

Siering has observed his look. 'We took them from a parachutist,' he says casually, and breathes the smoke deep into his lungs.

Kiepert still says nothing, in opaque situations he tries to let the others speak first.

'Damned decent stuff,' Siering continues and blows smoke out through his nose. 'So, to the matter at hand. A certain Mrs Wiegand lives in the town.'

Kiepert sighs, his humiliation has fled in an instant, making way for relief that Zeus's lightning bolt is coming down on someone else, even if that other person is a woman, and a woman whose humanity has often won his reluctant respect.

'Do you know what this is about?' Siering asks.

'Of course,' Kiepert replies, and closes a side door in his desk, 'we have often had dealings with her, or primarily with her husband.' He opens a drawer and takes out a file.

'I'm not interested in these scribbles,' Siering says, shaking his head, as the policeman tries to hand him the files, 'I want to know what measures you have taken so that we can advance this case.'

'Measures?' Kiepert is surprised, and holds the file indecisively in his hand. 'Wiegand had to report to the station every day, but he has been on the run since . . .' He opens the file and flicks through it.

'I know that already!' Siering roars. 'I don't need you to tell me!'

Kiepert is even more startled by this fresh outburst from the Untersturmführer than he was by the first one. He is evidently in an extremely bad mood and unpredictable, he thinks. He was quite peaceful a moment before and now he is raging again, something must have gone belly up for him.

'We informed Reich Security Head Office at the time that

Wiegand was on the run,' Kiepert says in a thick voice, weighing each word very carefully, 'and no measures have been imposed by them in the meantime.'

'No measures imposed! No measures imposed!' Siering imitates him. 'Everything has to be imposed on you lot, you have to shove your noses in the shit like a puppy so that you smell something.'

Kiepert swallows that one too and remains outwardly calm, even though a mild fury is rising up inside him. Son of a bitch, he curses inwardly, I could be your father.

Siering finishes his cigarette and immediately lights another from the glowing stub. 'This Wiegand is a very dangerous fellow,' he says in a slightly more subdued voice, 'he's been living in Berlin ever since his supposed flight, we'd just tracked him down, and then a fat fool of a sentry managed to lose his trail again.'

Kiepert nods. So he's slipped through your fingers, he thinks. 'I get it,' he says, 'and now you expect that . . .'

'Yes, that he's going to show up in these parts,' Siering interrupts, 'but that's not the real reason why I've come here. We had in fact presumed that . . .' He breaks off and turns towards the door.

An old man in a long, worn overcoat, high farming boots and a cylindrical black fur hat has come in and is standing in the doorway in a humble and expectant posture.

'What's all this?' Siering roars at him. 'Why didn't you knock?'

You don't need to, Kiepert thinks. 'What's the matter?' he asks.

'I did knock,' the old man says in an unmistakeable East German accent and waves his hand apologetically. 'I assume you gentlemen didn't hear me.'

'Get out!' Siering shouts.

The old man stays awkwardly where he is. 'I wanted to ask you . . .', he begins uncertainly.

'Get out!' Siering shouts again. 'Before I throw you out! Riffraff,' he says contemptuously to Kiepert when the door has closed again behind the old man.

Kiepert wants to put in a word for the old man, who arrived in the town a few days ago with a convoy of refugees, but chooses not to. How do individuals like this become so arrogant, he thinks? 'You were about to tell me the purpose of your presence here,' he says politely.

Siering lounges with his elbows on the desk. 'What was I about to say when that old brute came in?' he asks.

'You were saying that you'd presumed that . . .' Kiepert says, repeating Siering's interrupted sentence.

'Right,' Siering says. 'Yes, we presumed that Wiegand had run away to Russia, because there wasn't a trace of him to be found, but now we know that the bastard was in Berlin all along, if not actually here in Eichwalde.'

'I would rule out the latter,' Kiepert objects, 'he's far too well known here to dare to appear in this neck of the woods, particularly since his neighbour . . .'

Siering waves a dismissive hand. 'No matter, it was just a passing remark. What I want to say is this: from May 1941 Wiegand stayed in Berlin under a false name. Do you think it likely that his wife knew nothing about it?'

Kiepert shakes his head. 'No,' he has to admit.

'But the old cow has always disputed that,' Siering yells. 'If she's investigated, and at first that happened often, she never knew anything, she always played stupid, and our colleagues in the investigation service always believed the bitch.'

Kiepert is embarrassed, but he tries not to let it show, in the Third Reich pity and compassion are only to be granted to state-authorized objects, if one doesn't want to attract suspicion. Kiepert knows Mrs Wiegand and has often secretly admired her attitude, he has always treated her very correctly in an official capacity, and sometimes let her know with apparently chance remarks that he was acting not on his own initiative but on orders from above, which he by no means approved of.

'I'll get her to open that mouth of hers,' Siering rages again, 'you can rely on that.'

And what will I be doing? Kiepert thinks miserably. If he plans to do it on his own I want no part of it.

Siering stubs the cigarette out in the ashtray. 'You wrap yourself completely in silence,' he says, and looks at Kiepert through narrowed eyes. 'A very eloquent silence, most esteemed one.'

'How . . . how am I supposed to understand that?' Kiepert asks.

Kiepert rests his hands on the desktop and leans far forward. 'You understand me very well, my dear chap,' he says sharply. 'Don't you like us coming down hard on the rabble?'

'I must ask you, Comrade . . .' Kiepert begins.

'Oh, don't talk nonsense,' Siering interrupts him brusquely. 'Do you think I can't see what's going on with you? It's all down to your damned pansy politics if that mob start crawling out of the woodwork again, thinking their time has come.' He slaps the tabletop with the flat of his hand, making the pens clatter. 'But I'll make it hot under their arses.'

What a lovely chap, Kiepert thinks, appalled. 'Of course I will fully support you in your fight against hostile and defeatist elements,' he says.

'Extraordinarily sweet of you,' Siering sneers. 'I am greatly obliged!'

Kiepert's features tauten and he gets to his feet. 'I would ask you not to doubt my loyalty to the state,' he says firmly.

'Sit down,' Siering says in a calm voice and gives a broad, sarcastic smile. 'You don't need to tell me that you are a Party comrade, I see it that way too.'

Kiepert resolves not to be cornered any further, and to go on the attack. 'But that's enough now, Comrade,' he says resolutely and props his fists on the desk. 'I must ask you . . .'

Siering waves him casually away.

'Calm down,' he says, 'I will decide when it's enough, not you, and now let's get to the matter at hand. My instructions are as follows: Wiegand's house is to be put under the strictest surveillance immediately. Where is the property located?'

Kiepert sighs with relief. Moving on to the discussion of factual matters not only puts an end to the vulgar insults, it grants him a kind of rehabilitation, in that he is able to demonstrate eagerness and a set of beliefs. For a moment he thinks about Mrs Wiegand, whose small, delicate form he sees in front of him for several seconds, and is not quite able to suppress a certain regret, but in parallel with that sensation he also loses that justification that our lives are what we make of them, and that we must take the consequences of our own actions.

'The property abuts the administrative district of Zeuthen,' he replies, picks up a sheet of paper and draws a sketch, 'on the left there's a vacant lot, on the right and immediately opposite there are detached single-family houses.'

'And the entrance to the house on Wiegand's property?' Siering asks. Kiepert thinks for a moment. 'If I'm not mistaken,' he says after a short pause, and adds to his sketch, 'it is on the side, which faces the house next door, which is here.'

'That is a good situation,' Siering goes on, letting a cigarette slip into his hand from the blue pack. 'Take one,' he adds, and passes Kiepert the pack.

'If I may,' Kiepert says, and quickly strikes a match to light a cigarette for the SD man, then he too takes a cigarette from the pack and lights it. The pressure that lay around his head like a steel band a moment before has now made way for a cheerful sense of excitement, he has plainly been able to erase his initially unfavourable impression of the Untersturmführer. Would he have offered him a cigarette otherwise? And an English one at that? He smokes the cigarette, which not only tastes spicily of real Virginia, it also tastes sweet because he is inhaling the benevolence of the donor along with the taste of the tobacco.

'So I want Mrs Wiegand to be put under strict surveillance,' Siering says now, 'of course I don't want a sentry traipsing officially back and forth on his great flat feet. Put two men each in the house next door and the house opposite. Everyone who leaves or enters Wiegand's house is to be arrested and immediately taken to the Reich Security Head Office, no exceptions. You are to ensure the rigorous enforcement of this measure. Is that clear?'

'Entirely,' Kiepert confirms with a nod. 'Except . . .'

'Except what?' Siering snaps immediately.

'We have only four policemen in the whole town,' Kiepert goes on.

'Then use auxiliary policemen or town guards, but young, active men, not *Muselmänner*.* Are your men reliable?'

'I think so,' Kiepert answers.

'You think so, you think so,' Siering says irritably, 'leave thinking to the horses, their heads are bigger. You have to *know* something like that. Good God, man, have you been fast asleep for the last twelve years, if you don't know who's a hundred per cent reliable and who isn't? Aren't you aware of Gauleiter Stürtz's decree concerning the surveillance of national comrades for the sake of internal resolve?'

'Of course I am,' Kiepert defends himself, 'but this isn't a police decree, it's a Party decree, so the Local Group Leader is responsible for it.'

'Responsible, responsible,' Siering shouts again, 'that way you always shift the burden onto others. Who is the Local Group Leader around here?'

'Mayor Rutz, but he's . . .'

'Mayor and Local Group Leader in one and still a total mess?' Siering yells. 'You should smell some gunpowder in the air, you've had your arse behind a nice comfortable desk for too long, Christ, the things I would have to say . . .'

Thank God you don't, Kiepert thinks, and finishes smoking his cigarette. It no longer tastes right, the conviviality with which it was offered has rapidly fled.

'So put the necessary measures in place,' Siering orders, 'and then let's take a look at Mrs Wiegand and loosen that little tongue of hers. Come with me, Lieutenant!'

Kiepert hadn't expected that, he almost recoils and has difficulty controlling himself. 'Is my presence absolutely necessary, Comrade?'

Siering leaps to his feet and stands firmly in front of Kiepert, his arms pressed firmly to his sides. 'Do you feel sorry for this bitch? Can't bear to see blood, is that it?' he says menacingly and looks at Kiepert with a frown through half-open eyes.

---

* Literally 'Muslims', a slang term meaning apathetic idlers.

'Of course not,' Kiepert reassures him, 'I only asked because I have a lot of office things to get through.'

'Leave your paperwork,' Siering says contemptuously, 'you're all a bunch of ink-pissers rather than men of action. Right, so let's get a move on and pay a visit to our little sweetheart.'

XIX

Lucie Wiegand is standing by the chopping block behind the house, splitting wood, her hand lifts wearily, her blows fall at long intervals, without much force. Now and again she glances across the garden. The first buds are opening on the shrubs, the earth smells fresh, a cloudless, bright-blue sky stretches above her, the air is gentle and mild.

Lucie Wiegand sighs. Incomprehensible that nature should remain eternally the same, untouched by human misery. It contains comfort in its spring-like resurrection, but at the same time it fills us with despair that as civilization develops man moves further and further away from it, pointlessly crushing and stamping out the core of life, tearing open and ploughing up the maternal womb of the earth with bombs and shells, shredding and scorching the forests.

Lucie Wiegand stands there for a while with her arms drooping. There are moments when life is almost impossible to bear, and this is one of those. She got up at half past five this morning, she spent nine hours at the drilling machine at Schwartzkopff in Wildau and has just come home, now she has to do the housework, the garden needs attention, because not a single clod of earth has been turned, and there is an enormous sense of weariness that leaves her feeling hollow and makes every moment a torment and cannot drive her from her bed even when there is an air raid. When that happens she lies there holding her breath, but without any inner excitement, fatalistically surrendering, she gives a start when the anti-aircraft guns in

Schulzendorf thunder or the waves of night-time explosions come drifting in, but mostly she just goes back to sleep again, before the three long notes of the sirens indicate the end of the raid. When a bomb fell on Zeuthener Strasse months ago, the roof tiles clattered down and the windows rattled against their bars, she got up and waited for the next shock to come, but it didn't, the engine noises fell silent again and exhaustion forced her immediately back to sleep.

Just as Lucie Wiegand is raising her arm to split the log, she hears three short rings on the bell inside the house, walks around the side and sees two men standing at the gate.

Police Lieutenant Kiepert, she thinks. What does he want? It must be something special if he has come in person, and he's also brought someone else, in grey. A soldier? Then she gives a start. Kiepert's companion isn't wearing the usual grey. And the black collars? SS? She hesitantly walks along the garden path to the gate, having for a moment considered retreating back behind the house and not answering, but it's too late for that, the two men have probably seen her already.

'Can I help you?' she asks without opening the gate, she looks only at the police lieutenant, whom she knows, and who has always been relatively considerate towards her.

'Heil Hitler, Mrs Wiegand,' Kiepert says. 'We would like to have a word with you.'

Siering has taken a step back, not out of modesty or embarrassment, which are both properties that he does not possess, but because he likes observing people from the background first of all, spotting their weak spots, detecting their level of resilience from their movements and their posture, and from their faces the degree of their intellectual concentration. Admittedly his main weapon is brutality, but there are different ways of applying that, you can plunge down on your victim suddenly like a bird of prey and pierce their body fatally with your claws, but you can also grab your victim like a cat, let it go again to smell a crumb of hope before striking even harder, you can also lull and weaken your victim's attention like a wolf in sheep's clothing, before launching an even more devastating attack from nearby.

'What's it about?' Lucie Wiegand asks.

Kiepert waves his hand vaguely and turns half-way back towards the Untersturmführer.

Siering is still standing there motionless. So this delicate little woman with her strawberry-blonde hair, the fine, weary, pale face, is Wiegand's wife. When he saw her appearing from behind the house in skiing trousers and a light-blue pullover with a polo neck that makes her look even slimmer, he thought at first that she was a young girl. Siering is surprised, he doesn't know whether he is disappointed or glad, he doesn't know how he imagined Wiegand's wife, but one thing is certain: it wasn't like this.

Lucie Wiegand looks at the SD man for the first time. 'Won't you tell me . . .' she says, turning to him.

'We can't discuss it over the garden fence,' Siering says and looks frankly into the woman's face. He is barely impressed by her beauty and her delicate charm, he has always seen the people he is to interrogate as his adversaries, sometimes deliberately and sometimes inadvertently withholding from him secrets that must be torn from them by every available means, and helplessness or innocence, strength of character or conviction have never led him to soften his procedures even slightly, but have in fact spurred him on to yet harsher methods. And suddenly Siering knows how he imagined Wiegand's wife: as a tall, thin woman with an angular way of moving and a flat chest, with cool, probing eyes behind horn-rimmed glasses, a half-masculine woman.

Lucie Wiegand feels his cold, enquiring eyes on her as she opens the garden gate, her heart thumps in her throat as she walks towards the house and hears the firm footsteps of the two men crunching in the gravel, she feels a weird, terrible apprehension welling hotly up inside her and then turning into an ice-cold rigidity.

What's happened to Fritz? she thinks. Have they found him? And in that case what do they want from me? To arrest me? If that's it, they need only send one policeman, it's a bad sign that Kiepert has come in person and even brought an SS officer with him.

'Please, come in,' she says and opens the door to one of the rooms.

Kiepert has taken off his light-green cap upon stepping into the hallway, and now stands awkwardly in the middle of the room, while Siering has looked all around and immediately sat down, propped an elbow on the table and crossed his legs with their long, gleaming black boots, keeping his cap on.

Lucie Wiegand stands where she is. 'Please, Mr Kiepert, have a seat,' she says.

Kiepert turns down her offer and leans against the windowsill, he is determined only to play the part of the spectator, but at the same time he thinks to himself with bitter recognition that his decision is not crucial here, and that he will be called upon to provide active help if the SS man requires it.

For a few seconds the stillness is oppressive. There are three people in a room, two men and one woman. But they have nothing in common with one another apart from the fact that they are people, a product of the meeting of a sperm and an ovum, consisting of a particular kind and quantity of protoplasm, gifted with the ability to form emotions, affects and thoughts into sounds, called language, through their thorax, vocal cords and tongues, and to represent these with visible signs, called writing. The difference between people lies in the nature of this ability and the way in which it is used, raising barriers between them which, in spite of all their similarities, the identical nature of their biological functions and their dependency upon the same conditions of civilization, are impossible to overcome.

Here is a man in whom all the barbaric instincts that seemed to have been overcome by 2,000 years of Christianity, humanist education and fear of the law have erupted once again, turning him back with surprising swiftness into *homo primigenius*. Here is a woman who has not made life more comfortable for herself by closing herself away from the wretchedness of humanity, but who instead continues to fight to eliminate ancient injustices. And last of all, here is a man who does not belong to either of these two extremes and who allows himself to drift within a dualism produced by these two forms of conscience, the private and the public. He is the species of *homo sapiens* most widely present in the Third

Reich. It is true that his sense of humanity has not been entirely extinguished, but he – he believes – has been forced to yield to the pressure of the barbarians who hold the power. He doesn't realize that he himself is only practising a form of barbarism mitigated by politeness.

Siering studies his fingernails for a while and then looks up. 'We arrested your husband yesterday, Mrs Wiegand.'

Hang on, Kiepert thinks, he told me he'd got away.

Lucie Wiegand turns white as a sheet. So they've got him, she thinks, so close to the end of play. 'And you have come here to give me that message?' she asks, struggling to control her voice.

'Of course not,' Siering asks and takes the blue pack out of his pocket again. 'May I smoke?'

'Be my guest,' Lucie Wiegand says dismissively.

Kiepert purses his lips to keep from laughing. So this man can be polite, he observes, but it's only one of his tricks, he's trying to win the little woman's confidence first.

Siering awkwardly lights his cigarette and takes a few puffs in silence, but while he is devoting himself entirely to the pleasure of the cigarette he steadily observes his adversary, his eyes circle her like a hawk waiting for the ideal moment to swoop on his prey. It's a tried-and-tested piece of criminological knowledge that unexplained silence makes people more insecure and often makes them speak more quickly than penetrating questions.

Lucie Wiegand still stands expectantly between door and desk, she has some experience of dealing with the Gestapo, and therefore knows that gentle preliminary questions with polite phrases and silence are only ever the lull before the storm.

'So, Mrs Wiegand,' Siering says at last, 'we have come to ask you some questions.'

Of course, this is where things are going, Lucie Wiegand thinks.

'We haven't been able to get very much out of your husband,' Siering goes on, 'even though his situation would definitely improve if he spoke openly, and we thought you might wish to help him.'

Him, Lucie Wiegand thinks, you're the ones I'm supposed to

help, but you've made a big mistake, you won't learn anything from me. 'I can't help you,' she says.

'You haven't let me finish, my dear Mrs Wiegand,' Siering says calmly, taking a few drags on his cigarette. 'I don't want you to tell me anything about your husband, we don't demand that of you, we aren't the monsters you probably take us for. Lieutenant Kiepert here will confirm that I was very reluctant to come and see you. Isn't that right, Comrade?'

No, you bastard, Kiepert thinks.

'Yes, that's true,' he says and nods.

'Then listen, Mrs Wiegand,' Siering says amicably. 'I only want to know in which pubs or other meeting places your husband met with his colleagues, that is all.'

That's a lot, Kiepert thinks, and looks tensely at the delicate little woman standing like a statue in the middle of the room. Will she talk?

'I don't know,' Lucie Wiegand replies, 'I have no idea where my husband is or where he has been.'

'Don't misunderstand me,' Siering says with a hint of impatience. 'I don't want you to say anything about your husband, quite the contrary, I want you to help him, I promise you that he will get away scot-free if we catch the others, after all, it's each man for himself. Isn't it?'

Lucie Wiegand doesn't answer the question. He's not going to get me, she thinks, the whole thing is a trap, it's far from inept, but I can see the snare.

Siering quickly finishes smoking his cigarette and throws the stub in the ashtray. 'We're not going to get anywhere like this,' he says, his voice now a note harsher, and the friendly little wrinkles around his eyes have disappeared.

Aha, Kiepert thinks, off we go.

Lucie Wiegand looks through the window at the green lawn over the Untersturmführer's shoulder. 'You must try to get hold of the information you are after in some other way,' she says.

'When did you last see your husband?' Siering asks.

'My husband hasn't lived here since June 1941,' Lucie Wiegand says, avoiding the question.

'That's not what I want to know,' Siering says sharply. 'I asked you when you last *saw* your husband.'

'That was when,' Lucie Wiegand says.

'Nonsense, Mrs Wiegand,' says Siering, still calm, but raising his voice now, 'utter nonsense. Your husband has been living in Berlin for the past four years, and you haven't seen him? Who's going to believe *that*?'

Lucie Wiegand remains stubbornly silent, her hands locked firmly together. Stay strong, she thinks, don't give in, whatever happens next.

'I simply don't believe you,' Siering goes on, he uncrosses his legs and brings his foot down hard on the carpet and sits there with his legs spread, hands on his knees, head thrust forward, cap at the back of his neck.

Lucie Wiegand shrugs her narrow shoulders and glances briefly at Kiepert.

Embarrassed, the police lieutenant looks away. I can't help you, little woman, he thinks, he's stronger than me, much stronger, he has the support of evil made flesh.

Siering leaps to his feet and walks right up to the small woman. 'Are you going to talk now or not?' he asks threateningly.

'No,' Lucie Wiegand says just as loudly and clearly.

'You damned communist whore!' Siering roars at her. 'I'll loosen your tongue for you! This is the first instalment!' He raises his hand and strikes her in the middle of the face with the back of his hand.

Lucie Wiegand totters a few steps back and leans against the door frame, her small breasts heaving violently beneath her light-blue pullover.

Kiepert gives a start, as if he himself had been struck by the blow. He stares spellbound at Lucie Wiegand's face, where a dark patch is appearing on her forehead, and then at Siering's hand, which is imperturbably pinching a cigarette from the blue pack.

'So, my darling,' Siering says sarcastically, 'now you've seen that I'm not to be messed with. Sit down.'

He pushes a chair at her with his foot.

Lucie Wiegand doesn't move from the spot, her hands are clinging to the door frame and she looks steadily at the Untersturmführer. Her face is aflame and has become stiff as a mask.

'I said sit down!' Siering shouts, and lights his cigarette. 'Would you like one too, darling?'

Not a muscle moves in Lucie Wiegand's face.

I can't watch this, Kiepert thinks, and looks out of the window.

'So open up that sweet little gob of yours,' Siering says, walking up and down in front of her. 'You have visited him often in those four years, I'm sure you have, you're a young woman and you don't look frigid to me, you can't live without it, you still need it, I'm sure it's still fun, that old slap and tickle. Aren't I right?'

You really are a swine, Kiepert thinks with revulsion.

Lucie Wiegand is breathing heavily, she feels the tears rising up, but forces them violently back. No, she doesn't want to cry, she doesn't want to show weakness to this man.

'So, tell me, where have you been together?' Siering goes on, not taking his eyes off her face for a moment. 'On Friedenstrasse, on Gollnowstrasse, on the Landsberger Allee on Elbinger Strasse, on Löwestrasse, on Lebuser Strasse? You see, I'm well informed, my child. So tell me, where?'

Lucie Wiegand remains mute, she bites her lips and looks past the SS man.

'Or perhaps at Dr Böttcher's?' Siering fires the question like an arrow.

Lucie Wiegand can't quite avoid flinching, but she pulls herself together again straight away.

Siering has noticed her movement, and laughs triumphantly with his mouth wide open. 'Time to spill the beans, sweetheart,' he says, and waves his burning cigarette around in front of her face. 'Or else I'll resort to other methods, I've dealt with very different people, you little louse. I have highly efficient ways of opening that sweet little mouth of yours. Have you ever heard of the third degree?'

Lucie Wiegand presses her lips tightly together and closes her eyes until they are tiny slits.

'Well, what's it to be? Are we going to reach an agreement?' Siering presses.

Lucie slowly opens her mouth, moistening her dry lips with a quick movement of her tongue. 'No,' she says resolutely.

'I would feel sorry for you, my darling,' Siering says with a grin that spreads across the whole of his face. 'I'm sure you'd make a lovely little bed-partner if you weren't a communist whore. You're quite tasty, as a matter of fact.'

Kiepert turns back into the room, he can no longer hold himself back. 'Comrade,' he says, 'this isn't the way . . .'

Siering spins on his heel in an instant. 'What are you talking about?' he roars. 'Have you gone mad? There are more things at stake here than some little slut. Do you hear me?'

Kiepert bites his lips and doesn't say a word.

'Did you hear me, I'm asking you?' Siering yells.

'Yes,' Kiepert mutters between clenched teeth.

'That's what I'd advise,' Siering says, still in a menacing voice, and takes a few quick drags. 'So, now back to you, little one. So far you've only had to deal with wet dishrags like this one here,' – he nods to Kiepert – 'but I'm cut from different cloth, my darling. Don't imagine I'm going to be careful with you just because you're a woman.'

Lucie Wiegand opens her half-closed eyes and looks steady at the SS man.

'I want to know where your husband is, and you'd better believe me, I'll get it out of you, even if it means turning you inside out.'

He wants to know where Fritz is? The thought flashes through Lucie Wiegand's mind. That means they haven't got him. Her chest fills with a deep sigh of relief. They've been on his trail, they've lost the trail again and I'm to put them right, which is why this monster has come to Eichwalde.

Siering steps right up to Lucie Wiegand and points his cigarette at her as if it were a gun. 'So, where's your old man?' he asks, his face the image of fearful threat. 'Will you open your mouth, you filthy whore?'

Lucie Wiegand stares at him fearlessly. 'No,' she says in a firm voice.

'So you won't,' Siering says, drawling the three words without any particular emphasis, but with a terrible note of menace.

Kiepert bends far forward, he feels as if someone is pressing down on the back of his neck.

Siering, who is a good head taller than the small, delicate woman, bends down to her. 'What are you wearing under your jumper, sweetie?' he asks. His voice has shed its hardness, but there is a different tone in it, a repellent friendliness.

What's that question supposed to mean? Kiepert thinks. Is he going to . . . No, that's impossible.

Lucie Wiegand ignores the question; the words still echo inside her, they haven't got Fritz, they haven't got him, they're still looking for him.

'So you're not going to tell me, little one?' Siering says. 'Well pay attention, we'll get it out of you.' With a secure, hard grip he grabs Lucie Wiegand's hands, which she has wedged against the door frame, and pulls them powerfully backwards, then with his other hand he presses the cigarette against her arm, in an instant the ember burns through the wool to the skin, immediately there is a smell of burnt wool and singed flesh. Lucie Wiegand struggles in the SS man's tight grip, but she is unable to resist his superior strength. He holds her like a vice and presses the cigarette harder against her arm. Kiepert is paralysed, he was prepared for further blows, but he hadn't expected this. 'Comrade,' he says hoarsely and takes a few steps into the room, 'this is really unacceptable.'

'Shut your mouth!' roars Siering, but he lets go of Lucie Wiegand and throws his cigarette butt heedlessly on the carpet.

Lucie Wiegand sinks exhaustedly against the door frame, she shuts her eyes, her face is contorted with pain, but not a sound issues from her lips.

Kiepert has retreated to his place by the window again. I'm powerless, he thinks, of course I could . . . A thought rises hotly up in him, but he immediately rejects it again. For a few fleeting seconds he considered simply shooting the SS man. Mrs Wiegand certainly wouldn't give him away, but it's only a passing impulse, it would have called for courage and initiative and he doesn't have those.

'My dear chap,' Siering says, turning to face Kiepert. 'Let's talk later.' He sits down and crosses his legs. 'Well, now, my beauty,' he says in a voice filled with scorn and derision, 'are you going to talk to me?'

Lucie Wiegand opens her eyes and her face twitches. 'Yes,' she says firmly.

'Well, then, I knew it,' Siering says jovially, and lights another cigarette. 'Why didn't you do that before? You could have spared yourself the hole in your jumper and that tattoo on your arm.'

Kiepert listens. Is she going to tell him everything, he thinks? Poor little woman, it didn't take long to break you down. But her voice sounded so curiously firm, not like that of a person who is finally, after being tortured, ready to make their confession.

'So, what do you have to tell me now, my golden little darling? Open that sugar-sweet little mouth of yours.'

Lucie Wiegand straightens and presses her back firmly against the door frame, as if finding a support for what she is about to say. 'Even if you tear me to pieces, you won't get a word out of me, you bloody fascist scoundrel!'

Kiepert holds his breath, something terrible is about to happen.

Siering is startled for a second, but then he slowly gets up from his chair and is with Lucie Wiegand in an instant. 'You cheeky little bitch, you damned whore,' he roars, and slaps her face to the right and the left, grips her by the shoulders and drags her into the middle of the room, stands next to her breathing heavily and raises a foot to give her a kick.

Then the doorbell rings.

'Who is it?' Siering shouts.

Kiepert peers out of the window. By now dusk has fallen. 'There's a young man at the gate, as far as I can tell,' he says.

'Is he one of yours, Kiepert?'

'I don't believe so,' Kiepert replies.

'Believing is for priests,' Siering spits.

The bell rings for a second and then for a third time. 'Let's take a look at this little bird of ours, who wants to stroll into the red nest,' Siering says cynically. 'But how are we going to lure him in here, without arousing his suspicions?'

'He's on his way, you don't need to do a thing,' Kiepert says, sighing with relief at the temporary conclusion of the terrible scene that was playing out a moment before. 'In the meantime he's discovered that the garden gate isn't locked. I can see the young man quite clearly, I don't know him, he's not from Eichwalde as far as I can tell.'

Siering opens the door to the hallway and glances at Lucie Wiegand. She is lying motionless on the carpet with her head on her bent arms and her feet drawn up tight against her body, and two big tears run down her cheeks.

XX

At Eichwalde Station Lassehn is checked once again, this time by two armed men in plain clothes, who each wear a white armband with the inscription 'town guard'; they are patrolling the platform with a bored air and dutifully pounce on anyone who isn't local.

Lassehn shows his papers and is immediately allowed to pass, they've only glanced at them and then given them back.

Now Lassehn walks along Bahnhofstrasse. After a few days of the uninterrupted spectacle of devastation, the view of an undamaged city is as inconceivable as that of a well-fed person to a starving one. Everything here is peaceful, everything goes its own way, and perhaps the people are in slightly more of a hurry than they might have been in normal times. The shops aren't boarded-up caves, they still have display windows, the houses still have glass windows and red-tiled roofs, the streets are swept, you don't walk on broken glass or stumble over piles of rubble, the trees are sprouting their first leaves, in people's front gardens the buds of the shrubs are already far advanced, in the gardens to the rear the soil is being turned as if in certain anticipation of a good harvest.

War seems to have ignored the idyll of this small town just beyond the gates of Berlin.

The further Lassehn gets from the station, the quieter and more peaceful it becomes. If houses dominated near the station and the gardens were merely adjuncts, here the gardens assume greater importance, with the houses merely placed in the middle of them. Lassehn walks as if in a daze, he is almost numbed by the silence, he hears his own footsteps on the cobblestones, birdsong reaches his ear. The wind here stirs like a veil; it doesn't swirl up chalk dust and ashes, or carry the smell of burning into every corner.

While he walks along the streets in a slight stupor, he can't help thinking of Wiegand, for whom he is making this journey, and who has had to avoid these streets for years. Being excluded from one's actual sphere of life over a period of years, the constant temptation to reach into that sphere from one's shadowy existence strikes Lassehn as even harder, even more unbearable than the lurking peril forever pointed at his heart like the tip of a lance. Lassehn cannot feel the silence that seems to float among the gardens here as something pure. It is a silence that awakens in him something like a painfully consuming yearning because it is a silence in the middle of a hurricane of many deaths and mutilations, of hatred and wickedness. The silence is not a silence, but the taking of a breath before new hatred and new wickedness. That silence has often overwhelmed him when he stood at night on sentry duty and looked into the sky, where star flickered next to star and the moon poured its cold, blue light over the landscape.

That sky arches over all human beings, he thought then, over all human beings now lying in beds and sleeping bags, on bales of straw and on the ground, and who are immersed in sleep, who have interrupted their work to continue with their lives, whether damned or blissful, wretched or replete. Why can the peace of night not extend into day? Why is nature only an accumulator that enriches new energies which can then be transformed again into death and destruction?

Then Lassehn is standing at the garden gate that bears the aluminium sign 'Wiegand', and he rings, he hears the bell sound and waits. No one comes to open the door. He rings again and moves the latch more playfully than purposefully and the unlocked gate opens.

So she's at home, Lassehn thinks, heading towards the house along the gravel path. He knocks at the door, steps into a little hallway and audibly clears his throat, but the house remains completely silent, oppressively silent . . .

Curious, Lassehn thinks, and shakes his head slightly, all the doors are open, I rang the bell twice, but no one answered.

He takes a few steps further into the hallway and looks at a painting showing some wild ducks above a monotonous landscape of dunes with tufts of marram grass, then he clears his throat again.

'Come in, young man,' a man's voice says suddenly from a slightly open door.

She must have visitors, Lassehn thinks. He knocks twice on the door and opens it. 'Hello . . .' He is unable to finish his sentence, his heart seems suddenly to have leaped into his throat with terrible force. He finds himself facing an SS officer and a policeman. Damn it all, he's fallen into a trap.

The SS officer has exploited Lassehn's second of alarm to push the door out of his hand and shut it behind him, while the police officer in the green uniform leans with his arms folded against the windowsill. Lassehn can now tell that he is a lieutenant.

'Sit down at the desk,' Siering says imperiously. 'Take care you don't trip.'

Lassehn stands there hesitantly for a moment, he shivers slightly, his thoughts become confused, and he suddenly feels terribly weary.

'Didn't you hear me?' the SS man yells at him.

Lassehn takes a step in the direction he has been ordered and then stops again and tries to put his thoughts in order. Don't immediately give yourself up for lost if you encounter an obstacle, Klose told him, not everything is as desperate as it might seem at first sight, often it only appears that way because you give up, there's plenty of time left to die. Only now does he see what was previously hidden from him in the vague light of the room: a woman is lying on the floor, her hands laid protectively over her head and her legs pulled up tightly to her body. At that moment everything becomes clear to him, the woman can be no one but Mrs Wiegand, and the way she is lying there clearly indicates that . . .

'If you do not immediately accept my unmistakeable invitation,' the Untersturmführer says cynically, 'you'll be joining her down there.'

Stay calm, Lassehn thinks and walks the few steps to the desk, stay calm, don't be hasty, you've missed the opportunity to act at lightning speed in any case, it's not only about me, it's also about the woman. My God, what has this bastard done to her?

'So, at last,' the SS man says. 'Are you always so slow?'

Lassehn doesn't reply, he forces back the agitation that is rising up in him like effervescent water, he clenches his teeth firmly to take control of it. There is no point pretending, the situation is not propitious, the SS officer has occupied the door and the police lieutenant the window, and the second window is about six metres away. To get there he would have to cross the whole length of the room, but even if it were possible to reach the window, there would be no question of leaving the woman behind on her own.

'What do you want here?' the SS man launches into Lassehn.

'I want to pay a visit,' Lassehn replies. 'Is that forbidden?'

The SS man looks him contemptuously up and down. 'Who did you want to visit?'

'Mrs Wiegand, naturally enough,' Lassehn replies.

For the first time since Lassehn entered the room Lucie Wiegand moves, she lifts her head and looks at him confusedly, but since she is lying in the shadow of the desk and the room is already growing dark, Lassehn can't make out her face.

'Great,' the Untersturmführer says sarcastically, 'I don't think there's anything natural about visiting Mrs Wiegand. We are here to visit Mrs Wiegand as well, except that isn't as natural for us as it may seem to you.'

Lassehn gives the SS man a challenging look. 'What do you want from me?'

'We ask the questions,' the SS man reprimands him curtly. 'Why are you visiting Mrs Wiegand?'

'Because Mrs Wiegand is the mother of one of my schoolmates,' Lassehn replies, having been prepared for the question. It's lucky that Klose gave me a bit of background information, Lassehn thinks gratefully. Good old Klose, you've really thought of everything.

Again Lucie Wiegand lifts her head for a few minutes and looks at Lassehn, then she lets her head sink heavily back down on her arms.

'What's your name?' asks the SS man.

'Horst Winter.'

'Do you live in Eichwalde?'

'I used to live here.'

'God, how touchingly affectionate,' the SS man mocks, 'in spite of the terrible transport conditions the good friend comes from . . . from where?'

'From Reinickendorf.'

'From Reinickendorf to Eichwalde,' the Untersturmführer goes on. 'Touching, when you think about it.' He turns to the policeman. 'Do you know this young man, Comrade?'

The police lieutenant shakes his head. 'No, I don't know him, but that doesn't necessarily mean very much, because I've only been in Eichwalde since 1940, and then . . .'

'That's fine,' the SS man says. 'Of course you know this young man,' Mrs Wiegand?'

'Yes,' Lucie Wiegand says quietly, 'I know him.'

'Well, we might have expected as much. What was his name again?' the Untersturmführer says with a mischievous wink.

'Horst Winter,' Lassehn says quickly.

The SS officer draws his arm back and slaps Lassehn full in the face with the back of his hand. 'If you so much as open your trap if no one has asked you to,' he shouts furiously, 'you'll get another of those, but it'll be a fist next time.'

Lassehn has staggered backwards. For a fraction of a second he considers hitting back, but only claws his fingernails into the ball of his hand. He might have had a small chance of knocking down the SS thug if he had attacked straight away, but the cop is still there and above all the woman. An attempt to escape wouldn't just be pointless, it would also be mean to leave that defenceless woman behind in the hands of the bandits.

'Who sent you?' the SS man asks. Before Lassehn can even open his mouth he adds threateningly, 'And don't try to lie to me, or things will get very nasty for you.'

Lassehn doesn't reply, and looks cautiously around.

The SS man has noticed his gaze. 'You won't leave this room alive,' he says, drawing his pistol from his brown-leather holster, 'if you even think of trying to get away.'

Lassehn bites his lips, he sees that he has made a mistake, he should have answered, given some names and addresses, shown that he was willing, to weaken the SS man's determination. He will try to make up for that now, not all at once, and not too conspicuously to avoid arousing suspicion, for the time being he will have to contradict . . .

'Right then, spill the beans,' the SS man says in a tone that alternates between threat and advice, 'we know more than you can imagine.'

'Then you don't need me,' Lassehn says stubbornly.

The SS man inhales audibly, as if he is struggling to keep control of himself. 'This thing goes off incredibly easily,' he says and plays with the safety catch of his pistol. 'Will you speak now?'

At this Lucie Wiegand raises her head. 'No,' she says, 'no, no, no, he won't speak.'

'Shut up, you bitch,' the SS man roars and kicks at her with his foot. 'Just wait, my turtle dove, they'll teach you some lovely tunes to sing in Ravensbrück.'

The bastard, Lassehn thinks. 'Leave the woman in peace,' he says, 'I'll tell you everything.'

'Well then,' the SS man says. 'You have more sense than she does. Who sent you to Eichwalde? Wiegand or – Dr Böttcher?'

Christ, Lassehn thinks, he seems to know all kinds of things. 'What did you say? Dr Böttcher?'

'That's right, Dr Böttcher, you heard me correctly.'

'I don't know him,' Lassehn shrugs.

The SS man comes right up to Lassehn and presses the muzzle of the pistol to his body. 'If you think you can fool me, you've made a big mistake,' he says darkly. 'Who else sent you?'

'Someone called Richter,' Lassehn replies, and looks at the gun. The safety catch is on, he thinks, he's been playing around with it for so long that in the end he's forgotten to take the catch off.

Strange, the cop is completely passive, he's standing there as if none of this has anything to do with him. If I started shooting, would I have to kill him as well?

'Where is Richter?'

Lassehn replies and shrugs, 'I've always met him somewhere else.'

'Where is that?'

'Somewhere in the Prälat dance hall, or at Wollermann's on Alexanderplatz.'

'And Wiegand was there too?'

'Sometimes.'

The SS man pulls the pistol back a little and looks at Lassehn with a frown. 'And where does Wiegand live?'

Lucie Wiegand sits up. 'Don't tell him,' she exclaims. 'You mustn't give anything away.'

The SS man takes a step backwards and half turns towards Lucie Wiegand. 'Wait, you damned cunt!' he cries furiously, lifts his pistol and is about to beat her with the buttstock.

Then a violent kick from Lassehn catches him and knocks him down, at the same time Lassehn pulls his revolver out of his trouser pocket and shoots three times at the SS man, then he turns round and points his gun at the police lieutenant. 'Hands up!' he shouts. 'If you put up the slightest resistance I'll shoot you down, just like him.'

The police lieutenant is taken completely by surprise and immediately raises his hands.

Lassehn walks around the desk and glances at the SS man. 'He's gone,' he says, surprised that his own voice sounds so relaxed. Strange duplicity of events, never in his life has he deliberately killed anyone, and now over two evenings he has finished off two men, but what made him agitated yesterday leaves him quite cold today.

'Go and stand in the corner right now,' he orders the police lieutenant, 'with your face to the wall. I'll shoot if you don't follow each instruction to the letter.'

The policeman walks heavily into the corner and stands against the wall with his hands up. 'What are you going to do?' he asks, his voice quivering.

'I just want to get us to safety, that's all,' Lassehn says, he goes up to the lieutenant and takes the pistol from his holster, then walks back into the room and attends to Lucie Wiegand. 'Stand up, please, madam,' he says and puts his gun down on the desk. 'Pack a bag or two right now, you can't stay here.'

Lucie Wiegand stands in front of Lassehn, small and delicate, she barely reaches his shoulder, and gives him a long and urgent look. 'Thank you,' she says, reaching for his hand.

Lassehn hastily withdraws his hand.

'Oh, nonsense,' he says, embarrassed, 'let's not waste time on gratitude and sentimental gestures, we need to hurry so that we can get away from here as quickly as possible. Meanwhile I'm going to lock this one' – he points at the policeman – 'in the cellar. Will you show me where it is?'

Lucie Wiegand nods. 'The back door leads to the cellar,' she says. 'Kiepert was always very decent to me,' she adds with a pleading note in her voice.

'Come on,' Lassehn says to the policeman, 'I won't tie you up and gag you if you stay calm, but I have to lock you in the cellar for our personal safety.'

The policeman turns round, his face is pale grey, his upper lip trembles as if he were freezing. He glances at the SS man, who is lying crookedly by the door he was guarding.

'Come on, we have no time,' Lassehn says impatiently and pushes the door open. 'And I repeat that you will get three bullets in your body just like him if you try to make a fuss. Do we understand each other?'

'Yes,' the lieutenant says quietly, and stands uncertainly by the corpse of the SS man.

'Go,' Lassehn says. 'Or haven't you seen a corpse before?'

The policeman says nothing and steps over the body, his shoulders slumped, his arms dangling loosely and his head bowed.

As they go down the cellar steps, Lassehn says again, 'I warn you not to attract attention until we have left the house.'

The policeman stops in the cellar door. 'I'd rather you shot me,' he says weakly. 'Or do you think I can go on working after something like this?'

'I don't care about your work,' Lassehn says curtly. 'As far as I'm concerned you can say that an armed gang attacked the house, or come up with some other kind of cops-and-robbers story. Now, in you go.'

The policeman still hesitates. 'How can you imagine that . . .' he begins.

Lassehn isn't listening any more, he gives the policeman a shove and shuts the cellar door, bolts it and turns the key in the lock. 'That's him taken care of,' he says, and smiles at Lucie Wiegand.

She returns his smile. 'A good job well done.'

Lassehn waves her praise away. 'I hope it wasn't a mistake not to shoot the cop as well,' he says reflectively as they come back up the cellar steps. 'At any rate, let us hurry, madam.'

'Enough of the "madam",' Lucie Wiegand says simply, 'I've never expected that form of address, and in the present circumstances it sounds like sarcasm.' She shakes her head. 'Where are you going to take me? I don't even know where you're coming from and who sent you.'

Lassehn laughs faintly.

'That's right, we haven't talked about it, or had a chance to talk about it, the unusual situation dragged me into a kind of whirlpool, so that I didn't even introduce myself.'

They climb the steps side by side.

'My name is Joachim Lassehn.'

'And I'm Lucie Wiegand.'

They swap names like greetings, without bowing, without nodding, without phrases like 'allow me' and 'pleasure to meet you', everything is done quite naturally and in a comradely fashion.

'But now you must tell me, Mr Lassehn . . .' Lucie Wiegand begins.

'Forgive me for interrupting,' Lassehn says hastily, 'but time is marching on, we have to get out of here as quickly as possible, I'll happily tell you everything you need to know afterwards.'

Lucie Wiegand nods. 'You're right,' she says, 'but I'm ready to travel right now, my air-raid suitcases are always packed.'

'That's great,' Lassehn says, 'the quicker we get away from here the better, because I don't know if that man down there will try to make a noise, and I would like to . . .' Lassehn pauses and looks uncertainly at the little woman, who now walks to the door and opens it.

I don't want to have to shoot another one, he wanted to say, but he keeps the words to himself, they might sound as if they meant, or be interpreted as meaning, that it was a habit of his to kill people and talk about it in the cold-blooded, thoughtless manner of a National Socialist thug. Lassehn knows how much of an effort it was for him yesterday to shoot the Nazi block warden when he killed a human being for the first time without being ordered to do so, and even today, when the pure instinct of self-defence and the protection of a vulnerable woman had forced the gun into his hand, the death of this unknown Untersturmführer didn't leave him entirely indifferent. This SS officer – thug though he might be – was also a human being, who had emerged from his mother's womb, who had a short while ago still breathed and moved and spoken, and now . . . Damned sentimentality, Lassehn thinks in self-rebuke. What did he say when he spoke, and how did he move? Do you really need to justify yourself?

Lucie Wiegand touches him on the shoulder. 'Hello, Mr Lassehn,' she says and looks into his face with concern. 'What's wrong with you?'

Lassehn awakens as if from a dream. 'I'm sorry, my thoughts were . . .' elsewhere, he wanted to say, but it isn't true, he was here with them, in the room whose door is wide open, where the man in the grey uniform lies motionless.

'I'll just pack a few things in a little suitcase,' Lucie Wiegand says. 'But tell me one thing quickly. What's happening to my husband?'

'Your husband is healthy and cheerful,' Lassehn replies, 'but he had to get away from Lebuser Strasse. He sent me to Eichwalde to bring you news.' Lucie Wiegand's face brightens suddenly. 'Thank you,' she says. 'And now . . .' Her footsteps, which had dragged slightly a moment before, suddenly quicken.

'Can I help you?' Lassehn asks.

'No,' Lucie Wiegand says and blushes slightly, 'I just want to pack a few personal things quickly.' She pauses and frowns. 'Or rather,' she adds, 'you could bring up the two suitcases under the cellar steps. Will you do that?'

'Of course,' Lassehn says eagerly.

While Lucie Wiegand enters the room, Lassehn stands motionless in the hallway for a few seconds. There was something else he wanted to bring . . . right, that was it. He climbs over the corpse into the room and picks up the Untersturmführer's pistol. This might come in useful, he thinks

'Mrs Wiegand,' he says and knocks on the door, 'have you got room for the two pistols in your suitcase? We might need them urgently.'

'Of course,' Lucie Wiegand replies, and takes the two pistols. She flinches slightly at the touch of the cold steel and turns quickly away. 'It'll be all right,' she says and shuts the door behind her.

Lassehn immediately reproaches himself for having stirred unnecessary emotions with the sight and touch of the guns.

The house is very still, the only sound a rustle from the room where Lucie Wiegand is packing her suitcase. Nothing can be heard from the cellar.

Lassehn climbs down the cellar steps deliberately slowly and listens at the cellar door. The policeman is being very quiet, there isn't a footstep to be heard. Lassehn finds the two suitcases under the cellar steps and carries them up to the hallway.

At that moment Lucie Wiegand appears in the doorway, she has put on a coat, tied a brightly coloured headscarf around her head, and is carrying a dark-brown leather suitcase. 'We can go, Mr Lassehn,' she says. Her voice is quite calm, without a trace of excitement, she says it as casually as if she were telling him to go from one room into another.

Lassehn picks up the two suitcases again, he pauses for a moment and looks furtively at Lucie Wiegand's face. Terrible, he thinks, now this woman has to leave her house to go into the unknown. Everything her heart is fond of stays behind, small and unremarkable things, perhaps, but things that mean a lot in a woman's life.

Things she has grown with over many years, which are part of herself, and which she herself is now excising with the sharp blade of compulsory renunciation.

'What are you still waiting for?' Lucie Wiegand asks, and turns to look him in the eye.

An admirable woman, Lassehn thinks, and feels a great wave of respect and tenderness rising up in him, that upright posture, that resolute quality in her face, that clear gaze, even though she may be hurt and agitated below the surface. 'Yes, let's go,' he says.

By the time they leave the house the darkness is almost complete, they cross the garden and leave the property by the rear entrance. When they reach the adjacent forest, Lucie Wiegand stops for a heartbeat and looks back. Her house stands out like a silhouette in the darkening sky, loomed over by the tall, swaying shadows of the trees. Then she pulls herself resolutely away, and they disappear into the darkness of the forest.

XXI

Before Wiegand enters a house he first tends to observe its surroundings very closely. So he carefully lets his eyes wander around the northern side of the Frankfurter Allee as he approaches Dr Böttcher's house in the late afternoon.

The street isn't very busy, the Frankfurter Allee came to an end under a few violent and well-aimed blows from the British-American Air Forces, shops don't exist here any more.

There are only a few individual flats, and the street has forfeited its status as one of the city's principal thoroughfares, since its once-bright and shiny asphalt skin is filled with bumps and holes; it is a part of that Berlin whose face, in Dr Goebbels' words, bears heroic features because it bleeds from many wounds.

On the promenade, diagonally opposite house number 14, workers are busy temporarily closing the damaged roof of the tunnel of the underground and removing the loose wires dangling from the overhead tramlines. On the edge of the crater a man stands watching the workers. Something about the man's appearance seems familiar to Wiegand, that slightly loutish way of standing around, with the hands deep in the trouser pockets and the felt hat tilted slightly back towards the back of the neck, that almost imperceptible and yet unmistakeable attitude of tense expectation in the posture . . .

The man looks as if he is watching the workers with interest, but his eye keeps jumping to the pavement where there is nothing to be seen but the familiar view of the ruins, apart from house number

14, with a sign with a few words written in black letters on what
had once been white enamel:

Dr Walter Böttcher
Gen. Practitioner
Surgeries 9–10 a.m. and 4–6 p.m.
except Wednesday and Saturday afternoon

Wiegand wants to be absolutely sure, he strolls along the building
pit and looks the man fleetingly in the eye, then he knows. This
apparently harmless bystander is none other than the man with the
rucksack who followed him so persistently yesterday from Lebuser
Strasse to Petersburger Strasse, and whom he then shook off, so to
speak, when the air-raid warning sounded. It cannot be a coincidence that this man is now standing around here, in front of Dr
Böttcher's house. It is certain proof that the investigation has assumed
a much greater scale than might previously have been assumed, and
that Dr Böttcher has also been drawn into this investigation proves
that they have somehow tracked down his, Wiegand's, connection
with Dr Böttcher.

Wiegand moves away from the pit again. The man hasn't noticed
him, his eyes are focused on the front door of house number 14, he
isn't interested in the surrounding area. It hasn't occurred to him
that he himself might be under observation, he imagines that his
apparent interest in a pit would camouflage him sufficiently.
Wiegand smiles to himself, but then becomes serious again, he must
call Dr Böttcher straight away to warn him, but that won't be an easy
matter, in this bombed-out city there are not many telephones that
are still working.

Wiegand turns into Tilsiter Strasse. Here the destruction is less
extensive, and there must still be a telephone that is usable. But when
he enquires about the possibility of using one the only response is a
shrug and a shake of the head, the phones have no power or the
exchange is down. The protective shell that surrounds the sensitive
nerve fibres of the city is burst and shredded. Only on Kochhannstrasse, opposite the Schultheiss-Patzenhofer brewery, does he

find a tobacconist's shop whose telephone is working. He dials the six figures, but after only the second the hum of the engaged tone sounds, he sets the receiver back down on the cradle and after a while he tries for a second time, then a third and a fourth, but he can't get a connection. The humming tone is always in his ear.

Wiegand walks sullenly back up Tilsiter Strasse. He absolutely needs to talk to Dr Böttcher. He's to meet Schröter as they want to talk about the activation of their group and discuss the possibility of collaboration. But if Dr Böttcher is also under suspicion, an important central connection is lost, not only because his surgery was an ideal meeting point, but also because Dr Böttcher's work as a doctor explained why he was constantly travelling and legitimized him at every time of day and night.

Wiegand has reached the Frankfurter Allee again. The spy is still standing on the Promenade, turned half towards the pit and half towards house number 14. There is no question of entering the house without being seen by him, the house doesn't have a rear entrance, but . . .

That's one possibility. Wiegand turns from Tilsiter Strasse into Frankfurter Allee, walks along it to Petersburger Strasse, which he crosses, and then walks on the other side to Lasdehner Strasse. Lasdehner Strasse forms an acute angle with Frankfurter Allee. The courtyards of the ruins on Lasdehner Strasse abut the rear façades of the buildings on Frankfurter Alleee, and that is what Wiegand currently needs. He passes through a burnt-out, half-collapsed portal, climbs over piles of debris of what was once a rear wing, and stands in the courtyard of 14 Frankfurter Allee. Dr Böttcher's flat has another rear entrance in the side wing, which is seldom used and usually bolted up.

Wiegand climbs the back steps and gives his coded knock against the rear door.

A few seconds pass, then the bolt is drawn back.

'Hello, Wiegand,' Dr Böttcher says cordially and holds out his hand. 'A little out of your way?'

Wiegand steps inside and closes the door. 'Has its reasons, Doctor,' he says. 'Is Schröter here?'

'We're waiting for you,' Dr Böttcher says. 'Has something gone wrong?'

They walk along the corridor. Wiegand nods and greets Schröter, then outlines the situation in short sentences. 'They're after us,' he says, bringing his report to an end, 'there's no doubt about it.'

The men are silent for a few seconds.

'The first thing to do is find out who is under surveillance,' Schröter says, 'whether it's Dr Böttcher or you, Wiegand.'

'That's quite easy to discover,' Dr Böttcher says. 'It will become clear if I visit a patient later on.'

'Not necessarily,' Schröter objects. 'The surveillance doesn't need to apply to you personally, but more to your practice and the circle of your patients.'

'I'm the one under surveillance,' Wiegand says firmly, 'there's no doubt about that as far as I'm concerned. That man down there is waiting only for me. But what made them expect to find me here, outside your house, Doctor?'

Dr Böttcher shrugs. 'Perhaps they'd been observing you before, Wiegand?'

'Out of the question,' Wiegand says, 'I'm sure I would have noticed.'

'You're not infallible,' Schröter suggests.

'If Wiegand has been under surveillance before,' Dr Böttcher says, ignoring the dispute that the others are engaged in, 'that would mean that Klose's restaurant is also under surveillance, or has been for some time.'

Wiegand shakes his head. 'No, Klose's place has always been safe,' he says, 'they must have a precise point of reference to put a man right in front of your house. But what would it be?'

'Your visits to me are easily and credibly explained,' Dr Böttcher says. 'You're patients of mine.'

Wiegand stares at Dr Böttcher. 'Patients! That's the key word!' he cries. 'The sick note, Doctor, the sick note!'

'The sick note?' the doctor asks, perplexed.

'Your name is on my sick note, doctor,' Wiegand bursts out, 'I was written off sick in January, and of course I had to hand in my sick certificate to the personnel office . . .'

'That's quite possible,' Dr Böttcher says thoughtfully. 'It would be interesting to know who the Gestapo are tailing, whether it's Reichsbahn worker Adamek or the former Reichstag member Wiegand.'

'Someone called Adamek used to live on Lebuser Strasse,' Wiegand says, 'the investigation into Wiegand has probably been closed for some time, they don't keep files in evidence for four years.'

'I would assume that too,' Schröter says, 'they've had other things to do, particularly since the twentieth of July.'*

'I disagree,' Dr Böttcher says, 'the twentieth of July may have led them to seek out old files and issue new orders to investigate, but let's leave that aside for the time being. The important thing now is to discover whether my flat is under surveillance, or whether the man on the Promenade is just waiting for Wiegand. In the former case we'll have to change our way of working straight away.'

'This matter is of such fundamental importance that we must put it to the test,' Wiegand says stoutly.

'And how do you plan to do that?' Schröter asks.

'By simply walking past him,' Wiegand replies. 'If he follows me, I will know, if he doesn't then things will be clear as well.'

'You want to help him find the trail?' Dr Böttcher asks in amazement. 'That's not without its dangers.'

'I know,' Wiegand says, 'but it has to be, and you can also rely on me getting rid of him again very quickly. You will help me with that, Schröter.'

Schröter nods.

'I will,' he agrees, 'but for now let's deal with our agenda.'

'The only point is the collaboration between the groups "Ringbahn" and "Berolina",' Dr Böttcher smiles.

A smile passes over Wiegand's face as well.

'Unanimously agreed,' he says.

'Above all we need flyers,' Schröter says, 'our printer was bombed out last Friday. Can you help us?'

---

* A reference to the Stauffenberg plot, an attempt to assassinate Hitler on 20 July 1944.

Dr Böttcher nods. 'I can give you three hundred straight away,' he replies, gets up, takes down a painting from the wall and opens a safe in the wall. 'This is the one we have right now.'

Schröter takes the piece of paper that is handed to him. 'How do I behave in air raids? Produced by the Reich Air Protection League,' he reads. 'Very nice, with official signatures and everything, at first sight it looks very convincing. Right, let's see how I'm supposed to behave.' He reads through it.

To the German people and the German Army!

Filled with serious concern for the fate of our people, regardless of differences in creed and political affiliation . . .

'Hang on a second,' he breaks off. 'That's . . .'

'. . . the *Manifesto of the National Peace Movement*,' Dr Böttcher finishes the sentence.

'. . . of December 1942,' Schröter goes on and sets the piece of paper down on the table. 'Gentlemen, this is no longer current, and it's also far too long.'

Wiegand takes the piece of paper and scans it quickly. 'You're right,' he says, 'the manifesto may be a great synopsis, an appeal to the German people, it may be a document that will one day be compared with Mazzini's manifesto, but in a sense it is already passé.' He turns to Dr Böttcher. 'I assumed that something new could come out, Doctor, something that clearly and urgently addresses the current situation.'

Dr Böttcher shrugs. 'The intellectual vein of our Comrade E has been interrupted again, but I have already written a new proclamation, which I want to have set straight away, and which we will distribute as soon as the Russians attack on the Oder or the Americans cross the Elbe. The proclamation reads as follows:

Soldiers! Volkssturm men!

The final act in the drama of our people has now begun. A criminal leadership is continuing with the completely pointless struggle, even though it became clear long ago that our military adversaries are far superior in terms of both men and guns. The whole of Germany is now a theatre of war. The Allied air forces control German air space by day and night, and their armies of tanks are rolling inexorably forward.

Soldiers!

Time and again you have been rushed into completely pointless struggle, you have been made to bleed, the graves of your comrades are scattered across the whole of Europe. They have not died for Germany, they have died for the criminals of the National Socialist Party.

Volkssturm men!

In their military helplessness, and in impotent fury over their inevitable defeat, the Nazi criminals are sending you into battle as the last of the cannon fodder, just to extend their own pitiful lives by a few days.

Soldiers! Volkssturm men!

Do not allow yourselves to be abused any more. Every shot that you fire only extends the torments of your wives and children. Put an end to this bloody madness!

Dr Böttcher pauses. 'I think that is clear and objective, both in terms of language and content. What do you think?'

'I see nothing to criticize,' Wiegand says approvingly, 'but perhaps we could add a few positive words of conclusion, along the lines of: "Fight for a new, better Germany".'

'I can do that,' says Dr Böttcher. 'Could I ask you to take the manuscript to the printers? Tell them not to print anything else.'

Wiegand takes the sheet of paper. 'It'll be done today,' he says. 'Has Lassehn been here?'

Dr Böttcher nods. 'He brought the other flyers,' he replies. 'From here he went . . . to yours. I hope it works out.'

'He's a good lad,' Wiegand says, 'a little hesitant and uncertain, but also resolute and active.'

He turns to Schröter. 'A few days ago we took in a young deserter, and he's earned his spurs by now.'

'A worker?' Schröter asks.

Wiegand shakes his head. 'No, an intellectual, a musician, someone who's looking for a new way.'

'With us, of all people?' Schröter asks.

'Why not with us?'

'My dear Schröter,' Dr Böttcher cuts in, 'such discussions are completely pointless, now and in general. To be a socialist you don't necessarily need to have had a proletarian background, and in order to become an active fighter against Hitler's thugs you don't even need to be a socialist.'

'So?' Schröter says, outraged. 'What do you need to be?'

'A fighter for freedom, justice and humanity,' Dr Böttcher replies.

'I see,' says Schröter and waves his arms in the air, 'that is nothing other than socialism!'

Dr Böttcher casts a long look across the table. 'It's possible,' he says slowly, 'although this interpretation is a new one on me. I want to say something to you, Schröter, even though now isn't really the time for theoretical discussions. You must shed this proletarian arrogance, we don't want to replace the Aryan identity card with the proletarian identity card. The new Germany that will come with the fall of National Socialism cannot begin with dogmatic narrow-mindedness.'

'So that means we're to water down our ideas?' Schröter says obstinately.

'No one's saying that,' Wiegand says, joining in with the conversation. 'What the doctor means is the following. We don't want to replace the exclusive claim of the National Socialists with another exclusive claim, no one is to water down an idea, as you call it, not you and not anyone else either. When the war is over we will have different problems to solve, and we can only do so by common accord.'

'By common accord with who?' Schröter asks, and bends over the table.

'By common accord with the people who are working illegally with us right now,' Wiegand replies, 'bourgeois intellectuals, Catholics, pacifists, to use the old terms.'

Schröter leans back in his chair. 'I get it,' he says and laughs sarcastically, 'Weimar coalition, great coalition, Hindenburg front, Harzburg front, I'm familiar with the scale.'

'Christ,' Dr Böttcher says angrily, 'you seem to think it all has to happen that way again. I'm aware that history is a great teacher, and that people often stubbornly insist that its teachings should be ignored, but we want to be among those who learn from history. The blood-drenched educational demonstrations have opened our eyes.'

Schröter shrugs. 'Leave me out of it,' he says.

'Then we'll leave you out,' Wiegand says resolutely.

'Am I to understand that you are giving up your underground work?' Dr Böttcher asks.

Schröter taps his index finger against his forehead. 'You're not quite right, it's what I live for, the only thing.'

'Then I will say,' Dr Böttcher laughs, 'we agree, and we will agree just as much afterwards. Isn't that right, Schröter?'

Schröter hunches his shoulders. 'I don't know . . .'

'That sounds different,' Dr Böttcher says. 'In all modesty I might remind you that many – and not the least significant – leaders of the workers' movement come from the bourgeois camp that you seem to despise so much, I need only mention Marx, Engels, Lassalle, Mehring, Lenin and Liebknecht.'

'They are all notorious exceptions,' Schröter objects.

'If there were once such exceptions of undoubted greatness, to whom we may even attribute a theoretical and practical claim to leadership without further ado, why then should there not be people today who want nothing else but to fight with us against Hitler?' Dr Böttcher asks. 'You should not enter into a pact with the bourgeoisie, even though I, I should add in passing, doubt that the bourgeoisie will continue to exist after the war, either as a class or as a factor of power. But you should reach out your hand to those bourgeois who are honest and of good will and acknowledge their equal rights without prejudice.'

'Equal rights?' says Schröter, outraged. 'The path to socialism . . .'

'. . . is not walked according to a textbook or a firmly outlined itinerary,' Dr Böttcher cuts in. 'What was correct in Russia might be wrong in Germany. Precisely if you are a good Marxist, you should know that the economic conditions of a country and nothing else define the methods by which socialism can be turned into reality.'

'We don't want to reject elements that have been valuable to us in the past,' Wiegand says. 'In our underground struggle we have many fearless, loyal fighters in our ranks who do not come from the working class, and on the other hand – and I assume you know this too – many, sadly all too many, from our own ranks seem to have crossed over to the Nazis, flags flying. Is that true, or is it not?'

'Yes, that is true,' Schröter admits, 'but they were not class-conscious workers.'

'They were workers,' Wiegand says matter-of-factly, 'you can't insist on a distinction on the one hand, and dispute it on the other.'

'If you make common cause with a Catholic priest . . .' Dr Böttcher begins.

'I do,' Schröter says, 'I do, as long as he's against Hitler.'

'. . . then it doesn't make you pious and it doesn't make you an atheist,' Dr Böttcher finishes his sentence, 'and you can still work together. Must differences of a political or philosophical nature always lead to personal estrangement?'

'Not necessarily,' Schröter admits. 'What are you getting at?'

'I'll tell you in a minute,' Dr Böttcher replies. 'So I can assume that the common fight leads to a watering-down of Marxist ideology. Isn't that what you said?'

Schröter ignores the question. 'Because the fight against Hitler forces us together.'

'That's exactly what I wanted to hear,' Dr Böttcher says quickly, with a hint of triumph. 'And afterwards something else will force us together again, but it won't be a fight against, it will be a fight for.'

'For what?'

'For Germany.'

'For Germany?'

'Yes, for Germany. Is that so surprising?'

Schröter rocks his head back and forth. 'You know, when I hear the word "Germany" it always makes me shudder, because I always have military music in my ears and see fireworks in the colours of the national flag.'

'And I hear the *Lieder* of Schubert and the poems of Eichendorff, I see the forests of Thuringia and the valley of the Weser,' Dr

Böttcher replies. 'My dear Schröter, many of you – and you seem to be among them – are like the Jews. Just as the Jews scent anti-Semitism whenever anyone so much as utters the word "Jew", you always hear nationalism when the word Germany is spoken.'

'Words like "homeland" and "patriotism" are not the sole preserve of nationalists,' Wiegand adds. 'Or has it escaped you that the Soviet Union calls your struggle the Great Patriotic War?'

Schröter stares at Wiegand. 'You're not the same person you used to be, Wiegand,' he says.

'That's true,' Wiegand says, 'I've shaken off some of my dogmatism and gained in understanding. I can't see why those who proved their loyalty in the concentration camps should no longer be comrades all of a sudden, comrades in the broadest sense of the word.'

Schröter shrugs. 'You may be right, Wiegand, in fact you probably are right,' he says slowly, 'but that doesn't matter so much now. Let's . . .'

'. . . listen to the Wehrmacht report,' Dr Böttcher says. 'It didn't come through at two or at three, and at four o'clock a girl insisted on cutting her finger.' He gets up and turns on the radio.

'If the Russians would only get a move on,' Schröter says and gestures impatiently. 'The Americans have been remarkably slow lately.'

'Time to be quiet,' Wiegand says.

'. . . at the sound of the gong it was eight p.m.,' comes the voice from the radio. 'This is the repeat of the Wehrmacht report.'

From the Führer's headquarters, sixteenth of April.

This is an announcement by Wehrmacht High Command. In the border territory on the eastern Marches the enemy continued their attacks south-east of Mürzzuschlag and in Sankt Pölten . . .

Dr Böttcher, Wiegand and Schröter sit there, leaning forward. The words drip from the speaker with infinite slowness, like an oily fluid. Everything that is being said is important, certainly, but it isn't what they are waiting for, the words only brush past them like a fleeting breath.

. . . Sankt Pölten has been lost . . .

. . . In Vienna the Soviets have taken our bridgehead south of the Danube . . .

. . . road between Göding and Austerlitz pushed through our front line with superior forces . . .

. . . south-east of Ratibor the enemy breakthrough forced us to . . .

'Now it's time for the front on the Oder,' exclaims Schröter, and gets uneasily to his feet.

. . . After making futile advances yesterday, in the early hours of today the Bolsheviks launched a large-scale attack between the mouth of the Neisse and the Oderbruch after a violent barrage with heavy infantry, tank and air-force fighters. Bitter struggles are under way along the whole of the front . . .

'There we are,' Dr Böttcher says seriously, 'the battle for Berlin is beginning.'

PART II

Until Five Minutes Past Twelve

'If the war is lost, the people will also perish. This fate
is inevitable. There is no need to take into consideration
the basis which the people will need to continue even a
primitive existence. On the contrary, it will be better to
destroy these things ourselves, because this people will
have proved to be the weaker one and the future will
belong solely to the stronger eastern people. Besides, those
who will remain after the battle are only the inferior ones,
for the good ones have all been killed.'

Adolf Hitler
Führer and Reich Chancellor of the Great German Reich
(From the statement of Reich Minister Speer
before the Nuremberg war crimes tribunal)

I

Führer's order of the day, 17 April

To the soldiers at the eastern front –
Asia's last charge will collapse.

Führer's headquarters, 16 April.
The Führer has issued the following order to the soldiers on the eastern front.

Soldiers of the German eastern front!
For the last time our deadly enemies, the Jewish Bolsheviks, have launched their massive forces to the attack. Their aim is to reduce Germany to ruins and to exterminate our people. Many of you soldiers in the east already know the fate which threatens, above all, German women, girls, and children. While the old men and children will be murdered, the women and girls will be reduced to barrack-room whores. The rest will be marched off to Siberia.

We have foreseen this thrust, and since last January have done everything possible to construct a strong front. The enemy will be greeted by massive artillery fire. Gaps in our infantry have been made good by countless new units. Our front is being strengthened by emergency units, newly raised units, and by the Volkssturm.

This time the Bolshevik will meet the ancient fate of Asia – he must and shall bleed to death before the capital of the German Reich.

Whoever fails in his duty at this point in time behaves as a traitor to our people. The regiment or division which abandons its position acts so disgracefully that it must be ashamed before the women and children who are withstanding the terror of bombing in our cities.

Above all, be on your guard against the few treacherous officers and soldiers who, in order to preserve their pitiful lives, fight against us in Russian pay, perhaps even wearing German uniform. Anyone ordering you to retreat will, unless you know him well personally, be immediately arrested and, if necessary, killed on the spot, no matter what rank he may hold.

If every soldier on the eastern front does his duty in the days and weeks which lie ahead, the last assault of Asia will crumple, just as the invasion by our enemies in the West will finally fail, in spite of everything.

Berlin remains German, Vienna will be German again, and Europe will never be Russian.

Form yourselves into a sworn brotherhood, to defend not the empty conception of a fatherland, but your homes, your wives, your children, and with them our future.

In this hour, the whole German people looks to you, my fighters in the east, and only hopes that, thanks to your resolution and fanaticism, thanks to your weapons, and under your leadership, the Bolshevik assault will be choked in a bath of blood.

At this moment, when fate has removed from the earth the greatest war criminal of all time, the turning point of this war will be decided.

Signed: Adolf Hitler

Lassehn folds up the *12-Uhr-Blatt*. The time has come at last, the final battle is beginning, now things will have to be resolved. There is nothing left between the Oder and Berlin, no significant river, no mountain, no eastern wall, only the sandy plain of the Marches with a few lakes and some low ranges of hills, pine forests and heathlands, small towns and quiet villages, harbingers of Berlin, whose huge body stretches far into the landscape of the Marches and, with the ends of its transport network, reaches almost to the Oder.

The images of war rise up in front of him, tanks rolling over fields of wheat and sunflowers, artillery setting villages ablaze, platoons carrying out mass shootings, country roads with distraught people drifting along them carrying their pitiful belongings, and forests. More terrible than a disfigured human body, than a ruined house or an exploded bridge is a scorched and splintered forest, it is like a field of graves whose corpses are not covered by hills, but stretch their naked stumps from the earth in accusation, not decorated by a single leaf, flower or blade of grass, without the smell of resin and moss and blood, without the song of the birds and the rustling of beetles, without colour, nothing but gangrenous, charred, dead earth.

He shivers as if suffering from a violent fever, iron and blood have been sown in a strange soil, and now the crop is coming up here, tanks roll, planes roar over the soil of home, the artillery strikes, the villages and towns collapse into ash, the people travel along the country road as if whipped along by the Furies.

Lassehn sits in the S-Bahn, travelling to Charlottenburg again. He has a number of flyers on him, new ones, still slightly damp with printer's ink, they give off a strong stench. He feels as if everyone must be able to smell this odour that rises so insistently from the inside pocket of his coat, but no one pays any attention. Miracles could have occurred, and no one would have been aware of them, today people's thoughts have slipped beyond their own important selves and the trivial existences of their neighbours and out into the distance, they are turning to the east, where a wide stream is flowing through the Brandenburg March, the last barrier that the great force of a resolute and superior opponent is due to crash through. Just as a moving neon sign along the high façade of a building repeats the words of an advertisement uninterruptedly, so a thought keeps rising into people's consciousness. *The Soviets have reached the Oder for a major attack.*

This thought is indissolubly linked to a question whose answer will decide whether it's better or worse, life or death. *Is Berlin being defended, or has it been declared an open city?*

Admittedly the city has been put in a defensive state, anti-tank ditches have been cut deep into the surrounding land, communication trenches run diagonally across fields and allotments, one-man trenches have been cut into railway embankments, hills and stretches of woodland, machine-gun positions and anti-tank barriers block all access roads, anti-aircraft artillery has zeroed in on ground-level targets – that is all clearly visible, it cannot be ignored, and nor is it supposed to be. The inhabitants have witnessed the construction of the positions and obstacles from the outset, and smiled at them at first, the way one smiles at a pointless game, but soon their faces turned serious, when the game turned into system and method, barricade lined up against barricade, trench lined up behind trench. Still all the measures taken so far can only be seen as precautionary measures to feign determination to the enemy, and therefore to frighten him off; they have been like a gun that you carry to be on the safe side, without ever using it. But now it seems that one is forced to familiarize oneself with this gun, one must load it and keep it ready to be fired, because it could be that the city will really be defended.

Everyone is clear what it means to defend a city like Berlin. Almost three million people live in the crushed, shattered city, hundreds of thousands of women, hundreds of thousands of children, hundreds of thousands of old people, well over half a million foreign forced labourers waiting for the moment of their liberation, their long-suppressed feelings of revenge cranked up more and more as the Allied armies appear at the gates of the city.

It seems impossible that any of those responsible for the city will allow themselves to be involved in the combat. Had Rome, Paris, Florence and Brussels not been spared in order to preserve the irreplaceable cultures of those cities for the world (as they were told with vain and boastful gestures)? Was it not possible that Berlin, the heart of the German Reich, would be declared an open city to keep it from falling victim to complete destruction? Admittedly, in the history of the campaigns of this war there has as yet been not a single example of the National Socialist leadership failing to defend a city, to spare the city and its inhabitants, Aachen and Cologne, Breslau and Posen, Vienna and Königsberg were all furiously defended, even though the enemy was not seriously halted. But Berlin cannot be compared to other cities, which had at the time of their siege a hinterland to which the civilian population could be evacuated. The capital of the Reich no longer has access to a hinterland because the enemy army is inexorably approaching the city from east *and* west, and its aerial weapons are uninterruptedly flying their deadly circles above it.

There are no means of transport any more, there are in fact no streets either, because the railways have been exposed to the constant attacks of the bomber planes, and the streets are under surveillance from the low-flying aircraft.

The Soviets are now moving up towards the east of the city like a dark bank of menacing clouds. It is a distant storm, there is as yet no sound of thunder, but a whirling wind announces the approaching tempest, the lightning still lurks beneath the cloud cover, but an oppressive, sulphurous brightness is spreading over the city.

A stormy sultriness lies over the city. A quivering sense of expectation has taken hold of people, an oscillation between hope of some kind of miracle that has been repeatedly promised and presented as an immediate prospect by the people in charge, and paralysing horror at the prospect of a horrific end. In people's eyes, still apathetic and obtusely resigned only yesterday, all of a sudden there is a weary expression of anxious concern. The continuing air raids have become a daily habit, and as such they are endured almost like a natural necessity. People have become apathetic, lethargy has tangled the volutes of their brains far too much for them to be in a state of despair, because despair always assumes thought, a recognition of circumstances and an ability to assess the situation. But what is currently being prepared in the east, only eighty kilometres from the heart of the city, is something quite different, something new, it is breaking like a hurricane, it is rousing even the most indolent. There is not a single man or woman in this city who does not know what it means to defend an urban centre, street skirmishes, artillery fire, attack from low-flying planes. Some know of it from their own experience in two world wars, when French and Russian cities sank into rubble and ashes house by house, street by street, and the surface of the ground was churned up as if by an enormous bulldozer, the women and the others know it from the weekly newsreels, in which battle and its devastations are shown with a certain gratification, since the cities on the screen are foreign.

The danger that only rains down intermittently on people, and in between always leaves them time to take a breath, to repair the damage as best they can and to conduct a modicum of civilian life, has now become a constant threat, as the flood from the east has begun to rise. People think they can see the many thousands of black cannon muzzles raised in threat, roaring fire and slinging their shells at German positions, they imagine they can hear the roar and rattle of the tracks of the tank squadrons, which are now moving towards the bridgeheads like a crushing steel roller, they imagine they can see the quietly swinging propellers of the Soviet aircraft become whirring silver discs, opening their bomb bays and dropping their payloads on German supply columns, finally they imagine they can see the endless hordes of earth-brown Soviet soldiers, protected by the advancing tanks and sheltered beneath the wings of their aircraft, pouring across the land churned up and torn by their own artillery, and impetuously overwhelming it with loud hurrahs. And what do the German military leaders have to set against this enemy, which is still full of energy and very well armed? In October 1941 Hitler said: 'The enemy lies defeated on the ground, he will never rise up again.'

The divisions entrenched along the Oder and the Neisse have for three years staggered from one defeat to another, they have known nothing but retreats and lost battles, encirclements and envelopments, and they see the many gaps in their ranks being filled by weary and exhausted substitutes, sullen and malnourished, under-equipped and under-trained, and they also know that there is no field hospital behind them and no room to form a new line of resistance.

Lassehn's eye wanders over the ruined city. He had imagined his return to Berlin very differently, but perhaps it's good that it happens like this, that it had to happen like this. Curiously, he has always remained the same, the adolescent slightly wrapped up in himself, unaffected by the life going on around him, which didn't alter him even during his time in the army. But in the few days since he has been back in Berlin a change has taken place in him, he is tougher and more confident, his eyes and ears are more alert. He has met so many people during those few days! It started with Klose, then came Wiegand and Dr Böttcher, then came Mrs Buschkamp and Elisabeth Mattner, the red-faced man and the man with the horn-rimmed glasses, the little man on the S-Bahn, the SS officer and last of all Lucie Wiegand.

Immediately his thoughts leap to the outcome of the previous evening. Everything went well, after everything seemed lost. Even now his heart chills when he lives through that evening once again, the horror when he suddenly sees himself faced with the SS officer, and the paralysing second when all at once two people appear in the darkness of the property and yell a threatening 'Stop!' when he and Lucie Wiegand are about to entrust themselves to the protecting arms of the dark forest. Of course they hadn't stopped, they had run deeper into the forest, they had stumbled over tree roots and got entangled in overhanging branches, their feet had sunk into soft, slippery moss, the two heavy suitcases practically dragged Lassehn to the ground, then they climbed over a garden fence and crouched close together under a rabbit hutch. The two men had probably hesitated for a few seconds before following them, and that had given Lassehn and Lucie their crucial advantage. He had heard footsteps rustling in the undergrowth, and shouts, but then all was quiet. Apparently they had given up the search or carried it on in another direction, perhaps the policeman had broken out in the meantime and had hidden the corpse of the SS man for them, at any rate it had been quiet again for a few minutes.

For a while Lassehn and Lucie Wiegand had squatted under the rabbit hutch, it was very quiet, in the silence and the loneliness of approaching night the only sounds had been the panting of his lungs and the woman's quick breathing. Those few minutes, while their pursuers were close by and looking for them, were filled with more exciting tension for Lassehn than his first meeting with Klose, his encounter with the air-raid warden in Charlottenburg or the red-faced man in the 'Bayernhof', the clashes with the Nazi block warden in Klose's back room or the Untersturmführer in

Wiegand's house. On all those occasions he had always felt a degree of equanimity, because it had just been about him, but here he also had the woman to worry about, who was in some sense under his protection and he had to look after her. So they had crouched there, pressed tightly against one another. Lassehn had set the suitcase in front of him like a parapet, rested one arm tightly around the woman and held the revolver in the other hand.

But nothing had happened. When their lungs had calmed, the silence had engulfed them entirely. They didn't know how long they had crouched there when they got back up, and they had no time to think about it, their lives had just been returned to them, and required immediate decisions. They had left the garden and walked along a few streets. At Zeuthen Station only two carbide lamps were burning because of the electricity blackout, and beneath one of them Lassehn had looked into the woman's face. It was almost motionless, the corners of her mouth fluttered slightly, but otherwise there was nothing in her face but courage and resolution.

After that everything had gone smoothly. The journey on the steam train to Grünau and changing to the S-Bahn went without a hitch. In Schöneweide there was an interruption because of an air-raid warning, the usual evening flight of Mosquito bombers that forced them into the high-rise bunker at Schöneweide Station for an hour, but then there was nothing, they had done it.

Lassehn had registered the details with excessive clarity: stepping with Lucie Wiegand into Klose's back room, where Dr Böttcher, Wiegand and a few other men he doesn't know are sitting, setting down the heavy cases, exhausted and infinitely happy, Wiegand leaping to his feet and pulling his wife to him with a delicate, gentle movement, the conversations falling silent all of a sudden and everyone looking only at the couple, embracing in silence for a few seconds, her head resting against his chest and Wiegand's hands around her twitching back and reassuringly stroking her hair, the men turning away or busying themselves embarrassedly with something, Wiegand leading his wife to the sofa at last, asking questions and receiving answers, walking up to

Lassehn and shaking his hand firmly, Lassehn feeling as though with that handshake he had been accepted into a community as a member deserving equal rights and equal respect, Lucie Wiegand, now that she knew she was in safety, losing her composure and weeping out all her past torments, a little man with a sea-lion moustache coming up to him, looking at him insistently for a long time, shaking his hand brusquely and saying, 'Comrade', then Klose, in his bluff way, bringing the scene to an end with a joke and everyone getting back to their business . . .

Suddenly it occurs to Lassehn that he isn't travelling on the S-Bahn to dream and follow memories, but that he has a goal and a task to fulfil on the way. The train crosses the Humboldthafen and pulls into Lehrter Station. Lassehn takes a few flyers out of his coat pocket, looks around carefully and slips them onto the seat beside him, then he leaves the compartment, immediately disappears into the crowd and boards another carriage. At Bellevue and Savigny-platz he repeats the manoeuvre, and everything goes wonderfully smoothly. When he leaves the train for good in Charlottenburg there are a few more flyers lying around.

A soldier calls to him: 'Hey, you've left your newspaper!'

But Lassehn waves his words generously away. 'I've read them, Comrade, you can keep them!' After all, they're meant for you, he adds to himself.

As Lassehn leaves Charlottenburg Station and crosses Stuttgar-ter Platz, his thoughts run ahead of him, as if to show him the way. Now he must put a section of his life in order, or at least give it some kind of concrete meaning, it is no longer quite as urgent and important as it seemed two days before, but it still has to do with that bit of his life that is not entirely unimportant, and even though no one is interested in people's destinies these days, since everyone is sufficiently preoccupied with themselves and no one has time to address his own destiny, being focused entirely on the problems of the moment that he is living through, even though amidst the general chaos any order would stand out like a calm, still patch of water amidst foaming waves, Lassehn still wants to try.

As he goes down Kaiser-Wilhelm-Strasse again, he feels as if he walked here not exactly two days ago, but a long time in the past, because in those two days many crucial things have changed in him, and it is good that chance has granted him those two days of respite. If he had confronted Irmgard the day before yesterday, he would have done it like someone requesting help and indulgence, tottering along uncertainly and without a goal, and determined to take any opportunity to pull himself back up again. During these two days, however, he has not only found support and a goal, but also achieved a self-confidence that he had lacked for a very long time.

Lassehn doesn't even try to talk to Mrs Buschkamp, he doesn't want anything to hold him up, neither does he have a plan in mind, he strides quickly down the hallway, glances at the door of the concierge's lodge and resolutely climbs the stairs. The stairwell is as dark as a barn, the windows are boarded up with untreated planks, and sparse daylight pierces the cracks.

Then he is standing outside the door to the flat, which bears only the sign 'Niedermeyer'. For a moment bitterness wells up in Lassehn. As a rule, young women tend to be proud of their new names, but with Irmgard that doesn't seem to be the case, she hasn't yet considered it necessary to put up her new name, his name, on the door.

For a few minutes Lassehn pauses outside the flat. This is the moment for which he has been waiting for a year and a half, the moment he has desperately yearned for, which sparkled like a bright star in the dark night, unattainably high above him, and which then became a distant shadow, fading until it could barely be perceived. This moment was a single goal, and was supposed to compensate him for all the suffering and misery, for all the harshness and cruelty of war, which cut him off from everything that made his life worth living, which suppressed all that was good and allowed all that was bad and evil to spill to the surface, this moment was supposed to let him forget his nights of torment, in which a nightmare filled with blood and filth, corpses and destruction rolled over his chest like an enormous weight, or in which despair squatted on him like a nightmare, making him hold his breath with horror, not daring to move. Just a few minutes previously he had thought he had dealt with the memory once and for all. But now it grabs him and trickles into his blood with painful sweetness, the memory of that night, when his inner self, which had almost died, fled from the desert of loneliness and despair into communion with the opposite sex, when he drowned for the first time in a woman's blood, her body arching before him, drawing him in and violently taking possession of him, his consciousness extinguished leaving only warmth and softness, madness and intoxication. He remembered how weariness and new desire had come along, how lust and melting had followed one another, and everything had drowned again in the woman's mouth and her body.

Lassehn shakes the memory away and, like a swimmer rising to the surface with a few powerful thrusts, pushes the button of the doorbell violently three times. The sound of the bright bell brings him sharply back to the present.

The door only opens a tiny crack. 'Can I help you?' a woman's voice asks.

The aunt, Lassehn thinks. He can't make her out, as the stairwell is in complete darkness. 'I'd like to speak to Mrs Lassehn,' he says. Why don't I say my wife? he thinks with surprise.

'Who was that again?' The woman's voice is astonished and forbidding at the same time.

'Mrs Lassehn,' Lassehn repeats, and turns on the light on the stairs, having finally discovered the switch. 'Mrs Irmgard Lassehn.' My name doesn't seem to be very familiar in this house, not even my wife's aunt seems to know it. I'm not even sure my wife does. 'She lives here, doesn't she?' he adds.

'Cer-tain-ly, of course,' the woman's voice drawls. 'Who are you?'

Irmgard's husband! Don't you recognize me? Lassehn wants to say, but he says something quite different, words that force themselves upon him and seem to spring from some dark instinct. 'I've brought a message from her husband.'

The door is opened fully. 'Please, come in.'

Now Lassehn recognizes Mrs Niedermeyer, but it is more of an intellectual than a visual recognition. It is only the fact that this tall, slightly haggard woman with the thin hair parted in the middle and the dark horn-rimmed glasses is coming towards him here in the doorway of her flat that identifies her, in any other surroundings Lassehn wouldn't have recognized her.

'Is Mrs Lassehn at home?' he asks.

'Yes, yes,' Mrs Niedermeyer says, 'she's just lying down for a bit, as she's on the early shift.'

'I'm sorry . . .', Lassehn says with an apologetic gesture. A curious feeling, walking along this corridor again.

'Take a seat for a moment,' Mrs Niedermyer says, and opens a door. 'I'll just call my niece.'

Lassehn steps into the dining room and sits down on a chair. He is effectively visiting himself, he sits calmly here in the dining room and waits for his wife, even though he would have every right to go and see her in her bedroom. Lassehn shrugs to himself, he watches things developing with a mixture of excitement and indifference.

His eye moves around the room as if searching for something. Everything is unchanged, almost unchanged, it's all exactly in its place, even the picture of Hitler is still hanging on the wall, not a cheap little photograph hanging as a kind of alibi in the event of a visit from the block warden, but a big oil painting that shows the Führer in his loose brown coat with the collar open, without a cap and with that artfully contrived lock of hair over his forehead. Only the room itself reveals some small changes. There are a few cracks in the wall, stretching from the ceiling to the floor like thick, black brushstrokes, the stucco and plaster have fallen from the ceiling to reveal the bright-yellow straw of the false ceiling, the windows are nailed up with cardboard, and in one corner a pair of large air-raid suitcases stand ready to be grabbed. Lassehn gives a start when the door opens, but it isn't Irmgard. 'My niece will be right with you,' Mrs Niedermeyer says. 'I'll turn on the radio, it should be the news in a moment.'

Lassehn nods. 'Very kind of you,' he says.

'We're going through a crisis,' Mrs Niedermeyer says almost

with a hint of anxiety, 'but we will survive it, because survive it we must.'

You've borrowed that from Goebbels, Lassehn thinks and bites his lip to keep from smiling. 'Yes, of course,' he says.

'Even in the seven-year war things looked very dangerous for Prussia,' Mrs Niedermeyer continues, 'even then the Russians had reached Berlin, but Prussia still won.'

That's not true, Lassehn thinks, Hubertusburg was at best a setback.

'God is with us,' Mrs Niedermeyer says, raising her voice, 'he swept away the Tsarina Elisabeth . . .'

Now it's Roosevelt's turn, Lassehn thinks, or you aren't a real Nazi cow browsing in the field of the *Völkischer Beobachter*.

'. . . and now the war criminal Roosevelt has died just in time. That is the hand of God!'

Lassehn is by no means a believer, the notion of God has not found a place in his vision of the world, but there is still something in him that refuses to allow the name of God to be dragged down into the depths of such a discussion. He wants to leap up and throw his mockery like pepper in the woman's face. He doesn't do it, he can't do it, but it is still fermenting away inside him too much for him to take everything calmly and without objecting.

'You are leaving out one important difference, madam,' he says. 'Russia at the time was an absolutist state in which the Tsarina's will, her sympathies and her antipathies, were all-defining, just as she decided on the merits of war or peace. The United States, on the other hand, is a democracy, and its president is merely the executive organ of the popular will, so Roosevelt's death will not change anything about the politics of the United States, and hence the psychological effect of his death is greatly overestimated.'

At Lassehn's first words, Mrs Niedermeyer looks up in surprise. Admittedly her voice still wears an expression of conventional courtesy, but with the addition of a slightly sour trait like mildew. Someone casting doubt on an official interpretation of things is something so unusual that it almost takes her breath away, particularly since she isn't prepared for critical objections. She doesn't reply, and half turns towards the radio.

'. . . time for the report on the current situation.

The main event of the last twenty-four hours on our fronts is the major attack by the Soviets which began on Monday morning. On the lower Oder between Fürstenberg and Schwedt, and particularly on either side of Küstrin, severe fighting has broken out after heavy artillery fire with the oncoming Soviet infantry and tank squadrons. The main attacks are currently directed against the Seelow Heights. By conquering these the enemy will attempt to merge into a single bridgehead the previously separate deployment locations of Kienitz and Lebus. But the enemy has so far managed only local incursions, suffering very heavy losses.'

The previous day's Wehrmacht report had settled only for the general term of a major attack, but the complementary report is much more substantial. Lebus, Kienitz, Seelow, Lassehn knows the Oderbruch, these places are more than names to him, he has hiked through that area twice. Seelow is almost fifteen kilometres west of the Oder, from there it is only about thirty-five kilometres to the edge of the city and there is no chance of exploiting the space operationally or retreating, any backward step would give the Soviet tank armies further chances to advance and open the floodgates to their bridgeheads.

The speaker's voice emerges monotonously from the speaker, always uttering the phrases which have been used time and again, and which became threadbare a long time ago.

'. . . our grenadiers, engineers and tank gunners resisted the charge with all their might . . .'

'. . . only local incursions . . .'

'. . . defensive battle with a constant exchange of thrust and counter-thrust . . .'

'. . . some small breakthroughs . . .'

'. . . our tanks thwarted the breach . . .'

'. . . caught in the counter-attack . . .'

From the western front the same tired phrases, the same stereotypical reports which, in spite of some supposed successes on the German side, allow the enemy to press deeper and deeper into the country.

'. . . Saale estuary eastward thrusts have so far only had limited success . . .'

'. . . pressure from the Americans between Bernburg and Chemnitz strong again . . .'

'. . . at Bitterfeld the enemy is pushing towards the Freiberger Mulde . . .'

'. . . Jena-Hainichen road small advances by the Americans . . .'

'. . . failed attempts to advance any further into the territory around Brocken . . .'

My God, Lassehn, who can listen to all of this without fury rising into his face like a hot flame, without his hands twitching for the speaker's throat? Is there a single person in Germany who takes this literally? Haven't they always said: attack averted, incursions thwarted, advances held, resilient defence, nimble avoidance and successful counter-attack? Who still believes any of that, when it's no longer Tobruk and Benghazi, Leningrad and Kharkov, Caen and Le Havre, but Leipzig and Magdeburg, Frankfurt an der Oder and Stettin, Vienna and Bayreuth? Is there still a single person . . .

Yes, there is such a person, she's sitting opposite him, the one with the triangular badge of the NS Women's League on her dried-up chest, which heaves with a sigh at every favourable-sounding phrase, as if the danger has been seen off because our grenadiers are resisting the Soviet attack at Küstrin with all their might, because our troops are bloodily repelling the assaults of our arched fronts between the Ems and the lower Weser.

Lassehn would like to press his hands to his forehead in despair. He could understand someone – paralysed by horror – expecting disaster and willingly bowing their head to receive the annihilating blow, or someone dashing wildly into the fire to be consumed by the flames, but that someone – like this woman – should still be sitting there and sighing with relief goes beyond all comprehension, that is the true myth of the twentieth century.

My God, Lassehn thinks in despair, and now this music, the 'Glow-Worm Idyll' by Paul Lincke, the German master of note-daubing . . . And I lived here for eight days!

'This time the Bolshevik assault will come to nothing,' Mrs Niedermeyer says confidently, 'our best troops are in good positions between the Oder and Berlin, our leaders expected the attack.'

Lassehn can no longer contain himself.

'I admire your short memory, madam,' he says sarcastically.

'What do you mean?' Mrs Niedermeyer asks, slightly piqued.

'Didn't you take exactly the same tranquillizers before and after the last major Russian offensive?' Lassehn asks. 'I have the newspaper here, it's the *Völkischer Beobachter* from December 1944, a famous war reporter wrote from the Vistula front:

> Hard work has been done since the end of the Bolshevik summer offensive. The result is a network of fortresses and anti-tank obstacles of a depth and extent that we have never known in the east.

'And about the East Prussian front another propaganda corps man wrote:

> They are the best regiments ever seen in the east. The anti-tank ditches alone, which run up and down the hills on the East Prussian border territory, have a total length of many thousands of kilometres. The second Soviet offensive against East Prussia is coming. It will be an offensive without surprises.

'On 16 January, four days after the start of the major offensive, Wehrmacht High Command established:

> The assault did not come as a surprise to our troops. The attacking Bolsheviks ran quickly into our defence zones.

'But within only a few days the Russians were standing at the Oder and had encircled the whole of Eastern Prussia. Why should it be any different this time, madam?'

While Lassehn speaks and unfolds the newspapers, Mrs Niedermeyer has risen to her feet and nervously moved some chairs back and forth. 'This is mere pedantry. What are you trying to achieve, young man?'

Lassehn himself doesn't understand that he wanted to convince this woman, he just shrugs and puts the newspapers back in his pocket.

'I trust the Führer!' Mrs Niedermeyer says. 'We are too small to see through his intentions.'

Lassehn is close to exploding, but he doesn't get the chance, because at that moment the door opens.

II

Of middle height, slender but full-figured, confident and self-assured, Irmgard Lassehn, née Niedermeyer, comes in, wearing a colourful dressing gown over her pyjamas. Her hair is soigné, she hasn't neglected to wear powder and lipstick, and the high arches over her eyebrows are delicately drawn.

Lassehn rises to his feet as if pulled up by the strings of a marionette, and stares her in the face. So this is the woman, this is his wife. A strange mixture of feelings takes hold of him, astonishment, helplessness, resistance, estrangement, he runs through the full range of his feelings, but there is one that he can't find: affection. No, there is no affection. A moment ago, when he was standing by the door to the flat, the memory had set his blood racing, but now there is nothing between them. She is a complete stranger to him. She looks at him coolly, with a friendly but matter-of-fact expression, and with measured movements she closes the door behind her, after asking Mrs Niedermeyer, with a brief movement of her eyebrows, to leave the room.

'Heil Hitler!' she says, and raises her right hand slightly in a salute. 'Please, sit where you are!'

She really doesn't recognize me, the thought passes through Lassehn's mind, not even now that I am sitting opposite her, fully exposed to her view.

'So you've brought news of my husband?' Irmgard Lassehn asks, her voice is calm, almost indifferent, without the slightest tremor of anxious agitation.

'Yes,' Lassehn says, controlling his voice, while his heart hammers wildly in his chest. She asks in such an indifferent and matter-of-fact voice as if she were asking about a suitcase at a left-luggage office.

'So, what's happened to him?' There is no impatience in her voice, her beautiful, narrow face beneath the thin layer of bronze powder is still indifferent.

Lassehn hasn't yet worked out what he wants, something in him resists identifying himself, he feels as if he is being lured on a journey into the unknown. 'Your husband is alive,' Lassehn says, avoiding her questioning eye.

'Where is he now?' Irmgard Lassehn asks.

'Very nearby,' Lassehn replies ambiguously.

'Then why doesn't he come himself,' she probes, her voice now a little more animated. 'Is he wounded, or is something else holding him back?'

'That's not very easy to explain,' Lassehn says, evading the question; he wants to gain time, because only now is he beginning to understand the situation he has put himself in, that a return to reality is going to be more difficult the longer he continues this conversation.

'You have a slight look of my husband,' Irmgard Lassehn says. 'At first glance . . .'

'You didn't know him for very long?' Lassehn asks.

'Did he tell you that?' Irmgard Lassehn looks at him quizzically.

Lassehn nods; '. . . in those circumstances a face is easily forgotten,' he goes on, 'even if it was very close to you for eight days.'

'Did he tell you that as well?' Irmgard Lassehn asks again. 'I suppose he doesn't remember what I look like either?'

Lassehn shakes his head. 'He has often described you to me,' he says. 'I don't think he's forgotten.'

Irmgard Lassehn smiles faintly. 'You don't forget a wife, even if you were only married to her for eight days,' she says casually, as if describing a quite impersonal matter, 'but that's not really what I meant.' She pauses and looks past Lassehn. 'But that's not for now.' Her words sound slightly hesitant, as if she expects to be contradicted.

Lassehn gestures vaguely and leans slightly forward.

'Why not? I know your husband very well, we were quite close . . .'

She turns her face slowly towards him again. 'I meant,' she says, resuming the sentence she had just begun, 'whether he remembers what I look like, whether he would recognize me. But you can't know that.'

'Why not?' Lassehn says. 'We talked about it together.'

Irmgard Lassehn nervously clenches her spread fingers. 'And what conclusion did he come to?'

'He was sure that if you met him in some new place he mightn't recognize you,' Lassehn replies. He feels almost numb, something inside him is forcing him to keep the conversation running on the same track, it is as if he is hypnotized by the phenomenon of talking about himself, and hearing himself talk about himself, in the third person.

For a few seconds there is silence between them. Lassehn furtively studies the strange woman who is his wife and reaches the conclusion that he is familiar with neither the details of her face nor those of her body. A memory is sparked when he sees her bare feet, which she has slipped into a pair of sandals, the toenails carefully clipped and painted a deep red. Incredible that one can sit so calmly, almost indifferently, opposite a woman who welcomed you into her bosom for eight long nights, whose breath passed moaning into your mouth, whose body burned like embers against yours . . .

'You were a comrade of my husband's?' Irmgard Lassehn asks after a while.

'Yes,' Lassehn replies and looks her full in the face. 'We were comrades, very good comrades.'

'You stress that so oddly, Mr . . .'

'Winter,' Lassehn finishes her sentence. 'Forgive me, I forgot to introduce myself.'

Irmgard Lassehn notes the name with a brief nod of her head. 'You stress that so oddly, Mr Winter,' she repeats.

I really did, Lassehn thinks, not deliberately, because I would like to find out some things about myself from her. 'Oddly?'

'As . . . as if you were trying to hint at something,' she says, explaining her question, and there is a brief flicker in the back of her eyes as if something is lurking there.

'I just meant that . . . that Joachim and I talked about a lot,' he says stoutly, 'which is how I know some things . . .'

Irmgard Lassehn suddenly leans forward. 'What do you know?' she asks quickly, almost threateningly.

'I meant that I know you, madam, even though you are a complete stranger to me,' Lassehn replies. 'It sounds paradoxical, but that's how it is.' Inside him a feeling wells up, a strange mixture of cheerfulness and grief.

Irmgard leans back again and smiles ironically. 'A few years ago I happened to read a book by Leonhard Frank, *Karl und Anna*, and it was about two soldiers who were also good, very good comrades. Do you know the book?'

'No,' Lassehn replies. 'Why are you telling me this?'

'One of the two soldiers was married as well,' Irmgard Lassehn goes on, ignoring his question, 'and he told his friends everything about his wife, including the most intimate details of their conjugal life. Do you understand, Mr Winter?'

Lassehn nods. 'I understand, but Joachim didn't go into details of that kind,' he says, as if pardoning himself.

'So just how confiding was my dear husband?' Ironic wrinkles appear around her mouth. 'You can tell me everything, Mr Winter. You won't hurt me, or make me annoyed.'

'Why do you want to know?' Lassehn asks truculently.

'Psychological interest to some extent,' she replies.

The cheerfulness prompted by the tragi-comedy of the situation fades away. 'You speak of your marriage as if it were a trivial matter, madam,' he says irritably.

Irmgard Lassehn shrugs. 'You seem to be of the opinion, Mr Winter,' she replies, 'that an eight-day marriage establishes a lasting state, or that it is a guarantee of eternal love. You are remarkably naïve, and in that, incidentally, you are like my husband, who also saw the relationship between the sexes as a mystery.'

'Isn't it?' Lassehn asks.

Irmgard Lassehn smiles, showing her teeth. 'I see it as a biological matter,' she says, as if instructing him.

So that's what you're like, Lassehn thinks, and looks again at her feet, delicate, slender feet, immaculately white with a hint of tender pink, fine veins, smooth toes, slim ankles, springing on the tips of the toes and stretching their muscles. Lassehn sees these feet in front of him like a vision, the way they pushed themselves out of bed in the morning, established a connection with the world outside the bed, beautiful, slender, girlish feet. And that is what's left, no face, no body, no soul, just a pair of beautiful, slender, girlish feet.

Lassehn suddenly pulls himself together. 'I just don't understand why you married Joachim. You don't need to get married for the sake of the . . . biological function.'

Irmgard Lassehn gives him a superior look. 'The biological functions, Mr Winter, are closely linked to material things, in case you are not aware. To put it in concrete terms: a soldier who goes back to the front is closer to death than life, so a girl must logically expect that he can no longer fulfil the obligations produced by the relationship. Now do you understand?'

Lassehn nods. 'Completely, madam.' He feels anger rising up inside him, anger that is no longer far from hatred. So this is my wife, a synthesis of lust and a sense of commerce. Is that possible, is there nothing else there? Have I come here to argue about love and marriage? No, I'm here to gain some clarity . . .

'I don't see why we women always want to take the risk,' she goes on. 'We women are no longer the weaker sex, and in material terms we have also become more independent, but unfortunately nature has seen to it that in biological terms the greater burden falls on us, which is why we are allowed to stay out of harm's way.'

'So your marriage to Lassehn was, if I may put it this way, a safety valve,' Lassehn says.

'You could say that,' Irmgard Lassehn confirms. 'Under normal circumstances I probably wouldn't have married, a friendship would have done just as well.'

Lassehn keeps his arms clasped behind his back and avoids his wife's eye. 'I know from Joachim that he put much more into this marriage, it wasn't just an erotic experience for him.'

'Did he talk about it?' she asks, and smiles ironically.

'Of course, otherwise I wouldn't be able to claim as much.'

'Interesting,' Irmgard Lassehn says, and raises her eyebrows in surprise.

'You don't seem to understand,' Lassehn says almost bitterly, 'what that means. He gave you a soul, you only gave him your body, a very uneven – if you'll forgive me – deal.'

Irmgard Lassehn leans far back in her chair and crosses her legs. 'Do you read a lot of romantic novels, Mr Winter?'

Lassehn stares at her. The dressing gown has parted a little to show the beginning of her full breasts and reveal her slender neck, but nothing stirs in Lassehn. The breasts that seem to be breathing there under her dressing gown, the body hidden under the thin, colourful silk, are only part of a wax figure.

'If I may be allowed to ask a question, madam,' Lassehn says at last.

Irmgard Lassehn gestures her consent.

'Why did you marry him?' he asks, and quickly corrects himself. 'I don't mean the legal formality, but . . .' He falls into an embarrassed silence, having forgotten for a moment that he is facing his wife in the guise of a complete stranger, and that he therefore mustn't ask excessively probing questions.

'Well?' Irmgard Lassehn says encouragingly. 'Feel free to ask, I'm not a prude, and I'll also be granting you the pleasure of an erotic conversation.'

Lassehn gives himself a push. 'You know what I mean, madam,' he says, and pauses for a few seconds, but Irmgard Lassehn doesn't come to his assistance, she looks at him expectantly and rocks her crossed leg back and forth. 'Why you took Joachim, of all people . . .' Lassehn takes a deep breath and violently expels the question – 'into your bed?', he exclaims uncontrollably.

Irmgard Lassehn isn't angry, she still has a superior smile on her face. 'You seem to be of the opinion,' she says slowly, 'that I made a bad choice.'

'Not at all,' Lassehn disagrees, 'I meant something else.'

'Which is?' Irmgard Lassehn doesn't look at him, she rocks her foot back and forth, legs still crossed, and swings it from side to side, a motion designed to indicate her complete impartiality.

'I mean that you and Joachim are complete opposites, that you aren't suited to one another at all,' he says, 'and since I know that Joachim is very passive by nature, I must assume that you took the initiative.'

'You're not far off the mark, psychologist that you are,' Irmgard Lassehn says. 'So to answer your question, in which you seem to take so keen an interest: my husband was very much alone at the time, he was rather desperate, and I felt sorry for him, that was it, all the rest happened of its own accord. The fact that I married him, well, that was . . . how did you put it so beautifully? Oh, yes, a safety valve.'

'So not love?' Lassehn repeats the question and gives her a penetrating look.

'All these questions of yours are getting tiresome,' Irmgard Lassehn says, and throws back a lock of hair that has fallen onto her forehead with a violent shake of her head.

Lassehn senses that the conversation has reached a crucial point, and that the speeches, questions and answers that they exchanged were just the preliminary skirmish.

'But I haven't nearly finished,' he says harshly.

Irmgard speaks violently for the first time. 'What's that supposed to mean?'

'You'll hear in a moment!'

Irmgard Lassehn gets to her feet. 'I don't want to hear anything more,' she says impatiently, 'I've spent far too much time with you already. There's just one question that I would like to have answered, and then you can go. Where is my husband right now?'

'Your touching concern does you proud. Has that question only just occurred to you?' Lassehn mocks, then he too stands up and walks up to the woman, looks her attentively in the face and then says slowly, 'He's standing in front of you, Irma.'

'Stop this nonsense,' Irma Lassehn commands, pulling away from him. 'If you absolutely need something sentimental, then make yourself comfortable, young man, there are plenty of women and girls around who don't have a man and who would be happy to make you up a nice soft bed, pressing you to their forlorn hearts, but please leave me in peace. Or perhaps my husband has described his nights with me with such fire that you are absolutely determined to go to bed with me?'

Lassehn is hurled back and forth by wild emotions, hatred, rage, contempt, fury, his hand twitches as if in spasm, he has to fight with himself to make sure that it doesn't fly into her pretty, impertinent face.

'I am Joachim Lassehn,' he says, struggling to control his voice. 'Do you really not recognize me?'

Irmgard Lassehn bursts out laughing. 'So you've got the formula from *Karl und Anna*, and you want to follow that, you want to present yourself as the woman's husband because her fool of a husband has blurted out their marital secrets.' She laughs again. 'That's not going to work with me, no sir, not me.'

Lassehn stands there in confusion for a moment, suddenly seeing that a fiction, once it has become a concrete reality, can no longer be revoked, least of all by the truth.

'I really am Joachim Lassehn, Irma,' he says again.

'Don't talk such nonsense,' Irmgard Lassehn says impatiently. 'You do bear a certain resemblance to my husband, I grant you, and you want to exploit that now.'

'I don't want to exploit anything,' Lassehn says angrily. 'You needn't imagine that I'm after my so-called conjugal rights, you can happily go on using your bed on your own, or sharing it with whoever you like . . .'

'Shut up!' Irmgard Lassehn breaks in.

'. . . our marriage is only on paper anyway,' Lassehn continues unperturbed, 'and once this glorious war is over we will have a legal dispute to sort out.'

The words do make a certain impression on the young woman, but she persists in her refusal to acknowledge that Lassehn is her husband. 'You are not my husband,' she says, 'I just don't believe you.'

Lassehn shrugs, all at once he sees no point in identifying himself as Irmgard's husband, all of a sudden he doesn't understand what he's doing here, why he took this journey to Charlottenburg. 'In the end I don't really care whether you believe me or not . . .,' he begins listlessly.

'If you really are my husband,' Irmgard Lassehn interrupts, 'then I'm sure you have papers that will identify you as Joachim Lassehn.'

The papers are long gone, Lassehn thinks, I'm now Horst Winter from Strasburg in the Uckermark, I forgot that I'm an outlaw who can't get back to his former life, that in the moment when I became an outlaw I died to my old world, that I have to make my own life with my new papers, that I can have no relationship with my former self.

'My papers all went to hell,' he says. 'But I couldn't have guessed that I would need to identify myself to my own wife.'

'Just a moment,' Irmgard Lassehn interrupts him and opens the door. 'Aunt Else, come here, please.'

'What are you trying to do?' Without meaning to, he has addressed her formally again. Irmgard Lassehn doesn't need to reply, because Mrs Niedermeyer comes in and looks back and forth between the two.

'What is it, Irmy?'

'Take a good look at this gentleman, Aunt Else,' Irmgard Lassehn says, 'look at him very closely.'

'What's going on, Irmy?' Mrs Niedermeyer says, amazed. 'You know I don't enjoy pranks.'

'Please, examine him very closely,' Irmgard Lassehn says impatiently. Mrs Niedermeyer has stopped contradicting her, she is apparently used to submitting to the will of her niece, she looks at Lassehn with great attention and then turns back to Irmgard Lassehn. 'And now?' she asks.

'Doesn't anything strike you, Aunt Else?' Irmgard Lassehn asks.

'Not that I can think of,' Mrs Niedermeyer replies.

'This gentleman says he's my husband,' Irmgard Lassehn now says.

Mrs Niedermeyer gives Lassehn another scrutinizing glance.

'He looks not unlike your husband, Irmy,' she says, 'but that's all.'

'Thanks, Aunty,' Irmgard Lassehn says and smiles with a superior air. 'Leave us alone again.'

'Two to one, one-nil at half-time,' Irmgard Lassehn says triumphantly after Mrs Niedermeyer has left the room. 'What do you say now, sir?'

Lassehn shrugs. 'If *you* don't recognize me,' he says, 'then your aunt isn't going to, that much is clear. You could have spared her that test.'

Irmgard Lassehn waves away his objection. 'Let's talk in concrete terms and without beating around the bush.'

'My opinion exactly,' Lassehn concurs.

'I see that we agree for the first time,' Irmgard Lassehn says. 'Now tell me clearly and briefly what you want from me.'

'Certainty about my marriage, nothing more or less,' Lassehn replies.

'Don't start all that again,' Irmgard Lassehn says irritably. 'If you really are my husband, why didn't you say so straight away? Why did you go through that whole rigmarole?'

'I can't exactly say what it was that made me do that,' Lassehn replies, 'but when I'd taken the first few steps there was no going back, but I didn't want to continue because you didn't recognize me, you treated me like a stranger and talked about me in the third person. You gave me the certainty I needed.'

'Not that I was aware of,' Irmgard Lassehn says.

'You proved to me that our marriage, if we want to give that name to the eight days that we spent together, was only a small episode in your life, no more significant than any of your earlier friendships. You don't need to get impatient, our discussion will soon be over. I would just like to repeat the question I asked before: so there was no love?'

Irmgard Lassehn's mouth twists into a broad smile. 'What sort of question is that? With or without love, you got your money's worth, didn't you?'

She speaks to him informally for the first time, and it hits Lassehn like a slap in the face. 'Thanks,' he says, 'that was quite clear.'

Irmgard Lassehn walks up to him. 'If you really are Joachim Lassehn,' she says, 'then there's an unmistakeable distinguishing feature, too stupid of me not to have thought of it before. You have a small scar behind your left ear, it's in the shape of a spiral, and quite honestly that is the only mark that I remember.'

Lassehn recoils. 'I don't need to be identified by my wife,' he says bitterly. 'Stop it!'

But Irmgard Lassehn refuses to be deterred, she brushes his hair back behind his left ear and feels the spot, then she takes a few steps back and looks Lassehn up and down again. 'You really are Joachim,' she says quietly. 'It was mean of you to creep in here like that!' she suddenly shrieks. 'What were you thinking of?'

Lassehn stares at her. 'What were *you* thinking when you married me?,' he replies. 'When you took me into your bed, which was still warm from someone else?'

'I don't have to answer you,' Irmgard Lassehn says dismissively and throws back her head. 'Certainly not about my past.'

'And where is the child?' Lassehn asks all of a sudden.

'What child?'

'The one you were pregnant with when we got married!'

'How do you know about that?' Irmgard flares up.

'I know, that should be enough for you,' Lassehn says casually. 'Well?'

Irmgard Lassehn paces back and forth for a moment, then leans against the sideboard and fiddles with the belt of her dressing gown. 'In the eighth month I had a miscarriage when the house next door was hit by a bomb. Is there anything else you want to know?'

Lassehn shakes his head. The experience of those eight days, which previously burned within him every time it came to mind, has now shrunk down for him into the insignificant encounter that it was for Irmgard, it has lost the mysterious, marvellous power that forces the sexes together, it has shed all its aura of tenderness, and all that remains is a collision of two bodies. Lassehn listens within himself, but there is no voice of regret, he is not in despair, he is barely disappointed, he didn't even come here unprepared.

Irmgard Lassehn folds her arms over her chest. 'So what happens now, husband of mine?' she asks. Where does that leave us?'

'It leaves everything just as it was,' Lassehn replies, 'consider my visit today as something that didn't happen, live your life just as before, let's see what happens later.'

'Later?'

'Yes, after the final victory.'

There is a brief pause. Lassehn and Irmgard stand facing one another, their posture is by no means hostile, more one of hesitant politeness, of amicable negotiation, they are only three steps apart, but they can't walk those three steps because the distance is impassable, a high wall has been erected between them.

'When you got into the train for front soldiers on leave at Zoo Station,' Irmgard Lassehn begins at last, 'our marriage was basically over already as far as I was concerned, I went home, and everything was as it had been before I met you, nothing was left, and when I went to bed in the evening, something was missing, but it wasn't you, in fact, it was simply . . . You must think I'm shameless now, Joachim, but I'm telling you the way it is, it's just how I am, and many of my friends are no different. Have you got a moment?'

Lassehn just nods.

'Then I'll quickly tell you how I ended up like this, and you may see it as an excuse or an explanation, just as you wish. For a woman the first experience is usually crucial for her later life, and even if she manages to detach herself from it, she never rids herself of it entirely. And that was how it was with me. When I left school,

I went to do labour service with our whole class, at a camp near Lauenburg in Pomerania, that is to say we only slept at the camp, by day we worked with the farmers. Very close by was a pilots' flying school for Hitler Youth glider pilots who were being trained to fly propeller planes. You can imagine the rest, the pilots made a regular sport of invading us, as they called it. At first we defended ourselves, but in the end we let them do what they wanted. I don't mean to say that it was like that in all the camps, but it was in ours. Two of the girls hanged themselves when they realized they were pregnant, a few became incurably frigid, but the others, and I was one of them, were robust enough to survive it, it was how it had to be in the end, it was a part of everything, like eating and drinking, sleeping and the digestive process. There you have the reason why I see so-called love as a purely biological function. You're unlucky, my dear boy, you don't fit with our times, you're too soft, too romantic, there are no sufferings of young Werther these days, the sufferings of today's Werthers aren't treated with the soul, but with Protargol and sulphonamides.'

Lassehn has been listening without losing his composure. He has so far resisted the idea, but now he must admit to himself that for Irmgard he was just a man picked at random, that for her their marriage on leave was just an episode.

'You can't be thinking of continuing or resuming our marriage?' she asks.

'I didn't come here to continue or resume anything,' Lassehn replies. 'I was here a few days ago, but I didn't see you. It was probably just as well, because I might have been able to pick up where I left off, but that's over now, it doesn't work any more. And you've been a great help to me.'

'I have?'

'Yes, you have, by thoroughly destroying at last the legend that still lived in me,' Lassehn replies. 'And that's good, I couldn't live with you now, even if I wanted to, but I don't want to.' He produces a few dull chuckles from his throat. 'There are so many women and girls in Berlin who are walking around without a husband, and who would happily take me to bed. Isn't that what you said a little while ago? So why should it be you, just because you happen to be my wife?'

Irmgard Lassehn shrugs. 'Do what you like.'

'If we're just performing biological functions, it doesn't really matter in the end who with,' he goes on, 'always providing, of course, that racial principles are respected.'

'Stop that!' Irmgard Lassehn says sharply.

'Obviously I wouldn't do it with a Jewess or a Negress,' Lassehn says sarcastically, 'my Aryan body would certainly suffer as a result. But what is the situation, in fact? I can sleep with a Japanese woman, and she is of a foreign race, but she's allied with us politically and militarily. So we turn a blind eye to that?'

'What possesses you to talk about race!' Irmgard Lassehn rages. 'Race is the basis of all National Socialist doctrine, you can't mess with that.'

'Just look,' Lassehn says, 'I didn't even know you were in the Party. Next time, if there should ever be a next time, put your Party badge on your dressing gown so that we know straight away what we're dealing with.'

'I am in the Party,' Irmgard Lassehn replies, rattled, and for the first time her face blushes a deep red, 'but racial ideas are by no means restricted to Party membership, they're a universal property of our people.'

'I'm sure you've made an extensive study of the emotions of the mass of the people,' Lassehn smiles, 'so that you can deliver such a comprehensive judgement.'

'Let's finish this conversation here, anyone who doesn't grasp things through language of the blood won't understand with reason either. And besides . . . I see that you're in civilian clothes.'

'I was dismissed from the Wehrmacht,' Lassehn says quickly.

'I don't believe you,' Irmgard Lassehn replies, and looks at him quizzically. 'Since the twelfth of January no one has been dismissed, I happen to be well informed on that one, I'm a staff assistant at High Command. You can't pull the wool over my eyes.'

Time to get away, Lassehn thinks, it's starting to get dangerous. He thinks about the warning against getting involved in private matters, in 99 per cent of cases it leads to complications. And this is a bit much all at once: staff assistant, Party member, personal enmity.

'What do you think of me, Irma!' he cries with mock fury.

'You've abandoned your unit,' she says excitedly. 'Good Christ! In the hour of their greatest danger . . . I'm ashamed of you!'

'No need,' Lassehn replies, unmoved, 'everyone is ashamed on his own behalf, I'm ashamed of my cowardice in not putting an end to it before, you for being an accomplice with a wretched gang of criminals.'

Irmgard Lassehn furiously stamps her feet. 'You're crazy!', she cries. 'Only someone who has lost his senses could speak like that – or someone who is a traitor.'

'What you call treason is in reality the fulfilment of human obligation,' Lassehn exclaims, 'but you don't understand that, you can't understand it. Your conscience has been systematically dulled, numbed, confused, your ears have been tuned only to a single note, your eyes fixed on a single point, you think you are living when in fact you are being lived, you think you are thinking, but you are merely thinking machines . . .'

'Stop it!' says Irmgard Lassehn angrily.

A harsh smile forms on Lassehn's lips. 'That's your life,' he continues unperturbed, 'submitting to orders, disconnecting your own will completely, becoming a cog in the murderous machinery, that's your life, the absolute refusal to shape it meaningfully yourself and determine the course of your existence. You have become an apathetic and basically an amorphous mass . . .'

'I don't want to hear any more of this!' Irmgard Lassehn shrieks. 'I – don't – want – to – hear – any – more – of – this!'

'Does it ring in your ears like the trumpets of the Day of Judgement?,' Lassehn asks insistently. 'Does it break through the armour of emotionlessness that you think is invulnerable? Is there a spark of humanity in you that is fanned and burning you inside?'

'Whether you are right or not is quite irrelevant,' Irmgard Lassehn says, and looks at him menacingly. 'We are where we are and it doesn't matter how we got there. There's only one thing to do, which is to fight and fight again to avert the fate that threatens us.'

Lassehn smiles malevolently. 'Because you have committed a murder, in order to remain undiscovered you must commit a second to escape retaliation, you must line them up, murder after murder, there is no turning back until . . . yes, until it's your turn.'

'There is no agreement between us,' says Irmgard Lassehn.

'Yes,' Lassehn agrees, 'there is none. Where is my suitcase? I would like to take it with me.'

She looks at him, a hard, piercing gaze suddenly in her eyes. 'Personal concerns must now be silenced,' she says slowly as if to give her words a particular significance. 'I will give you up to the next patrol, I will not let you out of my sight. If we have reached a situation whereby the enemy is deep within our country, then it's the fault of people like you.'

Lassehn laughs darkly a couple of times. Then he says threateningly, 'My dear child, I have a revolver with six bullets in it.' He takes the gun out of his pocket and holds it in the flat of his hand. 'It would be a shame to damage that body of yours, which is so gifted in the art of love.'

Irmgard Lassehn takes a step back, her face has turned completely pale, as if the rouge and powder had been absorbed by her skin.

'Where is my suitcase?' Lassehn asks and puts the revolver in his right hand.

'In the hall,' Irmgard Lassehn says, her lips trembling. 'We put it . . .'

'Fine,' Lassehn says dismissively and walks slowly to the door. 'If you try to open the window and set your people on me, that would mean certain death for me. As a matter of fact I've brought a few of my own people with me, they're waiting in the hallway of the building and on the other side of the street, they're reckless chaps and excellent shots. It would be a good idea for you to moderate your behaviour accordingly.'

Irmgard Lassehn leans exhaustedly against the gable. 'Go,' she says, her voice fading away. 'Please go!'

At that moment Lassehn almost feels a little sorry for her, he turns round again in the doorway. 'How should I take my leave of you now?,' he asks. 'See you? No, I don't want to see you again, and you probably don't want to either. Good day to you?' He laughs again briefly. 'You won't experience any good days in the Third Reich once the Russian guns are firing at Berlin. So: Heil Hitler!'

III

19 April

'What follows is a speech by Reich Minister Dr Goebbels on the eve of the Führer's birthday.'

For a few seconds the only sound is the hum of the electrical current, then the nasal Rhineland voice begins:

'At the moment of the war when – so it seems – all forces of hate and destruction have been gathered once again, perhaps for the final time, in the west, the east, the south-east, and the south, seeking to break through our front and give the death blow to the Reich, I once again speak to the German people on the eve of 20 April about the Führer, just as I have done every year since 1933.

I can only say that the age, in all its dark and wounded greatness, has found its only worthy representative in the Führer. The fact that Germany yet lives, that Europe and the Western world, with their culture and civilization, have not yet fallen into the dark abyss that looms before us, is thanks to him alone. He will be the man of this century.

But if it is manly and German, as Führer of a great and brave people to depend wholly on oneself in this struggle, relying on one's own strength and certainty as well as the help of God in the face of an enemy who threatens with overwhelming numbers, to fight rather than to capitulate, then it is just as manly and German for a people to follow such a Führer, unconditionally and loyally, without excuse or reservation, to shake off all feelings of weakness and uncertainty, to trust in the good star that is above him and us all. This is all the truer when that star at times is covered by a black

353

cloud. Misfortune must not make us cowardly, but rather resistant, never giving a mocking watching world the appearance of wavering. Rather than hoisting the white flag of surrender that the enemy expects, raise the old swastika banner of a fanatic and wild resistance, thanking God again and again for giving us a true leader for these terrible times.

The war is nearing its end. The insanity that the enemy powers have unleashed on humanity has gone beyond all bounds. Fate has taken the head of the enemy conspiracy. It is the same fate that the Führer escaped on 20 July 1944, amidst the dead, the wounded and the ruins, so that he could finish his work – through pain and trials it is true, but nonetheless as providence ordained. The German people gave birth to him, they chose him, by free election they made him Führer. They know his works of peace and now want to bear and fight the war that was forced upon him until its successful conclusion. Who else could show us the way out of the global crisis but the Führer. His work is the work of order! His enemies can only oppose him with a devil's work of anarchy and the devastation of human beings and whole nations.

So if the world still lives, and not only our world but the rest of it as well, whom has it to thank other than the Führer? It may defame and slander him today, persecuting him with its base hatred, but it will have to revise this standpoint or bitterly regret it! He is the core of resistance to the collapse of the world. He is Germany's bravest heart and our people's most passionate will. I permit myself to make a judgement that must be made today: if the nation still breathes, if it still has the chance of victory, if there is still an escape from the deadly danger it faces – it is thanks to him.

We look to him filled with hope and with a deep, unshakeable faith. We stand behind him with fortitude and courage: soldier and civilian, man, woman and child – a people determined to do all to defend its life and honour.

We stand with him, as he stands with us – in Germanic loyalty as we have sworn, as we shall fulfil. We do not need to tell him, for he knows and must know: Führer command! We will follow! We feel him in us and around us. God give him strength and health and preserve him from every danger. We will do the rest.

Germany is still the land of loyalty. It will celebrate its greatest triumphs in the midst of danger. Never will history record that in these days a people deserted its Führer or a Führer deserted his people. And that is victory. We have often wished the Führer in happy times our best on this evening. Today in the midst of suffering and danger, our greeting is much deeper and more profound. May he remain what he is to us and always was – our Hitler!

Silence falls for a few seconds.

'So, now you know,' Klose says, and turns off the radio as the first notes of the Badenweiler March sound.

In spite of the time of the evening and the approaching air-raid warning, Klose's restaurant is quite full, but these are not random guests, not locals or passing trade. The houses in the immediate surroundings have been destroyed, and only someone with urgent business to attend to would be out and about. As no one tends to live in the ruined houses, and people who are on the road and already have the wail of the sirens ringing in their ears do not take the time to drink a glass of stale wartime beer, Oskar Klose's spring of Schultheiss beer on the street called Am Schlesischen Bahnhof should actually be empty.

It isn't. Klose leans on the bar with his arms folded and lets his eye wander around, but it is not the dismissive eye of a business-minded landlord, mentally adding up the number of pints poured and wondering whether it's time to change the barrel, as the pressure in the tap is already weak, and neither is it the impatient eye of a tired and haggard businessman who wishes his guests would clear the hell out so that he can close the place up and have a bit of rest, no: Klose looks at his guests like a father at his successful children who have gathered around him once again.

Sitting at the tables on the right-hand side of the restaurant are Dr Böttcher, Wiegand, Schröter, Lassehn, Lucie Wiegand and six other people, the light-blonde hair of a young girl being particularly striking.

'Having heard', Dr Böttcher says, leaning back in his chair, 'that victory will be ours because we have the Führer, let us now discuss the measures that we must take. We understand that our forces are far too weak to form an organized counter-movement, we lack weapons, we lack people, and above all we lack knowledge about how many resistance groups there are in Berlin. The obstacles in the way of sharing information or collaborating on a larger scale are too great to be overcome in the present circumstances. Today we do have a comrade from another group among us, Comrade Rumpel-stiltskin, but the connection with him and his group has only come into being by chance, and even in the future we have no option but to go on working in isolation and deliberately restricting ourselves.

'We are very well aware that *we* will not bring about the fall of the regime, that the push that throws Nazism from the throne must come from without. It has been clear to us for a long time that leadership can no longer come from within, and that realization, which began to dawn on many of us long before the war, has shifted the focus of our work, it could no longer be aimed directly at the removal of Hitler's dictatorship, as the balance of power was too unequal. The German people as a whole was sadly not an echo chamber for our efforts, it did not have the political insight to rec-ognize where the politics of the so-called Third Reich was headed. The war has changed little about that, the hope that many placed in the army was misplaced, not a single case of mutiny or the insubor-dination of a closed unit is known to us. This bitter realization has led some to withdraw in a spirit of resignation, but we, continuing our illegal struggle, have had to settle for the paralysis of very small parts of the Party's power apparatus. It was clear that our few flyers were not a match for the million-strong editions of the newspa-pers, and we were also aware that badly installed and inadequately equipped short-wave transmitters, constantly pursued by the Gestapo detector vans, could not drown out the big transmitters of the state propaganda machine. But we may claim on our own behalf that our work has not been entirely in vain. Every flyer, every broadcast, every word has been a thorn in the confidence, the self-certainty of the bourgeoisie, it has led many a worker to reduce his performance, it has weakened the fighting power of many a soldier. I would like to compare our work with the labour of ter-mites, which can hollow out a wooden house from the ground up and from within, and make it ready for collapse.

'If you ask me why I am talking about this now, and also touching upon the past, even though the present is a matter of urgency, my answer is this: because we have reached a crucial turning point. We are in the last phase of the war, the Russians are about to launch a thrust against Berlin, and there is no doubt that they will reach our city in a few days. Here is the *Nachtausgabe* with today's Wehrmacht report:

"From the Führer's headquarters, 19 April

Supreme Command of the Wehrmacht reports:
On the third day of the big defensive battle outside Berlin, the Bolsheviks threw men and materiel into the battle on a scale never previously known. Our brave troops, following the example of their officers, have withstood the mass charge by the enemy and thwarted all attempts to break through. South of Frankfurt our units maintained their positions against far superior Soviet forces. The Bolsheviks who had advanced on both sides of Seelow to the east of Müncheberg were blocked by immediate counter-thrusts. South of Wriezen our troops halted the attacking enemy after serious fighting. According to incomplete reports 218 tanks were destroyed yesterday.

West of the Lausitzer Neisse attacked the Bolsheviks with all available forces. In spite of stubborn resistance by our divisions, after heavy fighting with the loss of numerous tanks north of Görlitz and north-west of Weisswasser the enemy was able to drive narrow wedges into the space east of Bautzen and past the Spree on either side of Spremberg."

'I assume you hold the map of the Brandenburg Marches in your head, to know what that means. Wriezen and Müncheberg are only about fifty kilometres from the city centre, only twenty-five kilometres from the edge of the city, Bautzen and Spremberg means that Berlin is surrounded from the south. In five and a half years of war we have had ample opportunities to study the terminology of the Wehrmacht reports. From the history of the eastern, western and African campaigns we know exactly what turns of phrase such as "big defensive battle", "men and materiel on a scale never previously known" and "superior Soviet forces" should be taken to mean. As we can no longer use the expanse of territory as an operational weapon and – to quote Goebbels – can no longer use it like a boxer for footwork, it is clear what this means: the end. To show that the High Command has not only too optimistic a view of the situation but might be said to be deliberately falsifying it, I need only mention one example.'

Dr Böttcher pauses for a few seconds and takes a copy of the *Völkischer Beobachter* out of his pocket. 'A commentary on the Wehrmacht report says among other things: "Overall the enemy has lost over 260 tanks on the first day of the attack, or more than half of its deployment." More than half of its deployment, that would mean that the Russians entered the battle for Berlin with about five hundred tanks.'

Dr Böttcher curls his lips into a little smile and folds up the paper again. 'From a reliable source – namely Radio Moscow – I know that in the battle for Berlin the Russians have not more than five hundred tanks, but more than four thousand, that they have over four thousand fighter planes, that they began the battle with barrage fire from twenty-two thousand cannon, and that two army groups are attacking, the Zhukov Group, which is advancing frontally on Berlin, and the Konev Group, which is thrusting past Berlin to the south. That is the situation.'

'And what conclusions do we draw from that?' Schröter exclaims.

'I was about to come to that,' Dr Böttcher replies. 'I see our task as being to make the fighting troops, above all the Volkssturm, understand the futility of any further resistance, and even, where possible, of forming active resistance groups against the SS to avoid street battles. Unfortunately we must expect that the slogan of "fighting to the last knife" will find resonance among the Hitler Youth. If not many Hitler Youth follow that slogan, we must always bear in mind that a single rocket launcher can attract massive artillery or mortar fire. In such cases we should attempt to disarm the Hitler Youth, by force if necessary.'

Dr Böttcher clears his throat and looks from one to the other.

'Comrades! The hour of liberation approaches, but the few days that still separate us from it may well be the most difficult of our entire underground struggle. We must be on our guard against Gestapo spies and the hunters of the military police, we should expect desperate acts by the Nazi high-ups. The artillery fire, the bombs and the machine-gun bullets of our liberators threaten us just as much as anyone else, so we are doubly exposed to danger, but that should not keep us for a minute from carrying out all the things we have recognized as our duty. Afterwards Comrade Wiegand will assign you your special tasks.'

Klose draws attention to himself by pointing at the floor.

Dr Böttcher nods to him. 'Yes, correct. Until further notice the group will meet here at Klose's, since my flat seems to be under observation. As soon as the street battles begin, Klose has a well-built cellar at his disposal, our Comrade Klose has also, as a precautionary measure, set by a not inconsiderable supply of food, and also has places for us to sleep.'

'I still can't believe,' the blonde girl says, 'that there is going to be a battle for Berlin.'

'My dear Comrade Poeschke,' Wiegand says, 'consideration is a word missing from the vocabulary of the National Socialists, and neither do they use it towards the herd animals that they call national comrades.'

'But the people must wake up at last!' the blonde girl says in despair. 'When you hear people talking round about the place . . .'

Schröter waves a dismissive hand and looks at her almost with anger. 'Talking, talking,' he says violently, 'yes, people are talking, but that's all they do. When someone appears wearing the Party insignia, or some snot-nosed youth with a swastika armband, they immediately become small and ugly, they always start looking around for the nearest mouse hole, or else they smile politely, raise their hands and say "Heil Hitler!" No, no, my dear Comrade . . . what was your name?'

'Lotte Poeschke,' the blonde girl replies.

'No, my dear Comrade Poeschke,' Schröter continues, 'we

cannot depend on the activity of the masses. It's possible that one or other will come out when he sees us in action, but most of them will be crouching in their cellars, just as they did during the bombing raids, and even if they no longer believe in victory, they will go on shouting "Heil Hitler" and carrying out every order, and they won't stop until the first Russian is standing in front of them in the flesh. You'll see, that's exactly what will happen.'

'It's desperate!' the blonde girl says, and looks rigidly in front of her.

'There's only one thing I don't like,' says a grey-haired man who has until now been sitting there quietly, 'it's that the Americans and the British are being so calm along the Elbe. I could imagine them really letting go now, to organize a race to Berlin, and instead . . .' He takes a newspaper out of his pocket and unfolds it. '*DAZ* says this today, for example:

"In fact we need only carefully read the daily reports from Wehrmacht High Command from the last eight days, whose precision and manly openness are beyond dispute. Two things become clear: in many areas at present the same towns and spaces appear to be the target of fighting, but are still undefeated by the enemy; in other naturally significant areas the enemy is pushing successfully ahead, but, against deft and obdurate resistance, is having to beat back severe counter-attacks, and is in this way being worn down to such a degree and at such a rate that an uprising in the hinterland could be doubly dangerous. The consequences are already apparent: the outbreak of the Soviet offensive coincides with the moment when our Western enemies are showing the first traces of breathlessness."'

'Damn it all,' Schröter says furiously, and brings his fist crashing down on the table. 'That you should believe so much of what these people say! Sometimes they call it breathlessness, sometimes it's last reserves, sometimes differences between the Allies and sometimes running out of time, but it's always a fraud, whether it's delivered an octave higher or lower.'

'You shouldn't be so severe,' Wiegand says reassuringly. 'The suggestive power of the Nazi method is so great that it doesn't even leave us untouched. There are moments when you simply can't escape it, so . . .'

Wiegand says nothing. The door has opened and a man in a blue railwayman's uniform has come in, he walks up to the bar and orders a pint, drains it in one and orders another.

'What's up with you?' Klose asks. 'Christ, you look exhausted.'

The railwayman pulls a chair up to the bar and drops heavily onto it. 'What sort of association is this?' he asks quietly and points over his shoulder with his thumb.

'Oh, it's a little birthday party,' Klose says indifferently. 'So what's up with you? You look like a bridegroom after a long wedding night.'

'I've just come from Strausberg,' the railwayman replies, and takes a deep breath. 'Oh man, Klose . . .' He shakes his head like someone who doesn't want to acknowledge an unbelievable truth.

'Are the Russians in Strausberg already?' Klose asks excitedly.

'Not far away,' the railwayman replies, taking off his cap and wiping the sweat from his forehead. 'Their tanks are already on the ring road. It's all finished, it's over.'

'Do you think so?' Klose asks.

'Of course,' the railwayman whispers with a shy glance behind him. 'I work the Küstrin line. We couldn't get past Müncheberg even last night, they're in there already, Jeez, and the planes, they're over you like a swarm of bees, they practically take the chimney off the engine. And that's some artillery the Russkies have got, they're flattening everything.'

'And the mood?' Klose asks.

'Really bad,' the railwayman says, and finishes his beer. 'Give me another one, Oskar. You know, when our lads were still at Seelow, there was a kind of order in it, but that's all gone now. Man, they're not fighting troops any more. Wehrmacht, Volkssturm, OT work battalions, the Party, the Hitler Youth and behind it all the SS.' He shakes his head. 'And then you've got the Russians, fresh, rested, young fellows, well dressed, well fed, shiny guns and excellent training.' He pauses for a moment and adds almost apologetically, 'The things you hear, you know?'

Klose nods. 'And this is the enemy that Adolf said, in October forty-one, was on the floor and would never get up again.'

'And we believed him,' the railwayman says with a sigh.

'We did?'

'You didn't?'

Klose shakes his head. 'And what are you doing now?'

'How do you mean, Oskar?'

'Are you going to get back in your train and head east?'

The railwayman shrugs, a movement of helplessness and resignation. 'What else am I supposed to do?' he asks.

Schröter has risen to his feet and crept almost silently up to the railwayman. 'A bit of sand in the crosshead and the steering wouldn't be too bad,' he says thoughtfully.

The railwayman turns round, startled. 'What's the point of that?' he shouts.

'And what's the point of your keeping going?' Schröter asks him back.

'Who are you anyway? Poking your nose into someone's conversation . . .'

'I'm Otto Schulze, Gauleiter of Stralau-Rummelsburg,' Schröter replies and grins across his whole face. 'But to be serious for a moment, pal, have you ever thought about whether there's a point to your work?'

'Why should I care about the point of it,' the railwayman replies. 'I just get on with my job.'

'Blimey,' Schröter says, and smiles thoughtfully, 'your brain's been dried out by the heat in the driver's cab, if you can talk that kind of nonsense. If your train is out of operation it can't bring ammunition to the front, if you can't bring ammunition to the front they can soon call it a day down there, and once they call it a day the war's over.'

'Yes, and then the Bolsheviks will come!'

'They'll come anyway,' Schröter says quickly. 'You'll never stop them, whether you head over there or not.'

'Then it doesn't matter if . . .'

'Christ, are you really that stupid or are you just pretending? It does matter, pal, the sooner it comes to an end the better. Or do you think that's going to be fun: street battles in Berlin, tank advance averted on Frankfurter Allee, incursion thwarted on Thaerstrasse, attempted breakthrough thwarted on Warschauer Bridge, Ostkreuz Station firmly in our hands . . .'

'For God's sake, stop it!'

'That's what's coming, pal, just that. And why?'

'I don't know.'

'Then I'll tell you: because you knuckleheads do your duty to the very last . . .'

'If you'll allow me . . .' the railwayman says angrily.

'I won't allow you anything,' Schröter goes on talking undeterred. 'Because you're forever shitting your pants.'

'I have to think of my family,' the railwayman objects, running his right hand between his neck and his collar as if his collar was suddenly too tight for him.

'At last some good sense,' Schröter says approvingly. 'If you really are thinking about your family, then you must also do something to ensure that this damned war comes to an end before the battle reaches Berlin. Or do you want your wife and children, if you have them, to get a shell on the head right at the end, after they've survived the war from the air?'

The railwayman nods. 'That's obvious,' he says, and looks thoughtfully at the ceiling. 'But my train isn't the only one . . .'

'What does that matter?' Schröter says, and exchanges a glance with Klose.

'When there's *sooo* much sand!'

'You make it sound easy . . .' the railwayman says, still reluctant.

'Easy? No, but if we only wanted to do what was easy . . .' Schröter replies straight away.

The railwayman puts on his cap without a word and sets down some money on the table, then he gets up and walks slowly towards the door. 'Goodbye,' he says and puts two fingers to the peak of his cap. He turns round again in the doorway. 'Not a bad idea, that thing about the sand, let's see how it goes.'

'Great job,' says the young worker sitting next to Lassehn. 'Nicely done.'

Schröter waves his hand dismissively.

'Many a slip,' he says.

Klose turns the radio on again, having turned it off after Goebbels' speech. 'Let's see if the Mosquitoes are on their way already.'

'Why wouldn't they be on their way, today of all days?' exclaims Dr Böttcher.

'No one likes to be alone at night, because making love by moonlight is the loveliest thing, you know what I mean, on the one hand and on the other and besides . . .'

'Switch off that nonsense,' Schröter shouts irritably.

'But why?' Klose asks. 'It's nice if someone comes in. Otherwise you're sitting there like a funeral party.'

'No one likes to be alone at night, because making love . . .'

The music goes out like a candle, the singer's voice fades away into the distance, suddenly it isn't there, the sound of electricity predominates.

'Attention, attention, this is an air situation report. Small unit of fast fighter planes over Hanover-Braunschweig heading for the Brandenburg Marches. I repeat . . .'

'Well then,' Klose says, 'all according to plan, as it should be.'

'. . . it doesn't matter to me.
No one likes to be alone at night . . .'

The singer's voice is there again, an emotional, pronouncedly erotic voice, but for all its beauty and bell-like purity it still echoes with the shrill tone of the evening dance of death.

'*Woman of my Dreams*,' says the young worker beside Lassehn.

'That's the name of the film, colourful and trashy, practically dripping with the propaganda of the people's state.'

'Why do you watch such nonsense?' Schröter asks, and taps his index finger against his forehead. 'Don't you have anything else to do?'

'Slow down, there, Comrade,' the worker says. 'Cinema is a wonderful thing, so wonderfully gloomy . . .'

'You're thinking about things like that right now?' Schröter asks furiously.

The young worker smiles. 'Take care, let me tell you something, you might even learn something.' He winks at the blonde girl. 'Lotte and I go to the cinema as an affectionate loving couple, but we change seats a few times during the performance, and every time we get up, we leave something on our seats, a flyer, neatly stuck to the armrest. When the seat flips up you can't see anything, it's a normal seat like any other, neutral on the outside, but on the inside . . .' He whistles through his teeth.

Schröter nods appreciatively. 'I get it, and when someone flips the seat down at the next showing, the ordinary seat has turned into a very special seat, an enemy of the state, so to speak, and reveals its true face.' He laughs briefly. 'Good, son, very good. Has it caused you any problems?'

The young worker shakes his head. 'Not yet,' he replies, 'but we always leave the cinema before the end of the screening. Better safe than sorry.'

'Yes,' the blonde girl cuts in with a comically sad expression, 'and it means we always miss the happy-ending kiss. Isn't that terrible?'

Schröter chuckles and looks from the young worker to the blonde girl. 'Well, I assume you then act it out for real, the two of you.'

The young worker shakes his head.

The blonde girl's face, which seemed cheerful and carefree a moment before, is now full of shadows, it is as if the sun, which had been shining on her face a moment before, had suddenly been obscured by a cloud.

'Please don't,' she says quietly and turns her head away, to hide the fact that her eyes are filled with tears.

Schröter, startled, looks at her and rests his rough and callused hand on her arm. 'What is it, girl?' he asks. 'What have I said?' His eyes wander from the blonde girl to Wiegand and from there to Dr Böttcher.

Wiegand shakes his head. 'Our Lotte isn't a young girl any more, even if that's what she looks like,' he says quietly. 'She is a young woman and has a nine-year-old daughter. Her husband . . . I'll tell you later.'

Lotte Poeschke shakes her head and tries to dry her tears with the back of her hand. 'You can tell Comrade Rumpelstiltskin all about it,' she says, 'it's in the past.'

'I'm sorry if I touched a nerve,' Schröter says. 'Are you angry with me, Lotte?'

'No,' she says, and smiles through the last of her tears.

Schröter smiles back, even though he doesn't know why. 'What's the matter?'

'Our Lotte may be the bravest woman in Berlin,' Wiegand says gravely, 'but it's not a good idea to touch on it.'

Lotte Poeschke lowers her blonde head, her bright-blonde hair gleams in the light of the gloomy hanging lamp that has been lowered from the ceiling, and now Schröter sees that there are threads of grey here and there amidst the blonde.

Lucie Wiegand has stood up and walked behind her, she strokes her hair gently and presses her face against her cheek. 'Men can be a bit clumsy,' she says, 'and nosy as well.'

The blonde woman straightens her head. 'If you want to tell Comrade Rumpelstiltskin about it,' she says firmly, 'I don't mind, but I can't do it.'

Then Wiegand speaks, he speaks slowly, with careful, cautious words, because he doesn't want to run the risk of being over-dramatic or sentimental, and what he describes is this.

'Lotte Poeschke came from a well-to-do Jewish family, she was brought up in that traditional way typical of German Jews, that curious mixture of eccentric isolation and willing assimilation, open to German customs but still with its face turned towards Jewishness, not fully a part of the bourgeois world about which it had certain reservations, but not a part of the proletariat, with whom it shared the fate of the oppressed. Lotte Poeschke, still Lotte Joachimsohn in those days, found her way from the Jewish Wandervogel movement to the Young Workers' Movement, not to escape the monotony of bourgeois life, not as a snobbish little game, but driven by the social impulse of her heart. In the Young Workers' Movement she met the mechanic Poeschke and married him, to the horror of her bourgeois family, who were forced to acknowledge that her social attitude was not some kind of youthful aberration but had become the purpose of her life. After 1933 she immediately started doing underground work. There was hardly anything she didn't do, distributing flyers, working as a courier, sabotage, whispering campaigns, stealing guns, and for years everything was fine, fortune looked kindly on her, her innocent, girlish face, her wonderful smile, her bright blonde hair shielded her against suspicion and persecution. But one day the wings of death, which had only cast their shadow over her from time to time, suddenly hurled her to the ground. After the arson attack on the anti-Russian exhibition 'Soviet Paradise' in the Berlin Pleasure Garden, the whole group was arrested, including Lotte Poeschke and her husband. They were brought before the People's Court in Leipzig, the usual proceedings were rolled out over them, the indictment also delivered the sentence, the official defence counsels squirmed industriously before the judges' benches, the inevitable death sentences were announced and executed. Twenty-one times in a single day the prosecutor general read out the death sentence in a monotonous voice, twenty-one times young activists who had done nothing but fight for the cause of their oppressed people were tied to the block, twenty-one times the executioner's axe came down, twenty-one heads were severed in that one day, twenty-one times a stream of warm blood poured into the ground, twenty-one corpses twitched one last time. Only Lotte Poeschke was left, she had fallen ill on the day of execution, and since the law decrees that a sick person cannot be executed, the day of her execution was postponed, for a day, two days, a week, many weeks, by which time she had fully recovered. But the execution was not carried out, a new court decision would have been required and it could not go through because the files had been lost in the meantime. Whether they had been accidentally mislaid with the files of the other twenty-one, whether they had been destroyed in an air raid or whether they had been removed by well-intentioned court officials is unknown.

'The fact remains, however, that Lotte Poeschke, sentenced to death, was forgotten. She wandered from prison to prison but none of them wanted to take her. The legal machinery had fallen into chaos, Lotte Poeschke was not on remand, but neither had she been given a prison sentence, she had been sentenced to death for high treason, and the files containing her death sentence had been lost. But since the files also contained the evidence against her, the trial against her could not continue. The case of Lotte Poeschke threatened to fall into oblivion, in the end it almost lost the status of being a legal case at all, and all that remained was the legally neutral Lotte Poschke, who had no right of residence in any kind of penitentiary, who fell under no known rubric. As everyone knows, order must prevail, even among the millstones of the legal procedure. Just as the apparatus of the state legal machinery places the head of a mass murderer or a freedom fighter on the block and brings the axe down on his bared, clean-shaven neck, when all legal formalities have been completed, just as the court desk issues the relatives of the executed individual with a bill for the execution costs (precisely specified in terms of expenses according to §§ 49 and 52 of the Court Fees Act for the death penalty, postal charges according to § 72^1 of the CFA, costs according to § 72^6 of the CFA for the public defender, imprisonment expenses at RM 1.50 per day, costs for the execution of the sentence, postage costs for the dispatch of the bill of charges) and instructs them to pay it, so its crushing wheels could not intermesh if a single tooth was missing.

'Then some conscientious court employee discovered that the prisoner Poeschke was Jewish. To a certain extent it was a rediscovery, because the legally imposed first name Sara had also been lost, and this immediately took the Poeschke case to a quite different level, it swept away all difficulties concerning the allocation of powers. As the normal courts and penal authorities no longer applied to Jews, the Poeschke case and the individual at its centre were passed to the Reich Security Head Office of the Secret State Police, the Gestapo.

'Lotte Poeschke now found herself in the claws of another legal bureaucracy, and a new cycle began. She was put in the Jewish internment camp affiliated with the Jewish hospital in the north of Berlin. There were three kinds of prisoners there, the ones who were to be transported to the east and used as heating material for the incineration plants, the ones who were to be transported to Theresienstadt, a path to hell via the intermediate stage of purgatory, and those who fell under the heading of "N.r.", or "Not registered". Lotte Poeschke was not scheduled to be transported as she had to remain at the disposal of the Gestapo, so she was placed in the third category, and here there was a choice between the exercise grounds of Lichterfeld and Ravensbrück, one meaning a quick death in front of four rifles, the other a slow end through hunger, beatings, vivisection and illness.

'As the Gestapo camps were largely self-administered, Lotte Poeschke, a trained nurse, became a camp nurse. In spite of all her inner torments she set about her new work, because here once again she immediately had the opportunity to allow her warm heart, her cheerful nature, her humane temperament to flow freely. She always had a smile on her lips, and always a friendly word of support, and all at once she was the helpful angel of the camp. As a nurse she enjoyed a certain liberty, and even though there were occasional opportunities to escape she did not do so, because she did not want to put the stewards who had been pressurized into guarding the camp under pressure by fleeing. But one day she did disappear. No one knew how it could have happened, no one could be held to account for it. She exploited the confusion around an air attack and escaped along an underground passage which connected the camp to the hospital, and which was opened for the air raid.

'After four years in prison Lotte Poeschke was free again, but she did not remain afraid and in hiding. She resumed her clandestine activity, she began where she had stopped before her arrest, and she did so as naturally as if there were not four long and difficult years of suffering in between.'

Wiegand pauses for a moment and clears his throat. He was speaking at first in a matter-of-fact reporting voice, almost a monotone, but then his voice rose in volume from sentence to sentence. 'It all sounds so . . . so matter-of-fact,' he continues. 'We open a file, and it contains the words: Lotte Sara Poeschke née Joachimsohn, born on such and such, German national, no religion, recently resident in this place and that, height one metre sixty, hair blonde, eyes blue, distinguishing features none, prisoner number two-zero-one-hundred-and-sixteen, the dates of her arrest, preliminary investigation, main trial, death sentence, imprisonment, transfer, escape, but prisoner two-zero-one-hundred-and-sixteen is not only a piece of data in a file, two-zero-one-hundred-and-sixteen is a woman who breathes and feels, who has red blood flowing in her veins, who thinks a lot, she is a woman whose husband lost his head on the scaffold, who has her own head still on her shoulders purely by chance, two-zero-one-hundred-and-sixteen is a woman who *thinks*, about her husband and the other twenty comrades, who cannot banish the terrible memories or defend herself against the terrible images, in whose ears the footsteps of the condemned men still ring as they were led to the block, a woman who *thinks*, about her child, which is being dragged from pillar to post, without its father's protection, without its mother's love, exposed to humiliations and hunger, cursed and despised as a *Mischling*, a Jewish bastard, as subhuman. Four years between four narrow walls, with the rush of the falling axe constantly in her ears, grief for her husband in her heart, concern for her child at her back, a woman who *believes*, above and beyond her own fate in the greatness and power of the idea . . .' Wiegand moves as if struggling against his own words. 'Enough of this!'

'So this is our comrade Lotte Poeschke,' Schröter says, and clutches her hand. 'If all women were like you . . .' The door to the restaurant opens, and a man in the brown uniform of the Party's political leaders comes in.

'Heil . . . Heil Hitler!'

Klose returns the greeting with a few indistinct words muttered between his teeth.

'Your greeting doesn't sound . . . doesn't sound very enthusiastic,' the brown-uniformed man says, and sits down at the bar.

'I'm tired,' Klose mutters. 'You can't sleep a whole night through. We've had about enough of these airborne gangsters.'

'It's . . . it's coming,' the Nazi says uncertainly, 'just another few days . . . patience, a few days' patience, then we'll give the Bo . . . Bolsheviks and plu . . . plutocrats a . . . a . . . Cannae with our new weapons . . .' He brings the flat of his hand down on the bar, making the glasses rattle.

'What do you mean?', asks Klose.

'A Cannae, it's a kind of . . . just read the *Völk . . .* the *Völkischer Beobachter*, it's in there, the thing about . . . about the Cannae. A pint, please!'

Klose pours it and hands him the glass.

The man drinks half of the beer and shivers. 'Brr, that tastes like horse . . . like horse piss, hahaha.' He pushes back his cap and fans himself. 'I've got a question for you, National . . . National Comrade, a question.'

Klose gives him a questioning look. 'Go ahead!'

'I'm looking for block ward . . . block warden Otto Sasse,' the Nazi says. 'Ot-to Sas-se.'

'He lives here in the block overlooking the street, three staircases on the left,' Klose replies, and feels his heart suddenly thumping.

'I know,' the man says, 'I know, but there's been . . . there's been no sign of him for a few days, no one's open . . . no one's opening the door.'

Klose shrugs. 'His wife is in the Sudetengau, she's been evacuated,' he replies.

The Nazi drains his beer and pushes the glass over to Klose. 'Another one,' he demands. 'On Sunday he was still with the local . . . the local group, you know, the local group shut up shop, and since then he's disappeared, he's simply disappeared, gone,

gone away, he wasn't even there at the rocket . . . rocket-launcher training practice in Küst . . . Küstriner Platz. And Sasse is one of the most dedicated . . . dedicated men, yes, that's what he is. I was up at . . . up at Hühnerstiege, but there's not a not a soul . . . not a soul up there. And three days' worth of the *VB* untouched in his mail . . . in his mailbox, yes, three days'.'

'Hm, yes . . .', Klose drawls, 'can't help you there, I'm afraid.'

The man frowns and takes a small sip. 'When did you . . . when did you . . . last see him?'

'Maybe three or four days ago,' Klose replies, 'he didn't come and see me very often.'

The Nazi says nothing and finishes his beer in very small sips. 'You haven't got a schnapps there by any chance, a schnapps? This is horse . . . horse piss.'

Klose shakes his head. 'Nothing to be done, O valiant chieftain, bare ruined choirs where once the sweet birds sang . . .'

The Nazi wags a finger at him. 'You old . . . you old con artist. What sort of . . . of people are these?' he asks, nodding his head backward.

'I don't know these people,' Klose replies. 'Something to do with an engagement, I think.'

'They've got strangely . . . strangely tense expressions,' the Nazi slurs, and turns his whole chair round, 'it must be one hell of a serious . . . serious engagement, yes, deadly serious. Strange that they're . . . sitting around, when there could be an . . . an alarm at any moment.'

'That's exactly why they're sitting here,' Klose replies, 'because the bunker is only a few minutes away.'

The Nazi raises his hand and waves it around. 'Klose, there's something about your pub that . . . that doesn't feel quite right,' the man says, and looks sharply at Klose. 'Sasse comp . . . complained about you a few times at the local group, you fat pig. A few times, he did.'

'Wasn't aware of it,' Klose defends himself. 'My pub is clean, but of course I can't look under everybody's waistcoat and examine their heart and kidneys. And incidentally the Gestapo turned my place upside down only two days ago.'

'Your place?' the man says in amazement, and opens his eyes wide. 'Over in Mad . . . Madaistrasse there was a . . . a raid, in the hotels and pubs on Madaistrasse.'

'And on that occasion the gentlemen did me the honour too,' Klose says firmly. Total lies, but an outstanding performance, he adds to himself.

'I . . . I didn't know that,' the Nazi says, reassured. 'Well, all the better for you. Isn't that the . . . the siren?'

Klose shakes his head. 'No, that was a train in the station, but it's bound to be soon. It's already past nine.' He claps his hands. 'Ladies and gents, please get your things together, I'm about to close.'

The Nazi staggers to his feet and snorts violently, then he moves his hands like an orator who wants people to listen to him. 'One . . . one moment,' he says loudly and totters towards the table where the group is sitting. 'All . . . allow me to introduce myself, my honoured National . . . National Comrades, cell admin . . . cell administrator Emil Hoffmeister.' He clicks his heels together and extends his right arm. 'Heil to our Füh . . . Führer!'

The people around the table sit in silence. Dr Böttcher raises his hand slightly in a gesture towards a salute.

'Why are you sitting there like . . . like tailors' dummies?' the Nazi shouts, and props his hands on the table. 'Is this an eng . . . engagement? A funer . . . a funeral party is what you are, oh yes, a fu-ner-al par-ty. Haven't you got someone to tinkle the ivories or something?'

No one answers, they all stare angrily at the man in the hated brown uniform, only Dr Böttcher tries to lighten the silence with a joke.

'Open your . . . your mouths and say something, you, you . . . scoundrels!' the Nazi roars. 'I'm cell administrator Emil Hoff-mei-ster. One of you go to the . . . to the piano!'

'There's about to be an air raid,' Wiegand says and gets to his feet, 'we're off now.'

'Sit down, you screwball!' the Nazi bellows. 'One of you . . . one of you go to the piano. Will you get a move on?' He leans down and studies the faces. 'I'm sure . . . I'm sure . . . you can play the piano,' he says, and points a finger at Lassehn. 'I'm sure you can.'

Dr Böttcher waves a hand at Lassehn. Lassehn reluctantly gets to his feet and goes to the piano. He hasn't played for a year and a half, often he has stretched his hands out in yearning for the ivory keys and played scales and chords, arpeggios and chromatic scales in the air, but now he resists being forced, ordered to sit at the piano. But he can't make a stand, there's no point irritating the Nazi by resisting, he opens the lid and lets his hands rest uncertainly on the keys.

'Come on!' the Nazi yells. 'Play!'

Lassehn closes his eyes for a few seconds, then begins the first phrase of 'Les Adieux', but only manages a few bars.

The Nazi gives him a shove in the back. 'What . . . what sort of rubbish is that?'

'Beethoven,' Lassehn replies, 'Ludwig van Beethoven.'

'Not up to date, old Beethoven isn't,' the Nazi says. 'Play the Horst Wes . . . the Horst Wessel Song.' He draws a semicircle in the air with his hand and then raises it in the Hitler salute. 'And you all sing along, everyone, you hear? One, two, three!

Raise high the flag
The ranks are tightly closed
The SA marches
With calm and . . .

Why aren't you singing, you . . . you swine?'

'There's an air raid, pal,' says Klose, and rests a hand on his shoulder. 'Can't you hear it? The Mosquitoes are here!'

IV

It's one of the most astonishing facts that abnormal circumstances can become a daily habit if they occur in series. It isn't just that people's senses are quickly dulled, whether by suffering or joy, by acts of kindness and acts of cruelty; even their habits adapt to particular situations as soon as those become the standard. The original habits and sensations quickly weaken under the pressure of a new way of life. Weighed down by these unusual circumstances, they are obscured and soon become nothing but a vague memory. It is in the nature of modern man to invent a kind of system for his way of life that is far from any hitherto familiar norm, and to come to terms with things even in the desert of privation, his nerve system also reacts reliably to unusual things as long as they recur with a certain regularity. Habit is the full sister of intellectual sluggishness: it wraps mankind in a soft shell that hugs each fold and each twist of the brain, conducting the effector cells and influencing the receptor cells, in the end subjugating them entirely. Eventually it inverts concepts, the norm becomes the exception, the exception the norm, fear is no longer fear, torment no longer torment, danger no longer danger, an acute illness becomes a chronic state of suffering which is accepted as immutable. What appears physically as indifference and psychically as apathy is nothing but a mimicry of the brain. In the course of the war that becomes obvious. People get used to living in darkened rooms, to switching or reducing their food intake to a particular quantity of calories and a different level of vitamins content, to their male

375

relatives who have been called up for military service constantly being exposed to deadly danger, and when the war reaches far behind the front lines and the air becomes a theatre of war as well, the strength of habit can be seen most clearly: the *danse macabre* accompanied by the orchestra of sirens, anti-aircraft guns, aeroplane engines and bomb explosions becomes a daily round-dance and a natural event in the course of everyday life.

Only seven days have passed since Lassehn has been back in Berlin; they have been filled with all kinds of events, numerous meetings and with an activity that he hasn't even heard of before. This life, which at first lay before him like a deep, dark wood through whose shade no paths took shape, and in which thick and hostile undergrowth hampered his every step, assumed an almost methodical form with surprising speed, only now and again is Lassehn surprised by anything, and then only by himself. Everything has already become second nature: that he is on the move by day, collecting flyers and leaving them somewhere, in the underground or the S-Bahn, in public conveniences or mailboxes in apartment blocks, that his footsteps take him to Strasse Am Schlesischen Bahnhof in the evening, that he feels quite at home in Klose's restaurant, that Klose supplies him with food, and that even without asking particularly for permission, he throws himself down for the night on the sofa in the back room, and even that has become second nature, that he has papers in his pocket made out in the name of Horst Winter, who lost his life in an air raid and who is now saving lives from beyond the grave, that he has a loaded gun with him at all times and is ruthlessly willing to use it (as he has done twice).

Now Lassehn sits in tram 64, bound for Hohenschönhausen. At first he tried to look out of the window, but that is not possible, the few trams that are still travelling along the streets of Berlin in April 1945 no longer offer this possibility, because the windows are either painted blue, if they still have glass in their frames, and allow only a blurred vision of the streets, or else they are covered over with cardboard or wood.

On his seat he found the *DAZ* for 19 April and gave it a quick look. He is particularly repelled by the frantic optimism of this newspaper, which even prides itself on its independence. Every soldier knows that the peak of an attack is not reached on the first day, and that a provisional assessment of its success or failure is impossible after only three or four days, but the military commentator of *DAZ* is unaware of this, because he writes the following:

> We can already make one crucial observation with certainty: the hopes that our enemies have of suddenly overrunning the sections of the eastern front which they are attacking have not been fulfilled. Admittedly it is only to be expected that the enemy will pump additional fighting reserves into the focal points of its attack, the development of the first three days already allows us to assume that these reserves will be deployed less as additional forces and more as a substitute for the very high losses of these first three days of battle. In those places, after a brief flush of victory, they are now clear that one can no longer talk in terms of an 'Allied tank race to Berlin'.

When he had skimmed through the newspaper and then left it casually aside, particularly since reading in a violently lurching tram with the light from outside blacked out is a torment in any case, he has no distraction but his own thoughts.

He is on his way to Hohenschönhausen, to see that lady Elisabeth Mattner with whom he marched a few days after the daytime raid by the Americans from Wittenbergerplatz to Alexanderplatz, and who freed him in the 'Bayernhof' restaurant from the unpleasant company of the red-faced man. Lassehn received an invitation when he said goodbye to her at Alexanderplatz. Admittedly Elisabeth Mattner said only, 'Come and visit me some time, Herr Lassehn!', but it was more than a phrase, an almost rhetorical invitation. Her voice contained a promise, in her eyes there was a glint of flattering, unbridled wooing, her soft, warm hand rested in his for an unusually long time and pressed firmly against it. As Lassehn has always underestimated his effect on women, the friendliness of Elisabeth Mattner at first struck him as a kind of typically feminine politeness or sympathy, and he was almost ashamed of himself for undressing her and caressing her with his eyes and his thoughts as she climbed the steps in front of him in the 'Bayernhof'.

Later, when they had to stumble over mountains of rubble on Friedrichstrasse, he was helpful to her and supported her to keep her from falling, and when he took her arm he came into contact with her breast, which swelled full and firm from her suit jacket. Lassehn flinched with alarm, immediately loosened his grip and almost stammered an apology, but it soon turned out that it had not been a matter of chance. The next time they had to make their way over a pile of rubble, which was not particularly high and not very hard to climb over, Elisabeth Mattner asked for his support, and when he carefully took her arm, brought her breast into contact with his hand by turning her body quickly. In the end they walked on arm in arm, not like a married couple, with their arms loosely linked, but not like lovers either, with their forearms touching and their fingers entwined, to absorb a lot of warmth from the other person, no, Lassehn and Elisabeth Mattner walked together in quite a particular way. It happened as a man holds the arm of a woman whom he needs to support because she is unsteady on her feet or feeling faint, by putting his hand around her upper arm. But the fact that she kept her upper arm pressed tightly against her body meant that Lassehn's hand was caught between the warmth of her arm and the warmth of her breast.

Of course Lassehn's blood was suddenly stirred, but it didn't condense into a wild and impetuous longing. He had forbidden himself all desires, particularly since the woman's face had been entirely unselfconscious. In the end Lassehn gratefully accepted as a precious gift the womanly warmth that trickled from her breast into his body, and even temporarily forgot it via an interesting conversation about a musical subject.

When they said goodbye beneath the city-railway viaduct at Alexanderplatz Station, that invitation with the unspoken promise helped him understand something that had previously seemed unclear or a matter of chance as an intention or a test, a rehearsal or an examination, but had not yet fanned his blood into a flame of desire. Two things stood in the way of that, one the thought of Irmgard, with whom he had not yet had the chance to speak, and respect for the unknown Herr Mattner, the husband of Elisabeth Mattner, who is at the front in Italy and, as a paymaster, his comrade, even if he is his superior.

Lassehn is one of those young men who does not see the woman who smiles at him, or who is willing to transform sympathy into complete abandonment, simply as booty or as an object of pleasure, without introducing some kind of obligation or sense of responsibility, he always considers women and girls as the helpless, weak creatures in need of his protection that they ceased to be long ago. He has failed to notice that the long war years have made women hard and independent, that their emotional attitude has crucially altered, and traditional concepts have finally been overcome. Never before have women's lives been so geared towards the present moment, has the past disappeared into a grave without a trace, has the future been so opaquely veiled, never before has the impulse of the moment, the diktat of chance, so determined the rhythm of their emotions and so weakened their reservations. The wave of danger that crashes around them every day and every hour has burst the dyke of inhibitions, transforming the longing for tenderness into an eagerness for intense sensations. On the narrow threshold between life and death, when all around them material objects are burnt away and psychical supports are breaking away, the body alone remains as the vessel of a brief moment of happiness, which must be caught mid-flight like a butterfly, and which, like the butterfly, quickly loses its colour when you touch it. Happiness is now no longer a tenderly flowing adagio, since the sirens are wailing day and night, it is no longer a mildly fanning breeze beneath trees in the evening, since fire storms are raging across the city, no longer a word inspired by the classics, since a satanic desire for destruction is screaming down all reason, happiness has declined to become the fulfilment of physical needs, it is fodder and copulation, happiness can only be found in the hysterical hunt for cigarettes, real coffee and alcohol, for embraces and orgasms. The sexual act has become nothing more than a physical performance.

And now Lassehn is on his way to Hohenschönhausen, to pay Elisabeth Mattner that visit that was promised so casually and as if in passing. He is not going with the firm intention of embracing her, but neither is it his plan to escape such an embrace if the opportunity arose and he recognized her willingness. After his meeting with that strange and mysterious woman whose name is Irmgard Lassehn and who was his wife for eight days, Lassehn has undergone a transformation which may not be fundamental (since a character cannot fundamentally change), but the mystery of sex has revealed itself to him, and the only things that remain are calculation, deception and lust. But since no one can jump over his own shadow and Lassehn is used to justifying himself even to himself, he has convinced himself that he is connected to Irmgard by a formal legal bond but nothing else, and that Elisabeth Mattner can make up her own mind about how to behave with him. It is an attempt to free himself in advance of all responsibility, and assure himself of absolution, but also to expose himself to that unknown component of our lives that is called faith and is in fact only chance.

Lassehn gives a start when the conductor announces the Weissenseer Weg stop, he pushes his way to the exit, enduring some harsh words about himself, and jumps from the carriage, which has already set off again.

Now he stands in the encroaching darkness, and at first it seems as if he is in open countryside. For a moment he suspects that Elisabeth Mattner has duped him, but when his eyes have become used to the darkness he recognizes his surroundings. Where the tram pulled in there is a row of houses, some of which seem to have been partly destroyed, as if something has gnawed at them. A wide street passes in front of it, loomed over by the Eiffel Towers of high-tension power lines. This street is the Weissenseer Weg, it doesn't belong to any pattern because it isn't a city street, but neither is it an avenue, it isn't an arterial road, but more of a cross-country road, a wide road with two tram tracks running along its length, partly in the middle of the carriageway along a kind of promenade, partly off to the eastern side. To the right and left isolated houses appear, and open fields, the road surface is cobbled and tarmacked, but for long stretches the pavements are nothing but dirt paths. There is nothing more depressing than an unfamiliar area in the gloom of evening. Lassehn has never been here before, he doesn't know where he is, he memorized Elisabeth Mattner's address a few days before and remembers that he has to take line 63 to Berliner Strasse on the corner of Weissenseer Weg and then continue in the same direction, but nothing more than that. Lassehn stands there uncertainly, darkness and abandonment shiver over his skin. He can't make up his mind to take so much as a step along the course of the road, the question of the point of this visit is appearing too insistently in his mind. But then he shakes off his doubts, setting off with great determination, he walks past a ruined filling station and some dilapidated buildings, a few people slip away like fleeting shadows, and the bell of the tram penetrates the darkness from a long way off. Getting his bearings seems impossible, but in the end he finds the building he is looking for, climbs the two flights of stairs in the light of his torch because the light on the stairs doesn't work, and knocks firmly on the door bearing the brass plaque 'W. Mattner'.

A few seconds pass without anything happening in the flat. Irresolute characters tend to make their decision on the basis of accidental phenomena, and settle for explanations as to why things had to happen exactly like that. Lassehn is filled with a strange mixture of disappointment and satisfaction, but while he is still trying to work out whether it is disappointment over a failed adventure or satisfaction that it might be better that way, he hears a footstep.

Elisabeth Mattner is standing in the doorway, holding a candle in her hand and lighting Lassehn's face.

'Ah, it's you, Herr Lassehn,' she says delightedly, and holds out her hand to him. 'This really is a surprise. Please come in.'

'Good evening, madam,' Lassehn says, and takes her hand. He feels himself practically being dragged into the hall.

Lassehn is embarrassed, he almost regrets accepting the invitation, after all she is a stranger to him, and even her smile doesn't make her any more familiar. He lets her words run over him, trickling down on him like a light shower, as he sets down his hat and coat and follows her into a room. It is barely lit by the candle, and the woman's face is also distant and remote. Recollection makes colours look either too fiery or too dull, it is never an exact match for reality, and that is the case here, when the colours in memory's palette were too glorious. This is a pretty, friendly woman, but the erotic charm that previously emanated from her seems to have been lost. Lassehn is too inexperienced to know that a woman's sensual appeal does not emanate always and in every situation, that it must first be ignited and is to a great degree dependent on the mental disposition of the onlooker. The willingness to embrace can be present in latent form, but it needs a spark to trigger it. And that spark does not burn in Lassehn.

'You're so unusually silent today, Herr Lassehn,' Elisabeth Mattner says, and rests a hand on his arm.

'I'm sorry, madam,' Lassehn says, 'but I'm a bit muddled today. How have you been in the meantime?'

Elisabeth Mattner tells him a few details that Lassehn barely absorbs, he looks at her steadily like someone contemplating a photograph and examining it for familiar features. Elisabeth Mattner is in constant motion, straightening a doily or putting a crystal vase in a different place, sitting down for a few minutes or simply walking around.

'Would you like to play me something?' she asks at last, and points to the piano.

'I'd love to,' Lassehn replies, and immediately sits down at the piano. 'Is there anything in particular you'd like to hear, madam?' Elisabeth Mattner leans against the credenza, the flicker of the burning candle draws a grotesque shadow on the wall.

'Something tender,' the voice says quietly, 'something gentle and tender.'

Lassehn lets his hands rest on the keys for a few seconds, then he plays Mendelssohn's *Spring Song* and Schubert's *Serenade*, he plays with a very light touch, pianissimo, his hands only touch the keys very delicately, it is almost as if the keys were responding solely to his will. The notes float like cherry blossom through the semidarkness of the room. Lassehn isn't playing delicately because he can't play as he is ordered to, or as people might wish him to. He is more of an emotional player than an intellectual one, he can only ever express what moves him at that moment, and right now that is loneliness, yearning and some kind of unfamiliar pain.

Since notes do not possess the clarity of language and can be interpreted in different ways, Elisabeth Mattner hears his playing in her own way, as what she wanted to hear: as tenderness.

Lassehn, who sits at the piano and, even after the first few notes, has forgotten where he is, immerses himself in the music as if in a warm bath. He doesn't know that women's erotic sense is often only rolled up like a flag and unfolds completely if only a breath of tenderness catches it. And now he is provoking just that.

When the second piece is over, Elisabeth Mattner steps up behind him and leans the weight of her body over his shoulder, she brings her lips close to his ear and runs her hand over his hair. 'That was wonderful,' she whispers. 'You play wonderfully.'

Lassehn lowers his hands and turns his body half towards her. Suddenly everything that was there a few days ago has returned, suddenly Elisabeth Mattner is not a strange woman any more, he feels her hand again, warm and firm, her breast, soft and breathing, and her voice, quiet and tender. He sits there as if paralysed for a few moments, before desire wells up in him, but by then Elisabeth Mattner has straightened up again, she walks back and forth and says a few words, insignificant, trivial words.

Lassehn sits there trembling. What previously made him nervous excites him now, his eyes follow every footstep the woman takes, everything she does, her breasts tremble beneath the thin silk of her blouse with each tiny move she makes.

'Why are you looking at me like that, Herr Lassehn?' asks Elisabeth Mattner. Has she forgotten that she addressed him in a more familiar way just a moment ago?

Lassehn's throat is so choked with arousal that he can't speak.

Elisabeth Mettner brushes past him, and a mixture of perfume and the scent of her body confuses his senses.

Lassehn stands up. 'Madam,' he begins, and doesn't know what he wants to say, it is like a cry for help.

Elisabeth Mattner immediately stops and turns round. 'Well, what is it, my boy?' she asks. 'Are you always so irresolute?' Now, Lassehn thinks, now I must pounce, she expects me to. But he stands there and can't move, then he feels her arms around his neck and her mouth on his lips, at first it is just a tender, soft kiss, her lips are soft and warm, but then they become impetuous, they violently open his mouth, his teeth, their breath flows together and everything dissolves in an eruption of intoxication, there is not a thought within him now, only wild and reckless desire, frenzy, abandon. When thoughts flow back into Lassehn, he pulls away from the woman's embrace.

'Were you happy?' she asks.

Lassehn replies, stroking her hair. Was he happy? Is he still? Does happiness mean thoughtlessly slipping ecstatically into a woman's body? That feeling that ripped through his body and still quivers inside him, is that happiness? He doesn't know, he has gone mad since knowing that the happiness he thought he had found with Irmgard was nothing but an embrace, and everything else was merely an illusion. Has a wave of bliss put a pang in his heart? Strange that he has stopped calling her madam.

'What can I call you?' he asks, to keep the silence from becoming too insistent.

'Say Lisa,' she whispers close to his ear.

What does she feel? Lassehn thinks. Love? Lust? He would like to look into her face, but it is completely dark in the room, a total blackness that makes it impossible even to see outlines.

'I was very happy,' Elisabeth Mattner replies.

Lassehn is almost startled. Could there be something more here than the collision of two warm bodies? 'Do you love me?' he asks. It sounds stupid, clichéd, naïve, he rebukes himself and a moment later wishes he could pull his words back out like a fish-hook from water.

Elisabeth Mattner laughs quietly, a series of little chuckles. 'Silly boy,' she says and pulls him tightly to her, 'why do you always have to . . .'

At that moment light bursts into the darkness of the room with the force of an explosion. Elisabeth Mattner quickly pulls a blanket over her body. 'The electricity blackout has been lifted,' she says and blinks in the light, her voice is quite calm, without an undertone of arousal. 'There will be an air raid in a moment.'

Lassehn sits up. 'And what will we do then, Lisa?' he asks. The name doesn't fall easily from his lips, but he uses it so as not to insult her.

Elisabeth Mattner pulls the cord that hangs on the wall above the wide bed and turns the ceiling light off again. 'Nothing at all, my boy,' she says, and turns on the bedside lamp. 'We'll stay up here. Nothing has ever happened here at night.'

'Aren't you afraid?' Lassehn asks.

'Afraid?' she asks back, and slowly shakes her head. 'No, I'm not afraid any more, I overcame the feeling they call fear a long time ago, and a fatalistic surrender has taken its place. I don't know what you've been through, my boy, tank battles or assault raids or flights into enemy territory or perhaps even torpedo fire, but I would still say you're not much ahead of me.'

'You mean in terms of acts of heroism?' Lassehn asks ironically.

Elisabeth Mattner's face assumes a condescending expression. 'What rubbish, acts of heroism,' she says quickly, 'you don't believe in things like that, do you? Or do you?'

Lassehn shakes his head.

Elisabeth Mattner nods in response. 'I wanted to say that you, and all those of you who are at the front, are no more exposed to danger than we are. Anyone who has been through all those heavy day and night attacks, anyone who has stood beneath the bright sails of the flare bombs and in spite of the dark, rainy night could clearly make out every detail in their daylight glow, saw every corner sharply lit, anyone who checked the attics during an air attack and heard the stick incendiary bombs crashing through the roof tiles on all sides, anyone who felt the scorching breath of a wall of flame for hours at a time and pumped water into it as if they'd gone mad, and afterwards had to stand guard for hours on the roof, watched with horror the city burning all around and fought a desperate battle against the showers of sparks, who ran for their lives, wheezing and half blind, anyone who has done all that is no longer afraid, my dear boy, they have walked through purgatory on earth, but they have not been cleansed by it . . .'

'But?' asks Lassehn.

'It could be that there are people here and there who see it all as a trial or punishment from God, and who devote themselves to religion as a result,' Elisabeth Mattner goes on, 'but for most their moral conscience was consumed in the big fire, and the meaninglessness of all of life became so obvious that meaningless living is the only kind.'

'Meaningless?'

'Yes, meaningless, as if you've lost your mind, in a constant pursuit, always hot on the heels of life, to wring from it even the tiniest speck of happiness or pleasure or joy.'

'*Carpe diem*, Horace said,' Lassehn observes. '*Carpe horam*, that should be these days.' He bends his arm under his head and looks into her face, strange, it is no more familiar than before, that pretty, regular face under its white-blonde shock of hair, with the dark-red mouth and the little nose that doesn't get in the way when they kiss. Lassehn's eye runs over every feature of her face. He can read no arousal, no happiness and no pain in it, but something in it has changed, it has lost the artificially excited expression from a moment ago, it is filled with contentment and satiety, and somewhere, hidden deep in the eyes, lust still lurks.

'You look at me so strangely, my boy,' Elisabeth Mattner says.

'Don't always say my boy,' Lassehn says, somewhat disgruntled.

'Why not?' she replies, and runs her hand reassuringly over his hair. 'You aren't my husband. That is, you were a moment ago, but you aren't.'

'Stop it,' Lassehn says defensively and pulls away from her, 'I don't think it's very appropriate to . . .'

Elisabeth Mattner smiles thoughtfully. 'We're not children,' she cuts in. 'What does my husband matter? He's far away, and if he were here he would have to come to terms with it. I have something I want to tell you, Joachim, and you may take it as a justification or an apology, as you wish. When my husband was last home on leave, two or two and a half years ago, I can't remember exactly, he was only with me for eight days.'

Lassehn shakes his head. 'Only eight days?' he asks. 'From Italy?'

'All the way from Africa,' she replies.

'That's impossible,' Lassehn objects. 'Do you hear? Air-raid warning!'

'Let the sirens wail,' she says, and waves her hand dismissively, 'you can only die once. Death in bed may not be a heroic death, but with a man in your arms . . . Are you afraid?'

Lassehn shakes his head.

'Well, then,' Elisabeth Mattner says and smiles at him. 'Yes, you say eight days of leave from Africa is impossible. Of course that's true, but he tried to persuade me it could happen, he told me something about courier services, in very mysterious tones. And I almost took him seriously, until I found out that he'd spent another twelve days in Hanover, with his girlfriend, a member of the Wehrmacht assistance staff he'd met at the district air-force base. That's my husband, the company paymaster. You see, my boy, I've changed since then.'

Lassehn suddenly realizes that he doesn't know very much about women, he is filled with questions, and he has to force himself not to let them all come spilling out.

'Strange,' Elisabeth Mattner says, as if talking to herself, 'British planes are flying towards our city, and will soon spread their wings of death over our heads. The cannon will fire, millions of people will be crouching in bunkers, cellars, caves and trenches, with just the two of us in the middle, as you might say, between the planes and the ones under the ground, between heaven and earth, we lie naked in a bed, and all around everything is dark.' She reaches her arms out from under the bedcover and stretches her body with her eyes closed.

Lassehn stares in fascination at the blonde tufts in her armpits. 'There's something else I'd like to ask you, Lisa,' he says slowly, 'but you're not to take it the wrong way.'

Elisabeth Mattner is still lying there with her eyes closed. 'Ask away,' she says encouragingly.

Lassehn is still hesitant, because he doesn't know how to say what he wants to say in words that won't hurt Elisabeth Mattner. 'You're . . . you're certainly not a frivolous or flippant woman, and yet you . . . you made me come to you even though you don't really know me.'

Elisabeth Mattner opens her eyes and gives him a searching, penetrating look.

'My dear boy,' she says and smiles, her mouth closed, 'I too was once a virgin with curly hair, romantic, dreamy and longing for love, in my first so-called great love it was six weeks before I gave him his first real kiss, and another eight months before I went to bed with him for the first time. Believe me, I've always reined in my temperament . . .'

'They're shooting,' Lassehn says as she speaks, listening to the sounds beyond the window, 'not very far away.'

'That's the Friedrichshain bunker,' Elisabeth Mattner says, 'it doesn't matter to us. What was I saying? Oh, yes, I've always reined in my temperament, my boy, the incubation period between first meeting and intercourse has varied between four months and a year and a quarter, which shows unusual steadfastness for a hot-blooded woman, and you will have noticed that I am one of those. When I married seven years ago I had only had four friendships behind me. Not so many, is it?'

So her husband was the fifth, and that's not very many? Lassehn thinks. But instead of answering he nods, so as not to take the conversation down a side alley.

'I was always faithful to my husband,' the woman goes on, 'that is, until I found out about the story of what happened when he was on leave. Then I yielded to the desires that slumbered in me, and as tends to happen when desires reach the realm of the possible and the attainable and the walls of moral inhibition are blown away, then inconstancy knows no bounds. I don't wish to claim that that's generally the case, but it is for me.'

Lassehn almost holds his breath. 'So I'm . . . I'm not the first?' he says. 'I mean, after you found out . . .'

Elisabeth Mattner reaches her arms out to Lassehn and tries to pull his head to her. 'Why are you interested in that?' she says in a flirtatious voice. 'Isn't it enough for you that you can embrace me? You've possessed my body, as it is or as it was half an hour ago. Did it diminish your enjoyment that you weren't the sixth, but the twelfth or thirteenth?'

Lassehn gently frees himself from her grip. 'You didn't quite understand my question or fully answer it,' he says. 'What I was actually trying to get at . . .'

Elisabeth Mattner folds her arms under her head. 'I do know what you mean,' she interrupts him. 'My dear boy, we're at war, even here in Berlin, for years our lives have only been returned to us for a short time, for the breaks between one bombing raid and the next. You know, when you have death in front of your eyes every day, when every wail of the sirens could at the same time be your death knell, then you are seized by a hunger for pleasure, you want to drain to the dregs the brief respite granted to you, and that applies as much to love as it does to anything else. I call that the intensification of our feelings. Things that used to take months now take only days, and what once occurred over days now happens in a matter of hours. If I . . .' She breaks off and listens to the window. 'You hear that? The pre-all-clear!'

Lassehn nods, he has been listening with excitement, and staring at the red mouth that is talking so calmly, almost indifferently, about death.

The smile has faded almost entirely from Elisabeth Mattner's face, and a hard seriousness now sits in the corners of her mouth. 'If I meet a man I like these days, it isn't as it used to be. The first informalities, the first kiss, then nothing for a while and then maybe bed, no, my boy, today death and mutilation lie in between. The man you fancy in the afternoon might by the evening have been turned into a charred corpse the length of your arm by a phosphorus bomb, or shredded into a thousand pieces by an aerial mine, but it could hit me too. So why should I wait and invoke my moral inhibitions? Today everything is different, today it all happens as if in time-lapse, meeting, kissing, abandon, parting, it must all be savoured in one go before the next air raid. Don't you understand that greed for pleasure lurks behind you like fear, the fear that you might miss something, that you might not have lived your life to the full? What you might call moral degeneracy and intellectual neglectfulness is nothing but a narcotic for the soul.' Elisabeth Mattner shivers and pulls the bedcover up under her chin. 'Do you want to know something else?' she adds.

Lassehn shakes his head. Hasn't she satisfactorily answered all the questions he had been burning to ask? 'No,' he says. 'Or perhaps yes. So you're of the opinion that there is no room left for love in our time?'

Elisabeth Mattner stares hard at the ceiling. 'Love,' she says and sighs. 'What is love? Do you require love before you possess a woman? Isn't it enough for you to possess her body unrestrictedly and rest between her thighs?'

'At the moment of union that is enough,' Lassehn replies, 'but afterwards . . . It's like getting drunk, while the alcohol still fires me up, the wine still tastes good, but when I stop drinking I have a stale taste in my mouth, then I feel ill . . .' He doesn't finish the sentence, because the simile doesn't quite catch what he was trying to say.

'Have you always loved, have you always passed the psychical exam before you slept with a girl?' Elisabeth Mattner asks and turns to look at him again. 'Have you always allowed your affection, your sympathy, your friendship or whatever else it was to mature fully before you . . . well, and so on?'

Lassehn doesn't reply, the question hits the core of his insecurity. 'The all-clear,' he says, nodding towards the window.

'Why don't you answer?' Elisabeth Mattner asks and smiles quietly. 'You asked just now if I loved you. Now I ask you: do you love me?'

'I don't know, Lisa,' Lassehn replies, 'I really don't know, and the fact that I don't know torments me. Just now, when you opened yourself up to me, I felt your heartbeat close to my chest and your nipples pierced me like daggers, when our mouths shared the same breath, there was a purple cloud in my brain, and I thought I loved you, but when I freed myself from you and the cloud flew away, when my heart beat a different rhythm to yours, everything was merely flesh.'

Elisabeth Mattner slides to his side and draws his head down to her shoulder. 'Why do you torment yourself, my boy?' she asks softly, and seeks his lips. 'You'll never be happy if you dissect everything in your mind all the time, let your instincts take over and guide you, then you can still pluck some modest happiness, nothing more than that is listed on the menu of our lives.'

'Can you come to terms with the fact that that's how it is?' Lassehn asks, and presses his cheek deeply into the curve of her neck.

Lassehn feels her shoulders twitching. 'I've given up thinking,' she replies, 'thinking doesn't make you happy.'

Lassehn lifts his head and seeks her eyes. 'You've given up thinking, Lisa? Don't you understand that by doing so you are depriving yourself of the attribute that elevates man above the animals?'

Elisabeth Mattner laughs shrilly. 'Thinking elevates man above the animals?' she says. 'My dear boy, that's what the philosophers say, who sit lonely and godless in their rooms or sail high above the earth on pink clouds. No animal is so cruel, cowardly, cunning and wicked as thinking man. How do we elevate ourselves above the animals? By inventing flamethrowers, phosphorus canisters, gas chambers and poison gases? Oh, don't talk to me about man as a noble creation.' Her voice falls back to a whisper. 'Don't think, don't think whatever you do, just live, live.' She pulls Lassehn's head back down to her and presses her body close to his. 'Don't think, my boy, just love and live before it's too late.'

Lassehn sees the dark-red, thirstily open mouth and feels the warm glow of her body pressing close to him, the little flame of his resistance flickers out in a purple dream and he sinks back into her bosom, which she thrusts impetuously towards him.

When Lassehn wakes up, it is already pitch-dark in the room, he feels as if a sound has woken to him. He listens hard to the gloom, but hears only the ticking of a clock and the calm, even breathing of the sleeping woman who is lying right beside him and enveloping him in her warmth, otherwise it is oppressively quiet. Lassehn carefully frees himself from the woman, folds his arms under his head and stares into the darkness.

Don't think, she said, just love. Is that love? That collision of bodies, their wild seizing of each other, that whipping-up of the senses to unconsciousness? Is that love? Not the quiet, tender mutual immersion in one another that barely requires the body? He suddenly remembers a friendship in his youth, a memory that still makes the blood shoot to his head. It is only a small experience, a matter of seconds, but it is branded firmly on him. In the darkness of the room he sees Ellen Eggebrecht's pure little face in front of him, her slightly protruding, Slavic cheekbones, her delicate, transparent skin, her bright, clear eyes, her slightly arched, childish upper lip, her dark-blonde hair held behind her head in two simple braids. They had grown up together, they had always been quite unselfconscious with each other until . . . yes, until one day he bent over a book that she was reading and his face brushed her cheek. It was only a fleeting contact, a trace of warmth had passed from her to him, they looked at each other and blushed, he was flooded with a sweet and painful tenderness, not been startled by wild desire.

The memory is quite unreal, as remote as a fairy tale from long ago. The mouth of the woman whose eager breath had touched his face just now, her kisses with sharp teeth, darting tongue and devouring lips brushed him like a hot wind and didn't leave a trace, the softly flooding warmth of that sharp-smelling, girlish cheek, that random tender touch, is almost more present to him than the hot body of the woman who sleeps next to him, breathing calmly, a naked, soft, warm, wildly tender woman whose body has occupied his, and his body hers, demanding no love, just the satisfaction of the senses.

Lassehn turns on the side-table lamp and looks carefully at the sleeping woman's face. She lies there like a sleeping child, her hands folded under her cheek as if praying, her light-blonde hair that has fallen over her forehead like a wave, her nostrils quivering gently along with her regular breathing, which touches him like a warm wind, the crimson mouth cuts like a dark wound in the pale, tender skin of the face, that mouth that enticed him and brought the two of them together. Lassehn's eye lingers on each of her features in turn, grateful for the peace that she has brought to his dammed-up blood, for the comforting fact that in the middle of a desert of grief and tears a woman's body can still bring oblivion. Love, no, it isn't love, he has sunk into her body, he has lain between her breasts as if in a sheltering cave and sought refuge in her bosom.

Lassehn brushes the wave of hair from her brow and strokes her head gently. Then he gives a start, a whistling sound passes through the air, followed by an explosion. He knows straight away that it was this sound that woke him just now, and that it is artillery fire. Artillery? Of course, anti-aircraft fire has a deeper sound, and bombs don't make that drawn-out whistle. Where could artillery be firing from? But then a thought leaps on him like a cat. The Russians.

In an instant he stops thinking of the woman beside him. There . . . there it is again, that long whistle followed by an explosion. Lassehn sits up and listens, his senses taut, every pore of his body absorbing sounds. A few minutes pass, followed by another shot. There can no longer be any doubt: the Russians have begun firing at Berlin.

Lassehn leans down to the sleeping woman. 'Lisa,' he says, stroking her face. 'Lisa wake up!'

Elisabeth Mattner opens her eyes, her eyelids slide slowly upwards like a rising curtain, for a second she is dazed with sleep, then a smile appears on her face. 'What is it, my boy?' she asks, reaching out her arms towards him.

'We've got artillery fire,' Lassehn says excitedly.

Then the smile slips from her eyes to cover the whole of her face, like the sun shining over a field. 'What do we care about that, Joachim,' she says, and throws her arms around his neck. 'Come on, we're still alive today, who knows what tomorrow will bring.'

Lassehn pulls her hands gently from the back of his neck. 'This is serious, Lisa,' he says disapprovingly. 'There it is, you hear that?'

Elisabeth Mattner sits up, terrified. 'That's . . . but that's . . .'

'. . . artillery fire,' Lassehn finishes her sentence. 'The time has come, Stalin *ante portas*!'

The stillness of the night is suddenly interrupted, the house has come alive all at once, doors are opened and closed, footsteps thunder, excited voices sound. Elisabeth Mattner listens with her head raised, she folds her arms over her naked breasts and grips her shoulders. 'My God,' she says, her lips twitching. 'How is that possible?'

Lassehn laughs briefly. 'Strange question! Weren't you prepared for it? According to the last bulletins . . .'

'Just a moment,' the woman interrupts him, listening to the sounds outside. A car has arrived, it sounds its horn three times and then twice more after a pause, the door closes, but the engine goes on chugging.

Elisabeth Mattner glances fleetingly at Lassehn, slips quickly out of bed and starts hurriedly getting dressed.

Lassehn has been watching her admiringly, and immediately guesses the connection between her getting up and the signal of the car horn.

'What is it, Lisa?' he asks. 'Are you getting up already? It's only three o'clock.'

'Stop asking so many questions and get dressed,' Elisabeth Mattner replies impatiently. 'Something must have happened for him to turn up at this time of night.'

'Who is he?' Lassehn asks.

'You should get dressed,' Elisabeth Mattner repeats irritably. 'Or stay in bed, but stay calm. Do you hear me?'

'Certainly, madam,' Lassehn replies. 'But who is he? Your husband? In that case . . .'

'You're making me very nervous with all your questions,' Elisabeth Mattner says, and fastens her stockings with darting fingers. 'My God, what's up with him, turning up in the middle of the night . . . There he is!'

The doorbell rings through the flat three times, and twice more after a short pause.

'Who is he?' Lassehn persists, and starts getting dressed as well.

'A good friend,' Elisabeth Mattner replies, and puts on a dressing gown. 'You know him, by the way, he's that red-faced man.'

'Yes, I remember,' Lassehn says slowly. 'Isn't he a colleague of yours?'

'He's my boss,' Elisabeth Mattner replies. 'Ministerial director at the Interior Ministry.' She walks up to Lassehn and kisses him quickly. 'Stay calm, all right?'

Lassehn nods, then he is alone in the room. He gets dressed quickly and opens the door to the next room a crack, he is curious about why the red-faced man, the ministerial director, is out on the road at this time of night, and why he's driven to see Elisabeth Mattner, who is probably his secretary and whom he calls Lisa while she calls him fatso . . . No, that can't be, that flabby man and Lisa . . . Lassehn fights down the suspicion that assails him like a sudden coughing fit.

Then he hears voices in the next room.

'Hurry up and get ready, Lisa,' the red-faced man says excitedly. 'There's no time to lose, Secretary of State Kritzinger ordered the Thusnelda transport operation to begin half an hour ago.'

'Are things as bad as that?' Elisabeth Mattner says incredulously.

The red-faced man sounds impatient. 'Good God, are you living on the moon? Haven't you read today's Wehrmacht report?'

'No, the paper didn't arrive, and then there was the power cut . . .'

The red-faced man unfolds a newspaper. 'Listen to this, Lisa. I'll just . . . Yes, here it is:

"From the Führer's headquarters, 20 April

This is an announcement from Wehrmacht high command:
An extremely bitter battle is raging against the Bolshevik mass assault between the Sudeten and the Oderbruch. West of the Lausitzer Neisse . . ."

'That's not it. Yes, this is it:

"In the battle outside Berlin our brave divisions on either side of Frankfurt [an der Oder] have successfully repelled enemy forces, and re-established the old main battle line as a counter-attack. The situation at Müncheberg and Wriezen has intensified. In spite of tough resistance large enemy armoured forces successfully advanced from the area of Müncheberg further to the south-west and the south into the area around Tempelberg and Buchholz. Counter-attacks are planned. At Wriezen the Soviets threw recently transferred forces into the battle. Bitter fighting continues in the areas of Sterneberg and Prötzel. According to incomplete reports . . ."

'And so on, and so on. This is today's Wehrmacht report, my child, so the situation yesterday, and a day has passed in the meantime . . .'

'But counter-attacks have been planned,' Elisabeth Mattner objects. 'Don't you think . . .'

Lassehn hears the red-faced man clapping his hands together. 'So? What does that mean? Counter-attacks are always scheduled, even at Stalingrad we counter-attacked, at Falaise and Tunis, but whether they are successful is a whole other question. The Russians can barely be stopped now, at least not from Berlin, I have reliable reports that they are already in Fürstenwalde, Hoppegarten and Hohe Neuendorf.' He is speaking quickly, his words are tumbling over each other, his pompous, drawling speech has made way for a vulgar cadence. 'And you must have heard that the city is already under artillery fire.'

'Yes, yes,' Elisabeth Mattner says eagerly, 'at first I didn't know what was going on.'

The red-faced man stamps his feet impatiently. 'Come on, girl, don't stand around, get dressed and tell me which suitcase you want to take. The chauffeur can bring it downstairs.'

'I just need to . . .'

'Of course! What are you waiting for? Or do you want to be fucked by a Bolshevik?' He gives a short burst of laughter. 'That's what I'm here for, at least every now and again, at least until the meagre supplies run out.'

Lassehn feels numb. So that's how it is, the red-faced man and Lisa . . . He feels ill, the revulsion within him is so strong that he has to put his hands over his ears, but he can't escape their loud, agitated conversation.

'I can't come with you now, Georg,' Elisabeth Mattner says. 'This morning, let's say eight o'clock.'

'Out of the question,' the red-faced man says firmly, 'we can't take the train, the lines to the south and the south-west have been destroyed, Halle and Leipzig are lost already, my darling.'

'Right, so what's going to happen?'

'I don't know either,' the red-faced man says. 'But for now let's get out of here. It's clear that things have gone wrong, we've got to find a way of getting out of this madness safe and sound . . .'

'So how do you plan to . . .' Elisabeth Mattner asks, confused.

'My car is waiting down below, I've got enough petrol coupons. Get a move on, would you?'

'Where are we going?'

'To Eutin first of all, the district chief executives have been instructed to sort out lodgings. Later we might travel on to Holstein. Why do you keep staring at your bedroom door?'

'I'm not,' Elisabeth Mattner says.

'Don't play games with me, I know your tricks, my darling. Have you got somebody in there?'

Lassehn gives a start, he quickly releases the safety catch on his revolver and pushes the door open. 'Good morning,' he says, and looks the red-faced man defiantly in the eye. 'Delighted to see you again.'

If he had thought the red-faced man would be seized by a fit of rage and lunge at him, he was mistaken. The red-faced man returns his gaze with a superior, amused smile. 'Well look at this,' he says, 'aren't you the young man we picked up on Wittenbergplatz a few days ago, who then ran off with Lisa? Of course you are, I recognize you now, even though you're wearing a more respectable suit today.'

Elisabeth Mattner stands slightly to the side, tottering back and forth on her heels. 'Don't fight,' she says severely, 'we've got other things to worry about. Be sensible, Joachim.'

'So the boy's called Joachim,' the red-faced man says. 'Were you pleased with him?'

'Shut up!' Lassehn says furiously. 'You should be ashamed of yourself . . .'

'I'm not jealous, young man,' the red-faced man says, 'in the end Lisa can do whatever she sees fit.'

The conversation is torture to Lassehn, the assertive pose that he adopted just now when entering the room was not real and falls from him like a withered leaf. 'Lisa,' he says, agonized, 'I can't believe that you and this man . . . No, no, tell me it isn't so!'

'And why not?' the red-faced man says. 'Because I'm not as young as you and not so favoured in terms of my appearance?' He laughs, a deep, chuckling laugh. 'I have other qualities, young man, I have good connections in very high places and so on, and our Lisa – may I say that, or do you have some objection to the use of the possessive pronoun? – our Lisa values that, apart from her powerful need for love she has other demands, and you probably can't fulfil those, that's where us old fellows come in useful . . .'

'Shut up, Georg!' Elisabeth Mattner barks at him. 'You're being coarse. So what happens now?'

'What do you mean?' the red-faced man shoots back. 'You mean because I found the young man here with you? You know I'm not prissy. Now get a move on!'

'So the ministerial director can run away?' Lassehn asks sarcastically. 'While the ordinary people have to stay and fight?'

'I warn you, young man!' the red-faced man says menacingly. 'There's something very suspicious about you. Don't imagine you're taboo to me just because you've been to bed with Lisa!'

'I think you're a wonderful national comrade, dear sir!' Lassehn says confidently. 'Over the last few days something has changed very slightly, your throne is toppling, gentlemen!'

The red-faced man takes a step towards Lassehn. 'Why you little . . . I'll . . .'

'You won't do a thing,' Lassehn says, 'before you can make a single sound I'll put a bullet in your belly, taking away your hearing, your sight and the whole of your miserable existence.'

'Please, Georg, stop,' Elisabeth Mattner cuts in, and then,

turning to Lassehn: 'I think it's best if you go, Joachim, I'm really sorry . . .'

Lassehn is unperturbed. 'You don't owe me an explanation,' he says, and walks to the door. 'Bon voyage,' he adds, 'but don't imagine you will escape your punishment. Whether in Berlin or Holstein or anywhere else, we will catch up with you.'

Downstairs he feels as if he is waking from a bad dream.

V

21 April

The district around Silesian Station has changed crucially throughout these days. The flow of refugees that poured from the station
into Fruchststrasse, Langestrasse, Breslauer Strasse and Koppenstrasse to seep from here into the city centre has dried up, the
columns of handcarts, rack wagons, boxcarts, wheelbarrows,
prams, farmers' carts, bicycles, overladen cars and heavy trucks,
the dull grey mass of exhausted, desperate, half-starving and half-
crazed women, of stumbling, wailing old men and women, wailing
and whimpering children, have flowed away into the canals of the
ruins of Berlin. They have been fleeing the front, and have drawn
the front behind them as if by some magical force of attraction. The
thunder of the guns and the engine howl of the aircraft are like an
echo of their footsteps.

For a brief moment a strange stillness has settled, as if a riverbed
has run dry and the sandy, stony ground has been revealed. But then
other waves have come crashing in and washed the front into the
streets: the whole area has become a communications zone close to
the front. The streets are crammed full with vehicles of all kinds:
trucks, cars, Tiger tanks, mobile assault guns, anti-tank cannon, field
artillery guns, gun carriages, field kitchens, ambulances, the loudspeaker vans of the propaganda units, cars with radio aerials,
armoured cars. There are pyramids of rifles, mortars, machine guns,
ammunition boxes, and everywhere soldiers, soldiers, soldiers.

Berlin has always been a city of soldiers, but these soldiers roaming around Silesian Station district are of a kind that Berlin has not

previously encountered. Berlin knows soldiers in war and peace, marching off and coming home, soldiers victorious and defeated; it has seen the regiments exercising in Prussian goose-step at the imperial parades in the Tempelhof fields, it has seen them going off to war in August 1914, singing and draped with flowers, cheered by tearful crowds, and coming back four years later, beaten.

But almost in the same order as before, after a temporary weariness of all things military, it has befriended the new Reichswehr, which, in undying Prussian tradition, marched to mount guard at the monument to the fallen on Unter den Linden, and it became extremely intimate with the new National Socialist kind of Wehrmacht, proudly displaying its new achievements and amazing diversity at the Hitler parades on the Charlottenburger Chaussee. Finally, in 1939, the city experienced the unsung departure of the regiments from their barracks, without one of the many leaders of the boastful German Reich, normally so eloquent, deeming them worthy of an address and ensuring them that God was with them. Once again, in autumn 1940, the city was washed over by a mighty wave of soldiers when the troop transports rolled day and night, week after week, along the city railway and the various railway lines from west to east, towards a destination that was secretly whispered of but known to everyone. In the years that followed, countless personnel on leave arrived at the city and criss-crossed it, personnel who looked less like German soldiers than like Turkish porters, wheezing, sweating, dripping, with bent backs and transfigured faces as they dragged huge burdens, boxes, sacks, rucksacks, kit bags, suitcases, cardboard boxes, all kinds of luggage, soldierly souvenirs of the subjected lands.

None of these categories of soldiers exist in Berlin today, the city is now becoming acquainted with a new type of soldier that it has not seen for a long time, the weary, unshaven, dirty, battle-weary, starving soldier: the front-line soldier. They drift uselessly around or sit about in groups, rolling cigarettes or coming back again and again to the field kitchen, keeping out of the way of the officers where possible and calling out crude jokes to the girls. When shots ring out, they automatically head for cover and reappear when the danger is past. The officers give the appearance of being busy, they walk around hurriedly or with important expressions on their faces, they give orders or revoke them, they send out couriers and receive reports, but anyone who knows how to read their faces can see between their orders and instructions their deep insecurity, the nervous anxiety they are struggling to suppress.

The streets around Silesian Station have become an army camp, even the pavements are occupied, there are telephone wires stretched everywhere, in the hallways of the blocks of flats there are makeshift offices, and sleeping places and mobile first-aid stations have been set up in basements, shops, warehouses, factories, flats, under the arches of bridges and in tunnels, commanding voices, orders, curses, swearing, roaring, engine noise, the rattle of tanks, the clatter of typewriters, the whinnying of horses, music from loudspeakers, that is the acoustic backdrop of these days, sweat, the stench of petrol, a miasma of oil, gun smoke, the odours of field kitchens, a haze of tobacco, a smell of burning, clouds of smoke, chloroform, blood – that is the cloud of smells in which these days are enveloped.

Given the presence of these troops, known in good Prussian barracks as a band of pigs, the reports from the propaganda units are revealed for what they are: didactic dramas from the National Socialist propaganda primers for low-grade learners. Here all the propaganda reports, in which the lyrical element of descriptions of nature is an essential requirement (because they are designed to demonstrate the literary gift of the author and the human greatness of the German soldier in passing, but by no means inconspicuously), show themselves to be legends, they are stripped of their propagandist garb and all that remains are the only two things important for soldiers: food and sleep. In between there are orders and obedience and – if necessary – fighting.

But at first there is no fighting at Silesian Station, even if the Russian artillery fire is getting louder from hour to hour, and the low-flying planes are sometimes shooting so close to the rooftops that the red stars can clearly be seen on the white metal.

On the Strasse Am Schlesischen Bahnhof, between Klose's

restaurant and the Wehrmacht shelter, two four-man anti-aircraft guns have been set up, an anti-tank gun aimed at the freight-train tracks of the Eastern Station has been placed on the corner of Langestrasse and Fruchtstrasse, tanks with open turrets stand on Küstriner Platz and Mühlenstrasse, their guns aimed menacingly eastward, engineer units are busy bringing explosive charges under the railway viaducts above Fruchtstrasse and Koppenstrasse, and on the bridges over the Spree along Brommystrasse and Schillingstrasse. The entrances to Silesian Station, that iron-ribbed double atrium, are guarded by police sentries with sub-machine guns, their spread legs pressed solidly against the cobbles and the chin-straps of their steel helmets firmly tightened, because a general has set up his command post in the bunker under platform A. The general-staff map spread out in front of him no longer shows any Russian or Polish names, it is no longer on a scale of 1:100,000 or 1:250,000, and neither is it in fact a general-staff map. The magnitude of the task of leading the fatherland out of the war forced upon it and into the long-promised final victory is strangely in inverse proportion to the scale of the general-staff maps, so the scale of the map over which the general bends his worried head is 1:20,000 – it is merely a street map of Berlin.

In the midst of the army camp the meagre remains of civilian life vegetate like the sparse greenery among the rubble of ruined houses. In the course of the war it has shrunk more and more, almost all of the achievements of civilization have collapsed in turn, after the successful constriction of minds and souls. The fall into a primitive state did not happen all at once; the limitations and compulsory renunciations which were identified by the leadership with a telling wink across the Channel (where things are much, much worse), forced life slowly but inexorably into a tiny corner; every form of order was only provisional, every state merely temporary. Giving up on a certain quantity and kind of food is taken for granted, along with giving up on undisturbed sleep and a roof over one's head, after giving up on many different things had already been accepted, but with a strange perseverance among the ruins of the city, in the uncertain hours between the air raids and in the short pauses between work and sleep people had clung to a scrap of personal life. Now that the front line has come to the city, that has been erased, swept away by the fear of death. The war, hitherto a chronic illness with upsetting bursts of colic, now assails them with a burning, paralysing fever. The heroism, perseverance, spirit of sacrifice, Teutonic dedication commonly attributed to them are nothing but the primal survival instinct and, if there is still a thought in their minds, it is that of being liberated, of being *liberated from the war*, no matter by whom, no matter how, no matter by what, by the armies of Zhukov, Montgomery and Eisenhower, or by Hitler and his miracle weapon.

Only a very few look on calmly at the development of things, because they predicted the catastrophe when the crowd was still celebrating victories. One of them is Klose, he stands in the doorway of his restaurant with his sleeves rolled up and gazes out over the soldiers and the baggage train. Anyone who took the time to look more closely into his wide face with the slightly plump chin would discover, at the back of his eyes, an evil, hate-filled light, but who in these hours, as the volcano of war begins to pour its iron lava over the city, has time to look in other people's faces?

After a while the hard, piercing gaze vanishes from Klose's eyes and his face fills with a slack smile of nausea. He takes the one-page sheet from a newspaper seller, steps back into the restaurant and begins to read.

'Der Angriff, together with *Berliner illustrierte Nachtausgabe*
Saturday, 21 April 1945

The Führer's Sacred Mission
by Dr Robert Ley

Yesterday, when I came back to Berlin from the battle zone of Lower Silesia, I thought on the Führer's birthday about that strange, unique personality, about his fateful historical mission and his superhuman achievement for the salvation of the German people, and I would like to write my thoughts down here.

Right now, when incorruptible destiny, through the sudden death of Roosevelt, is driving the active individuals of this battle for the world into the foreground and demanding that we make the comparison with the rescuing of the Führer on 20 July, it is absolutely necessary to ask, beyond the day's events, about the demands made by destiny on the active individuals, whether friend or foe. In Roosevelt's case fate has spoken clearly and distinctly. Contrary to all reason, and thus contrary to destiny, he has begun the most criminal war of all time, brought monstrous suffering and unimaginable misery down on humanity. He has offended against God and man, which is why he was condemned, he had to die. In the case of Adolf Hitler fate clearly and distinctly declared its will. Destiny preserved the Führer from the shameful attack and granted him life to fulfil his historical mission. Let no one tell me: that is chance. No, that is fate. I believe in the Führer's historical mission, his sacred, saving mission to save the German people from downfall and lead National Socialist Germany to victory.

What would have happened if Adolf Hitler and his idea had not come? If Adolf Hitler had not come, the German people would no longer exist. Let no one imagine this only concerns National Socialism and its Führer. Were we wicked and corruptible enough to hand the German people, its life and its freedom, over to the Bolshevik and plutocratic hangmen, the Jews in Moscow and New York would accept us just as they accept any other traitors. But because the Führer and his party pursue and fulfil their historical mission incorruptibly and unswervingly, therefore they hate him and therefore they hate us.

In the most difficult situations I was always near the Führer. I also had the rare happiness of getting to know the Führer as a person. But only in the last weeks and months have I come to know him in all his greatness. The greatest thing about Adolf Hitler is his unshakeable faith and his unparalleled resilience. When everyone falters, the Führer never falters. When many hang their heads, the Führer's confidence remains steadfast. When no one can find a way out, the Führer finds it. He believes in victory and his mission: preserving Germany from its downfall.

The resistance of the German people cannot be broken, because Adolf Hitler cannot be broken.'

Klose slings the sheet of paper onto the table with a contemptuous laugh. 'That is . . .' he exclaims and shakes his head. 'Reading that, you're just speechless at the impudence.'

'You're insulting your intelligence to engage with such things,' Wiegand says, and picks up the newspaper. 'Why are you actually so annoyed?'

'Reading such nonsense would give you apoplexy,' Klose replies furiously and rinses a few glasses.

Wiegand glances at the page and smiles ironically. 'Did you expect anything else, Oskar?'

'Of course not,' Klose replies, 'but the brazenness of it still takes my breath away. In the past the Nazis have always packaged their nonsense very cleverly, but now the distance between lies and truth is so great . . .'

'. . . that it can no longer be ignored, is that what you mean?' Wiegand says. 'Yes, that ceased to be of any importance a long time ago, just as exhibitionists know of their criminal inclinations and still give them free rein, just as they keep on exposing themselves however many punishments they receive so Goebbels, Ley, Dietrich, Fritzsche and the others go on writing, regardless of the realities, and it isn't even entirely certain whether it isn't a similar psychopathic state. For us, maintaining distance from things, the discrepancy has become actually monstrous.'

'We know the drill by now,' Klose says, 'and it still makes us want to throw up. Where is Lassehn, by the way?'

'I've been worried about him,' Wiegand says, and gets to his feet. 'He was supposed to be fetching a few Volkssturm armbands for us, that's the best disguise at the moment.'

'That's right,' Klose says, 'they're grabbing every man who isn't actually crawling on all fours, and they're supposed to have issued the fourth Volkssturm conscription order.'

Wiegand paces uneasily back and forth. 'As long as nothing has happened to the boy.'

'It's no small matter being out and about right now,' Klose says, and dries his hands, 'there are checks everywhere, and then there's all the shooting . . . Have you any idea where he was last night?'

'He didn't say anything,' Wiegand replies, 'but I assume he was with a woman. Yesterday afternoon he asked my wife to iron the only good suit he managed to save.'

'He is a young lad,' Klose laughs, 'and these things have to happen even in wartime, but it seems to me that he's suffered a disappointment. His face when he came back at about six . . .'

'Right,' Wiegand agreed, 'he looked so pale, so tired, but not as if he hadn't slept, I would say it was a kind of psychical exhaustion. The boy has a good core that hasn't been eaten away by Nazism, I also think his character is faultless, but he's a bit too soft.'

'That's only half true,' Klose objects, 'the way he killed Sasse, and more importantly that SS cop out at yours, that was pretty good.'

'That's right,' Wiegand says and looks out through the big window at the street, 'but afterwards his nerves go. What he lacks is a solid political or philosophical foundation. But where is a young person supposed to pick up one of those, if he didn't get it at home?' He falls silent for a moment and listens tensely. 'The artillery is now thumping away almost without interruption, the explosions aren't very far away either. Just wait, soon . . . Oh hang on, we've got visitors.'

The door is pushed violently open, two dozen Volkssturm members force their way pushing and shouting into the restaurant. They are a curious bunch, most of them elderly men with greying hair, their movements angular, clumsy or ungainly, some of them have a pronounced limp, one of them even has a false arm. Their weapons consist of three rocket launchers, a bazooka and about a dozen M98 rifles, and some of them are unarmed. Not one of them is in uniform, the only identical thing about them is their red, black and red armband and their peevish expression. One of them is wearing an ancient pair of field-grey trousers with knee patches and quite a new officer's coat without epaulettes, another one is parading in a hussar's jacket and jodhpurs, Bavarian shoes and sports socks, two others wear the old dark-blue uniform of the Schutzpolizei, the others civilian suits, but they all feel obliged to give themselves a military appearance, whether through belts or shoulder straps, knee-length boots or work caps, knapsacks or haversacks, some even have bed rolls, rucksacks, gas masks, bayonets, hunting knives and holsters.

'Greetings, Comrades!' Klose exclaims. 'Just a quick snifter, and then off to fight the enemy!'

'Stop chatting!' says a tall, thin man whose wrinkled, shrunken neck protrudes high from the collar of his Litewka jacket. 'Just bring us a beer!'

'I'm right here, until supplies run out,' Klose replies, filling one glass after another and studying the Volkssturm men with contemptuous irony. 'Looking at you,' he goes on, 'I can't help thinking about what little Goebbels said in November at the big Volkssturm rally.'

'What did he say?' one of them asks.

'The truth, as always, only the truth,' Klose says, 'namely: "The Volkssturm is, by the Führer's will, a thoroughly modern force!" If you are the modern soldiers, I'd like to see the unmodern ones.'

'Stop your rabbiting. Have you got a few cigarettes?' asks another one, who is wearing a pair of smart riding boots and a patched and discoloured pair of breeches.

'No,' says Klose with a broad grin, 'but you can have a bockwurst and salad or a Wiener schnitzel, or a plate of decent meatballs . . .'

'Christ, stop it!' says a small man who is trying in vain to hide his crooked shoulder under a big windcheater. 'Or I'll fire my rocket launcher at your fat belly.'

'I wouldn't do that,' Klose replies, and skims off the long row of glasses with a single, quick movement, '*that* rocket launcher would be the one that would have saved Berlin by firing at the last T-34.'

'Is this a pub or a madhouse?' an asthmatic man asks, pulling furiously at the tips of his moustache. He is wearing a greasy blue postman's uniform with an old belt buckled under it.

'Why?' Klose says with a serious expression. 'What was it the Führer said? "However long the war may last, the final battalion on the battlefield will be a German one." I don't think you're taking the battle for Berlin seriously, gentlemen, it's about the survival of our glorious Reich. Gathered closely around our great Führer . . .'

The tall, thin man pulls a meaningful face. 'I've had it to there with the Reich, and the Führer can go and . . .' he says furiously, and makes an unambiguous hand gesture. 'We've had enough of this shit!'

'I don't understand,' Klose says, and shakes his head, 'how you're running about like you've just escaped from a cabinet of curiosities.'

'Easy for you to say, you old beermonger,' the crooked little man cuts in, and waves his arms in the air.

'Why? It wouldn't be a problem for me,' Klose says, and whistles through his teeth. 'Toot toot, and off to the middle of nowhere.'

'Or up he goes – hanging from a lamp post,' says the man in the hussar's jacket.

'That's exactly how it is,' agrees a man in a blue policeman's uniform. 'We have no option but to join in.'

'Great German heroes you are,' Klose says, and puts a set of glasses down on the table, 'instead of just bringing the whole thing to an end when your necks are on the line you keep going, in a way that's going to cost you your lives and take the battle into your houses, your flats and your cellars. But it's more comfortable to take commands and carry out orders even if they're a mockery of reason. Whatever you do, don't think, don't make any decisions of your own. You're a bunch of cowards, the whole lot of you!'

'Careful, fatso,' says the man with the smart riding boots, 'or you'll be dangling up there even before the Russkies light up your pub with their artillery fire. Listen!' he says, with an imperious gesture of his hand. 'Shut up for a minute!' Now their ears are all pricked for the sounds of the street, the artillery fire has become heavier and noisier, the explosions are coming at shorter intervals and the windowpanes rattle quietly.

'They're starting to fire at Silesian Station,' the crooked little man says.

'Every hour of battle means death and destruction for your

families,' Klose says seriously. 'Or do you think you can still halt the Russians?' The tall, thin man gives a weary, doubtful gesture and mutters a few vague words.

A middle-sized, dark-haired man with thick glasses now speaks: 'I still haven't completely given up hope,' he says, nodding violently, 'that the battle will not reach the end.'

'Poor mad fool,' Klose says, 'you believe what you hope. Let me tell you, the battle will bleed us dry if you don't call it off first. Here, read today's *Angriff*, and what they write about Magdeburg, that'll give you an idea. Here, take it – read it out!'

The man with the glasses hesitantly takes the paper and begins to read.

'Piles of rubble become fire-spewing mountains
Heroic battle of Magdeburg

Magdeburg, as the war correspondent of a major American news agency reports, is putting up more hate-filled resistance to the enemy invaders than the British and the Americans had expected.

When the American tanks rolled through the streets of the city, where after the heavy terror attacks of the previous few days no resistance was expected, the piles of rubble turned into fire-spewing mountains. The population, men, women and young people, had taken up position behind the ruins of their city to pay the hated enemy back for his scandalous actions with rocket launchers and rifles. Various islands of resistance, behind whose barricades the citizens of Magdeburg, including boys and old men, defend themselves bitterly and with wild ferocity, are effectively preventing the American advance.'

When he has finished, the men fall silent.

'Yes,' Klose says, and looks from one to the other, 'you can take an example from them, there are still some lads who entrench themselves when they have to, behind their own beards.'

'If only we knew what to do,' the tall, thin man murmurs, and absently drains his glass of beer.

'We should just shoot the bastards down,' says the man with the riding boots, 'bang, bang, bang, shoot them down, that's what we should do.'

'When you all end up in the grave,' Wiegand says, joining in with the conversation for the first time, 'today or tomorrow or maybe only the day after tomorrow, then your mass grave will have a swastika with the inscription, "Here lie the Volkssturm men Should, Would, If, But and If Only, out of their own indecision they died the patient heroic German death for the greatest of Führer of all times."'

Everyone turns to Wiegand, who is sitting in a dark corner.

'There's another one,' says the man with the hussar's jacket.

'But he's right,' says the crooked little man, 'he's right a hundred times over, but . . .' He lifts his misshapen shoulder and resignedly lets it fall again. 'Boy, they've really got us trapped.'

'We need to do some serious thinking,' says one man with a rocket launcher on his knees.

'Of course,' Klose says, 'but not too fast, first make a drawing and send it to Wehrmacht high command for appraisal and certification.'

'Drop the jokes, fatso,' the tall, thin man says irritably. 'It's not as simple as that . . .'

A mighty crash of thunder rings out, the house trembles for a few seconds, the front door flies open, the windows rattle, plaster trickles from the walls in white clouds, screams are heard from the street, the hoofs of a fleeing horse clatter on the cobbles.

'Bloody hell!' says the man in the postman's uniform. 'Now it's starting here, too!'

'Yes, try and find a quiet little place in Berlin,' Klose says scornfully.

'This is no time for joking,' the tall, thin man says furiously. 'I think . . .' He doesn't have time to finish his sentence and hunches his shoulders. A second shell arrives with a whistle and explodes, now they are coming in quick succession, shot after shot, explosion after explosion, accompanied by the rattle from the engines of the low-flying aircraft and the bursts of gunfire from their weapons. After a quarter of an hour the attack is over.

'Gentlemen, that was the overture,' says Klose,

'Damn it all, that was some heavy firing,' says the man with the riding boots, 'I've got to go and see what's going on out there.'

He passes through the door, which is still open, and collides with an SS officer. All of a sudden he is back in the pub.

'Attention!' he shouts loudly, clicks his heels together, and puts his hands against the seams of his trousers.

All the others leap to their feet and stand to attention in line with the regulations.

The SS officer studies them coldly. 'Report!' he says harshly. 'Are you making a report?'

The thin man steps forward and raises his hand in the Hitler salute. 'Platoon leader Albrecht and nineteen Volkssturm men, Hauptsturmführer.'

'Thank you,' the Hauptsturmführer barks. 'Where are you being deployed?'

'Küstriner Platz, anti-tank barrier on Müncheberger Strasse, Plaza and Eastern Station.'

'And what are you doing here?'

'We're off shift until eight p.m., Hauptsturmführer.'

'Nonsense, there are no shifts any more. There is no eight-hour day in the military, is that clear? There's plenty of work for everyone. Each man is urgently needed. Back to work, quick march!'

The thin man hesitates for a moment.

'Well, can we get a move on?' roars the Hauptsturmführer. 'You only have to say if you don't want to, there are still a few street lamps free, and we've got rope, too.'

'Patrol fall in,' the thin man shouts. 'Don't mark time, forward march.'

The Volkssturm men leave the pub in single file, with the Hauptsturmführer bringing up the rear.

Klose throws the washing-up brush in the basin, sending the water splashing. 'It's disgusting, Fritz,' he says furiously. 'Obedience is so much in their bones that . . . They'd almost decided to call it a day, but a few stars and stripes and the right kind of face, and they duck down and knuckle under, and it would have been an easy matter to kill that man, with all that banging and crashing out there no one would have noticed.'

'Certainly wouldn't,' Wiegand says from his corner, he is sitting there motionless, his chin pressed against his chest, his eyes half closed, a wrinkle of bitterness at the corner of his mouth.

Klose picks up the beer glasses and glances out at the street.

'Looks charming out there,' he says, half turning round. 'The anti-tank gun on Fruchtstrasse has been blown to hell, nothing but scrap metal and corpses, and the Wehrmacht shelter also took a blow, and they seem to have . . . Careful, low-flying aircraft!'

Klose leaps back into the pub. With a terrible roar a plane shoots low over the street, its shadow brushing the front window for a fraction of a second.

'This is getting cosy, then,' Klose says, and wipes the sweat from his forehead with his bare forearm. 'You're so calm, Fritz. What's up with you?'

Wiegand is breathing heavily. 'The Hauptsturmführer who was here a moment ago,' he says, 'that's . . .' He shakes himself like someone taking bitter medicine.

'That's what?' Klose says.

'My son,' Wiegand replies tonelessly.

Klose sits down on the nearest chair and slaps his hands on his thighs. 'Robert?'

Wiegand's voice is blank. 'Yes, Robert.'

VI

The Hackescher Markt and Silesian Station are exactly 2.2 kilometres apart as the crow flies. That normal member of the human species, *Homo sapiens per pedes*, or pedestrians and strollers who tend to walk upright and on level ground without being disturbed by sounds caused either by a perforated drum being rotated by an electric current and the air being fired from it by centrifugal force, or powder enclosed in metal cases being caused to explode by firing-pins – this species normally takes half an hour to cover that distance.

Lassehn is on his way to the Hackescher Markt. Line 1 is your best bet, Joachim (although only to Rosenthaler Platz), but it doesn't run any more, it's a very easy journey, you can't miss it, you walk down Holzmarktstrasse, then very quickly across Alexanderstrasse and under the railway tracks, where the 'Belvedere' used to be, on the Roland-Ufer you spit into the good old Spree and then you potter along Neue Friedrichstrasse, which follows the curve of the city railway from Jannowitz Bridge to the Stock Exchange, you turn right at Spandau Bridge, and you're already at the Hackescher Markt. The whole thing is a hop, skip and jump for a healthy young man, and if you stick to it you'll be there in just half an hour.

Klose said something similar, but Klose doesn't know everything. He knows a lot, because in his pub he hears everything you can imagine (and can't imagine), but he doesn't know everything because he doesn't like to move his heavy body any further than between the front door and the back room. Lassehn has already been walking for almost an hour, but he has only reached

Alexanderstrasse, because there are all kinds of obstacles and delays. Here an alleyway is closed because there's a danger of collapsing buildings, elsewhere sentries with rifles stand and stop people getting through, then there are attacks from low-flying aircraft and artillery fire that force you to take shelter; one street was impassable because the façades on either side were burning, across its whole width unbearable heat and stinging smoke seethed and a rain of glowing ash fell down on it. Three times he is stopped by army patrols and strictly checked, and in the end he gets lost, he is so confused by all the detours, he wanders among the ruins as if between huge labyrinthine fences and in the end he doesn't know where he actually is. The street signs have been destroyed, and there is no trace of them on the piles of rubble.

On Alexanderstrasse Lassehn considers using the S-Bahn, but he immediately rejects the idea, since public transport (if it is running at all) can only be used with special travel authorization papers of urgency level III. Since the Roland-Ufer is also closed, Lassehn tries to reach Schicklerstrasse, but that is impossible too, so he is forced back into a narrow street leading towards the east. A hurrying passer-by tells him he is on Kaiserstrasse.

He takes a few steps down the street, but if he thought he would find a dead and abandoned street he was mistaken. The street isn't empty, on the contrary, it is full of people, women are standing around outside a general goods store, but they aren't standing around as they usually do in dense, packed rows of three or four, with sulky, dull or patient expressions but quick tongues, no, they are standing in single file, pressed close against the wall, and pale fear is drawn on every face. There are flickering eyes in every face and pursed, twitching lips, because beyond the roofs the shells of the Russian artillery whistle and the engines of the red fighter bombers roar, shell splinters clatter into the street, each time it sounds like a harp string breaking. A firebomb has struck the roof of a house on the other side of the street, tiles clatter on the cobblestones and shatter rattling in all directions, in the beams of the roof the fire crackles and is already licking with fiery red tongues against the lower storeys. It is a gloomy, whitish day with low-hanging clouds, so the smoke is pushed deep into the street, and a light wind blows soot along. But none of the women leave the queue, they press handkerchiefs over their horrified mouths and put on air-raid goggles, they pull their headscarves, shawls and turbans more tightly around their heads and stuff each stray lock under the protecting fabric. There they stand, mute, with faces that look as if turned to stone, their hands holding shopping bags and nets pressed firmly against their trembling bodies, between fire and falling shells. Every sound, the whistle of the shells, the whirring of the propellers and the hiss of fire, makes them flinch, all for a miserable pound of semolina or groats, half a pound of sugar or flour.

'The fire should be reported,' murmurs one of the women with the wrinkled face of a prematurely aged worker.

'Where to? How? Who to?' her neighbour asks. 'Or do you want to go? Give up your place?'

'I'm not even thinking about it,' says the woman with the wrinkled face. 'And I lost my place anyway. Let the shop burn down!'

'Why doesn't he open up?' a young woman calls from the end of the row.

'He's waiting for instructions from the Reich Food Office,' another young woman calls.

'He's keeping us waiting until . . .' says a sturdy young woman in an overall.

The explosion of a shell pulls the words from her mouth, a stone fountain sprays up and rattles down, screams of horror ring out, dust and smoke roil above the place of impact.

Lassehn has thrown himself down on the ground, he has heard the whistling of the shell and shouted 'take cover', but the others haven't heard him, or have heard him too late. When he gets back to his feet he sees the women leaning against the wall, their faces distorted with fear, their mouths groaning. Only one lies on the floor, she is an elderly woman, a few strands of grey hair have come loose from under a brown headscarf, her skirt is lifted to her knee revealing black, knitted woollen stockings and stout boots with buckles. Her hands, big, bony, hard-worked hands with thick blue veins and broken nails, clutch several food cards.

Lassehn leans over the woman and reaches carefully for her shoulder. 'All over, Grandma,' he says.

The old woman doesn't move. Lassehn turns her carefully onto her back and looks into her old, sunken, grey face.

'What's happened to her?' a young woman from the queue asks, and approaches hesitantly. 'Is she . . .'

'I don't know,' Lassehn says, and shrugs. 'Perhaps she's . . .' Just fainted, he was going to say, but the words stick in his throat, he sees that the woman's coat is shredded just below the waist. It is only a hole the size of a thumbnail, but Lassehn knows this kind of shredded clothing, he knows what it means when the ends of the fibres seem to be turned inwards, he also knows what it means when a wound like that bleeds outwards. He takes the woman's arm and tries to feel her pulse, but he can't find her heartbeat.

The young woman is now standing beside Lassehn, who is still bent over the old woman and holding her hand. 'Say something.' The young woman is practically panting. 'My God, say something!'

Lassehn lets the old woman's hand slip slowly back to the cobbles and stands up. 'We've got to try . . . Isn't there a hospital or a first-aid station somewhere around here?'

'Perhaps in the air-raid shelter on Alexanderplatz,' the young woman replies. 'But how . . .'

'Won't you help me pick her up?' Lassehn asks, and looks her full in the face.

'I can't leave here,' the young woman replies, and looks searchingly along the queue as if to check that her place is still free.

'We might still be able to save her,' Lassehn says urgently, 'but she will have to be carried carefully.'

'Has she been hit, or has she just fainted?'

'I presume it's shrapnel in her abdomen, internal bleeding, if she isn't helped quickly . . .'

He pauses. The sound of marching comes from Alexanderstrasse, a platoon of SS grenadiers with rocket launchers, sub-machine guns and carbines turns into Kaiserstrasse, they are wearing steel helmets with SS runes pushed to the backs of their necks, and their jacket collars are unbuttoned.

Lassehn runs towards them. 'Comrades,' he says breathlessly, 'there's an old woman down there who's been hit by a splinter from a grenade.'

The SS squad leader, who is marching on the right of the platoon, gives Lassehn a fleeting glance. 'So? We're on duty.'

Lassehn runs along beside the junior section leader. 'She could still be saved,' he says, pleadingly. 'If you carry her carefully on the stocks of your carbines . . .' He points to the old woman lying at an angle across the pavement.

The Unterscharführer and a few SS men look at the old woman and shrug, none of them slows down for even a second, in their faces there is not a flicker that might suggest a spark of emotion in their cold and apathetic faces.

'We're on duty,' the junior section leader repeats. 'A few Bolshevik tanks are supposed to have broken through at Weissensee.'

'You can't make an omelette without breaking eggs,' a voice says from the platoon. 'That's always been the case.'

The platoon turns into Kurze Strasse, Lassehn is left behind. He has forgotten the shells that whistled over his head and the consuming flames in the street, and he stands irresolutely for a few seconds in the middle of the street, then with a shuffling step he walks back to the old woman.

The young woman stands there with her arms dangling and looks at the old woman. 'I think she's dead,' she says.

At that moment the body twitches as if in spasm, the legs stretch out as if to push something away, the hands shoot apart and a grey stiffness spreads over the old woman's confused face.

'She's survived it,' the young woman says, her lips trembling, then she turns round abruptly and rejoins the queue.

Lassehn picks up the food cards that have slipped from the old woman's hands, one card for adults and three for children. 'Therese Kaupisch, Berlin C, Elisabethstrasse 63,' he reads, 'Dieter Kaupisch', 'Rosemarie Kaupisch', 'Gudrun Kaupisch', an old woman who went shopping for herself and her three grandchildren and will never come back. A shell splinter has torn a hole in her body from which the life has fled.

Lassehn walks up to the young woman he was speaking to just now. She is leaning against the wall with her eyes closed, and her arms are crossed firmly over her chest. 'Can I entrust the cards to you?' he says. 'Do you want to buy something with them? The address is on the cards.'

The young woman takes the cards in silence and puts them carelessly in her pocket.

Lassehn looks along the queue, the gap left by the death of the old woman has already closed, the survivors have pushed forward. Then he turns and puts the old woman in the gutter, the way you clear away an obstacle. A man in the queue crosses himself and murmurs a few words into his ice-grey beard.

When Lassehn has walked a few metres into Kurze Strasse, he turns round again. There lies the old woman, the gutter is her coffin, the thundering cannon her death knell, a queue of people who have forgotten how to feel her funeral cortège. It is the conclusion of a hard-working life, the debris of an inhuman age. You can't make omelettes . . .

Then Lassehn is standing in Landsberger Strasse, which opens up broadly and extravagantly onto Alexanderplatz after a tight row of houses. Where Landsberger Strasse and Neue Königstrasse come together into an acute angle and two underground-train entrances form the threshold to the underworld of Alexanderplatz, three anti-tank guns have been set up. In the middle of the square, between the tramlines that glide apart beyond the traffic islands and curve towards the north and the south, there is a heavy anti-aircraft gun, with its cannon, painted with kill rings, aimed not towards the sky but towards Neue Königstrasse, which from Weissensee via Greifswalder Strasse forms one of the access roads to Alexanderplatz. Two field kitchens smoke in the ruined Tietz department store, a despatch rider speeds down Königstrasse from the City Hall and sweeps in a breakneck bend into Memhardstrasse to the Alexander barracks. A strange stillness has suddenly fallen over the big square, which is normally filled with seething life. The artillery fire falls silent or rumbles somewhere far away like a distant storm, the voices of the soldiers and the clatter of iron against iron are far too faint to be heard across the whole of the big square. Apart from the soldiers there is no one in the square. Since the sirens went off early in the morning no all-clear has sounded.

It has gradually become apparent that the alarm is a permanent state.

Suddenly a new sound penetrates the dark peace of the square. A low-flying plane, engines roaring, plunges towards the square, almost speeding towards the slender tower of the Georgenkirche, fires a few salvoes at the anti-tank emplacement and brings the plane back up over the hall of the railway station.

Lassehn has leaped into the hallway of a block of flats, a stray bullet hits the wall next to him and showers him with plaster. For a few seconds the big square falls silent again. Two orderlies appear from the underground shaft opposite the Tietz department store, they run with long strides, backs bent, across the square, to help an injured man. A cyclist in the brown jacket and short dark trousers of the Hitler Youth comes from Büschingplatz and rides along Landsberger Strasse, he pushes the pedals like mad, his torso almost lying on the handlebars, he leans the bicycle against the iron railings of the entrance to the underground and jumps down the steps into the depths. Then another sound enters the square, vague and indistinct at first, then increasingly clear: it is the grinding sound of tank tracks.

Lassehn looks along Landsberger Strasse, but he can't see far, thick smoke from a burning house is sent deep into the street, the outlines of the houses are almost invisible. A car stands brightly blazing in front of the Eden cinema, the penetrating stench of burning rubber blows up to Alexanderplatz, a man, two women and a little girl come running out of Frankfurter Strasse, panting under the weight of rucksacks and suitcases towards the bunker on Landsberger Strasse, the girl falls to her knees a few times, the man stumbles and loses his hat.

The barrels of the guns aim precisely at the cloud of smoke on Landsberger Strasse. 'Clear the street!' shouts one of the crew of the anti-tank gun.

Meanwhile the man with the women and the girl has reached

the entrance to the bunker, he sets down the two suitcases and wipes his brow with the sleeve of his coat, then goes leaping grotesquely across the carriageway to pick up his hat.

'Clear the street!' a gunner shouts again.

At the same moment thunder and lightning explode from the cloud of smoke on Landsberger Strasse, then thunder and lightning and, once more, thunder and lightning. A dark, resounding echo, explosions spraying debris high in the air, a hail of shell splinters, clouds of smoke, screams, then the big grey masses of two T-34 tanks emerge from the cloud of smoke, driving at an angle, firing shot after shot. The anti-tank guns start firing now too, but after only the first few shots the tank rolls over them. Several SS men with rocket launchers come running from Alte Schützenstrasse. Lassehn recognizes the Unterscharführer who was marching with his platoon down Kaiserstrasse a short while ago so he takes cover behind a pile of sand and sets two rocket launchers down in front of him. By now the first tank has driven around Alexanderplatz and is turning into Dircksenstrasse, while the other has turned right, cut across the tongue of pavement that protrudes sharply from the entrance of Frankfurter Strasse into Landsberger Strasse, and fires at the anti-tank gun that blocks the northbound carriageway of Landsberger Strasse. From Dircksenstrasse the first tank now opens fire on the anti-aircraft gun, but it is firing too high, the shells sweep over the square into the building of the Labour Office. Now the Unterscharführer starts firing, he hits the track of the T-34, picks up another rocket launcher and aims. At that very moment the tank advances towards him, the SS man pulls the trigger and jumps a few steps back, one, two, three seconds pass, then there's a cloud around the tank, sparks rain down, but the tank keeps going, it rolls across the traffic islands towards Landsberger Strasse, swings its turret round and fires shot after shot. Then all of a sudden it is engulfed in flames. The Unterscharführer throws up his arms in triumph, calls his men over with an imperious gesture, and they run after the tank, sub-machine guns at the ready.

The other tank, still standing on Frankfurter Strasse, now changes its direction of fire and starts shooting one round after another, and the anti-aircraft gun starts firing as well, the shots roar across the square, hitting the buildings behind the tank, ripping big chunks of stone from a block of flats, a balcony falls on the cobblestones, window frames swirl through the air, splinters of glass come down like rain. The second tank turns away now and rolls back into the cloud of smoke on Landsberger Strasse.

By now the SS men have surrounded the burning tank, the turret opens and three Red Army soldiers climb out. Lassehn can clearly make out their faces, two of them have young, broad, tanned faces, with eyes as clear as water and short, bristly, dark-blond hair, the sweat covers their low, angular foreheads like a thick layer of grease and drips like melted lard on their grey-green uniform jackets, the third is Asiatic, with slanting, narrow eyes, dark like a child's, sharp cheekbones and a hare lip, he wears a grey fur cap whose side flaps hang loosely down. They climb out of the turret one after the other, jump heavily onto the cobbles and raise their arms in the air.

The Unterscharführer walks right up to them and studies them darkly, then with a quick movement tears the decorations and medals from their uniforms.

'What shall we do with these fellows?' one of the SS men asked. 'Where should we take the prisoners to?'

The Unterscharführer turns halfway around to address him. 'Prisoners? Are you stupid?' he bellows. 'There are only the living and the dead now.'

'Don't do anything stupid,' the SS man says, 'you can't just shoot them down in the middle of Alexanderplatz, there are people all over the place, some of them are coming out of the bunker right now.'

'Just let me get on with it,' the Unterscharführer replies, and turns back to the Red Army soldiers. 'Clear off, Ivan,' he says and grins, with a gesture in the direction that the tank has just come from.

The Russians look in the direction he has just indicated, shrug their shoulders and protest to the Unterscharführer.

'Home, *domoi*, you,' the Unterscharführer says, and points again in the same direction.

The Russians look at each other, perplexed, and smile in disbelief. Aren't they taking us prisoner? Aren't they going to shoot us? Are they just going to let us run away? they might be thinking right now. But the war is practically over, they've almost conquered Berlin already, and Berlin is Germany.

They exchange a few words, then one of them points to himself and the two others and then points down Landsberger Strasse.

'We go?' he asks.

'Yes, Ivan,' the Unterscharführer says impatiently, he narrows his eyes and looks past the three Russians at the entrance to the bunker, where a few dozen people are standing and carefully keeping watch.

'*Spassibo,*' the Asiatic soldier says and reveals his white teeth in a broad smile, '*spassibo.*'

For a few seconds the three Red Army soldiers stand there in the oily haze and smoke of the burning tank, turn irresolutely on their heels, then walk a few steps, nod to the SS men and fall into a light running step.

'Fire!' the Unterscharführer orders.

The SS men suddenly raise their sub-machine guns and fire three salvoes in a row. Two Russians fall straight away, the third staggers on a few steps and then falls forward, raises his torso again and turns round with a puzzled expression, until a shot from the Unterscharführer's pistol finishes him off.

'The bastards tried to run,' the Unterscharführer says to a few people crossing the road from the bunker. 'I had no choice . . .'

Shot while fleeing, Lassehn thinks, so that's how it's done. He clenches his fists and feels tears of rage rising into his eyes. The death of the old woman on Kaiserstrasse, just a quarter of an hour previously, has almost been forgotten again. It touched him with a dull sense of grief, but the deaths of the three Russian soldiers leave him agitated and upset. The old woman's death was an accident or a misfortune, one might call it chance of fate, but this was cold-blooded, perfidious murder.

Lassehn studies the Unterscharführer's face. He feels anxious, the other man bears human features like his own, perhaps his lips are thin lines and his eyes the cold blue of a winter coat, but nothing else suggests that this man is a cold-blooded murderer. His hands are steady as he lights a cigarette, they don't tremble, there is only indifference in his face, and his voice sounds relaxed, without a hint of agitation, when he gives an order.

'Clear these fellows away,' he says. 'Chuck them somewhere in the ruins.'

Lassehn leaves the doorway in which he has been standing until now and crosses Landsberger Strasse. The hat is still there, a dark-green velvet hat with a grey cord, which the man with the suitcase lost, except the hat is still there, and a blood stain. The body of the man who wore the hat is lacerated, mangled, annihilated. He tried to save his hat and instead lost his life.

Lassehn crosses Alexanderplatz, walks past the still-burning tank and turns into Dirckenstrasse. What is it in these people that is different from me, that they can murder in cold blood like that? Just because others belong to a foreign race, have a different set of principles or wear an enemy uniform? Even if these people are separated from those around them by the SS runes, they are still human beings, upright-walking mammals, gifted with the ability to speak and associate ideas, born in innocence and growing up in a mother's care, the same seed has been placed in their mind as in mine, but the soil into which it has sunk must be a different one, more accessible to destructive ferments, which in the end overgrow everything that Christianity and humanism have over thousands of years of hard work forced, injected, instilled and impressed on the primitive mind of the barbarian. It is an incomprehensible trick of nature that it does not outwardly identify these people whose spirit denies thousands of years of human history by reverting to barbarism.

'But these are mere hypotheses,' Lassehn says to himself, 'where is the answer, my God, where is the answer?'

He goes on walking as if in a dream, but then he shakes off his inhibitions when an S-Bahn train rattles by not far away, high on the viaduct. He can find no answer to the questions that assail him, and now is not the time, as he must address the task at hand. He looks around to get his bearings. He has almost walked too far, because on his left, in the middle of the fields of ruins, the round hall of Börse Station rises. Lassehn sighs with relief when he turns right into An der Spandauer Brücke and the rectangle of the Hackescher Markt lies straight ahead. He doesn't guess that the most terrible link in the chain of today's events will be added here.

Outside the entrance to the Hackescher Hof, that big industrial building with a broad gate as an entrance, its grimness mitigated only by a few old brightly coloured film posters from the Imperial cinema, a number of people have huddled together, and excited voices are drowning one another out. Lassehn crosses the carriageway and walks past the gathering, he only wants to fulfil his task and not be held up any further, but his stride falters, and at last he stops.

He sees a young man being pushed through the crowd by a Nazi office steward with kicks and shoves. The young man is dressed in civilian clothes, his face is grey and pale, as if it had been dipped in ash, his fair hair hangs sweaty and dishevelled into his forehead. Every new shove makes him tremble like a young tree shaken by an autumn storm.

Lassehn is shocked. An underground worker? A deserter? A defeatist? A criminal? He releases the safety catch on his revolver, he might be able to intervene, but while he is still thinking his moment of opportunity has already passed. Three SS men come running up from Oranienburger Strasse, their hobnailed boots clattering over the cobbles. The young man stumbles into them in front of the Dresdner Bank, and a particularly violent kick from the office steward sends him flying to the ground.

The SS men stand where they are, they aren't wearing steel helmets but grey peaked caps with the death's-head insignia and have the Sicherheitsdienst diamond on their right sleeve.

'What's happening to him?' asks one of the SD man with the rank insignia of a section leader on the black collar of his uniform jacket.

The official, in a brown uniform, knee-length boots, wearing a Party insignia with a golden wreath, lowers his pistol and raises his hand in the Hitler salute. 'This is a deserter,' he says, 'such a damned . . .'

'Hang on a minute,' the section leader interrupts him, 'do you know that for certain, Comrade?'

'Yes,' the brown-clad man replies, 'very definitely, he turned up last night, secretly, silently and quietly, he was still in uniform, but I saw him . . .'

'Keep it short,' the section leader breaks in, 'we haven't got much time.'

The official nods. 'And then he tried to run away, in civilian clothes as you can see.' The section leader kicks at the young man, who is still lying on the cobbles with his arms raised protectively over his head. 'Stand up,' the man in the grey uniform says, 'and be quick about it.'

The young man tries to get up, he draws one foot underneath his body and straightens his torso, but his feet can find no purchase and slip back again.

'I said get up!' the official shouts, and kicks him again.

The young man supports himself on his hands, kneels down and then draws himself up with his final effort.

'Have you deserted from your unit?' the section leader asks.

The young man staggers like a drunken man, he tries to answer but his lips move without making a sound; only his Adam's apple goes up and down with a champing sound.

'Show me your papers!' the section leader demands.

The young man stands with his hands dangling by his sides, he doesn't even try to look for papers in his pockets, his eyes are still directed inwards, the white of his eyeballs gleaming spectrally in his ashen face, his upper lip with its thin growth of beard twitching spasmodically.

Lassehn stands in the middle of the crowd and feels that he has turned white as a sheet so he has to avert his gaze. He cannot bear the sight of his helplessness, his mute, quivering submission. He looks his neighbours in the face and is even more startled. He expected they would be standing there with bitterly raging expressions, twitching cheek muscles, sparkling eyes, clenched fists, ready to throw themselves at the torturers who were now their own torturers, but instead he is looking into faces that bear an expression that is a strange mixture of lascivious expectation and fear, and understands that this group is feeling the same emotions as spectators at a boxing match, for whom technical finesse is not enough, who want a tough and bloody exchange of blows and if possible a knock-out. It isn't hard to tell from the faces of the people that two hopes are battling within them, the hope that they will be presented with a sensation, and the hope that everything will be resolved for the best in the end.

'You're not answering me, you piece of filth?' the section leader roars. 'There!' His fist strikes the young man hard in the face.

The young man totters and immediately gets a push in the back from the official standing behind him, sending him staggering forward, blood pouring from his mouth and nose and dripping heavily on the cobbles, his upper lip thickly swollen, but he still doesn't say a word.

'Where is my son?' a woman's voice shrieks. 'Walter! Walter!'

A thick-set woman of middle height comes out of the gate of the Hackescher Hof and runs to the group. The spectators stand back and form an alley.

'What are you doing with my . . .' she begins talking hastily and breathlessly to the section leader and presses her hands to her panting chest. She doesn't finish her sentence, because her eye falls on the young man whose face begins to move for the first time.

'My God,' she says very quietly and brings her hands to her face. 'What have they done to you?'

The section leader looks at the woman through narrowed eyes. 'Are you his mother?' he asks.

'Yes,' the woman replies, and takes her hands from her face. 'Believe me, he's a good boy . . .'

'. . . but a bad German,' the section leader interrupts her. 'He has broken the oath he swore to the Führer, he is a deserter. In this, our fatherland's gravest hour, there can be no mercy.'

'He wasn't thinking,' she says, raises her hands and goes right up to the Nazi officer, 'I'm sure he didn't, and I'm sure he will go right back to his unit. Isn't that right, Walter?'

'To switch to the Bolsheviks,' the section leader says scornfully. 'Now clear off, and stop talking.'

The young man remains motionless, blood is still running from his nose, it runs over his mouth and chin and drips onto his suit.

'And you have aided and abetted a deserter,' the office steward says. 'We'll come back to that.'

'My mother doesn't know a thing,' the young man says, 'I told her I'd come home on leave.'

The woman starts crying, tears running down her cheeks and inundating her face, but she makes no attempt to dry them.

'Stop whining, you old witch,' the junior section leader says threateningly. 'Off with you!'

'What's going to happen to my son?' the woman asks anxiously and raises her hands pleadingly. 'Where are you taking him? Please tell me so that I can visit him.'

'Your son will be very close by,' the junior section leader replies, and there is a terrible menace in his narrow eyes.

'You can rely on it, very close, you'll find out all about it. Now go!'

The woman is still hesitating, her eyelids twitch helplessly up and down. 'Is that really true, officer?' she asks with a trembling voice. 'Is that really . . .'

'Go away now, damn it all!' the section leader orders. 'Or something will happen!'

'Go, mother,' the young man says, his voice surprisingly firm.

The woman takes a handkerchief out of her coat pocket and wipes the blood from her son's face. 'You did it for me, Walter,' she says, 'you will have to tell the gentlemen that when they question you, they're bound to understand, you've been a good soldier for six years.'

The young man pulls his lower lip deep between his teeth and turns aside. 'Go now, mother, please.'

The woman puts the handkerchief back in her pocket, then she walks through the ring of people with her eyes lowered.

The junior section leader watches after her until she has disappeared through the gate, then he gives a sign to the two SD men.

'Come on, apply the handcuffs!' he says in a harsh voice.

The young man's hands are twisted roughly behind his back and bound in steel chains.

'You know what's coming,' the section leader says, and looks searchingly around. 'Damn it, isn't there a single lamp post around here?'

The office steward shakes his head. 'The British have smashed everything to bits,' he replies, 'but over there you've got the tram stop outside the Scherl building . . .'

The junior section leader looks along the street. 'High enough,' he decides, 'that's fine. Come on, let's get going!'

The young man stands there and doesn't move.

The junior section leader looks at him scornfully. 'I could just shoot you down here, you scoundrel,' he hisses through his teeth, 'but I want you hanging visibly as a warning to everyone, and I've promised your mother that you'll be staying nearby. You see, I'm keeping my promise. Right, let's go!'

The junior section leader gives him a shove, his face twists into a repulsive grimace. The alley opens up again, the young man staggers forward and now they all shove him in turn, the three grey-clad men and the man in the brown uniform, as if they all wanted to play a part in the mistreatment of the deserter. With shoves, kicks and blows, the young man is driven down the middle of the road until he is standing by the tram stop.

A tram stop marks the point where trams stop to enable passengers to get in and out, it consists of an iron pole that is painted yellow and planted in the cobblestone pavement, it carries at the top a white flag made of iron with a coating of enamel, with the inscription 'Tram Stop', in the middle of the post an iron panel is applied; behind a pane of glass it lists the routes and timetables of the tramlines that can be used at this stop. Hitherto, tram stops have served no purpose other than to hold advertisements for cinemas, pawnshops and cafés. It was not until April 1945 that the National Socialist murderers managed to prove that tram stops could also be used as gallows. It is obvious that tram stops (like street lamps and shop grilles) are not comfortable gallows, with pulley blocks and trapdoors, but they can still be used to take human beings from life to death via strangulation.

Lassehn has stopped in the middle of the crowd which is standing on the traffic islands on Rosenthaler Strasse. All around is the half-ruined backcloth of the Hackescher Markt, it still bears the traces of the life that once roared across this small square from five channels, the Imperial cinema and the Hackescher Hof, the Caesar Lottery Company and the Commerzbank, the Bio-Cinema and Koester A.G., Oranienburger Strasse, Grosse Präsidenenstrasse, Mantow the stamp dealer's and Roesner's private school, Neue Promenade, Aschinger-Quelle, An der Spandauer Brücke, the billiard hall and 16th Police Precinct, Rosenthaler Strasse, Eckert Hats and the Scherl store, triangular traffic island with circular telephone box, tram and bus stops with narrow entry platforms, Börse S-Bahn station and Weinmeisterstrasse underground station, Wertheim department store and the Jewish community, Gestapo HQ and the old people's home, they all once cast their waves across the asphalt of the square.

The whistling and bellowing of the Russian artillery fire rings through the air, but Lassehn doesn't notice, he is frozen, he wants to turn round and run away, but he seems to be rooted to the spot, he is dazed, he sees everything as if through a veil. He suddenly remembers reading somewhere that criminals are hanged by opening a trapdoor under them or pulling away a support for their feet, so that the body suddenly drops with a jerk and death comes not through suffocation, but by breaking the spinal column. But here neither contraption is available, so there is only one possibility . . . No, no, something screams inside him, no, it can't be, we are in Germany, in 1945, and these are German people too . . .

Lassehn still hopes that . . . Yes, what? That they aren't actually going to go through with it? They are already putting the noose around the young man's neck, now they are throwing the other end of the rope over the enamel sign saying 'Tram Stop' and pulling it tight. The young man is still standing upright, the rope is still loose around his neck, the noose hasn't been pulled tight, a twenty-year-old or twenty-two-year-old or twenty-five-year-old heart is still pulsing with the fastest heartbeats of its life, the polluted but life-giving breath of the Berlin streets, a chemical compound of oxygen and nitrogen, called air, is still flowing into his lungs, the section leader could still call it off and say, 'Enough! But remember this, next time you're actually going up there', but none of that happens. Lassehn has not yet understood the terrible consistency of National Socialism, that oft-cited practice with which it first made its appearance, which began with murder and ends with murder.

A few seconds of unsettling silence pass against the roar of the guns. The boy stands there, his face stained with blood and his clothes drenched in sweat, his hands on his back chained with steel handcuffs and a noose around his neck. His face is rigid and waxy, as if he has already died and his eyes have been extinguished. There are two SD men behind him, the other end of the rope clutched firmly in their hands as if they are waiting for a signal to begin a tug-of-war, the section leader and the office steward stand there like referees who have to give a start sign, and there is a large crowd some distance away. The whole thing is a People's Court like those ordered by the Führer and Reich Chancellor of the Great German Reich.

The unbearable tension is discharged in the scream of a woman that rises, sharp and sudden, cutting through the silence like lightning from a clear sky.

'Shut your mouth, you hysterical old cow!' the section leader shouts. 'Come on!' he orders, and waves both arms wildly in the air.

The two SD men begin to pull, grip by grip, the iron pole sways but holds, the young man hovers in the air, his head at a strange angle, his legs dangling slackly, his face turning pink, then red, dark red and then blue, his lower jaw flaps down as if a hinge has been opened, a gurgling groan issues from his mouth, his tongue protrudes, swollen and bluish-red, bubbles of foam appear at the corners of his mouth, his eyes bulge from their sockets, no twitch, no rearing reveals the moment of death, the life rattles imperceptibly from his body.

The crowd disperses. No one is triumphant, the faces are serious, hard, angry, grim, thoughtful, but no one dares to say a word or raise a hand, they creep timidly away like thrashed dogs, but along with the boy who has just croaked his last, their own consciences hang on the gallows.

Lassehn stands on the traffic island for a few more minutes, sees the two SD men wrapping the rope around a few times and knotting it tightly, and suddenly there is also a sign there that they fasten to the buttonholes of the hanged man's jacket. Lassehn crosses the road and reads:

'I, the engineer Walter Deichmann, am hanging here because I was too cowardly to defend my home town.'

and walks quickly on. His throat is choking as if he too has a rope around his neck. He steps through the front door of a ruin to throw up.

VII

After it turns out that the air-raid wardens have blown their whistles, struck their gongs and drummed on the dustbins for the last time on the morning of 21 April, that no all-clear has followed this last air raid, and that the warning has by now become a permanent state, the city is definitively in its death throes. Admittedly the S-Bahn and the U-Bahn are still running on some lines, but they barely serve the population, those stretches have become military nerve fibres, and the stations are now places of refuge. The Russian artillery has moved into fire stations, from which they can fire on almost every part of the city, and the Russian Air Force is constantly flying over the city in superior numbers. The Zhukov divisions have victoriously taken the vast area between the Oder and Berlin, and the attack, which previously approached the city like a wide, co-ordinated wave, is now beginning to break up into many individual assault wedges of unequal length, pushing their way at very different speeds into the sea of houses to the east and the north-east. The German defence is no longer a solid line, behind which a central command post is observing the movements, ordering counter-measures and sending reserves to threatened positions. The battle is breaking up into a number of individual skirmishes that are only connected loosely or not at all, advanced posts are being stubbornly defended against the incoming Russian reservists, while important support points at the accesses to the city remain unoccupied. The defence of the city is breaking up more and more by the hour, each individual combat unit is acting independently, since contact with military command in Berlin is only possible at random if at all. In the city centre and in the zones that have not yet been occupied, Hitler Youth, Volkssturm men, engineers, Party members, factory guards and reserve policemen are being organized into new units, wretchedly under-equipped and sent forward even though the commanders don't know where the first line of fire is, the front line, the name they give to the nodal points, constantly moving, of the battle among the buildings. Heavy weapons are hardly being used, since there is either no ammunition or no fuel.

Oscar Klose's pub on Strasse Am Schlesischen Bahnhof is no longer a restaurant, since there is no longer any beer, and there are certainly no guests. The left half of the pub serves as a dormitory and guardroom for private soldiers, and in the right a field hospital has been set up. It smells of sweat, unaired clothes and chloroform, and all that remains of its former purpose is the sour haze of beer and the smell of stale tobacco. Klose has carefully removed all the objects that might be of value and interest to soldiers, and keeps himself to his two back rooms, in which he lives along with the Weigands and Lassehn. In the confusion of these days no one notices the increased number of residents, or it is explained by the flight of many city dwellers from the outlying districts to the inner city.

The air-raid cellar of the house, previously visited only sporadically when the sirens called for it, has now become a permanent quarters and a communal dwelling, a recreation room, dining room and bedroom all in one, a kindergarten, hospital and sickroom. Field beds, deckchairs, couches, mattresses, armchairs, stools, kitchen chairs, benches and boxes, as well as the floor, are places for both sitting and sleeping. Since the electricity is mostly out of action, the lighting is a candle, a paraffin lamp or a carbide lamp that a railwayman brought over from Silesian Station. Since the water pipes dried up, water has to be fetched from the hydrants, which are surrounded by crowds in the breaks between the attacks. In the little space outside the cellar, a makeshift stove has been made out of a few bricks. Particularly brave women cook in the ground-floor flats when the artillery fire or the air attacks temporarily ease off, and in the very first days of their cellar-based existence in the front-line city of Berlin the women still even manage to go shopping. People who are constantly thrown back upon one another in an extremely restricted space, enduring the inescapable presence of other people, are soon seized by an irritability that can quickly intensify into hatred. Other people's little foibles, normally only the subject of an indulgent smile, produce a kind of idiosyncrasy; minor differences of opinion, smoothed out in normal circumstances with a few clarifying words, grow into the obsessive insistence on being right at all costs; all disagreements which would previously have been ignored or would only have been expressed in occasional friction on the stairs, burst like ulcers that have been seeping away, invisible and barely apparent, under the skin.

Nerves, irritability, worry, concern, tears, rage and hatred swirl together among the people like the waters of a fast-flowing stream, but everything emerges out of fear, fear of the Nazi terror, fear of the artillery fire and the bombs from the planes, fear for the rest of their possessions, fear of the Russians, fear of a completely uncertain future, and only now and again are those fears overshadowed by the small concerns of everyday life, worries about food, about water, and about performing the most primitive functions.

Out in the countryside, in spite of the war, a lush spring is on the way, the days rise bright and beaming, the buds are springing open on the trees and bushes, the seeds are stirring in the soil, the birds fly through the clear air, but not the slightest hint of that makes its way into the cellars. Here the air is not only stale and polluted by the stench of unwashed bodies and unaired clothing, of flatulence and urine and babies' nappies, of burnt carbide and the smells of food, of the damp mildew of the cellar and gun smoke that forces its way from the street through all the cracks, the atmosphere too in which the people live together is saturated with ill will, nausea, envy, hatred and contempt.

Even more gruelling is the complete uncertainty, not only in relation to the future, but also about the immediate future, because there is no way of knowing whether the battle will last for eight days or eight weeks, they remember with horror that the defenders of Königsberg held out for weeks and the defence of Breslau is still going on. It is by no means out of the question that the battle will sweep back and forth and under the hail of shells they will be alternately exposed to fire from the Russian artillery and from their own. No less wearing is the complete inaction, the employed cannot (and do not want to) return to their workplaces, nor do the housewives want to do their normal work; apart from small tasks, the preparation and consumption of the meagre meals and visits to the primitive toilet, nothing ever happens.

Conversations falter after a few exchanges. Reading is impossible, since the lighting is too faint. The darkness of the cellar and the forced inaction leave room only for one thing, for waiting, waiting, waiting, for anything, for liberation or death, and it is still completely uncertain by whom and from what one will be freed, how and at whose hands one will be killed. They became used to staying in the cellar a long time ago, but then it was only ever for two, sometimes three hours before the sirens indicated the end of their imprisonment, they had become accustomed to that a long time ago, as one gets used to chronic pains, but this time they are not summoned back to the surface by an all-clear, to their flats or their beds, this time they are banished to the underworld, from which they cannot emerge without finding themselves in the hell of the world above. So about three dozen people sit in the cellar fifteen metres long and barely two and a half metres wide, they sit, crouch, squat, lie, everyone has his own particular spot in the midst of his possessions, and above them all there hovers the uncertainly flickering light of a candle, or else a burdensome darkness lurks, unbroken by a single shimmer of light, since the cellar is below the level of the street and the narrow skylights are blocked by boxes of sand. The words that were initially exchanged, short questions and dismissive answers, soon dry up, and apart from the noises that enter from outside, in the end the only sounds to be heard are those of air in motion, the fitful breathing of the short-winded, the coughing and moans of the ill, the snoring and groaning of the sleepers, the slurping and munching of the eaters, the wailing and weeping of the children, throats being cleared and sneezing and the internal sounds of bodies entering an abnormal state, all sounds of an intimate nature being played out now before everyone's ears and noses, intensifying discomfort to revulsion.

From the secure apartments, locked to the outside world with safety locks, bolts and chains, and with their inner, strictly protected secrets, people have been forced into a narrow and inescapable communality, all the more undesirable because it has come about forcibly and under the pressure of circumstances. A communality produced by random circumstances or external pressure rather than born of inner impulses will only ever last as long as the weight of external pressure weighs down on it. Mutual consideration and assistance are far from compulsory, and only occur when one's own claims and advantages are not violated or hampered. The impulse to self-preservation is stripped entirely of all veils imposed from without, extreme lack of consideration is the rule of the moment, and perceiving one's own fleeting advantages is a thousand times more important than yielding to any stirring of sympathy for others. The hard hearts that the National Socialist leadership demanded have now turned to stone, they are no longer capable of feelings, they are merely a part of the physical world.

Klose, the two Weigands and Lassehn have decided to avoid the shared air-raid cellar for as long as possible, Klose and Lucie Wiegand because of the terrible atmosphere of the cellar, Friedrich Wiegand and Lassehn because of the army patrols which are systematically combing all the cellars to put any halfway healthy men in fighting units of some kind. Admittedly Wiegand and Lassehn are now wearing Volkssturm armbands, and have armed themselves with carbines which they simply took from a house wall that they were leaning against, but Volkssturm men no longer have any business looking in an air-raid cellar, and if they do, they are entirely at the mercy or otherwise of the other people who live in the cellar with them. A word from a disgruntled neighbour in the cellar or a hysterical Hitler-worshipper can be enough to put a rope around your neck. So Wiegand and Lassehn prefer to stay in Klose's flat and to put on their Volkssturm armbands when they step outside.

The men are chafing under the inactivity, only Lucie Wiegand is busy enough, preparing food and trying to bring something resembling order to the male government of the house; and it doesn't matter to her if people laugh at her, she sweeps, wipes, washes and cleans as if it were the most natural thing in the world keeping a flat tidy in the midst of artillery fire.

'That makes no sense at all, Lucie,' Klose says, shaking his head as she runs the duster over the furniture, 'the plaster is coming off the walls like a steady rain shower, and you . . . You really are curious creatures, you women.'

Lucie Wiegand looks over at Klose with a strange expression on her face. 'You think so?' she asks. 'It does make sense, because at least temporarily it blocks out your thoughts.'

Dr Böttcher, who has just entered the room, gives her a shocked look. 'Do you really think this pointless work frees you from your thoughts, Lucie?'

Lucie Wiegand nods. 'Yes, that's exactly it, Doctor.'

Wiegand gets to his feet, walks up to his wife and looks at her. 'You've changed over the last few hours, Lucie,' he says seriously. 'Are you worried about the future?'

'Women have their moods,' Klose suggests. 'It'll pass.'

Lucie Wiegand leans against the window frame. 'Worries about the future?' She twists her mouth into a hesitant little smile. 'No, it's something else . . .'

'What?' Wiegand asks.

Lucie Wiegand waves his words away. 'Oh, it's not so interesting,' she says, and starts working again.

Wiegand takes her by the shoulders and forces her to look at him.

'Tell us, Lucie.'

Lucie shakes his hands away without saying a word. 'Perhaps I can help you,' Wiegand insists.

Again a little smile plays around her lips. 'You can help me least of all, Fritz.'

A look of surprise appears in Wiegand's serious face. 'I don't understand,' he says helplessly.

'It's better that way, Fritz.'

A hubbub of wailing and bellowing is heard through the door that closes the room off from the restaurant area, then comes the sounds of a mouth organ and the stamping of hobnailed boots.

'They're making a shameful noise,' Klose says, and points his thumb at the door. 'Yes, the soldier's death is a merry thing . . .'

Wiegand has reluctantly shaken off the interruption. 'Oskar, Doctor, Lassehn, please could you leave me alone with my wife for a few minutes, or even better, we'll go over . . .'

'No, no,' Lucie Wiegand says loudly, and immediately mutes her voice again, 'you can both listen, that's fine.' She sits down heavily on a chair and rubs her hands together.

For a long minute the room is silent apart from the sound of 'Lili Marlene' coming through the door, and from outside the crash of exploding shells and the uninterrupted shooting from the anti-aircraft guns.

'Fritz,' Lucie Wiegand says at last, 'I have to tell you this before you say anything terrible. You can't stay here any longer.'

'Right, young woman, what's up?' Klose asks in surprise. 'You aren't eating, you aren't drinking, are you ill?'

'Frau Wiegand probably has serious reasons for saying something like that,' Dr Böttcher says.

'Enough joking, Oskar,' Wiegand says, dismissing him. 'What's happened, Lucie?'

Lucie Wiegand closes her eyes for a few seconds. 'Robert is here!' she says almost in a whisper, with a frightened look at the door.

'How do you know that?' Wiegand asks.

'I heard him, through the door over there,' Lucie Wiegand says, 'and I've seen him too.'

'Where?'

'Here in the restaurant.' Lucie Wiegand stands up, walks to the door and pushes aside the curtain that covers the glass in the door. 'I heard a voice that pierced my heart like a knife, at first I didn't want to believe it, it struck me as impossible, unthinkable, but then, when I looked through this window, no doubts were possible, it was Robert.'

'Have you talked to him?' Wiegand asks calmly.

Lucie Wiegand shakes her head. 'How could I do that, Fritz!' she replies, and steps back into the room. 'It might put him on your trail.'

'And the lad is quite capable of having his own father arrested,' Klose adds. 'In the name of the Führer, Göring and the murderous Himmler.'

'But you'd like to talk to him, Lucie?' Wiegand asks, and a grim wrinkle appears on her forehead. 'And that's why I have to get out of . . .' He makes a hand gesture as if ushering himself out.

'You mustn't think that, Fritz!' Lucie Wiegand shouts. 'This isn't about me, but bear in mind that all that separates him from us is a thin, plain door, and one loud word could be fatal to you. Just one kick and the door will splinter . . .' She covers her eyes with her hands, her shoulders twitch.

'Yes, just a door,' Klose says, 'a door made of ordinary oak wood with a little bit of plywood and some thin glass, a door like millions of other doors, but on one side is hell and on the other . . . No, that's not right, I meant to say heaven.'

'On this side justice and on that side injustice,' says Lassehn, who has been sitting in silence up until now.

'Good man,' Klose says, 'sometimes education has a value after all.'

'You need to be particularly careful,' Dr Böttcher says.

Lucie Wiegand flinches, something flies violently at the door making the glass rattle. 'You're so calm, Fritz . . .'

'What should I get worked up about? The fact that Robert's here? I've known that since yesterday.'

Lucie Wiegand flares up. 'You knew?'

'Yes, he was here in the pub yesterday afternoon.'

'Did he see you?'

'Luckily not, I was sitting in a dark corner, and in any case he was very busy with a few Volkssturm men.'

'He has a wonderful turn of phrase,' Klose says. 'He was threatening us with hanging and so on. A charming child!'

'Oskar!' Wiegand says reproachfully, and looks quickly at the woman's eyebrows.

Lucie Wiegand looks at the floor. 'You don't need to worry about me,' she says firmly, 'I know exactly what . . . what he's like. I was about to say what my . . . yes, what my son is like, but everything in me rebels at the idea. My *son* – when you say that, there's always some pride and tenderness in the words, *my* son, that's the identification with him, that means he comes from my spirit. Oh!' – a sigh issues from the slender woman – 'How I wish I could be proud of him, how I wish I loved him, but I must be ashamed of him, and if I don't hate him it's only because I haven't yet quite erased the image of him when he was a child.'

Wiegand strokes his wife's hair. 'Dr Böttcher once told me the psychical structure was the most immutable component of the human being.'

Dr Böttcher nods. 'Yes, and it is already present and fully shaped before the womb expels the embryo. We must always come to terms with the constantly astonishing fact that while upbringing and environment may shape the intellect, they only strengthen or weaken the psychical and temperamental disposition, but can never crucially influence it.'

'So that means that no education, no influence ever reaches the actual core of the soul,' Lucie Wiegand says, 'environment, upbringing and school are fundamentally quite inactive ingredients.'

'To answer this question in the affirmative means to view the evolution of humanity with philosophical resignation,' Dr Böttcher replies. 'But if we do not wish to abandon ourselves, we must work on overcoming this dualism of soul and upbringing, or at least balance it out. And here I must correct you, Lucie, environment, upbringing and school are not in fact ingredients, they are counterweights. The complex of questions immediately becomes simpler once we employ the term "instinct" rather than "soul".'

'I understand,' Lucie Wiegand says. 'Instincts can be tamed, calmed, distracted, covered up, put to sleep . . .'

'One can, in so far as they are negative instincts, simply take away their opportunity to develop,' Dr Böttcher says, 'but of course that requires a highly developed society, from which we are far removed. Still, we had advanced a few stages in that direction, but at that very time we experienced a relapse that destroyed decades and centuries of efforts, and which is so immense that we cannot grasp its whole extent. The fetters which were imposed upon the instincts and held them down have been loosened, and where that was not enough, they were burst, the instincts themselves were goaded . . . You were about to say something, Lucie?'

Lucie Wiegand nods. 'Yes,' she says, 'our son Robert is unfortunately a telling example of how correct that is. Many of the features that we observed in him even when he was a child have reached terrible maturity. Many of those things we saw at first only as deviations and weaknesses which would fade over time and perhaps even disappear entirely. But what happened to us was what happened to so many, indeed most German parents, who had the upbringing of their children torn from their hands at a crucial stage, who had no power over them, and hardly any influence, who had to endure their children becoming judges presiding over them, and in their unsuspecting naïvety and trustfulness running after the brown-clad rat catchers, indeed fell silent in front of their children, or against their better conscience spoke pro when they were contra, if they didn't want to find themselves in mortal danger . . .'

'. . . and those who didn't,' Klose continues, and now there is not a single laugh line on his broad face, 'suffered the fate of . . .' He gets to his feet and takes a red sheet from a pile of newspapers. 'Read this, Joachim.'

Lassehn takes the red sheet of paper from him. He sees immediately that it is a poster, still rigid with stiffened glue, and reads:

> 'In the name of the people!
> The following, sentenced to death by the People's
> Court for high treason
> Erich Meissner
> Alfred Urbans
> Charlotte Urbans
> were executed today.
> Berlin, 12 September 1942.
> The Reich Senior Prosecutor at the People's Court.'

Lassehn looks awkwardly at Klose, who is still clutching the red piece of paper.

'They were betrayed by their children,' Klose says, 'perhaps unwittingly, in all likelihood innocently . . .'

'Innocently at any rate,' Wiegand cuts in. 'How can children be guilty? Is a cornfield guilty because it is hit by a hailstorm and doesn't yield a harvest?'

'You're right, Fritz,' says Klose. 'The three people whose names you have just read, Joachim,' he continues, turning to Lassehn, and taking the red sheet from him, 'were good comrades, fearless and steadfast, they often sat with us here in this room. In spite of all the torture, promises and threats they never gave anyone away . . .'

Klose breaks off, no one speaks, they are all staring motionlessly at the blood-red sheet of paper, saying nothing, as if words might desecrate the memory of the three executed comrades.

Lassehn is very shaken, he didn't know these three people, until this minute he never even knew of their existence. Involuntarily these three unknown people assume the faces of the two Wiegands and Dr Böttcher, but the features of Lotte Poeschke and the young fair-haired worker are mixed in with them. They sat here, in this room, around this table, people of flesh and blood, yes, blood, and then they were . . . A shudder runs through his body.

'Have you become fearful, Joachim?' asks Klose, who noticed him shivering.

'Fearful?' Lassehn asks. 'Why should I be fearful all of a sudden?'

'It just looked that way,' Klose answers, and gives him a penetrating look. 'You can still go back, Joachim, we're not forcing you to stay here.'

'No, Herr Klose,' Lassehn says firmly. 'How could there be any going back? And where to? To wilful ignorance, to bourgeois cluelessness? Anyone who has tasted the fruits of the Tree of Knowledge . . .'

Klose walks up to him and shakes his hand firmly. 'Good, my boy,' he says with a smile that bursts from his serious face, 'you can stay, then. I didn't expect anything else.'

Lassehn blushes slightly and tries to hide it by running his hand over his face. 'I would like to resume our conversation, Doctor,' he says. 'A moment ago you identified soul with instinct. Isn't that a materialization of the soul?'

'I didn't necessarily equate soul and instinct, Lassehn,' Dr Böttcher replies, 'they aren't equal, in fact, but they live in such close quarters to one another that it is impossible to separate the two. The soul isn't immaterial, by the way, Kant says the soul is an inner sense in connection with the body, and describes the reference to immaterial principles as a refuge of lazy reason.'

'I haven't thought enough about it before,' Lassehn admits, 'in my previous life I only ever allowed myself to be guided by random events, and apart from music there was nothing there in me.'

'Let us not forget the present by dwelling on the past and on theory, gentlemen,' Klose says, turning on the radio, 'if we are lucky, there will be electricity and we can hear the Wehrmacht report.'

The dial of the radio lights up, the hum of the electric current swells, and the voice of the announcer appears as if from a long way away.

'We nearly missed the latest Hitleriad,' Klose says, waving a hand towards the radio in a broad gesture. 'Please, ladies and gentlemen, hurry up, it has already begun.'

'. . . gap in the front line with successful counter-attacks. The occupation of Bautzen was stubbornly defended against the enemy, which was attacking with strong forces. Advancing westwards, the Soviets entered Bischofswerda and Königsbrück.

South of Kottbus the Bolsheviks brought in reinforcements to strengthen their attacks against the area south of Berlin, and with their spearheads they reached the line of Treuenbrietzen-Zossen south of Königs Wusterhausen. Street battles are being fought in Kottbus and Fürstenwalde. To the east and north of Berlin the enemy pushed amidst fierce fighting towards the outer defence zone of the Reich capital. Bitter fighting is under way in the line Lichtenberg-Niederschönhausen-Frohnau.'

'I'll fold,' says Klose.

'Don't switch it off, Klose,' Dr Böttcher says hastily.

'Let's see how far the other side . . .'

'. . . section Dessau-Bitterfeld . . . battles with varying success . . . slowly gaining ground . . .'

'. . . fierce fighting for the Mulde crossings . . . Bitterfeld lost . . .'

'. . . north of Chemnitz . . . local breakthroughs . . .'

'. . . area around Stuttgart . . . violent fighting . . . city surrounded . . .'

'. . . north of Tübingen . . . gain further ground . . .'

'. . . Gaullist units advancing towards the Kaiserstuhl . . .'

'Nice little menu,' Klose observes, and turns the radio off again.

'Give us the map, Oskar,' Wiegand says.

'A big situation report in the little general staff,' Klose laughs, and takes a brightly coloured brochure from the bookshelf. 'I would never have imagined that Ullstein's *Thousand Journeys Around Berlin* would one day find use as a general staff map for a battle for Berlin. Sacred Ullstein, how have you changed! *Sic transit . . .* What is it again, Doctor?'

'. . . *gloria mundi*,' adds Dr Böttcher with a smile, and opens up the book of maps.

'It's true, not that much Gloria around at the minute,' Klose says.

'The situation is quite clear,' Dr Böttcher says, wiping his glasses with his handkerchief. 'Our brilliant leaders learned nothing from the battle for Vienna, and apparently expected the Russians to attack frontally from the east.'

'Isn't that what they're doing?' Klose asks. 'Lichtenberg is . . .' Dr Böttcher raises a defensive hand. 'Let me finish, my dear Klose,' he says, almost in a reproachful tone. 'Of course the Russians are also coming from the east, but much more important are the two pincer arms that are arranged to the north and south of Berlin. The 1st Ukrainian Front under Zhukov is not only pushing its way into Berlin from the east, but is also encircling the city with its north wing and – according to the Wehrmacht report – has already reached Frohnau. To the south the 1st Belorussian Front under Konev, which was previously attacking in an east-west direction, after the advance of the first few days turned to the north-west – the line Königs Wusterhausen-Zossen-Treuenbrietzen – and is now advancing on Berlin along a south-north line, that is, Berlin is also being encircled from the south. There is absolutely no doubt that the two arms of the pincer, Zhukov's northern wing and Konev's west wing, will advance further and come together to the west of Berlin in a complete encirclement. This is the sober observation of the situation, only on the basis, I should add, of today's German Wehrmacht report, which is of course a summary of the situation yesterday.'

Dr Böttcher pauses for a moment and reads his notes. 'But the Wehrmacht report says much more than that, at least for someone who is not just reading today's report, but also remembers the previous few days' reports. The advance of the Konev army group from the Neisse over the Kottbus-Spremberg-Bautzen-Hoyerswerda line, and the subsequent switch to the Treuenbrietzen-Zossen-Königs Wusterhausen line, which also means joining the southern flank of the Zhukov group, means that the whole southern wing of the German front has been disrupted.' Dr Böttcher backs up his explanations with a few confident lines on the map.

Lassehn has been listening carefully to Dr Böttcher's words, and can't take his eyes off the map. 'If that is correct,' he says excitedly, 'and I have no reason to doubt it, that means that the German troops in the zone around Frankfurt an der Oder-Kottbus are enclosed and no longer available for the defence of Berlin.'

'Quite correct,' Dr Böttcher says, and puts his glasses back on again, 'As far as I can tell, that means no fewer than two armies, the Eighth and Ninth, with I would estimate at least twenty divisions. What did the Führer, the greatest general of all time say? *"I regret that I am only dealing with military idiots."*'

'But we mere mortals don't grasp that,' Klose says, adopting a comically regretful expression. 'Such a unique genius must measure things according to different standards, and he does so too. A thousand years lasts only twelve years, while the nine hours that the Anglo-Americans were due to remain on land in the event of an invasion of France has been somewhat extended. Add a thousand a twelve and nine . . . I'd need a moment's peace to add them all up. Calculating is witchcraft, gentlemen, and incidentally . . .'

'Someone's knocking,' Wiegand says. 'If those people in there would stop making so much noise . . .'

They all listen with great concentration. The knocking comes again, three times, a short pause, twice, silence, three times, short pause, twice.

'That's for us,' Wiegand says. 'Open up, Oskar.'

Klose nods and leaves the room, a few tense minutes go by, and then he comes back with . . . yes, it's a young woman or a young girl, she's panting excitedly and pushes back a blonde curl that has slipped out from under her blue air-raid warden's steel helmet. If her face did not show the soft, delicate features of a girl, if her eyebrows were not so thin and redrawn, and if she did not have a clear soprano voice, she might almost have been taken for a young man, because she is wearing a dark blue ski-suit.

'Hello,' she says, and looks from one to the other with her bright, clear eyes.

'Rumpelstiltskin has sent us this sweet fairy,' Klose says by way of explanation. 'So, my girl, what do you bring? Out with it!'

Before the girl can reply Wiegand speaks. 'Are you sure, Oskar, that she really has come from Rumpelstiltskin?'

'Quite sure,' Klose replies, 'there is no doubt, Fritz. So, my girl . . . what is your name, by the way?'

The girl laughs brightly, and then looks anxiously at the door leading to the restaurant. 'What's going on in there? Have you people quartered in there?'

'Only at the front,' Klose says. 'So, what's your name?'

The girl laughs again. 'My name doesn't concern you, people,' she replies, and takes off her steel helmet. 'They call me Redbreast, and you can too.'

'Nice name,' Klose says and strokes the girl's cheeks.

'So what's going on, Redbreast?'

The girl's face becomes serious. 'Rumpelstiltskin asks you to come and help him with a few determined men.'

'Help him?' Wiegand asks.

'I don't know exactly what he's planning,' the girl replies, 'but he wants to carry out an operation somewhere against the Hitler Youth, who are keeping some positions occupied. Can you send a few people . . .'

'Of course,' Wiegand says. 'Are you coming, Lassehn?'

'I'm there,' Lassehn says quickly and blushes to the roots of his hair, as it is the first time Wiegand has addressed him informally, and it feels like a distinction.

'Can an old fellow like me be of any use to you?' Dr Böttcher asks and smiles at the girl.

'You're exactly the right age for the Volkssturm,' she shoots back. 'Are you an orderly?' she asks, pointing at the white armband with the red cross.

'I would seem to be,' Dr Böttcher says. 'So let's just . . .'

'I'm here on my bike,' the girl says. 'Do you have bikes as well?'

'We do,' Klose says. 'So, to arms, in the truest sense of the word. You'll be surprised, Redbreast!'

The girl watches the men as they put on Volkssturm armbands and hang their carbines over their shoulders, and smiles. 'We've known this one for a while, Comrades,' she says, 'the lion's skin is the best defence against the lion.'

'Yes, come on, quick march,' Wiegand, says impatiently. 'Bye, Klose, see you, Lucie.' He shakes Klose's hands and strokes his wife's hair.

Lassehn and Böttcher say goodbye as well. When they are about to leave the room, Klose holds the girl back by the arm. 'Why do they call you Redbreast?'

'What a nosy old man you are,' the girl says, laughing in his face. 'But if you really want to know, fatso: because they say I have a pretty voice.'

'I see, I see,' Klose says, and winks across at Lassehn. 'If you need someone to accompany you, on the piano of course, then stick with this handsome young man, his name is Joachim.'

Lassehn turns away in embarrassment and leaves the room; when he pulls the door closed behind him he hears Klose whistling and recognizes the tune. It is the old Berlin song 'Give Me a Bit of Love, Love . . .'

VIII

Four cyclists ride along Fruchtstrasse, two Volkssturm men, an orderly and one wearing a ski-suit and a steel helmet. They are plainly in a great hurry, because they are pedalling very energetically, even though cycling is anything but a pleasure. All over the road there are chunks of stone, shards of glass and shell splinters, flashes of fire dart menacingly through the air. At first glance (and who has time to give some hurrying cyclists a second glance?) it looks as if a few men from the legendary Volkssturm are out on the road, apparently prepared to sink their claws into the soil of home, and to fight to the last drop of blood. They look so hearty that the motorized army patrol blocking Fruchtstrasse at the entrance of Küstriner Platz lets them through after a few explanatory words.

The rectangle of Küstriner Platz has been prepared for defence by the SS, its access roads, Fruchtstrasse, Rüdersdorfer Strasse and Königsberger Strasse and the Braune Weg, are all blocked by barricades and anti-tank barriers. Heavy machine guns and anti-tank guns have been put in position, heavy guns are aimed at the freight tracks of Eastern Station, three anti-aircraft guns aim their barrels steeply into the air. The Plaza music hall has apparently become a barracks with a command post, almost all of the gun operators are SS men, and around the anti-tank barriers there are Volkssturm men and a few figures in brown uniforms. Wiegand smiles quietly to himself as their bicycles twist amidst the swarming cars. The startled expression on the face of an NCO was clear enough, it's probably a long time since he last saw anyone (let alone a Volks-sturm man) who was in a hurry to get ahead.

When they leave Küstriner Platz and turn into Königsberger Strasse, they come across no startled faces and no friendly expressions. Instead the faces of the Volkssturm men are filled with irritable surprise, and one of them says in anything but a quiet voice: 'We'll be stuck here for as long as there are idiots like that around,' and another calls after them, 'Happy heroic death!'

'There can be no better praise,' the girl says to Wiegand, who is cycling along beside her.

'I agree with you,' Wiegand agrees, and laughs. 'Clothes make the man and uniforms make the hero. Where are you taking us, Redbreast?'

'You'll see. What's your name?'

'Fritz, if that's enough for you.'

'Completely. And the boy' – the girl turns her head back towards Lassehn, who is cycling next to Dr Böttcher – 'is called Joachim, I know that already. And the one with glasses you call Doctor. Is he really a doctor?'

'He is really a doctor,' Wiegand confirms. 'If you ever have a pain . . .'

The girl shakes her head. 'Rather not, I can manage without. Right, we're about to turn into Frankfurter Allee.'

Frankfurter Allee is under furious fire, uninterrupted wails and crashes, explosions splinter in all directions, smoke, haze and dust hang between the rows of houses, here and there a house is ablaze, another is collapsing in on itself, the tram poles are bent and broken, the overhead wires hang in tatters, deep holes have been blown into the cobbles, burning furniture lies on the pavements and in the road, the trees seem to have been uprooted by coarse hands. A weirdly menacing, dangerous wall has been built here on Frankfurter Allee, and they can only pass through it at intervals.

'We have to wait for a break in the firing,' Dr Böttcher says. 'Close to the walls. Now tell us where you're taking us, Redbreast.'

'Up Thaerstrasse,' the girl replies, 'so a little way along Frank-furter Allee . . .'

'I get it,' Dr Böttcher says with a smile, 'I know the area quite well.'

They are pressed up against the wall, the bicycles crammed close together. Shells are still flying at them, striking the houses, the promenade, the road, an armoured car is struck, a huge jet of flame shoots out as if from a flamethrower, where Komturei-Platz meets Hertie-Ecke a shell hits the horses pulling an ammunition wagon, and the horses rear up wildly, keeling over, kicking their heels like mad, whinnying loudly. Guts spill from a dappled grey horse as it tries to get back on its feet, pulls itself up, gets entangled in its own entrails, slips, falls, shows its teeth in a terrible scream. Suddenly, as if they have emerged out of the ground, there are people there. They leap over with bent knees, hunched shoulders, bent backs, with buckets, bowls, dishes, pots, cooking implements, and a wild scramble begins, pushing, jostling, shoving, thumping, everyone wants to be the first to reach the animals. They plunge kitchen knives, penknives, bread knives, even forks and pliers into the flesh of the animal, which is still alive. Above them the shells hiss and whistle, the warm blood of the animals is still flowing, but the people pay no attention, they see only meat, meat, meat.

Lassehn had at first turned away with a shudder, then he leaps resolutely between them.

'You bastards!' he shouts furiously, shoving a man aside, and kills both horses with bullets to the head.

A few eyes turn towards him for a fleeting second, but no one is insulted, no one takes time to be furious, they immediately turn back to their unexpected booty. Lassehn puts his revolver back in its holster and runs for cover again, because a Russian fighter bomber is plunging with wailing engines and rattling weapons, projectiles fly, stray bullets hiss like rockets, and the plane climbs back into the air, its engine singing. Two corpses now lie on the cobblestones among the dead horses.

Panting heavily, Lassehn leans against the wall of the house and closes his eyes for a few seconds. Then he feels someone taking his hand, and holding it tightly as if in a caress. He opens his eyes and looks into the luminous face of the girl, blushing slightly with agitation.

He abruptly pulls his hand back from hers and looks awkwardly to one side.

'Don't make a fuss, miss,' he says.

'What's up with you?' the girl asks and looks at him in astonishment. 'Why are you so polite? What's that all about?'

'I didn't know . . . I'm sorry.'

In spite of the seriousness of the situation the girl laughs. 'My God, you're a funny one, Joachim,' she says. 'It isn't just that you're allowed to, it's part of it. Are you new?'

'Quite new,' Lassehn admits.

'No time for chatting,' Wiegand interrupts them. 'The gunfire seems to be easing off. Let's try to get across Frankfurter Allee and reach Thaerstrasse. Just a moment.'

They listen tensely, but there really does seem to be a break in the firing. People begin emerging from cellars and ruins, the tunnel of the underground and the slit trenches of the Weberwiese, soldiers, Volkssturm men, women, children, horse-drawn supply columns get moving, the two dead horses are still surrounded, on the corner of Tilsiter Strasse the boarded-up window of a grocer's has been smashed, a few women are climbing into the shop, others force their way in immediately after them. Soldiers are standing there, laughing, encouraging the women, one of them even knocks the door open with the butt of his rifle and drags two sacks of sugar into the street, slits them open with his bayonet and scoops the sugar into the hollow of the women's skirts with his steel helmet.

Wiegand's face sparks with deep contempt. 'Let's get going!' he shouts. 'Get across the road. Don't stop!'

They run off, pushing their bikes in front of them, they balance them over the piles of rubble, glancing one last time at the gutted corpses of the horses and two dead men, who have been cleared aside like troublesome debris. After a few minutes they have reached Thaerstrasse and climb on their bikes. Here – hardly a hundred metres away from Frankfurter Allee – the picture is completely different. The curve of Baltenplatz opens up in front of them, and while the Russian artillery goes on firing at the main street, the war seems to slide by without fully unfolding its annihilating wings, the women still standing in front of the grocers' and butchers' shops.

'It's Sunday,' Dr Böttcher says in amazement.

'I'm surprised too,' Wiegand says. 'It must mean something . . .'

'It does,' the girl says. 'Don't you know there was a radio announcement that food is being distributed for the seventy-fifth and seventy-sixth allocation periods, and that the shops have to stay open today?'

'We had no idea,' Dr Böttcher says.

'They're giving out the survival rations,' Lassehn says.

'Come on, come on,' Wiegand urges as they cycle around Baltenplatz. 'Where to now?'

The girl reaches out her hand. 'Back into Thaerstrasse.'

They drive on. From the corner of Eldenaer Strasse to the Ringbahn the grounds of the abattoir stretch out on either side, rigorously separated from the street by high walls; then comes the confusion of summer houses and allotments, the meagre refuge of the land-hungry, earth-thirsty petty bourgeoisie and the workers, already run through with sparse greenery and the first white blossoms of the cherry trees.

The girl turns from Thaerstrasse into the allotment colony and jumps nimbly off her bicycle.

'So, gentlemen,' she says, and points to a summer house barely two metres from the fence, 'we're there. In we go!'

They dismount, walk around the summer house and lean their bicycles against the wall, then they step in through the low door, Lassehn even has to bend down.

'I saw you coming,' Schröter says, and pulls on his moustache. 'Good that you're here. Right, in you come.'

The summer house consists only of a room with a table, two benches, a few chairs, an old kitchen cupboard and a stove. A round iron frame hangs from the ceiling with a paraffin lamp dangling from it, the floor is roughly concreted and scattered with a few straw mats, and the walls are covered with render boards.

When they stepped inside two men had got to their feet, one wearing a grey overcoat, a grey forage cap with a black, white and red cockade and a Volkssturm armband, the other a shabby brown leather jacket, a blue peaked cap, breeches and leather spats as well as a Volkssturm armband. Their faces are obscured by the semi-darkness of the room, but they move into the beam of light from the window when they take a few steps towards the new arrivals. Lassehn glances quickly at their faces when he shakes the two men's hands; the one in uniform has a narrow, determined face, the other a broad face with a boxer's broken nose.

Schröter gestures to them to sit down. 'These are Comrades Münzer and Gregor.'

'Do we still need code names?' Dr Böttcher asks. 'Just asking in passing.'

Schröter rocks his head back and forth. 'Let's leave it like that for the time being.'

'And why not,' Wiegand says. 'Right to the matter at hand. Why did you summon us here?'

'Unfortunately our group has shrunk,' Schröter says. 'A few of our people who work at Knorr-Bremse didn't come home because they simply weren't allowed out of the place, the factory is now a workplace, a barracks and a dwelling place all in one.'

'The Nazi ideal,' Wiegand suggests.

'That's it,' says Schröter. 'You're right there. And as chance has decreed that the works manager had to go on an unpostponable business trip, the megalomaniac shop steward has appointed himself sole ruler, has had rifles and rocket launchers distributed to everyone who is a hundred per cent reliable, or who he considers to be so, and with the help of an SS unit has simply declared martial law, on the basis of some unknown emergency programme. At any rate, right now we can't bank on these comrades.'

Speaking with both hands propped on the table, Schröter glances out of the window at the carefully raked flower beds and the high scaffold of the beanpoles, but he can't see either of them, his thoughts are concentrated on what he wants to say now. He slowly turns to look back into the room, pulls the *Berliner Morgenpost* city map out of his pocket and unfolds it on the table.

'We assumed the task of protecting our district against an

annihilating, murderous battle.' Schröter is now speaking slowly and collectedly, he puts his words together carefully. 'We are apparently favoured by fortune, because we have . . . No,' he breaks off, shaking his head, 'first I have to tell you what I mean by our district, namely the area west of the Weissenseer Weg between Roederstrasse and Kniprodestrasse. Here we have three resistance points, first of all the assault guns at the crossing of Thaerstrasse, Oderbruchstrasse, Landsberger Allee and Landsberger Chaussee, the second one at the crossing of Kniprodestrasse and Storkower Strasse, and the third one at the anti-tank barrier just past Landsberger Allee S-Bahn station. The assault guns are presided over by Wehrmacht detachments and a few Volkssturm men, the anti-tank barrier is occupied almost entirely by a combination of Hitler Youth and Volkssturm, and at the bridge over the S-Bahn there is a Wehrmacht unit, the SS haven't turned up yet. That's the situation.'

'And where are the Russians?' Wiegand asks, leaning over the map.

'They can't be far off,' Schröter replies. 'If the wind is right you can hear the rumble of their tanks. From what I've been told they're coming from Marzahn via Hohenschönhausen, mostly along the Landsberger Chaussee, Grosse Leegestrasse and Berliner Strasse, their spearheads are already believed to be quite close to the Weissenseer Weg. Our task now' – Schröter is now choosing his words carefully – 'is to free up the way for our so-called enemies, so that the three strongpoints I mentioned won't offer any resistance, because it wouldn't just be pointless, it would be criminal, it would leave the houses and the remaining summer houses in rubble and ashes, and demand victims among the population, among old people, women and children. We've got to prevent that!' Schröter emphasizes his words with a few blows on the table.

'Your plan?' Wiegand asks.

'I'm coming to that,' Schröter answers. 'We have divided our groups into three sub-groups, one with Gregor' – he looks at the man in the grey uniform – 'must take out the assault gun on Storkower Strasse, the other, with Münzer, the one on Thaerstrasse and Oderbruchstrasse.'

'Take out?' Wiegand asks.

'Yes, take out, either by persuasion or by force of arms if that's the only way. It may sound violent, but it really isn't, of course we've already put out feelers with the gun teams and the few Volkssturm men and we're very clear that they're fed up, they don't want to fight any more.'

'But if there's an officer or some crazed corporal about, then the whole exercise and all good intentions are blown away in the wind,' Wiegand objects, 'obedience is so rooted in the bones of our soldiers that a single order from some little martinet is going to extinguish the will and conscience like a feebly flickering flame.'

'We know,' Schröter says. 'And it's to prevent such an order at any cost that we are deploying the three sub-groups, because we're well aware that a single shot from the assault guns or a rocket launcher will bring the whole artillery or a host of tanks or low-flying aircraft attacks down on us. If the Russians don't encounter any resistance, they won't shoot.'

'That's completely clear,' Wiegand confirms. 'And what about the anti-tank barrier at Landsberger Allee Station?'

Schröter sits down and pulls the map across the table. 'The anti-tank barrier at Landsberger Allee Station is the hardest nut to crack, in a way it's a double nut, because it isn't just about the crew at the barrier, a Hitler Youth motorized unit, it's also about the demolition squad at the bridge over the S-Bahn immediately behind the wholesale meat market. That squad is under the orders of a lieutenant of the engineer corps, and could consist of about a dozen men. So I see our task as being to disarm the Hitler Youth before they can fire a shot, and also prevent the bridge from being blown up.'

'And you've chosen us to do that?' Wiegand asks, without taking his eyes off the map.

'That's how it is,' Schröter answers, 'because our group has been decimated, unfortunately I have to . . .'

'Fine,' Dr Böttcher breaks in. 'Of course we're at your disposal. There probably isn't much point talking about it academically and making plans, we need to act on the basis of the immediate circumstances. If I understand you correctly, Comrade Schröter, you want us to be wolves in sheep's clothing.'

'Correct,' Schröter says, 'that's exactly the situation.'

'The problem, in essence, lies less in overwhelming the tank-barrier crew and the demolition squad,' Wiegand says, 'than in choosing the right moment. We mustn't act a moment too late, but also not a second too soon, not too late because we mustn't let the Hitler Youth and the other soldiers get a chance to fire, because then we'd have the SS or some other Hitler-loyal hangman on our backs. Our true task is to recognize that one minute during which we must hoist the white flag.'

'I see we understand one another,' Schröter says, pleased, and looks at his watch. 'It's half past five, we should get going.'

'How many are we?' Wiegand asks.

'You three and another two comrades,' Schröter replies.

'And me,' the girl speaks up.

Schröter looks over at her. 'This isn't a job for a girl, Redbreast.'

The girl smiles. 'In fact it is a job for little girls,' she contradicts him, 'if the little girl draws the Argus-eyes of the warlike Hitler Youth. I turn their heads . . .'

'. . . and meanwhile the rest of us wring their necks,' the man in the leather jacket finishes her sentence. 'She's right, bring her along.'

Schröter gets to his feet. 'Then let's get moving. We'll go one at a time, it's true that the summer houses are uninhabited, but better safe than sorry. Münzer and Gregor, you go first.' He holds out his hand. 'Good luck, Comrades!'

The men shake each other's hands firmly, then the man in the leather jacket opens the door and listens. The artillery fire thunders like an approaching storm, isolated machine guns rattle and air-craft engines hum in between. Then they leave the summer house.

IX

Blowing up the bridges over the Ringbahn is the last chance to hold up the advance of the Russian tanks into the city centre. One of these bridges crosses the railway tracks near Landsberger Allee S-Bahn station. Landsberger Chaussee runs in a straight line from the north-east between the allotment colony and the newly built blocks to the bridge, swings in a gentle curve above the deep crevice of the Ringbahn, and then reappears first as the Landsberger Allee and then as Landsberger Strasse, leading straight into the centre at Alexanderplatz.

The anti-tank barrier assembled from cobblestones, scrap iron and rubble has been set up behind the bridge, where the street reaches ground level again; there is a gap in the middle just wide enough to let the tram through. On either side of the barrier are a few run-down trucks which are ready to be pushed in front of the bridge when the barrier needs to be closed.

The barrier is crewed by ten people, a mixture of Hitler Youth, Volkssturm men and young anti-aircraft auxiliaries, and is loosely connected via couriers with the two assault guns on Thaerstrasse and Storkower Strasse. They have read the cowboys-and-Indians stories of the propaganda reporters, and received superficial training with rocket launchers, but apart from hunting knives and bayonets they have no weapons, and once they have fired the eight rocket launchers at their disposal they are defenceless. Their leader is a nineteen-year-old section leader who has a lot of goodwill and not a clue, who is firmly resolved to do what has been presented to him as his vital duty, and which he believes is: to fight to the last breath. He is in fact subordinate to the lieutenant of the demolition unit, but he is thrown back on his own devices, because the lieutenant doesn't care about anything, he has passed on his command to an NCO and withdrawn inside the abattoir, where he has found a case of bottles of vermouth which he is now downing in quick succession. The political leaders who originally ordered the crew to the barrier and issued wild threats in the cellars of the surrounding houses against anyone who so much as mentioned the idea of giving up without a struggle have by now withdrawn to the city centre.

When Schröter, Dr Böttcher, Wiegand, Lassehn and the girl reach the barrier, it is closed apart from a narrow gap for pedestrians. A Volkssturm man paces up and down in front of the barrier with a carbine over his shoulder.

'I've brought you three decent fighters,' Schröter says, and winks at the sentry.

'Excellent,' the sentry says. 'Squeeze yourselves through.'

Schröter is the first to force his way through the gap, he looks to the right and left behind the barrier and turns halfway back. 'Everything all right, Hans?'

'I think so, yes,' the sentry replies, 'they're all sitting in the guardroom apart from the two couriers, who are out and about right now.'

'And what about the demolition unit?'

'The lieutenant is drunk again, or still drunk, but the NCO has already put down fuses. The Russians can't be too far away?'

'They could be here at any minute. Where are the rocket launchers?'

'Thieme took them inside with him.'

'Thieme?'

'Yes, the section leader.'

Schröter thinks for a moment. 'Right, everyone through, and once again, the password is Stalingrad. You, Lassehn, listen carefully, don't go flirting with Redbreast, you can put that off till later.'

Lassehn's face flushes suddenly. 'Please, Comrade Schröter . . .'

'Fine,' Schröter says dismissively, 'I don't care, do what you want, but for the moment keep your mind on the task at hand. And you, Redbreast . . .'

'You old grump,' the girl laughs. 'Are you jealous?'

Schröter gives an impatient wave of the hand. 'Enough of the chit-chat, girl! Let's go!'

They force their way through the narrow gap. Even though it is the same street, they feel as if they are entering the inner city. Beyond the barrier the Landsberger Allee stands broad and empty, with its four-storey rented blocks, burnt-out and collapsed ruins loom here and there like broken tooth stumps between the houses that have not yet been destroyed or are only damaged. The street looks as if it has died out, only here and there does a shadow dart hastily across it. The rusty tram tracks stretch like dark ribbons, the light haze of early twilight has fallen, the evening is grey and without the glow of a setting sun. The houses stand there, cold and forbidding, each one a self-contained island, the flats are abandoned, only the cellars are teeming like an anthill, dominated by the fear and terror of uncertainty of what is going on up above, 500, 100, 200 metres away, at the gun placements, at the bridge, at the anti-tank barrier, in the one-man trenches at the railway embankment and on the anti-aircraft towers in Friedrichshain. People are no longer ducking away from the dangers that the battle is bringing towards them, the shadow of office administrators, block wardens and cell administrators, the Women's League leaders, the toadies and informers, but they are breathing a little more easily, in the whirr of aircraft engines and the thundering of artillery the fanfare of freedom is sounding.

Schröter glances at the deserted street. 'There's the guardroom,' he says, and points to a low building of red clinker bricks.

They step inside. The guardroom is the branch office of a bank, tables, benches and chairs stand in the cashier's office, straw is piled up behind the counter, four figures are sleeping with their coats pulled over their heads, one is busy heating a pot-bellied stove with wood and bundles of documents, two others are opening tins of meat, a Volkssturm man sits in an armchair near the door, his carbine between his knees.

'So, I'm bringing reinforcements,' Schröter says, looking around.

'Heil Hitler, Comrades!' From a niche in the background a lanky young man with curly blond hair appears, wearing a brown jacket with a cord around it, short brown corduroy trousers, stout boots and socks rolled down to the ankles. Vaulting nimbly over the counter, he holds out his hand to Lassehn, Dr Böttcher and Wiegand. 'Thieme, Section Leader,' he says by way of introduction.

Schröter and the others vaguely return his greeting and sit down at the table.

'Have you closed the barrier?' Schröter asks.

'Yes,' the section leader replies. 'Anything withdrawing from the east via Hohenschönhausen will head to the north and south, either to Weissensee or to Lichtenberg.'

'Then we are forced back on our own devices,' Wiegand says. 'Or are you expecting reinforcements from the inner city?'

'Of course,' the section leader says briskly, 'we can hardly hold the position all by ourselves.'

'The reserves should be showing up soon,' says Schröter.

'Are you in contact with the military commander? Are you in contact with any of the retreating units?'

'N . . . no,' the section leader says hesitantly.

'So how do you imagine this defence will go?' Dr Böttcher asks. 'Your few rocket launchers will be used up very quickly.'

'You're forgetting the demolition squad and the assault guns,' the section leader replies, 'and the political leaders who were first deployed here at the barrier promised they would supply reinforcements. But I don't know . . .' He falls silent, embarrassed.

Schröter has been walking around as if lost in thought, and when he discovers the rocket launchers he turns back to the section leader. 'What about the demolition squad. Have you communicated with the lieutenant?'

The section leader bites his lips. 'I haven't . . . had a chance to yet,' he says slowly. 'The lieutenant has severe neuralgic pains . . . and the NCO doesn't really know what he wants, he's only concerned about his bridge . . .'

'Everyone gets on with his own routine,' Wiegand says. 'Step by step along an already beaten path, an order's an order, regardless of what kind of order it is, whether it's lost its purpose (if it ever had a purpose) or if it's turned into its opposite.'

'I don't understand you, Comrade,' the section leader says, perplexed. 'Under the motto an order's an order, Germany has become strong and Greater Germany has been revived.'

'I don't know the people of the demolition unit,' Schröter says, ignoring him, 'but I do know that you can't trust them.'

The section leader bites his lips again and then quickly releases them. 'However that may be,' he says, 'we will do our duty for Führer and nation.'

'Of course we will,' Schröter says, 'but right now we want to set about organizing the defence. Or do you have anything like a plan?'

'Not right now, in fact,' the section leader replies. 'So far we've basically just been guarding the barrier, and I was only put in charge early this morning.'

Schröter nods. 'I understand, you're a bit inexperienced, and there's no shame in that, but you won't mind if we, and we're old soldiers from the First World War, take the subject in hand a bit?'

'Of course not, Comrade,' the section leader answers, visibly flattered by Schröter's respectful question, 'I'm even grateful to you for supporting me.'

'Good!' Schröter says, glancing quickly at Wiegand and Dr Böttcher. 'How many men do you have altogether?'

'When the two couriers come back, twelve.'

'And there are six of us, that works very well, two of you and one of us, each group gets a rocket launcher, and the two remaining rocket launchers stay in reserve. When the bridge has been blown up we'll have the demolition squad as well. Agreed?'

The section leader nods. 'Entirely. Do you want me to divide them up?'

'That's probably the best idea,' Schröter says.

The sleeping men are shaken awake, then the Hitler Youth and air-force auxiliaries arrive. While the section leader delivers a brief speech and divides them up, Lassehn studies the boys' faces. A hot feeling of rage rises up in him, not against the boys, who have been violently forced to become heroes, and whose thinking was twisted even before they were able to form an independent thought. They still have boyish faces, hardly one of them has fluff on his upper lip, but their eyes are hard and their expressions confident. Have they ever really been young, unburdened by duty and service, cheerful and intellectually curious? Are they still unaware that they are clay in the hands of liars, thinking machines, intellectual machines, that their senses have been dulled and can no longer distinguish between just and unjust, freedom and unfreedom, spirit and unspirit, Christ and Antichrist? Don't they sense that they are paralysed in their thinking, blind in their recognition, incomplete in their knowledge? How could they feel that? Does an animal born in a cage feel the lack of freedom, of hunting in the wild?'

Lassehn gives a start when he is spoken to. 'You're a man extra for now, Comrade,' the section leader says to him. 'You can take charge of the two couriers who are still on their way here, and perhaps our brave girl reservist. That'll be the couriers now . . .'

The door opens, but it isn't the two couriers who come in, but two elderly men, wearing the blue armband of air-raid wardens, steel helmets and gas-mask holders, one of them an old man with an ice-grey moustache, the other one a middle-sized, squat man, slightly younger, with a broad, bright-red scar on his right cheek.

'Good evening,' says the man with the scar, and looks curiously around.

'Heil Hitler!' the section leader says, and raises his hand in a salute. The two men mutter a few indistinct words.

'So who's . . . I mean, who is this fellow . . .' the squat man begins. 'Right, we'd like to speak to the person in charge of this place, the man in charge . . .'

'That's me,' says the section leader. 'What is it?'

'You?' the old man says, surprised, and looks the section leader up and down. 'Christ, you don't even believe that yourself. There were a few people from the Party here yesterday, a few old fighters, where have they got to?'

'They've been transferred elsewhere, and I've been put in charge,' the section leader replies.

'In other words they ran away,' the man with the scar observes, and purses his lips with contempt.

'How dare you!' the section leader says furiously.

'Don't get so worked up, kid,' the old man says reassuringly and nudges his companion, 'I didn't mean it that way.'

'I hope not,' the section leader says frostily, but, softening his tone a little, 'we need to stick together now, in our fatherland's most difficult hour.'

The old man nods. 'Yes, stick together, young man, that's why we're here.'

'Right then,' the section leader says, relieved. 'So if I've understood you correctly, Comrades, you want to fight with us . . .'

The old man gives a startled glance at the section leader and then looks at each of the others in turn. 'Fight? I don't understand.'

'Of course, fight,' the section leader confirms. 'Why else did you come?'

The man with the scar now pushes the older man aside. 'We're air-raid wardens from Ebertystrasse and Thorner Strasse, and we speak in the name of over a dozen air-raid wardens from Cotheniusstrasse, Paul-Heyse-Strasse and Kochhannstrasse . . .'

'So you're a sort of delegation?' the section leader interrupts.

'If that's what you want to call us,' the man with the scar says impatiently. 'And now I would like to ask you not to interrupt me any more, because what we have to say is extremely urgent.' He takes a deep breath and looks steadily at the section leader. 'We came here to ask you not to put up any unnecessary resistance. Our cellars . . .'

Bewilderment spreads over the section leader's face, and he looks around as if searching for something. 'I don't understand . . .'

'I'm talking now, damn it!' the man with the scar rages. 'Our cellars are crammed full of old and sick people, women, children and babies, we don't want them to go to the dogs just because you . . .'

'That's enough!' the section leader interrupts him. 'I'm going to pretend I haven't heard what you're asking me to do.'

'Chuck a hand grenade in his face,' one of the air-force auxiliaries said. 'Cowardly scum! You're a pack of traitors and defeatists!'

'Shut your face, you young pup!' the man with the scar shouts furiously. 'What do you know about what's happening? You're still wet behind the ears! I'm sure you're very proud that you're playing the soldier here, that you can act the strong man?'

'God, Horst, let him have it!'

'That's enough!' the section leader says loudly. 'Do you know I could have you put up against the wall?' he says, turning to the air-raid warden, 'but I'm not taking your request seriously, I'll put it down to your . . .'

'Right, that's enough!' the man with the scar rages, and raises his hand. 'A little brat like this wants to . . .'

Wiegand quickly grabs the raised arm and steps between the man and the section leader. 'Calm down, Comrade, calm down . . .'

The other man shakes his arm away.

'And as for you, and you and you and you' – he points to Schröter and the others – 'you're sitting around here and letting this little scoundrel order you about. You're a bunch of cowards, pitiful cowards! You should be ashamed of yourselves!'

'That's enough!' the section leader says loudly. 'Get out of here! I don't need to negotiate with you. We are here to do our duty, to stand for our oath of loyalty to the Führer and, if fate so decrees, to die.'

'You can decide to die if you like,' the man with the scar replies, 'but you can't decide for others. You're talking about dying like a blind man talking about colour. Good God, don't you notice that it's nothing but empty words?'

'Shut up,' the section leader says.

'I'm not going to let you stop me talking! The muzzle's coming off now, son!'

'I am standing here for our German people!'

'Very good! And we've been sent by the people,' the old man with the white moustache joins in. 'My colleague may have been a bit violent, and he expressed himself too coarsely, but he doesn't mean it. Listen calmly, lad, the people sitting in our cellars are all old people, women and children, do you want them to perish for nothing whatsoever?'

'You call Germany nothing whatsoever?'

'Chuck him out on his ear!' an air-force auxiliary shouts.

'Bullet in the arse!' cries another. 'Why are you spending so long talking to these doddery old fools?'

The old man gives the speaker a pitying stare. 'Father forgive them, they know not what they do, it says in the Bible,' he says almost solemnly.

'How do you little chaps think you're going to fight the Russians?' the man with the scar asks. 'They will come at you with tanks, guns and fighter planes, and if you so much as fire a shot they'll crush you like bedbugs.'

'I order you once more to leave the guardroom,' the section leader says.

'Fine, fine,' says the man with the scar, shrugging. 'There's no talking to you, or' – he nods towards Wiegand, Schröter and Dr Böttcher – 'with you lot either. These brats are just gormless, but you lot are cowardly and irresponsible, and that's much worse. But I'll tell you this, that when the first Russian soldier appears you'll be flying the white flag! You can be slaughtered for your beloved Führer as far as I'm concerned.'

'I might point out to you,' the section leader says, 'that according to Dr Goebbels' decree you are putting yourselves outside the national community by doing this.'

'Let's do that!' the man with the scar says. 'Let's just do that! You can't talk French to a cow, and you can't talk sense to a Nazi. We should have known that. Come on, Albert!'

'We'll come out with you,' Wiegand says quickly, and glances at Schröter. 'So that they don't do anything stupid outside, Section Leader.' He gives him a reassuring nod.

When they are in the street, Wiegand looks cautiously around, then he takes the man with the scar by the arm and says quietly, 'Prepare everyone in your houses for surrender, Comrades, but be careful not to fly the white flags too soon, follow our example and put a few reliable people in the hallways.'

The man with the scar and the older man stare at him in disbelief. 'I don't understand you. You mean we should . . .'

'Yes, you should,' Schröter says impatiently, 'you've understood correctly. How much effort do you think it took to keep our mouths shut in there? Man, we're not here to fight, but to stop the fighting. Have you ever heard of Rumpelstiltskin?'

'Of course, he's the . . .'

'Yes, that one,' Schröter interrupts him quickly, 'and this is one of Rumpelstiltskin's operations. You can be sure that it's going to work. Is that clear?'

'Yes! But there's one thing I still don't understand.'

'What? Come on, out with it!'

'Why don't you just fly the white flag and chuck those Hitler lads out of their shack?'

'Because we don't want to put ourselves in danger unnecessarily!' Wiegand says. 'Or do you think we want to have the SS on our backs? The white flag goes up when the Russians are here and not before.'

'After killing those boys first?'

'Nonsense!' Schröter says with a quick wave of the hand. 'What can those kids do about anything? We'll shut them in until it's all over. Right, now off you go, get everything ready, but don't talk about it. Good luck!'

'You're all right,' the man with the scar says, 'I'm sure you'll do it. Right, let's get going!'

The men shake hands, then the two air-raid wardens walk into the street.

'Those two were very brave coming here,' Schröter observes, watching after them. 'Courage hasn't quite died out.'

'It's comforting to know that,' Wiegand says.

'Did you talk to them?' the section leader asks.

'We made the position clear to them again,' Wiegand replies. 'Old men like that are sometimes odd, and you're a bit young, Section Leader, but you can rely on the fact that they won't do anything stupid.'

'Then everything's all right,' the section leader says, and sighs with relief. 'Thank you.'

'You're very welcome,' Schröter says and smiles, 'our pleasure.'

The section leader nods to him and turns round. 'Volkmar, you can take over from the sentry.'

While the boy is still putting on his bluish-grey coat, the door is pulled open and two Hitler Youth come stumbling in with their bicycles, gasping for air and waving their arms around wildly.

'It's kicking off,' one of them says, 'the Russians are already at Weissenseer Weg, there was hardly any resistance in Hohenschönhausen, and now they're slowly coming up Oderbruchstrasse.'

'And what about the demolition squad?' the section leader asks.

'We don't know,' the other courier says. 'Should we . . .'

'Let me just see what's going on up there,' Wiegand says hastily, 'and check that they aren't sleeping through all this. Lassehn, come with me, and don't forget your gun.'

'You're going to . . .' the section leader begins.

'. . . check that everything's all right,' Wiegand finishes his sentence.

Before the section leader can reply, Wiegand and Lassehn leave the bank and force their way through the barrier. In front of them the Landsberger Allee curves in a low arch over the S-Bahn towards the crossing by the Tax Office. There is a strange stillness in the air, there is no rush of trams, no squeal of brakes on the S-Bahn, no car horns, no bleating and grunting from the abattoir, no voices, no footsteps, no bicycle bells, the many noises of the city seem to have been erased, the only sounds that fill the air are the grinding rattle of tank tracks and the chirping of sparrows, planes rumble somewhere and guns thunder, but those sounds have nothing to do with this street. This street is silent and deserted. Berlin is a big city, and what is happening a dozen streets away is already a different war zone.

Lassehn and Wiegand run the 100 metres to the bridge. The guardroom has been installed in a restaurant by the entrance to the S-Bahn station, the door is wide open. Wiegand and Lassehn glance inside, but the room is empty and shows every sign of having been hastily abandoned.

Where is the demolition squad? With a few quick steps they are in the dark ticket office of the station. Bleakness and abandonment leap out at them, the only sound is the wind, which is knocking a loose poster back and forth. Where is . . . Then a few voices are heard, someone is speaking down on the platform.

Lassehn and Wiegand run down the steps, the platform lies in front of them, deserted and immersed in an unreal silence. The indicator is still showing 'Ring via Ostkreuz', and the men from the demolition squad are still standing on the platforms and staring at the bridge, which arches powerful and massive in front of them on the other side of the railway cutting.

'Shame about the beautiful bridge,' an engineer says.

'Shame is dead,' the NCO says, holding the detonator. 'Come on, start getting out of here, along the track towards Weissensee.' He looks at his watch. 'I'm detonating in two minutes.'

'No, don't detonate,' Wiegand calls, 'Our rearguard are still on the way.'

The NCO shrugs. 'Then they'll have to go up through the allotments or up Storkower Strasse, I've got an order to blow it up when the Russian tank spearheads have reached Weissenseer Weg, and they're there now, they may even be past it, I'm not bothered about anything else. Come on, clear off, or you'll go up with it.' He sets off at a slight trot, still holding the fuse.

Lassehn and Wiegand follow him 'Be sensible, Comrade,' Wiegand says.

'Leave me in peace,' the NCO says dismissively. 'I'm not here to reflect upon reason or unreason, sense or nonsense but to carry out an order. Or do you think I want to get a bollocking for non-obedience of an order? The hell with the bridge!'

'After the final victory everything will be built up again even more beautiful than before,' Lassehn says bitterly, and walks towards the NCO. 'You're not going to light it.'

'Shut up! Careful, take cover, I'm detonating!' He plunges the detonator down and throws himself against the railway embankment.

Lassehn and Wiegand leap over the electric tracks and throw themselves at him, but they're too late. They stare at the bridge and wait for the big explosion, which will be followed by a fountain of light, a tearing crash, a jolt, and then the middle arch of the bridge will go flying up into the grey sky.

But nothing happens, nothing changes. Unscathed, the bridge still vaults the railway tracks with a gentle curve. The strangely frozen stillness of an abandoned railway station settles over the whole area, a row of grey Dutch cooling wagons stands by the loading ramp by the big cooling house, on the siding a few wagons stand far apart.

'Misfire!' the NCO says, and pulls away from the embankment. He studies Lassehn and Wiegand with a few indecipherable glances and says, 'You stay here till I get back.'

'Let us go up and get back to our unit,' Wiegand says.

The NCO thinks and then nods.

'All right, then, but hurry up or . . .' He doesn't finish the sentence.

Wiegand and Lassehn climb onto the platform and walk quickly along it towards the bridge. The NCO nods in the direction of the steps. 'Come on, get out of here!'

Wiegand exchanges a glance with Lassehn. They climb the first few steps, but slow down as soon as they are out of sight.

'He's going to throw a hand grenade into the explosion chamber,' Wiegand whispers excitedly. 'Come on, shoes off!'

In great haste, fingers quivering with excitement, they untie their shoelaces, then run silently back down the steps and leap on the NCO, who is walking towards the arch of the bridge, holding a hand grenade in his threateningly raised hand. He is concentrating entirely on his task, and staring at the grey-green pillar covered with dark rust. He is swinging the grenade when Lassehn grabs his arm and twists it away from him, while Wiegand aims his pistol at him, ready to fire.

The NCO doesn't defend himself, he just looks at them darkly.

'You'll pay for this,' he says hoarsely.

'Save your words,' Wiegand says. 'Go and join your people, or even better, grab a few clothes and go home. Or haven't you had enough?'

'Of course I've had enough,' the NCO says, 'but you're seeing things from your point of view. If they grab me by the scruff of the neck because I haven't carried out my order, it'll be your fault.'

'Don't make such a fuss,' Wiegand says as they put their boots back on. 'There's nothing you can do about it if the detonator fails. Right, good luck.'

The NCO stands there with his shoulders drooping, then he turns round and walks along the platform again. 'They're right,' he murmurs to himself, 'but orders are orders, that's just how it is.'

Wiegand and Lassehn are no longer listening, they hurry up the stairs, always taking two or three steps at a time. The street still looks as if it has been swept clear, but the sound of the rolling tanks has come closer, and every now and again there is a hard, dry report.

'That worked,' Wiegand says, taking a deep breath. 'You hear the tanks coming in?'

'Yes,' Lassehn replies, 'the time has come at last. I hope the assault gun over there doesn't fire.'

'Wait and see. Come on!'

They walk quickly towards the anti-tank barrier. The section leader is already waiting for them.

'What's happening with the bridge?' he asks hastily.

'All fine,' Wiegand replies. 'The bridge will go up as soon as the first tank passes over it.'

'Great,' says a young air-force auxiliary standing next to him. 'I'm already looking forward to seeing how the Bolsheviks celebrate Ascension Day.'

'There's no reason to be gleeful,' Lassehn can't keep himself from saying, 'the Russians are people too, they have wives and children and fathers and mothers.'

'Christ,' the air-force auxiliary says, 'are you from last century? The louse is an animal as well, Dr Goebbels said.'

'That's enough remarks,' the section leader says. 'We're not here to talk, we're here to carry out the orders we've been given.'

With a few glances Schröter assesses the situation and winks at Wiegand. The anti-tank barrier has been manned again, two Hitler Youth, two air-force auxiliaries, the two Volkssturm men and Dr Böttcher are standing in a raised area behind the barrier, with the rocket launchers and carbines at their feet. 'Get them to fall in again, Section Leader,' Schröter says. 'You're still inexperienced, I'd like to give you a bit of advice.'

'Fall in again?' the section leader says. 'I'd rather not do that right now, listen to the tanks rolling, they're getting closer.' He pricks his ears. 'They can't be far from the Tax Office. Why isn't the assault gun shooting? He should have opened fire ages ago! Do you understand that?'

Schröter looks him carefully in the face, but he doesn't reply straight away, he has his ears pricked too, his eyes are narrowed to a slit, the tips of his bushy moustache quiver under the hurried panting of his breath. The rattle of the tracks on the cobbles becomes louder and louder but not a shot is fired, the assault gun is silent, the tanks aren't firing, they just rattle on.

'No, I understand this,' Schröter says firmly, and takes a few steps back. 'Listen everyone, Comrades from the Hitler Youth and the Volkssturm!' he calls in a loud voice.

They all turn round, Wiegand and Lassehn follow a wave of Schröter's hand, they step up beside him and take the carbines from their shoulders.

The rattle of the tanks becomes a roar.

'The big moment has come!' Schröter shouts, trying to catch his people's eye. 'Let us remember the heroes of Stalingrad! Yes, sir, of *Sta-lin-grad!*'

Lassehn, Wiegand and Schröter shoulder their carbines.

'Hands up, lads!' shouts Schröter. 'Enough of your war games! Hands up!'

The roar of the tanks swells to a thunder.

The Hitler Youth members and the air-force auxiliaries are completely taken by surprise, they don't understand the situation and laugh.

'He must be joking!' says one of the auxiliaries.

'He has a sense of humour!' says one of the couriers.

Only the section leader has turned pale, he is the only one who has looked into Schröter's grimly resolute face and understood that neither joking nor humour are involved here. He stands there as if ready to jump, his hands already reaching for Schröter's throat.

'Hands up!' Schröter shouts again.

Dr Böttcher and the two Volkssturm men pull the boys away from the barrier, and they raise their hands uncertainly.

'Right, to the guardroom!' Schröter orders.

'Never capitulate!' the section leader shouts, leaps to the barrier and grabs a rocket launcher, but immediately Lassehn is on him, encircling him from behind with both arms and holding him in a tight grip.

The first tank slows down and then drives on the pavement, further tanks break out of Oderbruchstrasse, arrange themselves in a diagonal line and roll slowly towards the bridge.

Ducking heads, hands still held high, the Hitler Youth members walk to the guardroom. Lassehn and the section leader are rolling around in the street, and the thunder of the tanks becomes a roar of iron.

Then a white flag is raised above the anti-tank barrier at Landsberger Allee S-Bahn station. And, just as lights previously went on in the windows, here and there, and over there, now white flags appear on the houses, here, there and everywhere. The dark, cold, forbidding street is suddenly swathed in white cries of joy.

X

The morning of 23 April breaks under an overcast sky. The light of the dawning day is merely faint greyness, which drives away the darkness only very slowly and hesitantly lifts the streets out of darkness, those streets which were once radiant with lights, and filled with countless people, which echoed with laughter and merriment, and which are now the most advanced supply lines of the front, and lead directly to death. The night has been relatively calm, it was an oppressive, anxious night that was spread out around the city, the night of a city on the front line. Every now and again artillery fire twitched into the silence like a distant storm, night fighters rumbled over the houses and dropped the projectiles from their weapons like exploding shooting stars, but beyond those noises, invisible, disturbing, menacing, were the legions of enemy soldiers, the columns of their tanks and the squadrons of their bombers were ready to charge at any second, to launch a hurricane of fire, to start the motors of the tanks and aircraft, to break over the city like a mighty wave and engulf everything.

The people in the cellars spent the night dozing, they didn't notice the change in the light, only the hands of the clocks showed that the daylight hours were over and the hours of night had begun, and that a new day had taken over from the old one. The minutes dripped away with infinite slowness, each one becoming desolate and running as viscously as oil, only hesitantly, reluctantly, have they lined themselves up into hours. Impenetrable darkness has spread across the cellars, they contain only breathing, wheezing, groaning, snoring, run through only by the wails of a baby or a cry caused by a nightmare, illuminated only for moments by the flickering of a candle stump. Lungs breathe like bellows, hearts beat like pumps, in brains thoughts melt formlessly into one another like molten lead.

The new morning remains outside, it doesn't penetrate the cellars through the iron doors. Exhaustion, stiffness, torpor, helplessness cling like shadows, and only the mechanical aid of the clock makes people aware that outside their catacombs light is flowing onto the city and seeping through the windows into the empty flats. With the new day, rising somewhere a world away, fresh torment falls upon the people, uncertainty grows, the waiting is protracted, the end of night brings no light, it does not revive the spirit, it does not stretch the limbs, with growing brightness the artillery fire resumes, the air attacks start up again, the front line, which had congealed on the dark edges of the night, starts moving once more.

In the kitchen of Klose's flat Lucie Wiegand and Klose are busying themselves and Lassehn sits on the windowsill, doing nothing. Since there is no gas left, a fire burns in the stove.

'Just past seven,' Lucie Wiegand says. 'Shall we let the men go on sleeping?'

'I think so, yes,' Klose replies, splitting a piece of wood. 'They're exhausted. I'll go and fetch water in the meantime.'

'I'll go,' Lassehn says and jumps to his feet.

'Be careful,' Lucie Wiegand warns, 'the shooting is starting up again already.'

'Being careful on its own isn't enough,' Klose says, 'you also need to be lucky, not every bullet hits a target. Go with God, Joachim, but go.'

When Lassehn has gone, Lucie Wiegand walks quietly down the corridor, carefully opens the doors and looks into the rooms. In the room immediately adjacent to the restaurant Dr Böttcher, Schröter and the new man who arrived with the others last night, the one they call Gregor, are still sleeping. The sofa where Lassehn slept is empty, Schröter is sleeping sitting up in two armchairs, his head hanging lifelessly to the side, the tips of his moustache stirring as he breathes. Dr Böttcher and the new man are lying on two mattresses, they have rolled up their coats and put them under their heads like pillows. Wiegand is lying in the bedroom, his arms crossed under his head and his eyes wide open.

'Awake already?' Lucie Wiegand asks, and walks into the room.

Wiegand slips from the bed. 'I've just woken up,' he answers. 'Good morning, Lucie. Are you working already?'

'Good morning, Fritz,' Lucie Wiegand replies. 'Making coffee, slicing bread, I have three men to feed.'

Wiegand pulls his wife to him. 'The mother of the underground brigade,' he says, stroking her hair. 'Are the others still asleep?'

'Yes,' Lucie Wiegand says, 'Lassehn has gone to fetch water. Who's the man you call Gregor?'

Wiegand shrugs. 'We don't know his real name, Schröter says he used to be, or perhaps still is, a lecturer at the university, and that he teaches canon law, he's supposed to have strong contacts with the old Centre Party, but we don't know exactly. At any rate he has so far proved one hundred per cent reliable, and that's the main thing. Where's Klose?'

'In the kitchen, tending to the fire,' answers Lucie Wiegand. 'I'm going into the kitchen.'

'I'll be right there,' Wiegand says. 'Is it possible to have a wash?'

Lucie Wiegand laughs as she walks down the corridor. 'Washing is a serious business these days, because water is scarce,' she says. 'You'll have to wait for Lassehn to get back.'

After greeting Klose, Wiegand falls heavily onto the kitchen chair. 'It's pretty noisy out there again,' he says, 'and a good number of planes seem to be on the way.'

Lucie Wiegand puts a few pieces of wood and a briquette into the stove, then she sits down too and lets her hands hang limply in her lap. 'Ah, Fritz,' she says in a low voice, looking through the window at the little piece of grey sky above the side wing of the building. 'Do you think we'll ever have our own house again, a regular, unworried life?'

Wiegand stares at her, stunned. 'Are you discouraged, Lucie? I don't recognize you.'

'A little sigh lightens your mood,' Klose says. 'Isn't that right, madam?'

Lucie Wiegand looks back into the kitchen and slowly shakes her head. 'Discouraged? No, it's not that, but I do need some rest, I'm desperate for peace and quiet, to be free of work, fighting and persecution. You get tired, Fritz, and then there's worry about the children . . .'

'I've always been in favour of complete openness, Lucie . . .'

'Your preamble is worrying, Fritz . . .'

'Very alarming,' Klose agrees.

Wiegand smiles faintly. 'Back when we met each other I didn't promise you anything, no bourgeois marriage, no home sweet home, bower of bliss, I wanted to let you know that my life is and will always be the struggle, and I promise you nothing even now, because it is certain that after the fall of the so-called Third Reich there will be even more work and even more of a struggle, except . . .'

'Except?'

'. . . we may be able to do it without the persecution.'

Lucie Wiegand smiles back at him. 'You are as you are, and I wouldn't have you any other way. Where could Lassehn have got to?'

'The fountains are besieged in the morning,' Klose reassures her, 'particularly early in the morning while the artillery fire is still weak. Then comes . . .'

Dr Böttcher appears in the doorway and blinks short-sightedly. 'Am I disturbing you?'

'Not at all, Doctor,' Lucie Wiegand says, 'it's not as if we're on honeymoon.'

Dr Böttcher comes in and shivers. 'I feel very uncomfortable, unwashed, unshaven, my clothes crumpled and – frankly – hungry too. I see, Lucie, you have already prepared a mountain of slices of bread. May I?'

'That's what I'm here for,' she says with a smile, pouring coffee into a cup and pushing it towards him.

Böttcher starts eating hastily and pouring coffee into himself, but his eyes will not rest, they blink uneasily, circle around the kitchen as if looking for something, they linger for a moment on the wall calendar and then return to an old newspaper lying on the stove.

'Is it good?' Lucie Wiegand asks.

Böttcher looks at her as if he hasn't understood the question.

'To look at you,' Lucie Wiegand says, amused, 'the question of whether it's good actually seems superfluous.'

Dr Böttcher nods. 'I'm sorry, Lucie,' he says at last, 'but I really don't know if it's good or not. That was always a great disappointment to my landlady, that I've never been able to tell her whether something tasted good or not, whether it was too sweet or too salty or anything else. I only eat to assuage my hunger, and I don't really care how and with what that happens, it's simply impossible for me to concentrate my thoughts on food. I know' – he raises his hands, defending himself in advance against a possible reproach – 'that this means not acknowledging the work of the lady of the house, and I do apologize for that. I am also aware' – he laughs briefly – 'because I am a doctor after all, that it is not healthy to read or think when eating, but then in life we often act contrary to our knowledge and understanding.'

'You look so . . . how can I put it? You look unusually lively today, Doctor,' Klose says. 'Even though I'm sure you haven't slept very much, or very comfortably.'

'Really, can you see that?' Dr Böttcher asks with a smile. 'Yes, I'm contented, even though my house has burned down and I should really be sad and out of sorts.' He thinks uncertainly for a moment, turning his hand back and forth. 'I said contented a moment ago, but that isn't really the correct term, it is an inner equilibrium that smooths the wrinkles from my face, and I also know why that is the case. Hitherto we have carried out our underground activities without visible success, we were barely able to touch people through our secret transmitters, and our words always dripped away into the darkness, they disappeared into the desert sands, our flyers only ever fluttered in the void, we were never able to observe their effect because we had to leave the people who received them before they had unfolded them, our acts of sabotage often seemed ridiculously tiny, like a mosquito bite on an elephant; we have never had any response, and in the end it was only out of faith in ourselves that we didn't despair in the face of the wall of silence that we were all running into. But last night something really happened, a success was visible, we had a response from many voices, and our activity, which was perhaps only a way of justifying ourselves, became a concrete action for the first time.'

'There you are saying something, Doctor,' Wiegand says, 'that I didn't wish to know until now, and if it ever did arise in me I would never under any circumstances have admitted it to myself. Our activity primarily gave us an alibi for ourselves, assuaging our consciences, and everything else came after that. We are, as we know, also egoists when we are selfless or loving without benefit to ourselves, but it is a special kind of egoism, which satisfies ourselves first and foremost, but . . .'

'Philosophy at break of day?' Lucie Wiegand asks.

'. . . leads to evening dismay,' Klose joins in. 'But now, gentlemen, answer one question for me. Why did you even come here? The war could have been over for you at eight o'clock in the evening.'

'I came back, if you really want to know, because . . .' Wiegand begins.

'. . . because your wife is here,' Klose finishes quickly, 'that's clear even to me, but I didn't mean you. I meant the doctor, Joachim, Schröter and the stranger.'

'Schröter and the stranger saw their task as being to strengthen our group,' Dr Böttcher replies, 'and I am one of you as well, particularly since my house is now a ruin adorning the Frankfurter Allee. You probably didn't seriously assume that I consider my work at an end once I have regained my own personal freedom?'

'No, I didn't assume anything of the sort, you old sawbones,' Klose says and laughs broadly. 'But Lassehn?'

'I told Lassehn he could go now, because no one was going to call him to account for desertion,' Dr Böttcher replies. 'He looked at me as if he didn't grasp the meaning of my words straight away, then he shook his head and said something along the lines of: "I'd almost forgotten my desertion, I stopped staying here with you just to seek refuge a long time ago. Now, for the first time, I'm carrying a gun for the cause of justice and against tyranny, and am I supposed to put that gun down before the struggle is finally over? Don't imagine that I'm going to do that!" No, we didn't imagine he could do that, but we also wanted to indicate that there was a possibility of leaving without putting himself in too much danger.'

'He's a great lad,' says Klose, 'he knows where he belongs.'

'Even if he doesn't know why and what for,' Dr Böttcher says. 'You can fight something from a nihilistic or negative point of view, but after the struggle that point of view must be replaced by something positive, otherwise nihilism or negation become a habit. Lassehn and all the other young people who despise the Nazi Reich seem to me like a building that has only a few weak supports, hatred, revulsion, disgust contempt, but no foundation. And we have to build that foundation very quickly.'

'Well, build it, then,' Klose says, and slides down from the windowsill, 'now I'm going to hunt out those two other gentlemen and give them the Sleeping Beauty kiss.'

'Someone's knocking at the door,' Lucie Wiegand says and dashes out of the kitchen, 'that will be Lassehn.'

It is Lassehn, he sets the two buckets down and takes a crumpled piece of paper out of his pocket. 'This is stuck up all over the place,' he says and unfolds the page. 'Listen to this:

"Remember:

Anyone who propagates or even approves of any measures that weaken our resistance is a traitor! He will be shot or hanged on the spot!

23 April 1945
Signed: Adolf Hitler." '

'This is anarchy,' Dr Böttcher says after a moment's silence. 'Conscription to the eastern front has spread anarchy among the soldiers and, with a stroke of the pen, erased that thing that the Prussian military was once so proud of: absolute deference to one's superior, and this proclamation is aimed at achieving the same effect on the civilian population. There is no mention of a court or a trial, or field courts or drumhead courts martial.'

'If we weren't such old friends,' Wiegand says, abruptly pushing away his coffee cup, 'I might be tempted to say that it took you a long time to realize that the Third Reich wasn't based on the rule of law.'

Dr Böttcher smiles. 'My dear Wiegand,' he says slowly, 'this fact is by no means unknown to me, but – yes, here comes the big but – previously it was a privilege of the state, the Party and its various organizations, to break the law, to lock people up without a legal arrest warrant and to kill without sentence from a court. Now that right to killing and violence has passed to everyone, there are no principles attached any more, everyone can act as his so-called national sentiment decrees. Anyone can kill, hang, shoot anyone without fearing that he will be called to account, and reference to this appeal will constitute sufficient reason. No accusation or verdict is required, assertion is both proof and death sentence. It is probably the first time in history that a state has officially given the right to kill, and proclaimed total lawlessness.'

'It's lucky the majority of people don't understand that,' Lucie Wiegand says.

Dr Böttcher laughs briefly. 'Lucie, have you ever experienced a situation in which the Nazis did not thoroughly explain and constantly repeat their goals and intentions so that even the stupidest person can understand? If their method of "drumming", as they call it, fails on this occasion, it is only because they no longer have propaganda methods fully at their disposal and – last but not least – because the people have sunk into a torpor, they have been sitting in cellars for days, tired, empty and defeated, and in no condition to do anything at all.'

Lassehn leans against the kitchen cupboard with his arms folded. 'Until now I have accepted as law everything that was proclaimed as such, I have obeyed not the political but the juridical terminology of the National Socialists. Just as the lives of German soldiers fall under the categorical imperative of "orders are orders", the lives of citizens are ruled by the motto "the law is the law". And just as orders must be carried out in military life, in the lives of ordinary citizens it has been the case that law is right and right is law.'

'Right always implies justice,' says Dr Böttcher. 'There is no other yardstick. Admittedly justice is a relative concept, but it cannot be reduced to a pragmatic goal, as the Nazis are doing by proclaiming that "right is what is useful to the people". We have experienced with horror where this vision leads, not only through the passing of laws that scorn any feeling of rightness, but by the fact that unwritten laws and the despotism of the Gestapo exist alongside this so-called common law, and that the only law that exists for them is the law of oppression, there is a widespread legal insecurity. Any law can be broken, sidestepped and thus effectively cancelled by the Gestapo. Often enough we have seen the Gestapo taking defendants who have been acquitted by a regular court into so-called protective custody, and thus simply abolishing the legal verdict. Ancient legal principles such as *in dubio pro reo* or the principle that no one can be sentenced twice for a single crime were dismissed as sentimental humanitarianism. The chief of the black hordes once stated this quite clearly when he announced: "We Nationalist Socialists have set to work without law. I have always assumed the position that I don't care if a paragraph is opposed to our actions. If others complained about the breaking of laws, I couldn't have cared less." The elimination of any sense of right by the openly proclaimed lawlessness of the superior and racial perspectives has contributed significantly to the bestialization of the German people. No defeat can be total and annihilating enough to halt this development, which has already advanced far too far.'

Dr Böttcher had begun speaking in his calm and academic way and then talked himself into a state of excitement, but now he smooths out the agitation in his voice and turns to Lassehn. 'You are holding something in your hand, Lassehn. Won't you show it to us?' he asks.

Lassehn nods and waves a newspaper in the air like a trophy. 'It's today's *12-Uhr-Blatt!*'

Klose pounces on him and grabs the paper.

'There are some wonderful things in it,' Lassehn says as Klose's eyes run over the newspaper.

'Read it out, Oskar,' Wiegand demands.

Klose looks up. 'Monstrous,' he says. 'If I didn't have it in black and white . . . Well, listen:

'The city will be defended until the end.

Fight with fanatical doggedness for your wives, children and mothers! We will prevail.

12-Uhr-Blatt Berlin, 23 April

Our home city of Berlin has become a front-line state. The Reich Defence Commissar and Gauleiter Dr Goebbels has therefore issued the following demands to all the people of Berlin:

1. All soldiers and Volkssturm men deployed to defend the Reich capital are to occupy the positions assigned to them, and begin fighting as soon as Soviet troops or tanks appear.
2. The civilian population is unconditionally to obey all orders issued by civilian and military authorities.
3. Arms factories, public utilities and the authorities responsible for the leadership of the Reich capital will continue to work.
4. Works security will ensure the internal and external security of factories. Provocateurs or insubordinate foreigners are to be arrested immediately, or, even better, rendered harmless.
5. Should provocateurs or criminal elements attempt, by hoisting white flags or any other cowardly behaviour, to stir unease in the population that is resolved to defend the city, and paralyse its resistance, all possible measures are to be taken against them. Every Berliner is responsible for his own house or flat. Houses and flats hoisting white flags have no right to the protection of community welfare services, and will be treated accordingly. The residents of such houses are therefore to be held responsible. The local Party authorities must guard staunchly against such behaviour and act accordingly. Such houses would be plague bacilli on the body of our city, and ruthlessly combating them is therefore the command of the moment. Traitors are to be shot down or hanged immediately. The only valid slogan is: the hardest and most fanatical resistance in all points.

Everyone knows his task at this moment.

Your mothers, your children and your wives are watching you, defenders of Berlin! They have entrusted you with their lives. Everyone knows his duty. The hour of truth has sounded for you. Let the men of Breslau be your model! They have not hesitated for a moment to deploy all of their courage and bravery and their faith in the Reich and the Führer. The city will be defended to the last. Form a solid community! Stamp out rumours! They only serve to poison the atmosphere and to undermine your fighting spirit. Let everyone act as if the welfare of our Reich capital depended solely on his actions! The whole nation has its eye on you, you defenders of Berlin, and trusts in you and the unconditional fulfilment of your duty.

Everyone knows that this hour is difficult. Thunder rolls and shells whistle over the houses of the workers. The Bolsheviks are storming the suburbs with men and *materiel*. If we have endured the bombs of the Anglo-Americans, we will not shy from shells. You Berliners are known for your quick-wittedness and your toughness. There is no doubt that these will now be on display.

So fight for your city! Fight doggedly for your wives and your children, your mothers and your parents! You are laying down your lives for a good cause.

The military defence of the Reich capital has been entrusted to a soldier who has proved himself time and again in this war in the leadership of troops and Volkssturm. He is the bearer of the oak leaf, Lieutenant-General Heymann. Your Gauleiter is with you. He declares that he will of course remain in your midst with his comrades. His wife and children are here as well. He, who conquered this city with two hundred men, will now activate the defence of the Reich capital with all means.

A great goal can only be achieved by great daring. Character is revealed, man proves himself, precisely in the time of danger and need. So do not stint in aiming your weapons against the enemy! Stand and fight! In that way we will finally prevail in the eyes of our wives and children and our home town of Berlin." '

When Klose has finished reading, he sets the newspaper down on the table. 'Every word a lie, a vulgar lie,' Wiegand says and picks up the newspaper. 'Every order is a crime, and between orders, threats, vulgarity, lies and cynicism there is always the usual sentimental stuff about wives and children, mothers and the land of home. They threaten and plead simultaneously. How else are we to understand this appeal from Goebbels:

"Appeal from Gauleiter Dr Goebbels

Everyone is to Join the Defence Front Forthwith

The Gauleiter of Berlin, Reich Minister Dr Goebbels, has issued the following appeal to the soldiers and men of Berlin.

In this fatal hour of the battle for the Reich capital, I turn to all the soldiers and men of Berlin who are not currently deployed to join the defence front of the Reich capital straight away. Soldiers and wounded men who can still carry weapons are immediately to report voluntarily to the commandant's office of Berlin, Johannisstrasse, near Friedrichstrasse Station.

I issue the same appeal to all the men of Berlin who have not been recruited to the Volkssturm or deployed for the defence of the city. I am convinced that every man who has a courageous heart and is determined to defend our Reich capital to the death against the cruel Bolshevik global enemy will respond to my appeal and also report immediately to the commandant's office on Johannisstrasse.

We will do our duty in an honourable and manly fashion, and serve as a model of brave resistance to the entire nation. Anyone who prefers contemptible cowardice to manly struggle is a scoundrel.

Soldiers, wounded, men of Berlin! To arms!

Signed: Dr Goebbels,
Gauleiter of Berlin."

'Why does he address the soldiers and men with an appeal and not an order? Because he knows very well that the reins have already slipped from their hands. But the whole thing is the most convincing proof that the authorities are taking their last breath.'

'Or their second-last,' Dr Böttcher says ironically. 'In spite of the general dissolution they are still convulsively trying to simulate something like order. Please, gentlemen, there are also official reports in the newspaper: "What groceries are there?" and "Directive concerning the consumption of electricity and gas" and – I must read this out to you, it's too good to pass over. Listen and be amazed:

> "Extension of the dog-tax stamps for the year 1942 in tax year 1945. New dog stamps will not be issued for tax year 1945. The stamps for 1942, which were still valid for tax years 1943 and 1944, remain valid for tax year 1945. For new applications in the course of tax year 1945 dog owners will accordingly receive tax stamps bearing the year 1942.
>
> Berlin, 13 April 1945
> The Senior Burgomaster of Reich capital Berlin
> Main Tax Office." '

'People think of everything!' Klose says. 'The only thing missing is the supplement that dog slaughter is compulsorily registrable, and that such and such a percentage should be factored in during the next distribution of meat. At any rate, order always prevails here, even in the middle of the greatest chaos.'

XI

The day is an endless chain of minutes, it proceeds fatally slowly and nothing changes. Russian artillery fire mounts and fades, the Soviet fighter bombers come down almost incessantly, firing their salvoes as they plunge, barrage balloons stand undisturbed in the eastern and northern suburbs of the city. In between there are endless minutes of complete stillness. Decimated and severely battered units crowd into the streets, the columns of vehicles and soldiers flooding back into the city, they cannot congregate at collection points or internal defences because there are none, and they end up joining the new recently and hastily constituted units marching towards some main battle line that doesn't exist either.

The battle is based on some nests of resistance, and the combat groups, rarely any bigger than a battalion, are also acting on their own initiative. Their commanders receive orders without knowing who has issued them, indicating attack objectives and then abandoning them again after a few hours. They defend unimportant strongholds until they are encircled, and battered gun emplacements are directed from one part of the city to another, without the chance to fire even a shot. The soldiers are weary and resigned and put up with everything, artillery fire and gunfire from on-board weapons, vermin and hunger, orders to advance and orders to retreat, they take the complaints of the civilian population with dull indifference, even though this time they are not insignificant Russian, French or Yugoslavian females, but women of their own people walking the ruined, burning streets with crazed eyes and desperate gestures and queuing outside shops to buy the last available foodstuffs while a few streets along the Russian armoured cars are already advancing and the low-flying planes dash away above their heads. Soldiers do what they are ordered to do, without thinking beyond the next minute, worry and apprehension about shelter, food and sleep is more important and more significant in the duration of the current minute than the thought of the great and inevitable fall that awaits them only a few steps away. Basically they have been falling for years, their bodies and their souls have already adapted to that fall so much that they will only reacquire a sensibility when they reach absolute bottom.

Among the defenders of the city there are many who have fought in the winter battle at the gates of Moscow, and who besieged Leningrad for years, who saw dozens of cities collapse and hundreds of villages going up in flames, and millions of people wandering about homelessly or vegetating in ruins, in the end it only awakened fleeting reflexes in them, as destruction and misery have been reflected too often and for too long in the retinas of their eyes. The receptiveness of their brains and the reaction of their emotions was exhausted long ago, the sensibility of their hearts is cut off so completely that they can no longer be horrified now that the war has returned to its starting point. They see one house after another sinking into rubble, women fetching water while under fire and chasing from shop to shop looking for groceries, they witness the enemy playfully overcoming one obstacle after another, they have precise knowledge of the suffering of a city under artillery fire, where the deadly wave of street battles is rolling towards them, but they endure it all as the disaster of an inevitable fate.

SS, military police and the recently instituted drumhead courts martial still hold together the remains of the collapsing and divided enemy with brutal terror. Within minutes death sentences are delivered and executed on the nearest lamp post or tram-stop pole, in the central military court on Rüsternallee in Charlottenburg a whole horde of officials are at work, military judges, staff lawyers, army justice inspectors and 'reliable' assessors, they do not deliver justice, they only carry out orders and every day, 'in the name of the German people', they deliver dozens of death sentences which are then executed as soon as the sentence has been passed. It isn't only external pressure that repeatedly kneads together the formless mass of companies and units, it is also the compulsion of orders that has been inculcated into them and conditions them, not making them fight resolutely to the last (but rather dodge fighting if possible), but making them obey to the last.

The situation is clear. The strategic plan of Russian army command is becoming obvious, it will succeed in a matter of only one or two days: the complete encirclement of Berlin. From Tegel via Reinickendorf, Weissensee, Lichtenberg, Köpenick, the Teltow Canal, Stahnsdorf to the Havel lakes, the circle around the city centre is already three-quarters closed, the arteries to the south and south-west have been cut off, the military corps still relatively capable of fighting in the south and south-east of the city have been cut off from their defence area, the Reich capital, and driven together in two large pockets near Halbe and Luckenwalde, where they are slowly being further constricted and confined. The only road still open is the military road, the big artery from the north-west via Spandau and Staaken, but it too is already under occasional fire from the Russian artillery.

In this situation the Gauleiter of Berlin, Reich Defence Commissar and Reich Minister for National Enlightenment and Propaganda, Dr Joseph Goebbels, stages his last bravura coup from the absolutely bomb-proof underground bunker in the Reich Chancellery: he invents the Wenck reserve army. After the planned dissemination of rumours concerning the advance of strong, fresh forces, the desperate mood of the population was to be brightened by a shimmer of hope, and strangely enough a flyer, which to judge by its textual composition must be intended only for the soldiers of that reserve army, has fallen into the hands of the civilian population. This flyer, a vaccination of last hope, reads as follows:

Soldiers of the Wenck Army!

An order of great import has summoned you from your marshalling area against our western enemies, and set you marching towards the east.

Your mission is clear: Berlin remains German! The goals set for you must be accomplished under all circumstances, because on the other side operations are under way with the goal of bringing about the crucial defeat of the Bolsheviks in the battle for the Reich capital and thus fundamentally to change the situation of Germany.

Berlin will never capitulate to Bolshevism! The defenders of the Reich capital have been inspired and are fighting with dogged obstinacy in the belief that they will soon hear the thunder of your guns.

The Führer has summoned you!
As in olden times of victory, you have joined the attack. Berlin is waiting for you, Berlin longs for you from the depths of its heart!

Schröter paces uneasily back and forth, his hands clasped behind his back, his forehead crumpled in a frown.

'I can't stand this inactivity any longer,' he says. 'Sitting here, having conversations and waiting while outside fire devours the city, street after street, house after house, flat after flat, and people sit in cellars as if in mousetraps . . .' He waves his hands wildly through the air. 'We need to do something!'

'Nothing imprudent!' Dr Böttcher warns, looking up from the chessboard between him and Lassehn. 'A few men like us can't represent a whole city, we have to restrict ourselves to this house or this street.'

'To hell with your prudence!' Schröter explodes. 'We can't just sit here and wait until . . . But what do you want?'

'What I want will depend on the situation,' Dr Böttcher says calmly. 'Every situation has its own natural logic, my dear Schröter. I've been outside for a few hours and I've seen the mood the soldiers are in.'

'And the mood is good?' Schröter asks menacingly.

'The mood is bad,' Dr Böttcher says quietly. 'But what does that mean? Soldiers are often in a bad mood, they curse and complain, but a sharp word or an order immediately brings them back into line. A soldier is like a devout Christian.'

Gregor, who was leaning against the stove with his arms folded, straightens himself up. 'How do you mean?' he asks.

Dr Böttcher smiles over at him. 'I have no intention of insulting you, Gregor, but the comparison that comes to mind is not without a certain logic. A devout Christian can sometimes despair (and even Jesus said, "My God, my God, why have you forsaken me!" at such a moment), but he will repeatedly return to his faith and take his bearings from it. A soldier, however violently he might rebel, will finally, when it comes to the crunch, obey the order, and that's why I don't believe in drawing conclusions from the mood of the troops.'

'Or at most that the fighting force of a demoralized army is likely to be reduced,' Wiegand says from the window.

'I agree,' Dr Böttcher says. 'And incidentally, the mood in a state like our Third Reich has no significance whatsoever. I remember very clearly many conversations I have had with my patients when reports of retreating movements at the front came at us with the force of an avalanche, I'm sure you will remember the opinion that was expressed even in our circles, to the effect that . . .'

'Just wait until German place names appear in the army reports,' Wiegand cuts in, 'then the mood will change pretty quickly.'

'Exactly!' Dr Böttcher says. 'That's what I mean. I still remember very clearly how all of us, even though we considered the mood factor on its own to be an unimportant quantity in our calculations, all fell for the magic of this moment, which I am sure is not insignificant. And what happened?'

'Nothing at all,' Gregor says. 'The man in the street, as the English say, has seldom had much influence in Germany, and in the Third Reich not at all, the mood of conscience and reason did not warn him, because National Socialism had imposed upon him the role of accomplice. We have heard the Wehrmacht report mentioning German place names as cold-bloodedly and as naturally as it once mentioned Russian and African places, and it is accepted with a kind of grimly humorous indifference that the Remagen bridgehead could only be extended step by step, just as we once received stereotypical phrases like "Malta was successfully bombed".'

'In physiology there is such a thing as a law of diminishing stimulation,' Dr Böttcher says. 'From "roast goose every day" to "bad news every day" it is basically only a small step, by which I mean that the psychical reaction, such as the mood, to a chain of setbacks and adversity arouses not rage, but only dull subjection, particularly in a people which is essentially addicted to obedience, and whose reactions can no longer be measured by human, only by mechanical standards.'

'May I add something?' Lucie Wiegand asks, resting both hands on the tabletop and with her eyes lowered. 'I don't see things with your scientific thoroughness, Doctor, or with your –' she glances at Gregor – 'objectivity, I see them in quite personal terms, I only listen to the voice inside me.'

'And what do you hear?' Dr Böttcher asks with a fleeting smile.

Lucie Wiegand's eyes are still fixed on the tabletop. 'A few years ago a shed of ours burned down,' she begins, 'and two rabbits died.'

'So?' asks Schröter.

Lucie Wiegand raises her eyes and looks absently at Schröter. 'I know exactly what you're thinking, Schröter,' she says, and nods very slowly. 'Only two rabbits, what does that matter?'

'They'd have faced the knife sooner or later anyway,' Schröter adds. 'Wouldn't they?'

'Of course,' Lucie Wiegand confirms, 'and it still went straight to my heart, I even wept, I couldn't sleep for a few nights afterwards, and every time I saw the burnt-out shed I was overwhelmed with grief. But now' – she shakes her head – 'I read about the terrible air attacks on Dresden, I walk through the burnt-out streets of Berlin, but nothing stirs in me any longer, my heart doesn't flutter with horror, no tears rise to my eyes. The death by fire of those two rabbits left me shattered, but the mass death of human beings leaves me entirely cold.'

'Between the burning of your shed and the destruction of our cities lie denunciation and ostracism, Gestapo interrogations and concentration camps, nights filled with bombs and deaths on the scaffold,' Dr Böttcher says slowly, 'events that have so absorbed your capacity for emotion that the destruction of people and cultural values, because of its indescribable extent, prompts only a fleeting reflex in you.'

'I am convinced, Frau Wiegand,' Gregor adds, 'that the fate of one individual, singled out from among the mass of the killed and the burnt, would still move you, while we can no longer make intellectual contact with the fate of the mass, the gassing of the Jews and the Poles, deaths on the battlefields or the suffering of the civilian population.'

Dr Böttcher returns to his chessboard, however he is looking not at the pieces but at Lassehn. 'Something has occurred to me, Lassehn. Weren't you saying this morning that you bumped into an old friend who is deployed somewhere near here?'

Lassehn nods. 'Yes, I wanted to bring him to see you, but so much has happened in the meantime, and you've been bombed out too.'

'What sort of friend is he?' Schröter asks.

'He's a lieutenant with an intelligence section,' Lassehn replies.

'And what's he doing now?' Schröter wants to know.

'He's got a unit over by the goods station,' Lassehn answers.

'Just you be careful, son,' Klose says, sitting by the radio, 'if you get caught they'll get the lot of us.'

'Don't worry, Herr Klose,' Lassehn says, 'he's not a Nazi.'

'. . . but he's a soldier!' Schröter says in a hostile tone. 'And an officer!'

'Calm down, Schröter, don't get so heated,' Dr Böttcher says calmly. 'Let's not reject this young stranger out of hand, even if he is an officer. Is he your age, Lassehn?'

Lassehn nods.

'So he's in his early to mid-twenties. That's the age group the Nazis had completely under their influence, but we have to depend on them and have to approach them at all costs.'

'And why is that?' Schröter asks.

'Because one day when we step down (and that moment cannot be so far off, because none of us are getting any younger), they will be the leaders,' Dr Böttcher says seriously. 'Because we know that our parties, when they are, as I hope, revived one day, will be outdated.'

'But the young workers . . .' Schröter begins.

'. . . have passed through Nazi school, the Hitler Youth and labour service just like all other young people, and like them they are now in the Wehrmacht and the SS,' Dr Böttcher says quickly. 'The young workers are no more immune than the workers generally. In my view there is only one option, and that is a general amnesty for German youth.'

'Quite right!' Gregor says. 'It would be nonsense to damn the young. You can't just eliminate a whole generation from the life of the nation, exclude it from the shaping of its own future. When this disastrous war is over, by and large among the young there will only be two directions: one will be unteachable and still National Socialist-minded, seeking the sources of mistakes in technical and military inadequacies, but not in the intellectual and political sphere, while the other trend, probably greater, will be nihilistic, intellectually and politically nomadic and vegetative, because the foundations of their previous life, their faith and their, for want of a better word, philosophy, have suddenly been pulled out from under them. It's clear that we can't just stand by and leave young people to their own devices, but neither can we' – and now his voice is raised, and he is turned towards Schröter – 'attack them with fully formed philosophies, programmes and dogmas. That would mean taking someone who wanted to learn to do sums and immediately plunging him into differential calculus, it would only increase his intellectual confusions . . .'

Schröter leans far forward. 'And what prescription do you suggest?'

Gregor's serious, ascetic face springs to life, a slight flush rises to his gaunt cheeks. 'The prescription, if that's want we want to call it, is not for the young, it's for us, and it's a mixture of impartiality and forbearance.'

'And self-criticism,' Wiegand says. 'Yes, Schröter, you heard correctly, self-criticism. Because the blame – in so far as we can speak of blame – for what happened, Germany's youth falling into the hands of Nazi criminals and failing to recognize the madness of their teachings, lies not with them, but with those who let it happen.'

'Mea culpa, mea culpa, mea maxima culpa,' Gregor says solemnly. 'Bring your friend, Lassehn.'

Lassehn gets to his feet and stands irresolutely in the middle of the room for a moment. 'Your argument with Tolksdorff will doubtless resolve many questions for me,' he says.

When Lassehn has left, the silence hangs in the room like a dark cloud.

'I hope you don't expect too much from this,' Klose says at last, and turns the buttons of the dead radio. 'Young people today are different from the ones who came back from the First World War. They were soldiers too, with Prussian drill and obedience in their bones, but they hadn't yet unlearned thinking, they weren't automata, and they wouldn't just have stubbornly carried out any order that was given to them. But young people today . . .' He gestures dismissively.

'Yes,' Gregor says from his corner. 'You're right, Klose, we were soldiers, but even in our grey uniforms we were individuals, and remained so, in spite of the unison roaring of the NCOs, and under the crust of mud and dirt we came back from France, Poland and Macedonia as rough front-line fighters, but we pounced like wolves on civilian life, to burrow deep into knowledge and discoveries and experiences, to occupy a space and fill it, to taste the real life that we had not yet encountered.'

'On the other hand young people today believe,' Dr Böttcher says, 'that they have been cast in a perfect mould, they see the true human in the figure of the warrior, and they don't think they have to find their way into civilian life, but rather fill civilian life with the habits of the barracks. Respect for intellectual achievement has been drilled out of them, intellectual Athens means nothing to them, the barbarian biceps of Sparta everything.'

The silence that had for a moment been lifted falls over the men again, every now and again the sounds of exploding shells can be heard, the groans of wounded soldiers come through the door, and the harsh, commanding voice of a doctor.

'Still no juice,' Klose murmurs, sitting by the radio.

'Get your crystal set working,' Schröter says, 'you can hardly bank on electricity any more.'

'You're right,' Klose says, 'but then we should take the thing into the back room. Walls have ears . . .' He points with his thumb to the connecting door.

Lucie Wiegand comes in and puts a tray covered with slices of bread down on the table.

'A little snack, gentlemen,' she says. 'Pease dig in. Where is Lassehn?'

'On a reconnaissance trip to an enemy wigwam,' Klose says and pulls his chair up to the table.

'Please, no jokes for once,' Lucie Wiegand reproaches him. 'Where is Lassehn?'

Klose looks at her, smiling, and then turns to Wiegand. 'Look out, Fritz, your wife's in love with Joachim.'

'Stop that nonsense,' Lucie Wiegand says irritably. 'I wish Joachim were my son, rather than . . .' She doesn't finish the sentence and turns round abruptly.

Klose glances quickly at Wiegand, whose face suddenly darkens. In an instant the shadow of Robert Wiegand has passed over them again, but Klose is already filling the gap with a coarse joke. They start eating, and when the door to the flat opens a few minutes later, the event has almost been forgotten again.

Then Lassehn comes in, followed by an officer in a grey uniform which reveals the work of a good tailor, with a peaked cap and black riding boots, which are dirty and dusty and certainly haven't been taken off for days. Lassehn tries to introduce the officer with a few obliging words, but an embarrassed silence follows.

In fact it is a strange meeting in that small, dark back room of a pub in the east of Berlin. There stands a Wehrmacht lieutenant with the Iron Cross First and Second Class, the gold German Cross, the eastern medal, the infantry general assault badge, and the Narvik Shield, with the insignia of Hitler's Reich on his uniform jacket and cap, and here, sitting in a semicircle, are a worker, a pub landlord, a trade-union secretary, a doctor and a stranger who is believed to be a theologian, in their shabby and unremarkable civilian suits, underground fighters against that very state whose uniform the officer wears, and between them, almost as intermediaries, stand a music student and a woman, both members of the underground, but also open to the young officer.

The men turn their hard, forbidding faces to the polite expression of the officer, and they sit there as if ready to jump.

'Please, sit down,' Dr Böttcher says at last, gesturing with his hand.

The officer sits down on a chair near the window, takes off his cap and looks at their faces in turn. 'I would like to reassure you, gentlemen,' he says in quite a coarse voice, 'that I have come here as a private individual, and anything said here I will keep to myself. So you don't need to fear any repercussions.'

Schröter chuckles to himself a few times. 'My dear man,' he says menacingly, 'if we thought anything else, you would not leave this room alive. That is the reassurance I have to give you.'

Dr Böttcher raises an appeasing hand. 'That is not a good introduction to a discussion,' he says. 'I think we've assembled in a friendly manner, isn't that right?'

'That's how I saw it,' says Lassehn, who is standing uneasily beside the table.

'Me too,' says Lieutenant Tolksdorff, turning the cap in his hands, 'I should add that I wasn't the one who introduced the abrasive tone.'

'You are completely right,' Dr Böttcher says, 'see yourself as a peace negotiator who has been taken blindfolded into the enemy fortress, and who will in due course be released again.'

The lieutenant lowers his head in agreement.

Then silence falls on the room again, the men sit facing one another like boxers in their rings, waiting for the bell to sound, casually leaning back on their stools, but with the potential speed of a coiled spring.

It is Lassehn who rings the bell.

'When we last spoke, Dietrich,' he begins, 'you said that it wouldn't come to Berlin being the front, that you were fighting to ensure that no more territories would be drawn into the war. Have I quoted your words more or less correctly?'

Tolksdorff nods. 'You're right, Joachim.'

'You see,' Lassehn goes on, 'that further resistance has only held up the enemy temporarily and has not spared the population the sufferings of war, on the contrary has increased them.'

Now Schröter intervenes in the conversation again. 'What excuse can you give, Lieutenant,' he shouts at him, 'for continuing this pointless war?'

Tolksdorff turns towards the little man. 'I could refer to orders from above,' he replies, 'but I can't do that any more. I have understood, albeit belatedly, that there is no longer a regulating will behind the orders that are issued to us.'

'Behind the orders stands the Satanic will for destruction,' Gregor says in his corner, his voice sounds quiet, as if he were only speaking to himself, 'the will to self-annihilation and the destruction of all order, our own end is supposed to be the end of a whole people, that is the only thing that the gentlemen who call themselves the government of the Great German Reich are still jealously guarding. If they had the chance to blow up the whole globe, they would do so with the heroic gesture of a redeemer.'

'It is a battle with the Hydra,' the officer says.

'Stop,' Dr Böttcher says excitedly, and raises his hand. 'Either you are misrepresenting your own new insight, or you don't have a new insight. It seems to me that you only see the hopelessness of military prospects.'

'Primarily,' Tolksdorff confirms.

'But that insight is already quite an advance,' Wiegand intervenes.

'And does your so-called military honour not decree that you should cease this senseless battle, or will it be replaced by a hara-kiri?' Schröter butts in.

'We're taking the conversation in the wrong direction,' Dr Böttcher says. 'If your doubt consisted only in an insight that military prospects were hopeless, as Wiegand says that would already be quite an advance, but it doesn't take us to the heart of the matter. You must learn, Lieutenant Tolksdorff, that they have succeeded in drilling out of you your ability to distinguish between good and evil, justice and injustice, and in consequence a fundamental element of your moral conscience has not only been deactivated but practically turned into its opposite. I am happy to attribute good faith and honest intentions to you. You knew or thought you knew what was good and right and noble. You were enthusiastic and confident, but today . . .'

Tolksdorff looks thoughtfully at his nervously interlocked fingers. '. . . And today there is no confidence and no enthusiasm in me, and no faith and certainly no knowledge of good and evil, right and wrong.'

Gregor rises to his feet and looks seriously at Tolksdorff. 'You have good eyesight, Lieutenant Tolksdorff,' he says slowly, 'and even if your brain was numbed, your eyes have not been blind, and your heart must have beaten wildly with horror. Did you not then become aware that you were acting on the basis of fatally false premises, and that good was evil and right wrong?'

'Yes,' Tolksdorff says quietly, 'but – and this is perhaps my great shortcoming – but I acknowledged that insight only in connection with the great military collapse.'

'That's exactly it,' Schröter says furiously, 'if you had won, then you wouldn't have cared in the slightest about injustice, oppression, murder and tyranny, you wouldn't have been bothered about the fact that other peoples . . .'

Dr Böttcher dismisses Schröter's speech with a reassuring gesture. 'So now how do you plan to draw conclusions from this insight?' he says turning to the officer.

Tolksdorff looks at Wiegand. 'I will tell you quite frankly: nothing. Because I don't know what to do.'

'So,' Wiegand continues, 'you will go on obeying all orders from now on, all of them?'

'I will try to soften them, weaken them or even sidestep them,' the officer replies.

'. . . But only carry them out if that was not successful,' Wiegand says. 'Is it not clear to you, Lieutenant, that having acquired that insight and recognition of your complicity, you can no longer be credited with negligence let alone ignorance? Is it not clear to you that every additional minute of resistance is prolonging the suffering of women and children?'

Tolksdorff lowers his head under the assault of Wiegand's questions.

'Good God,' Schröter says, and plunges his words into his opponent's weaker parts, 'just go into the bunkers and cellars and ask the women if they want to go on being defended! You will be astonished at what you hear! There's been a saying in Berlin for a long time: sooner a Russian on your belly than a house on your head.'

The officer looks up again. 'Over the last few days I have experienced quite enough,' he says, 'people speak very openly now, except when there's a Nazi uniform or a Party insignia anywhere around. Why don't a few thousand women get together and march on the Reich Chancellery, or to Herr Goebbels?'

'Ah no,' Schröter says, and pulls am angry face, 'that is a silly image, my dear Lieutenant. You are demanding this courage from women, but you heroic young men prefer to raise arms against the so-called external enemy rather than against the criminals among the ministers and generals. Do you think a heroic death is easier to escape than the claws of the Gestapo? You've got the guns!'

'I can't contradict you,' Tolksdorff says condescendingly. 'But I have arguments of my own. So I will ask you just as harshly: who was it who kept the munitions factories working? Did the workers on the shop floors not also hold guns, lathes, drills, rolling mills, blast furnaces, haulage levels, locomotive workshops? Are they not equally responsible for . . .'

'Stop!' Wiegand says irritably. 'That's not exactly how it is! You, Lieutenant, and all officers along with you, have assumed responsibility voluntarily, but the workers – in spite of the undeniable significance of their work – have no responsibility, and they did not volunteer to work in the factories. Yes, if you mean the foreman forcing his workers to work at crazed rhythms, the engineer coming up with improvements to the production line, the works steward reporting late or negligent workers to the Gestapo, the man from the factory troops insisting that even the tiniest amounts of waste should be picked up – they are all complicit and responsible, and if that's what you mean I could agree with you.'

'It is a mistake only to apportion one side of the blame,'

Dr Böttcher says. 'If we want to discuss the question of guilt, then here I would like to state my opinion, which is: the entire German people – apart from the small core of illegal fighters – is guilty, out of negligence, out of ignorance, out of cowardice, out of typical German nonchalance, but also out of arrogance, meanness, covetousness and a desire for superiority. It cannot be denied that its leaders are Germans, even if some of them are very curious, and of strange origins, from Latvia, Austria, Argentina, Egypt, the Führer even described one of his bodyguards as a degenerate homosexual, another as a crazed fantasist. Have people ever taken a good look at the people they are fighting for, or have fought for in the past?'

'That round-headed idiot with the Charlie Chaplin moustache, pulling his cap so low over his eyes because he can't look at anyone,' Wiegand says before he can reply, 'the cynical, scornful mug of Goebbels with his cardboard smile, that fat, bloated sybarite with the aura of the People's Court, Himmler's smooth, expressionless face with the cold eyes behind the rimless glasses, that inflated, unpredictable Ley, whose every word is a cliché, that cohort of fools blethering about Reich unity, gazing up like lickspittles and crawling around the Führer's unique genius?'

'I'm fighting for the German people,' the officer says, and scornfully purses his lips, 'and nothing else.'

'That's an error, Lieutenant,' Gregor says, 'I cannot accept your excuse. You are fighting for the oppression of your own people and foreign people, for the maintenance of the concentration camps, for keeping the gas chambers supplied with human detritus of inferior races, for driving God out of the German mind, that's what you are fighting for!'

'The Wehrmacht has nothing to do with that!' Tolksdorff says stubbornly. 'The Wehrmacht is a military organization, not a political one.'

'The Wehrmacht covers Nazi filth with its grey uniform,' Gregor declaims. 'I can't remember the Wehrmacht ever distancing itself from Party and government, apart from those brave men who left a bomb in a briefcase at Herr Hitler's headquarters, unfortunately, rather than shooting him right in the mouth, at the risk of being killed themselves. In terms of guilt, I see no distinction.'

'Today I can see with horrific clarity how wrong the path we took truly was,' the officer says quietly, looking out of the window, as if the path led directly to that gloomy courtyard at the back of a building in Berlin, 'but it can't all have been entirely in vain, the victories, the deprivations in the icy cold and in the blazing heat of the desert, the deaths of all those comrades, the amputated limbs . . .'

'No, it wasn't in vain, my dear friend,' Dr Böttcher says, 'just as nothing in matter is ever lost, and instead, without losing any volume, is only transformed, historical events are the same, in this case war and the sacrifices it involves, a process that turns itself into intellectual and political achievement. Democritus says, "Nothing that is can become nothing." The victims of this war were indeed brought to the most terrifying Moloch that has been visible in human form since the creation of the world, but they will not have been in vain, recognitions will rise from the corpses of the dead and the rubble of the cities, which will make a repetition impossible once and for all.'

The officer turns back towards the room. 'So you are of the opinion, Doctor, that there will be no more wars?'

Dr Böttcher smiles seriously. 'I am of the opinion that it is possible to avoid or prevent wars.'

Tolksdorff shakes his head. 'Music of the spheres, Doctor, after the First World War a wave of "No More War" went around the world, the League of Nations was founded and non-aggression pacts drawn up. And the result?'

'A failed attempt proves nothing,' Dr Böttcher replies, 'and in Germany there was, unfortunately, a "Let's-Have-War-Again-Soon" movement. Very quickly, the defeat of 1918 ceased to be the result of a bankrupt politics, it did not lead to a change of mind, oh no, armistice and peace were more of a pause for breath so that the defeated armies could gather and regroup. That was how it was that one saw only two lost battles in Compiègne and Versailles, no more than that, which had to be followed up by the great victorious conflict if honour was to be saved. You are too young to know what happened in Germany before 1933.'

'I don't know that, or rather I know it only in the official Nazi version, but I have an even more relevant objection to your thesis,' the officer says. 'Since men have existed, wars have existed too, and while men continue to populate this miserable planet, disputes between them will be resolved in belligerent ways.'

'That is the ideology of the eternal squaddie,' Dr Böttcher says. 'You, Lieutenant, should in fact be above adhering to it. First of all your assertion is not proved by anything, it is based on the pure theory of the immutability of the human being. Since people and peoples and the states that they have formed do not change significantly, their relations with one another, insignificant modifications aside, must also inevitably be immutable. That is your view more or less, isn't that correct?'

'You have expressed it exquisitely,' says Tolksdorff.

Dr Böttcher takes a deep breath. 'It is true that certain hereditary traits cannot be fully trained out of human beings, any more than they can from beasts of prey, they can be mitigated, weakened, even compensated for and finally allowed to atrophy. It is impossible, Lieutenant, for you as a rational human being to be able to assume that manly virtues such as courage, loyalty and honour can only be manifested through and in war, because our civilian life, as you soldiers think, is not varied enough and offers no opportunity to prove oneself. But I wanted to say something else. Just as one can mitigate and weaken hereditary traits or, to use the term, primal instincts, it is obviously also possible to stimulate them and breed them to disproportionate dimensions, and that has been done either by – and this is the philosophical variant – inventing the myth of the front-line soldier and the doctrine of the natural need for war, thus in the end relegating its causes to an abstract dimension independent of empirical considerations, or by loudly and ham-fistedly enticing primitive individuals and arousing them with the prospect of theft, booty and riotous living.'

'Are you trying to claim, Doctor,' Tolksdorff replies defiantly, 'that the Wehrmacht consists on the one hand of people with no sense of reality and on the other of robbers?'

'That would be an exaggeration,' Dr Böttcher replies calmly. 'I would put it like this: the military in Germany – and not only since the days of Hitler – has always been the ruling and dominant life form, everyone else had to make themselves subservient to you. In no other country on earth has there ever been such a discrepancy between the so-called fundamental ideals of the state and the universal spirit of its greatest minds as there is in Germany, and nowhere has the humanistic influence been inferior, even though crucial contributions to humanism have arisen from within our midst.'

'This development has now reached its supreme perfection in our Third Reich: the military has been declared the only possible life form,' Gregor says, and looks steadily at the lieutenant. 'To this exclusiveness, of which they were perhaps not entirely sure, that of race was added, declaring openly that a superior race, in the realization of its supposed mission, was not bound to the commandments of human morality as they are generally acknowledged. Since there was nothing to oppose this "truth" decreed by state and Party, no other opinion let alone an objection, for your generation, Lieutenant, the implications of this idea have been obvious from the outset. Your generation was rigorously schooled and brought into line, and the authorities were able to do this with unimagined thoroughness by making any other kind of thinking impossible for you, and excluding you and fencing you off from all philosophies, intellectual trends and political efforts that did not run a parallel course with National Socialism or could not be made compatible with it. Was that not clear to you?'

The officer contorts his face into a tormented smile. 'Clarity, Doctor ... Oh, it seemed so clear, so unambiguous, we were inspired, and now everything lies in shattered fragments before us.'

'But you pay reverence to each individual fragment,' Schröter breaks in.

'And since the whole giant building of this barbaric form of life, the so-called military philosophy, is tottering, you are left only with faith in a miracle that abolishes the laws of causality,' Wiegand adds.

Dr Böttcher waves them violently away. 'I have not yet finished, gentlemen. First of all I would like to present you, Lieutenant, with another example *ad absurdum*, before I return to your assertion concerning the natural necessity of war. The people of earlier centuries saw the plague as an unalterable fate, a scourge from God, and it is not today, it has been limited to a few small places where it is endemic, and it will one day be eradicated completely.'

'Thanks to the discovery of its source, and improvements in sanitary and hygienic conditions,' Tolksdorff says.

'In other words, thanks to scientific discoveries,' Dr Böttcher says. 'You seem to be of the opinion, Lieutenant, that wars are also unavoidable natural disasters, and thus resist scientific discovery. We are unable to prevent natural disasters, earthquakes, hurricanes, cloudbursts and sandstorms because they lie outside our sphere of influence, they are not based within ourselves, but wars – and this is a crucial difference – have precisely identifiable causes. We cannot say that the forces that cause them lie within the atmosphere or the earth's crust. Wars are produced in the human brain and nowhere else. All mysticism is charlatanry, presented to us by those who profit from war in one way or another. I don't intend to engage in a discussion of epistemology, it would take us too far from our subject and might also become too much like an academic argument.'

The lieutenant looks at his watch. 'I should point out that my time is unfortunately very limited. I am sorry that we have to have this kind of conversation on the hop, as it were.'

'I can't explain everything to you the way the doctor does,' Schröter says, 'my take on things is more emotional than rational, but I do know one thing: that I would never obey those criminals.'

'But I have sworn an oath of loyalty to the Führer,' Tolksdorff says. 'You can't just set an oath aside like an old newspaper, can you?'

Schröter laughs loudly. 'The oath does not bind you, if that is your only concern and your final reservation . . .'

'I would like to point out,' Tolksdorff contradicts him, 'that I took that oath voluntarily.'

Schröter is about to lash out at the lieutenant with a stinging remark, but this time it is Gregor who speaks after summoning their attention with a commanding gesture. 'First of all it should be said that you have sworn an oath to a man who deceived you and the whole German people about his true intentions, or in legal terms: that oath was demanded of you under false pretences, in fact the man to whom you swore that oath is not justified in demanding that you swear it. Is the legalistic interpretation enough for you, or do you believe in God, so that you feel bound to this oath before God?'

The lieutenant shrugs apathetically.

'Then let's leave that aside,' Gregor continues. 'In our times the religious content of such an oath is in any case nil, it has become an empty formula and been stripped completely of its actual significance, since the idolatrous cult of the Führer took the place of God. In fact an oath sworn on the flag also has only constitutional significance, and I should remind you that the man who demands this oath of unconditional loyalty from you is known as someone who breaks his word on a grand scale, who breaks solemn agreements and treaties as thoughtlessly as if cancelling a previously made engagement. Or what would you call the violation of the Non-Aggression Pact with the Soviet Union, with Denmark and Yugoslavia, the Munich Accord, his statements concerning respect for the neutrality of Belgium and Holland, his repeated assurances that he no longer had any territorial claims? There are many other examples, I have cited only the most striking.'

Tolksdorff is breathing heavily. 'I am so caught up in traditional thinking,' he says, 'that in all the monstrosities I am still looking for excuses, because I cannot grasp that there is such a division between words and deeds.'

'You are also seeking excuses for yourself,' Dr Böttcher says. 'I'm sure it's hard to see that you have become the victim of criminals and lunatics and sadists, as long as they have Führer and Reich Chancellor, Supreme Army Commander, Reich Marshal, Reich Minister or similar titles attached to their names. We do not doubt your personal honour, Lieutenant, but if we are to continue to believe in it, you must distance yourself from that rabble. You owe that to yourself, apart from anything.'

The lieutenant stares rigidly into his cap before he looks up again. 'But what will become of Germany, Doctor? There must be a way out. We are Germans, after all, and I assume that you too feel that you are part of the German people.'

'Why shouldn't I?' Dr Böttcher asks back. 'Or do you think we crave Germany's defeat as a kind of suicidal sadism? It is painful enough to have to acknowledge that the way to a better future leads only via the defeat of one's own people, and that it is better to plant the flag of right and the freedom of the individual on a pile of rubble than to put the seal on the eradication of man's individuality through blood and iron with a final victory. We are entirely aware of the unnatural quality of our situation, such that the success of our armies discourages us and that of enemy armies fills us with hope, that the devastation of foreign countries arouses our fury, while the destruction of our own grants us the certainty that our people will burn the false gods in the flames of their own burning houses. I would even dare to claim that we are the true patriots.'

'Even though you crave Germany's defeat?' Tolksdorff asks.

'Not even though, but because,' Dr Böttcher says firmly. 'You see, Lieutenant, here we are touching the core of the problem. The man from Braunau and his spokesmen have actually succeeded in equating National Socialism with what it means to be German, and to involve the German people in his own guilt, making it the spineless instrument of his barbaric megalomania, and in the end to commit all his criminal actions in the name of the German people and sadly also with their support, making them accessories to his crimes once and for all. Guilt becomes indivisible, or to put it in legal terms: it becomes complicity, and this in turn gives rise to the fear of the supposedly Old Testament revenge of the enemy, which Goebbels' propaganda describes in the most glaring colours with fake quotations and freely invented reports, shots to the back of the neck, deportations, slavery, eradication, sterilization and the like. Here you have the true explanation of the so-called loyalty of the German people.'

'It is terrible to have to see that,' says Tolksdorff. 'I must admit, there was a time in which I actually did see Germany and National Socialism as synonymous. It seemed so natural to me that it was beyond discussion . . .'

'Just as nothing officially proclaimed was up for discussion,' Dr Böttcher cuts in, 'whether it was a speech by the Führer or an article by Goebbels, a report by the Propaganda Department or an order from some little Nazi boss, a poem by Schirach or a politically valuable film by Harlan, it was all high-handedly exempt from criticism like the word of God, neither doubts nor counter-opinions were possible, the Führer and his lackeys were the measure of all things. But I interrupted you, I apologize, it's impossible to stay calm in the circumstances.'

'But of course I wasn't blind,' the lieutenant continues, 'the gulf between Germanness and National Socialism soon became clear to me, but then I took refuge in another interpretation, and that has stayed with me until the present day, and I think it is there that you should seek a reason for the loyal obedience you speak of: as Germans we must win this war – we thought that, with the small reservation that as human beings we were almost afraid of it.'

'That is a widespread view,' Dr Böttcher says, 'but it is easily refuted. How can there be a divergence between being German and being human? Something is out of line there, my friend. If German is not at the same time human, if I must first subtract the Germanness from my humanity, then I no longer want to be a German. But German has always been human, Dürer, Beethoven, Kant, Goethe and Leibniz have been German *and* universal in all of their works, there was no difference between their nationality and their cosmopolitanism. Or do you think that Beethoven, if he were alive today, would have written the closing movement of his Ninth like this: 'Be embraced, millions of pure-blooded German descent'? No, his kiss was meant for the whole world, and are you going to say that can no longer exist? All of your reservations, Lieutenant, have been empty vessels, you must have been able to tell from the hollow sound they made.'

'I am no match for your dialectic,' the lieutenant says.

'You can no longer ignore the truth, that's it,' Gregor says. 'Why do you still hesitate to acknowledge that? There is nothing more to excuse or defend, but' – Gregor stands and hurls his words into the room – 'you have one chance to relieve your conscience, and that is by preventing a calamity with a manly deed.'

'Which calamity, and where?' Tolksdorff asks and rises to his feet. 'I am ready.'

'Some calamity I don't know which,' Gregor replies, 'but it won't be hard to find an opportunity.'

'Tell us, seeing as we are effectively living on an island here, if we are in danger,' says Wiegand.

'I will happily do that,' the lieutenant says, 'but which danger do you mean? If the Russians come?'

'I'm not afraid of the Russians,' Wiegand says clearly, 'the Russians are coming to me and to all of us as liberators. The only danger threatening us comes from our own so-called national comrades, the military police and the SS.'

The lieutenant listens to the answer with a nod. 'But now I want to go.'

'Just one moment!' Klose cries. 'Tell us a few military secrets very quickly.'

'What do you mean?' the lieutenant asks, surprised.

'I mean today's Wehrmacht report,' Klose replies, and taps the radio, 'Goebbels' treasure chest has run out of juice again.'

'There isn't much to report,' says Tolksdorff, and takes a copy of *Angriff* out of his pocket.

'The usual old claptrap,' Klose says, looking at the newspaper. 'OKW, how small is your vocabulary. Listen to this, men and women of Germany:

"The battle for the Reich capital has been unleashed in all its feroc-ity. South of the city our troops intercepted heavy Bolshevik tank units on the line Beelitz-Trebbin-Teltow-Dahlewitz. The lost sta-tion of Köpenick was retaken in the counter-attack, and an enemy incursion along the Prenzlauer Allee was halted."

'According to this, the battle for Berlin is looking excellent. Attack intercepted, attack halted, retaken in the counter-attack, sweetness, what more could you ask? A few more days and it'll be: Bolshevik advance halted on the first floor of the Reich Chancellery, the second floor still remains firmly in our hands, there is still fierce fighting for the gentlemen's toilet on the ground floor.'

In spite of the gravity of the situation everyone laughs.

'Read on,' Wiegand says, 'the other fronts are of equal interest.'

'The others aren't that bad either,' Klose reads on.

"Between Dessau and Eilenburg, after fierce fighting our troops have built up a new and strong front line on the east bank of the Mulde.

From the Franconian Jura and to the north-east, scattered American tank units are advancing to the east, their spearheads have crossed the Naab at Weiden. The situation intensified yesterday in the region of Württemberg and Bavaria. Superior tank forces of the 7th American Army and Gaullist units reached our front after fierce fighting in several places and, advancing southward, reached the Danube between Dillingen and Donaueschingen. The defensive battle in Italy continues amidst fierce fighting with heavy losses on both sides. While the enemy was intercepted after gaining several kilometres of ground on the Ligurian coast and in the Apennines in western Tuscany, superior enemy forces made several deep incursions around Bologna, which were halted on both sides of Modena and north of Bologna. Between Bologna and Lake Comacchio the enemy was able, with heavy artillery fire and numerous aircraft, to breach our most important front line in various places."

'On the eighth of November 1918 Hindenburg, the general who became a national hero, demanded armistice negotiations at any price from the Emperor's government, even though his armies were still deep in enemy territory,' Gregor says. 'He had seen, as a responsible soldier, albeit too late, that the war was lost, and he drew the only possible conclusion from that. Our famous generals are fighting on under the thumb of a deranged hysteric, they are shameless enough to present their irresponsibility as courage and their cowardly weakness as an unshakeable will. If you still have a spark of honour, Lieutenant, call it off!'

XII

The night of 23–24 April passes peacefully. The artillery fire sub-sided towards evening, every now and again there is the sound of a shell being fired and striking home, a dull echo, afterthoughts like the last few rockets of a firework display, here and there another shot drops into the silence like a stone into water, and then evening has fallen. There are remarkably few planes over the city, only every now and again does an engine rumble, receiving as an echo the brief rattle of a light anti-aircraft emplacement chasing the glowing trails of a tracer bullet into the dark sky. For several min-utes the silence is broken by the monotonous clatter of armoured vehicles, of the dull trot of horses' hooves, but those noises disap-pear in the night, they sound and then fall silent.

When the new day breaks, the silence is shattered by a terrible cannonade. It is 5.15: the barrage of the Russian artillery that has taken up position in the suburbs around Berlin has begun. The sal-voes explode like an infernal storm, and dig as if with octopus tentacles into the streets and houses, mortars fire at surface targets, the Soviet Air Force flies mission after mission, bombers drop their payloads, low-flying planes swoop down on the supply columns that are wedged into the streets and unable to avoid them. The bar-rage lasts for forty-five minutes, then the Russian infantry and tank units launch their attack. From the south they cross the Teltow Canal and force their way into Neukölln, Britz, Lichterfelde, Zehlendorf and Neubabelsberg, from Tegel and Reinickendorf tank units advance to Wedding and don't stop until they reach

Nordhafen and the Ringbahn by Lehrter Station, additional tank units force their way from the north through Tegel Forest and over the Jungfernheide to the Spandau ship canal, cross it even though all the bridges have been blown up, and push in to Siemensstadt, violent fighting is under way around Fürstenbrunn, between Westend and Spandau, and around the embankment of the railway line to Gartenfeld. In the north-east and east of the city the Russian units have advanced as far as the big intersection of Elbinger Strasse, Petersburger Strasse and Landberger Allee, and are reaching the edge of Friedrichshain, always bringing artillery after them, putting the city centre under constant fire. As soon as a breach is made anywhere, the tanks immediately advance with infantry on board.

The battle is fought with varying degrees of severity and over different lengths of time. While little resistance is put up in the south of the city, and the few Volkssturm units there prefer to liberate themselves of their own uniforms, or clothing that resembles uniforms, SS units, the only ones adequately and properly armed, put up fierce resistance and pull the Wehrmacht and Volkssturm units with them into the murderous conflict. In Siemensstadt and Zehlendorf police units are fighting in complete isolation and with entirely substandard weaponry, some of them only with Italian carbines for which they have been issued with Greek ammunition.

The military organization of the defenders of Berlin demonstrates that they are inspired by fury and a desire for destruction. Their own artillery fire is directed mercilessly at the residential areas of the population. German aircraft bomb their own city, and bridges, factories, electrical substations, tunnels, gasometers and waterworks are blown up. The men of the fourth Volkssturm recruitment drive, tubercular, asthmatic, suffering from heart disease, epileptics, wearers of prosthetic limbs, diabetics, are all dragged ruthlessly along by the retreating SS units and the military police, women, old people and children are forced to construct new anti-tank barriers while still under heavy fire. The city is crammed full of people. In the residential zone, which air raids have reduced by 40 per cent, there are still almost three million people, including over 800,000 foreigners. The cellars, bunkers and underground stations are all overflowing, but still the battle continues relentlessly.

While the combat zone of Friedrichshain and the Schultheiss-Patzenhofer brewery on Landsberger Allee at the corner with Tilsiter Strasse is being defended, to spare the lives of the civilian population the Russians order the clearance of the quarter between Friedrichshain and the abattoir. Thousands of people climb from the dark catacombs, above the burning, smoking, shattered streets a clear blue sky arches with the brightness of a warm spring sun, but the people can't see it, not yet, the smoke and miasmas are still stinging their weary, reddened eyes, they are still too busy gathering together their few pitiful belongings in a few minutes, because they don't know whether they will be able to return to their flats, whether the shells of the German artillery or the bombs of the German planes are about to reduce to rubble what the enemy's weapons have hitherto spared. They are not valuable objects that are being collected together under the roaring of the guns and the orders of the Russian soldiers, beds, suitcases, food, household objects, because this part of the city is inhabited by people who are hardworking but poor, manual workers, office workers, lowly officials, small businessmen, pensioners and invalids.

The endless procession of refugees drifts eastwards along the Landsberger Allee and the Landsberger Chaussee towards Marzahn, Hönow and Alt-Landsberg, with prams, small transport carts, handcarts, old men and women on sticks, legless people in self-propelling chairs, children being carried and holding their mothers' hands, gaunt, careworn, exhausted people, consumed with fear, shaken with horror, but stirred by the will to live. To protect themselves from the shells of their own compatriots, they have all put themselves under the protection of the Russian troops.

When they step out of their narrow streets into the wide arterial road their hearts fill with hope again, not yearning or confident hope, but avid and blazing, like thirst, because only now do they notice the clear blue sky arching cloudlessly above the racked and tormented city, the bright sun that revives the chilled senses, the first tender green on the trees and bushes and the bright white of the cherry blossom. Nights filled with bombs, fire-fights, Gestapo terror are all left behind them. It is as if they were climbing out of the strange shadows that had clung to them for so long. Uncertainty still lies in front of them, but it no longer weighs so heavy, because they have brought their most precious belongings and the only real possession they have to lose, their lives, out of the dark confinement of the cellars into the new day. They do not guess that their few effects and their wives will become the booty of the victors.

The Landsberger Chaussee is a wide road, it runs between summer houses, gardens, fields and newly built estates out of the cramped conditions of the city and into the open countryside. The refugees are not the only ones travelling along it. On the northern side of the street the Russian army reinforcements are advancing into the city, tanks with infantry on board, trucks, utility vehicles, ambulances, gun emplacements, teams of horses, teams of horses, teams of horses, long, low farmers' wagons with stout, shaggy little horses under the *duga*, the round yoke. So two streams are flowing along the Landsberger Chaussee: eastward the women, the old and the children of the defeated people, westward the sons of the victors.

Then from somewhere, still a long way off, there comes a hum, as if a swarm of bees were on the way, but the volume rises very quickly and becomes a roar of thunder. The people in the street look in amazement at the unit flying in, there seem to be ten, twelve, fifteen, twenty planes, maintaining a level course towards the street . . . Russian planes returning from duty at the front? No, these are German Junker Ju 87 aircraft, they are suddenly huge, the black crosses on their wings are already visible. The refugees trek doggedly on. What do they have to fear from German planes? But then the unexpected, the improbable, the incredible thing happens – the German dive-bombers plunge with wailing motors at the Russian reinforcements, regardless of the fact that tens of thousands of German people are moving along the same street towards the hinterland. They are flying at their target and bombing it as orders decree. Again and again the Stukas swoop down towards the street, then rise roaring into the sky and plunge again like greedy hawks. When they fly away, hundreds of dead and wounded are left on the side of the Landsberger Chaussee, German people, mown down with German bombs and German aircraft cannon.

Where in the south of the city the Kottbusser Damm widens into Hermannplat and six major streets come together, the finest and most modern department store in Germany, the Karstadt building, stands, constructed as if for millennia, of heavy sandstone blocks, steel and concrete, seven storeys high, with two towers whose tops are seventy-eight metres above street level, and whose blue lights used to shine far over the city. The huge building no longer serves its original purpose, the general lack of goods emptied most of the sales rooms long ago, and ever since the Russian attack from the south reached the Teltow Canal, Wehrmacht operations staff and the artillery observation post of the anti-aircraft batteries in the Hasenheide were based here until the 'Nordland' SS division took over the building. They immediately began taking away the considerable food supplies, the trucks now roll constantly in and out. Just as one throws a dog a titbit, and the passengers on a luxury steamer enjoy making the natives dive for coins in the harbours of Alexandria or Colombo, every now and again the SS men throw a tin can, a tin of meat, a packet of biscuits out to the onlookers, and a wild competition begins to catch the morsel. Some things are left in the courtyard and in underground warehouses and 'given away' with casual cynicism, no attempt is made at an orderly distribution. A furious scuffle breaks out in the midst of the heavy fire from the artillery and the mortars, people are trampled and literally suffocated among groceries, others climb over the dead and wounded, wade through flour and sugar, pounce on tins of milk and meat, many collapse under the weight of the goods they have managed to grab, they wheeze and pant over their booty, unable to get up again, while people ruthlessly run over them. Suddenly the SS are there again, shooting wildly among the looters they themselves have enticed there.

Meanwhile over five hundred terrified women and children crouch in the cellar of the building. They have sought refuge here because the air-raid shelters of the Karstadt building are considered the safest in Neukölln, far below the ground and with a massive block of concrete on top. When the fire from the artillery and mortars intensifies and the Russian tanks are rolling into Hermannstrasse, the SS lay fuses and distribute petrol canisters among the individual storeys and parts of the building, and explosives in the cellars. No warning is given, either to those seeking shelter in the cellar or to the residents of the surrounding houses. The will to the complete destruction of all values which devastated great stretches of the country, left Warsaw in ruins and attempted to wipe the cities of England off the map does not even stop at their own capital city. All of a sudden the second floor in the wing on Urbanstrasse is ablaze, the fire leaps from storey to storey at furious speed, the petrol canisters burst open with a hiss, the flames spray as if from flame-throwers, windowpanes explode and shatter and the interior walls collapse. First the main façade on Hermannplatz is seized by the flames, then the wing on Hasenheide, and at last the whole huge building is burning all the way up to its towers, like a flaming torch. The iron joists glow and yield, at short intervals explosions go off in the cellars, the rattle and crackle of the flames is mixed with the shooting of the artillery and the rattling of machine-gun fire. The women and children in the shelters, already almost entirely encircled by fire, are fetched from the cellars by a few plucky men from the civilian anti-aircraft defence organization and, still under artillery fire, brought to the tunnel of the underground. A short time later the walls and ceilings fall in, and the proud, great building collapses like a felled primeval giant, a glowing, smoking pile of rubble, iron and glass.

The north-south line of the S-Bahn, a cross-connection between the furthermost points of the northern and southern curves of the

Ringbahn, disappears briefly below ground behind Humboldthain Station, runs underground to Stettiner Station and the stations of Friedrichstrasse and Potsdamer Platz below streets, squares and houses, and surfaces again only briefly behind Anhalt Station, before the line forks into two and rises to the stations on Grossgörschen-strasse and Yorckstrasse, and then runs beneath the Landwehrkanal at Schöneberger Bridge and Möckern Bridge. It is the nerve centre of the five-kilometre-long tunnel; it is protected against water penetration by the construction of a large watertight chamber.

The building of this stretch of track, which had been planned a long time previously, was used as a showpiece project by the Third Reich which, when Budapester Strasse was being rechristened as Hermann-Göring-Strasse, had already led to the loss of countless lives of workers. They were buried under slipping heaps of sand, crushed by falling beams and, as not even the magnificent state funeral and the oily speech by the individual who had just risen from a Viennese homeless refuge to become Führer and Reich Chancellor could conceal, had fallen victim to the inadequate preparation and over-hasty execution of the construction work and a boundless desire for prestige. Twelve years later it was the same creatures, not this time in the brown outfit of the Party, but in the field-grey uniforms of the Waffen SS, who went to work. What had then perhaps been inadequacy and neglect, born of the inferiority complex of the parvenu, was this time a bloody crime.

In those April days the platforms and control rooms of Anhalt Station were turned into an army camp, women, children and old people stand pressed tightly together in nooks and corners or sit on small folding chairs, not this time for the few hours of an air attack, but since the beginning of the battle for Berlin. Hearts thump, eyes flicker, faces are fearful, because up above the battle rages, the cannon roar, the mortars bark, the salvoes of the machine guns rattle, shell after shell shakes the roof of the tunnel, chalk dust trickles down, masonry falls with a dull thud, clouds of dust block the entrances, the smell of gunpowder and billows of smoke roll down the steps. People wait breathlessly, each one forced back in on himself, alone in the crowd.

Then a long train from the Anhalt-Dresden line draws slowly into the station, it consists not only of a red, green and yellow S-Bahn wagon, but also black and grey railway carriages with green and yellow camouflage paint and red crosses on a white background, an ambulance train led from the open platform into the safety of the tunnel. Even though the noise of battle is swelling and the falling shells almost bury the entrance, people are still sighing with something like relief: the tunnel, the platforms are apparently particularly safe, because if an ambulance train is being brought here with a lot of wounded people tied to their beds . . .

Hour after hour passes, one minute drifts vaguely by like another. The noise of battle, which became less insistent for a moment, swells again, the falling shells drum like hail on the street, but the ceiling of the tunnel holds. But then the SS appear, ruthlessly clear the railway station and drive the people into the tunnels. All of a sudden a distant explosion blasts air through the tunnel like a fountain, but no one pays any attention, all eyes are facing forward.

Suddenly a cry shoots up like an arrow: 'Water!' The people are frozen. Water? They still don't believe it, they look at one another, seek the same doubt in each other's eyes, the confirmation of the improbability, the impossibility. The water is already gurgling in, glittering darkly with little crests of foam, it is still shallow, washing only over the tracks. People start moving, become a raging, shouting, roaring, pushing, shoving crowd, shouts, weeping, prayers, curses, the laughter of people who have lost their minds. Where is their rescue going to come from? Where is the way out? The exits are blocked, the fire of battle rages above, fragments of stone rain down like a sudden shower. There is only one possibility: to reach, through the tunnel, an exit on Potsdamer Platz Station, to run away from the water, be quicker than the water, to run a race against death by drowning. The tunnel gapes dark and unfathomable, but there is no other way out, the people start walking, running, stumbling over the sleepers and ballast stones, they fall, pull themselves back up again, lie where they are, are mercilessly trampled underfoot, children are pulled from their mothers' hands, the wounded try to get out of the train, but the waves are now hurtling in like the Riders of the Apocalypse, they are no longer gurgling, they are rushing now, roiling noisily, reaching out a wet fist, engulfing everything. Another few shouts, some suffocated screams, then a ghostly silence falls upon the S-Bahn tunnel, a silence of the dead, a deadly silence, only the water gurgling, splashing and rushing, the shells sing their terrible song above the watery grave.

Women, children, old people, wounded soldiers drift restlessly like swollen blue corpses with shapelessly bloated bodies between Anhalt Station and Stettiner Station beneath the cobblestones of the city of Berlin, because the SS have blown up the tunnelling under the Landwehrkanal.

In a garden between Wilhelmstrasse and Hermann-Göring-Strasse, flanked by noble old houses whose classical façades contrast starkly with the pompous and overblown products of an inferior wave of building mania, in the middle of a patch of sparse grass there stands a rectangular greyish-green lump of concrete, to which has been added a semicircular feature resembling a wasp's nest and topped by a cone. This lump of concrete screens off the entrance to a cave which, in line with the new German linguistic practice, is described as a bunker; it lies two storeys beneath the earth, thirty-seven steps lead twelve metres down into an absolutely bomb-proof air-raid shelter. Situated as it is in this smart neighbourhood of Prussian private houses both old and new, this is no ordinary air-raid shelter, with rough masonry walls, damp and mildewed, sloppily whitewashed, supported by a few struts cobbled from tree trunks, roughly carved benches, inadequate lighting, with no heating and bad ventilation. Neither is it a people's bunker in which hundreds or thousands are crammed together into a very cramped space, with bare Prussian rooms, the size of a handkerchief, two bed-frames one above the other or primitive benches and narrow passageways, neither is it a makeshift shelter in draughty S-Bahn or underground stations. Far from it, this bunker is a masterpiece of the air-raid shelter architect's art, no expense has been spared in using the most precious raw materials of Hitler's

Germany – steel and concrete – and burying them deep in the earth, safe and secure.

This bunker, which lies beneath a concrete plate three metres thick (and for which there is enough material ready to add a further metre and a half) contains a number of rooms which differ from one another in terms of their furniture, and immediately reveal that they are only at the disposal of one user (and his retinue). It is an unusual, unique bunker. First come the rooms that might justly be described as 'spartan' – simple and utilitarian. They are not intended for private use, but as guardrooms, a telephone exchange and a sick bay, a machine room (with 120-horsepower diesel engine), doctor's room and pharmacy (not forgetting a kennel for the dog). Beyond this, after you pass through four heavy iron doors, a corridor leads past a kind of office to the actual private apartment, study, bedroom, boudoir, kitchen, bathroom, all furnished in a style both elegant and functional. The rooms are fitted with soft and precious rugs, the bathroom decorated with white tiles and equipped with a first-class ventilation system and electrical heating, comfortable upholstered benches, deep armchairs, lamps giving off a soft light, valuable paintings, movable tea tables, bookshelves, cosy nooks, a bar, a hairdresser's salon with a wide range of cosmetics, a sofa bed covered with heavy silk brocade, and stylish furniture in precious foreign woods complete the furnishings of this air-raid shelter. For a son of the working people, simple and unpretentious, who – as his spokesman announced – lives with ascetic self-denial between his camp bed and his desk, and indeed for his concubine, nothing has been left out that might relieve their sober, spartan life during those hours when hate-filled enemy pilots drop steel containers full of gunpowder, called bombs, down on the city. No bothersome noise finds its way into this hermitage, not the wail of the sirens, the hum of the aircraft engines and the roar of the cannon, neither the rush and whistle of the bombs nor the crash of the explosions, the clatter of collapsing houses and the crackle of flames, nor the cries of the victims and the curses of the people.

The air-raid shelter is in the garden of the Reich Chancellery, and is the private bunker of Adolf Hitler, Führer and Chancellor of the Great German Reich, but no longer from the Atlantic to the Volga and from the Arctic Ocean to the Suez Canal, no longer even from the Maas to the Memel or the Etsch to the Belt, from the Panke to the Havel and from the Isar to the Pegnitz. From this bunker Adolf Hitler, the Führer and general, sent by providence and chosen by fate, leads the defence of Berlin, just as two years ago he led the attack on Stalingrad and a year ago the defence of the Atlantic Wall from the Führer's headquarters in the 'Wolf's Lair' near Rastenburg. It is now that the purpose of that room that has previously been called a kind of office becomes clear: it is the briefing room. It is here that discussions have taken place since 22 April, which the Führer holds in the usual way: with his voice breaking, with a hoarse, rolling Balkan 'r', with the wild gestures of a ham actor, sweating and rolling his eyes, he develops his constructive plans and the others nod at his flashes of genius. The others – Reich Minister Bormann, leader of the Party Chancellery, Field Marshal Keitel, High Command of the Armed Forces, General Jodl, Chief of the Operations Staff of Armed Forces High Command, General Krebs, umpteenth General Chief of Staff of Supreme High Command by Führer's decree, General Burgdorf, Chief Adjutant of the Wehrmacht, SS Brigade leader Mohnke, Commandant of the Reich Chancellery, and SS Colonel Fegelein, contact man with Himmler, the Reich Minister of the Interior, head of the German police, Reichsführer SS and Supreme Commander of the reserve army. The extravagance of military luminaries no longer corresponds entirely to its object, which is already expressed by the maps that decorate each room, given that Fortress Europe has shrunk first to Fortress Germany and finally to Fortress Berlin, and in spite of all rough cursing, orders screamed until the Führer's voice broke and hysterical attacks, the Russians' concentric advance continues, and on this 24 April even Adolf Hitler acknowledges that the magnificence of his millennial Reich has come to an end and is reduced only to the district of Berlin-Mitte. He rages once more when Bormann outlines the ultimatum contained in Göring's letter, which reads as follows:

HQ 23.4.1945, 10.00 p.m.

Mein Führer!

Do you agree that after your decision to remain in Berlin to defend the city I now assume the leadership of the Reich in accordance with your decree of 29.6.1941 with full freedom of action both internally and externally?

If I have received no reply by 10.00 p.m., I will assume that you have lost your freedom of action. I will then take the conditions of your decree as given and act for the good of people and fatherland. You know what I feel for you in these most difficult hours of my life, and I cannot express it in words.

May God protect you and let you come here as soon as possible in spite of everything.

Your loyal servant
Hermann Göring

He curses the Reich Marshal and his Luftwaffe, expels him from the Party and shouts, '*The whole Luftwaffe should be hanged!*', but after that he is finished and says to his loyal followers: '*The cause is lost.*' Henceforth he is barely interested in any further news that reaches him, neither that his loyal follower, the Reich Marshal and Supreme Commander of the Luftwaffe, is trying to form an alternative government in Upper Bavaria, nor the telephone call from the Reich simpleton Joachim von Ribbentrop, who tells him in a joyfully excited voice that, according to information that has reached him from Switzerland, the conflict between the Western powers and the Bolsheviks, which he had always predicted, had now entered its acute phase. By this point Hitler has already worked himself up into a suicidal state, and reveals to his personal architect Speer that he has decided to defend Berlin to the last and, if the city should fall, commit suicide, and that he has also ordered the destruction of his corpse and the corpse of Eva Braun, '*so that nothing recognizable remains*'. But he is still riddled with suspicion, and anyone, even his closest colleagues, who enters the bunker must undergo a thorough search by SS guards.

During the early afternoon of 24 April, the newspaper *Der Angriff und Berliner illustrierte Nachtausgabe* is published for the penultimate time, with the headline: 'Berlin's heroic resistance is unparalleled' and contains the following editorial:

The Führer Leads the Defence of the Reich Capital

The defence of the capital is being led by the Führer, who has decided to assume the task of rescuing the capital from amidst the population of Berlin. The Führer is being kept informed every hour of the situation on all battle lines in Berlin and the surrounding area. He is personally intervening in the issuing of orders at all crucial points. Many officers, NCOs and teams have been brought from the battle lines to the Führer's command post so that they can report in person on their experiences. The Führer will be awarding decorations to particularly outstanding fighters in his command post. On all sides units are being brought to Berlin or led into the city centre so that the front line can be reinforced.

The editorial writer, Dr Otto Kriegk, says the following in the same edition:

The population of the capital, which works almost directly behind battle lines and provides all possible help, is firmly convinced of the fact that defence will be successful not in fighting on the current battle lines, but by repelling the Bolsheviks from the territory of the Reich capital. Attacks by low-flying aircraft with bombs and armaments, the impact of shells, the heavy fire of our artillery and our anti-aircraft guns have become quite natural. What the front-line soldier learned in terms of self-protection during the first battles, the men and women of Berlin have in recent days made their own. In the command posts and collective accommodation of the Volkssturm, in the quarters of the regiments and security units, plans for that which needs to be done to reinforce defence are being drawn up and executed with sober objectivity. The people of Berlin know that the defence of their city is conducted not only from within but also from without, and that to this end units have been made available which were originally being ordered in another direction. Everyone knows that the Führer is amidst the population of the Reich capital, and that the defence he has led now puts at his disposal forces that the enemy has been unable to factor into its calculation.

XIII

The battle is now getting closer to the area around Silesian Station. The impact of artillery shells is already mixed with the firing of mortars, and when the firing falls silent for several minutes, the rattle of machine guns can even be heard. The smoke and haze that lies like a thick, sticky vapour above the streets is kept down by the low-hanging clouds and forced back into the streets. The forms of civilized life are broken, the people crouching in the cellars were once used to washing and brushing their teeth every day, changing their socks and underwear at certain intervals, they were accustomed eating more or less well with a knife and fork, using running water, a gas tap and an electric switch, a bathtub and a water closet, standing behind a display counter or a workbench, sitting by a till or behind a school desk. None of that exists any more, now they sit there inactive and torpid, crammed together into a tight space, their shoulders hunched, their faces are pale green and sunken, their eyes, with red rims and deep circles, have lost their gleam, the smoke and haze that forces its way into the cellar has left a thick layer of dust on their faces as there is no water for washing, the men's chins, cheeks and upper lips are dark with the fluff of a six-day growth, since there is neither enough water nor enough light to shave, mothers' breasts are drying up since there is no milk, the last supplies, carefully distributed, are running out, and anyone who still owns a piece of bread or the end of a sausage eats it secretly because he doesn't know whether his neighbour is going to tear it out of his mouth. Since there is nothing to keep people busy, no distraction, only darkness, fear and waiting, day and night merge into an endless grey. During the day, whose arrival they know about only thanks to what they are told by more daring men and women, it is impossible to do anything different from what they do during the night, which is to sit vegetating apathetically on air-raid beds, benches and boxes, deckchairs and armchairs, letting the longing for salvation rise up, the way one might stretch one's arms towards a Fata Morgana, trying to block their noses and ears. The smaller the chance of keeping one's distance and concealing intimacies, or avoiding them, the more keenly every hour of troglodytic life throws up the problems of existence, the more evanescent the varnish of civilization, the more the veneer of good manners detaches itself from people, and the more furiously revulsion and nausea, envy and hatred rise to the surface. The darkness, the rank air become unbearable, but the battle is raging up above, the shells rattle down and the planes' weapons sweep the ground like a hurricane and push every attempt to leave the cellar ruthlessly into the grave of the living corpses. Many who have had the temerity to venture outside have not returned.

Klose's restaurant was cleared overnight by the first-aid unit, and Klose quickly used the opportunity to pull over the shutter and close the shop. So he gets the use of his restaurant back, and above all the use of his cellar, which not only offers better protection than the rooms on the first floor, but is also the place where he stores the supplies that were put by in anticipation of a siege and isolation from any ordinary provisions.

Dr Böttcher came back in the early afternoon. He had visited the surrounding houses, he did a medical round, in a sense, he leaped from hallway to hallway, he asked in the cellars to see if anyone needed medical help and helped, so far as possible. He prescribed the occasional spoonful of bromide or valerian, a few dozen tablets of Sulfadiazine, Redoxon or Albucid, and distributed reassuring words and advice. Dr Böttcher is exhausted, but even more than that he is depressed, because everything he has done has seeped like a drop of water into hot desert sand. No toxins and antitoxins, allopathic and homeopathic preparations can give suffering people the things they really need to heal: peace, quiet, silence, harmony.

'You look completely worn out, Doctor,' Wiegand says when he sees Dr Böttcher falling heavily onto a chair.

Dr Böttcher takes off his glasses and swings them helplessly back and forth. 'I wonder', he says, 'if it will ever be possible to remove the nervous, physical and psychical damage that human beings have done to themselves with this senseless war.'

'And what are people saying?' Wiegand asks.

Dr Böttcher looks up. 'Most people are apathetic, completely jaded, they don't even dare open their mouths any more if a Party boss is anywhere in the vicinity, and they won't do it until the last office steward has literally been replaced by the first Russian soldier. But I learned something that seems so typical that I have to tell you about it. I don't know if the latest rumour has reached you already . . .'

'Has Hermann Göring gone on the attack with a huge reserve army of paratroopers, to get rid of the Führer?' Schröter asks with a grin.

'A reserve army under General Wenck is supposed to be on the march,' Dr Böttcher replies, 'but before it can intervene in the battle for Berlin it would first have to engage with the Russian troops west of Berlin. According to today's army report' – he takes a newspaper out of his pocket and unfolds it – 'yes, here it is.'

In the battle for Berlin every inch of territory is being fought for. To the south the Soviets are advancing to the line of Babelsberg-Zehlendorf-Neukölln. In the eastern and northern areas of the city violent street battles are being fought. To the west of the city Soviet tank spearheads have reached the area around Nauen and Ketzin. North-west of Oranienburg the northern shore of the Ruppin Canal is being held against fierce attacks.

'Translated, tank spearheads in the area around Ketzin-Nauen means that the Russians have blocked the last major artery road to the north-west. And here is an article from which I'll read you some extracts.

"First Rapid-deployment Reserves from the West
Have Marched into Berlin this Morning

In the early hours of the morning, the Reich capital experienced
with joy and satisfaction the entry of strong rapid-deployment
reserves from the west, brought in to reinforce the defence force.
Under low-hanging clouds alternating with rain showers, through
which the last stars of the passing night blinked, trucks, tanks,
guns, utility vehicles and columns of infantry, heavily laden with
ammunition and equipment, drove down one of the major access
roads of Berlin, one of the supply routes, one of the paths that have
not yet been cut off or endangered by the Bolshevik tanks.

The attitude and mood of the people of Berlin just after these
images, which became visible before their eyes, has become even
calmer and more composed, and has completely overcome the first
shock after the incursion of the Bolsheviks into the city zone. We
witnessed genuine scenes of joy when reports came in of the entry
of these troops into those areas of fighting which have now been in
a constant state of combat with their troops. The words of a tank
driver with a laughing face early this morning said it all. He came
out with the slogan of today and the days to come: 'Let's get going,
this is where the fun starts.'"

'I think it's all bluff. These so-called rapid-deployment reserves
who are supposed to have marched in this morning are a total
invention; any troops being thrown into the battle right now aren't
coming from the western front, but from Spandau and Döberitz,
where they have been assembled in the Adler and Seeckt barracks.
These extremely questionable formations are made up of soldiers
on leave, convalescent companies, unemployed Luftwaffe ground
staff, Volkssturm men from the fourth recruitment drive, Hitler
Youth, reserve policemen, works security, factory guards, people
drafted into Organisation Todt and finally deserters who took
fright at their own courage at the last minute and joined up again,
they are badly armed and have hardly any heavy weapons. But I
didn't actually want to talk about that. How did I get on to that?'

'You were talking about a rumour,' Lassehn reminds him.

'Right, the rumour!' Dr Böttcher shakes his head and smiles for a moment. 'The rumour is: Germany has signed a truce with England and America, and is joining with them to fight Russia.'

'Nonsense!' Schröter shouts excitedly. 'The idea of taking something like that seriously!'

'Calm down,' Dr Böttcher reassures him. 'I know as well as the rest of you that it's nonsense, and I'm only mentioning the rumour to show how many – I'm not saying the whole German people – how many Germans are still reacting. I don't consider this reaction to the rumour to be unimportant, because it gives a deep and telling insight into the mentality of brains numbed by National Socialism.'

'Let's not spend too long on the preamble,' Schröter warns impatiently.

'I'm getting there, you overheated individual,' replies Dr Böttcher. 'You must take me as I am, I've got to wash myself down. Where is Klose, by the way?'

'He's fetching water,' Lucie Wiegand replies.

Dr Böttcher receives his answer with a nod. 'Then I'll get to the heart of the matter,' he continues. 'I was in a cellar, I was examining two children and distributing some medicine, but when I was about to leave the shells were falling so densely that I waited for a while. I listened to what people were saying without expressing my own opinion, and I must say, people were speaking quite frankly, they swore, they used all kinds of delightful epithets for our glorious leaders. "If only that bastard would kick the bucket," said one woman who was sitting beside me, and another young woman nearby remarked, "If only the Russians were here, so that all this shit would come to an end," others used similar expressions or nodded energetically. Of course I was only able to observe some of the people, as it was quite a big cellar with lots of twists and turns, but I didn't hear a single contradictory voice.'

'What you're describing isn't anything special,' Schröter says. 'Naturally, people have had it up to here.'

Dr Böttcher looks at him over his glasses with the indulgent look of a teacher at a student who hasn't learned his lesson well enough. 'Is it natural?' he asks. 'What I am going to tell you now does not make things nearly as unambiguous as you think, and I only described the mood in that cellar to . . . well, you'll see in a minute. When people were cursing fit to burst, a man suddenly came rushing in from the street, he wasn't a soldier or an old fighter, he wasn't even a Party member (at least he wasn't wearing an insignia), he was just a civilian, he was in quite a state and his words spilled excitedly out of him. This man brought the rumour of a supposed armistice with the Western Allies and the new coalition against the Soviets.'

Böttcher pants as if he is suddenly out of breath. 'I must say, the effect of this news was quite startling. Not only did the cursing suddenly fall silent, I could in fact feel a wave of joy running through the people, the same woman who had called Hitler a bastard a few minutes before was suddenly enthusiastic again, she didn't talk about Hitler but about our Führer, who would save Germany from the Bolsheviks at the last minute, others surrounded the man and wanted to know every single detail, whether the English and the Americans were already on the march, whether their air forces were already bombing the Russians and so on.'

'Depressing,' Gregor says. 'You might get the impression that the German people would still like to win, that they haven't recognized that only a total defeat can remove Hitler's dictatorship.'

'So who says that the great majority of the German people want to be freed of the Nazis? They want to see the war over, how and in what way is of secondary importance, whether with Churchill or against Churchill, whether with Stalin or against Stalin doesn't matter in the end. If Hitler were still to win the war they'd be happy with that, whatever the internal and external consequences.'

'Quite right,' Dr Böttcher says. 'The scene that I witnessed in that cellar, and which I see as typical, has proven to me once again that our people are rotten to the marrow. It pains me to say it, but unfortunately it's the truth, and history will pronounce it guilty.'

'Guilt, error and crime have led our people into the abyss,' Gregor says, 'even suicide is a crime.'

Schröter, wearing a pair of headphones, has been fiddling with the crystal set. 'Be quiet now!' he shouts. 'BBC London!' He listens with a tense expression, not a muscle moving, and scribbles a few brief pencil notes down on a piece of paper; when he takes off the headphones he looks around triumphantly. 'To keep it short,' he says, 'the Russians have taken Brünn and Pillau, the British and the Canadians are on the edge of Bremen and Hamburg, the French and the Americans are at the Austrian border with Bavaria, the Americans in Czechoslovakia are reaching Eger, in Italy the Allies have advanced to the Po, and' – he smiles like someone who wants to give a child a surprise – 'I've saved the best till last: the Russians have reached the Elbe and Torgau, and are united with the First American Army. Now?'

'Anyone who knows the dynamic of the Allied attacks won't be so surprised,' Dr Böttcher says thoughtfully. 'Today's army report basically says as much, but in the usual veiled and circumlocutory form, with the clichés about heavy enemy losses, halted advances and successful counter-attacks. Anyone who has familiarized himself with the terminology of Wehrmacht reports could always read between the lines, because by and large they corresponded to the facts, except that unfavourable events were paraphrased or minimized or withheld, and it is a favourite trick of Goebbels to dismiss unpleasant facts with a generous wave of the hand and to put them on ice for a while before either admitting them in instalments or mentioning them in passing as facts that have been known for a long time.'

'For journalists who have only dared to step away from the prescribed path by so much as a step,' Gregor says, 'the gates of the concentration camps were wide open to accept them lovingly behind the barbed wire. But no one dared to do that, or hardly anyone, because nowhere else was servility as great as it was among journalists.'

'One of the most charming of them is this fellow Dr Otto Kriegk, editorial writer of the *Nachtausgabe*,' Wiegand says, and points to the paper that Dr Böttcher has brought with him. 'Today's editorial is up with the best of them:

> "The Führer Leads the Battle for Berlin in the
> Most Active Manner

The battle for the Reich capital has reached a crucial point. Yesterday and during the night the Bolshevik attackers attempted, mostly in vain, to push their way from north, east and south deeper into the city. At some crucial points in the battle, with a very large deployment of men and *materiel*, they achieved some breaches, which the German defence is currently attempting to block. The Bolsheviks have also gained territory in the west around Berlin, attempting to establish a blockade some distance from Berlin. They have encountered heavy resistance from individual combat units.

The tactical behaviour of the Bolsheviks shows that they are slowly coming to understand the extent to which they will soon have to face a significant reinforcement of the German defence.

The German defence of the Reich capital has now deployed all available means and possibilities, so that army, Party and Volkssturm worked excellently together in Berlin. The Führer himself is leading the defence of our Reich capital.

Yesterday Gauleiter Dr Goebbels mentioned in a proclamation that it is a special honour to defend the capital, because the Führer has placed himself at the head of this crucial and heroic battle. The Führer is giving active leadership to the battle and will remain in the capital of the Reich until our goal, driving the Bolsheviks back to the east, has been achieved." '

'Even Goebbels could not have been more cynical or deceitful,' Lassehn says when Wiegand has finished.

'Oh, you innocent little angel,' Dr Böttcher says, 'this is all Goebbels, there is not a single article in Germany that isn't written precisely according to Goebbels' directives. Or didn't you know that the editors of the newspapers and news agencies had to report to Goebbels or Mr Dietrich to take their orders, because as we know we have the freest and best-informed press in the world? Goebbels once personally thanked the members of the press for their loyalty and readiness for duty.'

'I always find myself thinking of a comparison,' Wiegand says. 'If I tug my little dog on the lead behind me and almost choke him, he must follow me because I'm the stronger one, but it doesn't occur to me to stroke him and tell him he's a good, loyal little dog who's following his master like a good boy.'

'But the press pack, I mean, your good, loyal little dog, follows you even without a leash,' Dr Böttcher says, 'it follows you at a glance and cowers as soon as you raise your voice.'

'Our little dog is very well trained and adds new tricks to the already considerable repertoire of his master,' Gregor says, smiling faintly and then turning serious again. 'Our Nazi journalist always finds a twist to add a favourable commentary even to the most shattering facts. The *DAZ* of 31 January gave me a classic example of that when it wrote:

> "Precisely when you are aware that we are now in the third week since the beginning of the Soviet offensive, without operational counter-actions on the large scale having become visible, we must feel confirmed in our view that our leadership are taking counter-measures appropriate to the extent of the enemy attack."

So it wasn't our victorious counter-attacks that were the lifeline for this model OKW commentary, it was the fact that they weren't there.'

'If you read only the headlines, it would make you feel ill,' Schröter says. 'It all sounds so heroic:

> "This is how we master the situation"
> "Anti-aircraft gunners as anti-tank units"
> "Berlin anti-aircraft guns fire on tanks"
> "Hitler Youth engage in battle"
> "Berlin Police maintains M-Street anti-tank barrier"

"Morale exemplary in the Reich capital"
"Workers' representative shoots three Soviet tanks"
"Team of political leaders destroys mortar emplacement"

'Here, this article is particularly telling, it speaks for itself. Listen to this!

"The word of the people.

Not far from Schöneberg S-Bahn station, at the intersection of Hauptstrasse and Tempelhofer Strasse, the population found a soldier hanging from a lamp post on a washing line. He was not wearing his military coat. The people, acting as his judge, fastened to his belt a white cardboard sign with the inscription: 'I, Senior Lance Corporal Höhne from Berlin, was too cowardly to defend my wife and children.'

This unfamiliar picture in the streets of the Reich capital is profoundly justified at this time. A deserter has been hanged. Only a few metres away from him women and children stand outside the grocers' shops with bags and nets to collect the special distribution. They have to wait, because there is much work to be done in the shops. At home they have their emergency suitcases ready, but not to escape through the gaps in the front, not to be given preferential treatment and a free pass by talking to the enemy. This traitor hanging there, sentenced by the population, can do us no more harm. The dream of escaping soldierly duty, abandoning his people and knifing our troops in the back is over. Anyone who fears an honourable death will die that death in shame." '

'Good grief!' Wiegand exclaims. 'Just before their defeat and beyond, the Nazis show once again what they are: murderers of foreign peoples, and of their own people.'

'I've seen that with my own eyes at the Hackescher Markt,' Lassehn says, 'but I still persuaded myself that it was only an isolated incident, but after this article no doubt is possible. If it's even in the newspaper . . .'

'Lassehn,' Schröter says, 'they're still the same monsters! Whether they are driving Jews into the gas chambers, hanging their own soldiers or scribbling newspaper articles like this one, they're just using different weapons, sub-machine guns, the rope or the typewriter, it's all the same murderous intent!'

'Schröter has hit the nail on the head,' Dr Böttcher says. 'Barbarism plus modern technology as a vision of the world, that is National Socialism. And there's someone at the door.'

'My wife's in the kitchen,' Wiegand says as he listens to the knocking. 'It can't be Klose, he has a key and he wouldn't knock like that either.'

'Maybe it's that lieutenant of yours, Lassehn,' Schröter says, 'coming to get us for our exercise lesson.'

When Lassehn is about to reply, Lucie Wiegand comes into the room. 'Someone's knocking, but it isn't our signal. Shall I open the door?'

The knocking gets louder and more impatient, fists hammer against the door panel.

'Go to the front, Lucie, to the restaurant,' Wiegand says quickly, 'I'll open up. Come on, pistols at the ready, Lassehn, grab the torch.'

Wiegand walks along the short, dark corridor and opens the door a tiny crack, Schröter, Gregor and Dr Böttcher are standing behind him with guns in their hands. Lassehn aims the beam of his torch at the door.

'Who is it?' Wiegand asks.

'Open up,' says a deep, growling voice. 'Something's happened.'

'What is it?' asks Wiegand without opening the door any further.

'Does that fat pint-puller live here?' a man's voice asks.

'What about it?' Wiegand asks, still very cautiously.

'Are you a relative?' the voice goes on.

'Yes,' Wiegand replies, 'Klose is my brother-in-law. What do you want from him?'

'Want?' asks the voice. 'Nothing at all, no point wanting anything from him any more, he's . . . they've just got him.'

Wiegand pulls the door open and finds himself facing a big, broad man in a leather jacket. 'Where is he?' he asks quickly.

'He's by the pump on Fruchtstrasse, just on the corner, opposite the post office.'

'Can't he walk?' Dr Böttcher asks, putting his revolver away and picking up his doctor's jacket.

'Walk?' the man says. 'He's not walking any more, he's had it. Just as he was about to fill his bucket it happened, a splinter flew through the air like a butterfly, except a bit harder, and that's not the sort of thing a person's head can take.'

'Come on, we've got to go and get him,' Dr Böttcher says. 'Come with me, we may find a stretcher of some kind.'

'You'd be better off digging a hole in the courtyard,' says the man. 'He's dead as a doornail, you're not going to wake him up again.'

'Where is he?' Wiegand asks.

'I told you,' the man says, 'on the right around the corner near the post office. Had a good death, the fat fellow, one minute he was happy as a sandboy, the next he was gone. It's how I would like to go myself.'

'Come on,' Dr Böttcher says, and pushes his way past the man with the leather jacket. 'Hurry up!'

Lassehn, Wiegand, Schröter and Gregor follow the doctor and run across the courtyard and down the hallway.

'Even *you* can't bring him back to life,' the man calls after them, 'however fast you run, death is quicker. Sssssss, bang, and you're gone.'

Bent-backed, the men run along Strasse Am Schlesischen Bahnhof and then turn right into Fruchtstrasse. They almost trip over a body.

'That's Klose,' calls Lassehn, who is running immediately behind Dr Böttcher.

It is Klose, his legs are stretched out straight in front of him, and his torso leans, as if he is half resting, against the wall of a house, one shoulder slightly twisted, his eyes are unnaturally wide open, one hand is still firmly clamped to a bucket. A few metres away a few women stand by the pump, a man is pumping very quickly, no one looks up or around at the person lying on the step, no one makes a fuss about the fact that a person has just lost his life. In this orgy of destruction and annihilation death has become such an everyday event that their own lives are the only things they are concerned about.

Dr Böttcher kneels down beside Klose. He immediately uncovers the wound, a narrow trickle of blood runs from Klose's right temple and drips over his jacket. The doctor examines him quickly and then, still crouching beside Klose, looks up.

Lassehn sees a hopeless flicker in Dr Böttcher's eyes, sees his Adam's apple springing from his collar and moving up and down.

'Is he . . .' Lassehn begins and looks anxiously at Dr Böttcher. Dr Böttcher doesn't reply, he straightens slowly as if it is a great effort, bends over Klose and closes his eyes by resting his forefinger gently on the eyelids and pulling them gently down as if spreading a veil over the dead man's last gaze.

For a few seconds the men stand in a tight group around the corpse. Above them the shells wail and whistle, bursting against the cobblestones around them and tearing lumps of stone from the buildings, a house opposite is on fire, blazing beams fall into the street and send sparks flying in all directions, the endless rattle of machine guns forces its way quite clearly from the east, soldiers run along the road with clanking bayonets, gas masks and canteens, their hobnailed boots crunch on the broken glass, a field gun stands on the corner of Mühlenstrasse and fires at short intervals, a dog, a little black and white brindle terrier, runs whining back and forth, it hops on three legs, the fourth drawn up closely to its body, it tries to creep over to the soldiers but is always irritably chased away, orderlies carry a few wounded men to a car that has stopped in the middle of the street with its engine running, somewhere on the tracks a locomotive lets off steam with a hiss, but the men stand and see nothing of that, they stand there without moving, without saying a word, staring at the ground.

Schröter is the first to move; taking long strides he runs along the middle of the road towards the ambulance, he talks to the driver and then takes a stretcher from the vehicle. Lassehn leaps over to him and gives him a hand, then they put Klose on the stretcher. They both act as if under some kind of compulsion, no one utters a word, their faces have stiffened into the masks of waxworks.

Above them rages the noise of battle, conflagrations blaze around them, smoke and haze billow through the streets, a rain of ash falls down on them like warm, grainy dust, but they slowly put one foot after another. When they have almost reached Klose's house, a shell explodes in front of them. The blast throws Gregor to his knees, lumps of stone and iron splinters whirl around them and for several seconds everything is veiled in dust.

Lassehn is brushed by a splinter that slices open the skin of his forehead, his blood drips like red tears on the stretcher where Klose lies.

When Gregor is firmly back on his feet, they walk on and set the stretcher down in the hallway.

'Wait here,' Dr Böttcher says, and quickly crosses the courtyard with long, clumsy steps. A few minutes later he comes back carrying two spades and hands one of them to Wiegand. 'Let's both of us start,' he says. 'Come on!'

Dr Böttcher and Wiegand start digging in the narrow strip of earth in the courtyard, they throw up clod after clod, neither saying a word, their faces are tense and deeply serious, their eyes focused rigidly on the earth that is opening up deeper and deeper beneath their feet. Above the little rectangle formed by the walls of the houses there hangs a grey, overcast sky, gusts of wind violently drive black clouds of smoke, a heavy smell of burning penetrates the deep cavity of the courtyard, suffocating the smell of broken earth.

After a few minutes Lassehn and Schröter take over. Even now not a word is spoken, Lassehn and Schröter stand expectantly in front of Dr Böttcher and Wiegand and reach their hands out for the spades. All five now dig in turn, then they lay the dead man in the excavated grave.

They stand there bareheaded for another minute, Wiegand's

face twitching violently. The corners of Dr Böttcher's mouth are drawn down and his eyes are half closed, Schröter's hands are clenched into fists and his neck is craned, only Gregor's face is calm and motionless, shadowed by an expression of painful resignation.

'Our father which art in Heaven . . .' he murmurs.

When he has finished, the men begin to fill the hole. The glowing missiles of the smoke mortars streak above them with eerie wails.

XIV

26 April

The battle for Berlin has reached a stage that will later be described as the Sodom and Gomorrah of a modern city. Dawn breaks, its pale, gloomy light seeps onto the sea of debris: a new day is beginning. The cannon will begin to sound, spreading death and ruin over the city, the planes are darting overhead again like antediluvian pterodactyls and striking at everything alive with their iron beaks, soldiers will again be driven into senseless battle, killed or mutilated, women, desperately concerned about their children, wander the rubble-strewn streets in search of milk and bread, and are mown down by death's scythe. Millions of people go on cowering in cellars and underground tunnels, freezing, starving, feverish and terrified, buildings are split in two and fires eat through the streets, bridges sink like felled giants into the water of the rivers and canals, the first blossoms of spring are dusted with gunpowder and smoke, prayers, curses, screams, whimpering and death rattles rise into a sky that has pulled a dense wall of smoke over itself and the stars. Even though Berlin, the sea of rubble, has already collapsed into two zones, one part conquered by the Russians and one still defended by the Germans, the terrors for the population, which has already fled the fighting, are no smaller because the German artillery is firing, as it has been ordered to do, at its own city, and the German Luftwaffe is dropping bombs equally on the Bolshevik enemy and on the German national comrades that it was supposedly defending only a short time ago; but while there the last pitiful remains of the former tyrannical order are breathing their last amidst bloody chaos, here one can already make out the first signs of a new order, the first bread is being baked again and distributed from the trucks of the Red Army. But the Russian soldiers are not only liberators. Many of them are also looters and rapists.

This is all happening because a hysterical lunatic decided, in his urge to annihilate, ruthlessly to sacrifice the city, to postpone his own end by a few days and then 'fall in a heroic attitude on the ruins of Berlin'. He cowers in his bunker and remains in contact via radio, telex and telephone with General Jodl, Chief of the Operations Staff of the Armed Forces, Artillery General Weidling, Military District Commander, Lieutenant-General Reymann, Combat Commander of Berlin, General Braun, Head of Army Intelligence, Field Marshal Schörner, Leader of Army Group Mitte, and General von Henrici, Leader of Army Group Weichsel. Even though the hopelessness of the situation becomes clearer with each new report – in Berlin the Russians have advanced to Gesundbrunnen, from the south to Tempelhof and Friedenau, from the west to Spandau and Charlottenburg, from the east to Silesian Station and Görlitz Station, the Reich Chancellery is under direct fire, around Berlin one division after another is being defeated, Rathenow, Wittenberg, Prenzlau and Stettin are being conquered by the Russians, Regensburg, Ingolstadt and Augsburg by the Americans, Bremen by the British – no one tries to stand up to the lunatic. Between hours of complete apathy and raging delirium he is still every ounce the Führer, he summons General Ritter von Greim from Rechlin in Mecklenburg, who is injured when his Fieseler-Storch plane lands on the Charlottenburger Chaussee, and says to him, 'I called you because Göring has betrayed me'. He appoints him Supreme Commander of the Air Fleet and promotes him to Field Marshal, he orders and gets signatures, he appoints and dismisses, he receives delegates of troops fighting in Berlin and awards decorations, he moves flags about on a map of Berlin and the surrounding area and directs armies that no longer exist, he draws up a death contract with his confidant Martin Bormann and organizes rehearsals of their planned suicides. Goebbels, in his bunker under the old Reich

Chancellery, has been seized by a compulsion to speak incessantly, his children sing the song about 'Uncle Führer', Bormann, who has moved from his bunker beneath the Post Ministry to the Führer's bunker, writes in his diary and constantly enquires about the exact wording of the Führer's statements, Eva Braun gets on with polishing her fingernails, moving around frequently and saying repeatedly, 'It's better for hundreds of thousands of others to die than that He is lost for Germany'.

After a restless night, continually agitated by detonations and the rattle of machine guns, in the early hours of the morning an infernal storm crashes down over the area between Silesian Station and Jannowitz Bridge. When the guns fall silent, the barking of the mortars begins and the rattle of machine guns gets closer. It is no longer just a single rising and falling sound, each shot is now an independent bang.

'They're getting closer,' Wiegand says. 'Do you hear the machine guns?'

'Maybe the time has come,' Schröter says, and paces uneasily back and forth. 'I'd like to go out into the street to try and assess the situation.'

'Don't be ridiculous,' Wiegand says. 'Or do you want to be put in some kind of formation?'

'Of course not,' Schröter replies, 'but sitting either here in the room or down in the cellar is driving me quite mad. At any rate I've had enough.'

'We all feel like that,' Dr Böttcher says, 'but I've seen how they do it, Schröter. The military police patrol the streets like a column of dog catchers, and woe betide the man who looks in anyway fit to fight, they drag him off, and it doesn't matter whether they have papers on them or not, they're forced to be heroes, or hanged. It goes very quickly, a single derogatory word, a small betrayal, and the rope's around their necks.'

'That's exactly how they treated so-called witches in the Middle Ages,' Lassehn says. 'Suspicion was enough . . .'

'At least a witch trial was a legal process,' Dr Böttcher replies, 'of course it was very questionable, but there was still a court, there was even a book of laws, the *Malleus Maleficarum*, the judgment was announced by a committee, and besides, the witch trials were a few centuries ago, they were held in an atmosphere of profound superstition, but now, a hundred and fifty years after the Declaration of the Rights of Man, in the twentieth century, in a state that organizes every aspect of our lives, which has pressed every part of our bourgeois existence into exact laws and which is now in its death throes, which disregards all of its own principles and is thrashing about furious in all directions like a deer that has just been shot at, now some lout with a few stars or braids on his epaulettes or his collar can make life-or-death decisions and, with a casual gesture, adds one more to the hecatomb of corpses he is standing on, without being answerable to anybody. We are in the very final stage of National Socialism; the systematic contempt for people is becoming barbarous nihilism, legal uncertainty is turning into absolute anarchy.'

'What you just said is all completely true,' Gregor says slowly, 'it gets to the heart of the matter, but it is too intellectually felt, no, not felt, but grasped, because words are not capable of expressing what we feel. I am seized with a kind of impotent contempt, it makes me shudder . . .'

'You are intellectually overbred,' Wiegand says, 'so that you can barely feel anything more than a kind of scientific or political revulsion, but no hot, searing rage, everything first passes through the filter of the intelligence.'

'It would be worth discussing whether cool reason and hot hearts do not perhaps complement one another,' Gregor says, 'in fact whether they might not even be mutually dependent.'

'Let's not have any academic arguments,' Dr Böttcher says, 'perhaps with a Social Contract and a Communist Manifesto, first of all because this isn't the time, and secondly because someone's knocking at the door.'

Everyone listens.

Someone is knocking, three taps, short pause, then two.

'That's our sign,' Wiegand says and gets to his feet. 'Who could that be?'

'You'll see straight away if you open up,' Schröter says with an inviting gesture.

Wiegand leaves the room and comes back a moment later with Lieutenant Tolksdorff.

Tolksdorff is somewhat breathless, his face is flushed, his mouth is slightly open and his lips are shivering. 'Gentlemen,' he says hastily, 'you are in danger. The Russians are not far away, and . . .'

'The Russians aren't a danger for us,' Schröter interrupts him abruptly.

'I know that,' the lieutenant replies. 'Let me finish. The Russians are very close and that's why the SS are combing all houses from top to bottom and dragging off all the men, they look like men possessed.'

'You mean we can't stay here?' Dr Böttcher asks.

'That's how it is,' Tolksdorff replies. 'You are five healthy, sprightly men, and that looks damned suspicious. There's only really one possibility . . .'

'So where are the Russians?' Schröter interrupts.

'They're advancing in three groups, one coming down Stralauer Allee and up Mühlenstrasse, the second up Revaler and Memeler Strasse, and the third group is coming up the railway tracks from Warschauer Bridge.'

'That doesn't matter,' Gregor says.

'It matters a lot,' Schröter disagrees. 'Because if the Russians are already so close that they could be here at any minute . . . That's how it is, Lieutenant, isn't that right?'

'That's impossible to predict with any exactitude,' the officer replies. 'Apparently there's violent resistance on Revaler Strasse and on Stralauer Allee, the Russians will only advance slowly, but the middle group, the one coming up along the railway cutting is faster, the demolition of Warschauer Bridge hasn't halted them.'

'And how far away are they? Do you have any idea?' Schröter presses.

'These discussions seem pointless to me,' Dr Böttcher intervenes impatiently. 'The lieutenant didn't come here for a briefing.

You said just now that there was only one possibility, I assume you mean a possibility of keeping us safe from the SS hordes.'

Tolksdorff nods energetically. 'Yes, yes. And that one possibility . . .'

'. . . is to stay here and wait!' Schröter intervenes.

'No,' the officer says firmly, with a patient gesture of his hand, 'the SS will be here much sooner than the Russians, they're only a few blocks away, on the right from here. No, the only possibility is for you to put on your Volkssturm armbands and join my company (what they now call a company). I think that's your best protection.'

'And what happens then?' Schröter demands.

'Everything else will emerge from the situation,' the lieutenant replies. 'In the streets you always have the possibility of disappearing into the bushes just before the Russians get here, and in all the confusion no one will notice, but here they've got you on a plate, and you could easily get shot. The SS here is led by a Hauptsturmführer, he seems possessed, I would never have thought that a person could be like that, and the fellow's barely in his mid-twenties. I've never heard a word out of his mouth that wasn't roared or hissed like an order, not a word that wasn't ice-cold cynicism and bloody scorn . . .' Tolksdorff shivers. 'Do you want to find yourselves at the mercy of a monster like that?'

Schröter gesticulates excitedly. 'Listen, I haven't waited twelve years for freedom to be exposed to the shells and bullets out there, and to the orders of this SS officer.'

The lieutenant smiles. 'Not every bullet hits its target,' he says, and then becomes serious again. 'But if you want to stay here . . . It was just a suggestion, a well-intended suggestion, gentlemen . . .'

'We've got to decide quickly,' Dr Böttcher says. 'If the bloodhounds are already in the surrounding houses . . . Is there any point hiding in one of the flats?'

'They kick in every door that isn't open,' Tolksdorff says.

'And they steal stuff,' Schröter adds.

'You can rely on that,' the lieutenant confirms, and turns back to

Dr Böttcher. 'Make your minds up, gentlemen, we haven't much time, and every minute is precious.'

'I agree with the lieutenant's suggestion,' Dr Böttcher says.

'And the rest of you?'

Gregor and Lassehn agree with him, Schröter is still undecided.

Wiegand looks at the floor for a few seconds as if lost in thought. 'The Hauptsturmführer you were talking about before,' he says slowly, 'do you happen to know his name?'

'Yes,' Tolksdorff replies, 'his name is Wiegand, people call him Robert the Devil.'

'Then I can't come with you,' Wiegand says firmly. 'No, I can't do it.'

'Why not?' the lieutenant asks, astonished.

'This Hauptsturmführer . . . yes, he's my son,' Wiegand answers blankly.

'Your son?' Tolksdorff is flabbergasted.

'Yes, my son,' Wiegand confirms.

'That's no reason . . .'

'It's an excellent reason!'

'I don't understand,' Tolksdorff says, puzzled. 'Just because he's your son . . .'

'Yes, precisely because he's my son, lieutenant,' Wiegand replies. 'No one knows my political past, my unbending resistance and my deep hatred of National Socialism as well as he does.'

'But you're his father,' the officer persists.

'What difference does that make? Hasn't it occurred to you that it was one of the first tasks of National Socialism to break down all human relationships and put rigid principle in its place?'

'You mean that your son would take action against his own father? No, I can't believe that.'

'I know what I'm talking about, Lieutenant,' Wiegand replies firmly. 'A few years ago he once observed that they would be best off putting such an obstinate enemy of the state as myself behind bars for ever.'

'That is impossible to believe,' the Lieutenant says.

'You must come to understand, Lieutenant,' Dr Böttcher says, 'that National Socialism is merely the badge of an unscrupulous gang of criminals. What you previously saw only as military errors, a lack of discipline, occasional attacks or individual excesses, is in fact a monstrous system of murder and looting, a violation of the intellect and contempt for human beings, but we will talk about that in calmer times. So I agree with the lieutenant's suggestion.'

'Then let's go,' Schröter says, and takes his Volkssturm armband out of his pocket. 'But let me tell you this straight away, Lieutenant, I'm not shooting at Russians. If it comes down to it, I'd rather turn the gun on myself.'

'Do you think we'll be doing that?' Gregor asks. 'If we have to do any shooting then we're firing in the air, that's obvious.'

'And you need to hide, Mr Wiegand,' Tolksdorff says. 'I happened to hear that this restaurant is thought to be particularly suspicious, there's some kind of political functionary, Hoffmeister or something, who's constantly under the influence, he's forever going on about an office steward who's supposed to have disappeared suddenly under suspicious circumstances. Do you know anything about that?'

'No idea,' Dr Böttcher says quickly. 'So let's get going. Goodbye, Wiegand.'

'Shame we couldn't stay together,' Wiegand says, and shakes his outstretched hands.

A few handshakes, a brief bow, then the men run across the courtyard and through the hallway into the street. While still running, Lassehn glanced at Klose's grave, and for a fragment of a second he saw before him the affable face of the fat landlord – it seems an impossibly long time ago, and yet only ten days have passed since then – standing in front of him, broad and phlegmatic, and looking down at his revolver with a superior grin on his face.

But now isn't the time to get lost in thought. The little band crosses the street and, speeding up, reaches the station building. In the ticket room, in the corridors and waiting rooms there is complete confusion, flying columns of orderlies, field kitchens, impromptu offices, command posts, ammunition depots have been stored here, but everything is in the process of being moved, hasty, hurried, nervous, old bandages, broken medicine bottles, empty tins, bundles of files, steel helmets, gasmasks, bits of bread, broken chairs and tables, tangles of telephone wire, cigarette butts and tarpaulins lie around, all covered by the pale-grey clouds of the dust that trickles ceaselessly down from ceilings and walls, the smoke of the field kitchens, the sooty haze from the burning houses.

SS military police scour all the rooms, their eyes dart around like those of quick and hungry rats. 'All men to Küstriner Platz!' they shout over and over again. 'Apart from the seriously wounded and medical orderlies!' Their voices sound like hoarse barking.

'There's no point to any of it any more,' an old soldier says, 'It's all . . .'

A jab in the back shuts him up. 'Shut up, you old peasant,' an SS man says menacingly. 'Get moving, and be quick about it.'

The soldier takes his rifle away from the wall, he fiddles around slowly, buttons and unbuttons his greatcoat and looks furtively at the patrol, which has already walked a few steps further on. 'Bunch of bastards, damn them all,' he murmurs, and attends to his boots.

The Unterscharführer spins around and is right by the soldier in a trice. 'You're still here!' he roars. 'You thought once we'd moved on a few steps that would be it, is that right?'

The soldier puts his rifle over his shoulder and gets moving.

'I'm going,' he says. 'Can't we still . . .'

'You can do nothing at all, you dung beetle,' the SS man roars. 'Don't try to run away or . . .' He raises his machine gun and plays with the trigger, a repellent grin running over his brutal face. 'Bang, said the virgin and then she wasn't. Clear off you, rag-draped clothes-stand!'

Lassehn clenches his fists and bites his lips.

'Calm down, son,' Dr Böttcher whispers, having watched him carefully, 'just stay calm. I know it's hard to have a gun in your hand and not to be allowed to shoot.'

They walk down the corridors, past the waiting rooms and the Wehrmacht quarters into Fruchtstrasse. A young lance corporal shoves his way past them, he has a pronounced limp and is holding his perfunctorily bandaged hand up in the air. 'Come here, lad,' the Unterscharführer shouts. 'Where do you think you're going?'

'To get a decent bandage put on, sir,' the lance corporal replies.

'Balls with bells on,' says the Unterscharführer. 'That bandage is fine. You just want to skive. Are you shitting yourself because the Russkies are on the way?'

'No, Unterscharführer,' the corporal says. 'And besides, I've sprained my right ankle.'

'And besides you've got a fart stuck up your arse the wrong way, and you've got heartburn on top of that,' the SS man's companion, a Scharführer, mocks. 'Get going right this minute, or else ... We're not going to be hanging about, bang, said the virgin, and then she wasn't. Do you get that?'

'But the lieutenant expressly ordered me to ...' the lance corporal tries to object.

'Fuck your lieutenant!' the Unterscharführer says, and puts his finger to the trigger of his sub-machine gun. 'He has no say here. Come on, clear off!'

The lance corporal still hasn't given up. 'But the wound might ... The lieutenant expressly ordered ...'

'Shut your trap, you miserable little coward,' the Unterscharführer says. 'One more word and I'll fire a series of bullets into your arse and you can give up the idea of shitting for the rest of your life. So come on, jump to it!'

The lance corporal flushes deep red, he presses his feet firmly against the stone floor and doesn't budge from the spot. 'And if my hand has to be cut off because the wound wasn't treated in time ...'

'Like I give a tinker's curse,' the Hauptscharführer hisses. 'If you don't get out of here right this minute ... Christ, these people are driving me insane.'

Tolksdorff can no longer contain himself and walks up to the group. 'Chief Platoon Leader, let the corporal go to the bandage station,' he says vigorously.

The two SS men carelessly click their heels and raise their hands in the Hitler salute. 'Sorry, Lieutenant, but I can't accept your order,' the Hauptscharführer says, smiling in Tolksdorff's face with restrained hostility.

'What on earth are you thinking of?' Tolksdorff rages at him.

The chief platoon leader shrugs. 'I had express orders, Lieutenant,' he says, and turns back to the lance corporal. 'Get a move on,' he shouts at him, raising his sub-machine gun. 'There was some shooting a second ago.'

The lance corporal doesn't dare to contradict him again, but he still turns uncertainly on his heels and looks pleadingly at the lieutenant.

The Hauptscharführer registers his expression and smiles sarcastically. 'You needn't bother thinking about whatever you had in mind. Right, be off with you or you won't know what's hit you.' He gives the lance corporal a shove on the shoulder and then turns back to the lieutenant. 'I would also advise the lieutenant here to get to the front line as quickly as possible.'

The lance corporal has stumbled forward a couple of steps, but goes no further, he turns round again, stands to attention in front of Tolksdorff and puts his right hand to the steel helmet by way of salute. 'Please, Lieutenant . . .'

He gets no further. The Unterscharführer has raised his sub-machine gun and fired four times, the shots ring out like thunderclaps in the passageway and even drown out the fire of the artillery and the mortars, the lance corporal collapses and falls sideways, his helmet strikes the wall, his feet slip away with a scraping sound.

The chief platoon leader shrugs. 'I'd been patient enough with him,' he says calmly. 'What a coward . . .'

The lieutenant and his group are rooted to the spot for a few seconds.

'Why are you standing there gawping like a herd of cattle?' the chief platoon leader roars. 'Do you object to seeing cowards shot? You miserable shower! Come on, get him out of the way, and be quick about it, or this thing's going off again.'

Tolksdorff nods a command, Lassehn and Schröter lay the lance corporal on a bench. Dr Böttcher examines him quickly and breaks off the bottom half of his dog tag.

'And you and your men go to the front line, Lieutenant,' the chief platoon leader commands. 'Or what are you waiting for? Snow?'

Tolksdorff bites his lips and turns round abruptly. 'Come on!' he struggles to speak loudly, making it sound like an order, but he doesn't quite manage it, fury, shame and nausea block his throat, but there is also something else that takes his speech away, an impotent helplessness at being exposed to these beasts, who cold-bloodedly destroy human lives as others wouldn't even crush a beetle.

They leave the station, pass beneath the railway viaduct and go down Fruchtstrasse, past the big high-rise bunker and the warehouses, stagger among goods wagons and locomotives, over tracks and points. One-man trenches have been hastily dug here, machine guns set up in signal boxes and on goods trains, a few field-artillery cannon put in position, Volkssturm men, Luftwaffe ground personnel and a few railway police are sitting there too, and SS men are roaming all over the place with red faces and narrow eyes, mouths like slits, their steel helmets or caps pushed to the backs of their necks, sub-machine guns in their hands. They are running around like snappy dogs, their eyes are hard, they knock down any resistance, they crush any willingness, rip apart any refusal, they sling around hatred, meanness and murder, the words spray from their mouths like drool, rough, hoarse, gurgling, they don't speak, they grin, they don't walk, they creep.

The Tolksdorff group runs over torn tracks that protrude contorted into the air as if a giant's fist had begun to roll them up, they stumble over shattered sleepers, fallen lamps and signal posts, they wind their way through the confusion of burnt-out and ruined wagons whose iron structures cut strange figures in the bright-blue sky, the air above them bellows and whistles, shells rattle down, fountains of gravel spray up in all directions, goods wagons burn, smoulder, smoke, billow and blaze, the stench of burnt rubber sweeps across the area like a cloud of gas.

In the midst of the tracks stands an abandoned goods wagon, it has previously served as accommodation for railway workers and is curiously almost entirely undamaged, shell splinters have torn a few small holes in the roof, and a board has been broken from an end wall and the paint, once dark red, has made way for a faded bright red, but the particulars of the wagon are still clearly recognizable: Kassel 16,741 Gh, it says in discoloured white, 15.0 t/17.5 5, 21.3 m^3, 10,620 kg, and even the wire mesh that once held the accompanying document is still there, but all of those identifying marks have long since become irrelevant, because years ago the wagon took its leave from its colleagues from Königsberg and Leipzig, Munich and Essen, Breslau and Frankfurt and was pensioned off to Eastern Station. Its premature retirement has kept it from forming a train with its co-opted brethren SF France and FS Italia, PKP and CCCP, Nederland and BMB/ČSD; to some extent it has become stationary, and just as an old seal settles near a great body of water for the evening of its life, the veteran goods wagon has been put at anchor here in the wide expanse of Berlin's Eastern Station among the iron bands of the tracks and amidst the soot and smoke of the locomotives, and has placed itself at the service of the 63rd Road Master's Office. But now even the sign 'Equipment Room of the 63rd Road Master's Office' has lost its validity, because it now bears various military identifying marks, hastily jotted in chalk and only comprehensible to the initiated.

'In there,' Tolksdorff says, and points to the wagon.

Lassehn pushes the door open. A gloomy semi-darkness fills the wagon, the overcast daylight only comes in through the skylights and the holes in the roof. A few soldiers are sitting on a narrow bench, their feet stretched out, their backs resting against the long wall. One squats sleeping on a stool, his head resting against a lathe, all kinds of equipment are lying around, pickaxes, forks, wrenches, extension tubes, tar buckets, mallets, dowels, spirit levels, winches, crowbars, rail tongs, carbide lamps. 'Watch out!' one of the soldiers shouts when Tolksdorff comes in.

Tolksdorff waves a quick hand. 'Reinforcements are on the way,' he says, and turns to Dr Böttcher. 'It isn't exactly comfortable here, but I'm sure you weren't expecting anything else.'

'What happens now?' Schröter asks and shuts the door again.

The lieutenant shrugs. 'We'll see,' he replies.

'What kind of unit are you?' Gregor asks.

'Our task is to keep an eye on the incoming trains and the discharge of their cargoes,' Tolksdorff replies, 'that is, it was, because no trains are coming in now. And where would they come from? The last goods train we guarded has been burning since last night, and the unit is basically surplus to requirements.' He darts a quick glance at the soldiers. 'The people are more or less exhausted, and they don't want to go on.'

'Who does want to these days?' Schröter asks.

'Nobody,' Tolksdorff replies 'but they keep going along with it all, and that's exactly what . . .'

'Being a soldier's like being a dog,' Dr Böttcher says, resting on a heavy sledgehammer, 'he wants off the leash, but the more he pulls and tugs, the more the collar throttles him. He can only get out of the noose if he decides to jump at the person holding the other end of the leash, but he doesn't do that.'

'No, he doesn't,' Tolksdorff says quietly.

'There are some bread rolls back there in the corner if you're hungry,' one of the soldiers says without changing his position, he sits there with his eyes closed, his elbows resting on his knees and his chin in his open hands.

'Thanks,' Lassehn says. 'We're not hungry.'

'Don't be too proud,' the soldier says. 'Aren't you used to plain bread?'

'If you're enterprising,' another soldier says, 'there's a nice little food depot over at the Plaza, but the SS are standing outside.'

Lassehn makes a dismissive gesture.

'You're not so keen on the blackshirts either?' the first soldier says. 'Where have you come from?'

'From Stalingrad,' Schröter says, 'if you really want to know.'

The soldier still doesn't move, he just opens his eyes and blinks nervously at Schröter. 'Shut up,' he says, not loudly, not coarsely, he just murmurs the word with weary resignation. 'Stalingrad, I'm fed up hearing about it.'

'Why is that?' Dr Böttcher asks.

'Stalingrad,' the soldier says in a tired voice, as if talking to himself, 'I was there. I was lucky, I was wounded, they flew me out in a Junkers, that is, I smuggled myself into the plane in Gumrak, then they stitched me back together and chased me off to the front again.' He mutters briefly. 'What was left of the front, in fact, because it was moving backward. No harm done, I thought, the quicker we get back the sooner you'll be at home.'

'And where do you live?' Schröter asks.

The soldier slowly pulls himself away from the wall and opens his eyes. 'Not far from here, on Boddinstrasse in Neukölln, you know, the street that climbs gently from the City Hall on Berliner Strasse . . .'

'I know the one,' Schröter says, and nods to him, 'it continues to Hermannstrasse, and there's a big school on the left.'

The soldier almost becomes lively. 'I live directly opposite that, and I have a shop there, a cigar shop, not that big, but nice and clean, and it worked very nicely, thank you, six Bergmanns, a pack of Villager, a pack of Glücksmann, and a twenty-five pack of R6, a few better cigars, Ortolan . . .'

'Shut up, Ruppert,' one of the soldiers says from the corner, 'we all know about that, you've told us often enough.'

'He's forgotten Black and White and Neumann Hundred and One,' another calls.

The soldier gives the speakers a withering look. 'Yes, you see,' he goes on, turning to Schröter and Dr Böttcher, 'so I've come from Stalingrad via Rostov, Krementschug, Kamenez-Podolsk and whatever all those backwaters are called, back to Berlin, two or three thousand kilometres, I don't know how many, I didn't check, and now I'm sitting here at Silesian Station, and Neukölln is who knows how far away.'

'Stop it now,' someone calls from the corner, 'always the same line, like a preacher, it gets too much in the end.'

The soldier Ruppert ignores the interjection. 'I used to get on the number 1 at Andreasstrasse, went as far as Neanderstrasse and then took the underground to Neukölln City Hall, but now I'm sitting here, just a few lousy kilometres from home, but there's no number 1, no underground, you can't even get there on foot.'

'No,' Schröter says, 'you can't get there, the Russians are already in Neukölln.'

The soldier stands up straight.

'What are you saying?'

Schröter takes the newspaper out of his pocket. 'Here, Field Marshal, is the *Berliner Frontzeitung-Völkischer Beobachter, the Battle Paper of the War Community of all the Berlin Newspapers*, from 26 April.

'Give it here!' Private Ruppert says hoarsely.

'In a minute,' Schröter replies, 'but first you have to enjoy the lovely headline, let it melt on your tongue.

"It is here that the decision must be made"
"Reich Capital the field of destiny of the war".'

Private Ruppert pulls the newspaper out of his hands and scans the page. 'Where's the thing about Neukölln?

"The Führer's HQ, 25 April

On either side of the lower Weser . . .
From the Weser south-east of Bremen . . .
Not a single foot of ground has been taken in the battle for Berlin.
In the south the Soviets advanced to the line of Babelsberg-Zehlendorf-Neukölln . . ."

'You're right, Comrade,' he says as if he has been destroyed, and is about to lean back against the wall, but then he suddenly jumps to his feet. 'Damn it all to hell! Will this shit never end?' he roars. 'Now we're retreating again . . . No, I'm not joining in this time, I'm not joining in any more.'

'The lieutenant . . .' someone warns.

'What are you talking about, he's fed up too, you can tell by looking at him,' Private Ruppert replies.

'That's enough,' Tolksdorff says. 'Keep it down for a bit, Ruppert.'

Private Ruppert, mid-forties, tobacconist from Berlin-Neukölln, walks right up to Tolksdorff. 'Tell me quite truthfully, Lieutenant, as a person, not an officer: how would you feel if you were almost home, there was only a tiny bit of three thousand kilometres left, just a tiny bit, you could almost reach your arms out for your wife, who you haven't seen for almost two years, you can already see the colourful signs in your cigar shop, Saba, Juno, Hanewacker, you've got your foot close to the threshold you tripped over as a little boy, but you can't or you're not allowed to, or you just don't dare . . .' He shakes his head. 'Isn't that a real pile of shit . . .'

'There's nothing to be done about it, Ruppert,' Tolksdorff says, and turns away because he is ashamed of the banality of his answer.

'Why not, Lieutenant?' Private Ruppert persists.

Tolksdorff shrugs. 'I can't answer that one for you, Ruppert.'

Private Ruppert is still standing very close to Tolksdorff. 'I was only assigned to the lieutenant a few days ago,' he says, 'and I think the lieutenant is a decent chap, forgive me, a decent person, I meant . . .'

Tolksdorff smiles narrowly. 'Thank you. What are you getting at?'

Ruppert takes a deep breath. 'If I were to . . . Let's say, if I were to make myself scarce, would the lieutenant . . .'

For a few seconds the wagon is completely silent. The mortars bark outside, the machine guns rattle, many different noises collide with one another, crashing, bursting, roaring, clattering, hissing, cracking, splintering, shouts and cries, but here, in the disused goods wagon, right on the main battle line in Eastern Station, it is incredibly quiet for a few seconds. Here a soldier has asked a question which, in a flash, illuminates the destruction of a whole world.

'So, Lieutenant, you would . . .' Ruppert begins again.

'Nonsense, Ruppert,' Tolksdorff interrupts, 'as far as I'm concerned you can do exactly as you see fit.'

'Thank you,' Ruppert says, and sighs with relief. 'I will never forget this, Lieutenant.'

'How are you planning to do that?' one of the soldiers asks from the corner.

Ruppert laughs, what emerges is more a satisfied grunt than a laugh. 'Loaf, my dear Poppe, use your loaf. Here, take a look at this!' He giggles again and unbuttons his grey uniform coat.

Private Poppe gets to his feet and emerges from his dark corner. 'Blimey, Karl Ruppert,' he says in amazement, 'that's a railway-man's uniform.'

'Quite right, my dear fellow, it is a railwayman's uniform,' Ruppert says with pride. 'If the Russkies show up now, I'll chuck my coat away, climb up on some locomotive or other, or I'll go to a signal box and be a railwayman. And Bob's your uncle!'

'Terrific!' Poppe says admiringly. 'We should do the same. Where did you get these rags from?'

'From the signal box over behind the mail-loading platform.'

'So . . . you're organized, aren't you?'

'Of course! Or did you think . . .'

'There might be more clothes like this?'

Ruppert shrugs.

'I don't know, you'll have to check.'

Poppe and two other soldiers glance at each other in silence and then look at Tolksdorff. 'I would like to ask the lieutenant . . .' a tall, gaunt soldier asks hesitantly.

'Stop asking all these questions!' Tolksdorff says impatiently. 'Do what you like, I'm not stopping you.'

The soldiers stand uncertainly by the door for a few seconds. They have been given an answer as incomprehensible as if an inquisitor had expressly allowed a witch to cavort with Satan.

'Aren't you coming?' one of them asks the lance corporal who is still sitting in the dark corner of the wagon.

Corporal Schumann emits a grunt and waves dismissively.

'So you don't want to?' a soldier asks again.

'No,' the lance corporal replies, 'that would conflict with my vision of the world.'

'Look at the great German hero,' Schröter says, and takes a few steps towards the lance corporal. 'What kind of vision would that be?'

'You wouldn't understand, old man,' the lance corporal replies contemptuously. 'You've never been a soldier, have you?'

'I have, in fact, from 1914 until 1918.'

'Well, then you should know that soldiers don't do anything without an order. In fact, if the lieutenant were suddenly to say: on your feet, march, march, get civilian gear . . .'

'You're round the bend,' the tall, gaunt soldier says, and rests his head on the sliding door. 'You can't ask the lieutenant to do that. You're asking a lot of him already in . . .'

'Yes, it's enough that he's just let us go like that,' Private Ruppert says, finishing his sentence. 'Thank you, Lieutenant. So, come on, Arthur, let's get going.'

The tall, gaunt soldier pushes the door open. When he is about to step into the open he crashes back, turns half-way round and shouts: 'Careful!'

'What kind of robbers' cave is this?' a cuttingly harsh voice asks. 'Step aside!'

The soldier immediately steps back. In the doorway to the wagon stands Chief Platoon Leader Robert Wiegand, who thrusts his head forward and narrows his eyes. 'What's going on here?' he roars. 'Out of here, everybody, and be smart about it, if I might be so bold.'

The men leave the wagon one after the other. The chief platoon leader studies each one with a dark, contemptuous look, his lips are slightly parted and he forces his breath through clenched teeth.

'I demand an explanation from you, Lieutenant!'

'We went into cover here, Chief Platoon Leader.'

The chief platoon leader gives him a menacing look. 'We'll talk about that later,' he says after a moment, 'but there's no time for that now. Join your men. Right, get a move on, the Bolsheviks are already on our left flank, at the Plaza!'

XV

The Tolksdorff squad didn't manage to get away, they couldn't get rid of their uniforms or go into hiding among the ruins or be taken prisoner. They bumped into a battalion of SS storm troopers and were dragged into the battle for the Plaza as if into a whirlpool. In spite of their best efforts they were unable to extricate themselves so they had to join in with the fighting inside the Plaza, the retreat and the renewed storming of the building, and were then swept along by the wave of the retreating SS unit when the Russian mortars put the building under constant fire and the Russian snipers were already in the surrounding houses.

The Plaza went up in bright flames behind them, the fire ate through the wide spaces like an avalanche, until the big building was one great flaming torch. The advance of the Russian tanks over the tracks of Eastern Station from Warschauer Bridge had such momentum that the SS battalion was forced all the way back behind Jannowitz Bridge and only nightfall brought the fighting to an end.

The Tolksdorff squad was firmly wedged between the SS units that held them as if in a vice, they couldn't get either to the top or to the end of the retreating unit, and only the occasional remark by a section leader revealed to Tolksdorff that this fact was by no means a matter of chance. The squad is seen as unreliable, and on special orders of Hauptsturmführer Wiegand it is under strict surveillance. All of a sudden it is also clear to Tolksdorff that the Unterscharführer who shot the wounded man in the outside hall of Silesian

Station was not the liaison between his squad and the battalion, but a guard dog set upon him, tailing his every step and watching suspiciously for every order, every statement, every movement.

The Tolksdorff squad, made up of Dr Böttcher, Gregor, Lassehn, Schröter, Private Ruppert, Corporal Schumann and a further eight men, spent the night in the cellar of a burnt-out house on Stralauer Strasse, which is supposedly a part of the new front line. This front line is nothing but a loose, widely spaced chain of strongholds, which abuts the Spree on Alexanderstrasse, and which is supposed to cross Alexanderplatz to the north. What is happening beyond the Spree, south of the exploded Jannowitz Bridge, is as unknown as the course of the so-called front line north of Alexanderplatz, where it seeps away somewhere between the ruined houses.

The night sky which, filled with flames, had been a dark-red colour, has made way by morning for a pale-grey curtain of cloud below which thick black clouds drift away. With the first light of dawn the artillery fire begins again and the bright flashes of the volley guns twitch in the smoke-filled sky.

Lassehn sits between Schröter and Private Ruppert in a corner of the cellar, eyes wide open, staring motionlessly into the flickering flame of a Hindenburg light that trembles sulphurous, blue and yellow in the darkness and brings the faces out of the gloom like ghostly masks. Schröter leans his head against Lassehn's shoulder and sleeps with his mouth open. Private Ruppert stirs restlessly and twitches at brief intervals. He is lying on an old, torn mattress and has spread his coat over himself.

'Hey,' Ruppert whispers, 'what time is it?'

'After seven,' Lassehn replies.

Ruppert registers the answer and straightens up his torso. 'I've hardly slept,' he says quietly, 'thoughts are circling in me like poison. You know, Comrade, I used not to think about it too much, I've studied and worked, I've taken note of everything, because I've read a lot . . . You know, in a shop like the one I've got you always have a few hours to yourself . . .'

He's happily back in his cigar shop, Lassehn thinks. 'What have you read?' he asks, so as not to sit there in complete silence.

Private Ruppert purses his lips. 'Well, everything imaginable, pretty much at random, but mostly newspapers, of course,' he replies, 'but not much of it stayed in my head. When I really think about it, you know, there was nothing in any book or any newspaper about ...' He hesitates and blinks in the shimmering candlelight.

'What about?' Lassehn encourages him.

'I don't really know how to put it,' Ruppert goes on. 'Well, life, how it's organized . . . You know, when I used to read, revolution in Venezuela or strikes in England, war in Abyssinia or uprising in Bengal, I always said to myself: interesting, terribly interesting, and the best thing about it is that you're sitting here quietly and comfortably in your pretty little shop on Boddinstrasse and being involved in it without having to take any trouble and not really being affected by it. I just took note of it all and stuffed the news and knowledge into me as if stuffing it into a bag. But now . . .'

'And what about now?' Lassehn asks.

Ruppert straightens up completely and draws his legs up to his body. 'And now I've got the question drilling away inside me: why is it all like this, why are they having revolutions in Venezuela, why are they up in arms in India and can't stand each other in Palestine, and I'm squatting in this filthy basement hole . . .'

Lassehn half turns towards the soldier and looks at him with a cautiously serious smile. 'You have found the life that is being played out in the world interesting, but it didn't affect you, thank God it doesn't affect me, you must have thought. But it does affect you, you're just starting to think about it because life has torn you from the tranquillity of your cigar shop, has grabbed you with violent hands, gripped you by the throat and dragged you through the mud of the war. Isn't that the case?' Private Ruppert says nothing, he leans his back against the damp cellar wall, his eyes almost closed, his hair hanging tousled and sticky over his high, wrinkled forehead. 'So,' he asks after a while, 'why are we actually born?'

Lassehn shrugs. He looks into the candle, which is flickering uneasily, distorting outlines.

'To live, isn't that right?' Ruppert goes on. 'It's to live, isn't it?'

'Certainly to live,' Lassehn admits. What's he getting at? he wonders.

Private Ruppert pulls away from the wall again, leans towards Lassehn and grabs him by the shoulders. 'Certainly to live, you say,' he says, his voice trembling with agitation. 'Is it so certain, Comrade? Are we alive? Is this a life? Have you not removed yourself far from your real life, aren't you living here in the outermost tip of the shadow cast by your life, so very close to the border that you step out of the shadow into nothingness at any moment?'

Lassehn doesn't reply.

The soldier's agitated voice breathes hotly at him and revives all the questions that he has kept silent for so long.

'You say we're born to live,' Private Ruppert goes on. 'Don't we seem to be born to tear one another to pieces, to dismember one another and shoot one another down, to drench each other in blood?'

'Calm down, Comrade,' Lassehn says, and carefully removes Ruppert's hands from his shoulders.

'I can't calm down,' the soldier says, his whole body quivering. 'We are born because men love women, and we will die because people hate each other. How can love turn to hatred? We are begotten by people and destroyed by people. Do you understand why it is so, Comrade?'

'It isn't always the case that people die at the hands of other people,' Lassehn says, trying to calm him down.

'But now it is!' Ruppert's voice slides into ever greater agitation. 'Why does the peasant Ivan So-and-so shoot at the tobacconist Karl Ruppert? And why does the music student Joachim Lassehn stick his bayonet into the body of the metalworker Nikita So-and-so? Why does the peasant Ivan So-and-so not peacefully pull his plough in the Ukraine or wherever, and why am I not standing behind my counter selling cigarettes and cigars? Why can't I lead my calm, peaceful, clean, modest life, and sleep with my wife at night? Why can't I do that, Comrade, why?'

Lassehn shrugs and gestures vaguely.

'Must people live like that?' Ruppert asks, now in a furious state of agitation. 'Like pigs, worse than pigs? I was at Romny one time, halfway between Kiev and Harkov, and the front line ran through the middle of the marshes. We couldn't even dig foxholes, we sat behind tree stumps, we lay on the damp, cold, slippery ground and had stretched tarpaulins over our heads against rain and snow, without shifts, without reinforcements, without connection to other units we vegetated on that island of trees, and a few days later we were sitting in a bunker hole, you couldn't stand up straight, and you had to keep baling out water, otherwise you would have drowned miserably in there, and the Russkies were firing their shells right at the entrance, so you were in a dark, wet trap. The fact that we even got out alive . . . Is that a life, do you think?'

Before Lassehn can answer, a voice comes from the other corner of the cellar. 'Christ, you've got nerves of steel,' young Corporal Schumann shouts, 'if you can listen to that nonsense so calmly. Ruppert's talking out of his arse! Can't you tell that he's just greedy for female flesh, that his lecherousness has gone to his brain? He's constantly blethering on about his wife, and his wife again and on and on.'

Lassehn is about to say something, but Private Ruppert is ahead of him. 'What do you know about it, you little toerag?' he shouts. 'What you call lechery is only a yearning for peace, for a life of cleanliness and order, and tenderness, of course, and also a yearning for freedom. Do you have any idea what freedom is, you little know-all?'

'Don't get so worked up,' Corporal Schumann says, and they sense rather than see his indifferent gesture. 'Why wouldn't I know what freedom is?'

'Would you just shut up?' another soldier says. 'Get some shut-eye rather than rabbiting on.'

'How would you know?' Ruppert asks, ignoring the interruption. 'Where would you have encountered freedom? In the Hitler Youth, in labour service or even in the army?'

'Of course,' Corporal Schumann replies. 'My need for freedom has been completely filled, at least I didn't feel a lack of it.'

Ruppert throws his coat aside and is about to stand up, shaken convulsively with agitation. 'Is that part of your freedom too, twelve-year-olds running around with rifles?' he shouts.

'Don't talk twaddle, you old scarecrow,' the corporal says contemptuously.

Ruppert pushes himself up with both hands. 'I have seen that with my own eyes, I swear on God's name,' he says, raising his voice, and turns back to Lassehn. 'It was in Greifenberg in Silesia, a transport of women being taken from the prison in Jauer, on foot, of course, in the cold and snow, and twelve-year-old and fourteen-year-old Hitler youths with rifles were there as guards, and they shot a few of the women as well.'

'Christ alive, Ruppert,' the corporal says with a dismissive wave of the hand, 'don't get so het up about a few women, thieves, abortionists and all kinds of whores.'

'No,' Ruppert says furiously, 'they weren't criminals, they were political prisoners.'

'And you're getting worked up over riff-raff like that?' Corporal Schumann asks, and laughs scornfully. 'A shame they didn't all cop it. I can imagine what sort of women they were, communists, race defilers, nuns, Jehovah's witnesses and twentieth of July plotters, they're worse than murderers and arsonists.'

Ruppert's face turns purple, and a vein throbs menacingly on his neck. 'You stupid brat,' he hisses between clenched teeth, 'you're still wet behind the ears.'

'And you're old, and still stupid,' Schumann says dismissively. 'Have you ever thought, Ruppert, that the best people are dying at the front, and you're troubling your head over a few women?'

'A few?' Ruppert says furiously. 'It was a few hundred.'

'Either way,' Schumann says, raising his hand in the air and letting it fall again. 'Better off rid of them!'

Ruppert tries to get to his feet. 'You little whippersnapper . . .'

Lassehn grabs his hand. 'Calm down, Comrade,' he says. 'Lie down again.'

'Leave me alone!' Private Ruppert shouts, pulls away and is on his feet in an instant. 'That was your freedom, Corporal Winfried Schumann,' he shouts, and stands in front of Schumann with his legs apart, 'striding about like a Great Mogul among the intimidated population by day, and at night taking one of their women to bed, a different one every night, as if everything belonged to you and you were allowed to do whatever you liked and everyone cowered away from you like dogs, that was your freedom!'

'Damn it all, Ruppert, stop getting on my nerves!' Schumann says calmly. 'That was freedom for me, it was the only one I needed. Just a shame everything has ended up like this. Bad luck!'

'You be quiet now, Ruppert,' Tolksdorff intervenes. 'Let's not make life harder than it is already.'

'Freedom is like mountain air,' Dr Böttcher says, 'by unanimous consensus, mountain air is purer and healthier, and yet the lowlander can't simply endure it readily. When he stands on his balcony in the smoky city, he thinks he is breathing pure ozone. It's exactly the same with you lads and freedom, you can't take it, you have to get used to it first. Living the nomadic life as a mercenary isn't freedom, my dear Corporal.'

'But standing behind the counter in the cigar shop and pulling friendly faces for every Tom, Dick and Harry!' Corporal Schumann mocks. 'And always sleeping with the same woman, that's freedom too! No thank you to dried fruit, to freedom that smells mouldy, like mothballs, like nappies . . . You're boring conformists, you're ossified, you don't understand the new freedom at all!'

Beside Dr Böttcher the tall, gaunt private stands up, the round shape of his head making his thin cheeks look particularly hollow. 'Well, then let me tell you something too, you worldly-wise twenty-year-old philosopher, because you seem to identify freedom by following your nose,' he says loudly, almost threateningly, 'your freedom, which you are now mourning, stinks of blood and burning and swims in a sea of tears!'

'Damn it, Schumann,' says a young tank gunner beside the corporal, 'you're no match for the old ones. If we won the war they'd all be cock-a-hoop, they'd all want to cut themselves a slice of victory cake, even if it was baked on a funeral pyre.'

'Yes,' Schumann cuts in quickly, 'now that we're all up to our necks in shit, you suddenly discover your consciences, the stench of war suddenly rises into your sensitive noses. Is it so unusual for things to smell of blood and burning in a war?'

'And why is there war?' Schröter exclaims.

'Because the others don't want to let us live,' the corporal replies, 'because they envied us our rise to power. That much is clear . . .'

'Is it also clear to you,' Dr Böttcher says, 'that the steps on which this rise occurred are made of hecatombs of corpses?'

'Stop complaining all the time,' Gregor says with a placatory hand gesture. 'The corporal knows no better, he doesn't know that even before the war his Führer said: "I will never grant the same right to other peoples as I do to the German. It is our task to subjugate other peoples. The German people are called upon to become the new ruling stratum in the world."'

'That's completely fine,' the corporal says.

'Really?' Gregor says, raising his eyebrows. 'Do you think this is right too: "We need space that makes us independent of every political arrangement. In the east we need dominance as far as the Caucasus or Iran, in the west the French coast, Flanders and Holland. Above all we need Sweden and Norway."'

'I don't know what objections you could have to that,' the corporal says calmly, 'those are all territories that have been fertilized for years with German blood, and which even today bear the mark of German culture. It is our right to rule these territories politically as well.'

'The conquering expeditions of hordes of Teutonic nomads and the foundation of Hanseatic bank branches: is that what you call your right?' Gregor calls excitedly.

'Oh, give me a break,' the corporal says, disgruntled. 'You old people and us young people don't understand each other any more, we probably never did. Because you old people have closed yourselves off to the new consciousness, because you always have reservations, because you're trapped in your traditional ways of thinking, that's why everything went wrong in the end.'

'Since you seem to agree with the aims of your great Führer, don't let me deprive you of some more of his remarks,' Gregor says, clearly struggling to contain himself. 'How, for example, do you like this one: "If we want to achieve this, I am willing to assume responsibility for the blood sacrifice of the whole of German youth. I will not hesitate to take the deaths of two or three million Germans on my conscience."'

'Where did you get that one from?' the tank gunner asks.

'From a book published in Switzerland five years ago, whose author is no less a figure than the President of the Senate, Dr Rauschning,' Gregor replies. 'Listen carefully, Corporal, and you too, young soldier. Your great Führer, the patron of all civilization and the great friend of German youth, also said the following: "If I send the bloom of German youth into the storm of steel of the coming war without feeling the slightest regret, do I not have the right to eliminate millions of an inferior race that multiplies like vermin?" What do you have to say to that?'

The corporal shrugs. 'Adolf Hitler can't be measured according to the standards of your conformist bourgeois morality,' he says arrogantly. 'He's the right man, except that you old people . . . Well, see above!'

'You still believe in him?' Schröter asks.

'Of course,' the corporal replies quickly. 'And why not? Because he's run into difficulties?'

'You idiot!' Schröter says furiously. 'Why has he run into difficulties? Have a think about that one.'

Corporal Schumann waves his hand casually and stretches out again.

'You've run out of answers?' Schröter asks. 'All of a sudden your slobbering mouth is shut.'

'Oh, just bugger off . . .' the corporal says, and turns onto his side. 'None of it matters a damn any more in any case.'

The cellar sinks back into silence, with only the breathing of the men and the thin, flickering light of the candle.

Tolksdorff sits on a case by the entrance to the cellar, his elbows propped on his knees and his chin resting in his hands, staring at the small, guttering flame of the Hindenburg light. Pale, gloomy, grey daylight shimmers through the cellar door, which has been blocked with a twisted, rusting iron grille. Outside the guns thunder at longer and shorter intervals, the mortars hiss, a roaring hail of steel comes down on the city, a volley gun, wailing and booming, rains its projectiles over Jannowitz Bridge, the falling shells shake the cellar and send dust and plaster up into the air like geysers.

The blast from a shell falling nearby shoots deep into the cellar passageway and overturns the iron grille.

The sleepers wake with a start. 'Are the Russians here at last?' one asks drowsily.

'I heard a little birdie!' says the young tank gunner lying next to Schumann.

'Hellwig, check on the sentry and take over from him,' Tolksdorff commands flatly.

A young soldier gets to his feet straight away. 'Yes, sir!' As he lifts the iron grille to put it back in place, Lassehn jumps up to join him. 'I'll come outside with you,' he says, 'and get some fresh air.'

They climb the broken steps of the cellar stairs and take over from the sentry, who is leaning in an alcove smoking a cigarette.

'The Russkies are just over there,' the sentry says, pointing at the ruins on Alexanderstrasse, from where the tracer fire from a machine gun sweeps low over the ground, whips the tarmac and bounces back up again.

Lassehn and the young soldier stand in the alcove and look along the street. It is morning by now, but the flaming torches of the burning houses have formed a black wall of cloud that weighs heavy and dark over the bright blue of the spring sky.

'It looks like Stalingrad,' the young soldier says.

'Yes,' Lassehn says, 'like Stalingrad. Curious how our thoughts keep returning to Stalingrad. Stalingrad, it's as if the name is branded onto us . . .'

The young soldier Hellwig looks Lassehn quizzically in the face. 'Yes, Stalingrad.' The words drop heavy from his lips. 'Stalingrad, that gave us the first push, the crucial push, it threw us to the ground, psychically perhaps more than militarily, at the time we'd actually been beaten groggy, but we weren't out for the count and got up again at seven or eight, we still thought we might have a chance at least to go the distance, but now . . .'

'But now it's the KO,' Lassehn completes his sentence.

'Yes, the KO.'

'Not only of the war,' Lassehn adds, 'but of our whole existence.'

The young soldier gulps violently, he pulls his coat tighter around his hips and leans against the wall with his eyes closed. Sharp, manly features are already appearing in his young, almost boyish face.

'It's all pointless,' he says quietly, 'sentry duty, the war, life generally, sometimes you feel like firing a bullet into your head. What's going to become of us? Do you have a clue, Comrade?'

Lassehn nods.

'I do have a clue,' he replies.

'Which is?'

'I mean what we can become, what we must become: human beings.'

The young soldier laughs briefly. 'After being reduced to animals, we're supposed to become human beings? Never going to happen, Comrade. You can turn an animal into a creature that's like a human being, but never an actual human being.'

'Are you an animal, Comrade?' Lassehn asks insistently.

'I only exercise the functions of an animal, eating, drinking, digesting and sex, fight for life, shelter and warmth, that has swallowed up all our thoughts,' the young soldier replies. 'Those are the poles around which my whole life has been turning for years. Disgusting!'

'What do you do for a living?' Lassehn asks.

The other man opens his eyes and looks gloomily at Lassehn. 'A living? Machine-gunner, soldier, hero, aspiring mass-grave candidate.'

'Seriously!'

'That is serious!'

'So how old are you?'

'Supposedly I'm twenty-two, but I must be older, a lot older, our generation is old, ancient.'

'Twenty-two?' Lassehn asks. 'And you've never had a job? Did you become a soldier straight from school?'

'Yes, I even volunteered!'

'Volunteered?'

'Yes, volunteered, you're amazed aren't you? When I'd done my middle-school leaving exam and my labour service, I was just seventeen, and wanted to become a dentist. My old man even had an apprenticeship ready for me.'

'And why didn't you take the apprenticeship and volunteer instead?'

'Because I had to!'

'You had to? I thought you volunteered . . .'

'I did,' the young soldier says impatiently, 'it sounds crazy, but it's the truth. It's like that everywhere, voluntary compulsion. Or haven't you noticed that? Voluntary compulsion, with moral pressure or massive blackmail.'

'You'll have to explain it to me.'

'There's not much to explain,' the young soldier replies. 'When we'd done our year of labour service, the lieutenant turned up and delivered this big speech about the fatherland, a war that had been forced upon us and so on, and at the end he asked . . . Yes, not something like: who's going to volunteer for the Wehrmacht?, but: is there anyone who doesn't want to volunteer?'

Lassehn nods. 'So that's how it was!'

'Yes, exactly like that. Could you step forward and say: I'm not volunteering? You couldn't, even if you wanted to. Well, and that's how it was, you were half pushed, you half fell. And then the war impels you ruthlessly onward or backward or sideways, you're only staggering now, you can clearly see the abyss in front of you, very clearly, but you're too tired, too apathetic, too submissive to pull yourself back or change direction, you go on obeying because it's the easiest thing.'

'The war that was supposed to bring you freedom made you its prisoner,' Lassehn says.

The young soldier nods. 'That's exactly how it is. It was never so clear to me as when I had to guard some prisoners for a few days; in essence I had no more freedom of movement than the prisoners did, I was chained to an order just as they were, and actually the only difference was that I was in front of the barbed wire and they were behind it.'

'Although the terms in front of and behind are only relative,' Lassehn adds.

The young soldier nods again. 'Of course, you're right, Comrade. The concept of inescapability has finally rendered me completely apathetic, you obey, march, fight, and it no longer matters in the slightest whether it's at Lake Ilmen or the Müggelsee, in the Valdai mountains or the Rehberge, whether I'm patrolling the streets of Minsk or on sentry duty here in a bombed house in Berlin right now . . . What's the name of the street?'

'Stralauer Strasse,' Lassehn replies.

'. . . on Stralauer Strasse, Berlin, house number unknown, the Russians are two hundred or three hundred metres away . . . Damn it, we've been dead for ages!' He stands up and strikes his chest. 'Everything in here died long ago, even if the heart is still beating and the lungs still breathing, we're just wandering around like shades. You too, Comrade!'

He's reached the point where we were standing until a week ago, Lassehn thinks, he's still trying to discern a meaning in the frenzy of meaninglessness, he is still looking for a spot of light in the thicket of darkness, he hasn't yet found the goal that lifts him above his own small self. He takes two cigarettes from his pocket. 'Have a smoke first, Hellwig. That's your name, isn't it?'

The young soldier nods and flips open a lighter. 'How do you know . . . Oh yes, the lieutenant addressed me by my name. Allow me to introduce myself: Erhard Hellwig from Poggendorf in the district of Greifswald, twenty-two years old, machine gunner by profession. You?'

Lassehn replies.

'Music student?' says the young soldier. 'You're a music student as much as I'm a dentist. It's utter crap! What that soldier was saying just now, that stogie salesman from Neukölln, had something going for it.'

'You mean . . .'

'Yes, all we've ever done is military service. Work? We don't know it at all. A goal? We haven't got one. I understand that old guy very well, he wants to stand behind his counter like others at their workbench or threshing machine. We alone, if we are ever to survive this war, will be standing there with empty hands that can do nothing but shoot, load, stab, aim, drop bombs. We have learned to fire a sticky bomb, put a belt into a machine gun, we know what a wind correction angle is, and a dismounted line of sight, but what else do we know, and what else have we learned? One day we come back and only then are we supposed to start learning?' He shakes his head.

'How do you imagine your future life?' Lassehn asks.

'Not at all,' young Private Hellwig replies, 'I can't imagine anything at all, I just let myself drift, like a piece of wood in water. Perhaps I'll fetch up somewhere, then it'll be fine, but perhaps the stream will lead me to the sea, and I'll float around for the rest of my life, that's fine too, but perhaps a bullet will get me first, and I'm all right with that as well. I'm all right with everything. Anyone who survives this war will have done it by himself, an old soldier once said to me. That's exactly so.'

'No, you mustn't think that way,' Lassehn says helplessly, and he himself feels that his objection is weak and ineffectual.

'You mustn't,' the young soldier says and laughs briefly. 'Let me tell you something, Comrade,' he goes on seriously. 'I'm just frightened.'

'Frightened?' Lassehn asks, surprised.

'Yes, frightened of so-called civilian life, frightened of the life ahead of us, frightened of not being up to that life. You and I, and probably all of us thought we had solid ground under our feet, that we could absorb safety and confidence from the future, as an advance, so to speak, and now it turns out that our supports have broken like matches. Wherever we reach, our hands clutch the void, whatever we think about, our thoughts fall into nothing.'

They silently finish their cigarettes. At regular intervals the machine gun on Alexanderstrasse sprays Schicklerstrasse and Stralauer Strasse, the gunfire is now advancing from the Märkische Platz, beyond the Spree, mortars are firing into Neue Friedrichstrasse.

When there is a brief pause in firing it is unreally still for several minutes, only the fire of battle seethes in the distance, and suddenly Lassehn remembers standing here often as a boy, less than 200 paces away, listening to the thirty-seven bells of the parish church, every seven and a half minutes a few notes sounded, every quarter of an hour a chord, every half-hour a chorale and every full hour a chorale with prelude, and even then it seemed unreal to him how the pure, delicate tones of the Glockenspiel floated down from the top of the tower, how they were sprinkled over the troubled city like drops of holy water. Now the tower has been demolished under the fist of the war, the bells have melted to a shapeless mass among the burning pews.

'Tell me,' the young soldier begins again. 'Do you actually believe in God?'

Lassehn looks up in surprise. 'That's hard to say,' he replies.

'If you can answer that so fast,' the young soldier says slowly, 'it's already a bad sign. You can't answer a question like that either with a quick yes or a consistent no.'

'It's not quite as simple as that,' Lassehn objects. 'I don't know if your concept of God matches mine.'

'So in your view God is a very personal matter, attitude, vision of each individual?'

'Quite right,' Lassehn replies excitedly. 'Are you sure your idea of God corresponds perfectly to theological doctrine?'

The young soldier shrugs.

'I don't know, Lassehn, I have only a vague sensation of what is called God. But of course God must exist, because there must be something higher than man.'

'God is enclosed within my own breast,' Lassehn says slowly, 'only there, not above this sky to which the burning of the cities, the stench of millions of incinerated people, the cries of the tortured rise. God is only in my breast, Comrade, God is love, compassion, goodness, conscience, but not a supernatural being as you were taught in confirmation class, not a creature that you can invoke and pray to, unless you invoke the goodness within your own breast.'

'And if there is nothing more?' the young soldier asks. 'What if there are only innards, and no soul? What then?'

'If there really is nothing more,' Lassehn replies urgently, 'if no spark really lights up within you, then you are nothing but an animal.'

The young soldier stares steadily into the little scrap of bright sky that appears for a few seconds among the drifting clouds of smoke and into which the explosions hurl their bright-red mushrooms against the black background. 'God's ways are wonderful, we learned in Scripture, unfathomable, ineffable and beyond our understanding.'

'Yes,' Lassehn adds emphatically, 'and responsibility is thus transferred to the supernatural realm, because God is almighty, all-knowing, all-blessing, and ever-present, and if almighty God can't change earthly conditions, if all that happens does so according to His will and with His will, what can we humans change, since we are mere clay in His hand? If God is omnipotent, why does *He* not walk the earth with fire and a sword to eradicate all those who shame his name by invoking him and at the same time torturing creatures supposedly made in His image in gas chambers, air-raid shelters and trenches? Where are you, God, and what are you like, God, I ask, that you ignore the tears, the pains, the fears of human beings, that you allow them to plunge deeper and deeper into hatred, shame, guilt, suffering, enmity, misfortune, misery and desperation?'

The young soldier has been breathing hard while listening to Lassehn's outburst. 'But God is at the very least, in rare minutes, the only mainstay.'

Lassehn laughs bitterly. 'The only mainstay, a refuge between the fear of death and the torment of conscience or, as Goethe calls it, a supplement to our wretchedness. Precisely because human beings believe in a superordinated God – and that is particularly true of the Germans – who in the end organizes life meaningfully and justly, because everything is transposed to transcendence and withdrawn from our understanding, precisely for that reason God is not invoked within our own breast. Looking into heaven, which is mere material, prevents us from looking into our own breast, where the soul lives.'

'Now you've completely confused me,' the young soldier says, his voice a mixture of sadness and irritation.

'When old concepts collapse, there is always confusion until the new appears,' Lassehn replies.

Then they fall silent again. A second machine gun is now firing madly from Alexanderstrasse, the projectiles from the mortars are now lying on the intersection of Neue Friedrichstrasse and Stralauer Strasse, and hissing sprays of water rise every now and again from the dark river.

'The Russians are preparing to charge,' Hellwig says indifferently.

'Some are already coming,' Lassehn says. 'There!'

From the Roland-Ufer two shadows turn into Stralauer Strasse, they are covered by a cloud of smoke and only their outlines can be made out.

The young soldier raises his rifle, shoulders it and takes aim.

Lassehn pushes the rifle away. 'Are you crazy?' he says. 'They're the best thing that could happen to us, if . . .'

He doesn't finish the sentence, because at that moment a shell wails towards them and buries itself in the cracked carriageway. They fall quickly to their knees and wait for the next one, but subsequent shells fall further away.

When they get back up, the two shadows have become two people, they have passed through the veil of smoke and are now pressing themselves close against the shattered walls of the houses.

'Those aren't Russians,' Hellwig says, setting his carbine aside. 'I thought it was curious, as long as no one here is firing they won't attack.'

'No,' Lassehn says absently, staring with burning eyes at the two people who are now slowly feeling their way along the street. His heart is suddenly thumping violently, fear juddering through his body.

'They seem to be two Volkssturm men,' the young soldier says, standing on tiptoes the better to be able to follow their progress. 'No, a Volkssturm man and a woman.'

Lassehn can't make out the faces of the two people, they are black with smoke and yet . . . His throat feels as if it has been tied shut, he wants to shout out, but only a hoarse croak rises from his larynx.

'What's up with you?' Hellwig asks. 'You suddenly look as if you've seen a ghost.'

At last the vice around Lassehn's throat releases his voice. 'Wiegand!' he shouts, and puts his hands in front of his mouth like a funnel. 'Wiegand! Wiegand!' The two people stop, look around as if to confirm to one another that in the noise of gunfire and explosions they heard a shout.

Lassehn can no longer contain himself, he leaves his cover and, taking long strides, runs across the street.

'Wiegand!' he says, and hurries towards them.

'Lassehn!' Lucie Wiegand cries, and throws both arms around his neck.

XVI

When Lassehn enters the cellar with the Wiegands, the room is still filled with the silence of resignation. Tolksdorff sits motionless on the box by the door, leaning against the wall with his arms folded over his chest.

'Doctor, Schröter!' Lassehn says excitedly. 'Here come two good acquaintances!'

'Stop talking such nonsense,' says Wiegand.

Dr Böttcher initially looked with perplexity at the figures whose outlines are sharply drawn in the door frame of the entrance to the cellar, then jumps to his feet and walks towards them.

'I'm incredibly pleased you're here,' he says, and this time his voice lacks its usual cool composure.

'This is an extraordinary coincidence,' Schröter says, and energetically shakes the hands of both Wiegands.

'It's no coincidence,' Wiegand replies, 'we were looking for you. I don't suppose there's room for my wife anywhere here?'

Tolksdorff rises heavily to his feet. 'Hello,' he says flatly, and points at the box. 'Unfortunately this is the only seating I'm able to offer you, madam.'

'I still can't believe,' Dr Böttcher says emotionally, 'that you found your way here.'

'Why didn't you stop at Silesian Station?' Schröter asks, 'Or wasn't that possible?'

Wiegand smilingly dismisses the hail of questions. 'Slowly,

slowly, one at a time. And there isn't much to tell. We were sitting in Klose's cellar . . .'

'. . . thinking about you . . .' Lucie Wiegand chips in. 'We were terribly alone. But there's a special bitterness in having to part just when we need each other most urgently.'

'So we were sitting in the dark cellar,' Wiegand continues, 'which seemed twice as big in our loneliness, we heard the SS crashing about in the flat and in the shop, then the house was quiet again. The machine guns were already rattling outside, the mortars were spitting incessantly into the street. A few hours passed like that, we spent our time alternately sleeping and waiting. Then, towards evening, the house came to life again, running, shouting, screams, slamming doors. The Russians are here at last, we thought, but we decided to wait a little longer. The hubbub grew louder and louder, and then all of a sudden it was completely silent. There was still wild shooting outside, but not a sound inside the house. We couldn't work out what was going on. Whereas the cellar had previously seemed so enormous, and because of our loneliness the walls had moved infinitely far away that they no longer offered us protection, but instead left us exposed, now . . .'

'. . . now they were growing towards us, they were suddenly pressing in on us, so tightly that they almost took our breath away,' Lucie Wiegand adds. 'Years ago I read a short story by Edgar Allan Poe, in which he describes the ceiling of a prison cell falling with slow and deadly inevitability towards the criminal, that's more or less how we felt.' Lucie Wiegand shudders at the memory of those hours, and shivers as she hunches her shoulders.

'As my wife just said,' Wiegand goes on, taking his wife's hands, 'it took our breath away, and as we imagined the room shrinking the air supply also seemed to go into swift decline. But it wasn't our imagination, gentlemen, that was exactly what was happening, we were running out of air, and suddenly we caught the smell of burning. At first we refused to admit it, because after all everything smells like burning these days, but in the end the smell became so intense that we left the cellar. It was high time!'

'Because the house was on fire from top to bottom,' Lucie Wiegand adds.

'The rest is quickly told,' Wiegand says. 'At first we tried to reach the Russians, but we couldn't do that, so we went in search of you.'

'But how was it possible . . .' Schröter begins.

'. . . for us to find you?' Wiegand interjects. 'It wasn't by any means as difficult as you might assume, we knew that the whole area around Küstriner Platz was occupied by the Muchalla SS battalion, so we took it that Lieutenant Tolksdorff's squad was part of that. We asked around . . .'

'Didn't you stop and think, Wiegand . . .' Dr Böttcher begins carefully.

Wiegand says nothing and avoids his wife's eyes. 'It's time to go for broke,' he says. 'It's nonsense to try and avoid the decision.'

'Bravo!' cries Corporal Schumann. 'Exactly what the Führer says! What are you actually talking about?'

'Whether plum cake is better made with yeast or baking powder,' Schröter says cuttingly.

'You're incredibly witty, Grandpa,' the corporal fires back. 'Greetings from me, oh German heroine!' He gets to his feet and bows ironically to Lucie Wiegand.

'You're still very loyal,' Wiegand snaps at him.

'Gallows humour,' the corporal shrugs. 'So, what's happening out there?' he says, turning to Wiegand. 'Where have the Russians got to?'

'I even have a newspaper,' Wiegand replies.

'There are still newspapers?' Private Ruppert cries, and pushes his way into the circle. 'What does the *Völkischer Beobachter-Morgenpost* have to say?'

'That's quite a special newspaper,' Wiegand replies, 'neither *Völkischer Beobachter* nor *Berliner Morgenpost*. Here, take a look.'

Everyone peers at the little sheet of paper that Wiegand is holding in his hand.

Der Panzerbär
27 April 1945
Battle organ of the defenders of Greater Berlin

'Wonderful,' says Dr Böttcher, and looks at the coat of arms, 'the Berlin bear with a shovel and a rocket launcher. At least the headlines leave nothing to be desired.

"Bulwark Against Bolshevism"
"Berlin: Mass Grave for Soviet Tanks"'

'God almighty, don't talk so much,' one of the privates says, 'read out the Wehrmacht report if there's one in there. Perhaps they've thrown the Russians out of Berlin yet again, and nobody's told us.'

'Right then, listen to this,' Wiegand says.

"From the Führer's headquarters, 26 April

The Battle for Berlin

In the battle for Berlin, crucial for the future of the Reich and for the life of Europe, reserves were thrown into the conflict by both sides. In the southern part of the Reich capital heavy street battles are being fought in Zehlendorf, Steglitz and on the southern edge of the Tempelhof Field. In the east and the north our troops engaged in bitter resistance, bravely supported by units of the Hitler Youth, the Party and the Volkssturm, at Silesian Station and Görlitz Station, as well as between Tegel and Siemensstadt. The battle also flared up in Charlottenburg. Many Soviet tanks were destroyed in this fighting."

'This tells us,' Dr Böttcher says, 'that there can no longer be any question of surrounding Berlin, they went past that long ago, the city centre is surrounded, the suburbs have already been taken by the Russians. There may be the odd pocket of resistance here and there, but this report tells us quite clearly that the noose is tightening with deadly certainty.'

'And this noose is throttling us too,' Private Ruppert says.

'Cling together, swing together,' says Corporal Schumann, 'there's nothing you can do. Adieu, the glories of the cigar-dispensary.'

Ruppert walks quickly towards the corporal and raises a threatening fist.

'Ruppert!' Tolksdorff shouts, calling him to order.

Ruppert forces himself to retreat, his face is dark red, his gaunt, unshaven cheeks twitch violently up and down. 'Lieutenant,' he gasps, 'I can't go on . . . and all these flippant remarks from Schumann . . .' Schröter drags the enraged soldier deeper into the cellar. 'Pull yourself together!' he says severely.

'Letting this brat swagger like that!' Ruppert says, shaking his head.

'What's happening on the other fronts?' the lieutenant asks.

'Defensive successes all over the place,' Wiegand replies, 'but the other lot are still charging forward, Ulm, Tuttlingen, Bremen, Troppau, the whole Po valley lost . . . Total war is turning into total collapse.'

'Why don't they just call it a day?' asks the tall, gaunt private, speaking as always with a quiet, tired voice, as if he were talking to himself.

Schröter turns to face him. 'Hitler said he's going to fight until five past twelve. He will keep *that* word, you can rely on it.'

'Here is another very interesting report,' Wiegand calls, and waves the newspaper about. 'That must . . .' He pauses and turns round, because a shadow has fallen over him.

'There's someone coming,' Corporal Schumann says and stands up. 'I hope that's some supplies coming, because if you've got nothing to do at least you'd like to have a bite to eat, even if it's just your last meal before the rope.'

A pair of heavy boots thunders down the steps, rubble slides and falls into the cellar in a cloud of dust, then an SS man appears in the door frame.

'Lieutenant Tolksdorff,' he says and stands to attention, 'the Hauptsturmführer is waiting for you to come to the situation report. Please follow me!'

Tolksdorff rises heavily to his feet and puts on his steel helmet. 'Corporal Schumann, you take command in my absence!'

Then the lieutenant and the SS man leave the cellar.

'Situation report!' Private Ruppert says scornfully. 'He's off his head.'

'Perhaps he wants to introduce surrender negotiations,' says the tall, gaunt soldier.

'*You're* off your head!' Schumann rages at him. 'And now shut up. I won't have people saying things like this!'

'I'm not going to let you shut me up,' Ruppert says, 'not you, of all people.'

Schumann adjusts his coat and buckles his belt. 'Ruppert, I'll tell you once more . . .'

'Take a look,' Schröter mocks, 'a corporal from head to toe!'

'And you can shut up too,' the corporal says, turning to Schröter. 'The lieutenant is far too decent, he's given you too much leeway.'

'Hey,' Ruppert says menacingly, 'I have a hand grenade here, you can have it in the face, even if I go up with it!'

'Be reasonable, you people,' Dr Böttcher cuts in.

'Are you saying I'm unreasonable?' the corporal flares up.

Dr Böttcher gives a placatory wave. 'That's not what I meant,' he says evasively, and turns to Wiegand. 'Let's hear what else it says in the paper.'

'A very interesting report,' Wiegand replies.

"Berlin, 26 April

New Commander of the Luftwaffe.
Reich Marshal Hermann Goering Falls Ill.

Reich Marshal Hermann Göring has fallen ill with a chronic heart condition that has persisted for some time, and which has now entered a more acute stage. He himself has therefore asked to be released during this time, which requires the deployment of all available energy, from the leadership of the Luftwaffe and the tasks connected to it.

The Führer has granted this request.

As the new Commander-in-Chief of the Luftwaffe, the Führer has appointed General von Greim, at the same time promoting him to Field Marshal."

'He fell ill at the right time,' Private Poppe says. 'A shame you can't get yourself written off sick as an ordinary grunt.'

'Extremely interesting,' says Dr Böttcher, 'above all because it doesn't say whether he is holding on to his other offices. It's clear that the thing stinks. The Führer's deputy suddenly goes mad, and the Reich Marshal has a chronic heart condition.'

'Where does it say that about Göring?' Corporal Schumann asks, his voice now uncertain, having almost entirely lost its harsh edge.

'You don't believe it?' Wiegand asks him. 'Here, read for yourself, on page three. And here, you can check, this is *Panzerbär* and not *Pravda*.'

The corporal takes the paper and reads.

'Surely you're going to believe your own newspaper?' Schröter asks.

'The paper might just be some sort of forgery,' the corporal says, but his voice sounds flat and unconvinced.

'Who published it?'

He turns the paper round and reads under his voice: '*Der Panzerbär*, Publisher Fp.-No. 67,700.'

'You only believe what fits with your preconceptions,' Schröter says. 'Christ, will you finally open your eyes?'

The corporal turns round and crumples the newspaper.

'Is that checkmate, Corporal Schumann?' Ruppert asks.

'If it all goes to hell, I'm going down with it!' Schumann says furiously. 'Or do you think I'm going to stay here in this stinking hole to drown in my own swill, or be taken prisoner by the Bolsheviks?'

'But?' Dr Böttcher asks.

The corporal is stubbornly silent. 'I've got a plan ...' he says after a while.

Lucie Wiegand gets up and rests a hand on his arm. 'You're practically still a boy,' she says quietly. 'Why do you want to throw your life away?'

Schumann looks her in the eye with a dark, crooked smile. 'You wouldn't understand, young woman,' he says.

'Why not?'

'Because it's men's business.'

Schröter is about to object, but Lucie Wiegand dismisses him with a quick wave of her hand. 'I have four children, young Corporal, I carried each of them in my body for nine months, I shielded them with my body, I fed them with my blood, I bore them with so much pain that every time I thought I was going to die, so violent were the pains that raged in me and the spasms that shook me. And the same happened to my mother.'

'Why are you telling me that?' the corporal asks, still displeased.

'How can it be worthless, a life created in love, a life awaited in hope and longing and brought into the world in blissful pain?' Lucie Wiegand says insistently.

'Those are fine words, nothing more,' the corporal says, and turns round abruptly, then he walks to the basement exit and stares into the faint, fluid light of day.

'You have never yet loved, young man,' Lucie Wiegand says softly.

The corporal doesn't reply, he stands motionless in the doorway, a frail young figure in a worn, field-grey coat, hands deep in his pockets, with long and stringy fair hair that reaches down to the back of his neck.

'Can't you see by now . . .' Private Ruppert begins.

Corporal Schumann swings violently round, pulls his hands from his coat pockets and puts his steel helmet on his head with a practised movement.

'Leave me in peace, all of you!' he shouts. 'I can't see a thing!'

'You're not quite right,' Private Ruppert says, tapping his forehead with his index finger.

'Shut up!' Schumann roars again. 'Stand to attention, you hopeless old fool! Right, on your feet, that's enough dozing!'

'When a person goes mad, he does so from the head first,' a soldier says from his mattress.

'Get up, you lousy bastards, fall in!'

'The corporal is escaping into his ordering tone of voice,'

Dr Böttcher says ironically. 'Repressed feelings of anxiety lead to an over-intensification of the sense of self.'

'Stop talking such nonsense!' the corporal roars at him. 'You're to keep your trap shut just as much as everybody else! Right, on your feet!'

'You can kiss me where I'm prettiest,' a private soldier says without moving from the mattress.

'That's a refusal to obey orders, that's mutiny!' Schumann yells. 'You know what's at stake.'

'What you need is a cold bath,' Schröter says.

The corporal raises his sub-machine gun.

'The lieutenant has transferred command to me during his absence,' he shouts. 'I'll use this gun.'

Two soldiers get heavily to their feet. 'He's got NCO rage,' one of them says as he straightens his belt. 'Nothing to be done.'

'I'll wait one more minute,' Schumann says in a slightly quieter voice. 'If the platoon isn't in ranks by then I'm reporting you.'

'Best thing would be to go straight to the Führer,' Poppe says comfortably, and sits down slowly and awkwardly. 'This time, unusually, he's not living far from the front.'

'I forbid you . . .' the corporal says furiously and raises his sub-machine gun.

Schröter jumps over to him and knocks the weapon out of his hand. 'You've really lost your mind,' he says furiously.

The corporal doesn't defend himself, he stands there with his hands clenched, his shoulders twitch, his cheeks tremble, the corners of his mouth droop, his face collapses in on itself, then he bends his arm in front of his face and leans against the wall, a dry sob shaking his body.

'His nerves are shot,' Schröter says, and picks up the sub-machine gun.

The corporal lifts his head from the hollow of his arm for a few seconds. 'I wouldn't have fired at you, Poppe,' he says, 'you've got to believe that, the sub-machine gun still had its safety catch on.' A few tears run down his cheeks.

Lucie Wiegand runs her hand gently down his back. 'It'll all be fine again, son,' she says tenderly.

The corporal wipes the tears from his face with the sleeve of his jacket. 'Leave me in peace!' he says harshly, his lips twitching.

No one says a word. The collapse of the young corporal, his tears and his last attempt to resist an incomprehensible fate that dragged him from the heights of fame into this cellar in the shattered capital, have silenced everyone. The one standing there now, arms dangling, in the cellar doorway, staring into the flowing grey daylight, is a symbol of a lost, abandoned, betrayed youth.

Suddenly a spasm runs through the young corporal, he pulls himself up to attention, steps aside to leave the doorway free and shouts loudly, 'Attention!' Footsteps ring out, two grey shadows fall through the door, two large men bend down and come into the cellar. Lieutenant Tolksdorff and Hauptsturmführer Wiegand.

'Tolksdorff squad with fifteen men!' Corporal Schumann announces.

The Hauptsturmführer thanks him and peers into the dark cellar, in which the faintly flickering light of the Hindenburg candle and the thin grey daylight mingle into a gloomy twilight.

'Bloody dark down here,' says the Hauptsturmführer.

Lieutenant Tolksdorff peers tensely into the semi-darkness, his eyes seeking the two Wiegands. They have withdrawn unnoticed into the furthest corner of the cellar, which is totally plunged in deep shadow.

'Comrades!' the Hauptsturmführer says, his voice sharp and treading a thin line between joviality and command. 'The battle for the capital is being fought with great ferocity, but it is by no means decided, as our enemies imagine. This morning I was ordered to the Führer's headquarters, and stood face to face with the Führer, I received the Knight's Cross of the Iron Cross from his very hand, and my promotion to Sturmbannführer.'

There was something that struck me, Lassehn thinks, standing in the second row with Ruppert, Schröter and the young tank gunner, he's got the Knight's Cross around his neck, and he's even had time to add the fourth star to his epaulettes and collar.

'Comrades!' Sturmbannführer Wiegand continues. 'I regard this decoration and promotion as a decoration for the whole battalion, of which you too are now members, Comrades! Our situation is serious, but it isn't hopeless. The Führer is among us, and he confidently told those who were gathered around him today that the reserve armies are advancing on Berlin from all sides. It can't be long before the containment ring is broken through. But that will be the first step along the path on which we repel the Bolsheviks. We must rally closely around the Führer in Teutonic loyalty and form a solid kernel of resistance.'

He pauses briefly and lets his eyes wander over their faces.

'Comrades! I am depending on you. Remember your oath. Heil to our Führer!'

XVII

Time drips, heavy as lead, one minute is like another, one hour as monotonous as the next. The armed attacks become violent and ease again, they stretch out into a long, deafening barrage or come down briefly like a shower of rain, the artillery rumbles in the distance like an approaching storm or crashes like nearby thunder.

One ruined house is like another, one perhaps robbed of all its innards and only preserving its outward face, the other stonily collapsed in on itself. One cellar is like another, low-ceilinged, damp, filled with the smell of mildew and populated by rats, one perhaps rectangular, the other all crooked angles. There are cellars that are like crushed skulls, but between and below the ruins there are also cellars whose skull-ceilings have held and survived the pressure of the collapsing masonry.

In the first kind of cellar the skeletons of the dead still crouch, with limbs that are cramped, twisted, staved in and crushed, the rats dart quickly and greedily around, in these days of death they have eaten their fill, because there is a wide selection of human and animal corpses in cellars and tunnels, in courtyards and streets.

The second kind of cellar is inhabited by creatures which science identifies as Homo sapiens. In their way of life, however, they deviate considerably from the familiar pattern for this species; with the increasing duration of their cellar and cave existence they reveal the qualities that distinguish their habits from those of animals, and are evolving back to the species of primitive man which has just crossed the threshold of the age of human consciousness.

The Tolksdorff group of the SS battalion moved on from Stralauer Strasse to the city centre, as it was threatened with containment from Molkenmarkt, in the shelter of night they retreated down many streets and across many squares, climbed over piles of rubble and debris, stumbled over wrecked cars and tanks, fell into shell craters, forced their way across courtyards and through holes in walls, ran down burning streets and in the end lost their bearings. The dark of night flickers with the muzzle flashes of the volley guns, phosphorescing with a green glow over the jagged silhouettes of the ruins, and is illuminated completely for seconds at a time by the slowly falling parachute flares from the planes, which bathe everything in a repellently harsh light and violently hurl the destruction into the field of vision.

At last the Tolksdorff group found an empty cellar whose ceiling is only burst in a few places. In this cellar, they don't even know which street it is on, whether it is in the defence zone or already in the occupied territory or in the strip of rubble known in military terminology as no-man's-land, in this cellar the group spends the rest of the night. The cellars on the right and left are occupied by the other units of the battalion, which stay in contact by courier.

Not until the first waves of morning light break through the layer of haze and clouds of smoke that lie wide and heavy over the torsos of the houses and lighten the darkness a little is it possible for them to get their bearings. A toppled street sign shows that the cellar belongs to a house on Anhalter Strasse, and soon it also turns out that the retreat to this area was by no means random, because the battalion has been more or less selected to raise a blockade in the south of Friedrichstadt, to hold off the Russians advancing from Tempelhof down Belle-Alliance-Strasse towards the Hallesches Tor. The battalion has also been assigned the honourable task of taking over the immediate protection of the government district.

Only the faintest hint of the dawning day forces its way into the Tolksdorff group's cellar. Lassehn and the young tank gunner stand as a double sentry post in the gateway, whose arch is shattered and whose weighty pillars bear the traces of exploding shells. The ruins of this area date from some time ago, grass sprouts among the rubble and in the cracks in the burst asphalt, in the gutter and between the rust-red tram tracks, the grass the only colour in this grey, gashed, stony landscape.

'These were all once blocks,' Lassehn says thoughtfully, 'blocks of flats, flats with rooms, rooms with furniture, furniture with crockery and clothing . . .'

'. . . and in the flats and among the furniture, people moved,' the tank gunner concludes.

Lassehn looks at the young soldiers in their black uniforms. He has been a little noisy and boastful, and in fact the only one to take the side of Corporal Schumann. Since the collapse of the corporal he too has become meek and has held back, the superior irony with which he and Schumann had enjoyed irritating the older privates and Volkssturm men has made way for bafflement and insecurity.

'Yes,' Lassehn says after a while, and steps out from behind the protecting pillar, 'and once upon a time people lived there.'

'Once upon a time sounds as if it's an eternity ago,' the tank gunner says. 'If you stand at the edge of the city of Pompeii, now sunk in lava and ashes, you can talk about once upon a time, but here . . .'

'Yes, the ruins are still almost warm with the breath and bodies of the people who populated it,' Lassehn adds, 'and yet – if the people who lived six months ago or three months ago in that house over there' – he points at the house whose walls still loom high, yet enclose only a burnt-out cave – 'were now standing in front of them and letting their eyes wander into the corners and niches, it seems to them unimaginably long ago that they once sat in this corner in the soft chair under the warm light of a standard lamp and held a book in their hands, or embraced the body of a woman in the bed by that wall, or that in those four walls, which once perhaps enclosed a kitchen, a woman walked around, turning on a brass tap so that water gushed forth, she turned a knob on an apparatus and gas hissed, she turned a switch and light blazed, a bell rang, she lifted a moulded casing and an ingenious concatenation of microphone, cable and electric current allowed her to hold a telephone conversation. All of these outward signs of former happiness, of things formerly taken for granted, have been rubbed away and crushed, they have dissolved, the life that they once led within these walls has become as unattainable as a distant horizon, they try in vain to approach it, and even if they seem to be getting closer to it, it moves away from them, they can never catch up with it, all that is left behind is bare walls and a smell of burning.'

The tank gunner stares fixedly into the empty walls. 'Isn't our whole life like that, Comrade?' he asks, without averting his eye from the house. 'A façade without content?'

'Our life is like the other houses on this street,' Lassehn replies, 'even the façades have collapsed.'

'And what is left?'

'Only the raw, destroyed material and our hands, to shape something new from it.'

The young tank gunner takes his hands out of his pockets and holds them out in front of him. 'Our hands?' he says, and laughs for a moment. 'What can they do? They forgot long ago what they used to be able to do, and what they have learned in the last six years they will probably never be able to use.'

'Things turn up,' Lassehn says, 'as long as you want them to.'

'I don't know if I do want them to,' the tank gunner replies. 'I'm just tired, I don't want to hear anything more, no promises or anything, I don't want to be addressed by any speeches or any posters any more, I don't want to.'

'That isn't even despair coming out of you,' Lassehn says.

The tank gunner nods listlessly. 'It's true, there's no despair in me now, nothing but apathy and resignation, whether I'm standing here or walking around somewhere, whether I'm eating or sitting on the latrine, I always feel as if I'm lying down, unbelievably stiff, as if in a plaster, in a sickbed, staring into impenetrable darkness. That's how I feel.'

Lassehn steps back behind the pillar and lights a cigarette. He has felt the very things that the young tank gunner just mentioned, but he couldn't admit it, he has tried to suppress the questions in order not to have to provide answers. What the young soldier said the previous night also came dangerously close to touching him. We are like driftwood, he said. Hasn't there always been a whirlpool around us, which we couldn't escape? Wiegand, the doctor, Schröter, Gregor, even Ruppert, they know what they want, they are impelled by their own will towards a particular goal, but we have only ever been moved, and now that those who have previously moved us are no longer there, we drift aimlessly onward, we have become driftwood.

The gloom is turning more and more into day. Somewhere in the east, beyond the looming ruins, above the seething clouds of smoke, the sun must have risen long since, somewhere it shines clearly in a cloudless spring sky, warming the earth with its rays, only here it is overcast and sombre, on the horizon burning torches form a black, burnt-out wall of cloud which towers heavy and gloomy into the spring sky.

The artillery fire rages and whines in the air, the government district is under constant fire. Couriers run, backs bent, leaping like hares over the embankment, supply and ammunition columns dash at breakneck speed along the rutted streets, in which curtains flickering with flame are stretched and a heavy rain of shell splinters crashes down, while the wounded press themselves along the walls of the houses.

The Tolksdorff group also receives supplies and a few copies of the new edition of *Panzerbär*.

In the faint glow of the light the young tank gunner pulls a newspaper to him and reads the leading article under his breath.

'Sacred Word: Berlin

The capital of the Reich has become the capital of the battle. From Berlin came the Führer's orders which turned a deep German divide into a single Greater Germany, and gave the people the foundations of an exemplary social order. From Berlin came the Führer's orders that brought peace to Europe step by step. From Berlin came the Führer's orders which, during the war, in the face of all difficulties, brought the Europe that we had occupied peace and order, work and bread. Berlin was the capital of the profound German order, Berlin was the capital of the European order.

Today Bolshevism is striking at its hated Berlin. It wants to strike fatally at the head of the German order, of the European order. We dedicate ourselves to this battle. That is why the Führer is in Berlin. With us he bears all the burdens of the harshly embattled front city. He stands with us in our raging battle. Once more from Berlin come his orders in the fight for freedom that is making world history. In Berlin it will be decided whether in future Bolshevism will put all peoples under its yoke, or whether the peoples will keep their right to self-determination. In Berlin we will defeat Bolshevism once and for all. It stands in the most savage battlefield that history has ever known. Around it throng the most fanatical soldiers of all time.

The Führer is in Berlin. The global enemy will be defeated here.'

When he has finished reading he looks up, distressed.

'Why are you looking at me like that?' Lassehn asks.

'This language . . . I'm completely confused,' he says. 'There must be something in it.'

'Of course there's something in it,' Lassehn says, 'a common lie hangs on every word. Break the article down into its component parts, right of self-determination of the peoples, bringing peace to Europe, European order, and then think about it.'

The tank gunner shakes his head.

'And here, the headline of the army report: "Heroic battle for Berlin. Arrival of reserves from all sides." You hear that, arrival of reserves on all sides. And yesterday, according to *Panzerbär*, Secretary of State Dr Naumann said . . .' He takes the newspaper from his pocket. 'Here.

"Berlin, 26 April

The Secretary of State in the Reich Ministry for Public Enlightenment and Propaganda, Chief of Staff Dr Naumann, delivered the following speech on the radio on Thursday:

The Führer at the Head

At the head of the defence of Berlin is the Führer. This fact alone gives the battle for Berlin its unique and crucial face."

'That's not the right place,' the tank gunner says. 'Here, this is the bit I mean.

"The German soldiers fighting under the eyes of the Supreme Commander are convinced that their fortitude must be suitable to the situation, and that they will succeed in defeating this enemy where they have defeated him over the last few years. In the whole waging of the war they feel the personal hand of the Führer.

Supreme Generals Personally Leading
Units to Relieve Berlin

The Chief of the General Staff oversees every detail of the defence of Berlin. The victory of the Bolsheviks planned for 20 April has been prevented. But the word of the Führer will persist: Berlin remains German and Europe will not become Russian. Forces have already arrived in different zones and made themselves ready, supporting Berlin, bringing the Bolsheviks a conclusive defeat and thus fundamentally changing the situation of Germany. But the defenders of the Reich capital have taken heart at the news of the rapid arrival of battle-ready troops, and are fighting with stubborn defiance in the firm hope that they will soon hear the roaring guns of the approaching reserves."'

The tank gunner puts the newspaper away. 'There must be *something* in it. No one can lie like *that*.'

'You *can* lie like that,' Lassehn replies, '*they* can, but the worst thing about it is that you still believe them.'

The tank gunner sits down on the kerbstone of the doorway and rests his sub-machine gun on his knees. 'Even you don't know everything,' he says after a while. 'Let's see what it says in the army report.

"From the Führer's headquarters, 27 April

High command of the Wehrmacht announces:
The focus of the combat operations in North West Germany . . .

At the Elbe front the Anglo-Americans remained quiet . . .

At the centre of the fighting yesterday was the battle for Berlin. Shoulder to shoulder with all men capable of bearing arms our troops waged a heroic battle against the Bolshevik mass attack, defended every house and repelled the enemy with counter-attacks from the inner defence ring of the city.

From the zone to the south of Fürstenwalde our combat units thrust westward into the deep flank of the Bolsheviks operating in the south of Berlin, and broke through their main supply connection on the Baruth-Zossen road. Our zestfully aggressive young divisions reached the zone around Beelitz and stand there in fierce forest fighting with the Soviets." '

'Here comes the courier,' Lassehn cuts in.

'He'll probably bring the lieutenant back to the briefing,' the tank gunner says.

The courier darts them a quick appraising gaze and disappears into the house doorway. A few minutes later he reappears with Lieutenant Tolksdorff.

'I said you didn't know everything,' the tank gunner says, resuming the conversation. 'It says quite clearly in the army report that the reserve armies are advancing from the south and west.'

Lassehn shakes his head. 'Those aren't reserve armies,' he says, 'those are the divisions of the Ninth Army who have been encircled for a week, and now they're trying to free themselves.'

'You've got an answer for everything,' the tank gunner says irritably.

'And you've been placing false hope on each defeat,' Lassehn replies.

The young tank gunner shrugs wearily and pokes out his lower lip. 'I don't care about anything.'

For long minutes they don't speak. The air thunders and whines, aeroplanes dart low above the houses, their weapons rip a chunk of plaster from the walls, four-barrelled machine guns rattle, a few Tiger tanks rattle along the cobblestones, heavy anti-aircraft ammunition is fired on Wilhelmstrasse and the barrels are turned to fire horizontally.

'It seems to be kicking off here,' Lassehn says.

'As far as I'm concerned,' the tank gunner says indifferently, 'it'll have to come to an end sometime. Here comes our relief.'

They are relieved, they walk through the vault of this former hallway and climb a dozen crumbling steps down into the cellar. It is plunged into a vague semi-darkness, because it receives its light only through the hole in the ceiling. The hole is the size of a sheet of newspaper, but you can see through five storeys to the sky, the layers of beams have either been burned or stretch charred from wall to wall.

A few minutes after them the lieutenant comes back. He doesn't jump down the steps like someone hurrying to take cover, he climbs down slowly, almost clumsily, step by step. He waves Corporal Schumann away when he jumps up and shouts 'Attention!' into the cellar, he leans against the wall by the door and hangs his steel helmet on a hook. His blond hair hangs sweat-drenched on his forehead, he brushes it lifelessly back and runs his hand over his forehead, his chin lowered deep over his chest. He gives the impression of someone completely exhausted, his chest goes up and down in quick, spasmodic jerks.

Everyone looks in horror at the lieutenant, because it's clear to everyone that the exhaustion to which he has succumbed is not physical in nature.

'The Sturmbannführer has ordered us to the corner of Wilhelmstrasse and Anhalter Strasse to take part in the counter-thrust towards Blücherplatz and Belle-Alliance-Strasse,' he says, his voice quiet and toneless, without a commanding tone.

Take part in the counter-thrust, he thinks, counter-thrust to reconquer one block of flats from the many thousands of blocks of flats in Berlin, a block of flats that is supposedly strategically important. But how many times has he taken part in a counter-attack with his company, always being told it was strategically important, but in those instances it was always a commanding height or an important river crossing, and even there they always had to move to more favourable, previously planned reserve positions to be able to meet the pressure of the enemy more flexibly. And the furthermost point of the front, which still had to be widened at all events and regardless of possible losses to create a greater basis for the counter-attack, was cleared the next day, unnoticed by the enemy, to straighten the front line. Back then there might have been military necessities, although everything that seemed clear and necessary at the time has now been called into question, since he has gained distance and is overwhelmed by defeat, but the things that have been going on in this city the day before yesterday, yesterday and today, and which will be taken to their conclusion tomorrow and the day after – those things are the hysteria, cranked up into blindly raging delirium, of a megalomaniac individual.

The lieutenant's words are followed by a burdensome silence. Everyone knows what a counter-thrust means, in these streets raging with a hail of steel and blocked by curtains of flame, everyone knows that no counter-thrust will be able to loosen the grip of the mighty enemy even slightly, and everyone knows that a counter-thrust can only postpone the agony by a few short breaths.

'Out of the question,' Schröter is the first to say.

The lieutenant waves away any further objections.

'I have no intention of carrying out this order,' he says slowly, but in a clear voice. I shall never again in my whole life carry out another order that goes against conscience and reason, he thinks, I will never carry out any more orders.

Again there is silence in the cellar. This young man there against the wall is a human being like any other, but that has not been obvious until now, since he has previously covered his humanity with special sorts of epaulette, a few strips of silver braid and a few stars pressed out of light white metal have elevated him to a level that has made him unassailable from below and given him power that he would never have had in civilian life. None of the soldiers in this cellar is capable of appreciating the almost superhuman deed that this young man has just performed now that he has divested himself of his unapproachability with a few simple words, on the contrary, they think they see in his actions a snag in his normal brain activity, and even though they have no wish to take part in this pointless counter-thrust that has been ordered from above, the breakdown in the chain of command brings them face to face with an almost insoluble task.

'And what are we supposed to do?' Corporal Schumann says at last.

'Whatever you like,' the lieutenant replies wearily, 'you can follow the order, gathering on the corner of Wilhelmstrasse and Anhalter Strasse at ten-fifteen, or you can stay here or do something else. I've ceased to issue orders.'

'Clearly you haven't told the Sturmbannführer?' Dr Böttcher asks.

The lieutenant smiles very faintly. 'No, I haven't done that, it would have put not just me but the whole group in danger.'

Dr Böttcher and Wiegand communicate with a glance. 'Then we must leave this cellar immediately,' Dr Böttcher says.

'Straight away,' says Schröter.

Corporal Schumann looks, perplexed, from one to the other. 'What is going to become of the group, Lieutenant?' he asks.

'You can clear off,' Schröter says, 'only if you want, of course.'

'I didn't ask you,' the corporal snaps at him, and then looks at Tolksdorff. 'Lieutenant . . .'

'You are at complete liberty, Schumann,' the lieutenant says. 'Isn't that enough for you?'

Schumann shrugs. 'I don't know where to start, Lieutenant, I really don't know . . .'

'Just think very slowly, son, about what you want to do,' Schröter says ironically, 'at any rate let's slip away, because once they notice we're missing, they'll arrest us.'

'Then I'd rather go on my own,' Schumann says. 'What are you doing, Ruppert?'

Ruppert slowly shrugs his shoulders. 'That's quite a quandary,' he says. 'If they hadn't issued the order for the counter-thrust . . .'

'Oh, you poor sod,' Schröter says scornfully, 'want to play it safe, do you?'

'Come on,' says Dr Böttcher, 'let's go through the ruins, not along the street, we'll find some sort of dank cellar.'

Dr Böttcher, Wiegand, Schröter, Gregor and Lassehn head for the exit, Tolksdorff stands still by the iron door, his eyes half closed and his arms folded over his chest.

'And you, Lieutenant?' Dr Böttcher asks, touching him gently on the shoulder.

Tolksdorff looks at him as if he hasn't understood the question. 'Dietrich,' Lassehn says, and shakes his shoulder. 'Come with me!'

The lieutenant shakes his head. 'I'm fine, it'll soon be too late.'

Corporal Schumann is still standing irresolutely in the middle of the cellar, the light from the hole in the ceiling falls obliquely into his face, it is pale green, his eyes keep darting helplessly from one to the other. 'It's already twenty past ten,' he says, looking at his watch. 'For now let's act as if . . .'

Behind Wiegand, who is the last to go, the corporal and the other soldiers climb the cellar steps.

'Let's cross the ruins at an angle,' Wiegand says, 'there are still a few houses standing on Saarlandstrasse, we'll find somewhere.'

'You lot are fine,' Private Poppe says morosely, 'you just have to chuck away your Volkssturm armbands and you're civilians.'

'Right,' Schröter cuts in, 'we have no time to chat.'

They climb over a pile of debris, the grave of a collapsed house, Corporal Schumann and some soldiers are still standing uncertainly in the courtyard between the looming, burnt black walls of the empty ruin, the fire from the Russian artillery and the mortars raging incessantly over their heads.

'Where is Lieutenant Tolksdorff?' a voice shouts suddenly. 'What's going on here?'

Sturmbannführer Wiegand is standing in the gateway. 'Fall in!' he roars. 'Where is Lieutenant Tolksdorff?'

Corporal Schumann and the soldiers immediately stand to attention, Dr Böttcher and the others slow down slightly.

The Sturmbannführer looks menacingly around. 'And what

about you lot up on that rubble? Where do you think you're off to? Stop where you are!'

Schröter raises his carbine and lowers it again. 'Damn it all,' he murmurs to himself. 'This fellow would have to be Wiegand's son, wouldn't he?'

'Permission to speak . . .' Corporal Schumann begins.

'I want to know where Lieutenant Tolksdorff is!' the Sturmbann-führer yells at him.

'Lieutenant Tolksdorff is still in the cellar, Sturmbannführer,' Schumann replies. 'He has . . .'

At that moment a shot rings out in the cellar, followed by the dull sound of a falling body.

The Sturmbannführer purses his lips. 'Right, you at the back, over here. What are you waiting for . . .' He pauses, his mouth suddenly collapses lifelessly in on itself, his expression becomes stubborn, his hands, holding a sub-machine gun, start trembling, then he strides fiercely towards Wiegand and thrusts his head forward. 'You're here?' he says, a strange menace in his voice, his mouth tightenes again, his eye explores the faces. 'And you too, Mother?'

Wiegand breathes heavily and draws his wife more firmly to him.

'Now I'm starting to understand what's up with this group,' Sturmbannführer Wiegand says with a keenly incisive voice.

'Robert . . .' Lucie Wiegand says quietly.

'No sentimentality,' the Sturmbannführer interrupts.

'No,' Wiegand says, 'no sentimentality.'

'Now you have the chance to prove yourselves,' the Sturmbann-führer says, 'all of you, in line . . .'

Ruppert, who has thrown off his field-grey coat, takes a step forward. 'You mad dog!' he roars. 'Make your war on your own!'

The Sturmbannführer raises his sub-machine gun. 'I order you . . .'

Ruppert takes a step back, pulls the hand grenade from his belt and throws it at the Sturmbannführer. Explosion, double, ringing echo, splinters flying around, clouds of smoke and dust, nothing else. The man who was standing there a moment ago is gone, as if the earth had opened up and swallowed him. If someone had looked more closely . . . But no one looks at the spot where a young man in an olive-green uniform had been standing a moment before, with a steel helmet and SS runes, holding a cocked sub-machine gun, no one looks around for the traces of this young man.

'I'd been saving that one,' Private Ruppert says triumphantly, 'for a special occasion.'

XVIII

One cellar is very much like another, the earth was dug out, a hole
was cast in concrete or walled around with bricks, a low ceiling,
without light or warmth, held down by the weight of a house.
What escapes the eye in the flats, where it lies within the walls or is
covered with plaster, in the cellars is laid bare, ugly and undisguised, gas pipes, water pipes, sewage pipes, the intestines of a
Berlin apartment block, but what was once only an unnoticed
appendage, a storage space for old furniture or other junk, is now
the centre, the refuge of life.

What remains of the Tolksdorff group has moved into one such
cellar. It lies under a house that burned down only a few days previously, the ashes on the cellar ceiling have not yet turned cold,
bluish-yellow flames still flicker here and there, the bricks and
breeze blocks crackle almost audibly. The cellar has apparently
been cleared in great haste, and a few air-raid beds, old suitcases
and boxes stand around. This cellar is part of the side wing of a
house on Saarlandstrasse. The front part of the house is still standing, offering the usual view of a Berlin house of these times, with
torn-out plaster and bullet holes, with the window frames splintered and the roof blown away.

Saarlandstrasse, formerly Stresemannstrasse and before that
Königgrätzer Strasse, the main thoroughfare between Hallisches
Tor and Potsdamer Platz, with a station for long-distance, suburban
and local trains, with overground and underground railways, trams
and buses, countless taxis, cars and lorries, cyclists and hordes of

pedestrians, with a theatre and an ethnological museum, Hotel Fürstenhof and Hotel Excelsior, Anhalt Station and Haus Vaterland, the Europa skyscraper and the Philharmonie – this once-magnificent street, bursting with life, has now become the front line. From the south the Russians have thrust their way from Tempelhofer Feld down Belle-Alliance-Strasse to the Hallesches Tor, from the west they are advancing along Potsdamer Strasse, and in the north SS units are still putting up resistance on the east-west axis, by the Reichstag and the Brandenburg Gate. But the red flag already waves on the dome of the Reichstag. This strange front line only has some freedom of movement in the east towards Wilhelmstrasse.

Heavy artillery and mortars hammer uninterruptedly at the apartment blocks on this street, aeroplanes dive at them, artillery fire and the bombs from the planes dig up the stony ground, incendiary bombs turn houses into conflagrations, and down in the cellars people cower, the faint little flames of their will to live on the point of flickering out.

The former Tolksdorff group still consists of fourteen men, Dr Böttcher, Wiegand, Schröter, Gregor, Lassehn, Privates Ruppert, Poppe, Kebschull, Hinzpeter, Behrend, Manthey, Dulinski, the young soldier Hellwig, the tank gunner Reithofer, and last of all Lucie Wiegand.

The great silence has sunk inside them. Outside rages the fire of battle, the wail and crash of the shells, the crazed rattle of the aeroplane engines, the firing of the anti-aircraft placements, the rattle of stones whirl wildly around. The cellar totters and sways, the foundations tremble under the impact of the exploding shells, the earth seems to be spinning, but the fifteen people are sitting motionless in this cellar in the middle of the unfettered hurricane of iron and dust, they feel as if they were entirely removed from their lives, as if they were sitting in this cellar as if on a raft drifting rudderless in a stormy sea.

Who are these people who have been blown together into this cellar by the storm of war? And what are their thoughts in this moment, on 29 April 1945, at 11 o'clock in the morning, in this dark cellar under a bombed-out house on Saarlandstrasse in Berlin SW?

Here is Dr Walter Böttcher from Berlin East, 14 Frankfurter Allee, fifty-six years old, general practitioner by profession, widowed, with a cool, superior mind and social empathy based on a sense of responsibility, a former member of the Social Democratic Party and district councillor, the intellect behind the 'Berolina' resistance group. He sits with his legs crossed and his arms folded over his chest, half leaning back, and thinks about the hand grenade of Private Ruppert, which shredded the Sturmbannführer like a bundle of rags. A young man has dissolved in front of his mother's eyes into a pasty muck of flesh, blood and fabric fibres.

Here is Friedrich Wiegand from Eichwalde, district of Teltow, forty-six years old, book printer by trade, compositor, later trade-union secretary, persecuted for twelve years by the Gestapo, living as an outlaw for four years, the most active member of the 'Berolina' resistance group. He sits relaxed in an armchair, memorizing Russian words to be able to speak to the liberators in their own language.

Here is Lucie Wiegand, née Rückert, his wife, forty-two years old, small and delicate as a young girl, but strong in spirit and will, she met and married Friedrich Wiegand at the age of eighteen, as a shorthand typist in the printworks of *Vorwärts*. She sits there upright, rubbing her fingertips very gently against one another, she is thinking about her son Robert, who was lifted from the earth by a hand grenade barely twenty-four hours before, and she doesn't really know whether the feeling that stirs her breast is grief or relief.

Here is the man who is called Gregor and whose name is Dr Josef Grabner, who lives in Berlin-Frohnau, forty-one years old, devout Catholic, lecturer in ecclesiastical law at the Friedrich-Wilhelm University in Berlin, who has lived underground for over a year, because it was discovered that he had been reproducing and distributing the encyclicals of the Pope and the speeches of Count Galen, the Bishop of Münster, member of the 'Ringbahn' resistance group. He lies on a couch with his eyes half closed and wonders whether it will be possible to guide people to a new faith since they have already had to walk through purgatory on earth.

Here is Richard Schröter from Berlin East, Petersburger Strasse, sixty-two years old, divorced, precision mechanic by trade, dogmatic and fanatical Marxist, the driving force behind the 'Ringbahn' resistance group, cunning and skilled. He paces restlessly up and down and looks at the entrance to the cellar, through which a grey light falls into the cellar, thinking, I'll fire at any uniform that appears there, whether it be SS or Wehrmacht, Hitler Youth or police, I'm not going to be dragged out of here until the Russians arrive.

Here is Joachim Lassehn from Berlin-Lankwitz, twenty-two years old, married on an eight-day conjugal leave, music student, soft and sensitive, but hardened by the pressure of a supposedly great era. He is reclining on a lounger and letting the rondo of Beethoven's Third Piano Concerto play in his head, with the curious switch from minor to major and from two-four to six-eight in the presto.

Here is private Karl Ruppert from Berlin-Neukölln, Boddinstrasse, forty-three years old, married and the father of two children, businessman by trade and owner of a small tobacconist's shop, a modest man who loves peace, order and cleanliness, and who has ended up in an almost psychopathic state. He is crouching on a crate, as if about to jump, and thinking: the Russians should be here soon, they will put me in a car and drive me to Boddinstrasse, or they just need to let me walk, then I would ... yes, from the Hallesches Tor along Urbanstrasse, across Hermannplatz, up Hermannstrasse, perhaps a good half-hour's walk.

Here is Private Arthur Poppe from Forst in the Lausitz, thirty-eight years old, married without children, weaver by trade, a quiet, rather ponderous man, who does his work conscientiously, but without verve or personal initiative, member of the compulsory National Socialist organizations the German Labour Front and National Socialist People's Welfare, otherwise politically completely indifferent. He has rested his head on his left shoulder and is thinking about his wife, not knowing where she is at present, he thinks of her, seeing her nimble hands quickly and deftly moving the crochet hook.

Here is Private Emil Kebschull from Wendischfähre near Bad Schandau, fifty-one years old, married, father of a grown-up daughter and twice grandfather with no son-in-law, unskilled labourer, called up during the war into a Dresden armaments factory and trained as a lathe operator, after the bombing of the factory moved to a regional defence unit. He sits there stiffly listening to the noise, his eyes focused on the ceiling, his head constantly moving as if he were following the course of the projectiles that fly over the cellar ceiling with an unpleasant hissing, wailing, piping, screeching, whining.

Here is Private Paul Hinzpeter from Cosel in Upper Silesia, forty years old, married, father of a sixteen-year-old son, section leader of the Hitler Youth, ironmongery salesman by trade, Party member before 1933, then tax commissioner, constantly declared indispensable until the Russian occupation, later assigned to a Volkssturm battalion which was blown up on the third day after it was organized, a phlegmatic, stubborn and indifferent man. He sits with his face pinched in a half-lying position in two wicker armchairs and thinks, deeply worried: what if we really do lose the war, what then?

Here is Private Ernst Dulinski from Nedlitz near Potsdam, thirty-six years old, married and the father of three children, bricklayer by trade, former member of the Red Front League and immediately arrested by the SA after 30 January 1933, released again after being beaten half to death and finally converted into a patient citizen by marriage to a girl from Osthavelland with limited aspirations, but never quite shedding the smell of the Commune. He is thinking about the freight train that came into platform C of Kottbus Station on 20 February 1945, crammed with many hundreds of refugees, and which he had to help to unload, frozen corpses and almost lifelessly petrified people, and a shudder still runs through him even now when the phrase 'frozen meat commando' darts through his brain.

Here is Private Bruno Behrend from Landau, Saarpfalz, thirty-two years old, single, engaged to a war widow, owner of a good haberdashery in Kaiserslautern, representative of the Pforzheim jewellery industry by trade, a lively, agile man, quick and sharp, former sergeant in a supply unit, demoted for embezzlement and transferred to a punishment battalion, finally pardoned and assigned to an infantry unit. He lies on an air-raid bed, his hands folded in the back of his neck, and thinks: the jewellery industry is going to be dead after the war anyway, we'll have to start something completely new.

Here is Private Walter Manthey from Altefähr on Rügen, thirty-five years old, widowed, father of two small girls who are being brought up by their grandmother, gardener by trade, owner of a seed-cultivation centre, a hard-working, knowledgeable, slightly cumbersome man, a soldier since 1941, suffered from frostbite on his feet near Rzhev, was painstakingly reconstructed and reactivated at the beginning of the Soviet offensive. He leans against the posts of the air-raid beds and thinks about his garden, which he has dug over year after year and not seen for three years, and the fruit trees which need to be pruned and cut back this month.

Here is the young soldier Erhard Hellwig from Poggendorf, district of Greifswald, twenty-two years old, middle-school student, aiming to become a dentist, did not become a soldier entirely voluntarily, a young man who has become unstable, who has always been driven along against his will, with a deep dislike for everything military. He lies on the upper air-raid bed and tries to sleep, but can't, he thinks constantly of his little home town and a girl he kissed last time he was on leave, autumn 1943, on her beautiful, dark-red lips which were at first firmly and defiantly closed, and then opened, soft and warm and moist.

Here is the young tank gunner Ulrich Reithofer from Cham in the Upper Palatinate, nineteen years old, son of a brewer, flag-bearer in the Jungvolk, cadre unit leader in the Hitler Youth, Party member at eighteen, by no means a fanatical Nazi, more someone who joins in because everyone's joining in, a rather brutal, surprisingly confident boy who unhesitatingly believes everything he is told. He is sitting sideways on a kitchen chair, restless and edgy, not because the air from shell fire is roaring, he is thinking of Corporal Schumann, who disappeared after Ruppert threw the hand grenade: if he reports what happened we're up the creek, we'll be strung up in an instant.

The minutes flow sluggishly on, the artillery fire becomes stronger and stronger, lumps of masonry crash into the courtyard, clouds of dust and smoke are forced through the open cellar door.

'Unbearable, sitting here and not knowing what's going on around us,' Schröter says, and irritably stamps his foot.

'You can't go out there now,' Wiegand says. 'They'll nab you straight away.'

'I know,' Schröter replies, 'I'm staying here, but still . . . There seem to be a lot of people in the next air-raid shelter along.'

'And?' Dr Böttcher asks. 'What do you mean?'

'We should make contact with them,' Schröter answers.

Wiegand shakes his head. 'An air-raid community like that is like a closed society, they don't want to see a stranger . . .'

'. . . and men, even soldiers,' Gregor adds. 'They'll hand you over just to have a bit of peace.'

'I could go over,' Lucie Wiegand speaks up.

Wiegand waves his hand quickly. 'It's too dangerous, Lucie.'

'I'm going,' Lucie Wiegand says resolutely, 'if the firing eases off a bit.'

'I'll go with you,' Lassehn says, 'if you . . .'

He doesn't finish his sentence. A whistling hiss approaches at great speed, the roof of the cellar is hit, shakes and sways, a fountain of dirt sprays as far as the doorway, but no explosion follows.

'A dud!' shouts Private Kebschull, and leaps to his feet.

'Right, outside!' Wiegand shouts. 'Quickly, quickly!'

They all jump to their feet and run up the cellar steps. The courtyard is full of smoke and haze, the stirred-up ashes whirl around as if in a black snowstorm, the looming ruin now has cracks as wide as the palm of a hand, it sways, bricks are already coming away from the top edge of the wall and falling with a dull thud in the courtyard.

'Come on, come on!' Wiegand spurs them on.

They run into the courtyard, climb over a shattered wall and find themselves standing in another courtyard surrounded by undamaged front and rear houses. A hallway at first offers them some shelter, they stop with panting lungs and thumping hearts. A shell tears a hole in the wall of the house to the rear, and at the same moment a bomb from an aircraft drops through the smoke, pulls the air apart like a curtain and falls into the ruin in whose cellar they were sitting less than a minute before, it sways like a sail, leans over and collapses with a terrible crash, stones and iron splinters whirl around, the blast knocks the men over, they fall in all directions like skittles and are almost unconscious with breathlessness. For a few seconds everything is wrapped in smoke and dust, the narrow courtyard is like a smoking fireplace. Only after endless minutes does the heavy grey cloud disperse.

'Damn it all, where's the air-raid cellar?' Schröter shouts.

By now Lassehn has discovered the cellar door below the staircase to the front building. 'Here!' he shouts. 'The door beside the hallway!' He tries to open the door, but it doesn't yield, he hammers against it with the stock of his carbine. 'Open up!' he shouts. 'Open up!'

The door is opened, only a crack, but Lassehn pulls it from the hand of the man standing behind it and throws it wide open.

'Stop!' yells the man, whose blue and white armband identifies him as an air-raid warden. 'Stop! The cellar is full! No one's coming in here!'

He stands on the top step, legs wide, and spreads his arms.

Lassehn pushes him silently aside, and lets Lucie Wiegand walk ahead of him.

'The cellar isn't for you!' the air-raid warden says furiously. 'The woman can come in here, but you can't!'

'We'll ask you about that in a minute,' Schröter says. 'Come on, everybody down there, and shut the door!'

'There's no room for soldiers here!' the air-raid warden barks, and grabs Private Ruppert. 'You lot should be up there, clear off, or . . .'

Ruppert gives the air-raid warden a shove in the chest, making him stagger back and clutch the banister to keep from falling down the stairs.

'What else?' he asks, and grabs him by the front of the jacket. 'Come on, what else?' he asks threateningly.

The air-raid warden, a middle-aged man, middle-sized, broad-shouldered, tries to free himself from Ruppert's grip. 'Let me go!' he pants.

'What else? Come on, what else?' Private Ruppert repeats his question and discovers the Party insignia on the air-raid warden's jacket. 'What else, Comrade?'

'Don't cause trouble, Ruppert,' says Private Manthey.

Ruppert loosens his grip, but still stands threateningly in front of the air-raid warden. 'I want to know, what else? Are you going to set the SS on us, or the military police?'

The air-raid warden straightens his jacket and studies the soldiers with a crooked, angry expression. 'Is that a way to treat people?'

Ruppert now lets him go completely. 'Everyone downstairs?' he asks. 'Then shut the door, Hellwig!' The young soldier Hellwig shuts the door. 'It's quite smart in here,' he says as he goes down the stairs, 'you've even got electric light.'

At the end of the cellar steps, in the room just outside the actual air-raid cellar, the troop gathers, they have all arrived safe and sound, although Private Poppe's upper arm has been torn open by a shell splinter.

'It's not so serious, Poppe,' Dr Böttcher says, and presses him down onto a sandbox, 'it's bleeding copiously but otherwise it's harmless.' He cuts away the torn fabric of the coat and jacket, trims the edges of the wound, dabs the area with iodine, parts the tissues with small metal clamps, and wraps a layer of muslin around it.

'So, dear boy,' he says as he packs away his instruments. 'That will do for now.'

In the meantime a big man with rimless glasses has come out of the iron door that separates the actual air-raid shelter from the room outside and has watched Dr Böttcher's manipulations with great interest.

'Bravo!' he says appreciatively. 'You've done that like a proper doctor.'

Dr Böttcher looks at him over his glasses and struggles to suppress a smile. 'That will heal in no time.'

The man with the rimless glasses looks at him, perplexed. 'Are you a trained orderly?' he asks.

Now Dr Böttcher smiles. 'A medical doctor, sir,' he replies. The other man now smiles as well, his severe face brightening suddenly. 'Then we are colleagues,' he says, and extends a hand to Dr Böttcher. 'Dr Heinrich Wiedemann.'

Dr Böttcher shakes his hand and says his name.

'How does that work?' Dr Wiedemann asks. 'You being a simple Volkssturm man?'

'It has its reasons,' Dr Böttcher says abruptly. 'Tell me, do we have to stay in the outside room? Is there no room in the cellar?'

'Even if there was room,' the air-raid warden cuts in, 'that cellar's not for you. Do you think I'd risk going down for facilitating an escape and so on?'

'And there you have the shit,' the tank gunner says to Lassehn. 'It's obvious, it stinks for seven miles with the wind in the other direction.'

'Listen, my dear man,' Private Ruppert says, and walks right up to the air-raid warden, 'the SS and the Gestapo have chirped their last, you shouldn't rely on those fellows, or you're stuffed.'

'But . . .' the air-raid warden wants to object.

'There's no but,' Ruppert says in a superior and condescending voice, 'and you should throw that badge of yours somewhere where no one can find it.'

'You can leave that up to me,' the air-raid warden says stubbornly.

'Fine, we will,' Schröter says.

'Christ,' says Private Hinzpeter, 'don't be so obstinate, the Third Reich is over, a blind man can see that. Here you've got an excellent opportunity to give yourself an alibi.'

'An alibi? How do you mean?'

'Look, if you find room for us,' Private Hinzpeter says eagerly, 'then you'll have done something . . . Just the thing that . . .' He falls awkwardly silent and remembers his own Party membership.

'Come on, out with it,' the air-raid warden says impatiently.

'Well, among us there are a few . . .' He looks shyly at Wiegand, Dr Böttcher and Schröter. 'Well, a few people who might be able to do something for you later on, I mean.'

'I don't know what you're talking about,' the air-raid warden says.

'Just shut up for a bit,' Schröter says. 'If you're reluctant, you great air-raid Nazi, there are a few tried and tested methods.' He aims his rifle at the air-raid warden. 'Hands up!'

The air-raid warden immediately throws his arms in the air. 'For God's sake . . .' he pants.

Schröter laughs briefly and lowers his rifle again. 'Do you know what I mean now, Party Comrade air-raid warden?'

Dr Wiedemann rests a hand on the air-raid warden's shoulder. 'I'm sure there's room here somewhere, Herr Zimmer,' he says, 'where you could put up the men. It'll probably only be for one or two days, perhaps even just a few hours.'

The air-raid warden has brought his arms slowly back down again. 'Well, there might be a room,' he says, 'the boiler room.'

'Up to the boiler room,' says Dr Böttcher. 'Right then, show us the boiler room.'

The air-raid warden looks doggedly at the floor and doesn't move from the spot.

'Along the corridor,' he says, pointing to the corridor, which leads past a number of rooms fenced off with lathes. 'You can't miss it, the boiler room.'

'One of you stay by the door,' Dr Böttcher says, 'so that the air-raid warden here doesn't get the idea of . . . Will you go first, Lassehn?'

The boiler room is not very spacious, with a big stove and two water-boilers, but it is almost directly below street level, the sky-lights are blocked with sandboxes, and even the electric light is on.

Dr Wiedemann has followed the troop to the boiler room. 'The Russians will be here by tomorrow at the latest,' he says, 'perhaps even tonight.'

'We don't know very much about what's going on,' Wiegand says. 'Do you know more?'

'Only vaguely,' Dr Wiedemann replies. 'The Russians are already at Belle-Alliance-Platz, they are even supposed to have got as far as lower Friedrichstrasse and Wilhelmstrasse, on the other side they are already behind Anhalt Station and close to Potsdamer Platz.'

'So we're right in the middle,' says Private Ruppert. 'Damn, if only we'd stayed on Stralauer Strasse it would all be over already.'

'Of course,' Dr Wiedemann says, 'the army report is already mentioning Alexanderplatz.'

'You've got an army report?' Schröter asks quickly. 'Radio or newspaper?'

'Newspaper,' says Dr Wiedemann, 'here's today's *Panzerbär*.'

Schröter takes the paper.

'Those miserable hacks,' he says contemptuously.

'Heroic Struggle.

Strike Forces Brought in

Day and Night.

The Battle for the Heart of the City Rages.

Diversionary Attacks Under Way.

From the Führer's headquarters, 28 April

Wehrmacht High Command wishes it to be known:

In the heroic battle for the city of Berlin the fateful battle of the German people against Bolshevism is once more being played out in front of the whole world.

While the city is being defended in a struggle on a unique historical scale, our troops have turned our backs on the Americans at the Elbe to relieve the defenders of Berlin by attacking from without.

In the inner defence ring the enemy has penetrated Charlottenburg from the north and the Tempelhofer Feld from the south. At the Hallesches Tor and Alexanderplatz the fight for the heart of the city has begun. The east-west axis is under heavy fire.

Airborne units are supporting the fighting, with great self-sacrifice on the part of their crews. In spite of heavy fire from anti-aircraft guns and fighter planes, reserve strike forces have been landed day and night and ammunition dropped. Over the past four days our fighter pilots and ground-attack pilots have destroyed 143 aeroplanes, 58 tanks and over 300 vehicles. In the zone south of Königs Wusterhausen, divisions of the 9th Army have continued their attacks to the north-west and fought off concentric attacks from the Soviets against their flanks throughout the whole day. The divisions deployed from the west have thrown back the enemy amidst fierce fighting on a wide front, and have reached Ferch.'

'Bloody hell,' the tank gunner says anxiously. 'That looks awful. If the Russians are really beaten back, we're up to our necks in shit.'

'Yes,' says Private Behrend, rocking his head back and forth. 'Shouldn't we report to a troop? What do you think?'

'I think,' Schröter snaps, 'that you're a bunch of spineless wets. But if you want to, clear off!'

'You're a hardliner,' says Private Kebschull, 'I suppose you're a communist, a museum piece from before thirty-three?'

'Shut your trap,' Schröter rages at him. 'If I'm a museum piece, then I'll tell you where you've sprung from.'

'Which is? Let's have it!'

'The Nazi bumper book of criminals, if you want to know.'

'Gentlemen, calm down,' Dr Wiedemann says pacifyingly, 'the war will be over very soon. What the Propaganda Department says is nothing but an old fraud, they just write it to perk you up a bit.'

'But there would be absolutely no point to that,' tank gunner Reithofer says dubiously.

'There is a point to it,' Dr Böttcher says, 'namely that of dragging an entire people with them into their own disaster.'

'That's impossible,' says Private Behrend, shaking his head. He picks up the newspaper, scans the front page and then turns it over.

'There are more articles in it about the deployment,' says the tank gunner, who is looking over his shoulder. 'This one, for example:

"Where the Führer is, There is Victory!
Clarification of the State of Battle Due Shortly

The German strike forces penetrating the greater Berlin area from outside are already dangerously close to the enemy. They are doing severe damage to enemy reinforcements and putting ever-greater pressure on the rear of the enemy with their inexorable advance.

It is clear that the Soviets are trying with all their strength in the final hour to attain their goal, the occupation of Berlin, so as not to be fired on from both sides. So the enemy is pushing with all his strength against the inner defence ring. He is trying to find weak spots in our defences where he can break through, because he does not have sufficient forces to turn an encirclement into an attack in all directions.

In these circumstances various focuses have emerged in the battle, with the temporary consequence of complex and critical situations which have been eased thanks to the solid deployment of the defenders and partly through counter-thrusts.

If fighting continues with the same courage, the picture around the battlefield of Berlin will soon be fundamentally transformed. The resoluteness with which the Berliners defend their city springs from the fact that yesterday over 40 tanks and during the last five days a total of 300 tanks have been destroyed. The Luftwaffe has once again backed up the battle on the ground with a heavy deployment of fighter and ground-attack planes.

Our task is clear. We are staying where we are. The Führer is with us. Where the Führer is, there is victory!"'

'Did you expect the other articles to say the opposite?' Schröter asks. 'Where is the Führer's victory? Since the Führer has been there, there has been nothing but defeat after defeat!'

'Liars are liars,' says Dr Böttcher.

'What do you think our chances actually are?' Wiegand asks, and picks up the newspaper. 'Read the second part of the army report. Deep incursions near Prenzlau, Regensburg and Ingolstadt lost, southwards advance between Dillingen and Ulm, which is to say towards Augsburg and Munich, withdrawals beyond the Ticino, which means from the Po Valley into the Alps . . .'

'This is the most devastating defeat ever suffered by a German army,' Gregor says, 'and you want to prolong the madness by another few seconds?'

'We don't want that, we're not that stupid,' says Private Behrend, 'but we don't want to perish during those last few seconds either.'

Dr Wiedemann looks around a few more times, starts to speak, falls silent, but then speaks after all. 'There is one other interesting thing,' he says, 'it isn't in the paper, but I've heard it on the radio. Mussolini was arrested by Italian partisans while escaping near Dongo on the twenty-seventh, and shot by firing squad yesterday afternoon.'

'Bravo!' shouts Schröter. 'And where are the German partisans?'

'We've got heroic women instead,' Dr Wiedemann says. 'I'll read you a little cutting from an article.

"Women at the Front Line

In Neukölln an elderly woman with a packed rucksack reported to a police station. In the end she went to the distribution office housed in the same building and said, 'I would like to join the Volkssturm, if you'll give me a rocket launcher. I've got to fight the Bolsheviks.' "

'Touching,' says Schröter, 'I suppose that means we're saved.'

'It would have to be Neukölln,' murmurs Private Ruppert.

'So to cut a long story short, are we going or are we staying here?' asks Private Kebschull.

'Oh, it doesn't matter either way,' says tank gunner Reithofer, sitting down on a bench, 'whether we get it in the neck in here or out there, you can only die once.'

'You're right, lad,' says Private Kebschull, sitting down beside him. 'So let's stay.'

'Unstable pair,' Dr Wiedemann says to Dr Böttcher.

'What else can you expect from these people?' says Dr Böttcher. 'They're always looking indecisively and anxiously upward, waiting for orders, uncertain when there aren't any, always ready to carry out every order, but never thinking or acting independently, as they are unacquainted with the compulsion of conscience and the force of reason.'

Dr Wiedemann nods. 'Anything else is a rare exception. I was recently involved in a case that is not only harrowing from a human point of view as well as being medically interesting, but also demonstrates how people, peaceful, gentle, calm, quiet people, can be drawn into a tragic sequence of events. It is a destiny of our times.'

'Tell me,' says Dr Böttcher.

XIX

The Story of the Tram Conductor
Max Eckert

'But all that yet remains we find,
Embodied in the strength of those who stay behind.'

Frank Wedekind, from the *Brettl Songs*

A day dawns, as countless days have broken before it, with the sun hauling itself up to the horizon and climbing over it. Its rays send their light to the earth, and give no hint about what will happen in the interval between the rising of the sun and its setting below the horizon. In those hours, when the light flows down upon the earth or seeps through dense curtains of cloud, the internal clocks of two billion people run unstoppably on. For many that clock will stop and for some it will be rewound, everything is still in darkness. The morning that welcomes them once night is over is like any other morning, no clue to the catastrophe hurtling towards mankind warns their souls.

On 3 February 1945 the tram conductor Max Eckert left his flat in Berlin-Reinickendorf, 144 Residenzallee, to go on his early shift. He is a conductor with the Berlin public transport service and travels on line 141, the first one setting off just after five o'clock from the tram station in Pakower Allee. Shortly after four in the afternoon Eckert, after clocking off, goes back to his flat. So far the day has passed like every other, he has done his duty, he has fussed around the passengers and tried to stick to the timetable even though there was quite a long air-raid warning, but there's certainly nothing unusual about that. Much more unusual is the fact that his wife and sixteen-year-old daughter aren't at home. That never happens, in fact, and if it ever has happened there has always been a note on the kitchen table, in which his wife has told him in a few lines that she has gone to the cinema or to visit friends, and he just needs to heat up his dinner. But today Eckert finds nothing there, neither his wife nor his daughter, neither a note nor his dinner. The flat has been spotlessly cleaned, because Frau Eckert is an excellent house-wife, the beds in the bedroom are carefully made as ever, even the quilts are smoothed over them, but in the kitchen nothing has been prepared for dinner. The flat has clearly been abandoned by his wife that morning, and now, in the afternoon, she hasn't yet returned. It's completely incomprehensible, so an unsettling feeling wells up in Eckert, before it occurs to him that there was a daytime raid by the Americans around midday which, as far as he was informed at the end of his working day, was concentrated on the city centre, and there again Eckert has the explanation for his wife's absence. Twice a week she goes with their daughter to consult a doctor in Ritterstrasse, their daughter suffers from stubborn eczema which so far has resisted every kind of treatment, and the doctor in Rit-terstrasse has been recommended to them as particularly good. And in fact the girl, since she has been in treatment with this Dr Wiedemann, has made a considerable recovery.

So at first Eckert is reassured. He knows that the underground D line from Neukölln to Gesundbrunnen, which his wife usually takes, has been disrupted, and that the tramlines that connect the south and the centre with the north have been halted because of the air raid, so his wife and daughter will have to make the journey from Ritterstrasse to Reinickendorf on foot, and would probably have to take significant detours as well, since from experience there are always numerous road closures and diversions after air raids.

Eckert heats up a dreg of coffee that he finds in the pot and pre-pares himself a sausage sandwich, then he reads the midday paper, but soon notices that none of it means anything to him, at least not in his present state of mind, because as his eyes glide over the pages and grasp the occasional headline like 'Today the German Nation Is More United Than Ever Before', '718th and 719th Knight's Crosses Awarded' and 'Volkssturm Proves Itself Once Again', his senses are entirely focused on the sounds coming up from the stairwell. As soon as a footstep is heard, his whole body tenses, he is ready to leap to the door as soon as a key is placed in the lock, but the footsteps always fade away before they reach the second floor, or else they go past his door and carry on up the stairs, once they pause on the second-floor landing, but then the doorbell rings at the neighbours' flat. Eckert paces back and forth, hands clasped behind his back, he glances occasionally out of the window, but even that does not distract from the heavy silence of the flat and the agonizing wait. The street is, as usual, busy with bustling, scurrying people, crowded trams and clattering lorries. Fear of the coming night, the wail of sirens and the doom hurtling towards them, is already making people shiver.

Two hours pass, twilight falls and flows through the window-panes into the kitchen. Eckert turns on the radio, but the speaker remains mute, and when he turns on the light switch the bulb doesn't come on. A curfew has been imposed upon the district again. So once more he is once again deprived of the consolation of light and the distraction of music. Eckert taps his way back to the wicker armchair and slumps into it. The minutes creep along even more slowly, because the torment of waiting has now been joined by the shroud of darkness. Eckert sits motionless in the kitchen and waits, his hands rest on his knees and he looks at the wall that retreats further and further the denser the darkness becomes. He has only one thought inside him, it fills him entirely and threatens to blow him up. His wife should have come home long ago, it doesn't take more than an hour and a half, two hours at most, to get from Moritzplatz to Residenzstrasse, the alarm went off at about 14.00 hours – as a transport worker he thinks only in the twenty-four hour clock – so his wife, even if she had to make a few detours, should have been home by about 17.00 hours, but it's now 18.30, and she still hasn't arrived.

Eckert is a matter-of-fact, sober man, he doesn't care for high-flown words, he is neither sentimental nor romantic, he would be amazed if anyone tried to identify the emotion he feels for his wife as 'love'. It's more a solid affection, an unqualified fondness, a habit tried and tested and found to be good, but these three components, affection, fondness and habit, are a solid bond, more lasting and sustainable than the rosary of eternal love and fidelity. So during these hours, brushed by a dark apprehension, he is not moved, it is more the fear of having lost a valuable possession that is a part of himself. It is the last possession left him, his wife and daughter, since his two sons have been lost, as one might imagine one has lost a watch before working out that it has been magicked away by a conjuror. The younger son, who served with the Luftwaffe, was taken from him even before the war, after his letters, which seemed to be assuming a secretive turn, began coming at ever-greater intervals and finally stopped altogether, until one day a communication arrived saying that he had crashed during an exercise, and that he had been fatally injured and buried with full military honours. Only much later, when the veil of secrecy concerning the 'Condor Legion' had been lifted, did Eckert learn that his son had died in the Spanish Civil War, the great dress rehearsal for the Nazi Luftwaffe. His older son, a model maker with Borsig Rheinmetall in Tegel, a calm, clever young man with a slight artistic inclination towards wood-carving, was swallowed up by the war: he came back from the Kazakh steppes with frozen hands and feet, a helpless, amputated bundle of humanity with black stumps for limbs which, when given its first opportunity to move independently, fell from the fourth floor into the street and smashed to pieces on the cobbles. So, from an apparently firmly established cycle of life, two pieces were broken, like two good teeth from a healthy set, and each time it was like a deliberate strike to the heart, which stirred in him not so much pain as rage, since the death of his sons was accompanied by the raw bawling of marching songs.

So he was left only with his wife and daughter. All his care and affection were now focused upon them, but this life cycle too is endangered daily and hourly, as all human life cycles are. They draw tighter and tighter, they ensnare hearts, the menacing shadows grow blacker and deeper, but the power to which they, yielding and devoted, must bend is not super-terrestrial, it is not the almighty power of God, not the violence of a natural disaster beyond the human will and human prescience. It is the tyrant's reach for life and certainty, happiness and peace, so from the loss of life and goods grief and resignation do not mature into an inescapable fate, they turn into rage and fury.

During that hour, spent motionless in an armchair in his dark kitchen, Eckert understands why the grief for his lost sons has not completely overshadowed his life, and from that understanding, rage, fury and hatred rise from the unconscious into the consciousness, the inner unease of waiting becomes an explosive disquiet that needs to act. He stands up and pushes the chair away with a violent jerk, shakes off his thoughtfulness, puts on his grey-green uniform cap with the cockade and the golden oak wreath awarded for twenty-five years of service, he pulls on his heavy, dark-grey uniform coat and leaves the flat. He doesn't yet know, in fact, what he intends to do, but he needs to do something, the waiting has become unbearable and is hollowing him out inside, he is oppressed by the silence and emptiness of the flat, and by the darkness. He stands uncertainly outside the front door of the building and then walks slowly along Residenzstrasse to Osloer Strasse. Here he stops again. The outlines of the electricity poles and the endless lines of the wires cut thin, ghostly figures into the arc of the evening sky, the lights are already burning outside the Gestapo's Jewish assembly camp in Schulstrasse, and a sentry with a red armband and yellow star is walking up and down in their murky glow.

Eckert turns irresolutely on his heels and is about to go back to Residenzstrasse, which now lies there lifeless and swathed in grey. The blacked-out windows of the houses are like clouded coffins with living creatures moving in them, hoping to outrun death, trying to outwit it by having their air-raid packs – their gas masks and protective goggles – ready to hand, by listening to the radio air-raid warnings and numbing all their senses but their ears. But then Eckert slows his pace, no, he can't go back to the empty silence of his flat now, but what's he supposed to do?

He stands alone on the street corner and looks helplessly around. All the energy that twitched within him a moment before has vanished, a paralysing indecision is starting to take hold of him again. Then his eye falls on the telephone box outside the school in Osloer

Strasse, and at the same moment the start of his paralysis returns. Making a phone call, that's what he's got to do now. He strides quickly towards the rectangular little cabin with the red iron frame and the thick matt-glass panes, opens the door and picks up the receiver. It happens so spontaneously that only now does it occur to him that he doesn't know the doctor's phone number. The phone book is in shreds, and it's so dark in the kiosk that it's pointless trying to find the number anyway. He steps out of the phone box and closes the door behind him. For a few seconds Eckert is downcast and leans against a street lamp, but then he turns resolutely into Schwedenstrasse, he knows there's a big restaurant on the right, halfway between Osloerstrasse and Exerzierstrasse, he'll call from there.

He enters the restaurant with a curt greeting, orders a glass of beer and requests the telephone book. The doctor's name is Wiedemann, Wiedemann is his name, there are lots of people of that name in the Berlin phone book, four dozen at a guess. Slowly and conscientiously his finger glides from line to line, architect, artists' equipment shop, painter, tobacconist, then he finds him, at the foot of the first column. 'Wiedemann, Dr med., Heinrich, dermatologist, Berlin SW 68, Ritterstr. 44, 17 48 64.' Eckert walks to the phone and turns the dial, one, seven, four, eight, six, four, the engaged tone hums, Eckert hangs up and tries again a few minutes later. It's fruitless again, even after the first two turns of the dial the deep hum of the engaged tone drones into the receiver. Three more attempts, at short intervals, produce the same result.

The landlord sees Eckert's helplessness and tells him that all connections through the central and southern exchanges have been disabled, the air raid . . . Eckert has stopped listening, throws a fifty-pfennig piece down on the metal counter and leaves the pub. An urge has welled up within him to speak to Dr Wiedemann today, he himself doesn't really know what he expects from it, but the urge is irresistible. On the corner with Koloniestrasse he jumps onto the 88, rides as far as Gesundbrunnen and then switches to the underground. 'Train travel irregular', he reads mechanically, 'interruption between Alexanderplatz and Kottbuser Tor', and climbs down the deep shaft to the platform. 'Train stops at Alexanderplatz!' Only as far as Alexanderplatz, Eckert thinks. He wants to get to Moritzplatz, that's – he calculates quickly, Jannowitz Bridge, Neanderstrasse, Moritzplatz – three stops further, but none of it matters any more, if the underground only goes as far as Alexanderplatz, then he'll go from Alexanderplatz to Moritzplatz on foot, even if it means creeping on all fours.

People who, like Eckert, are suddenly swept into a manic compulsion can become so unyielding as to turn into murderers, they can commit deeds which in the whole of their previous lives they would not even have imagined. At first, however, Eckert is peaceful, as he encounters no resistance, he is only uneasy and roused, he is still suppressing his dark apprehensions, those apprehensions are still nothing more than dull sensations.

Eckert hangs on a strap and doesn't let go of it even when the seat immediately in front of him becomes free at Bernauer Strasse, he is so completely fixed on his goal that he can't see or hear anything, the word circles incessantly in his brain: Moritzplatz, Moritzplatz, Moritzplatz. He knows the area well, because he used to work very close by, in Sebastianstrasse, in a mechanic's workshop, before he joined the Berlin tram service. Moritzplatz, the intersection of Prinzenstrasse and Oranienstrasse, it's a four-cornered square, with the big Wertheim building (he's never been able to get used to its new name, Awag), and opposite, with the Tam cinemas and function rooms, where he once attended many a *Bierfest* and whirled many a brazen Berlin girl on the dance floor, with the branch of Aschinger on the corner of Oranienstrasse, with its blue and white Bavarian tiles, oddly, but still Berlin's gastronomic trademark, and the Dresdener Bank on the corner of Prinzenstrasse, with the unchanging Pleite Café opposite Prinzessinnenstrasse, from which the red vans of the post office roll unceasingly. Moritzplatz, it isn't just the name of a place, for Eckert it's a concept, even though the square has changed considerably over the last few years, since the four underground exits were added and the roundabout was introduced.

At Alexanderplatz Eckert leaves the underground, he knows the subterranean labyrinth very well, and leaves it by the correct exit opposite the teachers' union building. By now it's 20.00 hours and air-raid time, outside the bunkers at the point formed by Neue Königstrasse and Landsberger Strasse a cluster of waiting people has formed, trusting in the dependable punctuality of the English pilots and waiting for the alarm to sound so they can be granted access. A velvet-soft sky stretches over the city, many stars gleam and glimmer. Since there is a new moon it is quite dark, Alexanderplatz is a wide, dark field with high black backdrops, the street lights hang apparently unconnected in the air, the blacked-out trams glide across the city viaduct with a dull rumble and squeaking brakes.

Eckert strides into the urban canyon of Alexanderstrasse. It is empty, as if it has died out, the policeman by entrance A of the main police station opposite Kaiserstrasse leans bored against the grille, he holds a cigarette in the hollow of his hand and smokes furtively. Eckert's footsteps sound dull, no echo comes from the ruins on either side, behind the empty windows the stars gleam against the dark outstretched canvas of the night sky. When Eckert catches a glimpse of Jannowitz Bridge behind Blumenstrasse, the sky is no longer dark blue and velvet-black, broad, red patches are rising from the south, the glimmer climbs almost to the zenith, and if it weren't night one might for a fleeting moment mistake it for sunrise. But the thought doesn't occur to Eckert, he has been through all the big daytime and night-time raids and knows exactly what that red wall of clouds means: the city is still burning, nine hours after the raid.

Eckert is stopped at Jannowitz Bridge. The crossing is blocked, a policeman explains to him that he can under no circumstances go into Brückenstrasse, under no circumstances, it's completely impossible, the whole district beyond the Spree is closed off. Eckert's unease turns into agitation as he sees himself being forced away from his goal, but he is still in a state in which every thought, every word and every action is controllable and subject to his will. Before his agitation turns into action, forcing his way through, the sirens fling their fearsome voice into the silence of the night. The policeman nods towards Waisen Bridge, where a yellow and orange sign indicates a public air-raid shelter. Eckert walks a few steps in that direction and stops behind a shattered advertising pillar, he doesn't even think of seeking out an air-raid shelter, the alarm can only be helpful to his intentions, which he will implement beneath the cover of the alarm. Once the bombing begins the policeman will presumably take cover with the others, and the bridge will be left open. Eckert waits patiently. The arches of Jannowitz Bridge are etched like a huge spider's web against the dark sky, on the right looms the massive tower of the Märkisches Museum, while on the left the façade of the ruined, burnt-out building of the Josetti ciga-rette factory rises jaggedly like the battlements of a fortress.

Eckert feels no fear, just a nameless dread. Even though he can't see what lies beyond the Spree, he knows it is hell over there, its fires still spurting into the sky, engulfing everything. Time flows thickly on, the sky is still deeply dark, but a deep, even hum can be heard, quietly at first, then more and more distinctly. Then a grand spectacle unfolds against the black background, red pyramids, composed of countless licking little flames, appear out of the dark sky, gleam in all directions and float gently to earth, and immedi-ately there are other signs there, three yellow balls that turn white after a few seconds and are then absorbed by the darkness once more.

Eckert is rooted to the spot, he has never watched it before, but he knows that the red pyramids, known as Christmas trees, mark out the targets for the bombers, and the bright spheres are the markings of the fighter planes, and then suddenly the spotlights are there, they stretch spectrally into the darkness, with their long, white arms they feel their way around the sky, unite into a single beam and then fan out again. When one of the spotlights goes out the darkness returns all the more heavily, and when another shoots up behind the savings bank, a small, bright, silver patch appears in it: a plane. Immediately all the other spotlights pounce on it, inter-sect and almost stumble over another with excitement, they persistently follow the tail of the plane, which continues evenly and unwaveringly on its course. Then the silence is suddenly interrupted, a hard, dry report roars out: the anti-aircraft guns have started firing. All around the plane there are orange flashes of light bursting on either side, above and below, then a glow rises on the eastern horizon, explosions throw their bright-red mushrooms up into the dark background, a few seconds later there is a rumble like a nearby thunderclap.

Eckert can't tear himself away from the spectacle, but eventually he does get moving and cautiously approaches the bridge. It is unguarded now. Eckert wraps his coat tighter around his body and runs over the bridge, he pants a little as he goes up the gentle incline, but then he has reached the summit of the bridge and his legs run all by themselves. The closer Eckert comes to the crossing with Köpenicker Strasse, the hotter the breath of the flames strikes him, and smoke billows in his direction. It's too dark for Eckert to make out details, but he can tell that no houses here have been left standing, the flames still lick from windows and skylights, from shutters and cellars, the storm whips them up and down, pushes them down and draws them back up again. The street is like a path across a scree slope, stony and uneven, the traffic lights and street lights are bent, the overhead tramlines dangle loosely. Eckert cuts his cheek open on a wire, but barely notices, wipes away the pumping blood with his glove and at last presses his handkerchief to the wound, he stumbles on across the debris, every step is dangerous, because the rubble still lies loosely around, deep holes have opened up in the thoroughfare. Eckert doesn't pause for a moment, the idea of turning round barely occurs to him, it is as if an invisible fist were pushing him forward. Darkness and fire, rubble and debris embrace him, the gas spits from burst pipes with an unpleasant hiss, water spouts from cracked conduits, high in the sky the anti-aircraft shells explode, British Mosquitoes and German fighters circle, but Eckert stumbles on into the field of rubble. When he falls his hand touches a soft, sticky mass, the blood halts in his veins and seems to congeal, he is shaken by a feverish shiver, an unfathomable terror seizes him and brings a cold sweat to his forehead. His hands, which he stretched out to protect himself as he fell, have plunged into a slippery mass from which a sickly smell of blood rises, and he senses rather than knows that he has touched the smashed body of a human being. For a few seconds he lies there as if paralysed, he feels as if he has reached into the bloody face of unbridled war, then he draws himself wildly up and staggers on, with just one thought, Moritzplatz, Dr Wiedemann, his wife, his daughter. At last he just stumbles on, every stone and every hole is a cunning and treacherous trap, and when the three long notes of the pre-warning sound, he has only got as far as Dresdener Strasse, and again and again he is surrounded only by mountains of fire and rubble, the miasma of blood and the smell of burning. He can hardly see a thing, because his eyes are sticky with blood and soot and dust, but he makes it as far as Ritterstrasse, he knows the area well, and he also finds Dr Wiedemann's house.

When he almost falls into the main door of the house, the last inhabitants are coming up from the air-raid cellar. A woman stops and pauses for a moment as if frozen when she glimpses him, then cries roar loud and shrill from her, a young woman crouches down on the lowest step of the stairs and starts whimpering quietly, a child throws its hands over its face and weeps silently.

Eckert looks terrible, like a corpse that has risen from some terrible mass grave. His face is torn on the right cheek by a dreadful gash, blood still seeps from it, his coat is drenched with blood, dusty and torn, human tissue is trapped in the buttons of his right sleeve, from the soot that covers his face two wild, crazed, bloodshot eyes stare. Eckert wants to say something, but he can only gurgle, the words well into his mouth, he takes another few steps then his knees give, he tries again to pull himself up, but at last his feet are pulled away and he collapses.

When he comes to he is lying on a sofa, a man with severe rimless glasses is bending over him and running a wet object over the wound on his cheek. The bespectacled man asks him to lie still, not to move, as the wound needs stitching. Eckert lets his head fall back again, he suddenly has an ice-cold feeling on his cheek and he is aware of delicate, painless needle jabs. Who is the man with the rimless glasses? A doctor? Of course a doctor, it must be . . . 'Dr Wiedemann?' Eckert struggles to say.

The other man nods, he has finished stitching the wound, walks to a basin and methodically and ponderously washes his hands. 'How do you know me?' he asks over his shoulder.

The fact that the man who is now in the same room with him is actually Dr Wiedemann, to whom he has made his way across rubble and debris, over bomb craters and corpses, through fire, gas and water, immediately revives him, he swings his legs carefully off the sofa and tries to stand up, but Dr Wiedemann pushes him gently back down onto the sofa. 'Lie where you are,' he says in a friendly but resolute voice. 'You are in quite a dire condition,' he adds. 'Where have you come from?'

But Eckert is not in a mood to answer questions, the questions he needs to ask burn within him. He carefully slides himself back against the cushion. 'My name is Eckert,' he says.

Dr Wiedemann looks at him quizzically.

'Eckert, Max Eckert from Reinickendorf,' Eckert repeats. 'My daughter is a patient of yours, Doctor.'

'Right,' says the doctor. 'Now I understand.' He looks closely at Eckert. Fluxus salinus, he thinks, so this is the father. 'And what brings you to me at this late hour?' he asks.

Eckert takes a deep breath. At last he has reached his goal, he doesn't yet guess that it is only a stage on the way. With short, hurried words, without full stops or commas, he tells his story.

Dr Wiedemann has been listening to him quietly without interrupting him. 'Yes, your wife was here at my surgery with your daughter this morning, Mr Eckert,' he says when Eckert says nothing. 'I had your daughter under the sun-ray lamp and gave her an injection of Detoxin. Your wife was in a great hurry, because the arrival of the bombing units had already been announced, she left here at about a quarter past eleven, and she probably didn't make it home because the sirens were already going off about ten minutes later. She might have sought refuge in a bunker somewhere, or in the underground.'

Dr Wiedemann studiously avoids mentioning the fact that a bomb has crashed through the roof of Moritzplatz underground station and killed an as yet unknown number of people who were standing inside the station, neither does he mention that after the first wave of bombers the whole district between Moritzplatz and Köpenick Bridge, Hallesches Tor and Friedrichstrasse Station was in flames, and that during the very minutes when people were escaping from the basements of the burning houses and factories and into the streets the second and third wave were flying in and once again dropping enormous explosive and incendiary payloads on the same target area.

'At about sixteen-thirty hours my wife and my daughter were not yet home, Doctor,' Eckert says, agitated. 'Something has happened, I can sense it like a certainty in my blood.'

'Calm down, Mr Eckert,' Dr Wiedemann reassures him. 'Perhaps your wife was so upset by the raid that she stayed with friends.'

'We don't know anyone around here,' Eckert remarks curtly.

'Or perhaps she couldn't face the long walk,' Dr Wiedemann says, trying to diminish his fears.

Eckert won't have any of that, either. 'Think about it, Doctor, four and a half hours after the alarm they still weren't home,' he says urgently. 'Four and a half hours!'

'There is little point engaging in speculation,' Dr Wiedemann observes. 'But while you have been out and about, your wife may have come home, it's after half past nine. So you have been out for more than three hours. While you are talking to me here, she may be sitting at home worrying about you.'

Eckert sits up stiffly. That possibility hasn't even occurred to him, he has roused himself into too great an anticipation of disaster. 'That may be so,' he says quickly, takes his legs off the sofa and stands up.

'Where are you going now?' Dr Weidemann asks.

'Home,' Eckert replies. 'That should be obvious.'

'Out of the question,' Dr Wiedemann contradicts him forcefully. 'In this state, in the middle of the night? Haven't you had enough trouble getting here?'

The battle between going and staying lasts for several minutes, in the end Dr Wiedemann wins, after promising to take Eckert to Reinickendorf in his car early in the morning. He secretly stirs a powerful dose of bromide into the coffee, and it isn't long before Eckert is sound asleep. Dr Wiedemann is a doctor whose job is also a deep calling, and for whom suffering human beings are not divided into private patients and members of the public health scheme. Of course it is not only his humanity that is the crucial factor, there is also his special medical interest, as he graduated with a dissertation about dermatitis with particular reference to fluxus salinus, weeping eczema, but he can hardly be blamed for that, it is only active in his unconscious, because he has realized that Eckert has entered a severe mental and psychical depressive state, that an almost manic compulsion is threatening to explode from within, and he has made up his mind to treat the man quite delicately.

At seven o'clock the next morning, while Eckert is still fast asleep, Dr Wiedemann gets his car from the garage, which has remained miraculously unscathed in the middle of all the destruction, and then, as promised, drives Eckert to Reinickendorf. To reach Residenzstrasse he has to take an enormous detour, via Schöneberg, Friedenau, Charlottenburg and Moabit, as the previous day's attack has caused unimaginable damage and deviations keep sending the car further and further west. They don't reach Residenzstrasse until about nine o'clock. Dr Wiedemann goes up to the flat with Eckert, now feeling uneasy himself. Even if Ursula Eckert is only one of his many patients, she and her mother, who has always come with her, are after all people that he knows personally, and a personal fate always speaks to one more directly than the most terrible misfortune on a mass scale.

Eckert's hands are trembling so badly that he can't open the door to the flat. Dr Wiedemann takes the key from his hand, unlocks the door and pushes it violently open. With a few glances he can tell that the flat is empty: Frau Eckert and her daughter have still not come back. He knows what that means, and it is quite clear from Eckert's face that he does too. Still he tries to offer him some words of comfort, but Eckert doesn't even listen to him, he takes a few quick steps through the flat, stands reflecting for a moment in the kitchen, mechanically straightens a chair and then resolutely leaves the room.

He doesn't say a word as they go down the stairs side by side. He doesn't rush down the stairs, his hands are plunged deeply into his coat pockets, and he carefully takes one step at a time, but that slowness is itself stranger than raving and shouting. Only when Dr Wiedemann opens the car door does Eckert voice the request to be driven back again. Dr Wiedemann doesn't dare refuse him, he also thinks it right not to leave the petrified-looking man on his own for now. On the way back to Ritterstrasse Dr Wiedemann tries several times to engage Eckert in conversation, but it doesn't work, so in the end he lets it be. When the doctor stops on the corner of Ritterstrasse and Prinzenstrasse to allow a procession of firemen to pass, Eckert quickly opens the door, gets out, nods fleetingly at the doctor and flings the door shut behind him. It happens with such swift and skilled movements, of which Dr Wiedemann would not have thought this rather awkward and measured man capable, that he is taken by surprise and unable to hold him back. He just catches sight of Eckert resolutely heading straight for the field of rubble.

And now begins the odyssey of tram conductor Max Eckert, on 4 February 1945, the day after the most annihilating air raid by the Americans on Berlin. Admittedly the ruined district has been closed off within a wide radius, but Eckert is still able to penetrate the devastated streets, his conductor's uniform stands him in good stead. He is clear that there is only one possibility now of his wife and his daughter being alive, which is that they are locked in some basement somewhere. In Schmidstrasse, near the intersection with Neanderstrasse, a bulldozer is at work because there are thought to be living people under the rubble. Eckert crosses the area between Köpenicker Strasse and Moritzplatz, but again and again he returns to the bulldozer and watches as the sharp jaws of the grabber eat their way into the mountains of rock, swing round and spew out their bites to the side again. He pursues the progress of the work very closely, he is often in Schmidstrasse, and normally travelling. What he only vaguely perceived during the night, what could only be guessed at in the darkness, is now, with bright daylight falling down upon it, revealed as an inferno of unparalleled horror. Among the collapsed and still-burning houses are shattered trams, cars and lorries, dead humans and horses lie on the ground, body parts, mortal remains, heads without bodies, bodies without heads, trunks without legs, legs without trunks, undefinable piles of burnt, charred, shredded human flesh, desperate, wailing, half-crazed people are wandering around, many of them staring with uncomprehending eyes and pointing feebly at the smoking, crushed, devastated buildings which barely twenty-four hours ago still provided shelter and warmth and a pitiful remnant of independent life, some dash through smoke-filled doors and climb on unsteady walls to secure the wretched remains of their possessions from the piles of rubble.

When it becomes clear that no one can still be alive in the basement in Schmidstrasse because it is full to the ceiling with water, the digger stops work and is withdrawn. When it is dragged away by a tractor, Eckert undergoes a sudden transformation. Until now he has still fed the faint flame of his hope, but now he is certain that his wife and his daughter have died here, somewhere in these streets. If until now Eckert has been agitated, but still relatively calm and level-headed, now he has been gripped by an idea that won't let him go, that spurs him on: he must find his wife and his daughter, regardless of where and how. He looks each body in the face, turns over every corpse lying on its belly and studies its ravaged features, he checks the clothing on the severed trunks and picks up skulls in his hands, he climbs among the still-smoking and smouldering ruins, he clambers into collapsed basements, forces his way down half-buried passageways. Again and again he crosses the field of rubble from Köpenick Bridge to Schmidstrasse, from Moritzplatz to Alexandrinenstasse, from Michaelkirchplatz to Neanderstrasse, he clears lumps of rock aside with his bare hands as if he thinks he might be able to reveal the entrance to a basement, he digs through buried basement windows, he has already seen hundreds of corpses and helped recover corpses from Moritzplatz underground station, he has gazed into the faces of charred and blackened human beings and not even been able to establish whether they were men or women, but it has all been in vain. He has not been able to find his wife and his daughter.

He is utterly discouraged and starving, his hands are smeared with ptomaine, he is close to complete collapse, but he is still wandering around the field of rubble. He knows that his wife and his daughter have died, but he also wants to know how they perished and where their bodies are. If they had died of tuberculosis or cancer or some revolting illness, it would have been a death that he would have experienced along with them, that would have been established in the people themselves, that would have corresponded to traditional views of dying. Then he would have walked behind a corpse and thrown three handfuls of earth into the open grave, he would have known where a mound would be heaped and later a marble headstone raised, but like this he doesn't know anything. He can't grasp that the two of them are simply no longer there, vanished, trampled, scattered, simply no longer there. The imagination of this simple man is then sparked by the gruesome, terrible images that he has seen that day and which are still before his eyes. He sees his wife and daughter sitting on a bench as they always sat in the shelter of their building, with their shoulders hunched and their arms pressed tight against their bodies, knees together, with quivering jaws and darting eyes, clutching damp cloths, ready to press them to their mouths at any second, goggles pushed up on their foreheads, prepared to bring them down over their eyes, he sees them sitting there, every fibre of their bodies attuned to the slightest noise from outside, the singing of the engines, the thunderous roar of the anti-aircraft guns, the whirring, droning and whistling of the bombs plummeting towards them. He sees them sitting there for only a second, even before they can conceive a thought, before the event hurtling towards them can spark a reflex in their brains and enter their consciousness, in that second the basement ceiling coming down on them like an elemental fist. It happened without them seeing, hearing, feeling anything, even though hundreds of alarms had prepared them for it.

It could have happened like that, but it could also . . . Eckert can no longer halt his imagination, again and again it feeds on the molten streams from the corpse-scattered field around him. He is, like everyone else, trapped in the world of empirical thought, and lacks the experience of those whose mouths are sealed for ever because they are already beyond Lethe, but the imagination distorts outlines and darkens the colours of the images.

Might it not also be that when everything was burning, heat, anxiety and breathlessness assailed them when the way out of the basement was blocked by scorching flames, when the hole in the wall suddenly opened up and the fire in the next-door basement blocked that escape route too? Might it not be that the flames leaped at them with greedy, clutching fingers, darted glowing tongues into their flesh and turned them into ashes or arm-length stumps of charcoal, or that smoke and fumes hurled them to the ground and slowly choked them to death? Might it not be that they had time to think lots of thoughts and feel terrible emotions, sudden fear, oppressive anxiety, deadly terror, ungraspable dread, paralysing horror?

Might it not also be that they were buried in an avalanche of rubble, trapped in a dark grave, and that the water began to spout from a burst pipe, ran and ran, unstoppable as a waterfall, spilled over the basement floor, rose, slowly but steadily, climbed up the people, held them in its wet clutches, blood rose to the brain and paralysed it, flooded the lungs and halted the breath? Or perhaps a pipe was bent and the gas started flowing, an invisible, deadly cloud began to spread over the basement, first floated to the ceiling and then fell back down on the people, made their eyes flicker and struck up an unbearable roaring noise in their ears, enfolded them in a stupor and gently led them into a state of torpor, sealed their tissue and drove their breath away, turned their blood bright red and discoloured their mucous membranes?

Might a lump of rock not have pulled them down and fixed them to the floor as a wrestler holds his defeated opponent on the mat, perhaps the burden pressed down on body or legs, but did no more to them, it only held them tightly, let them breathe, think, feel and even speak, but held them in a stony grip and made the place where the block of stone had struck them the last and unalterable site of their lives, so that only a great miracle could have swept it away and freed them, so that their lives under the stone clamp in the dark vault of the caved-in basement gasped their last and their bodies ceased to function with tortuous slowness?

Or perhaps nothing happened to them except that they were trapped in a subterranean vault, that they were still walking around in it, conferring and knocking against ceiling and wall, but no one heard their knocking because huge mountains of rubble were spread above them, that now, while he, Eckert, climbs over scree slopes, they are still alive and hoping to be freed, but that hope is becoming ever thinner and more fleeting, despair and madness are inflamed in their brains, the more hunger and thirst and darkness take hold of them, the more unlikely it becomes that someone will find their stony grave and free them from it?

The tram conductor Eckert stands on the threshold of that world to which there is no access, which no human eye has looked upon, whose wall can be penetrated only by the mind, and of which there is no likeness, only a cold, grim uncertainty.

He knows the word 'missing', but so far it has meant nothing to him, he has read it and spoken it, but associated nothing more with it. In his life he has used many words thoughtlessly and superficially, without filling them with a concept. One of those is the word 'missing', it has slipped smoothly from his tongue in the past, but now it stands before him as if in physical form, a monster, gigantic, with gaping jaws and crushing teeth, with scornfully grinning, bloodshot eyes and long, rapacious arms: missing. Now he knows what it means to bump into the void, to let thoughts, hopes and longings circle around a deadly uncertainty: missing. Never having complete certainty, sending your thoughts time and again to the basements and tunnels, caves and craters, time and again hypothesizing that they might have been crushed by boulders, drenched in water, numbed by gas, slung into the air by exploding shells, gnawed by rats, whether their cries slowly faded gasping away, or whether the life fled quickly from them: missing.

Even in those days of utter chaos a man like Eckert must stand out. A police patrol picks him up at last and tries to persuade him to leave the disaster area first by calling out to him and then by grabbing him with a practised grip. Eckert desperately defends himself, but the police are stronger than him, so in the end he gives in and allows himself to be led away with a policeman on either side.

One of the officers, a young man with a smooth, vacant face, claps him approvingly on the shoulder and says quite casually: 'It's bad, old man, but take comfort from the fact that you can only die one death.'

Eckert doesn't listen at first, but then the words trickle into his consciousness. What did the cop just say? You can only die one . . . Eckert stops in front of the policeman and looks him in the face, at once desperate and menacing.

His threatening gaze makes the policeman uncomfortable, he pushes Eckert away with a dismissive gesture and asks, 'What's up? Why are you staring at me?'

Eckert doesn't avert his eyes, he goes on looking at the policeman. 'You can only die one death, you say?' he mumbles. 'Yes, of course, only one death.' His voice gets louder and finally rises to an animal roar. 'Yes, only one death, but it matters what kind of death it is, whether you die, just die, because syphilis slowly eats you up, or because one day your heart gives out, but this is not dying, burning, charring, choking, drowning, cut down or crushed, shredded or pulverized by the blast . . .'

'Fine,' the policeman says, and takes a step back. 'Could all be, but come with us for now.'

'You've got to understand,' says the other policeman, an older man with a coarse face, gesturing with his eyes to the other man, 'that you can't go on creeping around the disaster area. Who are you looking for?'

'My wife,' Eckert replies, 'my wife and my daughter, they must be here somewhere.' He points to the ruins with his right hand. 'Here or there or over there, somewhere. Perhaps they're dead already, but perhaps they're still alive and we're standing on their sarcophagus right now.'

'It's ridiculous looking here, you won't find them alive,' says the older policeman. 'And that's enough looking now. We don't want to take you along. Go!'

'Where to?' Eckert asks. 'Can you tell me that?'

'Home, of course,' the younger policeman says. 'Where else? Or have you been bombed out?'

Home? The word stings Eckert's consciousness like a goad. Home? Into the dead, empty flat, where every item reminds him that his wife and daughter were still living there two or three days ago? Being there is almost worse than searching in this field of corpses.

'Be reasonable,' says the older policeman, and puts his hand on his shoulder. 'Go!'

Eckert, who has already turned his back on the policemen and begun to walk away from them, jerks round. It's as if something inside him has torn open, as if the crust that has hitherto covered his soul is breaking open and everything that has been repressed for years and repeatedly held down is spilling to the surface through the crack. The images run rapidly through his brain: the loss of his two sons, the fate of his wife's sister, who married a Jew and was beaten to death in Sachsenhausen, the arrest and cold-blooded destruction of Dean Lichtenberg (because Eckert is a devout Catholic), the total conversion of the people to materialism, the appeals to God from the mouths of rapacious murderers, the insane prolongation of a war lost long ago.

'Heil Hitler, you say, here, in the ruins of Berlin?' Eckert roars, and lowers his head like a bull waiting to attack. It may be, it's even likely, that the young policeman only gave the Hitler salute out of habit and without giving the matter any particular attention, but Eckert can no longer consider that possibility, his brain has been deluged by a red wave, all reflections are extinguished, hate, rage, fury, contempt, despair fill every cell and every pore. This man with the green uniform and the cap, right now he is the system itself, from beneath the peak of the cap pulled low over his eyes there grins the repellent grimace of the hated devil of Braunau, the Antichrist.

With one leap Eckert is on him, both hands grip the man's throat, they press tightly, almost compressing the throat, the young policeman has almost lost his balance under the attack, he totters and falls to the ground, but Eckert doesn't let go. He is in an intoxicated state, his surroundings have vanished into the ground, all that remains is him and beneath him the other man, that devilish grimace with the little black moustache on the upper lip.

The other policeman was so surprised by Eckert's sudden outburst that he missed the moment to intervene. He draws his gun from his side pocket. 'Let go!' he roars. 'Let go this minute!'

The voice reaches Eckert as if from a long way off, the blood rushes in his ears, wild and unruly, his hands tighten their grip on the throat, the young policeman is dazed, his face has gone crimson and is already turning blue.

The other policeman tries to pull Eckert away, but he can't, Eckert's hands are like iron fetters around the young policeman's neck.

'Let go!' the older policeman roars again. 'Or I'll fire!' He lashes out at Eckert, but Eckert doesn't release his grip, he presses his adversary's head deeper and deeper into the gravel, his breathing is coming in pants. His lips start foaming. Then the older policeman kneels down next to Eckert, puts the pistol to his temple and pulls the trigger.

A short, sharp bang and a dull crackle and it's over. Eckert's head falls sideways, his body arches, then slides down and rolls a few metres down the steep scree.

Not everyone who has devoted his life to Führer, nation and fatherland has been given an official obituary. What follows is a report from Police Commissioner Wilhelm Schikorra from the 13th Police District:

On 6 February 1945 local patrolman Günther Dietzer and I were patrolling the incident site in the 13th Police District. At around 16.15 hours we noticed a very unkempt man was rummaging around the ruin of the building 12 Annenstrasse. He was later identified as the tram conductor Max Josef Anton Eckert, born in Bielefeld on 18 November 1894 and living in Berlin-Reinickendorf, 144/II Residenzstrasse. When first instructed to leave the ruin, Mr Eckert violently resisted. At last we managed to persuade him to leave the ruin without applying force. The local patrol man Officer Dietzler gave the Nazi salute as he did so. Hereupon Mr Eckert turned round and shouted: 'Heil Hitler, you say, here, in the ruins of Berlin?' At the same moment he jumped at Officer Dietzler's throat, threw him to the ground and choked him very violently. Dietzler was completely dazed from the fall and the choking and hence not in a position to defend himself. I therefore ordered Mr Eckert twice and loudly to let go of Dietzler. Since he did not comply, and other attempts to release Dietzler from the immediate threat to his life were unsuccessful, I resorted to the use of my firearm. Mr Eckert died on the spot.

This is case III Ic of the Police Administration Law of 1 August 1931. Paragraph 53 of the Criminal Code is also invoked.

Berlin, 7 February 1945

Signed: Wilhelm Schikorra
Police Commissioner

That is the story of the tram conductor Max Eckert, which may seem like the trivial fate of an unknown little man. It took place amidst the mayhem of an event that shook the continents, it was only a drop in a sea of blood and tears, but even the greatest events are composed of small and very small incidents, and only together do they constitute the large whole. The death of the tram conductor Max Eckert is only one small piece in the terrible mosaic of this vast war. Many died more pointlessly, most of them without the triumph of going for the throat of the hated adversary. Eckert died because his tormented and trampled soul discharged itself with the violence of a volcanic eruption. Neither did he die in vain or pointlessly, because every death in the struggle against tyranny goes on working, even if it does so invisibly. It is not the end and the conclusion, it is a new seed and a new beginning.

It is five minutes past twelve. The city's breath is suffocated beneath the vapour of smoke and haze rolling through the streets, its veins are opened, the tortured body bleeding its last. A pestilential miasma cloaks the jungle of ruins, mountains of human bodies and animal corpses, the wrecks of burnt-out, blasted tanks and vehicles, heaps of debris, bottomless craters, leaning house walls, exploded bridges, blazes block the streets. The battle still rages in the city centre, on the Kaiserdamm and around the high-rise bunkers in Friedrichshain, by the Zooloigical Garden, and in Humboldthain by Gesundbrunnen Station, aerial battles are being fought between Russian fighters and German supply planes, while new companies have been assembled of the wounded and the scattered, old Volkssturm men and fifteen-year-old members of the Hitler Youth, thrown into battle inadequately armed or with instructions to grab the weapons of the fallen.

Wilhelmplatz lies empty and dead beneath the furious fire of the Russian artillery, only the breadth of the square recalls its former purpose, the parade ground of enthusiasm, the hysterical enthusiasm of a people seduced, and the compulsory enthusiasm of the helots, nothing recalls the torchlight procession of the SA on 30 January 1933, the marches of the Luftwaffe regiments to musical accompaniment, the compulsory presence of school classes at the visits of illustrious guests, the choral calls of 'We want to see the Führer!' and the slavish cries of 'Führer command us, we will follow you!' nothing more is there, banners, insignias and standards, torches and Turkish crescents have vanished from the granite slabs of the square. Only ruins line it now, the Hotel Kaiserhof, the Dreifaltigkeitskirche, the Finance Ministry, the Reich Transport Office, the Reich Chancellery, the Propaganda Ministry.

The Reich Chancellery is under constant fire, piece by piece the shells eat away at the masonry and unmask the fraudulent display of fake marble, thin sandstone slabs and cheap pink bricks. As on a target, the bullets of the low-flying planes drill into the plaster, walls and ceilings begin to tear apart, mirrors shatter, crystal chandeliers crash and splinter to the parquet floors.

In the underground bunker beneath the garden of the Reich Chancellery, the Führer Adolf Hitler sits on a wooden box. His face is twisted and distorted, his features slack and feeble, his skin pale and covered with bright-red patches, a spasmodic twitch tugs at the corners of his mouth every few seconds, his eyes are bulging far from their sockets and red-rimmed, his gaze is blank, his hands are trembling, his hair is damp and clammy, and the sweat stands out in fat droplets on his brow.

The leader of the Great German Reich, sitting there, ugly and crumpled with anxiety, does not look like a happy bridegroom, who married his long-term lover the previous evening and entertained his guests with sparkling wine. The wedding ceremony was only the prelude to the gruesome, trashy operetta staged according to the orders given by the deranged petty-bourgeois from Braunau, just as he ordered millions of people to be hunted into misery, poverty, death, despair, hunger, fire, gas chambers, mass graves, gallows, prisons, concentration camps, military hospitals and the Labour Front. This Führer, who exerted his tyrannical power over the continent of Europe, who had all the means of power and all the sources of information at his disposal, who played with generals as children play with pebbles, who had a whole people lying at his feet in hysterical ecstasy, a people who had taken all gifts from his hands as if they were gifts from God and who listened to his words as if they were the word of God, this great Führer is now sitting in the underground bunker on a plain wooden box and asking his chauffeur, 'Any news?'

But his chauffeur is not in a position to tell him the news he wishes to hear, that the reserve armies are close by, or that Field Marshal Ritter von Greim has effectively struck in the battle for Berlin with the remains of his Luftwaffe. It can no longer be kept secret that Russian tanks coming from the Brandenburg Gate have reached Potsdamer Platz, the Tiergarten and Weidendammer Bridge, that on the Reichstag, whose blaze twelve years ago went on to rage across the whole world, the red flag of the Soviets now flutters, that Russian tanks are also moving from the south along Wilhelmstrasse northward towards the Reich Chancellery, that Russian infantry are advancing along the underground tunnels at Friedrichstrasse. Neither can it be kept secret any longer that all around the entrance to the bunker a devastating artillery fire is coming down, that the earth is being stirred up, and black fountains of soil are spraying into the air, that the trees are ragged and the walls around the garden of the Reich Chancellery have been laid low. Two days previously he had fetched SS Group Leader Fegelein, Eva Braun's brother-in-law, from his flat and had him shot because he had attempted to withdraw back into civilian life, in a nocturnal address he had made all the inmates of the bunker take an oath of loyalty to commit mutual suicide, was still preoccupied with defence and relief, intoxicated with the final victory, and had said to Field Marshal Greim: 'Do not despair, it will all be fine.' But then the mood had changed again, and he had raged once more like a lunatic through the corridors and rooms of his bunker, when he received the news that his most reliable supporter, Reichsführer SS Heinrich Himmler, had made contact with the Western Allies via the Vice-President of the Swedish Red Cross, Count Folke Bernadotte, and offered the unconditional capitulation of Germany to Great Britain and the United States, the will to total destruction blazed up in him once more. He immediately stamped out the tiny spark of reason, forbidding any radio communication with the special train 'Steiermark', Himmler's headquarters, had, through his Party clerk Bormann, the words 'Foreign press reports new betrayal, Führer expects unshakeable loyalty from everyone' broadcast to the four winds, and ordered Schörner from the south of the eastern front, Dönitz from Holstein, Vietinghoff from Italy, Wenck from the Elbe front and Stumpf with the air fleet to relieve the Reich capital, but since then two long, fearful days have passed, and he has had only refusals or no answer at all, which has led Bormann to say 'betrayal everywhere'. There is no longer any way out, the Führer Adolf Hitler realizes he is surrounded and besieged from the air, he is caught in his own trap. He has not left his bunker for days, and he is not leaving it now, he crouches cravenly deep in the earth below concrete metres thick, he knows that his end has come, that the thousand-year Third Reich that he proclaimed is over, that it is already five minutes past twelve, that the solders whose young gullibility he duped and enslaved with vain gestures and boastful words, whom he despatched six years ago to conquer a world, who toppled cities on his orders and made whole landscapes go up in flames, have now returned from the icy nights of Norway and the roasting desert of Egypt, from the wide steppes of Russia and the unconquerable wall on the coast of France home to the capital of the Reich, but still he does not fall to the scythe-wielding skeleton, he wants the last stalks to be mown down, he wants everything to be harvested this time. He dictates his political and private testament and sends three men with copies to Dönitz, Schörner and to the Party archive in Munich, he appoints Dönitz his successor, draws up a new list of ministers and makes Bormann his executor. And since he lived as a fraud, so he behaves in his final hour, when he orders an announcement to be made that he fell in battle at the head of his soldiers, but he seeks death not in the bullets of the enemy, he creeps cravenly from his accursed life, he orders his chauffeur to get hold of 200 litres of petrol, he bids farewell to his henchmen and withdraws to his room, and while the guards dance with the secretaries to gramophone music, he turns his pistol upon himself and fires into his blasphemous mouth, his wife poisons herself, their corpses are laid by Dr Goebbels and Bormann in the garden of the Reich Chancellery by the emergency exit to the bunker and have petrol poured over them. Under the thunder of the Russian guns and the raised, bloodstained hands of his accomplices, the bodies of Hitler and his lover blaze in bright flames. The stench that has spread across the whole of Europe under his tyranny also accompanies him on his journey to hell.

Towards morning the artillery fire swells again to a monstrous volume, the big house rocks and trembles under the massive explosions, the foundations seem to shake, the air is run through with an incessant rage and roar, a flaming sky arches above the city, and still dust, lead and fire rain down upon it, columns of fire burst up amidst showers of sparks when the shells from the rocket launchers explode. Blood-red and overcast with grey, the sun rises over the horizon in the east, and casts its rays over the mown-down city that smokes, smoulders and burns from a thousand wounds, which from all sides is ceaselessly hammered by all calibres, by rocket launchers, field howitzers, anti-aircraft guns, mortars, tank guns and anti-tank guns, on-board weapons, heavy machine guns, mine throwers and bomb shafts.

When the dull light of day pierces the clouds of smoke, the air-raid warden comes to the boiler room. He greets them abruptly and turns to Dr Böttcher. 'I would like to warn you, gentlemen!'

'Warn us?' Dr Böttcher asks, and gets slowly to his feet. 'What about?'

'The SS are close by, they are sitting in the Europahaus and the Excelsior,' the air-raid warden replies, 'the battle is now concentrated on Saarlandstrasse.'

Dr Böttcher listens to the noise, but the thunder of artillery fire is too great for him to make out fire from handguns.

'You can believe me,' the air-raid warden says, 'I'm telling you the truth.'

'You just want to get rid of us,' says Wiegand, joining them, 'isn't that right?'

The air-raid warden gives Wiegand an angry look. 'That too, of course. You're digging a revolting hole for us with your people. If the SS come they'll say I've helped you, then they'll wring my neck, and when the Russians come, there will be a battle.'

'Where is Dr Wiedemann?' asks Dr Böttcher.

'Over in the public air-raid cellar,' the air-raid warden replies, 'look over there to the right. That seems to be him now.' Dr Wiedemann comes through the door.

'Gentlemen,' he says excitedly, 'the situation is becoming critical, the SS are crammed together into the tightest space, they are defending every house, every hallway, every courtyard, every cellar . . .'

'I told them,' the air-raid warden interjects, 'but they wouldn't believe me!'

Dr Wiedemann explains the situation in short and hasty words. 'The Russians are on the western side of Saarlandstrasse, the eastern side is still occupied by the SS, but the Russians are also behind them on Wilhelmstrasse. The front line, as it is still called, even though it is also the rear line, runs right through the block. The walls to the courtyard that abut the courtyards on Saarlandstrasse and Wilhelmstrasse, and the firewalls that divide the houses on Saarlandstrasse and Wilhelmstrasse, that is today's front line. They are fighting bitterly over the walls that connect the courtyards, over the cracks in the cellar walls, with unparalleled ferocity, the SS are ignoring the fact that there are hundreds and thousands of women and children in the cellars.'

'So we need to act quickly,' Wiegand says firmly. 'If I have understood you correctly, Dr Wiedemann, we only need to get over the walls of the courtyard to the back and we will be with the Russians.'

'Just clear off,' the air-raid warden says angrily. 'You can join the Russians or the SS or the Zulus as far as I'm concerned, just get out of my cellar.'

'We can get through a hole in the wall,' Lassehn says.

'Quite right,' Dr Wiedemann replies, and shrugs slightly, 'but of course I can't guarantee it . . .'

'Of course not,' says Wiegand, 'but your information is very valuable to us.'

'We could be unlucky and end up in a courtyard that is still occupied by the SS,' says Private Poppe.

'You could slip on a pile of sand too,' Schröter says dismissively. 'I say we should try to get across to Wilhelmstrasse.'

'That raises an important question,' Gregor says. 'Are we going with or without weapons?'

'Without, of course,' Lassehn says quickly.

'No of course about it,' Gregor says. 'If we bump into the SS on the way, I'm not going to be dragged off as I was at Silesian Station and later on Stralauer Strasse.'

'Quite right,' says Wiegand, 'My thoughts exactly. This time we'll fight on, I say we bring our weapons with us. The important thing will be either to make use of the weapons at the right moment or to get rid of them at the right moment.'

'So with weapons,' says Dr Böttcher.

'And what about you lot?' Schröter says, turning to the soldiers.

'I don't really know,' replies Private Kebschull.

'You have a good old think,' says Schröter, 'take your time.'

'How come you're so wired up?' says young Private Hellwig, 'This isn't a game.'

'I'm glad you've worked that out at last,' Schröter shoots back.

'Think very carefully about what you're doing,' the air-raid warden says antagonistically. 'Wenck's tank armies reached the western edge of the city last night, and are advancing towards the city centre, the Bolsheviks are already in retreat and are even supposed to have been encircled. And you want to . . .'

'I've always said,' Private Hinzpeter joins in triumphantly, 'the battle for Berlin is nothing but a trap set by the Führer for the Bolsheviks, a really big trap like the one Hindenburg set for them at Tannenberg, into the bog and then roaring down on them. Mark my words, in a few days Berlin will be free again.'

Schröter looks him scornfully up and down. 'Good God,' he says slowly, 'you don't seriously believe that?'

'He's dozy enough for a whole company,' Ruppert says with a broad grin. 'They shat in your brain and forgot to stir it. I could do a few things to you!'

'You're not up to much yourself,' the air-raid warden says furiously. 'Your comrade is right, Berlin is just a trap, a huge trap, and we will bury the Bolsheviks under the rubble, and whatever is left will be chased into the sea.'

Dr Wiedemann smiles thinly from the corners of his mouth. 'You are allowing yourselves to be deceived today as you have been deceived before, but you have learned nothing from it,' he says. 'Every great defeat has been turned into a brilliant chess move by the Führer. After we were thrown out of Africa, a representative of the OKW said this to the press:

"The clearance of Africa has been part of our strategic plans for months. Now it is strengthening fortress Europe to an enormous degree. We never wanted to stay in Africa, but to keep the enemy away from European soil until we had made the continent of Europe impregnable."'

'But a few months previously,' says Dr Böttcher, 'Rommel had grandly announced in the Sportpalast:

"We are at the gates of Alexandria, and hold the key to the Suez Canal in our hands. Wherever the German soldier stands, there he stays."'

Dr Wiedemann nods to him. 'And after the defeat of Stalingrad, Dr Dietrich said something along these lines at a press conference:

"Were it not for the genius and the unique brilliance of the Führer, we might be up against something very serious. But Stalingrad is only one of the Führer's many brilliant chess moves, with which he paves the way for German victory."

Isn't that enough?'

The air-raid warden frowns disgruntledly and says nothing.

'It doesn't need to be true,' says Private Hinzpeter.

Dr Wiedemann shrugs. 'Yes, if you only believe what you want to believe, you're beyond help.'

'So think very hard, we're off in a moment,' Schröter adds.

Dr Böttcher, Wiegand, Gregor, Lassehn, Schröter and Lucie Wiegand leave the boiler room.

'You could stay here, Lucie,' Wiegand says to his wife, 'you're safe here, and in good hands.'

Lucie Wiegand smiles at her husband and ties her turban tighter. 'You don't think I'm going to duck out now, do you, Fritz?'

'That's not ducking out . . .' Dr Böttcher begins.

'Fine,' Lucie Wiegand says quickly, 'then there's nothing to think about.'

They slowly climb the cellar steps.

'Wait!' calls Private Ruppert. 'I'm coming too!'

Lassehn carefully opens the cellar door and peers into the court-yard. The sky is a great vault of smoke, soot and smouldering haze, the artillery fire has become weaker and moved away a little, now the dominant sounds are the roar and rattle of tank tracks, the clatter of machine guns, the hard, dry reports of sub-machine guns, the brief cracks of rifles. Bullets whistle through hallways, ricochets whirr around.

'The courtyard is clear,' Lassehn says.

'You've got to get through the hallway of the rear building, across the second courtyard and over the wall of the courtyard, and then you'll be in the rear courtyard of 116 Wilhelmstrasse,' Dr Wiedemann says.

'Thanks,' Dr Böttcher says, and shakes his hand.

'Break a leg,' says Dr Wiedemann.

Lassehn opens the door completely. They dash up the last steps of the cellar stairs, run across the courtyard through the dark hall-way of the rear building, the second courtyard, surrounded on three sides by grey rear buildings, opens up in front of them, and there is the wall, the border between friend and enemy, but this time the terms have been reversed, the enemy is in fact the friend, and the friend is the enemy.

'Slowly,' Wiegand warns, stopping close behind Lassehn.

But the second courtyard is empty too. As if under a spell, they all slow down and stare keen-eyed at the wall, the fateful wall, that leads to the free country of the enemy.

'In that case . . .' Wiegand begins, but he says no more.

Six SS men swing over the wall, their hobnailed boots clatter on the stony floor, one of them stumbles and loses his sub-machine gun, behind them a few bullets whip into the masonry.

An icy shudder runs through Lassehn. To be caught like this at the last moment . . .

Wiegand seems quite calm, his face is a single taut muscle. He did flinch for a second, but he doesn't move backward, which could be understood as flight.

Ruppert is about to open his mouth and say something, he has already turned halfway around, but Gregor grabs him hard.

'Be quiet!' he hisses.

'Where do you think you're going?' an Unterscharführer says, slightly breathlessly.

'Over there,' Wiegand says, and points to the wall. 'Reconnaissance mission.'

'You can't go there,' says the Unterscharführer, 'the Russians are there already.'

That's why we want to, Schröter thinks grimly, and then these bastards have to go and get in our way. Just a . . .

'Clear off,' an SS man says. 'Where have you been deployed?'

'Here,' says Wiegand, 'between Anhalter and Hedemannstrasse.' He turns round and winks at the others. 'Right, everyone, back, march, march!' He says goodbye to the SS men abruptly and sets off.

They stop in the hallway leading to Saarlandstrasse.

'Bad luck,' Wiegand says curtly, 'but well done, it could have been worse. Great that none of us ran away, because that would have been that.'

'What now?' asks Private Ruppert. 'Back to the boiler room?'

'No, my dear Neukölln stogie salesman, now that we're on our way, we're going to keep going. If we can't go up, we'll have to go down.'

'How do you mean?' Ruppert says in disbelief.

'Look, the houses all have gaps in the walls, and we'll go through those,' Schröter replies.

'Fine, Schröter,' says Dr Böttcher. 'I've thought of that as well. Right, everyone back to the cellar, our good old Party comrade the air-raid warden will show us the gap in the wall that leads to Wilhelmstrasse.'

The air-raid warden is standing in the room outside the cellar in animated conversation with Dr Wiedemann, his face is bright red, he is gesticulating wildly with his arms and talking uninterruptedly at the doctor.

Dr Böttcher delivers a brief report, then turns to the air-raid warden. 'Where is the gap that leads to Wilhelmstrasse?'

'Leave me alone,' the air-raid warden says grumpily. 'There are more important things.'

'Like what?' Dr Böttcher asks.

'Hitler's supposed to be dead,' Dr Wiedemann says and shrugs. 'Whether it's true . . .'

'Hope so,' Schröter says, and gives the air-raid warden a violent nudge in the ribs. 'Come on then, you tried-and-trusted Party comrade, show us the mousehole, we want to go to the funeral of your great Führer.' He lifts his rifle and holds it right under the nose of the air-raid warden. 'You know I'm not going to put up with any nonsense?'

'That's . . . that's . . .' the air-raid warden pants.

'Do what you like, my love,' Schröter says, 'as far as I'm concerned you can think what you like, I couldn't give a damn, but you're going to show me the gap.'

'And if I don't?'

'Then you will die a hero's death for your Führer on the spot,' Schröter says, playing with the safety catch of his rifle.

'This is violence!' the air-raid warden gasps.

'Of course!' Schröter says fiercely. 'What else?'

The air-raid warden opens his pursed, colourless lips very slowly. 'Then come with me,' he says furiously.

They walk down various dark passageways.

'If you take us to . . .' Schröter says threateningly and lights his face with the torch.

'Stop that,' growls the air-raid warden.

Then they are standing by a wall. It is a wall like a hundred thousand other cellar walls, casually whitewashed, brick on brick, hung with cobwebs, and yet it is a very special wall, with a big, dark patch in the middle, on which it says in black capitals: 'Passageway to 116 Wilhelmstrasse.'

Lassehn grabs the pickaxe that hangs on a hook beside the passageway and starts striking the wall. At first there are only fragments of plaster and bits of brick, then a small hole appears, soon whole bricks are breaking away, the hole grows quickly. Lassehn works furiously, the pickaxe rains incessantly down on the wall.

The cellar on the other side is in deep darkness, a smell of mildew envelops him. Wiegand shines his torch: it is empty. Then the hole is big enough for them to climb through. Wiegand stands in front of the hole and stares into the darkness, pierced only by the narrow beam of light from his torch, he stands there motionless for several seconds. It is incredibly quiet down here.

Then firm footsteps ring out, suddenly there are strange sounds in the cellar. Standing in the beam from Wiegand's torch is a Russian soldier, in a long, grey-green coat and wearing a white fur hat with a red Soviet star blinking brightly from it.

Wiegand takes a deep breath, then climbs skilfully through the hole in the wall and walks up to the Russian soldier.

'Tovarich,' he says in an excited voice and raises his hands in the air. The Russian soldier looks at him calmly, then twists his lips into a contemptuous smile and replies, 'Nix tovarich. Give watch. Davai!'

The End

'Here and now begins a new era of world history
and you can say you were there.'

Goethe, after the cannonade of Valmy (1792)

2 May

It is 5.30, the rays of the rising sun pierce the wall of cloud that
stretches grey and bleak across the ruins of the city. On Vossstrasse,
which connects Wilhelmplatz and Hermann-Göring-Strasse, a
massive blanket rises slowly into the air, it rises clumsily and reluctantly like a drawbridge allowing access to a besieged fortress. This
concrete blanket, which is lifted on Vossstrasse by hydraulic power,
opens access to a cave, the last command post of the last Berlin
Combat Commandant. It is surrounded on all sides, a detachment
of Russian officers has taken up position, they raise their cocked
sub-machine guns and aim at the entrance to the bunker, but they
don't need to make use of their weapons, because the first to appear
is a soldier. Unshaven, rumpled, gaunt, he carries on the tip of his
bayonet a scrap of white cloth. Only then do the others appear,
Weidling, General of the Artillery, Supreme Commander of the
Defence Zone of Berlin, in an immaculate uniform, with the collar
fastened at the top and the Knight's Cross, gold epaulettes with two
stars and a row of medals, and only the untidily wrapped ankle
garters reveal the unusual haste with which he has put them on,
Ministerial Director Hans Fritzche, Goebbels' protégé and imita-
tor in word and tone, in a perfectly fitting elegant suit with sharp
creases, and last of all the senior editor Dr Otto Kriegk, intellectual
opinion maker and agitator of the Hugenberg company, in the
olive-grey uniform of a leader of the Labour Service, with woven

silver epaulettes. For a few seconds they stand there in silence and blink like owls into the light that falls upon them, then they clamber awkwardly into an armoured reconnaissance vehicle that stands ready a few metres away. The doors are closed, the vehicle sets off, turns into Hermann-Göring-Strasse and crosses Potsdamer Platz, it bellows its hoarse signals through the ruined streets, dashes down Saarlandstrasse, past the horrific skeletons of Potsdam and Anhalt Stations, hurries along Hallesches Tor and up the slope of Belle-Alliance-Strasse to Tempelhof. The vehicle drives recklessly over rubble and through potholes, it rattles its passengers against one another and bounces them off walls and ceilings, but no one says a word, their lips are pressed tightly together and their eyes half closed, every now and again the general takes his glasses off and rubs them clean, the broadcasting liar fiddles nervously with his tie, the opinion-making hack has collapsed entirely in on himself.

Then the car brakes hard, the doors are pulled open, General Weidling, Fritzsche and Dr Kriegk get out, they are standing outside a house on the Schulenburg-Ring, one of the many streets of Tempelhof where there are rows of uniform new buildings. They slowly climb the stairs while an unpleasant, damp, cold wind blows through the empty windows of the stairwell, the sun has disappeared behind grey clouds and a fine rain is beginning to drift down. The general looks fleetingly at the street, then he steps inside a flat on the first floor, is led down a corridor and stands in a room. It is a nice middle-class gentleman's room with a desk and a bookcase, a leather sofa with a still life above it, a few chairs and a filing shelf, a nice middle-class gentleman's room, but it isn't a smooth gentleman sitting behind the desk, it is a medium-sized, powerful, squat man with a wide, reddened face, short, light, bristly hair, watery-blue, determined eyes: General Zhukov, the conqueror of Berlin. He rises to his feet for a moment, points to a chair and sits down again. General Weidling brings his hand correctly to his cap and then takes it off, sits wearily down and furtively looks the other man in the face. This Zhukov, he may be thinking now, is not a general by blood, upbringing and privilege, he is a broad, almost corpulent peasant who wears a general's uniform, a man from that incomprehensible country. He is now sitting behind a desk in this small, almost petty-bourgeois flat in Berlin-Tempelhof and pushing the capitulation document across the tabletop. The desk is otherwise completely empty, nothing interrupts its smooth, light-brown grain. There is only this white sheet of paper.

General Weidling gulps violently a few times, cleans his glasses again and unscrews his fountain pen. His hands trembling a little, he begins to sign, but then pulls the pen back. It has probably occurred to him that he may know the contents off by heart but he doesn't know the text, he darts through it quickly and then brings the pen to the paper. It is six o'clock in the morning and very quiet in the room, the shorthand typist by the window has interrupted her work and turned round, the Russian officers bend their heads down, even Fritzsche and Dr Kriegk can't escape the tension of the moment, only General Zhukov sits there quietly, leaning back in his chair, his eyes resting on the hand of the German general holding the pen. The general seems to sense their gaze, he glances up for a second and then looks at his own hand, which lies in front of him, half clenched into a fist, like a worm-eaten fruit, then he moistens his lips and resolutely writes his name below the document. Berlin has capitulated.

A few words are exchanged, then the general leaves the room. He quickly goes downstairs and doesn't worry about his companions, he still has a task which he would like to put behind him as quickly as possible, and climbs back into the armoured reconnaissance vehicle.

This time the door is not quite closed, the general can look through the open crack at the streets they are driving along, and he sees the endless columns of marching Red Army men, troops of tanks, batteries of artillery, bivouacs and the long rows of the defeated trudging dully into imprisonment. He also looks at the steaming field kitchens, besieged by the population, and the trucks to which hands are no longer outstretched in the Hitler salute, but reaching for bread distributed by the soldiers of the victorious army.

This time they are going to Johannisthal. In a former film

studio, the general stands by a recording machine, and here he dictates his last order into a wax cylinder machine:

'Berlin, 2 May 1945

On 30 April 1945 the Führer abandoned those who had sworn loyalty to him. On the Führer's orders you still believe you must continue to fight for Berlin, even though the lack of heavy weapons and ammunition and the overall situation makes fighting appear pointless.

Every hour that you continue to fight prolongs the terrible suffering of the civilian population of Berlin and our wounded. In agreement with high command of the Soviet troops I therefore request that you cease fighting.

Weidling

General of the Artillery and Commander

Defence Zone Berlin.'

The New Beginning?

Dr Böttcher, Wiegand and Schröter slowly climb a wide flight of steps, the central staircase of a primary school which has suffered no damage apart from broken windowpanes. It is a cool, rainy day, the wind blows through the open windows, every now and again a piece of glass falls to the floor or a window frame rattles. On the clothes hooks where once children's coats, caps and lunchboxes hung, there now hang steel helmets, sub-machine guns, gas masks, ammunition belts, and the steps that once echoed with the sound of hundreds of children's feet when the bell rang for the beginning or the end of class, now echo with the hurried steps of solid, hob-nailed boots, the corridors and rooms that once were filled with the cheerful chatter of many children's voices now whir with strange sounds. The primary school has become the base of a Russian military commandant.

The men stop outside a door on the second floor and greet others who wait with serious faces. On the door the sign 'conference room' can still just be read, and above it a piece of cardboard with Russian writing is fastened with a drawing pin.

Then everyone enters the room. At a big table sits a Russian major with his back to the window, his hair is greying at the temples, he has several days' growth of beard, his eyes are red-rimmed, his eyelids lie thick and heavy, the deep wrinkles of exhaustion are etched around his mouth and eyes. On the long side of the table sits a young staff sergeant with a narrow, dark head. He has a few sheets of paper in front of him, and holds a fountain pen.

With a heavy, weary gesture the major points to the chairs that stand around the table. When the men have sat down, he looks attentively and questioningly around at the faces. A few seconds pass like that, a few guns echo in the distance, hurrying footsteps in the corridor thunder back and forth, but here in the military commandant's room it is quiet.

'Gentlemen!' the major begins at last. 'You have been described to me as reliable and trustworthy, and I should like to ask you whether you are willing to assume the temporary administration of this district.'

The major speaks excellent German, with a slight accent, a rolling 'r', strictly separating the syllables in a staccato fashion.

'The task before you is an incredibly difficult one,' the major continues, 'it cannot be accomplished with bureaucratic methods. You must supply the population with food, water and electricity as soon as possible, and I promise to help you do so, as far as it is in my power.'

'I am sure of it, Major,' Schröter shouts.

Dr Böttcher and Wiegand say nothing.

The major looks at the sergeant, whose pen is gliding rapidly over the paper.

'As the mayor's office you can occupy some rooms in this school for the time being. I will issue the order that they be freed up for you. Sergeant Yenakiev will give you papers which will allow you to pass unhindered, and you will also be given armbands to identify you to the outside world.'

Again the major lets his eye wander over the men's faces.

'I expect you to use all your strength and all your knowledge to overcome the misery of your people. Go to work without hesitation. I expect your first report by this time tomorrow. Thank you, gentlemen.'

When Dr Böttcher, Wiegand and Schröter go back downstairs, they stop by an open window. From here their eyes wander far over the sea of houses, over fields of rubble and fires, over torn streets and churned-up squares. The big city lies before them, mown down by the scythe of death, extinguished by the flaming torch of war, stamped down by the feet of the armies. A hurricane of destruction has torn down everything in its path, but there is still a breath within it, the blood in its veins has not yet frozen, the will of its people is not completely broken. Heavy clouds of smoke rise into the gloomy sky, jagged ruins obscure the horizon, here and there a church tower rises up like an extinguished torch, everywhere the roofs show their bare beams, cracks and breaches gape in the walls, panes of glass are missing from the windows. Down below in the street, mountains of debris have piled up, street lights and tram masts have collapsed, the cobbles have been blasted, the tracks torn up, the overhead lines dangle, the shops are merely empty, looted caves, desperate, hungry, weary, homeless people wander around, soldiers stagger dull-faced and dead-eyed to the assembly centres, while the cries of the women being raped echo from the houses.

Dr Böttcher shudders when he turns back to Wiegand. 'It's almost too hard,' he says. 'Those cries will follow us for a long time to come . . .'

'Oh come on!' Schröter interrupts him. 'You have too gloomy an outlook.'

'I wish that were so,' says Wiegand. His face is sceptical.

Then they go downstairs. In the street they encounter a fine, thin rain. They turn up the collars of their coats and walk out into the ruined city.

A van with loudspeaker has stopped at the corner. It is announcing the capitulation.